Deception by Proxy!

Deception
by Proxy!

❖

John K. Sutherland

Copyright © 2010 by John K. Sutherland.

Library of Congress Control Number: 2010907504
ISBN: Hardcover 978-1-4535-0907-4
       Softcover 978-1-4535-0906-7
       Ebook   978-1-4535-0908-1

All rights reserved. No part of this book may be reproduced or transmitted in any form or by any means, electronic or mechanical, including photocopying, recording, or by any information storage and retrieval system, without permission in writing from the copyright owner.

This is a work of fiction. Names, characters, places and incidents either are the product of the author's imagination or are used fictitiously, and any resemblance to any actual persons, living or dead, events, or locales is entirely coincidental.

This book was printed in the United States of America.

To order additional copies of this book, contact:
Xlibris Corporation
1-888-795-4274
www.Xlibris.com
Orders@Xlibris.com
79304

Contents

Chapter I: Good Advice Is Sometimes to Be Ignored 7
Chapter II: Lady Seymour! 15
Chapter III: Revenge Bites Back Hard as It Often Will! 32
Chapter IV: The Elusive Cousin George! A Mistaken Identity? 40
Chapter V: Underby Manor. A Promise made 47
Chapter VI: A Contract Kept, an Untimely Bereavement 59
Chapter VII: Questions. An Enlightening Conversation with One Corpse, a Vigil Over Another 68
Chapter VIII: Painful Readjustments, a Conversation Overheard 79
Chapter IX: The Letter! 94
Chapter X: Some Confidences Disclosed 98
Chapter XI: The Squire and the Mysterious Stranger 108
Chapter XII: A Promise Kept, a Violent Blatherskite Dealt With, the Service, a Gossip 112
Chapter XIII: A Helpful and Silent Observer 129
Chapter XIV: Two Strange Men Arrive, Secretively Confer, and Depart 132
Chapter XV: An Armed Protectress Disarmed, Rearmed—Confusion! A Revealing Journal 135
Chapter XVI: Surprising Disclosures—We Are Watching and Learning 147
Chapter XVII: Buying Some Time! 155
Chapter XVIII: The Elder Thackeray Countered and Repulsed, a Murderous Listener! 160
Chapter XIX: The Revelation and an Embarrassing Reassessment 171
Chapter XX: The Tour of the Estate, a Stolen Kiss 181
Chapter XXI: Tearful Reappraisal and a Motherly Confession 189
Chapter XXII: A Revealing Encounter 196
Chapter XXIII: Difficult Questions and Foundations of a New Relationship 208
Chapter XXIV: We Are Forever in Your Debt 232
Chapter XXV: Change of Plans and Preparations! 244
Chapter XXVI: Brooklands 258
Chapter XXVII: Time Is the Great Healer 272
Chapter XXVIII: Truth and Consequences 276
Chapter XXIX: The Observers and the Most Disturbing Question 300

Chapter XXX: The Unusual Plights of the Kitten and Annis 309
Chapter XXXI: A Young Conspirator Is Run to Earth
    and Expresses Herself Candidly 324
Chapter XXXII: The Inestimable Value of a Thunderstorm! 329
Chapter XXXIII: Charlotte Tells a Secret, a Plot Is Born 339
Chapter XXXIV: That Night! The Grand Deception! 350
Chapter XXXV: At the Dock 356
Chapter XXXVI: Once Aboard the Lugger . . . and So to France 361
Chapter XXXVII: The End of the Seamew in Deadman's Slough 368
Chapter XXXVIII: Truth and Consequences Again 377

Chapter I

Good Advice Is Sometimes to Be Ignored

When Major William Devane arrived at his mother's house shortly after leaving the city, he discovered that he had not only missed her, as she had deserted the city for Bath some days earlier with no indication of when she might return, but had also missed his sister Elizabeth too, as she had left for Brooklands.

Once he had turned his horses over to his mother's stable lad, he entered the house and was warmly greeted by an old retainer whom he recalled from five years earlier. His mother's butler informed him that he had been expected some days earlier but that his sister had become impatient of waiting for him.

"I would have been here last week, Horace, but I needed to see my horses safely transported, so I landed only this morning."

"Yes, sir. Your mother did expect you last week I think, and then when this week came and you were still not here, her disappointment got the better of her, and her nerves demanded that she go to Bath for a few days."

"So she still has nerves then? I thought I had destroyed them all! She has you well trained, Horace!"

"Yes, sir. Also, your sister has gone to Kellands lodge, to your cousin for a day or so, before she goes on to Brooklands."

As his late father's estate, Brooklands, was some distance beyond Kellands, it made sense for him also to ride to his cousin's estate first, even as the greater part of his baggage went off ahead of him to Brooklands. He would be sure to catch up to his sister in one of those places.

"She thought she might remain there for a day or so, but if not, she will leave directions for you there too, in case you arrived unexpectedly as you now have, sir. There is a letter she left for you here too and another addressed to you from Lord Seymour. *That one* came a day or so ago. Her ladyship's man said that her ladyship regarded it as urgent, I believe!"

"I have been away five years, Horace! What can there possibly be that is urgent on the very day I arrive some weeks late and from someone I barely know and have seen but once, to my knowledge, in my entire life? I shall read that one later. Besides, he is no relative of mine. I believe my mother is vaguely related to the old Lady Seymour, and that is as far as it goes. I would not put it past her ladyship to have written this herself for some reason. She seems to be devious that way."

"I believe Lord Seymour is not in good health, sir. If you will pardon me for pointing it out, but you are related to both Lord Seymour and his late wife through some very distant connection. It is his daughter, the present Lady Adelaide Seymour, your godmother, who sees to her father's affairs now, and that is why she saw it delivered to you."

"So what might she be up to now?" He was well aware of his godmother's very limited affection for him. "No matter. He had his stroke even before I left, so I would say he is hanging on quite well. Probably still as grouchy as he always was from what little I hear. Why my godmother might want me anywhere near him beats me, for she couldn't stand me fifteen years ago. And from what Elizabeth said to me in her last letter, her animosity for me seems not to have diminished!"

"Situations change in five years, sir, as do people."

"I suppose you are right about that, Horace. But I don't think that I have. I'm still me! Lady Seymour also still dislikes me intensely—so my sister hinted in her letters. No change there from what I hear."

"She dislikes everyone, sir, except your mother and sister."

"They still meet in that little coven of theirs each month, do they, and burn little effigies of me?"

The older gentleman cleared his throat as a sign of disapproval that he might speak of his mother that way. "I don't think I would put your sister into that same class of people, sir!"

"Yes. A little unkind to call it a coven, for my sister is not a witch any more than my mother is, though she engages in some very strange dealings with equally strange people, I hear. Elizabeth wrote me and told me of some of their scheming and plotting for my future. But I cannot speak for Lady Seymour. She always did try to practice an air of being threatening to me, even the one time I consciously met her. That is the way she seemed to me as a small boy, which is when I last saw her. At that time she would quite happily have had me spitted and roasted!"

The butler ignored that comment. "I believe the matter may be important, sir. At least her ladyship's man, Maltby, who brought it, thought it was."

"It always is when they want you to do something for them. Why is Lord Seymour now taking an interest in me? He never did before, and I am sure that I have no expectations there!"

"Others might recommend that you should go and ask him, sir. However, Maltby was . . . ," his voice dropped, "In confidence, sir, I must add, he was quite of the opinion that it was all her ladyship's doing and that she was in a strangely aggressive and awkward mood where you were concerned. He was of the opinion that it was *she* who wanted to see you and suggested to drop a word of wisdom in your ear, that it might be wise to ignore her letter for the moment and give her the bye."

"He did, did he? I wonder if she knows of his treachery!"

"Yes, sir! No, sir! I think I tend to agree with him, for your sister said the same thing by way of warning to me before she left, and she also left you a note to that effect on the hall table with the instructions that I was to ensure you got it and read it *before* you left here."

"This sounds exciting, Horace! Did he say why she wanted to see me or might be aggressive toward me? Though why it should concern me, I am at a loss to understand. Besides, when was she *not* ever aggressive to me?"

He stammered a little in his reluctance to explain further. "Well, sir, I . . . I am not sure I should say anything. It is not my place to give credence to what her ladyship might believe."

"Oh, come now, Horace! I know she already believes the worst of me as she has for many years and is the one who continues to spread vicious rumors of my behavior even after all this time. Surely it cannot be something new that we have not had to deal with in the past for I have been away for five years?"

The old gentleman blushed. "No, sir. It was something to do with a young lady some years ago."

William smiled cynically and raised an eyebrow at the older man. "The situation sounds dreadfully familiar, Horace! When was it *not* about a young lady? But which specific lady? Did she say? I seem to recall that there was more than one lurking in my past!"

"Her ladyship's niece, sir! The same young lady as was in this house some years ago. With you! In a somewhat distraught condition from what I saw and from what your sister said just before you were sent off because of that other . . . !" He waved his hand slightly as though to conjure away the memory. He was clearly not comfortable relating such questionable goings-on involving the other sex.

"Ah yes! Relax, Horace. I do remember some of it. I did not realize that the young lady was her ladyship's niece at the time." He thought for a few moments. "Well, I wonder what bee she might have in her bonnet over that. Surely it all settled down and was forgotten after I left, once it was fully explained to her?"

"Well no, sir, it wasn't! What I mean to say is that none of it *was* explained to her at all. It seems that what actually befell the young lady at the time was never accurately related to Lady Seymour, and she still lays the whole at your door. There was a . . . a . . ."

William watched with some amusement as the old retainer struggled with both his embarrassment to relate such a tender topic and to find the words. "Yes, Horace. No time to be niffy-naffy about anything! Spit it out!"

"There was an offspring of that time, sir! So Maltby told me." He breathed out heavily, having got it off his chest.

"There was?" William seemed more amused than surprised.

"Yes, sir! The young lady gave birth while you were away! A girl! I am sure it would have been a surprise to everyone, had they known of it. But it was never widely mentioned, thank the Lord!" It clearly embarrassed him to raise such a tender topic. "Maltby and your sister seem to have known of it, however, as well as your mother and her ladyship of course! I believe that *that* is what has been festering at her ladyship for the last few years and why she holds you in such animosity!"

"Yes, seeing her nearest and dearest violated in that way and then deserted, leaving her with child—four or five years old by now—and by one such as I, would have that effect on her, I expect. Although she did not see any of that particular defilement, I can vouch for that, and she only learned of it much later! Looks like me, does it? The baby?" He looked at the older man.

"I cannot say, sir. I have not seen it!"

"Strange that *that* should be one of the first things to greet me with when I come home after such a prolonged absence." He was thoughtful for a few moments. "I wonder why Elizabeth never mentioned that birth to me! Yes. You are right, Horace. I should most certainly give her the go-by in that case. She would sic her dogs onto me anyway or lay a trap for me! Thank you for the warning."

He regarded himself critically in the hall mirror, and changed the subject somewhat too easily for Horace's peace of mind. "More importantly, Horace, did my sister leave some clothes for me here? I told her that I would need some changes to my threadbare wardrobe," he inspected his sleeve and did not like what he saw, "so I hope she was able to do something, for she mentioned that some of my own that I left behind and even some of my father's clothes would be here for me. Would it also be too much to ask if there is hot water enough for a bath?"

"There is a choice of your older clothing upstairs, sir. She selected some of your father's too, which I suspect will fit you now." He cast a critical eye over the son's less-than-complimentary attire—carelessly dressed—but then he had just stepped ashore. "Your father always dressed so *well*, sir. One of the best-dressed men in London all of his life, in or out of uniform!"

William frowned good-naturedly at the older man. "Don't rub it in, Horace! I am painfully aware that I do not present a spectacle of sartorial resplendency. Nor smell too good either, I imagine!" His nose wrinkled for a moment.

"No, sir! There is also ample hot water for a bath. She said that you had made the comment at how you so missed a hot bath and were looking forward to one when you set foot ashore. If you were to try some of your father's clothing on first, sir, I suspect that Mrs. Priddy will be able to make enough changes while you are bathing, to tide you over until you can see your own tailor. She is a formidable needlewoman and is aware that you have arrived."

He looked critically at William's boots. "I will see what I can do for your boots in the meantime if one of your father's many pairs does not fit. That looks somewhat like a hole in the side of that one, sir, and there is a cut or two marking the leather, and they have not been looked after as they should have been!" He sounded mildly offended.

"No they haven't! The vicissitudes of war! As for looking like a hole, that is because it is one! The cuts are saber cuts. Fortunately, I was not wearing them at the time that the ball did its damage. Someone else was. A Frenchman! Dead now I expect! The ball did not go right through as you can see, and whoever was wearing them at the time was undoubtedly unhappy!"

"They seem to be a remarkably serviceable pair of boots that have seen better days. I can do nothing about that hole, sir, but the scratches and other slight damage I can do something about while you bathe."

Sometime later, after a hot bath and seeing himself better attired in one of his father's slightly altered coats, he was about to ride away from his mother's house in a much better frame of mind, cleaner and far better dressed than when he arrived, when his surviving uncle on his mother's side drove up.

His uncle reined in his horses and looked his nephew up and down. "Hoping I'd catch you here, dear fellah! Good to see you survived the planned reception at the dock. First of many such hurdles I expect! If you'd come back a day or two earlier I doubt things would have been so pleasant for you!" He glowered at his nephew. "Yes, I am well! Thank you for asking! I'm your uncle! You do remember me, don't you? You haven't been away that long. Or did the war addle your brain and you are speechless?"

William had asked nothing of his health, and he did recognize him, but his uncle would not let him open his mouth to say anything. "I am sorry, Uncle David. Army manners—listen, shoot first, and enquire second! I did recognize you! I take it you are well?"

"So you do remember my name! No, I ain't well, so damn you for asking!"

His nephew smiled. Yes, this was the irascible uncle he remembered!

"Just came from Bath! Your mother expects to be there for some time. She sends you a message in the expectation that you had landed, and hoped I'd catch you before you took off. Wants to be sure to warn you to steer clear of your godmother for a while!" He winked at his nephew.

"Another one warning me off? My God, Uncle David! What does she have planned for me? But yes, I intended to do that myself."

"Wise! Very wise! She is a very fiend from hell where men are concerned, her own family included, but especially where it concerns you! I heard that baby looks too much like you for any easy denial on your part!"

His nephew was taken aback by that comment. "Not another warning me of that? Who does not know about that baby, I wonder?"

"Never mind that, me boy! History and old grudges! She means *you* no good, I can tell you that. She led her father a merry old dance before he had the biscuit!"

"I thought the letter supposedly came from his lordship, Uncle, and that it was he that requested my presence, but Horace said that she, and not her father, had sent it."

"Horace had that right! Lies, my boy, lies! All lies! His lordship never requested it! Don't be fooled by that! I told you, he's dead! She means you mischief because of that Trevelyan chit and that baby! I don't know the truth of it either way and wouldn't care if I did! She intends to castrate you one way or another boy, or to shrivel you up somehow, flay you, skewer you, eviscerate you, and send you off to the nacker's yard. So don't get sucked in to anything with that arch-wife!" His nephew was already well aware of that, for his sister had hinted as much.

He knew better than to take his uncle too seriously. "You're *looking* well, Uncle, even if you may not feel it!"

"Too late, brat! You're five minutes off the pace! I thought we'd already got that out of the way! I may look well, but I don't feel it! Damned toothache! Why I came to town! I'll see my own tooth puller and not that damned fellow in Bath! By the way, congratulations on bumsquaddling old Windy Winthorpe! There was a mob thirsty for your neck or your blood, waiting for you at the dock until yesterday. He was making a lot of unflattering noise about you there for a while until more friendly voices came into play. Especially Cadogen's. Pity we can't do the same for that Seymour woman and her gossiping about you and the rest of us and dragging our name through the mud!"

"Cadogen? My old colonel? He's dead, surely? That was what we heard in Portugal! Suffered a cannonball through his tent I heard, while we were off somewhere!"

"No! He survived that and everything else that went with it, fortunately for you, for he rose to your defense rather well and got the dock cleared. That cannonball blew his arm off. He spent six months in Greenwich getting patched up but he was never fit for duty again! White hair now but a tongue on him still that would take the barnacles off a boat! I was privileged to hear him sound off about Winthorpe two weeks ago when he came to your defense. He had a lot more to say too, about him and about his sheer incompetence and stupidity in getting too many of his men killed. He was of the opinion that he should never have been put in charge of the latrines, never mind fighting men, and especially not soldiers the like of you, who knew where their duty lay. As that utterance was made in the officers' club, in the midst of company that was well acquainted with both him *and* Winthorpe, *and* which was highly influential with the military, it had its effect, but by God, it took it's time! Winthorpe's not been seen since! Gone into hiding, I expect, to lick his wounds. Cadogen also had some very nice things to say about you, me boy, and he has the ear of Wellesley." He dropped his nephew a knowing wink. "Wellesley, no less! Any time you want a promotion, it's there for you I would say, after that." He began to realize that he had blabbed on for too long.

"Ah well. You don't need your head swelled any more by whatever he said, but I tell you, your credit in the military is raised very high indeed! Better be off to my club before I say something I might regret. Oh, while I remember! I got a whiff that your mother wanted to see you married off. Don't know what put that maggot into her head! She couldn't do it before, and she won't be able to now, I expect. If she tries to get you to offer for that Collishawe chit, run for the hills. She'd sour you and emasculate you faster than your godmother ever could. Women of that kidney are the worst kind of whores, but they are all whores one way or another! They can any of them be bought! It's just a case of finding the right price! Her price is low right now! Wrong side of thirty, and she squints!"

"Rather an unkind thing to say about the cream of London society, Uncle!"

"True though! Those women are all the same. They are disturbing and disturbed. We can neither live easily with them nor survive comfortably without. Don't ask me to explain it! Do not expect to have a rational conversation of longer than about two minutes with any female before it devolves into a welter of emotions. They are all about feelings of the heart and commiseration, tearfulness, happiness, palpitations and trembling and blame, and *never* this and *always* that! Maddening! Beautiful and charming—but *not* that Collishawe female—even as they drown you in their tears or eviscerate you and unman you with their simpering ways! They animate at length about such trivia as buttons, cotton, muslin, silk, and gossip! They pride themselves upon their hair but with no wit worth speaking of lurking beneath it! Put them in front of a mirror, and they are lost for an hour or two admiring and preening. One of the women of the other kind who understands what a man really needs is worth tying oneself to. Find her! Marry her!" He suddenly thought better of that. "Or perhaps not!"

William was rather amused by the outspoken animadversions of his uncle. "But then, marriage is not in my future, Uncle! You warned me off not two minutes ago!"

"Just remember that, me boy. Say it every day when you get out of bed as I do, and when you get into it. If there's anyone there to hear you, they won't care about that, or they wouldn't be there! More than they expect from you anyway, or they'd not be anywhere near you in the first place! But then what has marriage got to do with being happy or contented? Usually the opposite I found! Mark my words, boy, keep clear of that old witch or she'll kill you like she was rumored to have done her father *and* her brothers before him. *He* didn't deserve it, but *they* did! Rumor has it that they meddled with her when she was a young girl, just like you did with that niece of hers, and she found some way to see them off—her and that protective butler of hers! She'd do the same for you! She may have held a grudge against her father for not putting a stop to it himself!

"Her father's not been seen for years now, and no one knows where he is or can track him down. I'm betting she did for him! I don't know what to think for certain, but his lordship seems to write a lot of letters these days that I swear he never wrote at all, but not nearly as many as he used to, nor in his usual cutting and meaty style, which is why I said what I said. I doubt he's in this world at this time, but it's no use me saying anything. We used to exchange letters all of the time, but they dropped off a lot some years ago. And the ones I get once or twice a year now, never cover the same ground that we used to cover. Lost their flavor and his sharp edge and their salty language! I'd swear he never wrote the ones he is credited with now, but a woman did from what I can see. Fond of the women his Lordship was, but one of his closest acquaintances . . ." His mind drifted off for a moment. "Flori— ah, dear Flori, most obliging female—got turned away and not allowed to see him! Even if he'd been dead, there'd have been a sudden revival in the old boy when she walked in on him! She could do that to a man, she could! Still can! But turned away she was!" He was momentarily lost in thought.

"I must thank her ladyship for that though, for the delightful Flori looked me up instead, and we manage to rub along a lot more than well enough and she fired up that old spark in me. Another reason for my trip to London!" He winked at his nephew. "Might even be time for me to get married and make a respectable woman out of her, but then she always was very selective about who she associated with and might not go for it." He frowned at his nephew, recognizing that he had already said too much and had even managed to contradict himself about marriage. "But don't go blabbing that to anyone!

"But turning Flori off like that." He shook his head. "It would have killed him if he'd known! If he'd been alive! So I firmly believe he's dead! It has nothing to do with that stroke. She did for him just like she'd do for you given the chance, so keep away. Something havey-cavey going on there and you should keep clear of it all! She's playing a rare game, and after what she believes of that Trevelyan chit, she's either out to castrate you or kill you! But I told you that. Same deal in the end. Women do that to us all in time. Not Flori though! But it would happen to you overnight with that Collishawe female. Bugger all use for anything after that!"

He seemed a little red around his neck. "Seems you're struck dumb and you've got nothing to say for yourself, so I'll be off. But keep quiet about what I said." He nodded and winked at his nephew as he put a forefinger to the side of his nose in some Masonic kind of a signal. "Wouldn't have said anything about that . . . that meddling thing and the other . . . ," He realized he'd overstepped the lines a little. "So keep it to yourself, except I thought to give you a pointer to what she might be capable of! I'll go and ask Flori if she'll have me once I get this damned tooth out."

His nephew watched him drive off into the city and set out for Kellands as he went over in his mind as much of what his uncle had said as he might remember.

Chapter II

Lady Seymour!

The butler frowned in some surprise as he opened the door on the visitor. He did not give in to his first impulse to swear at him as he might a tradesman at the wrong door and to tell him to take himself off! If the young gentleman was fool enough not to listen to good advice and to present himself where he was not likely to get a good reception, then more fool him!

He smiled pleasantly instead and, as little as he felt it, spoke in welcoming tones. "Her ladyship has been expecting you for some time, sir." He led the way into the house, noting that the major did not have a hat and saw that his hair was a little windblown. He would likely not take kindly to having that commented upon, as she certainly would.

"Did you not call in at Mountjoy Street, sir?"

"Yes, I did!" He smiled and spoke gently. "Relax, Maltby! I received Horace's recommendation to pay no social visits today, as well as the similar advice of another, and the wise words of both my absent mother and my uncle too. My sister also recommended it in her letter. So much concern for me already! It quite warms my prodigal heart! But then I am a contrarian soul, which is why I am here. My curiosity is piqued! Five such recommendations in one day, and all within an hour of my returning to England, are too much for me to ignore. Not only that, but when my instinct is to retreat in the face of insuperable odds, I advance. And when to advance into an easy circumstance, I retreat. It appears to have served me well so far against most enemies and saved me from many traps."

Maltby was not impressed by his dubious logic. This was his godmother he was speaking about, not the action on the Peninsula. "It might have been better to listen to so many wise advisors, sir. Her ladyship is not feeling quite at ease with the world. However, you are now here. May I recommend, sir that you not engage in any heated argument with her if you can avoid it? She has a most agile brain and wit and will box you in if she can, and she tends to learn far more than one might like from the unguarded tongue in such exchanges and is capable of leading the conversation where you might least like it to go." He recognized that his words might just be as water off a duck's back for all the effect they had upon the major. He had heard of

15

his stubborn, bullheaded qualities. They had undoubtedly served him well abroad, but would not do so, here.

"Yes, Maltby. I know! I do the same myself with others. How interesting! A kindred spirit!" He paused before the hall mirror and straightened his cravat and then tried to get his hair to lie down a little less rebelliously on his head, but with no success. "Yes, I fully intended to ignore the summons and ride on as those much wiser than I recommended, but after a visit to an even wiser man, occupying his confining throne on the common—Gentleman Jack, late highwayman, windblown and desiccated, communing with me from a higher plane or a lower one as he sat in his cage—I decided that I would not evade such a challenging confront . . ." He recovered from using that word and found one just as evocative— "contretemps."

He made one last attempt with his hair and then gave up. "I found, Maltby, that I was suddenly in a distinctly rebellious mood—completely out of character for me, of course," Maltby knew that it wasn't! " . . . and decided to ignore the good advice that was provided me and made up my mind that I could not avoid my fate, whatever it might be at her ladyship's hands. I seem to remember my father telling me constantly never to evade an unpleasant situation but to remove it somehow, if I could not easily deal with it any other way."

"Oh, dear!" The older retainer had blanched to hear that.

"Do not fear, Maltby. I am not usually a violent man, at least not with ladies on this side of the channel, despite what seems to be believed of me. Especially not with her ladyship, though at one time she would have beaten me within an inch of my life or skinned me alive, if I recall her words correctly, after the issue with her dog!"

"Yes, sir, I recall. I think she reluctantly forgave you of the issue giving rise to those feelings, sir. A little late perhaps—just a day or so ago—after so many years, when she found out the truth of it, but the other . . ."

"Yes, the other! I take it that you refer to the unfortunate Miss Trevelyan? Three times now at least, I have heard about that in just one day. I wonder if she dare throw that at my head. The portents for my unscathed return, though less than they were with Winthorpe and his neck-stretching delegation at the dock out of the way, do not look promising."

The butler seemed a little taken aback that he so easily mentioned the young lady's name. "Yes, sir, the other is still nagging at her. Justice denied, she thinks, and does not choose to listen to those who might know better."

Major Devane looked at him in some surprise. "But does anyone know better, Maltby? Do you? Or has everyone managed to persuade themselves that the Devane features of the infant are so very obvious, and unerringly indicate that I must have played a part in its existence? I had hoped someone—at least her aunt—might at least have *questioned* the Trevelyan girl about what had happened! No, Maltby. Justice *was* done in that regard! I shall tell you what I mean some other time, though I doubt I shall enlighten her ladyship about that today. Not if she is in an argumentative mood. I shall let her stew a little longer."

The butler was puzzled by his words. "Yes, sir."

"Relax, Maltby. I am probably as curious about her as she is about me, and I felt it better to get this meeting out of the way. I bear her no ill will—strange as that might seem considering her persistent attempts over the years to blacken my name—nor shall I fight with her more than she deserves, if for no other reason than that my mother and sister both seem to love her and so therefore should I, but I do find it a challenge!"

"Thank you, sir." He was still not fully sure what he might believe. "On another matter, please forgive my asking, sir, but is Colonel Walters still on the continent?"

"Yes, he is. He still has his hands full tidying up. But it is almost all over by now. He said he would not be able to leave for at least another month, but it was getting to the stage where if he did not leave, he might face an unpopular revolt. They want their country back and don't care whether it is the French or the English they remove to do it. Enemies become friends for a while. Friends become enemies so quickly too! But what do you know of the colonel?"

"My brother is with him, sir. His aide-de-camp. Joseph Aspden."

"I know him! They saw hard action in the early going. Touch and go for a while."

"Yes, sir. He wrote often when he was able. Told me a lot of your exploits too. I believe your father was very proud of what you were doing over there."

"Thank you, Maltby, I doubt I would hear that from many others."

"I think your regiment saw even more if it than he did from what he said."

"At times we did, but I was not with them for very long. The new colonel was an ill wind—old Windy, aptly named—and got too many men killed needlessly, so I waged my own war out of his way and against him too. I should never have rescued him from the French as I did, for he then accused me of kidnapping him! I don't think there were any of us that had an easy time of it, but we were seen as liberators, tolerated quite well until the last of it. So we were treated almost as one of their own eventually and much better than the French, of course, who got short shrift at the end."

He showed him into a large drawing room.

His godmother was sitting close by the window, reading. She had clearly seen him ride up but was not about to acknowledge him until she was good and ready. His sister had warned him of her general animosity toward him in each of her gradually more revealing letters, except she had not mentioned Miss Trevelyan or the infamous love child.

"Your godson, William Devane, ma'am!"

She turned and scrutinized him coldly. "Well, you took your time! You were expected weeks ago! Obviously, you managed to escape the violent welcoming committee at the docks!" She sounded disappointed. "Though possibly not the other one."

He did not need to ask about "the other one." Every ship was met by women of that kind, intent on relieving the returning soldiers of their rewards. "I am pleased to see you too, ma'am. I did not entirely escape a welcome of sorts! But of a different kind! Some damned thief tried to make off with my saddle even before I had set foot ashore!"

She had not heard anything he said, for she was too busy inspecting him. She was relieved to see that he did not intend to cavort about the countryside in uniform and to bowl over the local women with new-found and short-lived wealth; his panache, and exaggerated tavern-tales of heroism and unlikely exploits as seemed to be the usual style of some of the returning soldiers. The most action many of them would see or choose to boast over might be their exploits with the lusty women in the bawdy houses in Lisbon and London, which had seen more men in and out of their doors in the last few weeks than for any of the last few years! Unfortunately, they often brought something more virulent than gold back with them: the French pox! She had also heard that some brought mistresses; even wives and children!

She waved off the butler from fussing near her as she took in more of her visitor. Her butler went over near the door but did not leave, apparently awaiting further instructions.

She raised her spectacles on a ribbon about her neck and looked him over in finer detail. He had changed a great deal from when she had last seen him, but that was to be expected, for he had been no more than eight or nine years old then, maybe older. He had filled out and grown considerably more than she expected.

Some of the more lurid tales of him and his reputation that had intruded over the years now began to make sense to her. It was clear that the military had not been a total loss for him, for he was not inclined to slouch but had a defiant, almost aggressive look about him. There was a hint of both arrogance and pride, common with young men who thought more of themselves than they should. He also had a sharp eye that would have lesser men avoiding him. He even seemed amused by her scrutiny but said nothing.

It was one of her favorite tactics to remain silent and have others nervously start the conversation.

It appeared that there was not an ounce of fat on him as far as she could see. He moved easily as his eyes took in everything around him. It was evident that he would soon need to see a tailor, as his shoulders were somewhat snug in his coat, though it hung a little loosely elsewhere. He had not yet run to the belly that his father had developed over the years, but he would, once he settled down to the easy life that he had inherited.

When he did design to notice her scrutiny, he did not seem uncomfortable under her steady, undoubtedly hostile gaze, for she had no intention of making him feel as though he might relax. He seemed to regard her in turn with a look that seemed to vary between one of being curious at her scrutiny to one of amusement, with a smile playing about his lips. He was well aware of her intent, and returned measure for measure, look for look. He had steady and unwavering gray eyes that gradually took in her and then the details of the room, just as she looked him over. He did not rush over to greet her as others closer to her ladyship and caught up in the same situation might, for as far as he was concerned, she was a stranger to him, though not so much to his sister if her letters had laid out the situation correctly.

She decided not to take him to task for being insolent in scrutinizing her in the same kind of detail as she was scrutinizing him, but she was intent on putting him down and keeping him in his place. "You don't much favor your father!"

"Thank you, ma'am! That is a relief to me to hear! I began to fear that my general appearance might have struck you dumb for a moment!"

She didn't much like his apparent ease with the situation. "No! Your father was a true gentleman! He knew how to dress as well as how to behave in society." She could not resist those digs at him.

"You don't take after your mother either! But there are some things to be said in favor of the military, I expect, for it does not let you get too soft I see. Though there are some habits that you undoubtedly would learn over there that you should get rid of as soon as you will."

He smiled at her. "I doubt that *those habits*, as you describe them, could be any worse than the ones I supposedly learned in my own country of birth, ma'am, before I was shipped out!"

She snapped back at him, not liking his easy ability to respond. "Don't play the innocent with me! You men are all alike in that department with your rapacious appetites while you sing your songs of innocence! You might try to remember occasionally, that a man's reputation is the only thing he carries with him through life. It is worth protecting, and yet it seems that you have done everything you could to sully yours in the worst way! So what do you say to that?"

He looked at her steadily. "My father tried to instill the same thoughts into me too, with little success I am afraid! I may still have the bruises! However, my reputation is safe with me, ma'am, no matter what others might think of it or say to try and influence it. I shall look after it and defend it as I see fit and necessary."

She was not amused by his easy response or his relaxed manner. Her voice hardened. "But it is others who decide what your reputation shall be, and based upon how you behave in society and with others! You should think of that!"

"Alas, ma'am, I gave it no thought at all until you raised it now. I have been out of society for the last five years. But if I had been worried about what others thought of me, or concerned myself with how others might see me, what a poor specimen I would be, living my life according to how others choose to dictate!"

His calmness was getting through to her. The interview was not supposed to be progressing like this! "A rebel, eh? You should care what others think!"

He picked up a small china figurine from the table, examined its fine detail for a few moments and then replaced it, before he decided to answer her. "I am sorry to be a contrarian, ma'am, but I don't! We are all saddled unavoidably with our *perceived* reputations whether we deserve them or not. I believe you also have an unenviable reputation."

"But what kind of a reputation do *you* have?" she had snapped a little and had to rein in her growing anger. "On the other hand, I earned mine!" She did not like his relaxed attitude, or his ready responses to her when he should have been silent, if not tongue-tied. "If I had your reputation, I would be ashamed of it! But I see you were not being complimentary." Her face was a little flushed.

Her butler noticed with some amusement, though careful to not let it be seen, that she clearly felt annoyed by his relaxed composure and easy repartee—a foreign feeling for her as she tended to overawe her visitors and have them tongue-tied or to blather incautiously and incoherently even, and not to have them turn the tables upon her as the major seemed to be capable of doing.

She forced herself to calm down and to recover her composure before she continued. "You will need to watch your language, I suspect, and your social ways too, with a better class of lady around you. And remember that you are not still in the company of those lightskirts that I hear are the camp-followers. I am surprised that the army did not rename one of its regiments to celebrate that kind of nefarious antisocial activity considering what I hear of that. Lightbobs or lightskirts, all the same to me, and to them, likely!"

He remained silent, recognizing her efforts to establish position by putting him down. He decided it would be pointless to try and correct her on anything. Better also not to be too aggressive himself, and fire her up even more.

Her eyes flashed. "Yes. Outspoken, ain't I? I'm not one for evading plain speaking when it is called for! When did you land? Or did you *sneak in* some other way? A few days ago I warrant, to avoid the reception at the docks. Maybe you have been here a week or more and been frequenting the wrong places since, with the hordes of women at the docks for the last few weeks, plying their profession! They can smell the gold coming up the river and weighting down the pockets of those returning, and intend to get it one way or another. Or both, and usually do! Easy targets and easier pickings, the lot of you! Hard to tear yourself away, I expect, from those alluring offerings!"

"I am sure you are right, ma'am." It seemed that he thought nothing of the kind. "However, I landed this morning and somehow managed to avoid those more personal negotiations with certain ladies plying their profession. Indeed, there were many women at the dock initially I recall, though some seemed to be wives and loved ones of the officers. But then you are speaking of ladies of that other stripe, but I could have been wrong. I did not obviously notice any of *them*, but it was probably too early or too late."

She tried a different approach. "Oh, come in and sit down, boy! I won't bite you! Yet! I wish to look at you, and the light over there is none too good."

He walked over to the window area, where she might see him a little more closely, but did not immediately sit.

"So you saw your mother, I assume?"

"No! My mother is still in Bath, ma'am, recovering her nerves after anticipating and agonizing over my arrival. I may have to join her there soon myself for the sake of my own nerves if my reception continues as it started." He had a wry smile on his face and did not rush to clarify himself for a few seconds. "I meant on the docks! The welcoming party that intended to stretch my neck for me; and that damned thief! My sister had already gone ahead of me to Brooklands, I think. I did not realize that my arrival might be an excuse to evacuate the city!"

"Turn!"

He slowly turned his frame that she might inspect him from top to toé.

"Well. Better than might be expected, I suppose, considering . . ." She did not really think so.

"You should also not place items in the pocket if you expect a coat to sit well upon you and to maintain its shape."

She referred to a slight bulge in an outer pocket.

"A pistol, ma'am. London seemed a most violent place when I left it, and I find it has not improved." He walked over to the butler and produced his pistol and gave it to him with a smile on his face as some measure of reassurance that he was not about to resort to violence of that kind on her ladyship. He seemed almost to be enjoying himself, whereas her ladyship was not.

Maltby placed it gently on the table by the door.

"My meeting with the unfortunate weather-beaten gentleman, caged on the common, and one or two other things since I landed suggest that I am right."

She raised an eyebrow. He had been the cause of some of that violence. "Did you not wear a hat? Gentlemen wear hats."

He smiled briefly. "Unfortunately, as you seemed at pains to point out, I am not yet a gentleman again, ma'am! I certainly don't feel like one at the moment. I am a dissolute soldier, so you told me, without respectability or worthwhile reputation, returned from abroad with my pockets weighted with gold to attract those ladies of *unquestionably* questionable virtue! Everyone knows what soldiers are like—hither and yon! I expect it will take a few days for me to get rid of the military stigma and try to behave in the manner that is expected of me around the ladies—the other kind, though they are all of the same stripe in the end—get rid of my pay, settle down, and grow into a new role since I doubt I can enter my old life quite so easily. But then I do not feel inclined to do so."

He continued speaking as she still allowed him the floor. "As for a hat, I sent it on ahead of me, and I do not have access to another one just yet. My father's would not fit me well, so the wind that ruffled my hair a little, would have soon seen it gone."

"You should sit down and take some refreshments. You look uncomfortable."

He smiled at her. "I feel uncomfortable for some reason!" She was not surprised. She had no intention of letting him get away with anything. "But then I have not felt comfortable any moment for the last five years. War does that to a man, so I expect I am still carrying those feelings about with me. But if you do not mind, ma'am, I need to stretch my legs. I have been cramped up for too long aboard ship or jounced on the back of a horse and am still restless."

"As you will!" He did not look uncomfortable, the way he almost seemed to lounge about. He was too damned relaxed and not at all shy to say what he was thinking.

He stifled a yawn behind his hand and then smiled at his lack of manners. "I beg pardon, ma'am. I have not had a good night's sleep for several days. We had a rough crossing, and I had my cattle to see to." He recalled why he was there. "But I believe his Lordship wished to see me. As I'd heard a rumor somewhere that he had died some years ago, I was most curious to see if he was capable of communicating from the grave. Or was that a ruse to get me here?"

Neither of them appeared to notice that the butler had gone suddenly pale.

"No. He didn't! Send for you, that is! I did! He can't even remember his own name these days, never mind hold any other thought. He might as well be dead! But who told you that he'd died?"

"Forget now! Rumor around town, I expect."

"Already? You say you only landed this morning? I believe I might be able to expect that after his stroke and staying away from his usual women—that Flori creature—and his usual haunts. I am sure that you and she might have much in common. You'd like her I think, despite the difference in your ages!" She was in an argumentative mood. "Are you sure you haven't been . . . ? No! You'd deny it anyway. You all do! I sent you that letter. His Lordship is not at home at present."

He did not seem surprised, but refrained from commenting.

"I believed you were more likely to respond to a request from Lord Seymour than from me." Her eyes glinted.

She was right. He said nothing for a few moments and withheld the needling comment that he was almost tempted to make about her being devious. She had no sense of humor when it might be turned back upon her. He did not ask why she wanted to see him. She would undoubtedly tell him when she felt like it. If she dared! She did not approve of him in the slightest! No matter!

"Am I to take it then, that contrary to the rumors, his Lordship is still in passably good health, ma'am, apart from not knowing his name and the . . . er . . . other?"

"As well as can be expected. He had a stroke some time ago and tends to stay out of everyone's way. But I can't stop rumors. I ignore them!"

"Yes. That's usually the wisest and safest thing to do, I believe! To respond to them tends to give them credibility!"

She continued, "I wanted to see for myself how you might have turned out. I did not like the reports I heard of you just before you went away." He decided not to respond and ask what those reports might be, and set her off again. "Your mother will be relieved at your return and the prospect of you settling down."

"I am sorry to continue to be argumentative, ma'am, but it does not seem that my mother is at all relieved by the prospect of my return. She cannot yet know for certain that I have landed, though she soon will! From what I hear, I think it is expected—she expects—that I might settle down in some way, rather than return to my old ways. I am sure my mother hopes so and is still making plans for me as she was before I left. I expect she cherished hopes of seeing me married off and settled as soon as possible after my return. But then, such relationships and even marriage, are all a process of negotiation for position, comfort, security (for the lady and possibly her future children) the transfer of money or wealth, whether for a temporary alliance of a few hours (those other ladies again!) a few months, or of a marriage for a lifetime! I sometimes think that ladies too easily profess love in the hopes of ensnaring some unsuspecting suitor and trapping him into marriage. But love of what? It is all the same process, whether from whores or Duchesses as my uncle pointed out! I do not feel the need to negotiate my freedom away with such finality just yet." He had rambled on, much longer than he intended.

"What a jaundiced view of women and marriage you seem to have, to regard them *all* that way! Negotiation indeed! No wonder you would not look favorably upon that state."

She decided to fire her broadside at him and see if he could respond to that as easily as he did the rest. "So is there not a foreign lady in your life? So many young men seem to have become attached to those foreign women. No Constanza?" She paused and watched for a response to her suddenly dropping that name into the conversation. She noticed only a slight raising of an eyebrow, a possible tightening about his mouth—another partial smile perhaps or a grimace? "But then there would be no question of marriage there, would there be?"

He decided to deal with it head on. "So you heard of Constanza?" She was a little put out, that he did not seem too surprised, or was even uncomfortable to have that name thrown at him. His expression was hard to interpret. "You surprise me, ma'am!" He was surprised, in a way, for he had expected the name Trevelyan instead! "But Constanza, you say?" He sighed audibly. "I could not expect *that* to remain secret for so long from one such as you, ma'am, with your fingers of influence and intrigue woven so finely throughout the fabric of society!"

He stared off into the distance as he recalled that name, and continued to give voice to his thoughts. "The fair and fast Constanza! So that is now in the rumor mill along with all of the others, is it? But a little late I would have thought! That was all of two years ago now." He smiled and looked at her strangely, almost in a measuring kind of way, debating how much or how little to tell her.

She tried to encourage him. "Not a very English name, is it? I don't think I know of any English ladies with that appellation." She waited with bated breath to hear what he might have to say.

He did not seem to hesitate or even seem to wish to avoid it. "No, ma'am. She is—was—French, but of Spanish ancestry. I am amazed you stay so current! But married to her? There are those who would suggest that I was, in a way, considering how closely we had become entwined while we were thrown so closely together, or felt that I should have married her, but I can assure you that I did not. It was merely a convenient fleeting relationsh—association, for our mutual pleasure and intense satisfaction, however short-lived. At least I found it most pleasurable and of great benefit as long as it lasted, but I think I was too much for her, for I was unused to one so delicate and fragile such as she in my clumsy and inexperienced hands. Clumsy male that I am, I taxed her to the full and vigorously put her through her paces without mercy before I lost her from my protection!"

He noticed her sharply indrawn breath and that her knuckles had turned white as her hands gripped onto the arm of her chair. Those kinds of casual, outrageously revealing descriptions about something so sensitive, one would never normally hear from any gentleman, but then he seemed to want to agitate her!

He noticed that Maltby was grimly smiling over by the door. He was probably equally offended!

She was quite agitated at his second round of ungentlemanly admissions and had a stony look on her face for a few moments before she recovered a little. "I hear many things, but I had not heard those . . . unsettling aspects of it all! Is she in London still? Hidden away in some little love nest, I expect, as you all seem to do. For I heard you brought her here!"

"Yes, I did bring her here, didn't I?"

He admitted it! There was a look of angry triumph on her face as though her suspicions of him were once again proved correct.

He shrugged in dismissal. "Where she might be now, I cannot say! She changed affiliations and hands too much for my liking after I was sent back into war. I began to feel betrayed. I would have liked to have kept her by me much longer, for we did eventually develop a wonderfully comfortable understanding of each other. She was quite a tidy little package when I knew her. But all things must change. Much too hard used, knocked about and damaged to interest me now, I fear! I might have forgotten her entirely but for you raising her name like that!"

She was astounded at the lack of finer feeling that he showed or at his stark candor about so cavalier an affair!

"But I am sure you did not summon me here to speak so revealingly of such sensitive and deeply personal things!"

He noticed that her fingers were drumming upon the table beside her in some agitation at his expansive and insensitive admission of his execrable behavior. He accepted a cup of tea from the servant but shook his head over the offer of cake or biscuits.

"Thank you, no. Not at the moment. Perhaps later." It took the old lady some time to settle her seething anger at him over his dreadful admissions, and to relax enough to stop grinding her teeth, and to feel like any further attempt at polite conversation. He wondered with some amusement that he did not show to her, how she might respond to all of that. She was unlikely to be tongue-tied for long. He noticed that her butler was smiling a little, but out of her sight. Perhaps he knew much more than she did about the Constanza affair!

A little dog came into the room and began to growl at him until his mistress uttered an uncharacteristically severe and snappish admonishment. Her butler noticed, and knew the reason. She was unnerved by her errant godson's assured poise and his relaxed and even easygoing banter and manner and his dreadful admissions, for he did not seem as cowed or as likely to submit to being browbeaten as she had expected or hoped. She would likely learn nothing except what he chose to tell her, and that was likely to be more than she expected, by far, and in descriptive terms she would not like. He smiled. The major was a knowing one! He was proving to be quite a surprise to the old dear, as well as to him, and more than a match for her.

William was surprised to see how closely the little dog's sharp features and attentive eyes resembled those of its mistress. He had heard it said that dog owners often tended to come to physically resemble their pets (or was it the other way around?) but had never seen the truth of it until this moment. She probably had the personality and character to match, for she seemed to be baiting him as she scowled and growled at the situation. Yes, they had much in common!

He squatted and gently called the dog over to him. To her ladyship's surprise and consternation, the little dog cautiously went over to him to be fussed over gently and to have her hair mussed and her head and neck and back gently scratched, enough to drive the little dog wild with gyrating about to get the best out of his efforts and licking furiously at his hands to encourage him to continue what he was doing.

He spoke in affection terms to the little dog. She had half expected him to either ignore it or to discourage it in some other way. "No half measures with you, is there you little trollop? You are like most of your sex. A little attention from me and you are entirely ready to sell your soul to have yourself the focus of affection and even to be roughed up a little! Yes, I know I am a rough and callous rogue and do not deserve any attention from one so fine as you." He reached over and took a small piece of cake from the tray that the maid had left on the table beside him and gave it to the dog without asking if he might do so. The little dog looked up at him with large trusting eyes and took it gently from his fingers after only a little hesitation.

"I try not to spoil her!" His godmother spoke very sharply. He put it down to his earlier statements which had clearly rattled her.

"Oh, I very much doubt that, ma'am!" He chuckled. "I am sorry. I am being contrarian again! All females like the attention and like to be pampered and spoiled as they work their way closer into one's good graces! I am sure that she deserves to be spoiled, even by one such as I. I always had a tender spot for animals, and they for me. They tend to be more constant and to love honestly, and respond unreservedly with never more than minimal expectation. They are also rather more reliable in their affection than humans, I found." He could not resist adding an afterthought. "They don't engage in idle gossip either!"

After that telling comment, delivered in a notably harder voice, he returned his attention to the dog as she fawned over him shamelessly.

"Ah! So you wish to wash my hands for me too, I see. As well as my boots? Thank you!" The little dog fussed excitedly around him. "Perhaps there are some remnants of pig fat left on them from their previous owner or even from my recent habits!" He knew there could be none, for Horace had done a remarkably good job of bringing them back from their neglected state.

His godmother shivered in revulsion and spoke harshly to her dog once more, only to be ignored.

"Her tail seems to have recovered quite well again, ma'am, after being shaved!"

"That was this dog's great-grandmother!" Her tone had been a little too snappish again. She did not like his apparent and lavish affection for her dog, which was more than amply returned. The dog had no ability to recognize his utter lack of worth.

"Of course, it would be, wouldn't it?" He might almost have been enjoying himself at her obvious discomfort. He had known it was not the same dog, but seemingly could not resist another gentle rub. The dog did not wish to leave him alone, fawning over him outrageously until he stood up and then ignored her.

His godmother knew he would be the same with other females too. As he had done! Even by his own admission concerning that most recent affair that she knew of! Pay them outrageous personal attention as he had, and then leave them to suffer the consequences in the hands of others. As he already had with her niece and then that other one, the Chisholm female, and now Constanza! Who else might there be, whether in London or abroad? She would make contact with more of her friends in the city and find out what she could of that. There would be nothing hidden for very long. Rakes like him left a trail that would be easy to follow. He seemed to be picking up exactly where he had left off!

"So why did you send for me, ma'am?" He was growing impatient with the sniping and hoped to provoke her to disclose her real reason for wishing to see him, wondering if she dared to bring up the Trevelyan name.

"I wanted to see you for some inexplicable reason that escapes me at this moment." She regretted it already, which was clear by her generally curt manner and her expression. He had not changed one wit over the years! "Nothing strange about that! I try to follow the course of all of my godchildren, and you are the only male among them." *Thank God!* "However, it is almost sixteen years, I believe, since I last saw you!" She sighed. "One hopes for improvement, but in some things, there will inevitably be disappointment!" She still regarded him as a lost cause. "I seem to remember you as an ill-behaved child, and I wanted to see how the man had turned out and improved," her voice hardened slightly, " . . . or worsened!"

He smiled easily at her. "Still ill-behaved, but worse likely." She undoubtedly agreed with that! "Certainly, I am more outspoken, so I will need to ask your forgiveness for that. I probably never could improve nearly well enough to suit even my *least* severe critics." He smiled at her again. He obviously regarded her as one of the other kind.

She raised her spectacles once more and scrutinized him more closely, wondering what she could have missed to comment upon.

"No, ma'am, no horns and tail yet. Just a matter of time though!"

She dropped her spectacles into her lap. She did not like his easy flippancy.

"I believe I still have most of my body parts too, despite several attempts to part me from some of them. Unlike my father. The navy is not kind to a man in time of war. Society is generally not either, it seems, even in times of peace." He was referring to his own history, obviously.

He had given her a small opening. "Society usually deals quite well with those who go against it and, in her own ways, sometimes not at all kindly but always deservedly." She had a barely perceptible angry inflexion to her voice. "But you were not in the navy! Your father wanted you to be, however. It might have made a man out of you!"

"Ouch!" He smiled at that attempted barb. He had her measure and knew how to deal with her. "Yes, he did, didn't he? I did not deliberately disoblige him. I had a desire to see more of the continent from the land side of things once Nelson put paid to the enemy's ambitions at sea. I also discovered that I preferred the chance of mixing in a more comfortable and genteel society, however rare that might happen, than I was ever likely to find on board a ship. I've lived too long cooped up on board ships and needed a change."

She knew he was gauged to be a good sailor and would probably have made his mark in the navy. "At least you did not turn out to be foppish or a dandy going the route that you went. I see you rode in on horseback alone, followed by that other. A foal?"

"No, ma'am. A mule. My packhorse." He decided that he had spent more than enough time with his godmother. It had been a waste of time to be sidetracked as he had been, and he would bring it all to a close and be gone as soon as he might to find more congenial surroundings.

"But I believe I can set your mind at ease, ma'am. I am neither married as seems to have been feared, not to Constanza nor anyone else. At least I don't think that I am!" He had to think about that for a moment. "Nor am I encumbered in other ways at this moment with any other female, but it is difficult to recollect some of the things one did." He seemed a little unsure of that. "Nor do I have children—that I acknowledge or know of, if that is what you mean—littering my path, though others seemed to expect or believe that there might be for some reason!" He looked at her with a smile on his face, perhaps challenging her to bring up that other. She didn't. "I was most careful to escape those lures and snares of social intrigue, but then, after a while, it all becomes so commonplace and boring once the fighting ended. So I decided to return home and try to find a more challenging and exciting existence."

There were some further lengthy moments of silence. The ball was in his godmother's court.

"You caused your mother a good deal of anguish, and your father too, with all of your violent exploits before ever you went to war! Set society quite on its ear for a while! Your sister has good things to say about you though!"

"Yes. No doubt." She had always risen to his defense for what little good had been achieved. "Most foolish of her to swim against the tide of studied opinion like that!

I must ask her to tone down her praise of me to create the wrong impression as she undoubtedly does."

"So when might we expect your mother to return from Bath? Surely you know that?"

"Perhaps never, ma'am! Her man told me that even in my absence, I had caused her enough nervous indisposition, so she felt she had to go. And it seemed to grow stronger in her, the closer I got to England. I shudder to think what it will be like when she returns and finally meets me face to face and in the flesh again and undoubtedly hears all of the new gossip and rumors that appear to have begun already. She may find herself completely prostrated!"

He had wandered over to the mantelpiece to warm his hands by the fire before he left and was admiring the large painting of a battle at sea. He still seemed far more relaxed than she liked. He shivered gently. "Someone wandering over my grave somewhere! I had forgotten how cold and inhospitable England can be, but it is nonetheless comforting in some small degree to find that it is just as I left it and remembered it."

She corrected him. "It is not cold or inhospitable to those who respect her rules!" She had spoken snappishly yet again and had given rein to her feelings once more, without intending to, for his complete ease with everything rubbed her the wrong way.

He did not argue.

She made an effort to recover and changed the topic of conversation to the painting he seemed to be admiring. "It is most impressive, isn't it? His lordship's favorite."

"Very detailed and most cleverly done. How do they manage to make it look so real, with the waves and the smoke from cannons, all frozen in time? Yes, I do like it."

He backed away from the fire, beginning to feel the heat through his clothing, and sat beside the fire.

The servant refilled his cup, and this time, he did accept cake and biscuits. The dog did not seem any the worse for having eaten a little, but snuggled at his feet. He nibbled at them and dropped an occasional small piece that was much appreciated by the dog, if not his godmother, who decided to say nothing about it. Better to stick with the present topic.

"My father and yours were both in the navy. Yours collected ships models and other memorabilia for his failing years. I think it was far safer than toying in the muslin line and less expensive too. Mine collected paintings and would have liked to have collected more personal things to surround himself with." She was undoubtedly referring to the incomparable Flori female that his uncle had inherited by default. His uncle might do worse than marry her from what he had heard of her.

"They are all through the house."

"I had not realized Lord Seymour was in the navy, ma'am!"

"No, of course not. How could you know? He served before your father's time but still managed to outlive him. I expect you will manage your own estates now that your father is dead, and take your place in society once more if you can settle down and get rid of whatever strange notions being abroad filled you with, and those other of your views about marriage and about ladies."

"Yes. I believe it is expected of me. Good God! Am I agreeing with you, ma'am? Yes, I am! But I expect it will all seem so very flat for a while." He probably had not had time to consider what he would do.

"You probably can't wait to get into the various establishments, perhaps even the clubs and gamble it all away and make a general stir with the ladies again. I should warn you, however, that the clubs are quite particular over whom they welcome these days."

She was back to baiting him again, seeking some other chinks in his armor.

"I would hope so from what I hear! But then I am not surprised after they welcomed some 'respectable' women into their inner sanctums and found that their respectability was barely skin deep, if that. Still, one searches for a husband using whatever talents and wiles one has, and the clubs are a fruitful source of frustrated husbands and would-be puppet masters. However, I find that I am particular over the quality of the society that I keep most of the time, though I do make exceptions," he stared at her as he said that, "So it is not all one-sided."

She did not believe that, except in a possibly negative sense. The clubs would be too slow for him!

"Though, as I do not gamble, I shall have to run through my inheritance in some other way. Nor do I feel any urge to frequent the other establishments of ill repute as seems to be generally expected of a returning soldier with my questionable pedigree. My father limited my allowance quite severely to ensure that I did none of those things that are the usual downfall of undiscriminating young men, and so I did other things left to me to cause my downfall instead. Gambling, orgies, and whoring may have been far safer than what I encountered." He continued before she might take exception to his outspokenness again. "I have no intention of joining any clubs, nor even London society. I saw enough of it in my last year in England to decide that we had little in common with each other. Too violent by far!"

That caught her attention. It was a case of the pot calling the kettle black.

"I believe I shall rusticate! In any case, I was safer abroad than at home, despite our violent little disagreement with the French. I seem to have survived so far! I am not so sure I will survive English society after that, considering the reception that I have had since landing!"

Could that have been another barb aimed her way? She decided to let it slide. "You should not shun society! But I should warn you that society has a long memory for some things and may decide to shun *you*! Though it may well have forgotten you, if it ever knew you at all, for you were only at the fringes of it if I recall. It does not tend to take much note of wild twenty-year-olds, even ones that behaved as badly as you did, so you may not be entirely obstructed as you undoubtedly deserve."

He would be obstructed if she had her way.

She continued in the same aggravating way. "You seem to have very little to say after being away for five years other than to disagree with most of what I might have said. I also seem to have led most of the conversation except for a few rather startling interludes."

"My naturally awkward disposition, ma'am! But I thought I was being uncharacteristically garrulous! For me anyway, for I did try to enliven the conversation, as seems to have been expected of me and to keep it alive. But I always preferred to listen more than to speak. Why, I think I have spoken more English in the last ten minutes than I spoke for the last two years I was in Spain and France."

He dropped the final piece of cake for the dog. "My mother described me as taciturn, though others said uncommunicative or moody or ill-mannered when I ignored them. Others thought I did not have the wit to converse rationally. They were all right about me, depending upon my mood or theirs! But then, ma'am, I am here at your request, to be looked over and critically evaluated and undoubtedly found to be wanting in some way. I do not think that you invited me to have me speak so much about nothing in particular, which I thought I had done at length, as to have me listen to what you may have to say to me since we last met. Did you find out what you expected to find out?"

He was most relaxed and confident of himself and seemed to be playing with her. There was a gentle smile, almost a smirk on his face. Perhaps that was his usual expression!

"I think I found out what I needed to know!"

"I'm sure you did!" She liked none of it as he could tell from her face and general attitude. He didn't care what she might think. "There! I am so shallow I can be read in a matter of minutes." He smiled at her.

"Why do *you* think I sent for you?"

Did she hope to provoke him into mentioning the Trevelyan name, where *she* could not? "Perhaps to assess me in some way or for some purpose known only to yourself? To note my weaknesses, my deficiencies in dress and character, to take me down a peg or two—as you did, I think!" she hadn't been able to do any such thing, though she had tried. "To throw me into disarray with your legendary rapier wit and sarcasm. To throw my various and legendary indiscretions at my head, as well as to exercise your dreaded outspokenness in general, that has London society scurrying for cover as you approach! I doubt that it was to give me the thrashing you promised me eighteen years ago or to skin me alive, as I think I also overheard, but I cannot be sure. Perhaps to throw that Constanza affair at my head? Or was there some other indiscretion that you had in mind? Did I cover most of them? Was there anything else you wished to roast me about, ma'am?"

He interpreted the offended look on her face and waited for her to throw the Trevelyan name at his head. He had tried to invite it. She didn't! He continued, "Yes. I incurred a great deal of displeasure of my parents and others too. You are right, ma'am; impudence was another of my many faults, as well as a similar outspokenness to match your own, so you will have to excuse me if I seemed a little too brusque, but then I took my lead from you, didn't I?" She seemed tongue-tied herself as he rambled on. "I regard myself as assertive, whereas others maintained that my manner was not so much assertive or outspoken, as both abrasive and rude. But then I did not think about why you may have sent for me, ma'am. Nonetheless, like you, I was curious. I am pleased to have been able to make your acquaintance again."

She doubted that.

"I shall also beg your leave and depart, ma'am. I have some little distance to go still, and I find I am in need of somewhat warmer, more friendly and familiar surroundings to relax in!"

Having fulfilled what he felt might be an obligation to her by meeting with her, he bowed to her gently, turned to the door, picked up his little gun which he dropped back into his pocket, smiled at Maltby, and saw himself out of the house.

His horse and its companion mule were awaiting him, as he had given instructions to water them, but not too much, and to give the charger only a little grain, and the mule, fresh hay only, as he would not be staying above half an hour. He regretted staying even that long!

He rode away with much on his mind and even feeling a little down as well as angry with his godmother and with himself for rising to her bait. His reception in England so far, had been less than he had desired but probably no better than he might expect. He was likely to be burdened by too many reminders of his past history, no matter what he did or where he went.

They all had memories that were too damned long about events they knew little about. He found he was longing for company that might be more in tune with his own feelings. His sister would have uplifted his spirits, but she had not been in London. His cousin would be another. With any luck, he would find both Elizabeth and George waiting for him to give him some reason to feel comfortable again.

After he had gone and she had seen him ride off, Lady Seymour gave vent to her spleen.

"He was impudent! Insolent! Disrespectful! Unfeeling! Awkward! And ill-mannered, except that he seemed to try to turn every situation I threw at his head to his advantage! There was also that infamous admission about that woman . . . that . . . that . . . Constanza! What did he mean by that last set of remarks? I was hospitable enough! There were two other similar comments at least that I noted."

Her butler felt it wiser not to answer that question or point out her own numerous attempts to put him down, but let her go on. She would settle down eventually and might then hear other viewpoints. He found he rather liked Major Devane!

Chapter III

Revenge Bites Back Hard as It Often Will!

William was smiling grimly with much on his mind as he rode off from his godmother's house. He realized he had been particularly stupid to have ignored his uncle's advice as well as that of his sister in her letter, for they had both recommended to avoid Lady Seymour and certainly not to respond to her request that he should be sure to visit at his earliest opportunity after landing.

His godmother would probably agonize and fume over what he had said to her of his views on many things and what he had not said. Unfortunately, he had not been as guarded in his words as he might have been, for she had deliberately set out to annoy him. It was quite a pity that she would choose to get the wrong impression, though every word had been the truth although designed to mislead her. Especially about the fair and fast Constanza. She had started noticeably when he had unexpectedly expanded upon that particular topic, rather than to try and sweep it all aside or ignore it. He smiled grimly. If she tried to make trouble for him there, it would come back and bite her hard. After that, she may have choked upon daring to raise the Trevelyan name into the conversation.

She could think of him what she would. He did not particularly care. He was resolved not to be touched by anything she might do or say or think. But she had a stranglehold on segments of her society and could get away with almost any invention she might make to discredit anyone.

He was so immersed in thought, he missed the signs that his horse gave of others approaching until they were upon him and a shot was fired, missing him, but not by much. He noticed two men.

There was nothing slow about his reactions, however. His instincts from his recent experiences in war served him well, and he turned his horse and charged his attackers as the first man tried hastily, and clumsily, to bring up a second pistol to fire at him and was somewhat unnerved by the unexpected response as the horse and rider were bearing down upon him so fast.

With the assailants' horses moving nervously from the unexpected noise, his attackers were unsteady in their seats. The second man had never even raised his gun to fire but had dropped it, unused to such a weapon it seemed, and was struggling with what seemed to be a strange and unruly horse under him, scared by the gunshot and determined to get rid of its rider and to run.

William's own horse had no such problem, however, being used to such activity and such loud noises; and he had a steady seat to bear down upon his first attacker. As they came abreast, he launched himself at the man in front of him who was struggling with his second pistol. With his hand on the man's throat and the other on his gun arm at the wrist, his momentum carried them both off their horses to the ground as the second gun discharged. They both fell heavily into the milling feet of the horses but with his attacker beneath him and receiving the worst of the fall from his bone-jarring encounter with the ground. The man did not move, and there was blood beginning to ooze from his nose and mouth as he coughed and fought for breath. There was a look of horror and terror on his face. The horses began to calm and wander nervously off from the men on the ground, now that their moment of extreme panic was gone.

The second attacker was lying almost as still as the first, with the wind knocked out of him and seemed to be momentarily unconscious.

William regained his feet and checked that he had not been shot and was relieved to see that his horse was unmarked by any injury. There was a powder burn on his coat sleeve but no other damage to be seen. He picked up both pistols that he could see from the ground and put them to one side, wary that either man might be able to produce another.

He must have angered his godmother over the years, far worse than he thought might be possible if she was intent on engaging in such desperate measures to see him stopped, but then he had provoked her outrageously, and had done so deliberately.

His first attacker was helpless, unable to move, gasping to draw breath, and from the look of him had sustained more serious injury than a broken bone or two that one might have expected from a fall. The horses were still excited and somewhat restless from what had unfolded, but were soon calmed. His own horse stood there with the mule, calmly grazing off to one side of the road. They had become well used to gunshots over the years. He secured the second man's horse, which was still fidgeting nervously, ready to take off.

The injured man that he had knocked from his horse was watching him with a growing fear in his eyes that William had seen many times. There was far more blood than might be expected from such a fall, and he could see that a sharp upended piece of slate that was used to mark some position on the side of the road was now obliterated by blood. The edge of the rock had sliced into his neck as he had fallen, and blood was steadily pumping from the wound. He clearly did not have long to live.

William recognized him. "Julius, you young fool! Why could you not have got to know me even a little before you decided to be revenged like this? You and your brother were too hot tempered and impetuous by far, and it has now brought you to death's door like it did him!"

His former assailant said nothing, but his head slowly rolled to one side as he expired. It was unlikely he had heard William's comments, considering the look of absolute fear on his face, knowing that his last few seconds were here. Nothing focused the brain so well as feeling the certainty of death creeping over you.

There was nothing William could have done. Maxton had brought it upon himself. "Damn the man!" Less than one day ashore and already met by one violent problem after another!

He turned to the second man, recovering now, and noticed that it was the man "Sharkey" from the dockside—the man who had tried to steal his saddle. The man was now sitting up and taking note of the change of circumstances and a little the worse for wear and groggy.

William was forced to revisit his first and fortunately mistaken impression that he had considered what had just happened might have been a plot of his godmother. She was probably capable of it or was surrounded by those who were, but these were other enemies.

He spoke impatiently to the man. "Why am I not surprised to find you in his company?"

The man on the ground swore at his predicament. There was a distinct accent to be heard.

"French?" William asked.

"Oui! Yes. French." The man glowered at him defiantly, uncertain what to expect but sure that death could not be too far off for him too.

"And what were you doing with this blackguard? Is he a friend of yours?"

The man he addressed was angry with himself for his failure. "Helping him to kill you of course! We would have succeeded but for this ill-trained horse!" He scowled at him and looked at the body against the rock. "So you are a double murderer now as well as a horse thief! I almost had my saddle back at the docks."

"The fall killed him! Though I did cause that to happen to protect myself! But your saddle?" William was puzzled. "Explain!"

"My master's saddle! It is embossed with his family crest—Desrosier. That is also his horse!" He stared over to the animal, noting how well-looked-after it seemed, for he had not seen it closely while it had been on the deck of the ship. "I vowed I would meet the man who murdered him and took them from him and kill him myself. I knew he was an Englishman, for my master told me so as he died in my arms. But it appears it is not to be."

"There are many Englishmen, monsieur. What makes you think I killed your master?"

He gestured impatiently in frustration at this stupid Englishman. "You have his horse!"

It was clear that protestations of innocence would be met with the same disdain from this man as from his own relatives, so he did not try. "His saddle too, it seems! So how did you know where to wait for me?"

"After you had shot at me and made me to return the saddle, I overheard you telling the man at the top of the building at the docks some of your business after you landed, and I heard your name—Devane—and I related it to this man to enlist his help." He looked at the body. "He had been waiting for some days for you to land, but he missed you when you actually did come in. He knew the countryside where I did not. He failed and died for his efforts. I also failed. So shoot me and have an end of it! I died when my master died!"

William pursed his lips and weighed up the man. "Even you seem to have built up a great anger with but one aim in mind, I think! Anger is a very destructive emotion, monsieur, for it most surely destroys those who harbor it, more than those it is directed against, as this man found out a little late; though his brothers pointed the way for him, having also died violent deaths. Those who live by the sword . . ."

The Frenchman scowled. He did not like this philosophizing Englishman. "A man who will not protect his property deserves none!"

"I *was* protecting my property and my life! But no, it is not to be. I shall not shoot you! You have come close enough to dying on three occasions today I would say, and I came close to being involved in two of those. I shall not have your blood on my hands in addition to that of this man. There has already been more than enough of that spilled already."

The man on the ground looked up in some surprise to be suddenly addressed so fluently in his own language, for his opponent had switched to French as though it were his first language. William continued, "I take no pleasure in killing anyone, not even one such as this." He gestured to the fallen body. "Not today anyway. But then, I did not steal either the horse or the saddle that you believe I did steal, so your intent might be forgivable, were it true."

The man on the ground did not believe him.

"However, I think I knew the man that did kill your master and stole it, and he was certainly not a Frenchman but even more English than I am and no friend of mine! I find I do not wish to kill you. He . . ." he pointed to the man on the ground, "was already another one too many. Your purpose might have been excusable, had it been justified. His was not. Your anger would have been better directed at him, not at me."

"I do not understand." He clambered unsteadily to his feet and wiped his clothing off where grass was clinging to them.

"He *is*—pardon, *was*—the last surviving son of a once moderately well-respected family. At one time, it was. I was forced to deal with his elder brother some years ago, fatally, and this one seems to have felt that killing me was the only honorable thing to do by way of revenge for that, no matter that five years and more have intervened.

"From events that I was unavoidably caught up in several years ago, there were two men, maybe three, who vowed to see me dead. Both Englishmen! I dealt with one many years ago—his brother—and I shot another one from the back of that horse . . ." he nodded toward the charger he had been riding, "as he was about to kill me. I inherited his horse and belongings in the midst of battle by that move, but the only thing of value was the horse, the saddle, and his pistol that I still carry!

"This man . . ." he stirred the dead man's feet with his own, "the third of those—though there may be more still after my blood—is Julius Maxton. The last of that family's offspring, except for daughters. Three sons dead now, and I was responsible for the deaths of two of them, including this young fool! At least it will be laid at my door instead of his own. I think I saved your life, though I would rather not have killed him to have done it! His father will wish to be revenged upon me for this too, if he was not already fired with that desire."

"You saved my life?" The Frenchman did not believe that. "How can that be?"

William laughed cynically. "I see you do not know the Maxton family. *You* did not bring *him* along. *He* brought you along with *him* to help kill me and then for you to take the blame afterward. Two guns are more likely to be effective than one. But after I had been put away with, he would then have shot you and let anyone who came upon the scene assume that you had killed me and that I had managed to kill you before you could escape. He would have ridden off and no one the wiser. That family does not like to leave witnesses to their violent escapades!"

The man was pale. "He would have done that?"

"I believe so. He was too full of vengeful thoughts to be grateful to anyone that he might use to his own end. I do know the family very well, where you obviously do not!"

There was a dawning understanding in the man's eyes as he looked from the man on the ground to the man he would have happily killed. He remembered what he had seen in the man's abrasive manner and dismissive attitude when he had first approached him to give him news of Major Devane. "Yes. He would have shot me! Why did I not see that?"

"You were blinded by your own anger and thoughts of revenge, I expect. As he was."

"Yes. I was!"

William looked at him, seeing the change in his attitude. "Do you still wish to kill me, Monsieur Sharkey?"

"No, monsieur." He was stroking the horse's neck and receiving some affection from the horse in return. The horse remembered him! "My reason is no more, and he is well-looked-after. I am no longer angry, except with myself at being so stupid and being used in that way. But who was the man you shot off my master's horse? I should know his name so that I might see that all is brought to an end, if I can."

"Trencham! The late . . ." he clarified his comment, "the *dead*, right honorable, Viscount Trencham!"

"Right honorable?" The Frenchman snorted in contempt at that thought. "I do not think so! He was a coward, for my master was shot in the back. I would have done the same for you. That would have been bad, but it would have been justice, I thought! But I do not know him!"

"No? You were lucky there too! He was worse than any Maxton, as I had earlier found out to my own cost, for he almost cost me my life some years ago. He would not have hesitated to kill you, whereas I do not like to kill too readily. Fortunately, I did not hesitate *then* as I might have done, for I recognized him from long ago. He was far from being an honorable man.

"But, monsieur Sharkey, please do not repeat his name in England, for there are those who might wonder at you knowing him at all!" He gathered the horses together before they wandered too far. "Above all, do not couple it with mine if you do. I do not need more vengeful relatives hounding me down. He has too many, and all just like him! There might still be others out there that I do not know about. As you obviously know who I am, might I know who you really are, sir, since you wished to kill me? A man should know the names of all of those."

"My name is Charquis. Jean Charquis. I once served the Desrosier family. But I find I no longer wish to kill you, even if I had the means, for you have my pistol."

"Good! Charquis! Sharkey!" The name of the would-be thief that he had heard at the docks as he had arrived now began to make sense to him. "What of the horse and saddle? I shall be loathe to give them up. I still have some distance to go, and I would not choose to be aboard either of those two broken-down windsuckers or my mule."

The man flashed a glance at him. He seemed to know horses, at least a little, and had handled his own—his late master's horse—surprisingly well for an Englishman and much quicker than anyone might have expected.

"However, as I have grown attached to this horse and him to me, I am more than prepared to purchase this horse and saddle from you for a handsome price, if that will bring a lessening of your murderous intent and closure to this."

Monsieur Charquis looked strangely at this man who might have killed him and possessed them anyway and was now offering to pay him for them! He did not understand these English. At one moment, they could be so arrogant and stupid, and then at another, quite understanding and honorable too. But then this man seemed to be very French himself the way he spoke French, and in some ways better than he himself did, so that might explain it!

"I have no claim on them now, monsieur. There is none of the immediate family that I served alive now, not with the war and the terror earlier, at least none of the direct family, merely some distant relatives who do not know this horse or his horses. The Desrosier family, near Lyon. My master was famed across all of France and further for his horses. They know nothing of them. They will all be sold or eaten now, for there is much suffering and hunger in France at this time! It is a great shame! But you seemed to have gained this horse by killing a fellow Englishman, not one of the enemy! I would not choose to argue with such a man who kills his own countrymen. But why do I say this when that is what we civilized French have been doing to each other for many years now?"

"You are not my enemy, Monsieur Charquis. I am almost as French as you are. As I said, he was trying to kill me at the time. My war was not with the French. I have too many relatives still over the channel living there, even some near Lyon. I was at war with Napoleon's ambitions and wanted to stop him before he might have designs upon coming over here!"

"So you said, monsieur! But no, I had no patience with what was happening to France and other countries under Napoleon. We, and they, had been bled white to keep him supplied with food and horses and new recruits to die in his army—I lost a brother and a nephew—and for his ambition."

"Well then, Monsieur Charquis, in the interest of not leaving behind a scene that might upset ladies or casual travelers, let us get this body aboard his horse. The rain will soon wash the blood away. It is unlikely to bleed much more from the indication of what he has lost already, and I shall suggest—if you do not mind—that you will ride with it into London and turn it over to the authorities, if you know who they are."

Monsieur Charquis had looked startled and had gone a little pale at that insane suggestion. "I know who they are!" He glanced in disbelief at the man before him. "I think I would like to not do such a foolish thing with such a corpse as this! I am too obviously French, where you are not, and this body is of an Englishman! You English are at war with France! I doubt I would survive, if I was to be so stupid myself, for I have heard of your prisons and your strange code of justice with hanging a man to die a slow death from strangulation or having his head torn off. Napoleon, for all of his other failings, did at least give us a code of law that was better than what we had. We also have the guillotine! Most quick! In England, the authorities, as you call them, took enough of an interest in me as they do in all foreigners, especially the French at this time."

"As you wish. Yes I suppose it might be a little foolish of you to show up with the body of an Englishman, and you would have many questions to answer! They would likely not believe anything you said!"

The Frenchman looked at Mr. Devane as other thoughts went through his head. "Monsieur, as the horse was hired in a small village a little way from here, we could just let the horse find its own way back. They will see to him. His own horse threw a shoe and is also stabled there at this time. I would prefer to head for the coast and return home without the lengthy inquisition reserved for foreigners on this soil, especially a Frenchman who happens to encounter a body that he cannot explain—a body of an Englishman—and who might be too closely linked with it, for I was seen in his company in too many places now."

"Yes. You are undoubtedly correct! That is probably the wisest course of action."

The man looked relieved that his suggestion met with approval. They both cooperated in raising the body across the saddle without getting bloodied, and as they tied him down there, a small pouch fell from an inner pocket of his coat.

William picked it up, felt its weight, and tossed it across to the Frenchman who caught it, almost losing it to the ground in his surprise. "Gold coins, I expect. A small down payment for your horse and your trouble I think. It will get you back to France in some comfort. You deserve to be rewarded for your unfruitful efforts on his behalf that would most certainly have been fatal for you, had you succeeded. It almost was for you anyway had I responded as I might have done even just a few days ago, though I did intend only to scare you at the docks this morning."

"I was suitably scared, monsieur!" He had thought his last moment had come!

"Then, Monsieur Charquis, as Julius Maxton has no further use of it, you should take it. You will certainly need it more than I will. When you get a mile, a little over a kilometer, down this road, there is another that branches off to the East. Turn the other horse loose to head for his stable. You may need to slap him off or he may try to follow you, which I think might spoil your plans if you are discovered to have a horse following you with a body strapped over the saddle."

The man listened. He already knew all that but was loath to interrupt this surprisingly lenient gentleman.

"Take that other road. The coast is barely half an hour along from there, and you will easily find passage to France from the dock there. If not, then ask for a Mr. Stuart at the small inn there—the Swan—if he is still there. And tell him my name—Devane—that he should help you. He will see you get to France safely if one of my family suggests it. He will remember me well, I think. His wife is French, and he will treat you hospitably knowing you are unlikely to be a spy. If you choose, you can turn your own loose when you reach the top of the slight hill and can see the village."

He handed him the pistol he had dropped. "You may also need this in this land of blackguards, as I am rapidly discovering for myself."

"Thank you, monsieur. I am glad I did not take my—your saddle now and even more glad that I did not kill you, or I might also still be lying here and he the only one riding away. But then, perhaps he is, but to another place! Fate appears to have had a different ending for him as well as for me."

"Perhaps even for me, Monsieur Jean Charquis!" He smiled at him. "I am glad I did not kill you for the attempt either time! I have more than enough blood on my hands!"

They both of them rode their separate ways, each with an uncomfortable feeling that England was not quite as welcoming as they had hoped or expected. For William at least, it was proving to be even more violent and less predictable than the conflict he had just left. One expected to find violence with the enemy but not with one's own countrymen and relatives. Three unpleasant encounters in just one day! With a fourth just avoided, considering the earlier reception committee of Winthorpe's henchmen at the dock. At least in the Peninsula, he had known who the enemy was and where they were and what they would be counted upon to do. Here, he could not be sure about any of it!"

CHAPTER IV

The Elusive Cousin George! A Mistaken Identity?

William arrived at his cousin George's estate of Kellands an hour or so later to find that he had missed his sister by a few hours only, for she had already left for Brooklands, some distance to the North. Equally disappointing was the fact that he had also missed his cousin by only an hour, for he had taken off to the coast to take passage for France on one of his many trips over there to purchase horses and whatever else might catch his fancy. He began to wonder once more, if news of his arrival back in England, had encouraged an exodus of all of his nearest relatives from their usual haunts so that they might avoid him.

Nonetheless, he was made welcome by his cousin's butler, Henry, who recognized him and made him feel entirely at home.

He learned that his cousin was not expected back for at least a week or two, but Henry had been told to show William hospitality whenever he might arrive, for he had been expected for some time now.

After seeing his horses stabled and fed as well as groomed, he partook of a light supper and settled himself to begin a letter to his sister relating what had happened to him since he had landed just hours before. He also touched upon the unfortunate meeting with their godmother, Lady Seymour, and even a clumsy attempt on his life that had left one of his attackers dead, and all barely ten minutes after he had left her estate to ride to Kellands. So far, the omens surrounding his return to his native shore had not been good ones. He would give it to her tomorrow at Brooklands when he caught up with her unless he missed her again.

Later, he sat back with another glass of port wine and a book as he stared into the roaring fire. He began to feel welcome, warm, and more comfortable for the first time since arriving in England that same morning. He was prepared to be bored to tears for the next few weeks—and planned on enjoying it, provided more troubles did not descend upon him. He could return to the city at a later date, see his tailor and unearth some of his friends, see his mother when she returned from Bath, and get other business out of the way.

Some little time later, as he dozed in front of the fire, not noticing that his book had fallen to the floor, the servant interrupted his peace with the strange news that a messenger had just delivered a letter addressed to William Devane, Esq.

"A message?" He looked up in some surprise. "For me? Not for George? Are you sure, Henry?" He blinked away his confusion and sleep as he looked at the servant proffering a platter with a letter on it.

"Yes, sir."

"Thank you." He picked the message off the salver, read its direction, and turned it over. He saw no sign that it was from anyone he knew. "There cannot be more than two people in the whole of London who might know that I am here, and it did not come from either of them."

It was marked MOST URGENT in large letters. Everyone that he knew, was aware that his cousin answered to the name of George and not William once they had settled on how they would be identified to the world, for though his elder cousin had been christened William George and he had been George William, they discovered that they had not liked their first names so well and had exchanged them. The family had not objected, though occasionally there still was slight confusion in some of their more distant relatives.

He had never received more than two letters in any month even from his sister, and none from other relatives who regarded his extended absence with some relief, and then to not only receive several when he landed, but also to receive another and at his cousin's estate of all places, seemed unlikely. No one might know that he would be there. But then that might not be true either. Far too many people seemed to know much more about him than he was aware of, and having spoken with his sister's butler and his mother's and others too, none of his plans had been secret. Even Maxton had known where he might be waylaid!

A lot had happened behind his back and around him, and there had been too much going on concerning him even before he had arrived home. His acquaintances would know that he would be either at Mountjoy Street or most likely at Brooklands or on his way there rather than at Kellands. The news seemed to have been widely broadcast that the prodigal had returned and to lock up your daughters and valuables.

No. It was *not* meant for him! He preferred to believe that it was meant for his cousin. A slight mistake in intention. He easily persuaded himself that it was obviously meant for his cousin, though what trouble he was in, for a letter to be marked MOST URGENT, did not brook thinking about. It nagged at him. He sighed in resignation. There would be no rest nor peace until he had seen to it himself; no one else would or could with his cousin absent, and it might need a response or to be dealt with. Or it might really be for him. George would not mind, for his cousin would have done the same for him. He broke the seal and read the brief missive.

He looked first at the bottom to see who it was from. It was from an Eliza Barristow. Now where had he read or heard that name before? He could not recall, but it rang a bell, and it was indeed urgent, or so it seemed, from the language involved. He did not drop it on the tray for his cousin to deal with when he returned from France but decided that it appeared to be of such an urgency—if the lady was not prone to exaggeration and making a great deal out of nothing—that it perhaps could and should be dealt with sooner. It seemed to be somewhat stained and smeared here and there with water damage, for the ink had run out into the small lacunae. Could they be tear marks? The first few sentences were smeared this way, as those tears had fallen onto them after they had been written, whereas the later part of the letter avoided those same kind of spots and wrote around the damage. Yes, they were tears! He had better see what he might do. He re-read it.

> *Dear Mr. Devane,*
>
> *I realize that this will be most sudden for you to have to deal with. Please accept my apologies for disrupting your evening with you so soon returned from abroad. A great tragedy has suddenly befallen us, and I have no one else to turn to. Complete and utter ruin faces us! As time is of the essence, I beg that you set out for Underby at once and rescue us.*

"At once" was strongly underlined.

> *·I beseech you, sir, that you will not delay a moment longer. Soon after you receive this, my carriage will come by for you. Do not set out on your own, or you will likely be lost, and I fear that if you do not arrive tonight, that all will indeed be lost to all of us. I will tell you all when you arrive.*
>
> *Your most grateful,*
> *·Eliza Barristow*

He was not sure what to make of it. He did not know the lady! There were a lot of emotions seemingly in play as she had written this, if the damage were tears and not rain spattering. But it had been a fairly clear day, and the letter had been sealed. What understanding did she mean? What had George been up to?

His cousin might know enough to throw some light on the matter, but he was not here. The sly dog! He had given no hint of being in any difficulty about anything. But no matter, the situation had clearly become urgent in some way. Indeed, the lady—Eliza Barristow—was clearly in some difficult situation or felt herself to be, considering her desperate tone. How was he to deal with this? What had his cousin been up to in his absence? A carriage would soon be arriving, and by now his cousin was not likely to be found on this side of the channel, and there was an urgency that needed a cool head, presumably.

He could not ignore it and possibly create a greater problem for his cousin. They had occasionally changed places when it suited them both and responded to the other's name. Well, the evening had threatened to drag on, for he was restless. He no longer felt like reading, and there was no one to talk to with his sister gone off to Brooklands. He could have retired, but with so much on his mind after the visit with his godmother and the incident later, he doubted he would be able to sleep, although it seemed he had, for Henry had woken him up with that letter. He decided that he would respond to the plea for help, and his cousin might feel some obligation to return the favor when he arrived back.

As he had no idea where the Barristow estate—Underby Manor—was, he was not motivated to set out on what would undoubtedly be a fool's errand by himself, in hopes of meeting the promised carriage, and indeed was half inclined to not believe anything that seemed to be happening. He had the feeling that he should ignore it or, indeed, to run instead in the other direction.

He wondered if his cousin were not playing him some kind of prank or other, as he was noted for his little surprises meant to bring some life into a gathering or to startle someone from lassitude or complacency.

But how could George have got this lark prepared so soon? If it were a lark! George had not known that his cousin was to arrive on that particular evening, although he had been expected much earlier in the week, and the letter was from someone even further from London than he was. It was from a lady who expressed herself strangely and from the heart. Maybe it *had* been meant for him.

He tugged on the bell pull and spoke with the servant who responded quite promptly to its summons.

"Henry. What do you know of the Barristows?"

"I do not think I am familiar with that name, sir. Although . . ." he thought a little further "the name does seem familiar. But then Mr. Devane, your cousin, deals with so many families with his horses and other ventures. Oh! One moment, sir. There was some correspondence a month or more ago I believe, with a gentleman of that name. I think the letter is still on his desk, and I do not believe it was anything too private. I do know he had reached an understanding of some kind with Mr. Barristow. I got the impression it was to do with some horses, but he was a little secretive about it, as he usually is, until sometime after it is all finalized. I believe his business with that gentleman was concluded successfully, for I did not hear otherwise."

"Might I read it then?"

"Yes, sir. If it is still there."

They looked at the untidy desk in his cousin's study and then risked opening the drawers onto even worse disorganization but could not easily see it. They gave up.

No matter! It seemed that he might be of service to his cousin. Certainly there was nothing amiss that could come from him responding to the most urgent request and straighten it all out with Mrs. Barristow when he saw her and explain that his cousin was abroad for the moment.

Almost an hour later, a similar letter with considerably more detail from Mrs. Barristow was delivered to Lady Seymour by the same messenger on his way to London.

She uttered some choice words when she read it and immediately sat down again, tore up the brief letter she had begun earlier to that same friend, Eliza, concerning William Devane's visit and then started afresh with new purpose and urgency. "Damn the boy! Why would he be at Kellands, of all places, where he might most readily be found?"

She wrote in furious haste, oblivious to the frequent sputtering of the pen and smudging of ink. She had rehearsed so often in her mind what she had long intended to write, that her presentation of it was orderly and quite reasonable, if far too untidily written; but there was the need to get her thoughts down on paper and quickly. If possible, she would see her letter go out of the door that night and if not, then by first light in the morning!

"Oh, Eliza, my heart goes out to you and your girls! Now how best can I help you? Well, I can put paid to that one overreaching ambition of his mother – to see him respectably married—that I should have most strenuously objected to when I had the chance!"

She continued writing. "Letters! Letters! Letters! I have never written so many letters in the course of one day as I have on this day! But this must be stopped. Hopefully Eliza would not find William at Kellands! If she did not find him there, she might not waste time looking for him at Brooklands but might search further afield, even to London. Damn the boy! Why could he have not stayed away another five years or got himself firmly married to one of those foreign women as he should have done, perhaps even to that . . . that Constanza, rather than inflict himself again on English ladies and have saved us all from this. Better still, why could he not have got himself killed?"

Almost a half hour after he had read the message, William heard the sounds of a carriage in the driveway. When it came to a stop, he could then hear the sound of labored breathing and the fidgeting of the horses, which had obviously been pushed to their limit.

The driver asked but one question as both the butler and William approached. "Mr. William Devane, sir?" The horses were severely winded and flecked with foam. A stable hand was standing at their heads, holding them steady.

"Yes, that's me." He turned to the servant. "That's all right, Henry, I'll see to it!"

The driver of the carriage passed the back of his hand across his brow. He could not believe his luck. "What a relief to find you here, sir, or I'd have been tooling into London and around half the countryside looking for you, and I am needed back there! Mrs. Barristow had said that your sister felt reasonably sure that you would break your journey at Kellands rather than go on to Brooklands after you arrived! Mrs. Barristow also said I might change horses here to either go on or to return with you."

William gave a sign to the stable-hand at the horses' heads, who immediately set too, uncoupling the somewhat distressed animals from the carriage as their replacements were even then being put into harness in the stable.

Within ten minutes after seeing the concern of the driver, who was wondering why William was not, even then, ready to leave with him, William was astride his own horse and following the carriage off, as the steaming horses were being cooled off by walking around the yard before being stabled. The fresh horses were straining at the harness to be off, and the driver did not seem too inclined to try and stop them.

William began to think that a wiser course of action might have seen him heading back to London or on to Brooklands instead of following this apparently mad man, who did not care what kind of a scorching pace he set!

The light carriage, with fresh horses of his cousin's, bowled along at a ferocious clip. More than once, the carriage was running on two wheels. It seemed obvious that it was just a matter of time before the carriage would lose a wheel, break an axle, or even overturn, as the wheels bounced around in the deeply rutted road and seemed likely to throw the driver off his seat if it were not completely overset. He was driving as though pursued by all of the demons of hell at his back. It was to be hoped he hung on, and he seemed to; for if he was thrown and broke his neck, the chances were that those horses knew their way back only to Kellands and not to where the driver wanted to be. Fortunately, its weak lights, once it had become somewhat darker, were clearly visible; and the driver had been forced to slacken his pace a little or risk greater chance of upset, so William had not had to follow so close and to risk becoming generally spattered with the mud thrown up high by the wheels.

He would be splashed enough with mud from his own horse's hooves, but mostly just his boots, he hoped. The smaller animal, Pat, was able to keep up with the pace, as she had no burden on this occasion. He dared not leave the mule behind, or he would risk finding himself unseated when Boney, his horse, realized his companion was not following him; for they had been stable-mates for long enough now and would not be separated. William's portmanteau and other gear were undoubtedly being thrown around in the carriage bowling along ahead of them, but better *there*, than to be bounced off into the black of the hedgerow or into the muddy road from the back of his own horse or the mule.

Also, fortunately, there were no others on the road at that time of night, or there would certainly have been an accident on the narrow, dark, and tortuous road.

His conversation with the coachman had been brief and to the point as well as somewhat reassuring. The man spoke well of the Barristows between draughts of the beer he had thirstily gulped down as the horses had been replaced, and had conveyed a sense of urgency but would give no other details. He was obviously concerned over their plight and itched to be returning without delay.

Never having shied away from any adventure in the past, William was not about to do so now, but had been loath to part with his one means of escaping from a situation he was unsure about and did not like. He would ride his own horse and follow the coach. The coachman had not evinced any surprise at that or at the mule that was to keep up with them.

The letter from Mrs. Barristow had intrigued William. She expressed herself well, as a lady in a desperate situation might plead. He decided that if he could help her in any way, he would; for he had never refused the plea of any woman, even though responding to such pleas had twice led him into serious trouble, even of a life threatening nature. Again though, there was that nagging thought about who the intended recipient of the letter had been—himself or George?

He also wondered what kind of situation demanded such urgency and at such short notice. His cousin might not thank him for interfering, but with *him* likely to be out of the country for at least a week and possibly two, he could at least assess the situation and deal with it in the least damaging way.

Chapter V

Underby Manor.
A Promise made

William was relieved to see the carriage ahead of him slow down as the steaming horses were walked for a minute or so along a fairly narrow lane, overhung with trees, before they were turned into a broad driveway, dimly illuminated by the bright lights shining from most of the windows in the house.

These horses too, were labored in their breathing at the pace that had been demanded of them. His cousin would not thank him if they had been injured in any way by the exertion demanded of them on such poor roads by their reckless driver. If any of them had pulled a tendon or went lame after this, there would be some accounting to be made.

William was surprised to see that Underby Manor, the home of the Barristows, was not at all ramshackle, shabby, run down, or what he had begun to half expect and fear. The name had sounded dark, even sinister, and ominously depressing for some reason; though that came from himself, considering what had already happened to him that day. What possible good might come from this new twist and turn of events?

What little light there was to see by, thrown out by well-lit windows and smoky flambeaux lit in front of the house, perhaps in anticipation of his arrival, showed a very large and ancient rambling structure with blackened timbers in the usual half-timbered Tudor style, alternating with the external whiter covering of mortar between the timbers and showing up in brighter contrast, even in the darkness. It showed every sign of prosperity and being most well-looked-after despite its age. Perhaps in the more revealing and honest light of day, and to closer scrutiny, it might show its age and true character, much like certain ladies once they leave the protective and obscuring darker shadows that provided them with a kindly anonymity.

As Major Devane walked his horse up behind the carriage, there was activity behind the windows as the new sounds from the driveway intruded into the apparent upset of the house, though another carriage was preparing to leave even as he rode in. Fortunately they had not arrived a little later and encountered each other on the much narrower and tortuous road and in the dark. The doctor was even now just

47

leaving, and the light from the interior of the house flooded across the stone step out of the opening door as he left.

As the doctor's carriage drove off and as the one that had led William to where he now found himself was led around to the stables, the stable hand that had seen the doctor off, took his horse, which was breathing quite heavily at the exertion demanded of him. The mule was standing with heaving flanks, observing all, while recovering her wind too.

William gave instructions to the stable hand concerning the stabling arrangement of his horse and mule, letting him know that if he got it wrong, he faced the risk of having the stable demolished by the mule. His portmanteau, which had been in the carriage, had been promptly retrieved by a maidservant even as he had dismounted, and had preceded him into the house.

A lady of uncertain years and a little untidy in her appearance in the dim light outside of the door came forward to greet him and to make him welcome, and he barely noticed another servant removing the more obvious mud from his boots with a dampened cloth before he scraped off the bottom of his boots and then entered the house. The older lady had seemed a little surprised to see him, but obviously was much relieved to see him arrive the way she fussed over him. Perhaps she had not been so very certain that he might be at Kellands.

He met her with a sinking heart and began to wonder what his cousin might have inadvertently got him into, but did not utter what was in his mind. "Lord, what have I let myself in for now?" He had, some time earlier, regretted giving in to his sense of adventure and responding as he did. Whatever transpired after this could only be his own fault!

"I am relieved more than words can express that you have come, Mr. Devane, and not a moment too soon I fear!"

Her welcome was sincere! She seemed not to doubt who he might be. His arrival had seemingly lifted a great burden from her. No doubt he might feel the weight of it himself in short order, whatever it might be.

She looked at him, showing obvious gratitude shining from her moist eyes as she took his hand and was, for the moment, speechless. She wanted to say much more to him, but her tremulous voice showing her ill-concealed emotions would not allow her. Also evident, though fleeting, was her curiosity, despite her noticeable anxiety and fidgeting; for she had never met him before, to her knowledge, and he could not remember having met her. He rather surprised her for a moment with his steady intense eyes, adjusting to the higher level of light flooding from the hallway. He looked almost wild, but then he had been out of the country until just that morning (for so she had heard) and would have had had little time to settle himself anywhere; and he had not had an easy time either abroad, or in getting here, for Underby was well off the beaten track.

"Please do come in. I must ask you to excuse our disorganization and the mess at this time." She noticed that he had to bend a little to avoid bumping his head in the low doorway but did not seem to notice his still questionably clean boots or his rumpled clothing or untidily windswept hair.

"We have no time to stand on ceremony, sir, so I hope you will forgive us. Three years of planning and preparation and all to come to naught through some fateful accident." She sniffed and dabbed at her eyes with her apron as she struggled with an inner grief that threatened to burst forth but was held under tight control for the moment. Her apron showed disturbing signs of smudges of what could only be blood upon it, with similar marks upon her dress and cheeks, yet she herself did not seem to be the source of it. She had been crying for some time and trying to control it, and the effects on her face were obvious.

"Oh, what a turmoil to lay upon you! Such haste is most unseemly, I know, and for such an occasion too, and to be abhorred in every way; but fate deals with us in some cruel and unavoidable ways! Whoever would have thought that such a thing might happen as it did? I dare not give in to my female weaknesses here!" He knew that allusion to female weakness could be most misleading. Women—some women—were by far the stronger of the two sexes in the face of the worst upsets and emotional adversities.

Her mothering instincts caused her to reach up and to straighten his neck cloth a little, and to pull his coat a little more tidily on his frame, almost as though he were her own son. He did not resist, though he was a little amused, but not taken aback at her familiarity. His father's coat was of the highest quality, but it had been made for his father and not for him and still needed some minor changes that he had not had time to allow Mrs. Priddy to complete.

"There is much to be done before we may rest tonight, though there will be little of that I fear. I doubt there can be any consolation in knowing that she is relatively unknown to you; yet if there had been a better knowledge of each other, the hurt might be as hard for you to bear as it is to us, for she has been a good daughter and a more kind and helpful one to both her father and me would have been hard to find. Such a loss as we all face will be hard to endure."

It began to sound ominous! *She is relatively unknown to you.* What had cousin George been up to? He was relieved to find that he could not hear the protesting crying of any newborns, but the blood upon her apron was from either a new birth or . . . that alternative seemed the more palatable of the two at the moment!

She led him deeper into the large house, and he noted that the inside of it was as tasteful in every way as had been suggested by the outside and what little of the grounds he had seen in the dim light, though there was a hint of untidiness about it all. "Yes, Molly," she interrupted the maid in her surprise at seeing so large a man taking up so much room in the hallway. "Take that bag up to the bedroom we prepared, and make sure that the sheets are properly aired out and that there is an additional blanket. The nights have been none too warm of late."

She turned back to him. "I must offer you my hospitality for at least the night, sir, and hopefully for much longer if you can bear that thought. There is no way of you returning to Kellands this evening even if you were inclined to do so, with the rain starting again, and I am grateful beyond what words can express that you were able to set out so promptly. I was not sure where I might find you or if you could be persuaded to come if we did. All of the horses are exhausted and my servants, too, with the events of the day. But you will not find us wanting for hospitality, and after your ride there is some refreshment being laid out for you in the parlor while we prepare."

Prepare for what? he wondered.

She fussed restlessly. "Please forgive the disarray. Before this tragedy befell us, we had embarked upon some needed renovations. If only we had delayed another week!" She turned to the coachman, who had now appeared in the doorway. "Thomas. You know as well as anyone might, where to find Simpkins in the village. I know he returned from London, but I expected him here before now. I hope he did not get lost." She sounded a little exasperated as well as anxious. "Of all the times to take up a new position and not know his way about! He is aware that we would need him at some time this evening, and that time is now certainly come!"

"Yes, ma'am." The servant she had addressed as Thomas went off down the driveway at a brisk walk, unmindful of any fatigue he may have been feeling from his recent jaunts about the countryside and his miraculous survival driving that carriage as he had.

William's hostess was clearly laboring under an immense emotional burden and could not stay still for very long before she was giving instructions in other directions. She was younger than he had assumed. Her hair was a little unkempt and across her forehead where some strands of it had come adrift from a coil upon her head, but that was understandable. Her clothing was of a high quality, though bloodied, and she was gently spoken despite what seemed to be a desperate situation. The ruination she had hinted at was not to be seen in either her home or her own appearance, except for the blood stains, nor might be suggested in any obvious way considering the number of servants scurrying silently about the place, or the light that bathed everywhere from numerous candles.

"Unfortunately, sir, our loss is shortly about to become yours also, for you will be a widower all too soon and I, a widow!"

He was surprised but said nothing. A widower? He felt a sinking feeling spreading over him once more. He had not liked the sound of that!

It seemed that a wedding—his cousin's perhaps—had been planned! Now what was it George had said in one of his rare letters about being married to a French lady? He could not rightly remember his exact words. He could say nothing at the moment until he knew more, and now was not the time to bring forth any suggestion of the undoubted mistake that had been made, both with him and his cousin George. There were too many emotions in play already. But did they not know his cousin better than they seemed to and recognize that the man standing in the middle of the hallway was clearly not him? It did not sound promising.

He was not about to discuss or question the arrangement with such obvious tragedy hanging close by and risk greater upset to this lady, nor protest anything about what seemed to be a planned marriage, involving him at this particular moment, under such circumstances. At least not until he knew more. What had his cousin been up to? Perhaps he had known of this and decided he should be on the continent to avoid it all? A little reflection suggested that that was unlikely to be the case. George had a keen sense of humor, but it never involved such a tragedy as was becoming more obviously laid out by the minute.

It was far stranger than William might have initially assumed. What woman did it seem he was to marry with some haste? What circumstance made it all so urgent? How could it be that he would soon be a widower, unless . . . ?

He would let things move forward as they would, and observe and listen. It might never get to marriage at all if the circumstances were truly as desperate as they described. In truth, he would have rebelled and ran in the opposite direction at the thought of marrying any woman he had never seen, nor even had anything less than an extensive understanding of her character and ambitions, and certainly not so hastily even then, if at all. Yet it seemed that fate now ordained otherwise, for his horses had been put away, his luggage taken up to his room, wherever that was, and he was not sure that he could desert this distraught lady in her moment of sorrow and need, where she had been so overjoyed to see him arrive. He was trapped! He recalled his uncle's words about the Collishawe woman. But these were Barristows and not Collishawe. Scant relief there, however!

He resigned himself. He had encountered worse situations and had muddled through them before. Now was not the time to become difficult, though he *would* if the need were there.

"May I know what happened, ma'am, and what you intend, if you have time and can relate it? I am sorry that my cousin . . ."

Her mind was rushing along furiously for she did not realize she had cut him off as she did. "Aye, there is time to talk for the moment, but only briefly, and you need to know of the tragedy." She cast a glance at a young girl sitting in a chair in the parlor and staring out of the window into the dark and steered him away so that they would not be easily overheard by her.

She held him close by his arm. "Oh, sir, my husband and elder daughter were in a carriage accident this morning when it overturned upon them both some miles away." He felt her tremble and sensed her pain at that admission of events that had so devastated the entire family. He wanted to reach out and to comfort her but realized that he ought not do that with such emotions in play and with him a relative stranger.

"The doctor has been here all afternoon but was just called out to another accident and will be back when he can, or not. There is nothing more he can do here anyway and was merely giving us some comfort in his presence; impossible under these circumstances and with such a black outlook. He says that we can hold out no hope for either of them. The internal damage to them both is too great and the blood loss too, and my husband is not expected to regain consciousness!'

She raised her apron and wiped at her eyes as she recovered herself.

"My daughter . . ." her voice faltered, "has other injuries internal to her, and she is coughing and breathing blood and becoming weaker by the hour and is drifting in and out of consciousness. There is nothing of good news in anything that faces us at this time other than your arrival! I only dared leave their sides when I heard that you had arrived, and I must return to them and join my younger daughters who are sitting with them."

It was not the time to ask for assurances that he was the one she expected to be here or for any more than she had already told him.

There was the sound of movement on the stairs beside them. The lady looked up to see who might be coming down them.

"Annis! My second daughter, sir!" He watched as the daughter descended the stairs. Her mother took in the look on her face. "Good news is not to be expected in any of this either, I fear. I must go!" She quickly went over the stairs and mounted them.

That there was no good news to impart was obvious from the look upon the younger lady's drawn face as she slowly descended the staircase and then sat down on the stairs and buried her head in her hands as though burdened beyond belief. She raised her head and took her mother's hands as they met and comforted each other, but he could not hear the words that were exchanged. Their tenor was obvious. She had been crying as had her mother, and she still was, for he could see the glint of candlelight on tears as she moved her head.

She appeared to be no more than about twenty years of age; and though she had been crying and still was, she had a determined, if pale, look upon her face as she turned her head to look at him below her; and he found that her large dark eyes blinked away the tears and drilled into his own as though to lay bare and to read his very soul in that first moment of tragic meeting!

He decided at that moment that he had no need to rush off. In fact, he surprised himself by wondering at his complete lack of backbone and character to have even considered such a thing when surrounded by those who seemed so much to need his presence. He must see this through. There was much more to this than he could likely take in, in just the few moments since his arrival. Besides, it was dark and he knew nothing of where he actually was and had nowhere else to go, with Brooklands some way off.

His eyes had never left the young lady's face as she had stared at him. Then she turned to face her mother and spoke to her as her glance flickered occasionally over to him. It was clear that he was the subject of their exchange but that his presence might not sit easily with the daughter at this moment of tragedy.

He had the feeling that she resented him, his presence, and everything about him but could not know why; though with a little reflection, it soon became apparent. She was probably thinking why this unseemly haste? What was the purpose? Why now? Perhaps even, *why had he not appeared sooner?*

Why hadn't George mentioned any of this to him in any of his letters? Perhaps he had not known! But then his last letter from George had been some five months earlier, and too much can happen in five months!

They seemed not only to know something of him, but also to have expected him sooner. It was all most puzzling, as they clearly seemed to know little or nothing of his cousin nor of him.

Both ladies ascended the stairs with some alacrity, leaving him standing in the hall. He could not go wandering by himself and decided to wait.

Barely two minutes later, Mrs. Barristow came down the stairs again, her eyes a little brighter with purpose.

"Sir," Mrs. Barristow descended the stairs and approached him—"it seems that my husband has regained consciousness! We were able to let him know what happened and what we were doing even now. It seemed most confusing to him for a while, but I think he understands the gravity of his situation now, if he didn't earlier. I told him some of what I had been able to do before the doctor left and before he drifted off again, and now he requests to see *you* above all others and would not be put off, though how he knew you had arrived . . ." She did not dwell on what she did not understand. "He knows he has little time and insists that he would like to speak with you. Please wait while I go and see him again and prepare him a little. I shall not be long."

A servant led him into the small parlor and wiped at his boots once more and brushed off his clothing a little. He washed his hands in the bowl of water brought for him and then he sat down to a tankard of beer as he mulled over the events of the last few moments. The rest of his day since landing at the docks had slipped entirely from his mind.

He could hear sounds of activity from somewhere above his head. The girl sitting by the fire had her legs drawn up with her in the chair and was observing him with curiosity upon her pale and sad face. She was probably about six or seven years of age. She did not like being left out of everything as she must be, to protect her. She must be the youngest daughter perhaps. She seemed troubled by what was happening about her and could not have liked being left out of it.

"Hello." He decided that he should break the ice with her and try to take her mind off what would be difficult for one so young to deal with. She had been crying too, caught up in so much tragedy and about to see some of her family stripped away from her. It would be more than a child might easily deal with in the short term, and yet she would probably be more resilient than her elders.

"Hello," she responded. "Are you William? Mr. Devane?"

He was pleased to see that she was not shy. He smiled at her. "Yes. I am. Who might you be?"

"I am Sophia. I am the youngest, for so they keep reminding me. You are very suntanned! They will not let me see my father or Bella! Annis thought you would not come to such a hasty summons, as you had not appeared before now either, though you have been expected for years, I think. Mama thought that you might come if you got her letter in time. I think your arrival helped Mama a great deal, for she seemed unable to deal with any of it until she saw you step into the house."

"And why did Annis think I would not come?"

"I do not know! But you are not old, are you?"

"No, I am not doddering long-tooth old, though I am much older than you."

She digested that. "You are not fat and bald either."

"Not yet! Not the last time I checked in a mirror."

"I heard her say those things—that arranged marriages with strangers usually involved someone old, fat, and bald, often with bad teeth and bad breath, and usually unpleasant manners and mannerisms. She said it to Charlotte so that Mama did not overhear her. But I do not think they were talking of you. Your teeth look healthy. But she said *that* before any of this happened. But I also heard Mama say that she knows you to be a much better man than the vicious rumors of you might suggest, though she also said that she had never met you either. What are vicious rumors?"

"Your mother sounds most wise and probably too trusting." *What vicious rumors?* he wondered. *Already?*

She was not sidetracked by his comment. "Please, sir, what rumors are those, and why will they not let me see father or Bella?" She seemed close to tears. "Everyone seems to have forgotten me."

"Rumors are just another word for gossip! Usually untruthful and hurtful gossip!" He left his seat at the table and moved across to her as he knelt in front of her and held her hands as he looked up at her. "I think that they may be trying to protect you. They most certainly have not forgotten about you. If you were my sister, you would be impossible to forget! I do not know what rumors your mother referred to either. There are many floating around concerning me, few of them true, and I think you know that rumors are generally to be viewed with caution and should not easily be believed."

"Yes, sir, I know that."

A maid entered the small parlor bearing a tray and set the table for him. There was hot coffee and a hearty stew to assuage his hunger and a plate of fresh bread. He was not sure he should eat at a time like this in the midst of so much upset. There was nothing to dampen his appetite, however, though he was sorely aware of the mood of despair throughout the house and felt a little guilty that he might be able to eat or think of partaking of refreshment at such a time as this with others, even now, dying above his head and with the youngest girl watching him intently.

"Will you join me while I eat, and keep me company?"

"If you wish?"

"I wish! You can help me eat some of the bread and cake if you would like." He led her over to the table and brought out a chair for her so that she might sit with him.

It was not long before Mrs. Barristow appeared again, surprised to see her daughter eating a little with their guest as they chatted away. Sophia launched herself from the chair and held onto her leg.

"You can see him later Sophia, and Bella too. Be patient, my dear." She stroked her daughter's hair. "We have not forgotten you."

Sorely disappointed, she returned to her chair.

"I am sorry to interrupt your meal. But please, sir, follow me. We have little time for what must be done, and you may finish that off later." She led him out of the parlor so that Sophia would not hear her yet again. "He will not be put off, but we did tidy him up a little and clear some things away. He insists that he will speak to you alone." She put her hand on his arm as they were ready to mount the stairs. "Please, sir. He is very weak and has survived longer than was anticipated, but he always was a stubborn man, and I love him!" Her voice broke at the dreadful emotional burden she was carrying.

"I will try not to tax him nor upset him, ma'am, and I shall call you in if he seems to need you."

She sniffed and wiped away her tears. "Thank you." She led the way up the stairs and into the master bedroom, dimly lit and dark, except close by the bed.

Her husband lay propped up into a sitting position in a large bed in the middle of the floor with yet another young lady, clearly another daughter, sitting by him, this one about fifteen or sixteen years of age. She was also sad and tearful and loathe to leave her father in the company of a total stranger, a complete unknown to her. But her mother firmly indicated that she was to go and saw her out of the room as she closed the door behind them all, leaving him alone with Mr. Barristow.

William walked over to the bed and looked down upon the man. He had a very pale face, drawn with pain. A bottle of opium by the bed suggested that he was being medicated, though probably not heavily enough. His eyes were sharp and intense, fighting off death and holding onto consciousness.

"Closer!" He waved his finger.

William sat down and leaned over him. He was fighting to hold off that shadowy reaper, he knew lurked just beyond the light, inching ever closer and waiting to pounce on him. There was a film of drying blood in the corner of his mouth.

"I fear I do not have long to live. I do not know you, but I knew your father well, as a true friend, and your mother." He fought for breath and his eyes flickered over to a glass of water by the side.

William picked it up and held it for him to drink a little to wet his mouth as he gently supported his head. He recovered and seemed to brace himself to ensure that he did not falter or give out before he had completed his task.

"You know why you are here?" His voice seemed stronger.

"Yes, sir. I think so. To marry your eldest daughter if that is what is required. But . . ."

The dying man did not wait for him to finish but seemed to call upon an inner last reserve. "It is required! Urgently! This was not planned to unfold this way. I have nothing to give you by way of dowry other than a daughter, who despite what is said to me to spare me further anguish, may not survive. There will also be trouble!" He breathed more heavily at that thought. "Not a fitting dowry for anyone to shoulder in repayment for a kindness!" William was used to trouble. "But you will be doing me and this family a service we might never be able to repay. I won't be able to in any case. Dreadful way to do this I know . . . and completely flies against everything proper for you . . . and against everything that is desirable . . . cannot be avoided at this time."

He fought against the weakness that was creeping over him and desperately grasped William's hand to be sure he was still there, but he also seemed to be finding peace at last where there had been none until this gentleman had arrived. He rallied briefly. "I did not believe it might be accomplished so well and so soon, though almost too late. Though it is much to ask of any man, for she is a stranger to you, I know, though I love her dearly as I do all of them." He paused and swallowed hard. "I hoped it would not get to this stage so quickly and unexpectedly, but we are not masters of our own fate." He closed his eyes and breathed a few times and then opened them again. "What would not have been achieved better with another year or two?" He seemed to be losing his strength with each passing minute and was fighting to talk more than he should.

He drank a little more.

"I need you to remain here afterward, if you can." He seemed to be pleading, for he knew he could not force his will upon this gentleman sitting by him, known to him in so many ways it seemed, despite never having seen him and yet unknown in others. His eyes moved about the room closing in about him, taking in its closeness and familiarity that he would soon lose, but he was not yet finished.

"There are those who will try to overturn what we must do and put my family out and usurp this property, and I cannot stop them now, but you can and must. Violent men who have no respect for a woman unprotected by a man! I have no right to ask this of you, for you do not know me, though I feel I know you. I fear the consequences to those I love if you do not! Will you do that for me and for them, sir?"

"I will."

"Your word." He had to have it, it seemed.

"I give you my word as a Devane and the son of your friend. I shall not desert them. I shall protect them to the best of my ability."

"Thank you!" He seemed able to relax at last as he sank deeper into his pillows and closed his eyes for a moment. He opened them again as though ensuring that he had not imagined this man sitting beside the bed. "You will do! Like your father! We served together on the Hyperion many years ago now. A staunch friend! I needed to see you, to look into your eyes and know that you were just like him, for you are! If she lives you will do well together."

William would have liked to learn more, and how he had known his father, for he himself had never met this man nor even heard the name until today. But his father had indeed served on the Hyperion. There seemed to be no mistake. He accepted then, though he did not understand it, that the letter had truly been intended for him and not his cousin. It was all most strange. How had this got to this stage without him knowing anything about it? There had been vague references by his sister in her many letters, concerning various deliberations about him and marriage, but she had not mentioned any name that he could recall, probably recognizing that it would be premature, as well as ill-received.

The dying man sank back even more deeply into his pillows, seeking some physical relief that was not at hand for such a broken body, and pointed weakly to the door. The interview was over, and he wanted his family about him now for his final moments.

"I will get them, sir." William opened it and saw Mrs. Barristow and her daughters immediately enter. They must have overheard very little but had heard his footsteps approaching the door. They moved quickly over to the bed to provide comfort to the man lying there, and to be there for the last few moments of his existence, for he did not have long.

Mrs. Barristow turned to him. "Sir. Will you please send up my youngest daughter now? We should all be present at this time."

"Yes, ma'am." He returned to the parlor, aware that he should not assume that her words might include him.

"Sophia. They would like you to go up now to see your father."

She was out of the door and scrambling up the stairs as quickly as she might, skirts flying, even before he had finished speaking. "Papa!"

Now why had he promised what he had, and trapped himself? He knew well enough. A woman's agonized plea was burden and obligation enough, but a dying man's request must never be denied if it were possible to fulfill it!

He saw that as the youngest girl had fled from the room, a thick folder she had been going through had slipped to the floor and was spilling its contents. He noticed also that his plate of stew had been cleared away. It would have been cold anyway.

He picked the folder from the floor and set it in the embrasure that Sophia had been sitting in and saw that he should try to keep it together and not have it shed pieces of paper everywhere to perhaps waft into the fire.

He opened it and saw that it was a well-thumbed family record that many families often kept of their children and progress through the years. It was originally a large bound book of blank pages, but that the binding had not been well done and had come adrift, releasing the individual quires.

There were the records of all of the daughters, and drawings, very well executed drawings, of the children as they were growing from baby to infant and then to child and even young women for the elder three girls. There was a section for each, and in order, as they had been born. The first entries were of the young married couple themselves and were dated from late in the previous century, even as they newly married. There was a sketch of her husband as a younger man, and the features did bear a resemblance to the man dying upstairs. Clearly, Mrs. Barristow had kept the journal, for it was all as neat and as well-written as a young lady might do it, and the writing was as he remembered in her letter to Kellands. Besides, few men were such accomplished artists or had an eye for the minor and intriguing details that all women seemed to dwell upon, and that gave such a journal a personality and an existence.

The first entry for their daughters was for "Arabella Jane Barristow; December 6, 1791. Six pounds and five ounces, twenty-three inches. Bella. Light thin hair. Most difficult birth! Not sure she would ever appear, but then as the sun rose she practically delivered herself with much screaming after leaving me wondering why she made me work so hard for so many hours."

There were many similar entries tracing her sleeping habits. She had been a quiet baby and had grown well. There were several drawings of her on every page tracing her progress, her ills, her smile; with notes beneath them describing her christening, her first real words, her first steps, and various adventures and illnesses that all children seem to need to encounter as they grow, including falling downstairs, learning not to torment the cat—a lesson accompanied by some scratches—and that roses, for all their beauty, always have thorns.

After twenty or so pages, with the last few blank, there was the start of an entry for "David John Barristow, July 24, 1793. Our first son! Died a few minutes after birth! Devastating loss to us all!

On the next page was the entry for the second daughter; Annabel Mary Barristow, January 28, 1795. Annis. Eight pounds! Black hair, even at birth! Soon after she appeared, she startled us all by screaming loud enough to clear the attics of bats and let the neighbors know that I had delivered. A good sign. An easy birth despite her size. Colicky!

This was followed by similar notes of progress and drawings as there had been for the first daughter.

He tidied the loose papers away as he saw where they belonged.

They had lost only the one child. Their only son and heir. A major loss to them as to any family!

Charlotte and then Sophia had appeared later, with there being quite a few years between the last two daughters; for Charlotte was now sixteen, while Sophia was only six.

Chapter VI

A Contract Kept, an Untimely Bereavement

By the time Simpkins, the reverend new to the area, arrived somewhat out of breath at his exertion following Thomas, William was just finishing off a newly presented plate of hot stew and much of the bread. They waited in the parlor for the ladies to appear or at least give them some direction as to what was now expected of them.

William took the needed step of introducing himself to a man about his own age and found that he was not a complete stranger to the gentleman, for he seemed to know something of him and his family from other sources, and clearly not too much to his disadvantage. Once beyond the initial introductions and decrying the unfortunate turn of events that had brought them both to this house and at this time, they somehow put the existing circumstance to one side and launched into a quiet discussion of smuggling, much to William's surprise, for he had not raised the subject. The reverend seemed to know more of him than was desirable yet had not seemed disapproving of that illegal activity.

Within minutes, there was a steady procession of servants from the upstairs, which quite cut off their conversation, seeing the reverend fall quickly back into his expected role of sober and somber cleric. The last to appear was Mrs. Barristow herself, also a little breathless, carrying various items of clothing, some still stained with blood. She nervously bundled them into the ready hands of a servant without anything being said, though both were heavily choked up with emotion and futilely fighting back the tears that were evident.

She dried her eyes on her bloodstained smock and turned to her guest and the reverend. "Gentlemen—Mr. Devane, Reverend Simpkins—I see you have met, and I hope you have introduced yourselves to each other for we have no time to waste. You were able to obtain the special license, I hope, sir?"

"Yes, ma'am, I did. I explained the circumstances to my bishop not three hours ago, and he kindly supplied what we needed."

She sighed. "My husband is slipped off again now for the last time and will not live much longer I think, but we cannot yet mourn nor dwell upon that at this moment. He will soon be in good hands! Now we must see to the rest before that is too late.

Please follow me." She led the way up the narrow stairs again. The servants were aware now that the very large military-looking gentleman in the parlor, in company of the new vicar, was there to marry Miss Bella before she might die, but could not fully understand it at all and were not aware why it had to be done so hastily or why it had to be done at all with her on her death bed. There had been the occasional rumor that Bella was soon to be married but that her fiancée, who was not yet her fiancée—all very confusing—was abroad and in the war.

But *that* rumor had been bandied about for the last year or more and had gradually lost any credibility as it did not seem to be well known, for there were a string of other suitors who would not have either been easily tolerated nor would have been paying attendance had they known of any such *firm* engagement. She had been seen to turn off one of the local beaux after another, though gently and with consideration for their feelings. It began to seem that she might not marry at all, for it was very rare that the family ever went as far as Basildon, never mind London, which is where a young lady as beautiful as Bella should be able to find a suitable husband. It was also rumored that her intended had been killed abroad, though no one said anything of it to confirm it or deny it.

Mrs. Barristow turned before they got to the stop of the stairs and spoke as an afterthought to a servant in the doorway below. "If we need anything, Molly—though I doubt we will at this late stage—I will ring or send one of the girls. Thomas is sitting with Mr. Barristow and will alert us if he recovers consciousness again."

"Yes, mum."

She turned to William. "We should not waste further time, gentlemen. We have little enough of it as it is." She continued upstairs on suddenly heavily stressed and loudly complaining stairs with three adults upon them, and led the way into a nearby area of the house, where the floors sloped even more noticeably, and into a small room—they were all small and with low ceilings—brightly lit with candles, though the bed itself was in some measure of shade to protect the patient from the discomfort of too bright a light, even that from a candle.

It was obvious that Mrs. Barristow was exercising considerable discipline upon herself to stave off the growing sense of helplessness and overwhelming sadness and the need to see all of this brought to an acceptable if unfortunate end. Only then might she be able to remove herself from this painful reality and to dissolve into tears. But this was the wrong time and place. She was needed in another way that now demanded her full attention. She drew upon that inner strength that all women have in abundance when the situation is the most hopeless and they are needed in other directions.

The patient, a young lady, was awake and watching with conscious awareness of what was intended perhaps, as they entered her room. Her attentiveness was a good sign, if it were possible to believe that any good might exist in the midst of such pain and approaching finality. There was the untidiness and smell of a sick room, even overlaying the cloying smell of smoky candles. There was but one girl—probably another sister—administering to the needs and wiping the face and mouth of the young lady lying propped up in bed. There was blood upon the invalid's lips and blood leaking a little from her nostrils, and there was a bloody towel across the coverlet over her abdomen. A bloody basin and other soiled towels had been moved off to one side. Her injuries were obscured by the coverlet over her but were clearly most serious for there to be so much blood evident.

Her helper moved to join others in the shadows, out of the way of her mother and the two gentlemen who had entered the room.

William could see that there were dark lines under her eyes and the drawn look of pain across her face and in her expression—as there had been with her father—as she labored and breathed with difficulty while attempting to hold a cloth up to her face to avoid any blood being thrown about if she were to cough. There were other young ladies in the room—Sophia and the girl who had tended to her sister. That must be the third daughter—Charlotte. It was not difficult to see their resemblance to their sister and to their mother, and there may have been another—Annis—perhaps overcome by what was happening and behind the other two, but it was difficult to make out figures and faces in the shadows.

Their mother spoke. "Now, young man, William, we have come this far and need to complete this task, or all of this will become history around us, and we shall very likely lose . . ."—her voice caught—"but you need to hear none of that at this moment!"

Now was not the time to be asking for any kind of explanation of the circumstance. He almost regretted giving in to the impulse to see this adventure unfold, for it was clearly much more a tragedy than an adventure, but his difficulties with this were Lilliputian compared to theirs. It was obvious that he might indeed be a widower before morning. He might lose a wife he had never before met and knew nothing of, but they would lose a sister and a daughter as well as losing a father and husband. Now was not the time to ask questions and expect a rational answer nor to become difficult over the strange situation that was already tragic enough without it being added to. He had given his word, but even if he had not, it was not the time to shrink from what seemed to be needed!

The deep tragedy of the events that so clearly and painfully surrounded him reminded him too well of those similar situations that he had just quit on the battlefield. He had felt helpless *then*, and he felt helpless *now* to do anything but what was needed of him to ease the obvious pain of such a cruel loss—two of them—to this family of bereaved women. He suddenly felt a great loss himself, in that he had never met the young lady before this circumstance occurred, nor had had a chance to make her acquaintance. He suddenly felt that he would like to have known her, for beneath all of the pain her face was well shaped and in any other circumstance, perhaps even this one, would have been described as beautiful. There was clear intelligence in those bright eyes. She and he were but two ships that pass in the night, unknown, and who was to know with what unfulfilled promises aboard! What might have been possible in life with a slightly different course and a possibly different outcome to this?

The only obvious things to him in the dim candlelight were her long and loose dark hair, untidily framing a very pale face—still marked a little with blood that her sister had missed—and drawn with pain as her father's had been. She may have been his one true love if such a one existed. But all of that was nothing but the romantic dreams of foolish women who threw themselves headlong into seeking that *one* supposedly true love, which might not exist, yet his sister Elizabeth, seemed to have found hers. But for him, nothing could come of it now, even if she were that one special person! Nonetheless, he resolved that he would make an effort to find out more about her from her family when a better opportunity was presented, and time had had a chance to allow their grief to fade and their thoughts to be less tragic. Now was not the time to express reservations, caution, or to hold back from what was needed; but those thoughts never entered his head. It would have taken a poor specimen of manhood indeed to deny them this final completion to what seemingly must go forward without delay and for whatever reason.

Undoubtedly, they might just wish to see him gone as soon as maybe, after all of this, so it might be difficult to keep his promise to their father, but he would do as much along that direction as he was able until the problem might be resolved. To welcome a complete stranger into their home at the best of times was trial enough, but at a time such as this, with all of the other baggage going with it, it was unthinkably painful for everyone. But afterward? When the grief and sorrow could be given free rein and with him in the midst of it, both he and they might wish him long gone.

He might have reservations about what he was about to do, but it all paled into insignificance compared to what they were feeling. Besides, he would soon be free of it all, for from the looks of her she was not long for this world!

He seemed caught up in a dream and became aware that the reverend had opened his book and was droning on in some formal way as the young ladies gently sobbed and cried behind him as they held tightly onto each other for what little comfort and support they might find in each other's embrace. Her mother had a hand laid lightly on her dying daughter's shoulder as though to keep her in touch with this world she would soon be forced to leave. To lose one member of a family was traumatic enough, but to lose two at the same time was unthinkably devastating. The older girl holding Sophia close, appeared to be much more mature than the sixteen years of age that the record downstairs had indicated. With the responsibilities likely to drop on them all, they would all be changed in ways that no one should have to encounter at so young an age. They were all far too young to lose their father or a sister so close in age to themselves. Their mother stood rigid and pale beside them all, a link between the living and the dying, striving to hold her daughter in this world for as long as she might—the bulwark against all buffeting seas. She would be the strength that they would need now to move forward.

He had made his promise to their father and would provide whatever help they might allow him to provide and in whatever way was necessary moving forward. He had nothing else that needed his attention so very urgently that he needed to rush away to attend to his own affairs.

He noticed that the other daughter, Annis, was no longer with her sisters but had left the room as quietly as she may and without disruption of any kind, explaining her position behind her sisters earlier. She had seemed to not fully approve of this union from the little he had seen of her as she had looked at him. As the eldest girl now, or soon to be, she would likely be with her father at this moment, though perhaps from the look she had directed at him as she came down the stairs earlier, she may not have felt up to attending such a hasty and possibly ill-conceived wedding with one such as him. If they knew anything of him at all—and they seemed to—from what Sophia had let slip, she may have had cause to doubt the wisdom of even such a fleeting alliance. From the intensity of the glance she had directed at him, William had the feeling that Annis, may have known more of him than he might be comfortable with.

It seemed most peculiar to him, but the dreadful loss to all of them, so obviously surrounded by such tragedy, began to hit *him* hard also. It was a strange feeling and entirely foreign to him to commiserate with others so deeply. He had viewed death many times with only men about him, and that was sad enough, but he had remained detached from it out of necessity so that his judgment might not be impaired or slowed down—a reality of war, bottling away his feelings, his grief, his anger at the futility of war, even as the dying man, with stark fear in his eyes, had lain in his arms surrounded by relative strangers, and knowing that his last minutes on earth were now here.

Now, he could let go of all of that pent-up anger and frustrated anguish that had fermented in his own bosom, unexpressed, and bottled up for too many years. He had never seen it so poignantly or painfully displayed as within *this* tearful family of women and girls, who strove so hard and bravely to hold back their undoubted pain and emotions in the presence of strangers and with the formality of the ceremony, however abbreviated and simple it needed to be. He had seen many men die, friend and enemy alike, and felt some pity for them all, for they were all the sons of women like his own mother. They, unlike these ladies, lived with death every day they arose from their beds.

These gentle women by comparison, not caught up in war, could give in to pain and grief and tears in a way the others did not. This feeling was borne of love. The other had been used to stoke up anger. His heart went out to them all, especially the girls, at their intense and hard-felt grief and loss. Adults grew closer to death with age and recognized that they would one day need to deal with it. But not so suddenly nor tragically as this! He felt a lump rising in his own throat then, felt his lips start to tremble completely beyond his control, and had to blink back a tear himself at the wall of sudden and starkly-felt emotions surrounding him on all sides but did not entirely succeed as he felt first one and then another escape down his cheek. It was a most strange sensation. He had never been caught up in anything quite like this before, nor to such a degree in any of the previous five years. Such luxuries as sorrow and grief and gentle mourning had been foreign to him until now. *Then*, he had felt anger, pity, and frustration and had been caught up for a while in vengeful actions—coldly and calmly thought-through; pitiless, ruthless, and devastatingly effective, with no fear or consideration of death!

He noticed then, through the haze clouding his vision, that the young lady lying in the bed, dying, had fixed him with an intense stare, much like her father had, knowing death was near, and with a furrow across her pale brow. That brief moment of horrified clarity just before the end! She was fighting her own battles and demons. She seemed momentarily confused, and must wonder who he might be and why he might be here and even why he might be shedding tears, for was he not a stranger to them all and to her. Did she know what was happening even?

Then he feared for a moment that she was dead even before the knot had been tied, defeating all of their efforts. He began to feel cheated! A most strange response, considering his earlier feelings concerning a marriage he had had no warning of or desire to participate in. He was relieved then to see her blink, to see her glance lessen in intensity and flicker off to her mother and then to her sisters, who had their heads bowed and were keeping their own feelings under as much control as they could but with little success.

It seemed that all of the years of holding back any show of emotion as he had held one after another of his comrades as they died, was now suddenly let loose. How many of them? He had lost count over the years. He felt the tears coursing down his face and dripping to the floor and could do nothing about it.

She suffered a few moments of painful coughing as she held a towel over her mouth and then settled uneasily once more.

His heart went out to them all. He responded as he knew he must. He took her hand, sensing the feverish temperature and trembling and the weakness. He felt suddenly overpowered by the heat in the small room from numerous candles hurriedly moved off to the side before they had entered. He felt anxious to be out of it and heard his wife-to-be, haltingly, in a grating voice and with obvious difficulty, give her responses. She was conscious of what was happening and knew that her death was not far off—a feeling no one needs to be conscious of, though he had seen it often enough himself in the Peninsula as he had cradled one after another of his own dying comrades! He had tried to comfort them as they knew full-well that their last conscious moments on earth were also here before them and in some strange foreign field far from home with nothing he or they could do about it! So much to think about and say, but too little time to say anything before death removed all of their memories and heartaches and feelings and even most of their entire history as though they had never even lived.

His heart went out to her, where it had not been able to go out to even his own comrades in the heat of the moment and in the rush back to battle. He knew that his own end would eventually be the same. A brief pain from a saber cut or thrust, or a lead ball or flying pieces of wood or metal. Perhaps a fall from a horse. A helpless bed upon the grass, perhaps surrounded by others in the same state. Stony, angry faces of silent pity surrounding him and looking down upon him one last time before turning away. They were the faces of those who would follow him to the grave, and all too soon. Knowing it! This might be how they would end in a few hours, days, or not at all. Regrets? Would he be missed? By some, perhaps! Would anyone notice his passing? Too few! Fading consciousness—all enveloping and final death! Oblivion! There would be memories of him that might survive with others for a little time but not very far beyond that generation that entered the world with him. But by some trick of fate, he had survived, whereas better men, more deserving of life, had not! He was here to face the tragedy of death yet again!

From somewhere, rings were produced and according to custom he had encountered in his reading, he placed the one he was given, first a little way upon her thumb, then a little way upon her forefinger, then the same upon her second finger and then finally slid it fully upon her third finger. He omitted the religious words that usually accompanied that gentle custom, seeing the reverend suddenly looking at him with a puzzled look on his face. It slid on her ring finger easily and was clearly the property of others as it was too loose fitting—probably from either her mother or her father. He placed his hand close to hers. With difficulty, she attempted to slide the ring she had been given upon his ring finger, dropping it once into the coverlet from her weak fingers. He retrieved it for her, put it back into her hand, and then gently assisted her.

He listened as the reverend Simpkins pronounced them husband and wife and told him that he may now kiss the bride. Simpkins had hesitated briefly after that, feeling that it was perhaps inappropriate with the young lady's condition, but then realized that it could not matter now. It should be done to bring some formal finality to it all. William leaned over and placed a gentle kiss upon his wife's lips as she looked up at him and into his eyes with a sudden flush upon her face and then he placed another upon her forehead. There was a taste of blood, and salt from one of his own tears, albeit faint, in his mouth. She had flinched a little as he had unexpectedly kissed her. He hoped he had not caused her pain!

His bride's hand lay weakly on the coverlet, starkly pale on the darker fabric. He was then given a pen, dipped it into ink, and signed the register that the reverend offered to him, and then watched as his bride attempted to focus upon the page and tried clumsily to sign her name too. She fought to dredge up the strength to do so while he held the book for her to sign which she was able to do once she became focused upon it. Afterward, she relaxed back into the pillows. She could now die with the knowledge that she had somehow saved her family . . . but in what way and from what?

With that final act, as the quill dropped from her fingers, there was a sudden spatter of rain and leaves blown against the window, causing everyone to pause a little in wonderment. Her mother had looked up startled, and glanced toward the room next door where her husband lay with her other daughter in attendance, wondering if this might be some sign of his passing as his soul sought to escape. There was no sound from the other room of that daughter alerting them to anything untoward with a cry or other noise. The uneasiness soon passed. Wind was wind, and it had picked up, as a shower had moved through the area and had blown rain and leaves against the window as it had often done in the past. It was all natural, one did not need to seek spiritual meaning in any of it!

As their momentary alertness and bewilderment subsided, her mother and sisters sobbed in some relief at that moment as though a massive burden had been lifted from them, but it was nothing that he needed to be concerned about. The relief could almost be felt pervading the entire room. Mrs. Barristow lifted her head and silently thanked him with her eyes as the tears rolled down her cheeks. In another world not so far behind him, all of this would have fired him up to go out and to kill relentlessly, ruthlessly, without mercy, like the Berserks in all of their ancestry and without concern for his own safety, but there was nothing he might do here except fight back his sudden feelings and control his emotions lest he upset these women even more than they were.

"Charlotte! See the reverend has a glass of port or some other refreshment before he leaves, please. There are those who believe that those who are . . . a toast to their memory and to their life . . . to ease them on their way. Unless, sir, you are like your predecessor who abjured all forms of alcohol?"

The reverend cast a strange look at her and spoke gently. "I have no such strictures, ma'am, and I have no objection to those older customs or beliefs. They all serve a purpose that I shall not question. I will raise my glass as needed, but I should not stay longer. I have preparations to make for tomorrow." His predecessor, Reverend Coles, had no such feelings against imbibing alcohol either. He did not know how they had managed to obtain that impression of him, for the old vicar had a reputation of sometimes digging a little too deep into the wine and whatever else was offered.

"Of course."

Mrs. Barristow seemed now relaxed and to some small degree much more contented in all of her pain, having achieved her main goal of seeing her daughter married and, apparently, their future somehow secured.

"Charlotte, see that Mr. Devane, your sister's husband now . . ." she hesitated as she said that and her voice caught for a moment as she looked at him in gratitude " . . . goes to the living room or the parlor. The parlor is the more comfortable at the moment, and we shall join you shortly, sir. At least for a while."

Her voice dropped so that she might not be overheard by the young lady lying back on her deathbed. "I fear there is not long to go here. After that, Charlotte, you may return here and join Sophia and me, and we shall see to your father and sister and make their last moments as peaceful and comfortable as we may."

"Yes, Mama."

They had tied the knot with too little time remaining, for the news soon spread throughout the house that the elder daughter died not ten minutes later after slipping back into unconsciousness. Their father had died sometime during the brief ceremony that had seen his daughter married to a relative stranger! Perhaps his passing *had* caused his daughter at that moment to drop the ring she had been putting on his finger, and the suddenly gusting wind and rain had truly been a sign of some kind, of his passing.

Later that evening, it had been a tearful gathering in the parlor once all of the surviving sisters were there, following their preparations of their father and eldest sister. They seemed to need to do it themselves rather than have the servants involved in such deeply personal matters.

William felt immensely out of place—an interloper, a fraud in the midst of all of their outpourings of pain and grief and had been relieved to have excused himself and gone off to bed in some area of the house near where his dead bride and her dead father now lay. It would obviously be an uneasy and restless house all night. Sleep would come easily to no one. He would rather have been a hundred miles away than in this place at this very moment, but he could not desert them.

Chapter VII

Questions. An Enlightening Conversation with One Corpse, a Vigil Over Another

Indeed, he could not sleep! He tossed and turned fitfully, unable to find comfort in a strange bed; though he had slept in hammocks and on straw ticking, in stables, and on hay with less difficulty. Perhaps the bed was too comfortable considering where he had found sleep over most of the previous five years. Certainly the social setting was much different. The company of women, ladies, young ladies—and so close—he was not used to. Had he actually married one of them? Yes he had, and promptly seen her snatched from him too!

His thoughts were a jumble of confusion, trying to find some meaning in the fog of what had just transpired. It was too much to try and fathom how everything had so suddenly rolled along like a gigantic snowball, picking him up in its roll.

Was he really married one moment and then a widower the next? He was used to being caught up in a not easily escapable circumstance in battle, where he knew how to deal with what was happening, even the totally unexpected; for extreme violence and quick thinking usually would solve most problems with expedition. But not here in a family setting. War, even with all of its unexpected qualities, he understood clearly enough. This kind of intrigue and gentle inexorable maneuvering and dealing with heart-rending anguish and gentle feminine emotions could confuse, fog, and enmesh a man more firmly and securely than any ambush or becoming mired in a swamp; for it was subtle and had achieved its end before a man had time to think about what was happening or to back from it, if he might!

His head was feverishly going over the events of the last few hours, trying to make sense of it all. Had he been mistaken in the matter and could his cousin have been the intended groom? As far as Mrs. Barristow had known, they could be brothers with the same father. It might be easy to confuse him for his cousin, for they had shared the same father in so many ways, and there was a notable resemblance in facial features, if not in stature. Nothing he could do about any of that now, anyway. What was done, was done. Besides, the young lady would have been dead long before George might have been able to respond, considering where he was.

From what his sister had related to him in her letters, it had seemed that just such a fate had been planned for him by his mother; though from his guarded conversation with Lady Seymour, it seemed that her thoughts had not been along those lines at all, for she had obviously disapproved of him and found him to be lacking in every way as she always had. Perhaps he should not have led her along as he had done. It had been unwise to give her more ammunition to use against him! Too late now to change any of that, but now was not the time for any regrets either, though the Maxton death had been unfortunate and not intended. He found he really did not care what his godmother thought of him any more than he had as a child.

He wondered for a few brief moments if he had not been caught up in a devious and clever conspiracy hatched by his relatives to marry him off. Could Cousin George have been part of some plot and had known what would happen? A moment's consideration convinced him that no such conspiracy might also include the untimely deaths of two individuals. His cousin had known none of this; everything had been tragic and unexpected!

He had seen gratitude and relief in the face of Mr. Barristow, looking his last upon the world and the faces he loved, and true anguish and grief in their faces. He had married a woman that had been on her deathbed with blood leaking from her mouth and nostrils. These were good people whose world as they had known it had come to an end—losing a husband, father, sister, and daughter.

He had learned of his fellow man the hard way and had rapidly learned who it was that one could trust and believe and who not. Perceptions were misleading and rarely told the entire story. They had been hard lessons at first, for he had been as green as grass. Mrs. Barristow was a true lady, with never a mean thought, unkind word, nor devious plot in her formidable womanly arsenal. He would trust that perception at least.

But his godmother was not one he might trust other than to serve him ill if she could! That again! There had been that about her that made him a little uncomfortable as they had met. She had seemed to set out to provoke him for some reason and get under his skin and loosen him up, having got him there on false pretenses, and had tried to read more of his character and about him than perhaps he should feel comfortable about.

What had he got caught up in?

Less than a day ashore after a five-year absence, and already he had seen three people die or had been soon to die, all in his presence. Not only that, but he had also married and was a widower, all within ten minutes. He had seen more of life unfold in a day than most might see in a lifetime! What curse had he brought back with him? Further, he had too easily promised enough to a dying man to ensure he might never get to Brooklands before the month was out, or back to London as he had intended.

As the hours unfolded, he heard the others retire reluctantly and uneasily to their undoubtedly equally restless beds considering what their minds would dwell upon, and then he lay there as the clock struck each hour as sleep still eluded him. His life suddenly seemed to consist of only this one last day, for his mind went repeatedly over his encounter with his godmother—wearisome enough—and then with Maxton and then getting caught up in this. Everything was occupying his mind too strongly for him to rest. He could hear one of the night birds moving through the espaliered branches outside of his window and an owl somewhere, then a fox screaming and other myriad noises rustling outside of his open window that he could not easily identify, along with the constant scurrying patter and prying of rats in the attic above his head. It had not been so long ago that he had learned to relish them for what little meat they carried, but he would relate none of that to any of this family. Those times had gone and would not be missed.

When he was a child, he recalled his mother calming him at night when he could not sleep or had a nightmare. She had told him that if he was ever afraid in the dark, he just needed to look at the cat that invariably spent the night at the foot of his bed. If the cat were not disturbed by some noise, then he need not be either. He had lost his fear soon after that.

That was also when he noted a cat actually lying down near his feet on the bed, taking advantage of his warmth with the cooler air blowing across the bed from the window, wide open. It seemed like a good omen in the midst of such ill goings-on. When the rats then also began to fight and to let out eerie screams like those of a child, and the cat left to investigate that and other noises, he decided that he also had had enough of rest for the moment. There were too many unanswered questions racing through his head and he needed to refresh earlier impressions that refused to let him rest until they had been answered. He struggled to understand what had filled his day thus far!

As the clock below stairs chimed the quarters, then the halves and then the hours, and let him know that it was two o'clock, he arose and dressed and made his way along the landing in his stocking feet, realizing that he broadcast his presence and progress with every step, as the boards creaked loudly beneath his weight. He did not need a candle. There was light enough from the windows letting the moon in, for the rain clouds had cleared, and most of the rooms obviously had some light in them for he could see the flickering of candlelight under the large gap at the bottom of some of the doors.

Pausing at a doorway, he heard a male voice within reciting some religious text. He recognized Thomas's voice and one of the Psalms. This was the master bedroom that he had been in earlier, where Mr. Barristow was now laid out awaiting what little future above ground was his. It was hard to orient himself with such a darkened corridor where previously it had been quite well lit. He made his way in his stocking feet down the equally complaining stairs to the parlor.

A light still burned there from a single candle on the table, and he was surprised to see Mrs. Barristow with her head down on the table, sleeping the sleep of emotional exhaustion, almost as drained of life as her husband upstairs. A large comfortable chair by the parlor fire had been placed there for her to sleep in, but she had been as restless, it seemed, as he had been, and could find no comfort in it.

He chose not to awaken her if he could avoid it, but she seemed in danger of sliding off to the side and to the floor, risking injury as well as a rude awakening, so he could not ignore her predicament. He gently sat her up and then lifted her easily into his arms and walked over to the chair made ready for her and carefully deposited her in it. Apart from a slight change in her breathing and some mumbling from the depths of what little consciousness she had, she gave no sign that she was aware of anything that might be different. He placed a small soft cushion beneath her head, and carefully put a blanket over her, made up the dying fire with as little noise as possible, and then returned upstairs.

He must have gone off in the wrong direction; the house was not so very large, but it was a veritable rabbit warren, for he found himself in the corridor opposite the one in which his own bedroom was located. He retreated and found again the master bedroom. He paused at the next door along the corridor, this time before the door to the bedroom of the lady he had just married. There was a light showing under the door. He entered quietly and moved across to the bed to look down upon his late and short-lived wife, seeing only a pale face on the pillow, barely illuminated by the one candle sitting on the dresser. Her face showed no sign of blood now and even had a look of peace and contentment. He could now see that she was somewhat heavily suntanned as though she had led an outdoor lifestyle. She was neither laid out as he might have expected to avoid problems once rigor mortis set in—he had seen enough of the awkward problems that rigor caused when limbs had to be broken in order to bury someone if there had been the rare luxury of a coffin—nor was she covered over completely as she should be.

He almost jumped when the body let out a faint sigh and adjusted her position. He held his breath. She was alive! He stood still for a few moments and puzzled over the situation, realizing that he was in a strange house, whose arrangements he knew little of, and that few things were what they seemed. What he was thinking could not possibly be true. He must have become disoriented, for it could not be the same room; and yet it was, for there was a smudge of blood on the headboard that he had earlier noticed, and there was a bloody towel almost out of sight, under the edge of the bed, perhaps laid there to try and counter the forces seeking to pull life from the body. He had seen others place a knife, a sword, or even a gun under the bed of a wounded man as a means of sympathetically countering the injuries he had incurred from one of those weapons. The towel left there must have been an accidental oversight, as this young lady was well, and clearly alive—the healthiest corpse he had ever seen, and he had seen many. She would be most alarmed to find him wandering the house, and in her bedroom.

He recognized her now. This was Annis, the young lady, the daughter who had seemed to judge him harshly for whatever reason. But if that were the case, where was his bride who had occupied that same bed a few hours earlier?

He quietly—as far as the groaning floor would allow him—backed from the room and gently closed the door, relieved to find that he had not awoken her and that there was no one else to see him. He regretted his decision to go for a walk with so many young women in the house who might be afraid, or worse, if he blundered into their rooms, making all of the noises that the floor made with his passing.

He walked back along the corridor and stopped before the door on the further side of the master bedroom from which mumblings could still be heard and beneath which a light also shone. He tried the door gently and cautiously opened it and put his head inside, ready to back out if it were occupied by any other. In this case, there, presumably, was the daughter's body properly laid out as he expected on top of the bed, and this time the entire body was covered by a sheet—also as expected. As before, a single candle was on the top of the dresser in this room too.

He walked silently over to the bed in the dim light and gently pulled back the sheet from her head and upper body. She was now in a clean nightdress, free of blood. She had been moved over to this room and laid out while the other room had been tidied up. There was that lifeless, pale face, also free of blood this time, which had been wiped away. Here was the lady he had earlier married!

He gently put his hand on her cheek and was surprised to feel how cold and lifeless she now seemed, though he should not have been surprised. He looked down at her for some time and then retrieved the candle from the dresser, bringing it closer, and observed her more closely, taking care not to drip wax upon her pale face or on the bed in which she lay. He felt even more like an intruder, violating their expectation that a stranger such as he was, would not risk giving alarm to any of these women. They would trust him not to wander the house and possibly risk blundering in where he should not be, as had happened just a few moments before, and especially not with young daughters in the house and *him* such an unknown quantity.

They knew nothing of him at all and certainly knew nothing of his disruptive past nor what caused his father to drive him from these shores five years earlier. At least he hoped not. He doubted they would feel so much at ease with him if they knew any of his difficult past. He was thankful that they didn't know, or they would not feel so trusting or easy in his company, for how could they know that they had nothing to fear from him?

He had met this lady for the first time just a few hours earlier, had married her, and was now able to view her properly for the first time without all of the uncharacteristic emotions that had attended his previously being with her. Yes, he had cried easily, and from the heart at their pain and grief. There was no shame in that. It had been honest emotion. From the little he had seen of her and her sisters, they were all to be described as beautiful women, despite their faces showing signs of grief and anguish. He felt a lump rising in his throat again at the thought of it all, and how utterly desperate they must feel to be so burdened by such losses that even *he* began to feel yet again on their behalf; for he had lost something himself that he would never be able to experience again, or recover.

He felt the tears begin to flow again for a few moments, though he could not understand why they came so easily now where they had never come for him in any of the last five years of endless death. He recovered his composure and spoke to her gently, no matter how strange it might seem to be addressing the dead, for he felt a bond with her that he had never experienced before with any living woman. Not even his sister or mother. Most surprising, considering that he had married her barely a few hours earlier. He had never before in his life considered marriage, seeing only a disagreeable change in what was expected and required of one—loss of freedom and a change in lifestyle, and rarely for the better considering what he had seen. What might have been had she lived?

He spoke gently. "For what little comfort it may provide you, Arabella, Bella, my wife, I honestly do wish I had come to know you long before any of this happened. Who knows? My presence *then* may have turned you aside from *this* day and *that* fate. But what trouble were you and your family faced with that you must needs wed a relative stranger—me—in such haste, and one with such an unenviable history as I?" He sighed. "Not only that, but you on your deathbed to do it!"

He brought a chair over to the bed and sat down beside her as he considered how best he might move forward without losing the trust of these vulnerable ladies. He gently took her bruised hand in his, for rigor had not yet started; and much to his own surprise when he later considered his actions, he actually conducted a lengthy, one-sided conversation with his former bride. He told her far more about himself than he had ever shared with anyone in the previous five years, indeed ever. If there were any vestige of consciousness remaining even after death and in that transition to the other life, she would at least be comforted by knowing something—albeit one-sided—of the stranger she had married, from both words and caress. Or maybe nothing of any credit, considering what the general impression of his own relatives was of him.

Strangely, he gained some comfort from it, as foolish as it obviously was, for he believed in none of that intermediate, tenuous state betwixt life and death or of the passage of a soul, if the soul existed even, or even might move—called away upon the death of the body. Death was death! He had seen more than enough of it first hand for a hundred lifetimes and had felt it touch him more than once. No consciousness of any kind afterward, despite those who claimed the ability to converse with the dead. It was devastatingly final, and there was nothing to look forward to afterward. Dust to dust, indeed!

After about five minutes he replaced the candle and the chair, put her arm across her chest again, covered her and retraced his steps to the master bedroom, feeling more confident at what it contained, knowing that Mrs. Barristow would still be safely downstairs. He pushed open the door and entered. Thomas sat there with his eyes wide with fear as the door opened and a ghostly face appeared around it. There was the corpse laid out on the bed, covered fully as was the corpse he had found in the previous bedroom.

William smiled sadly and with understanding. "I see you are not used to sitting vigil upon a corpse?"

Thomas let out an explosive breath after holding it in terror as the door had swung in and a pale face, illuminated in the ghostly candlelight glow within the room, had appeared. He laughed quietly and nervously, but without humor at his own embarrassed fear.

"No, sir, I am not! Death is a fearful thing, even upon someone I knew and loved as I did this man, but I remember him as he lived and not as this one who is a stranger to me now. His soul is gone, and the man I knew is no more. I am not used to this for I was never called upon afore for this duty."

William approached the bed. "I could not sleep. I was bidding farewell to my bride! A sad moment to meet someone and then see them die so soon after, with neither of us knowing anything of the other. If you wish, I can stay here and keep your vigil, as I cannot sleep either. I have watched over many such as this as they quit this life, and to keep animals off, though in less comfortable circumstances."

"Well thank you, sir, I would appreciate that, but I shall not leave him. I promised the girls and their mother that I would keep him company at this time, and that he would not be left alone on *this* night, or they would have had to have done so themselves. It would not have been right putting such young ladies in such an unenviable and awkward predicament, for they would probably be more feared of this than I am, but then again, I'm feared enough for all of 'em, I think."

"May I see him once more?"

"Well, sir. I expect you can. You have that right, I think. I doubt he'll complain. Though there is nothing special to see other than that great scar on his neck, though he has a stubble on his face that will need to come off I see."

"Yes, the hair continues to grow for some time. Quite surprising at first." William gently pulled back the cover and saw his late wife's father for the second and probably the last time in his life. He looked to be at peace without sign of the pain that must have been his lot in the last few moments as the carriage rolled upon him, and then accepting a stranger to marry his daughter dying in the next room. Then the final anguish, seeing his wife and daughters looking upon him tearfully as he slipped into unconsciousness and onto the path out of this life. He touched his hands and was surprised at how cold he seemed also, even as his deceased daughter had been, but then William was sweating for some reason, so everything would seem cold to his touch.

"You say you've done this afore, sir?" Thomas looked at him with wide eyes, though less scared now.

"Yes. Many times." He re-covered the man who had become his father-in-law, and regretted that here lay another individual that he wished he might have known even a little. He moved back from the bed and sat down.

"I recovered the bodies of many of my friends and others from the battlefield on several—no—on too many occasions and laid them out ready for burial; even the French too, where their living counterparts were long gone, stood guard over them to keep away the dogs, and . . ." better not to speak of that, he realized; he was back in a different society now, "and even buried them with whatever little of the service I could remember. Often, the French and English in the same common grave. Soldiers all, following the same commands and deserving the same sympathy I thought. There were those who thought that was wrong, as they would then continue their interminable fighting in the grave and get no rest, so they got around that by burying a weapon or two with the English so that they might at least have an advantage if it unfolded that way and *earn* their future peace. It was all a thankless and disturbing task."

He suddenly remembered that one of his duties sometime in the near future was to visit the families of some of those he had seen die in his arms or under the surgeon's knife or on a lonely and filthy cot far from loved ones as their lifeblood oozed steadily from them into the filthy bedding of straw or into the soil. He needed to pass along his memories of them or their final words or wishes. Death had come peaceably to none of them! They had raged inwardly at the injustice and suddenness of it all as he could see from their wild eyes filled with fear. He had promised himself that he would let their loved ones know of their death and that they had been attended to, no matter how poorly, just as he had earlier promised Mr. Barristow that he would look after his family.

He recognized that relating some of his own experiences might take the man's mind off his own fears. "I have fought in many places, so many that I cannot remember them all—Portugal, Spain, France—small towns and villages whose names I no longer remember and lost many friends to the enemy. Even onboard ship, when we were being moved about by sea to avoid an awkward trap they had laid for us on land, and encountered enemy ships then, in another trap, trying to sink us and sniping at us from the rigging. They got quite a surprise at the hail of lead in the return fire from marksmen that soon brought them down and emptied their decks and gun ports, but it was easier to dispose of the bodies then of enemy and friend alike to get them out of the way. A fast trip over the side while the battle raged. I seem to have led a charmed life I would say, for I walked away with nicks and surface scars and nothing worse than wood splinters, a few saber cuts, and minor wounds, where many a better man did not. War was kinder to me in that way than my own society was before I went away. My mother once told me to stay away from ships and the sea. It seemed that too many of our family were drowned, and it was likely to be my fate too, so my mother said, if ever I went out of sight of land."

He leaned back and stretched his legs out ahead of him. "My father survived the experience though, but I did go to sea many times with him, and alone too, despite her concern. I did not tell her. The sea shall not get me, I think. It's had enough chances, and father Neptune threw me back ashore each time. I began to think that I did not so much lead a charmed life as one where even death did not want the likes of me! It seems that I shall either be shot in battle or on my home soil, or hanged instead, as others predict for me. But I seem to have missed that fate at the docks by just a few days, I think, and another of those unexpected welcomes just a few hours ago. Some welcome home!"

Thomas looked at him sharply at his last comment, but he was looking elsewhere. "I think I'm all right now, sir. The night was dragging too much for me, and I found my mind was playing tricks on me as though he were alive and moving. I could swear I saw him flinch once or twice!"

"You probably did!" Thomas looked startled at him. William explained. "Bodies will do that as their muscles relax or stiffen, even long after all life has gone. I have heard them belch as well and even sigh. When I have seen bodies burned on a funeral pyre, I have seen one or two of them even sit up in the flames and groan as though they were still alive and continue to moan dreadfully, but as one of them was without a head I knew that it was not so. The heat of the fire contracts their muscles and can cause them to make other noises too."

"Well, I never knew that! I am not normally a superstitious man, but for a while there . . . ! Thank you, sir! I thought I was going mad and that my mind was playing tricks on me!" He looked around into the far shadows with some concern. "Or that there was another power in the room."

"No. The dead cannot hurt us, Thomas, and they should not frighten us. They may need our presence to make that final passage in peace, and we should not deny them that, though I have difficulty believing it. Only the living need us or can hurt us. There is nothing to fear from the dead. They can neither deceive nor lie nor do us violence when we least look for it. One can trust *them*, where one might not trust the living man! As for any other power, I think you will find none worse than your fellow man more capable of inflicting death and destruction. I have seen no evidence of any other evil power that one might need to fear, and I have been in many situations where malevolence would thrive and grow if there were any such evil force beyond that which the living can provide in abundance. My grandmother used to say that we were our own worst enemies and that there was no one we would ever be likely to meet that was worse than ourselves and what we could be. I think she was right."

"You look tired, sir."

"Yes, I have not slept for too long, for I had a rough crossing from France before I received your mistress's letter . . ." he thought for a few moments " . . . many hours ago now, at least two days I think since I slept. I have not yet slept in England for five years! Strange thought! I think I am somewhat overdue."

"You should get back to your bed then, sir. I'm fine now. Just speaking to one such as yourself about my foolish fears put me right. I need to say my good-byes properly as is fitting, and without fear I think." He listened as the clock struck somewhere below. "Well there now! It will be getting light soon and there will be someone along to spell me. What rank were you over there, sir?"

"I was a major."

"You have that bearing about you. I did notice! Also, that horse you came in on? He's a rare size, but then you'd need a horse like that to carry a man your size too. Strange that that mule is so attached as he is."

"Yes. But the mule is a she. They will not be separated without a fight for whomever is trying to separate them. Much like many another relationship I think, except that there, there is often fighting leading to the separation, not a consequence of it."

He stood. "Good night, Thomas. I doubt that this new day or any following one will be much better than the one that has passed for this family for a long while, though time will eventually ease all of the pain, and they will get easier."

"I hope so for all of our sakes but mostly for theirs. My heart goes out for them all. They did not deserve this, and the best of 'em ripped away!" He shook his head in disbelief. "Bella was a rare fine lady. The master was a good and kind man too. I do not know how they or we will all go forward now. Four young women to fend off who knows what? Do you intend to stay, sir?"

"Should I? Yet I must! I promised Mr. Barristow that I would. I feel like a square peg in a round hole as though I were intruding badly into their grief where I feel none by comparison, though I am much saddened by their loss."

"Aye. I know the feeling, sir. I am relieved to hear you are to stay. I was fair worried about what lay ahead without the master. It tears the heart out of me to see how it's affected all of them since we first learned of it, and helpless to do aught but stand by and see that nothing worse comes about. If you can stay sir, then you should do so. It will be a hard time for everyone for some time, and they may not give in to their grief too much if you were around, as they might, though they will need to do that too and get beyond it, and the sooner the better.

"They will need a man's guiding hand now and to keep others at bay, at least for a short while; for there are those who would try to take advantage of them, lurking close by as they have been before, and I do not have the authority or the strength to fight them off at my age. I am a known entity to them, and to be neither feared nor respected either, whereas you are not, and that will be an advantage for you. The girls and their mother will need to be distracted too and guided in ways they cannot know at this time. It will be hard for us all I think, and hard for you too; but if you could stay for a while, it would help a lot I am sure."

"Thank you, Thomas. I intend to stay but only as long as I am needed. I shall speak with you tomorrow when I have rested, about these others that I was warned of. But if you perceive that they would be better off without me, despite my promise to their father, please let me know. I am unlikely to see what you might see and I would hate to overstay my welcome here because of a promise to a dead man. I have made too many of those promises and have so far been able to keep few of them, but I will if I can. The living, need me more at this time. I have a knack of bringing out the worst in too many of my own relatives even, and I doubt I am better with relative strangers. My promise was to take care of them, and that may better be done at a small distance if I am not fully welcome or needed."

"From what I have seen of you, sir, you would never be made to feel unwelcome here. They would be hurt if you lodged anywhere but here now. They are too kind to show such mean-spirited qualities when you have been so helpful to them, though I do not know what lay behind any of it. As for the others—aye, I shall tell you of them right enough, for they will be likely to descend upon the family now and try to put them out and cheat them. I am too old to stop them."

Once the major had returned to his room, Thomas took up a quiet conversation with his former master. "Well, sir, I believe that you might now rest in some peace if you saw what I saw, and I know you did with you lying there listening. Nothing wrong with your mind despite the other injuries. If anyone thinks to strut in here and make the womenfolk uncomfortable or try to put them out, they will find their plates rather full, I would say, with that young man. We shall do all right, sir, and God help those Thackerays! But then, *he* won't be planning on doing anything of the kind I would say!"

Chapter VIII

Painful Readjustments, a Conversation Overheard

Within seconds of William's head touching his pillow once more, he was asleep.

When he awoke just after dawn, fighting down the sudden fear that he was still in enemy territory and had overslept and put himself in danger from a sudden surprise attack, he found the youngest daughter sitting in her nightdress in a chair in his room, her legs hugged close to her and up under her chin, with her feet resting on the edge of the chair. No enemy here!

He relaxed as his thumping heart began to settle once more and watched her.

She seemed to be waiting for him to awaken. He observed her for a few moments as she had turned away to see outside of the window before she realized that he was now awake. She had a nut brown complexion and freckles standing out on her face. The effects of the sun and an open-air style of life seemed to characterize the entire family and showed their love of being outside. When he stretched and smiled sadly at her, though saying nothing, she quietly unwound herself from the chair and left without saying anything either.

Although he was typically an early riser—even before dawn, despite his lack of sleep that previous night—the youngest girl had beaten him to it and had then disappeared.

He dressed, retrieved his toilet kit from his bag, picking up a towel that had been left for him on the dresser, and went downstairs. Mrs. Barristow was no longer to be seen in the parlor where he had left her. He pulled on his boots, noticing that they were cleaner than when he had removed them on the previous night. There were sounds of an active kitchen from deeper in the house, but no one was obviously to be seen. He quietly let himself out and decided to shave and wash himself before others might appear.

He walked over to the trough and proceeded to lay out his gear before he stripped to the waist and prepared to shave. He had propped his small mirror at the back edge of the trough and had filled his pewter cup with water and raised a lather, which he spread across his whiskers and under his neck. He would not be able to sharpen his blade as there was nowhere obvious to hang his strop. He had almost completed shaving when he had the feeling of being watched. He gave no sign that he might be aware of it but continued what he was doing as he adjusted his position relative to his mirror to see behind him. He could just make out a figure standing at one of the upper windows watching him, but he could not make out which of the family it might be.

He rinsed off his razor in the overflow from the trough and then began to wash himself in the cold water—much colder water than he had grown used to in Portugal and Spain, but then this was England and he was lucky that he did not have to break ice off the water before he might do anything.

He dried himself, put his shirt back on, and after leaving his toiletries by the side of the door to pick up when he returned, he strolled off to walk about the kitchen garden and then moved further afield into the larger garden behind the house and then even further about the grounds to get his first look at the entire house and garden in daylight. The gardens were all extensive and well kept, yet there did not seem to be any gardeners involved in doing so—at least not just yet. It was still probably too early with everything still damp from the previous night's rain and the overnight dew. The house itself, though very old and from a much earlier time, showed no signs of neglect or of being run-down in any way, so his few remaining fears of the night before had been groundless. It was all an exceptionally well-kept and prosperous property.

On his return to the house, he heard hammering from the coach house and found Thomas busy putting two coffins together. Without a word, he joined into what he was doing and helped him for an hour or so to the point where they were almost finished. He quite surprised the older man, who had not expected any help, by showing that he knew what he was doing without being told and was no stranger to a plane, a drill, or any of the many tools lying about, nor the finer points of joinery. Clearly, he might be described as a jack of all trades, having learned by bitter experience, to fend for himself and his friends, to make life easier and more comfortable under the worst conditions while on campaign. There was a lining for the coffins already prepared for the two still upstairs, to rest upon. Others must have been busy working at that for much of the previous night.

"We are almost done, thanks to you, sir. If you do not mind my asking, where did you learn to work with wood? One does not expect a gentleman to know such things."

"William will do. I dislike formality. There are those who might argue with that description of my being a gentleman. I expect it will take me some time to learn the rules again. I spent most of my youth, when I was not with tutors, with my father's grounds men, joiners, masons, or at the dock with my father's sailors. None of them tolerated an idle youth watching them, and had me working with them. In short order, they soon trusted me enough to help them. I was a fast learner."

"You learned well, I would say. I had not expected to be done before lunch." His eyes drifted into the rafters above, as pieces of hay were dislodged from the planks above. "So you decided to show up at last, did you, my mousing friend?" He castigated the cat. "The Captain, as we call him," he explained to William. "Captain Cat! Sad day for all, my furry friend, though you are untouched by it all. No, we are *not* making a comfortable bed for you to discover when we leave." The cat was sitting above their heads and licking his paws while perched precariously on a narrow piece of wood. He had seemingly fed well. "They were busy looking for him last evening."

"He spent part of the night on my bed, but we were both restless. Did you manage to get any sleep."

"Yes, sir, William, I did. Mrs. Barristow came in shortly after you left and told me to go and rest, as she knew what I needed to get done today. She was a little surprised that you had come and sat with me and grateful of it, I think. But if Captain spent the night with you, then you were rare privileged, for he is most often found with the girls and usually keeps clear of those who are not well known to him, especially men. He ignores me except when I feed him a mouse or two from the feed bins when they fall in there and can't get out, but he gets enough of those for himself."

At that moment, a rider could be heard coming along the roadway at a steady canter, breaking only to a walk as he turned into the gate and approached up the driveway. His horse had not been pushed too hard, but he had clearly come some distance with the mud thrown up onto the horses legs. William thought he recognized one of Lady Seymour's own grooms. Now what mischief was the old dear up to?

Thomas put his hammer down. "I'd better see what it's about afore he wakes the rest of the house up. If we didn't already with our hammering!"

William watched as some few words were exchanged and a letter handed down. "Thank you. I will see she gets it."

The rider listened to what was being said to him, undoubtedly the offer of some refreshment before he returned, but he shook his head, and then turned and left as he had arrived. Lady Seymour had obviously told him not to impose upon the family, for a messenger from any distance away might expect some refreshment before he returned.

Thomas looked at the folded paper and turned it over. "From near London no less!" He squinted at the nearly illegible name on the folded paper.

"From Se . . ." he struggled to decipher the scrawl, "Semont? No . . . Seymour, Lady Seymour!" He did not say what seemed to be going through his mind, but the look on his face said it all. "Aye, bad news travels fast, but she was told of this last night by the lad, as were others. He must have left at first light to have got it here by now, and his instructions were to return promptly. I'm surprised he didn't get lost!"

"Well, I wonder what urgency demanded that he be here with this so early and leave just as soon as he arrived and without wetting his whistle? No doubt sends her commiserations but is unlikely to provide much comfort to them, considering what has already happened, but she means well I expect. He should have stayed, for grub's about to be served up from what I can smell." They put the liners inside and then gently covered the coffins to keep the cat out. "You go and eat, sir. I'll join you shortly. I'd better see missus gets this first."

William retrieved his gear from by the door and entered the house, with Thomas not far behind.

"A message, Thomas?" She took it from him. "The first of many, no doubt! Good morning, William!" She put a hand on his arm to warmly thank him again.

"Ma'am." Her eyes were red and swollen from far too many tears, but she strove to be civil and attentive to what was required, no matter how little she might feel to be that way.

She looked with some difficulty at who might have sent it and recognized Lady Seymour's hand. She sighed heavily; there would be many more like that as the days wore on. She dropped it on the hallway table, unopened.

"I cannot handle this at the moment! You should both come and eat a little. There will be a more substantial breakfast later when the girls are able to get about. I shall not disturb them just yet. I could hear you working out there, and you cannot work on an empty stomach. I fear I overslept, but I shall leave the girls longer. They must be exhausted too."

A little later, as he was about to go back to the coach-house, he encountered Annis coming down the stairs. He was pleased to note some gentleness in her attitude toward him for she did try to smile.

She had obviously spent a tearful night, as he could see that her eyes were reddened with crying and were somewhat swollen. She seemed quite different, and appeared to have retreated from the more severe and critical, even angry reception that he felt had been his on the previous day. However, that may have been her helpless response to the injustice of what was happening about them, and *to* them, and her sorrow had been directed at all and sundry about her, rather than targeted at him as it had seemed to have been.

"Good morning!"

Her eyes took in his easy and careless manner of dress, with his shirt sleeves rolled up to his elbows and the neck open. He had obviously been making himself useful somewhere. His eyes were direct, and his hair seemed almost to be even more unruly than it had been the night before when she had first seen him.

"Yes, sir. I expect it is, but alas, I can see nothing that is good about it?" She perhaps was gently taking him to task for his thoughtless adherence to custom! It was understandable considering the grief that they all had to bear.

He swore inwardly at his forgetful ineptitude and his speaking without having thought of the impact of anything he might say under the circumstances. "Indeed, yes. I am sorry. I did not intend to be clumsy that way. It was a manner of expression."

She inclined her head to acknowledge his apology. "You should call me Annis, sir, as everyone else does."

"Thank you, Annis. My name is William. I am sorry that a complete stranger to you such as myself, and one so gauche and stupid, has intruded so badly upon you at such a time as this."

"It cannot be helped. We must all put up with some inconvenience it seems. You must pay me no mind, sir, and I beg your pardon. For I spoke rudely and with lack of patience when you meant only good! I think your intrusion was welcome and perhaps even necessary for all of our sakes."

He smiled. "I am also sorry that I blundered into your bedroom last night, for I think I may have disturbed your rest."

She acknowledged his second apology but could not meet his eyes, for her own were somewhat misted. It seems she had known of his presence. He continued. "Please forgive my clumsiness. I shall stay out of your way as much as I can."

She looked at him and blinked back her tears. "You married my sister, sir. We must also be complete strangers to you too, so I suspect we must learn to live with a little discomfort with each other's presence for a while until other plans are made. But do you intend to stay? I am sure we do not expect it of you under such awkward circumstances as these must be for you. There is no setting that is likely to be less relaxing or comfortable for you, than to be privy to the grief of so many women in such a confined circumstance as here, when you do not need to be. You were not obliged to do what you did, yet it seems to have been a great help to us. Mama was much relieved, and I must thank you for that, though in what way you helped, I do not understand. We should not ask more of you. You must have a good deal to do on your own behalf without having to deal with our grief, and that must have sidetracked you so suddenly from more important things."

It was difficult to gauge her mood or opinion. She seemed to be offering him reasons and an excuse to go, if he needed one. A few hours earlier, he might have been relieved to have been offered that excuse, but no longer.

"If I am not in the way, I will stay and try to be useful as I may be able to. For a while, anyway." He said nothing about his promise to her father. "I have no need to rush off, provided I can locate my clothing before I destroy what little I have with me."

She could see a small separation of the sleeve at the shoulder where he had strained the seam in some activity that morning or even earlier.

"My own late father's estate has been well managed for the past five years and certainly since my father's illness over the last years and, indeed, since his death some time ago now. I could be mistaken, but I doubt I am needed there. I may prove to be of more use here at the moment."

He seemed gentle and well spoken, but she already knew that from the little she had seen of him on the previous night. But to shed tears at their loss as he had—for even her sisters had noticed it and commented upon it with some confusion—was quite surprising. Most men would never dare show such feelings openly and could not feign tears or emotions as some women could.

Somehow, he was different from other young men she had encountered. He was more mature, more assured of himself, and had not appeared too uncomfortable with their grief but had joined it! He had also spent some time privately with her father at her father's request, and she could not help but wonder what they might have discussed that was so very important, with her father as close to death as he had been, and him a complete stranger to them all. She did not know him well enough to ask him directly about any of that just yet.

"At least I hope I may be of some use, though at the moment I am at a loss to know what it might be. I expect I shall stay, unless I appear to be overstaying and trespassing where I am not needed. But then, your mother will let me know if I am, I think."

"Yes, I expect so."

"I find myself in a rather awkward quandary. If it would not be too much to ask, may I request that—when there is a more suitable moment, and it is far too early I know at this time—that you tell me something of your sister when all of this is behind us, though I know I ask far too much of you to consider it at this time. It would be truly a tragedy if I were the only one who knew nothing of my wife." He deliberately avoided referring to her as his *late* wife. "I find that I need to know much more than I do."

She was surprised a little at his request that he might like to know more of her sister, for he had come out of nowhere and might depart just as quickly and conveniently without becoming any more deeply embroiled in their grief. Why he might want to learn more of her dead sister was a little puzzling, for there had been no affection on such short and tragic acquaintance. He would be wise, and it would be better that he departed at the earliest opportunity and leave them to grieve in peace. He had done what had been required of him, and if he left as quickly as he came, it might be better for all concerned. However, it did not seem that that was likely to happen as soon as it might, for her mother wished him to stay.

"Yes, sir. I shall do that if you wish it. But when that might be I do not know, for there is much to occupy us over the next few days."

"Of course. I understand."

"Please excuse me. I need to help Mama." She had heard the sounds of activity from the scullery and her mother's voice.

He stepped aside and let her go about her business.

Sometime later, while he was in the small study continuing his letter that he had started at Kellands to his sister, he overheard a subdued conversation between Annis and her mother, complaining about a relative—a male, and one who believed that he was directly in line to inherit the estate now that their father was dead. They were concerned that this gentleman was sure to call upon them now that their father could no longer deflect him as he had needed to do in the past to defend them from him.

He listened and learned more of their remarkably poor opinion of the individual. His name was Thackeray; and they seemed to dread his anticipated appearance, for he had the reputation of being a most unpleasant individual, with little respect for a woman. Thomas had told him of the man and his father while they had both worked in the coach-house and had painted an unenviable portrait of the pair. It seemed that they had been the ones that Mr. Barristow had felt concern about.

He decided that, if possible, he would probably help them to avoid him and his father, though how to do so was not yet clear, unless they obviously tried to intrude where they were neither welcome nor wanted. He felt guilty overhearing such a personal exchange of views but felt that it would not harm to listen and to learn what he might.

Unfortunately, the conversation turned to him at that particular moment; and though Annis's voice had dropped, knowing that he might not be far away, he could still hear what was said.

"Mama, I know you try not to think ill of anyone, but Mr. Devane is also an entirely unknown quantity to us. We know so little about him. He may turn out to be quite as bad as either of the Thackerays."

"Hush, my dear! No, he is not! I did learn something about him from his mother and his sister, remember, even if you did not? Your father said only good of him at the last and had known his father very well some years ago!"

"Yes, but knowing the father is no indication of the merits of the son, Mama! You and Bella may have learned a little of him from his sister, but you did not share what you knew with me, and I was not always privy to your conversation. I doubt that his mother or sister are disinterested enough to share any of his failings with relative strangers."

"They are not strangers to me Annis, but are like sisters! But then no, you are right. We do not know him quite as well as we should, I expect, but we were given precious little choice in doing what we had to do! Whatever his failings may be as you say, they are the least of my concerns at this time. Before you wonder about him being let loose in a house with four vulnerable and grieving females and no male to protect us, I will have you know that I am aware of many of the various earlier accusations that had been raised against him before he went off to war, and I firmly believe them to be without merit. I had the full details from his sister." He could sense her looking hard at her daughter. "He is not a threat to any of us in *that* way!"

Annis chose not to argue the point with her mother. "I suppose it must be some small consolation to realize that he cannot possibly be as bad as what we know already of the younger Mr. Thackeray! For *he* is insufferably arrogant, rude, offensive, insulting—even stupid—as well as dangerous for us. He is an extremely dull kind of person, who cannot take a hint but is likely to try and inflict himself upon us without our father to discourage him now. I did not like him creeping about the house as he did when he was last here and snooping into everything. So, better the devil we know a little about than the one we know everything about!"

"Oh hush, Annis. Let us not visit there. We have troubles enough without anticipating more, and they are just begun, I fear."

Annis felt very strongly about something. "But there is no adjective scathing enough to use that can do sufficient justice to his poor character, for he is all that I said and worse! He bullies everyone he can, and ignores common decency. He can blunder in where he has no business and openly interferes in situations that do not concern him, for he tried to go through father's desk until he found it locked after that. He was not suited after making that discovery.

"Now that father is not in his way he will strive to work behind our backs in ways sure to achieve what he wants without any of our interests or needs being protected. He is a weasel! He last came with some obscure intention of asking Papa's advice upon something, but his clumsy and stupidly transparent intent was obvious to father, and he was firmly steered off and sent away. I doubt that Mr. Devane will put himself out so very much to discourage him. Why should he? He knows nothing of us."

"He married your sister, my dear! He blindly trusted me to allow that to go forward, as I trust him, but not so blindly. He did not have to do that. I think that counts for far more than you might believe."

"I hope you are right, Mama. That Thackeray individual and his father cannot be trusted. They may even more openly try to sell off that large piece of ground to the squire. Squire!" She went off on another tangent. "He has no right to call himself that, for Papa is—was—by far the bigger landholder and is . . . was, better considered in the local area."

"Gently, my dear, gently! Do not get yourself worked up over nothing. We have enough on our plates at this moment. Too much to deal with easily, I fear! Now is not the time for argumentation and brangling! A rose by any other name, my dear."

"A midden by any other name, more like!"

"Oh, Annis! If it makes him feel good and important to puff himself up in that way, I am sure it cannot affect us in any way, call himself what he will. Your father was more amused than offended by it and gave it no thought and nor should you at a time like this. You should remember that if you cannot say something nice about someone . . ."

"Then say nothing!" She interrupted and finished off what her mother had taught her many times. "Yes, mama, you are right. I am sorry. I am not making things any easier."

"He always hoped your father would give that field to him, in the expectation that it would eventually come to him anyway, no matter how many times your father told him that there was no question of the succession—when there may have been, for his persistence put your father's back up over it—and you know what a complete schemer the squire is to get what he wants. I fear it will all be revived again now!" She paused. "Oh dear! Here was I telling you off and I fall into the same trap. But indeed it is not all misplaced, for it is true. I expect he will have broken the fence down again, claim that his cows did it, and has seen his cattle stream into that pasture already, thinking that no one would notice or dare say anything now that your father has gone and no one to defend our interests."

"He did that once before, Mama, and father had to go and see him about it and tell him to remove them, or he would shoot them and be well within his rights. They had a dreadful argument about who owned that land, but it was settled well enough—until the next time. Which is probably now! I believe Thackeray may have come that time with the expectation of developing a relationship with Bella and ensuring his so-called 'rights' through marriage—so he did start out to be as well intentioned as he might be or at least strove to give that impression, but I don't believe he seriously considered marriage. She turned him off most severely when he persisted, and yet he persisted further, despite what she said to him before he was shown off by Father. He wandered the house the only night he spent here, snooping in and out of everyone's bedroom. *That* was too much when he startled Charlotte, and she raised the house telling him to leave her room instantly in a loud enough voice that could be heard out to the road I expect, so you and father insisted he leave before first light. His intentions cannot have been honorable."

"That was your father that showed him off, dear! But we cannot know he intended any mischief. He was just used to getting his own way. I am so relieved they did not come to blows, for there were some harsh words spoken. But we cannot lock ourselves away nor lose a year in mourning, with all of our futures hanging in the balance and still to think about and resolve. Mourning is a luxury for the rich and foolish who can afford to see a year of their life pass them by. Your father was most adamant in his words about that, for he had no patience with such folly as he told me at the end. Made me promise!" William heard her sniff loudly and could almost see her brace her shoulders to fight on.

"Get over it, and get on with life," was his way of expressing things when the going got rough, and there were times when it was most hard and difficult for us in the early going, but we weathered it all. We will weather Mr. Thackeray and his father too, just as we will weather this turmoil, and I do not think that you will find Mr. Devane to be quite as bad as he might have been painted by others, for I do know more than just a little of him."

"I really do not know enough of him, Mama, to be negative, or otherwise, but we should be on our guard. I suppose we can expect them all to descend upon us now and try to turn us out on one pretext or another."

"All? I don't think so. The Thackerays—father and son both—are the only ones. I doubt that any other half cousin—or whatever the relationship was—will be likely to show up now, for the one that might, has taken an interest in a rich widow over Lonton-East way and seems to be meeting with some small success from what I heard."

"Mama, I should tell you that Mr. Devane wandered the house last night too!"

"I know, my dear! He could not sleep either. I do not know how I did sleep, but I must have done. For I was at the table one moment and then in that chair by the fire the next, with the fire made up and a blanket over me and a cushion under my head, and I did not get there by myself."

"Oh! Then that was kind of him mama! But he did come into my room too and most others in the house from what I could hear with floors creaking and doors opening. I think he expected to find Bella, but when he didn't, he soon left! Most strange! I do not know what he expected to find. He also spent some time with

Thomas. He was comforted to see him, I think. I could hear them next door talking together. I could not sleep and listened to some of what was said, yet it seems that I did sleep, or at least dozed off, for I do not know when he left."

"He visited Bella too, so I hear!"

"So he did eventually find her, did he?" Her daughter sounded surprised to hear that. "Why would he need to do that?"

"He had just married her, my dear. He was curious and could not sleep. Yes. I doubt you might approve of that either! But neither did I get the impression that anyone felt in any danger from him." For some reason, that feeling did not surprise her. She recalled again her surprise and sudden brief contentment at finding herself in the chair she had intended to spend the night in, and with a blanket over her and not at the table as she had last remembered. "It does not surprise me that he could not sleep either, with all of our grief keeping him awake and other strange noises in a house he did not know, and comings and goings and what had just happened to him. It was a pity we had to embroil him in our grief as we most certainly did."

"Yes. But he shouldn't have wandered like that." Annis was speaking. "But I suppose that was different and might be excused as you say. I would say he had no motive that might be questioned. Not from what I observed, for he looked quite sad and then confused when he saw that I was not Bella, whom he expected to find in that bed. But then, men are all the same, always showing off, seeking to intrude and dominate and overrule, and show how superior they are. Though father was not like that."

"He was your father! We depended upon him far more than you seem to know. William is not like that either! A family of women without a man they might trust to look after their interests is like a rudderless ship. You may not like it any more than I do, but this is a male-dominated world where a woman by herself counts for very little. But what would you know of men to be so cynical?"

"Only what I saw of London society and the little social interactions here in the village. Those Thackerays! They were the worst by far. Insufferably arrogant, encroaching, and argumentative!"

"Annis, I can assure you that William is nothing like the Thackerays. If you look for comparisons, I think you would be wiser to think of him more in the mold of your father. We may be as dependent upon him in that way now. I can only hope that he does not resent what has happened and feel that he must rush away. In truth, I am not even sure what we accomplished by doing what we did. But we should be careful of what we say! The servants mean well, but we must be careful!"

"Yes, Mama. No! He is nothing like Thackeray. Maybe worse! But he is nothing like father either! Thackeray had the house in turmoil with his outrageous explorations. Especially after one of the house keys was found to be missing Father had told us to place a chair under the door handle to our bedrooms soon after, and I know I did that time, but I forgot last night. But yes, William is different, I will grant you that. For some reason, I did not feel threatened by him as I might have been, when he walked into my room. He had not expected to see *me* there, and he was suddenly confused and almost hurt, I thought. I also remember that he shed tears with us as we all did when he married . . ." She could not easily continue for a few moments. "He looked so sad and confused, for he held a candle to look down at me, and I tried to make it seem as though I were asleep. Then after he had later gone to the other bedroom next to mine where father was laid out, I overheard him comforting Thomas a little, and Thomas was obviously very relieved by his words, so I must thank him for that. No, he is not all bad, I will grant you that, but that is no reason to be so trusting of him so soon!"

"I am afraid we are not out of the woods yet, my dear. There is at least one aspect of this that I find most uncertain . . ." She sighed heavily, " . . . that the marriage might be challenged and overturned."

"How so, mama?"

"Because it was not properly done at the last! It was not consummated as it should have been, and society seems to place such store by that. There are those who say that there is no marriage at all in the proper sense until . . . no matter! It is a delicate subject! Oh why could she not have lived for a few more days, weeks, and preferably lived on as she should to avoid all of this? But it did not happen. That could be grounds for challenge and annulment, and would be, if these upstart Thackerays get wind of it, and then we would be back where we started and them buzzing like hornets about us."

Just as they seemed unaware that William was close by and overhearing more than he was intended to hear, so was Sophia sitting quietly in the window embrasure of the parlor, drinking it all in and not sure what any of it might mean but able to sense that her mother was obviously worried about their very future in the home that was all they had known since they were born.

"Better call everyone to breakfast, my love, though William and Thomas already ate a little before they went back to the coach-house. How I am to eat anything, I do not know, yet I must!"

Annis began to see more than her mother might of those circumstances. Perhaps it might be better if that marriage were overturned! A problem had nagged at her concerning that marriage and the estate. Exactly who did their property belong to now? If it passed to Bella upon her marriage and her father's death, did that not mean that it had now become the property of her husband? Perhaps they had disinherited themselves in their foolish rush to see Bella married. She felt a headache coming on and could no longer think about such a disturbing possibility and would certainly never dare raise it with her mother. Perhaps it would somehow sort itself out as her father had always told her it would, when she had worried over so many other things and then found that they had never been quite as bad as she had feared.

Mrs. Barristow encountered William sometime later as he entered the house from finishing off in the coach-house with Thomas, as they both returned for a proper breakfast.

"I took your coat, sir, if that is what you are missing. Molly is seeing to it at the moment. There was a burn mark and a speck of older blood on the sleeve and another smudge on the side. I feared at first that the blood might have come from . . . our tragedy."

"No, ma'am. They both came a little earlier than that."

"Well, Molly will do what she can. Neither mark was so very obvious, but blood must be seen to before it dries if possible and, if not, then before it gets too old. What a pity we did not notice it last night when you arrived, but it was not to be, with everything going on as it was! I just hope she was able to do something with it. Nothing serious, I hope?" She looked a little concerned, though she had much more that needed to occupy her than a speck or a smudge on his coat.

"No, ma'am. Nothing serious. A small and unfortunate disturbance just outside of Inchdene yesterday afternoon. Of little consequence and soon resolved."

During their more formal breakfast some little time later, he noticed that he was being regarded with some interest ranging from outright curiosity to perhaps reserved judgment by all of the daughters, but mostly in a kindly and curious way. They were not sure what to make of him just yet, for he was almost as much a stranger to them now as he had been last night. If they expected to find him unused to the gentle manners at table after being on the Peninsula, they would be disappointed. He had washed up most carefully before appearing at the table and had tidied himself up as much as he might, considering his limited wardrobe, even to the extent of brushing his unruly hair with little success. He did not slurp his hot coffee or drink noisily from the cup; he used a napkin—in fact, he had assisted Sophia with hers as well as helped her cut her ham—and he did not eat with his knife or his fingers. Nor did he reach across the table and load his plate beyond reason as another relative had done when he had been there, but had passed plates as required and had made sure that Sophia was looked after, and even the others too, before he began himself. He ensured that all were fed as much as they desired to partake before he or Thomas might consider any additional servings for themselves, for they both had the appetites of hungry men. One never knew how they could eat so much and not get fat. All of these things were carefully noted.

They were not to know of the violence of hungry men, half starved, or the not-so-rare fights over the distribution of food that had sometimes accompanied their impromptu dinners during campaign, over a share of the meager rations that had been perceived to be excessive on someone else's part.

So began an informal mental cataloguing of those small personal observations of the one upon the other four, and of the four upon the one, as they curiously learned of each other.

The youngest girl seated next to him was still a little shy of him, regarding him with the greatest curiosity, but then he had recognized that she had followed him around after he had returned to the house the first time after helping Thomas and had seemed not to leave him since but had always been close by. He did not mind.

He found it somewhat amusing, but recognized that she needed to be distracted as much as he might be able to achieve, so he had spoken kindly to her and showed her what he was doing and why, and had even got her to help him a little where she might be able to. He began to feel a sense of belonging rather quickly when he noticed that she stood very close to him and that her hand had gently intruded into his own from time to time. He began to pay her more attention.

"You will need to forgive my daughters' attention, sir. They are not used to a relative stranger, a gentleman, dining with us, even though he is . . . even though you are now their brother-in-law."

He liked that thought, and that appellation. "Pay it no mind, ma'am. I used to receive the same scrutiny when I was pied-a-terre, that is, I was billeted with different families in the early stages until the action picked up, and then I found I sorely missed the usual comforts of table and the kindly attention."

They seemed to listen attentively to everything he might say. They had even watched as he and Thomas had washed up before sitting down at table, almost as though they had never seen a grown man washing before.

It was a little off-putting to be at the focus of such interest. He knew he would have to get used to it, and it far beat the alternative that he had left behind him and had almost forgotten in this new setting. He had lived with his fellow soldiers in rough conditions for the last few years, devoid of all family life and civil, gentle exchanges. He had had to get used to their coarse language and pointed, sometimes personal, banter and hectoring, and their indifference to good manners and formality; for with the need to cooperate and pull together and fight for each other's safety under the most taxing and severe of conditions, there had been little formality in their closely confined society. In the heat of battle, with ever-present violence and death, ranks soon disappeared. One ate when one might. They were often so hungry that no one inquired too closely what it might be, but accepted it and ate it appreciatively, often on horseback as they moved under cover of night. Beef was not available, yet it had seemed like beef to hungry men, though there had never seemed enough of it to feed everyone. He had never believed he might relish horse meat, but tough as the meat was, and relatively tasteless, it was not to be scorned, and there was an abundance of it at times after some of the furious exchanges. Changes of clothing were not to be thought of, though in the rainy season or by the larger streams, there was an abundance of water to bathe with and wash out their clothing.

The society at Underby, by comparison, was a most pleasant change. To be surrounded by so much gentle and even refined beauty in a proper and more relaxing and peaceful setting without fear of snipers, was most restful, despite the recent upset, and he was naturally curious himself. He had never been at a gentle table before with more than just his mother and sister, and now he was surrounded by three beautiful and mature ladies and a young girl. He even seemed to be the centre of attention from time to time when they thought he might not notice, and was being waited on by gentle females rather than his gruff comrades. The society of women had been very thin over there, and those few had often been as violent as the men, and very different from the women he had been used to at home.

However, the intensity of their scrutiny at this table was at times disconcerting, though they tried to make it not so very obvious. Had he cut himself shaving perhaps, or missed some hairs on his neck or under his chin, as he often did in his usual rush to shave? Perhaps he was not dressed as formally as they were used to—and he certainly wasn't—for his good clothing had gone ahead of him. He did not mind being dressed at this time in only his trousers and shirt with its sleeves rolled up to his elbow and open at the neck, for he had been helping Thomas, who was also dressed that way at table too. It was to be hoped his sister was still at Brooklands to see that what he needed would be sent along.

"My daughter mentioned some damage to your shirt, sir. If you do not mind, I can sort out some of Mr. Barristow's things for you. He has no use of them now, and some of his larger shirts may fit you."

"Thank you, ma'am, but please do not go to any trouble for me. When I can, this afternoon if possible, I will send off to my sister for some clothes from Brooklands. I am working on a letter for her."

Annis inquired at that moment. "What are your plans, sir—William?" That was the first time she had been able to use his name without prompting, and it had not come easily for her. "We can have no further calling upon your time or patience after helping us as you have." It seemed that Annis still had reservations about his need to be there.

Her mother leapt in and looked pointedly at Annis. "You have already been more help that you might realize, William! Again, I must ask you to excuse my daughter, sir. She can be abrupt at times and speak without consideration of what is needed." Annis blushed at being corrected in that way. "You are not required to desert us so soon, and we do not expect it. You are more than welcome to stay for as long as you wish. I am sure you have as many questions to ask of us as we will have of you."

Annis flashed her mother a glance that was not entirely approving. William noticed her glance and a slight tightening about her mouth. She did not seem to approve of him.

"Thank you, ma'am. I would like to help where I can, and I can see where there is much that I might do, but Annis is right to be cautious. I am little more than a stranger to you, and I would not care to be an additional burden at a time like this to any of you."

"You would not be a burden, sir. More of a welcome deflection and distraction at the moment, I think, as you have been already with many things, including my youngest daughter. I hope she will not make a nuisance of herself in that way. We need some point of stability in our lives."

He smiled down at his young companion and gently nudged her leg with his own to reassure her. "She is good company rather than a nuisance. She reminds me that I am once more in a more gentle society than I ever seemed to remember. But in any case, I have no significant calling upon my time elsewhere that cannot wait and provided I do not trespass or impose upon your hospitality too much, I think I would like to be of use in some way that I can see might be of benefit to you. I have seen some things where I might prove to be useful, though I will ask your permission first, of course. There is a pigeon cote in danger of coming off the barn roof with the next strong wind, and there is an old tree about to shed some more branches into your gate with the next wind as it did last night."

"Yes, there are some things that one does not notice readily when one lives with them all of the time. Please do what you believe is necessary."

"Thank you. I expect you will be receiving visitations and condolences from many people. So if necessary, as I am not really *family*, I can keep clear, but I will be close by if you need me."

"Yes, I expect so. But you are now *family*, William, no matter how recent that is, nor how tenuous at the moment it might seem. You married my eldest daughter and are now a part of *my* family! But we should not subject you to our grief more than we have already. A most strange predicament and situation for all of us. You took a step blindly, based upon more trust than any of us had a right to ask of you, considering how little you knew of us. We are very much in your debt. You are a recent and welcome addition at a difficult time when all we have seen are losses. I think we would like to get to know you better once this turmoil settles down as it inevitably will. Life does go on despite all the upsets, as Mr. Barristow was fond of saying."

Annis had to be satisfied with that and decided not to persist in her cautioning her mother.

"Those who are my friends will be at the service either this afternoon or this evening and the funeral tomorrow or, if they miss those, will not stay long anyway and will confine themselves to the usual hours at such a time. They will be made as welcome as we can." She looked at Annis as she said that, "for they will offer their help honestly and with genuine sincerity and concern. Others may not, but may seek to see what can be turned to their own advantage. It is them I most would like to avoid, but it will be difficult. I do not wish to give offense."

Chapter IX

The Letter!

"Mama, you do know that there is a letter on the hallstand for you? I think it was delivered early this morning."

"Yes, Annis, I know. I saw it dear! From Addie—Lady Seymour. I have neither the patience nor the inclination to struggle through it at this moment. If you have time before lunch, please open it my love and see what it says. I do not have the time, for there are so many things I must see to before this afternoon and this evening."

"Yes, mama. But I shall have to read it later also. I see that Ellie Davenport and her mother are coming up the driveway to visit us. They must know the turmoil that we are in and that we are not receiving visitors at this time. Why are people so inconsiderate?"

"Be patient, my dear. They do not mean to be unkind or inconsiderate as you say but are being neighborly and seeking to help. We'll need all of that, I expect. Perhaps they cannot attend either this afternoon or this evening and feel that they should approach us now."

Annis read the letter with some difficulty much later that morning in the privacy of her room after their visitors had at last departed. She had not realized that her godmother was such an untidy writer, although to be fair, it had obviously been written in haste. It was grammatically acceptable, except perhaps to a strict grammarian as had been the Reverend Coles who had taught all of the girls their lessons, for he firmly believed, unlike many of his persuasion, that girls should also be afforded as good an education as boys. But he would have taken great exception to the untidiness; for there were many blotches, even deletions, underlines, the occasional smudging of ink, corrections, and some minor additions, even in the margin—all of which interrupted the flow, and made it more difficult to understand, though the import of it was clear enough once she got into it.

> *My dearest Eliza,*
>
> *It is difficult to know where to begin. Too much is happening of a dreadful nature to upset us all. I was devastated to hear of your tragic circumstance and am only sorry that I cannot get there as quickly as this letter. It is to be hoped that it is not as tragic as you fear. I shall come to you when I am able.*

> But to get to the point quickly, and I hope I am not too late. In this matter of Bella marrying William Devane that all of us had discussed when we met earlier, it should never [never, was strongly underlined twice] *have been* [the next word was unreadable at first, but then became obvious] *considered at the start and must NOT be allowed to happen*. The consequences of his continued presence among you and your other girls might be unbearable to you and the entire family.

She sighed heavily. "Too late now. The damage is done, for he has already married her. But how can this affect anything, for he no sooner married Bella than she was taken away from us and him? What consequences might she be referring to?"

> I should have laid all of my reservations out to both you and his mother earlier, I know, but I did not wish to cause his mother any distress with my devastating and long-held opinion of her son, though I think she already knows it. I honestly never thought this plan of marriage would ever get this far, or I would have spoken sooner.
>
> My objections to this possible connection going forward are numerous and persuasive. I provide details of such disastrous incidents that few in society know about, it seems, and those who do know have said precious little about! The less his name is linked with any part of your family, the better it will be for all concerned.
>
> Most of my objections come from the time before he was banished by his parents but obviously led up to that action. I doubt that warfare and fighting for his country will have improved him any, for I understand it often does quite the opposite. Violent men are forever violent! It might have been better for all if he had not returned, for he was nothing less than a brawler, a libertine, even a—I hesitate to say the word, but it must be laid out without any timidity—rapist, and worse, if that were possible. Yet, it is worse, for I have firsthand knowledge of one such affair to a relative of my own. Who knows what else there is that I have NOT heard about!

There were many more paragraphs of much more detailed and damning revelations, which gradually deteriorated in their readability as the writer's emotions had gradually overcome her. They concerned, even more, the iniquitous and highly disreputable William Devane, with hints of other scandals that were just unfolding since his return and some even concerning what had happened over on the Peninsula, though her godmother seemed to know few details at the moment.

She read it through and then read it again to glean some deeper understanding of it that she may have missed by struggling with some of the untidiness. She found she was trembling with an additional burden of growing anger, trepidation, and uncertainty over what had been let loose in their midst. She screwed the letter up in her sudden agitation and stared off into the distance out of her window. What should she do? She dare not show it to her mother! There was nothing that anyone could do right now, except to see him gone at the earliest opportunity, rather than press him to stay!

She straightened the pages and read it yet again with a sinking heart. At the end of the letter, she let it drift from her nerveless hands to the floor and sat in deep thought for some time.

They had let a viper intrude into their lives! But what *could* she do? He had behaved in only seemingly helpful ways considering their current plight. His words had been kind, his behavior above reproach – what little she had seen, but his history as laid out by their Godmother (for she was godmother to both the Barristow and Devane children) suggested a villain waiting for his chance to strike in some way. But in what way? If their Godmother were indeed correct, then none of them were safe from him. How could his own sister not know him? Elizabeth was a good friend to her mother as well as to her late sister and would not have deliberately misled them if such a danger were so imminent or obvious. But then his sister was at least five years his elder and might not know his full history for she would not move in the same social circles that he might, and men sought different pursuits than women and strove to hide their teeth, and less creditable behavior from mothers and other relatives.

She would not broadcast this litany of vitriol through the house and possibly risk warning him that he had been found out, for there was more than enough upset as it was. She would keep a close eye on Mr. Devane but did not know for the life of her, how she might be able to deal with him.

She also resolved that she would soon write to her godmother and let her know what kind of a turmoil they had landed themselves in and ask her advice on how to extricate themselves as quickly as they might, and with the least harm.

"What did Addie's letter say, my dear? I might have time to read it now."

"Oh, nothing very important, Mama." She must keep it from her mother at a time like this. The damage had been done and there was nothing to be gained by revealing any of this sad history at such a time. Their troubles were more than enough without adding fuel to the blaze. It was to be hoped he was soon gone, and she would try to see that brought about. Either that or . . . she would need to protect her own family from him. She decided to say nothing of the disclosures.

"She commiserates with us all at some considerable length. We do not need to go through all of that. It appears that she has that secretive recipe for the lemon tarts from Mrs. Devane—and will tell you of it when she comes, as she says she will soon, and also gives you her secret to her marmalade. I thought we already had that first recipe."

"We do. But I did not wish to tell her that."

"Why do they all assume we want them around us at such a time as this?" Her impatience and frustration with everything was rather obvious.

"Oh hush, Annis! They mean well! They are only trying to be helpful and to lend some support."

"Oh well, that's good then, I expect." She did not believe it. "Though what there is good in any of this, I cannot see! Anyway I have put it down somewhere and cannot lay my hands on it at this time."

"No matter. Probably not important at all!"

"No, mama." She resolved that she would see that one of her father's pistols was by her bed from this moment forward and would have no hesitation in using it if he dared enter her room again or that of her sisters, and she would instruct her sisters to keep their door locked at night. Her mother was in such a peculiar and foolish state of mind that she would likely be inclined to believe nothing ill of this man anyway.

Chapter X

Some Confidences Disclosed

William saw the table cleared from the noonday lunch and decided that it might be a suitable time to find out in what way he may have helped them the previous night and how he might help them going forward.

"Please forgive me for asking, ma'am, but if you have time, if it is not asking too much, I would like to know in what way I have helped you by what I did last night. For I know nothing of the affairs that required any of this, and I am naturally curious."

"Oh dear! Of course you are, and we will need to address it sooner or later!" She took a deep breath as she gathered her thoughts. "I am not entirely sure myself, sir, but I will tell you what little I *think* I know. We can retire to the parlor and discuss it there and let the servants clear away. The girls have their own things to do at this time, and they do not need to overhear any of this."

She saw that both Annis and Charlotte disapproved of that plan but did not go against their mother's wishes. They would learn enough from her later if she chose to tell them, and she usually did.

He followed her to the parlor, where she sat herself in front of the fire. "Now, where to begin? We lived here with Mr. Barristow's elder brother until he died, and then Mr. Barristow inherited it from him and took on management of the property, though he had been doing most of that already. His brother had said nothing of the confusing history of the property by way of warning us, for on his death we discovered a veritable mountain of papers concerning at least ten or twelve earlier properties that had gradually become *this* estate, and we ourselves added to it and created more confusion, I think. There seemed to be a history of confusion and controversy about most of them, as with any property." She was pleased to note that he was an attentive listener.

"The real confusion, however, concerned this smaller core property of Underby, on which the house stands, from long before the other additions were made to it. In his brother's papers was an old copy of a will from long ago in which *this* was a property passed along family lines, from father to son and so on, which is how it came down to us. Though I do not know how the Barristow's came to be the recognized owners, for ours is not a French name as far as I am aware.

"We had no surviving son, and regretted that omission most especially yesterday. We had briefly discussed, perhaps even flippantly joked, about what might happen if I were left alone, but nothing was ever clearly resolved. With no son, we left ourselves open to challenges by other male descendents, and we have seen those already. They might be able to contest not just Underby but the entire property."

It was clearly a worrisome situation that she faced. "By rights, I think the property should come to me, for there is nothing unusual about any of it. But nothing is certain, and it might just go the wrong way. However, there seemed to be a strange clause in there from the original Norman-French which had survived to more recent times, and that nagged at us both. It made no sense to us then or now. It seemed as though one of the original owners, some considerable time ago, had sought to keep some undesirable male, still resident in France, out of the succession and had somehow written some strange clauses into the will that seemed to apply to all subsequent owners. We could make no sense of it other than that in the absence of a direct male heir in the *resident* family, the property may be transferred to the eldest daughter, provided that she were married at that time. The intent seemed to be to make sure that there was a male in the immediate family, even someone not a direct heir, rather than having only women. As I say, we could make neither hide nor hair of it, and it seemed more of a peculiar curiosity of the original French, that we felt we had time to deal with. Until this! Indeed we had consulted lawyers from time to time, but they seemed of no help whatsoever and could clarify nothing for us. A needless expense! Or so it seemed at the time.

"Failing that, it passed to the next legal male heir, unless of course, I am the next legal heir of my husband, though, as I said, that does not seem so certain at all anymore." It seemed confusing to William too. "We had often thought about it and its meaning and what we would do if anything happened to my husband. We laughed over it then and noted that we should ensure that Bella should marry and possibly avoid having it all thrown in disarray if there was ever a question raised of the true succession. As I said, we joked at the time, but I am not sure that I can joke about it now, faced with possibly losing it to some most undeserving and very distant relatives who feel that they have every right to it, even though my husband assured them that they did not." She seemed to be referring to the Thackerays. "Your marrying Bella as you did may have saved us from that difficulty. Or it may not have, for unfortunately, she died immediately after. The marriage might mean nothing now as far as that will is concerned."

She studied his face to see what he might make of it, but could read nothing in his expression.

"I know it all seems very complicated. Certainly, it is to me even. I hope you can forgive us, William. It seems that we rushed forward and maneuvered and coerced you into a marriage that might have achieved nothing! How could I have been so stupid! I should have told my husband much more clearly about Bella's outlook and admitted it to myself even and saved you from being caught up in such a promise to us, but I dared not overload him more than he already was. We all hoped that none of it might go as it did, and that some miracle would intervene and that they both might live despite what the doctor said, for he has been wrong before. Would that, he had been wrong this time too!"

He tried to reassure her. "No matter, ma'am. In the heat of the moment, I doubt that anyone might think clearly about it. What is done is done. I was not harmed by it, and I don't think anyone else was either." He said nothing about there being much more to this than anyone other than he seemed to have realized. If any of the Underby estate had come to Bella by her father's death, with William marrying her—a strange circumstance indeed—then none of them appeared to have considered that upon marriage, all of a woman's property became the property of her husband! His! Yet he did not see the validity of any of it. In the normal state of things, Mrs. Barristow now was the most likely owner of Underby and not him. He said nothing. She did not need to consider that possible upset to everything, as temporary as it would certainly be!

Mrs. Barristow seemed not to have considered any of that herself and continued as she had begun. "Yes, and old wills get contested all of the time, and I am sure that this one will be. But we will at least buy ourselves some breathing space, though how we may have done so, I cannot know. However, I fear what the outcome will be. The other heirs have been constantly nipping at our heels for the last few years." Something else still seemed to nag at her. "The other—larger— concern that my husband had was in the description of the property, for the designation 'Underby Manor' has gradually come to apply to the much larger estate. We could lose *everything*, without any part of it being retained by us for our use."

William mulled over her words. It all did indeed sound strange and most unusual, but his knowledge of legal matters was almost nonexistent. "Ma'am. It sounds strange and confusing indeed! It does not sound regular, though I am not familiar with such things as wills, especially from Norman times, except that my grandmother had full title to all that *her* husband had, including her London house, for she left it mostly to my sister. It may be that it passed to you in any case, no matter what we might have done. However, I know someone who is most familiar with such things and should easily be able to sort it all out. Might I suggest that you allow me to consult my father's . . . now my own lawyers in London about this, to unravel this confusion? They are highly recommended and are widely respected throughout the city for fair dealing, unlike the usual run of lawyers that one hears about. I was just with them, briefly after I landed, and they seemed most enthusiastic about helping me with my own affairs of property. My family has trusted them for many years, and I believe we have never found cause to be concerned over their actions on our behalf. Perhaps I can persuade them to assist you in this one."

"Oh, Mr. Devane! If you would do that for us, sir . . . We did not know who to consult or who might be relied upon. We seemed to encounter only the worst of that breed. In that regard, I know that Mr. Barristow had accumulated and put together many documents concerning this estate in his study as well as in some small chests stored in the attic. At least those documents he could find, for they seemed to be in so many places when he first took on that task. They were all to do with old wills and many estates, which were consolidated into this one, along with papers dealing with bequests, charters, royal . . . land grants, rewards for services rendered the crown, or confiscatory punishments for supporting the losing side" She threw her hands up in confusion. "What is not there?

"As I said, the present manor and its grounds are the melding of many other large estates and countless smaller properties, some with their own retinue of would-be claimants and problems of clarity of ownership. Now we can expect some of these old claims to be revived once more now that we are all thrown into confusion with his death. He found them all confusing and frustrating enough at the best of times and had put off dealing with them. Now, it can no longer be put off! If you would not mind unraveling that, I would be most grateful to you." She looked at him with tears starting in her eyes. "But this other . . . I hope we have not blighted your future prospects in any way, and we clearly have no right to expect you to remain after what happened."

He took her hand. "Pay it no mind, ma'am. There were no rosy prospects in my immediate future other than for more trouble to descend upon me considering the various welcomes I got when I landed. You welcomed me where others did not. I was needed at that time. I also did marry your daughter! Suddenly, that does mean a lot to me, and I confess I do not fully comprehend it." She seemed grateful for his kind words and could say nothing. "I had never believed that I might ever marry so soon or in such a way or with such thanks or expectations of achieving miracles. So we shall just have to see what miracles we can work. There are no urgent calls upon my time elsewhere now. I shall draft a letter this very afternoon to my lawyers, with your approval of what I might suggest they do and see that it goes off with another letter to my sister at Brooklands for some of my clothing."

"There is one other thing that you could do for me, sir, if you do not mind. Though I should not load all of my troubles upon you."

He smiled at her. "I would be pleased to help you in any way that I can, ma'am."

"Thank you! I think we have time to discuss this a little before we need to depart for the service. And if I ask it of you now, you will know how to deal with it, for it will slip my mind again I am sure, if I do not tell you of it now."

She struggled to find the words to begin. "I find that I am caught on the horns of yet another dilemma. That will, is one thing, but there is another issue that I will need to understand as soon as I may. In brief, I do not understand the true nature of the financial position in which we find ourselves. My husband was a careful manager of the estates, but I left him to deal with all of that himself while I managed the house and the home garden and marketing, and neither of us thought that anyone else might need to know any of the broader estate also. So I am not entirely sure of the state of our financial affairs, though they always seemed very solid for Mr. Barristow to expand the estate as he did. There is a ledger on his desk that contains all of those transactions and accounts that I am aware of concerning tenants, income, expenditures and so on, and that might be a fairly simple and straightforward task for someone familiar with all of that, but I am not. I do not have a head for figures of that complexity or import. The finer details of my own kitchen I can understand well enough, but not that!

"As far as the existing estate itself goes, its boundaries are fairly well defined after that Inclosure Act, with the possible exception of the side field." She hesitated for a few moments. "There is some dispute of the claim of a close neighbor, Mr. Pendleton, but that is still relatively minor. My husband saw to the broader affairs of the estate and often took Annis with him, and though I am aware of some of it, I did not expect that I would be so soon thrown into the thick of it!"

She rummaged in the pocket of her dress. "These are the keys to the desk and other places where he stored his papers. Better that you have them now." She passed over keys to the desk and to the other trunks to him to begin his task when it might fit in with other things he had taken upon himself.

"I believe they are all unlocked at this time. When you finish working, it might be wise to lock everything up. There are others who may seek to remove them or change things if they have the opportunity to do so."

Annis, who had overheard most of what her mother had proposed when she had brought them both a tray, tried to interject a note of caution as she poured them tea. "Oh, Mama! I am sure I can sort things out much easier than anyone unfamiliar with them might. They are most boring papers. Only father understood them fully, though I have quite an extensive knowledge of the estate as I often accompanied him. I am sure much of it might not be at all clear to a stranger."

Her mother sighed at her daughter's over-cautious attitude. "Then rather than oppose this, you will help him, my dear. You make it all sound so simple, and I know that it is not."

"Mother!"

"Please, Annis. There is so much we need to understand now for ourselves and with some hurry, I think. We are given little choice in the matter, except to deal with what we find *now*. I never thought I might encounter this and never so soon or with such urgency!"

"Yes, Mama." She sounded resigned to having to do so, and decided that it was undoubtedly for the better that she would be close by, for she could then keep an eye on him and see that everything that was done, was done properly and honestly. Unfortunately, he now had the keys to everything important. Mrs. Barristow watched as Annis left the parlor.

"Annis is only trying to be helpful I think. I must trust someone at this time, William. It may as well be you. I would like it to be you. You do not have the shiftlessness of one who might not be trusted—not like some of our own relatives—and Thomas related a little of last night and how you helped him in that too. He said that he was ready to lose his mind until you appeared. Apart from that, we do know more than just a little of you, as I said, for Sophia found your name and other things about you in one of the newspapers, and you even show up in the navy list, which Mr. Barristow occasionally got. Most unusual to see an army major listed in those. It seems that you were not only highly regarded by the navy but also became somewhat of a hero. Yet Thomas said you were a major in the army, and he believes that you are a man to be trusted, but I think I already knew that from your sister and from what I have seen of you."

Annis, who was lurking just outside of the parlor door, itched to leap into the conversation at that moment and interject a note of caution but didn't. Her mother was putting everything into the hands of someone who might seek to ruin them in every way imaginable.

"Yes, ma'am. I am—was—a major. I did not realize I was in the navy publication."

"And why not? I am sure that it is not a common occurrence for an army major to commandeer a French warship, and in its home port too, and make off with it under their noses. I gather it impressed the admiralty from what my husband said, for he did relate a little of it. He said that your father was most proud of that, and him a well-decorated navy commander, for your father was still alive when you did that, and they frequently exchanged letters and mentioned you often. They are all in there somewhere."

"I did not know." It was obvious that there was a lot he did not know. "But yes, ma'am. I returned with that ship to London. The navy threatened to sink me off Southampton, where I would have headed, so we had to give them the slip. There were some red faces at that when they found out that an army major had out-sailed and escaped the British navy for a while. I think they would rather have sunk me out of sight of land than have *that* embarrassing circumstance happen."

"Your father said something similar I think. He was beside himself with pride over that, a poke in the eye of the navy, and from a son of his! He must have taught you to sail!"

"Yes, ma'am. He taught me to sail when I was a boy and even let me command a small sloop—his, mine now—from time to time not so very long ago, so it was all second nature to me. There were times when I lived on board that small ship and did not set foot on land for a month or more. My father's . . ." He stalled and corrected himself. "My late father's estate is on the coast not so very far from here."

"Yes, I am familiar with your father's estate. Is it true that you were a smuggler then?"

He looked up in surprise. "Yes, I was! But I thought only my closest relatives knew that, but then you would have heard it from them, I expect. That was one of the many reasons my father sent me off. It had become too well known, and his own careful efforts in that regard needed to be abandoned as a result of my clumsiness. So my father was a smuggler too, while trying to preserve the dignity of a naval officer with a son like me careening across the map. I was a somewhat unruly youth and had grown worse the older I got, it seemed. How did you know that?"

"We have few secrets, sir, and I am sorry to say it but nor do you, unfortunately, from our intimate little gatherings and other disclosures. I hope that does not make you uncomfortable. Surely we are also closest relatives ourselves now?

"I should confess to you a little more openly how I know so much of you, and it was not all from either your mother or your sister. I should warn you that I have most inquisitive and alert daughters. Nothing is hidden from them. It can be quite unnerving at times. I also think you were the one who carried me and put me into my chair and draped a blanket about me while I slept, and all without waking me. And I thank you for that, for the house can be draughty, and the table was hard. You must have caught me at the only moment I did sleep, for I am normally wide awake at the slightest movement.

"However, the other . . . When you did find Bella and even speak to her . . . yes, I know of that too and am most touched by it, more than I can tell you." She sobbed a little at that thought and hesitated, unable to contain herself. "When you did that, I think you did not notice two very silent, at first frightened of course, but then attentive and curious young ladies sitting off in the shadows. They could not sleep after that set of events, any more than any of us could and had gone to keep Bella company. They listened most attentively as you shared your secrets and innermost feelings with . . . with their sister." She broke down into tears at that moment, no longer able to restrain herself.

William knelt by her and gathered her into his arms and let her weep a while. Annis resisted the impulse to rush in and displace him. He was being kindly, no matter how poor his character in other ways.

"Oh my! Emotions. Emotions. You men are lucky in some ways to be able to control them and put them aside, but I cannot. I have struggled to bottle them up around the children when I felt like tearing my hair out." She dabbed at her eyes. "They dared not let you know they were there, for they knew so little of you and did not wish to earn your anger at being discovered. But they were soon quite impressed and even touched I think, and gained a favorable impression of you. Though they did not entirely hold back their tears, they stayed silent enough that you knew nothing of them being there. Two sisters who had slipped out of their makeshift beds to keep their sister comforted. After their initial concern, they were most entranced by your conversation, even curious, and were obviously very touched by it. Please do not think ill of them for not letting you know they were there and for telling me of some of what you said."

"I don't, ma'am. I won't. One is not responsible for what one overhears. I regret nothing that I disclosed! I spoke from the heart. Others might be quite surprised to learn that I have one!"

Her eyes shone at his kind words. "You have gained two adoring admirers by what you did and said so kindly to their sister. Do not be offended. I told them that whatever they had heard was in total confidence and to relate it to no one, not even me. I told them that your feelings would be most bruised if they betrayed that trust, and their sister would not rest easy as a result of it. But that was after they had blurted some of it out and confessed to where they had heard it. I will ask you to try and forgive them."

"Yes. I had no right to do any of that." He analyzed what he had confided to his dead bride and recognized that he had not divulged anything beyond a sketch of himself and nothing that might be too revealing or disturbing to anyone who might have overheard him. He resolved to be more careful in his confidences without checking next time, for an audience of young women seemed to be everywhere. He was well aware that the second daughter was lurking outside of the door to the parlor at that moment so that she could overhear their conversation without interrupting her mother.

"Nonetheless, I am glad that you felt able to do that."

"So am I. But I felt an overwhelming sadness that I had never met your daughter or, indeed, yourself or your husband before last night. From what I am finding out, I very much regret that deficiency, but I knew nothing of any of you, and now I am finding that I wish I had. Too late for Bella and your husband, I know that. But not too late for the others, if they will not mind and will allow me to trespass a little and try to share or even displace some of the burdens. But it is a lot for me to ask on such short acquaintance."

Annis did not like the sound of that. An encroaching and crafty schemer with a silver tongue whose intentions were undoubtedly of the worst kind from what little she knew of him. She wished she had paid more attention to both Bella and his sister when they had been discussing him!

"However, I think I am the one who must ask your forgiveness, ma'am. I could not sleep, and I had no right to wander about the house as I did and possibly cause concern to you and your daughters, for you know so little of me. I would have gone outside into the garden or have walked further afield, but I was in my stocking feet for fear of clumping about the house and waking everyone. I made enough noise, anyway, and I thought that the added noise from the doors being opened might also have awoken others."

"The doors are never locked, and the hinges are well greased as both Mr. Barristow and I were early risers. But the roses might have caused you some discomfort had you stepped on one of the branches that had been laid down by the wind last night. I think my daughters are already aware that you are not to be feared. I think they are beginning, even at this early stage to regard you as an elder brother. Oh dear. Quite a frightening thought for you possibly!"

"Not at all, ma'am. The one sister I do have was quite protective of me, and I do love her dearly, for she saved me from some rather severe punishments. Perhaps I can return that favor to the sex generally."

Annis doubted that such protection—as he described it—would be his intention. How could her mother be so trusting of a relative stranger whom all reports, and that letter, painted in such a scathingly poor light?

"They will be very shy with you at first. But that will soon pass, I expect, and you will then heartily wish to be rid of them and be elsewhere. Their father and Thomas and various stable hands were the only males they were familiar with. You are now being cast into the mould of a strange elder brother who has been abroad and seen many things and encountered some unusual adventures that young ladies might never learn of other than by eavesdropping. I am beginning to think that we are most privileged to have had you enter our little family in some way for however brief a time."

"I am beginning to think, ma'am, that the privilege has been mine that you allowed me to be here."

She was relieved by his relaxed responses in the face of so much curiosity. He, for his part, recognized that she found relief in filling her mind with small and recent details and chattering on about them and being in the company of others, rather than sitting alone and having her grievous situation alone occupy her mind.

"The girls were quite taken by your confessions of being a smuggler. Mr. Barristow was fond of Brandy as am I on occasion, especially when we can pour some of it on the Christmas pudding and light it. My daughters and I also like French lace. With the ruinous taxes on those and on tea and other things from abroad, especially with embargos. And in wartime, we never discouraged anyone with a living to make, supplying people with those things they most wanted and at a favorable price even if it was an endeavor the government did not approve of and tried hard to close off. Bad laws deserve to be broken!"

Annis raised the subject with her mother when they were alone later, and William had already begun on his task. "Mama, do you think it wise to let a complete stranger become privy to our financial affairs so easily, indeed, to our very existence? We are putting ourselves more deeply into his hands at every turn. It cannot be wise! We know nothing of him."

Her mother rounded on her and seemed quite put out by her lack of trust. "You may not! I do! As you get older, you will learn who it is that you might trust and who not, and soon, too. Mr. Devane is one that I choose to trust. He may have been rambunctious in his earlier years and was clearly most difficult for his mother, but then everything can be made to seem difficult for her, dear soul, but he is a man I understand well. So like your father was."

Annis decided that she could not argue with her mother in her present mood and recognized that she should not yet produce their godmother's letter. It would be too upsetting to her mother on top of what had already happened. It could stay misplaced for the moment. She would take matters into her own hands as might be needed.

"But we should not spend any more time discussing this. We need to get ready for this afternoon. Little as I like the process, we must put a strong front upon it and be there to see it all through as it should be. There will be more than enough time to think upon it all later. Too much, I fear. Better let Charlotte and Sophia know that they should be getting ready."

"Yes, mama."

Chapter XI

The Squire and the Mysterious Stranger

After the small service later that afternoon, attended mostly by servants, friends, and some of the locals, William excused himself and walked out alone to take in the local area and to give the ladies time to recover their composure after walking them home and before the demands of what would be a much-better-attended evening service, with others coming from further afield, also robbed them of their night's rest. He also needed to think about recent events; what he had learned, how he felt about them, and how he would move forward. Nothing like this had ever happened to him before. How could it have? Certainly his life had been profoundly affected in ways that he might never have believed possible even just a few days earlier.

On his return to the Manor sometime later, he noticed two men conversing in the lane. He saw a thickset individual who dressed somewhat strangely as though aping some new fashion trend but not quite achieving what he might have intended, for he looked more comical than well dressed, and therefore could more accurately be described as ill-dressed. However, it is the man within the clothing that should attract the attention and not the clothing upon the man, though the one does give some often amazing insight into the other. The ill-dressed man was conversing with one dressed more casually as a working individual, and who had to be the squire, their immediate neighbor. He was curious to meet this man and get some hint of his character, as he had been somewhat well criticized by Annis and her mother.

He saw the younger man tip his hat and ride off before he quite got to them. Just as well. He had no stomach for would-be dandies. The man was a poor rider with an awkward seat and obviously had too severe a bit in the horse's mouth, for the horse threw its head in pain as his rider was too hard on its mouth. He was a bruising rider who probably considered himself quite adept at it. He appeared to lack a sense of balance to go along with his lack of dress sense, though much of the former might have been attributed to the style of saddle which seemed rather odd. The horse would soon be rid of him if he were not more considerate and gentle.

"Good morning, sir." The squire greeted him affably enough. He seemed to be a pleasant enough individual and perhaps not quite as devious a character as the Barristow's may have intimated, but it was too early to judge.

"And to you sir."

"You must be a stranger hereabouts, for I do not think we have met before?"

"We have not met. I am a newcomer to the area. My name is William Devane. I shall be spending some time in the vicinity, I think."

"And I am Wilfred Pendleton, sir." They shook hands.

"Yes, I thought so. You appear to have a most prosperous estate, and some fine pedigree cows I would say." William admired those he could see. "I am sure I should know the man who just rode off. There cannot be so very many men in London—I assume his address and manner could only be the product of a certain segment of London society—with such a characteristic seat." He was striving to be diplomatic, but the smirk on the squire's face spoke volumes of what he also thought of the man. "I feel I might know him, but I cannot quite place a name to him. Is he local?"

"Not yet. He expects to be very soon if he has his way, but I am not sure that he will. A recent death in a distant branch of his family has apparently just left him with a nice property . . . if he is to be believed, but he tends to exaggerate, so I am not sure what to believe. His name is Thackeray. Joshua Thackeray. He is a somewhat strange individual."

William said nothing in response. The squire did not like Mr. Thackeray either, that much was obvious. Trouble had seemingly arrived for the Barristows a little faster than others would be aware of. He leaned against the fence and looked about himself.

The squire noticed the man's large and very rough hands and his deeply suntanned face. He decided that Mr. Devane would be one who would not miss too much going on about him. A man used to hard work and the outdoors but also a gentleman, possibly fallen on hard times, he thought, considering his somewhat less-than-perfect clothing, which showed some signs of being worked in, his refined speech, and his relaxed nature. Normally one would never see *them* engage in any kind of work if they did not have to, and they always took better care of their clothing and their hair than this man did. He guessed he was a returning military man, a second son, with little prospect of an inheritance and with his prize money weighing heavily in his pocket.

"You'll be staying at the Maggot, will you, sir? The inn?"

William smiled. "Unfortunate choice of names for an inn, I would have thought! No. I am staying with a local family."

"Yes. It used to be called Maginot, after a French family, I believe, that owned it for some time. But the sign was modified by some of the locals for a lark, and the new name stuck. Good food too, and very nice people who run it!" He puzzled for a moment. "No Devanes locally that I know of, though there is a family of that name some way off I recall."

"No, I am not local." William has no intention of going into his pedigree, and changed the subject. "It appears to be good farmland hereabouts, and your cattle look to be healthy and well fed."

"Well, this we are standing upon is of the best, sir. Good alluvium and deep, I think. It should be under oats or corn to get the best out of it, but it is in dispute with a neighbor at this time. My father farmed it for many years and then it was the subject of disagreement about ownership after sale of another property, and that is where it still stands. It is a shameful waste to keep it in pasture year after year, and neglected and overgrown like this, but there is still no resolution to it, and not likely to be now until other things are settled. I try to keep the thistles down in it and see that it is grazed, but my late neighbor was quite angry about that and would have shot my cows in here, when he was alive. Still, I am sorry to see his family now left without their father for although I disagreed with him he was a good man, if stubborn. I'm not sure how I can help them with this difficulty for things have been difficult between us for some years now."

Mrs. Barristow had described her husband as stubborn too. William smiled. He liked the way the squire expressed himself honestly and openly. He clearly had no idea that his listener knew that the disputed field belonged—in the eyes of the law at least—not to him but to his neighbor and that he was trespassing to have put his cattle loose in there, when he had.

The squire pointed off to the far distance. "A little further off on the higher elevations, it is not so good, for the soil is somewhat thin, and there is sandstone a little too close to the surface. It is all very hit and miss and good for little other than trees or pasture and raising sheep. If you read the ground carefully, you can see where it is good crop soil. There are areas where there are good stands of timber too, especially in some of the gullies, good hay ground, and pasture for sheep everywhere. Are you thinking of taking on farming, sir?"

"It is very possible. In fact, more than likely."

The squire discovered he was being looked at rather intently by cool gray penetrating eyes that met his own, from a face with a smile on it that seemed to speak of a broader knowledge of all things local, than he was admitting to. He would have to find out if there really were no Devanes in the immediate area.

After some moments of perfunctory conversation from which little was derived by either party, William bade the squire good day.

The squire watched him walk off and saw him enter the Barristow Driveway some way off and suffered a small pang of doubt about the gentleman as he recollected in whose field his cattle were now grazing. Of course, he may just be paying his respects to the family over their bereavement. No matter. He would now reopen his case with his lawyers, to see what clarity might be brought to bear on that ownership issue, for it was still not properly settled. He was prepared to consider making Mrs. Barristow a generous offer for the land to get it behind them once and for all, but with their tragedy as it was, it was not a good time to do any such thing.

A small carriage arrived at Underby some hours later with a letter for William from his sister. There was also a small trunk that contained some of his better clothing that had come from the continent with him, though not suitable for social visitations or mourning, but it did augment his meager stock of clothing.

Elizabeth would have been quite surprised at the sparseness of his wardrobe, when she went through his belongings to sort out some clothing for him. Her letter expressed her deep shock at the recent events that had befallen the Barristows, and expressed feelings of both sympathy and surprise at the additional news of his marriage and his sudden loss, for the Barristows were among her best friends, and the girls were always so fun-loving and intelligent. But to lose the elder daughter, and the father too, was more than anyone could be expected to bear.

She had written:

> *Please give Mrs. Barristow and the girls my condolences. I shall break away at the earliest opportunity. Let me know if and how I may help. Married and a widower in one day! How tragic for you as well as for them! Most sad for us all! My heart goes out to the Barristows, and I must find out how I may help them. Of course, I shall maintain your confidence. More later. This is far too much to digest easily, and I need to see this gets to you today as you requested along with what little of your clothing I could find. I dare not leave at this time as I am expecting John, or at least a message from him or some news. I dare not risk missing either him or any message, considering how long we have been apart, but I shall come when I may.*

William recollected that he had such a letter in his pocket for her from John, but had forgotten to enclose it earlier with all else going on about him.

Chapter XII

A Promise Kept, a Violent Blatherskite Dealt With, the Service, a Gossip

William walked to the church with the ladies for the early evening service in somewhat better attire than he had for the earlier one and noticed the man he had seen with the squire, riding some fields off.

His peculiar but characteristic, inelegant, even clumsy riding style gave him away as Mr. Joshua Thackeray. From the direction he was heading, it was as though he were going to the Manor, for there was little else beyond there for at least another four miles. He would perhaps be aware that the house might be empty of the family at this time as they attended service and might see to turn that to his advantage from what William had heard from the Barristow family's scathing commentary concerning this individual, and certainly enough to regard him in an unfavorable light.

At that moment, William decided that he should make some excuse to return to the Manor and see what the other man had planned that had him riding in that direction. There was nothing beyond it worth visiting and had he been on his way to visit the squire, he would have been headed on a slightly different track.

Fortunately, the others had not seen him riding in the distance.

"Please excuse me ma'am for a few minutes, there is something that I need to see to. I shall rejoin you as soon as I can." He turned and walked back along the lane toward the Manor without waiting for a response.

Mrs. Barristow and the girls watched him go. "I wonder what he could have forgotten? No matter, I expect he will join us again quite soon."

Annis suspected that once they were all well out of the way, he might snoop in other ways to find out what he might, except there was no need for any of that. He already had the keys to everything important and could go over it with her mother's blessing and approval at his leisure, and he had already begun that task earlier.

On his return to the Manor, he found that the gentleman had preceded him by no more than a minute or two, and had bullied his way past the servants, pushing one of them aside with a threat from his crop. William had seen that threat as he had crossed the lawn. Mr. Thackeray was even then in Mr. Barristow's study going though the papers on top of his desk, having found the drawers to be locked.

William's shadow fell across the desk, and the man looked up from what he was attempting to do. He noticed a modestly well-dressed gentleman filling the small doorway. An imposing presence, smiling calmly at him.

"Mr. Joshua Thackeray, is it not? I saw you with the squire earlier, I think."

He showed his surprise. "Yes, it is, sir, and who in tarnation are you to barge in here? Who are you? Who let you in?"

William did not show any anger at his obvious ill manners. "Strange! From what I saw, I got the impression that it was you who had barged in. Who I am does not matter for the moment. Somewhat more to the point, why are *you* here? What gives you the right to be taking an interest in these ladies' affairs or the private matters of the late Mr. Barristow?"

Joshua Thackeray bristled at his questioner. "You take too much upon yourself, sir. I am not accountable to you, but then I might ask you the same. Who do you think you are to question me? I am his nearest surviving relative. At least my father is, and have been used to visit here as I wished." Clearly an untruth, designed to put off any questioning of his presence. "My father will follow me in a day or two. This will soon be my estate—indeed it is mine at this moment as the only direct relative after my father, and so you see I have every right to protect my interests . . ." he saw the raised eyebrows of his inquisitor, " . . . and those of the ladies of course. I think that you are the one trespassing, sir. Or did that crafty squire put you up to this to try and cheat me in some way and keep me off the property until he had cheated me out of what is mine? I would not put it past him."

He called out for the servant girl. 'Ho! You! Whatever your name—Polly, Molly. See this fellow off before I do so myself, and then you can bring me some refreshments. Haven't eaten all day! You can make up a bedroom for me too. I shall be staying. Why are these drawers and the cabinet locked? They were not when I was last here."

"It's all right, Molly," William said in a low voice while focusing solely on the intruder. "Just ignore us entirely and everything said, and go back to what you were doing."

"Yes, sir." She was well aware who she was about to listen to, and it was not about to be that giblet-grinding-blatherskite, Thackeray, who had pushed her aside as she had thought to resist his ill mannered intrusion. He had never been welcome here when Mr. Barristow was alive, and he was not welcome here now. She was pleased to see that William was not about to be either overawed by his bluster or put off by his transparent lies. Thackeray would be wise to change his mind on certain things, especially if he thought he would be welcome to stay, or he would likely find himself poisoned, but if not poisoned, he would most certainly find himself severely ill.

"They are locked because of when you were previously here, I suggest. Your prying was perhaps as unwelcome then as it is now."

Thackeray, effectively tried to ignore him. "Well, locks are easily broken." He rummaged on the desktop for an implement to do so. "I need access to the papers that my relative kept here."

"No! You don't need to see them at all. They do not concern you. You will not be staying!"

Mr. Thackeray raised his eyebrows and laughed nervously at the sheer impudence and certainty of the man and then frowned. He saw that despite his questioner's comments being made in a low and controlled voice, he had been serious. "Oh, it's trouble you want, is it? I'll have you know that I—my father, that is—is having the magistrate seeing to the transfer of the estate at this very moment. It should have been ours long ago for it passed to the Barristows—both of the brothers—in error, and it is about to be dealt with fraudulently again. We did not feel disposed to argue at that time, but . . ." he looked directly and defiantly at the gentleman in the doorway, "you would be advised not to interfere with the workings of the law, sir."

"I suggest you put those papers down, Mr. Thackeray! The law is not on your side now, just as it was not on a previous occasion, as I briefly learned from Mrs. Barristow, and those same papers denied to you."

The man behind the desk began to feel rattled and annoyed by the persistence of this unknown upstart in front of him, for he knew nothing of him, despite the servant girl seeming to know him and even taking his orders. He had never seen him before and he could have no claim upon the property. The apparent gentleness and polite good manners behind the request, stated in the same low voice, seemed to invite an objection, for it suggested weakness to one who was not familiar with a certain kind of assured gentleman—one who increasingly smiled and whose eyes became a little harder when met by increasing intransigence—and did not know enough to be terribly alarmed by it as he should have been.

He chuckled in mild disbelief at what he seemed to be hearing from a complete stranger to him and undoubtedly to the family. "Why should I, you meddlesome upstart? You had better leave before I throw you out! Why are you here at all? What do you know of any of this? Take care, sir! I'll have you know that I have wrestled bigger men than you to defeat and—"

The large man before him moved much faster than he expected. His words were cut off as his ear was grasped most firmly, as in a vice; and he found himself pulled off balance, and was then being viciously and forcefully pulled across and around the desk in a most indecorous, humiliating, and painful way fit only for dealing with a recalcitrant schoolboy. As the other surprisingly large and rough hand closed on his wrist and his arm was twisted behind his back, the papers drifting to the floor as he was forced to let go of them. He moved himself clumsily around the table before he risked loss of his ear as well as a dislocated shoulder. He complained loudly at the pain and threw his free arm around to try and encounter his opponent and get a grip on his hand to stop the pain as he was pulled across the corner of the desk.

There was a scurrying of listening and attentive servants from just out of sight behind the scullery doorway, as both men passed noisily, and with much cursing from one of them, from the study and down the corridor amidst a good deal of resistance and even more pained protest from the one being dragged indecorously by his ear—helplessly being dragged along, and unable immediately to do anything about it. Mr. Thackeray unwisely thought to slow his ignominious progress by grabbing onto the door frame with his free hand and planting his feet. It was a mistake to do that!

He cried out in pain even more, as he felt his ear being gradually and unquestionably being torn from his head along with his hair too, for the man had let go of his arm and had now taken hold of his scalp and was tearing that from his head too as he pulled him to the door. The pain was unbearable. He let go, grabbed the hand holding onto his ear with both of his own to lessen the pain, and with a bellow of rage, rushed toward his tormenter, intent on running him into the door frame, or bowling him out of the open front door and landing atop him and, at the same time, freeing one hand to feel in his pocket for the small pistol that he knew would soon decide who would prevail.

However, he was the one thrown hard against the door frame as their relative positions were suddenly changed, and his hand was wrenched from his pocket as he was easily disarmed; his small gun sent spinning off to the floor by the door.

He then found that his opponent had momentarily let go of him entirely and had not only stepped a little to one side but then had taken hold of collar and the seat of his trousers and had rushed him toward the open doorway and then had added to his momentum as in the manner of throwing a sack of grain. Caught severely off balance yet again, he went sprawling into the rough driveway.

He looked up and saw his tormentor slowly and methodically strip off his coat with some deeper purpose in mind and began to roll up his shirt sleeves with a look on his face that suggested he held little regard for the man he was looking at most sternly.

And he was looking down at him!

With a bellow of rage and pain, once he regained his feet, he launched himself at the man before him. A second later, he felt as though his head had been hammered from his shoulders as his face ploughed into the dirt once more. He tasted both the dust and grit of the driveway and something else. He had tripped! That must have been it. He had tripped. But he had not tripped! He was being manhandled as though he were a nothing, a nobody, and he knew that he was not that. There was a taste of blood in his mouth and an intense pain from his neck and jaw. He also discovered that he could not clearly see his attacker, for his eyes refused to focus; and in any case, he was facing down the driveway, not sure how he had turned about like that.

It was then that he felt that he was being dragged across the driveway, and then felt an even tighter constriction at his throat and middle as he was lifted bodily by the collar of his shirt and his middle and was dropped unceremoniously into the horse trough. *That* was surprising enough—to be handled as a child, for he weighed the better part of fourteen stone.

He lifted himself out and sagged back against the stone edge of it, with runnels of water streaming from his clothing and pooling near his feet. It seemed that he ached in ways and places he had never felt before. His face hurt, especially his cheek and jaw. His ear was ringing, and his eyes had difficulty seeing much of anything as clearly as he would have liked, but the cold water had cleared his brain a little.

His attacker seemed to be talking to him, quite relaxed and he still spoke gently.

"You shall take yourself off, Mr. Thackeray! You are not welcome and have no legitimate business here, and you will not come back to pester these ladies ever again." There was no mistaking whom he was addressing, yet the voice was as calm and as controlled as before, as though he were talking of the weather or of something entirely inconsequential in the market place. "You will leave this family alone from this time forward, for if you do not, I shall be seeking *you* out, supposed legal claim or not. We will both regret it if I do!"

As Mr. Devane spoke, he watched with interest and mild amusement the gradual change in Mr. Thackeray's expression, position, and attitude as he seemed to gather himself for an ill-advised and clearly signaled offensive. He was obviously a swaggering blowhard used to getting his own way and who won most of his fights only in his own mind and by thunderous bluster and a loud voice and did not like to be so easily bested, while others—women—those he had intimidated just a few moments before, stood in the doorway and looked on with obvious smirks on their faces and the gentle sound of their low laughter to inflame him to unwise action. He would make them pay for that when he had dealt with this fellow.

It was no surprise to Mr. Devane when the attack came, for he had anticipated it, and had moved quickly forward to meet Thackeray, as he charged at him once more. This time, unexpectedly again, the attacker was stopped dead in his tracks by the most punishing blow to his face he had ever experienced, exceeding the force even of the earlier one, as the entire momentum of his opponent's body had been behind it. Not only that, but it was also followed by a half dozen others just as hard and ruthless to both his head and his body and driving him back, except he found that he was now being held firmly by the neck of his shirt in an iron grip and could not escape the brutal and relentless punishment being meted out to his face before he was then let go. Severely winded and fighting for breath, with a taste of blood from his broken lips and his mouth and other places, he sat down hard with a gasp of pain, his legs refusing to support him. He sobbed in frustration. He was not sure how this could be happening to him.

His opponent turned away, recognizing that the man on the ground had been thoroughly humiliated, with the fight and any remaining dignity knocked out of him, and would not persist further and risk an even greater beating and further embarrassment.

"Thomas. Please bring Mr. Thackeray's horse for him. He has decided to cut short his untimely social visit for some reason, and to leave the vicinity and the locale immediately for a more relaxing and healthful location. But first, we should exchange that foolish and far too severe a bit in the poor horse's mouth for a different one. Take the one I was working on this morning."

"Yes, sir!" The horse had not been put away as Mr. Thackeray had demanded but had been loosely tied to a metal ring by the trough. It might have been instructive if one had been able to ask the horse what it had thought of the proceedings. Thomas followed his directions and changed the bit, marveling that Mr. Devane could exercise some gentle wit and humor over the predicament that would have had most other men presenting a most ferocious aspect. Yet he was smiling and speaking gently and politely as though nothing serious had happened. He did not seem to care that Thackeray was also known for carrying a murderous little knife that he was fond of using when someone's back was turned to him. But it looked like Thackeray might have got the measure of Mr. Devane, and had more sense than to go looking for it. The major was a knowing one about things like that, which was clearly why he had survived as long as he had.

Thomas had felt the hairs rising on the back of his neck when he had seen it all beginning to unfold, recognizing that though they had lost their former master, there was not much that would unsettle or distract *this* gentleman from whatever he decided to do. He remembered his now prescient observations, spoken to his dead master the previous night, concerning what he had seen and felt concerning Mr. Devane! He had correctly assessed Mr. Devane by his kind words and actions that previous night and just that morning too, and had found nothing to cause him concern for the ladies or their future. Had not Mr. Barristow given his blessing to the union between him and his daughter? He had also heard that his late master had seemed to trust him to see all of the womenfolk safe in that last tragic meeting, and he was doing just that.

William turned and rinsed the blood off his hands in the trough. Most of it seemed to belong to the man sitting on the ground nearby, who had seemed to have lost all interest in almost everything other than his own circumstance. Mr. Thackeray's nose was flowing freely with blood and his cheek was opened and sending more of it dribbling onto his clothing. His eyes seemed to be closing already, and his lips had no feeling to them. His scalp hurt unbearably, and he sensed that his cheekbone had been broken, if not his jaw. He reached up to find out if he still had an ear. He was also getting rid of at least one tooth from his broken face as, some minutes later, he struggled unsteadily to his feet, stumbling once to his knees as he spat blood and other things through his broken lips. He would later discover the rumpled and stained effects of his ducking upon his clothing and many further effects upon his body from being sent sprawling into the dust of the driveway. But that would be later. Much later!

He wisely decided not to provoke his soft-spoken, powerful but surprisingly agile and deceptively polite opponent any further, for he could not see him clearly anyway. He accepted that he was unlikely to prevail in any fair fight against this man. From the relaxed and confident way he had handled himself, the same would likely be true in an unfair fight too. He had seen his pistol removed from his hands even as he had reached for it, and he would not dare risk trying to find either that or to go searching at his belt for his knife. It was amazing that his arm had not been broken, the way it had been twisted up behind his back, but he would wonder more about that later once he had time for the more serious pains from his face to die down.

He noted that his crumpled hat had been unceremoniously and contemptuously tossed out of the door by one of the female servants and to his feet. He picked it up and put it upon his head. An unwise move, for the pain shot through his head again.

Mr. Devane, turned back to the house and retrieved his coat from the hands of the housekeeper as he watched the man clumsily try to get to his feet once more.

She had picked his coat up from where he had dropped it and had swept any dust and leaf fragments off, that might have clung to it.

"Thank you, Mrs. Rogers."

He shrugged into it with a little help, taking care not to transfer blood from his hands onto the fabric. She had seen the entire incident and was both robbed of words and, at the same time, had been overawed and horrified by the level of violence that had so suddenly erupted and then had just as quickly died away as though it had never happened. Yet there was a man sitting all bloodied in the driveway, struggling once again to climb to his feet and completely at odds with the world. Then, for the man responsible for that vicious, though provoked attack, to speak so gently and calmly to her afterward as though nothing untoward had just happened, was quite surprising to her. It seemed that what had just passed was of no more concern to him than if he had just bade a gentle farewell to visitors. He had, but it had been far from gentle, and then he had spoken just as softly to the man he had mercilessly beaten too.

She noticed then, that he was even thanking her kindly for assisting him as he smiled upon her. She was rendered quite speechless for some moments.

William watched with disinterest as Mr. Thackeray unsteadily recovered his feet once more, straightened his clothing as best he could, and then after several attempts to do so, after the manner of a severely inebriated man, mounted his horse most indecorously and with difficulty, and made off down the driveway. He was somewhat unsteady in his seat, more so than was usual, and with various new pains that he was just discovering. He felt as though he might have been kicked. The horse would appreciate its changed circumstance however.

Mr. Devane noticed then that the housekeeper, Mrs. Rogers, was wrapping a narrow strip of clean linen about his knuckles even as she was unabashedly shedding tears as gratitude shone from her eyes. She buttoned up his coat, recognizing that he would not be able to do so easily for himself.

"Thank you, Mrs. Rogers." He placed a gentle hand on her shoulder, taking care not to mark her dress. "Better if this is not mentioned at this time to Mrs. Barristow or the others to upset anyone further. I should hate to think that they might be regaled with a description of such poor behavior of mine and such violence at such a delicate time as this, but it had to be, I'm afraid."

"Yes, sir. It did! I'll let the servants know to relate nothing of what happened to that excuse of a man."

He smiled at her polite and restrained description of Mr. Thackeray. Had he known of Molly's description of the man—'giblet-grinding-blatherskite!' He might have admitted to preferring that.

On his return to the church barely ten minutes later, he noticed that their neighbor was busy rounding up his cattle and removing them with some urgency from the field.

The squire had seen Mr. Thackeray ride by most unsteadily and had not needed to see more than the condition of his face or disheveled clothing even at a distance—and his precarious seat which was apparently not solely related on this one occasion to his innate clumsiness with his horse—to realize that there seemed to be things rather suddenly happening of a most violent nature that he'd rather not be too close to; and he suspected who might be to blame for that, for he had been speaking to him barely a few hours earlier. He felt a sudden discomfort up his back. He hoped things might not have gone from bad to worse, yet it seemed that they might have done. Civilized discourse and reasoned action was one thing, but what he suspected had just taken place was neither of those.

Mr. Thackeray had not seemed likely to be able to see him, or to see anything, the way his face was puffed up, so he had had no need to inquire after his health, for it gave all indications of being decidedly poor and unlikely to improve for some time. He had spoken to that same Mr. Devane earlier, and heard his gentle voice and seen his steady smile and intent and focused expression as he had looked deep into his eyes, as that same Mr. Devane had conducted a gentle conversation, all innocent-like. From what he could now see, that same Devane individual seemed to move easily enough and without injury and with no mark on him that might be seen at that distance, despite Mr. Thackeray being a known brawler with lesser men, even taking pleasure in injuring them and always ready to blow loudly about it. Better not invite trouble from that quarter at this time. Mr. Barristow had been firm, at times very stubborn and determined and had cost him money for damned lawyers, but he had never been inclined to be so violent with such little likely provocation. It seemed as though things had indeed changed, and for the worse!

William caught up with the ladies once more, just as they were ready to enter the small church, having waited for a few moments for him as others went in before them.

Mrs. Barristow took in his slightly ruffled appearance. "But, Mr. Devane, there is a smudge of blood on your cheek! You should not have rushed as you appear to have done, for your hair is a little more askew than it was. But your cheek . . . you have been careless again! Allow me to wipe that away for you."

"Yes! Foolish of me. I'm sorry, ma'am. Carelessness! I should have checked."

"Come here and lean down a little." He submitted to her gently, as she moistened a corner of her handkerchief in her mouth, as his sister or mother used to do when he had still been in knee britches. She got him to lean closer to her, wiping at his cheek in a decidedly motherly way. He found it most amusing and thought-provoking that anyone might wish to pamper him in that way but did not object or pull away. It was kindly done and filled him with a regret that his own mother might not have been so considerate of him. He then recalled that he used to fight with her when she had tried to show him any such concern or affection. He was remembering how poor and hurtful a son he had been while growing up and did not like the feeling of guilt it filled him with.

"Oh dear! And a few little splashes on your shirt too." She dabbed at them. "Not very old either. We will see to those later before they become more permanent. Now what have you been up too?"

He made no immediate response. She seemed to regard him as an errant and mischievous son.

She looked at him with a weak smile on her face. "Well, well. You did not need to return to shave in such a hurry you know? We are none of us at our best at a time such as this, and no one would have noticed anything amiss."

Annis had been looking at him with some alarm for the few moments since he had returned and had noticed other things too. She knew he had shaved earlier that morning, for she had watched him a little from an upstairs window. He was an early riser, and he had even shaved by the trough outside, stripped to the waist, with a small mirror standing on the higher lip at the back, as there had been no hot water taken up to his room at that early hour, and he had not gone into the kitchen to find any. She had watched with great interest as he had even washed himself in the trough as though he was entirely used to doing it that way, and yet in other ways he had seemed to be a gentleman used to doing things in a much more civilized way, for his table manners left nothing to be desired. She then noticed, where her mother did not, his bandaged hand, out of sight of her mother and a little behind him to be out of sight to others too, and with a few stains of blood beginning to seep through. There were obvious signs of redness and scrapes on his other hand too.

After what she had read of him in her godmother's letter, she began to fear for the welfare of at least one of the servants, indeed for the safety of the entire household, but dared say nothing. She regretted not showing that letter to her mother now so that everyone might be aware of his potentially violent nature but would dig it out and lay if before her when they returned and see him gone from their midst. Meanwhile, he would be with them at the church and could not get up to any mischief while she was watching him.

The viewing was prolonged, with a steady flow of numerous friends of many years passing the open coffins and commiserating at length with the family afterward.

After the throng had conveyed their sympathies and offered their support and condolences to the widow and her daughters, they departed almost as quickly as they had come. No one was comfortable with tragedy and sorrow of such a magnitude.

William absented himself at that point but was not immediately missed by Annis.

Eventually, only one other lady remained behind. She had deliberately let everyone else depart before her so that she might have Mrs. Barristow to herself.

"My dear friend. I am disconsolate over your loss. A daughter and a husband, both at the same time."

Annis was annoyed at the intrusion, where her mother was not. Mrs. Chepstow was the village busybody, for they all have them to go along with other questionable notables like the renowned village idiot, of which there seemed to be several, and the would-be dandy, as well as the squire!

She also fancied herself as a person of some importance and above most other of her acquaintances, as she had wealthy relatives in town who, on occasion, would invite her to accompany them to Brighton or to Dover as the mood took them so that she could help them manage their three young and generally uncontrollable sons—for so she had described them to their parents on more than one occasion. Or so she said!

"But then I also heard that Bella was just married last night also in some haste. Most strange."

Mrs. Barristow hid her annoyance. "Yes. It was a long standing intent to see her soon married, but with the accident, it was brought forward, as her fiancé had then arrived."

"Ah, I think I see." She did not understand. It seemed to be strange dealings. "I did not know."

"No. How could you?" Mrs. Barristow would have turned away and left the conversation there, but her inquisitor would not let go so easily.

"Well. It has the village astir with speculation and gossip, I can tell you. Was that the young man with you at the service this afternoon and just now?"

"Yes."

Annis looked about her and saw that William was no longer in view, and that was why Mrs. Chepstow had dared broach any part of it. She had waited for him to leave before she pounced upon her present, vulnerable audience.

"I have seen him before, I believe. Some years ago in London. Is he not the son of Captain someone or other? Some estate not too far from here. But his name . . . Oh, I cannot remember it!"

"Yes. He is from not so far from here." Mrs. Barristow did not, however, mention a name that might arm her inquisitor with information to continue, yet Mrs. Chepstow was not put off.

"Well, if he is the same man, and I think he must be, do you think it wise to have him in the same house and under the same roof as your daughters, without a living wife to perhaps steady him and sidetrack him from . . ." She expressed herself with slight gesturing to her daughters about her and a pointed look upon her face to convey her unspoken meaning of implied impropriety. She sniffed. "Well it is none of my business how you decide to run your own house now, but one should be very careful. There are all manner of dreadful scoundrels ready to take advantage of a widow and her grown daughters."

She gave every appearance of being horrified and, at the same time, critical of the possibility that he was let loose around young ladies in the same house, without some other male to control his likely predations. "His reputation may not be so very well known in most circles as he has been away for some time after his family banished him abroad, for that is what they did, but I did hear of some of the things he did before he went abroad. Now what was his name?" She struggled to remember it. "I doubt he should be trusted around your girls, especially not the elder two, perhaps not even around the youngest."

Her eyes lit up suddenly as she recalled the name. "Devane! Yes, that's it! Devane. William Devane. Very violent man!"

"Yes, I have also heard the same vicious gossip and the same scathing rumors! I knew all about him and his *alleged* reputation before ever he set foot in the Manor, and the gossip is entirely wrong about him. You may tell *that* to those who choose to spread any of these disreputable tales about him for all the difference it will be likely to make! I would rather not hear any of it!"

But Mrs. Chepstow was not to be put off so easily. "The gossip is not only that he seduced—too kind a word for what I believe actually happened to the poor girl—one of the Trevelyan girls, but there is another most disturbing rumor that he actually might have killed that elder son of Lord Maxton some years ago in a duel, about the same time, over another female. For *he* has not been seen ever since that time, though that is not widely known or even confirmed, but it sits out there still, despite the Maxton son being rumored to have gone off to the continent almost immediately afterward."

She continued. "Speaking of the devil, for the elder Maxton as well as his entire surviving male brood has that reputation, his remaining son was also murdered by a highwayman at Inchdene not more than a day ago. At least, so I heard just this morning, so now there are none of them remaining to comfort the father in his old age, nor to protect the daughters when he dies!"

Annis had perked up at the mention of that village name, for it was also mentioned in Lady Seymour's letter, and she remembered William having also mentioned that place to her mother. Her starting, however, provided the older lady with an excuse to continue.

"Why, yes, miss. Ugly goings-on! The stable hand at Inchdene related how a horse that Mr. Maxton had rented from them turned up in the stable yard with Maxton's body tied across it, all bloodied with his head a terrible mess and no sign of his companion. Cruelly beaten to death he was, with a broken neck and a smashed-in head, and who knows what other injuries. Terrible, terrible thing to have happen, and that it seemed like the devil himself must have dealt the blows that killed him and crushed his skull! He said that Maxton had rented the horse when his own had thrown a shoe. Maxton's companion—a Frenchman, I hear—must have witnessed everything that happened. He could not be found, however, and there is suspicion that his body is either still out there, perhaps torn limb from limb, or that he may have fled the country in fear or guilt or both, after that."

Annis intervened to save them from more lurid and bloodthirsty tales. "Mama, we must go. It is getting somewhat chilly here, and we have much to do." She shivered. She did not like the disreputable Mrs. Chepstow with her gossiping tales. But what she seemed to know may not have been so far wrong, considering what she herself now knew.

They turned away and moved away from the village gossip, robbing her of her audience. "Oh, Annis, I do wish Mrs. Chepstow was a little more restrained in her comments and did not relate such gossip, as she undoubtedly will, throughout the village."

"I am afraid we cannot stop her, Mama. But perhaps she may be right in some of it, for there is never smoke without fire!"

"Oh hush, Annis! Not you too?"

They walked on in silence, each with her own thoughts to disturb her, but each feeling very differently about what seemed to be known.

Within fifteen minutes they had turned into their own lane and then followed Charlotte through the gate, seeing her take off at a run and then stoop in the driveway to recover something she had perhaps dropped.

"Now what is your haste, miss?"

"Mama! Look! I found some gold sovereigns—four of them—lying loose in the driveway along with a pocket watch and two teeth, and there is blood and even some hair on the edge of the trough. I wonder what happened? May I keep them?"

Annis knew she had been right to fear for the worst and looked about for who might have suffered such a beating. Thomas had not been the recipient of it, as he was close by, speaking with her mother for a few seconds and then going about his work. He did not look to be suffering in any way and certainly showed no sign of injury. There, in the garden, was Molly hanging clothes out, and Mrs. Rogers could be seen through the window preparing for their supper, but then he would not beat a woman and expect to be welcomed anywhere. No one seemed to be the worse for wear. She wondered if the squire might somehow have earned his displeasure. She would feel little concern for him in that case.

Her mother responded to Charlotte's question. "What was that you said, my dear?" Her mind had been in another place as she had been speaking with Thomas about something that she had meant to point out earlier.

"May I keep them?" Her fist clenched upon the coins and the watch, expecting that Sophia or Annis even, might suggest that they be given up and try to claim a share.

Her mother saw only the small bouquet of wild flowers that she had picked from the hedgerow on the way home.

"Of course, you may keep them, my dear. What a question to ask!"

Annis took note of the teeth left lying on the ground. Fortunately, her mother had not seen them. They appeared to be human teeth! She shivered. There was some story to be told, and she had better find it out for herself.

She then went to speak with Molly, who also seemed confused by her questions and, for once, seemed almost blockish—frustratingly so, and seemed unable to disclose anything. She then found Thomas, who had returned to his work in the stable. She was relieved to note, in better detail, that none of their own servants seemed any the worse for wear, but all had a different look about them and were even secretive about something, but they did not appear to be afraid of anything as she had first feared. Rather, they appeared to be quite contented and even happy—if that were possible in the present circumstance—but also a little furtive about something.

"Thomas, what went on here to leave those teeth and blood in the drive? Is everyone; are the servants all right?"

"Why, yes, miss. Why would we not be in good fettle?" He seemed equally evasive.

She felt a little frustrated to be learning nothing when there was a story waiting to be told. "Why is everyone so secretive all of a sudden? Surely you cannot deny the evidence presented in the driveway for us all to see?" She broached the presence of the teeth again and the sovereigns and watch in the driveway and demanded to know how they had got there.

He had not liked to be asked, and frowned. "I knew I should ha' moved 'em when I had the chance! Nothing to concern yourself over, miss!"

It could not so easily be swept aside. "But I am concerned, Thomas! I need to know what happened!" The reluctant and somewhat unsatisfactory account she eventually winkled out of the unusually close-lipped Thomas told her enough to start with. She found out that Mr. Thackeray had paid a visit while they had all been in church, except for Mr. Devane of course, who had returned to see what his intentions might be. One part of the puzzle had now fallen into place. So that was why he had returned as he had.

Thomas heartily wished he'd thought to remove those signs of violence before the family returned, for he knew they would not be ignored.

Annis then heard a similar disjointed tale from Molly, who gradually became more expansive once she realized it could not be denied.

What was related was a tale of a most violent encounter, which Molly stressed she should not repeat to her mother. The way it was told all seemed to reflect well on Mr. Devane, if the servants were to be believed. However, the violent nature of it all was to be abhorred and left too many unanswered questions.

"Oh please, miss, don't tell your mother. It was but a minor incident and best forgotten." She was not likely to get more out of Molly at the present time, so she returned to Thomas. "Despite what you told me, Molly tells a slightly different tale, and it does not present the appearance of only a minor incident at all, Thomas." There was obviously much more to it than had been initially related, and Annis had no intention of letting it rest until she knew it all, but Thomas had decided to say no more and had excused himself to get on with his work.

When she approached Molly yet again, it was almost the same story. But she persisted. Gradually more was dragged from her. Molly was quite happy to initially play down what she later opened up to confess that she had been most privileged to have witnessed. She seemed almost choked up with emotion as she recalled and retold it all, for she had seen everything that had gone on. But she was adamant that Annis's mother should learn none of it, for she seemed keen to protect the girls and their mother from being upset by what had really transpired.

"Molly. I must hear it all, or I might never rest easily with him under the same roof."

"Oh, do not say that, miss! Mr. Devane thought that it need not be more widely known to upset anyone any further." Annis believed that. "And I promised him, we all did, that we would say nothing, and I would not like to betray that confidence more than I already have." She seemed ready to break into tears.

"Do not worry, Molly. I was not about to let this rest without knowing. We *must* know it all, can you not see that? For our own safety. I promise that I will say nothing to my mother, but I do want a better account of what happened than just to hear that there was a *minor* incident, when I think it was not minor at all. Especially when I see human teeth in the driveway, hair on the trough edge, and when Charlotte finds sovereigns and a watch lying there too, amidst the blood, and you seem to regard it all as a great and wondrous thing to have had happen."

"Very well, miss, but I do not feel easy betraying what I know. As for those teeth and other things, we knew they were there, but none of us was going to touch any of that, miss." She sniffed and wiped at her eyes. "Anything that man had about him, even gold, was cursed, I would say, especially considering the condition he left in . . ." she chuckled and then remembered herself. "So we left them lying there. I doubt he'd come back to try and claim them, anyway. Not after the beating he got!"

With a little more encouragement, Molly went on at length and in considerable detail about what had unfolded, becoming more expansive and expressive as she warmed to the tale.

To Annis's surprise, Molly recounted the violence she had witnessed in tones of such admiration that she was quite taken aback. Molly's excitement was evident in her expression and the nature of her actions as she related the way in which Mr. Devane had spoken very gently and in a low voice to that Thackeray man.

"Oh, miss! I was terrified for him—for Mr. Devane—at first for he did not seem to know who he was up against. I'd heard tales of that Thackeray man's skullduggery with others and knew him to be a most dangerous kind of man and rough with women. But he more than met his match in Mr. Devane. I felt the hairs rising on the back of my neck over it, and Thomas said how he'd felt the same way. Within no more than a minute, it was obvious what would happen even though that Thackeray man seemed *not* to know— stupid man to argue with a man that smiles when he is angry, as well as when he is contented with life. Though you would never have known he might have been angry at all when he most gently thanked Mrs. Rogers after, as she bandaged his hand. All bloody it was! She was crying, as we all were, I do not mind admitting to that! I was breathless over it all, for I sensed what was to come. But Thackeray—the fool—had no wit about him and did not know what we did. Then before we knew it and with no more to do or hesitation, Mr. Devane had unceremoniously dragged him by the ear, and lord knows what, out of the house amidst considerable protest and noise—from that Thackeray individual of course—for Mr. Devane said nothing after his first gentle words. We fled for fear of our lives and being run down. He even disarmed him of that little pistol and sent him sprawling in the driveway. We were terrified. All the ill we had heard of that Thackeray person and his vicious ways and how he could be trusted to injure anyone who dared stand up to him had us quite concerned at first."

She faithfully related the subsequent actions of both parties—the hammering of that stupid man to the ground and then his being lifted into the trough as though he were a child and then Mr. Devane hammering at him again, and Thackeray helpless to do anything about any of it as though he were a mere stripling. Her voice had broken several times in the telling of it, for she had felt it so strongly. She punctuated her words with emotions of her own as her eyes sparkled, and she bubbled over with tears of relief and gratification that it had happened as it had, and that she had been privileged to have been present to see it; for she had never seen the like in all of her life, and *she* had been in some rough company before she came to work for the master and had seen many brawls when she'd worked in those inns! She had spoke the last without pausing for breath or slowing down and then fell silent, having emptied her budget of it all.

Annis had no difficulty reconciling Lady Seymour's lurid description with the man that was living with them, from the violent aspect of it all, but did have difficulty with the character that was being related by both the excited Molly and the admiring Thomas and then even by the tearfully admiring Mrs. Rogers—a lady who rarely showed her emotions over anything, except in the last few days.

What she heard related from all of those she questioned, was so very clearly at odds with his generally gentle behavior of the last day, and yet, what could one possibly know of anyone on such short familiarity? This rough and extremely violent man, worshipped now, it seemed, by the servants, had stooped and meekly submitted to her mother wiping a drop of blood off his cheek with her kerchief moistened in her own mouth *after* he had grievously injured Thackeray in such a bloodthirsty brawl. He had submitted to her as though he were merely a young boy who might not harm a fly—one of her own children, in fact—and he had not objected in any way or pulled away. He had even thanked her kindly for it afterward, grateful for the unexpected attention. It had been someone else's blood on his cheek and shirt! She recalled that he had smiled kindly at her mother as though she had been his own mother doing it while his bloody and bandaged hand, hidden a little behind him, had eventually dropped a little blood onto the ground from the end of his fingers. She had seen him scuff that evidence into the dirt with his feet before entering the church with them and had then taken care that no more fell from his fingers.

But then, he would endeavor to hide his true colors from everyone as he worked his way into their confidence. Who might know what he was capable of if confronted in the wrong way or time? It seemed that Thackeray had got the beating he had deserved, but he had also served another purpose—he had forced the true character of Mr. Devane into the open. She began to wish that Lady Seymour had come in person rather than just sending her most inflammatory letter and accusations along.

But then this account of calm and yet terrifying ferocity that had appeared to have made Molly's blood run cold, and that transpired barely minutes before William showed up at the church, had also fired Molly up with such defensive awestruck admiration for it all and the man who had done it.

Thomas had been much less effusive and had managed to play it down rather more, but the same story had been there to see and the same admiration, though not so openly expressed. She returned to Thomas wanting more details still, and managed to winkle more out of him. She was confused but relieved in the knowledge that she now had the entire tale and not sure what to make of it.

"Better not tell your mother, miss. It might upset her."

"Yes, that's what Molly and Mrs. Rogers said too when I asked them. You should have told me all of it at the outset and saved me from this inquisition. Don't worry. I shall say nothing. So how should we deal with this, Thomas?" She was unsure of how to go on, never having encountered such a situation in her life before. "Should we all be in fear of our lives from this man?"

"He won't be back again, miss!"

"I meant from Mr. Devane!"

He could not hide his surprise from her. "Him? Not from him, miss! Far from it!" He leapt to his defense in no half measure. "Why, just you ignore it all and try to forget it. It won't never happen again, I can promise you that." He chuckled as he thought about it again. "Not from what I saw." He looked sharply at her. "Oh no, miss. You need not fear about Mr. Devane. I'd stake my life on him! Certainly you need not worry about seeing Mr. Thackeray around here again! Not after what I was privileged to see. Not for a very long time, at any rate. Not in my lifetime! Not if he has any sense!"

When she entered the house, there was a subtle difference in the way everything had almost imperceptibly changed. The looks on the faces of the servants were different—sharper, brighter, and they tended to move with a little more purpose and alacrity. Something had certainly changed, but in a positive way for once.

She also could see that there was a not totally *subtle* change in the way in which they looked at Mr. Devane.

She noticed over the next few hours that he responded kindly and with a gentle smile to any small attention given him during supper and afterward, and even openly thanked them for their help in whatever way they had given it and told them that he really did not need to be waited upon quite so well.

He did not behave like a tyrannical being or a usurper, for his every word was kind and gentle to them. But then he had never uttered an unkind word about or to anyone within her earshot that she was aware of, nor did he order anyone about as some men seemed to do, but always deferred either to her mother or even to her, and thanked all of the servants for even small attentions. She could not fault him for his manners but was afraid what it might portend. Her godmother's account still lurked in her mind. The greatest villains always had the sweetest smiles and disposition with those they needed to confuse, while they worked their way into their trust and confidences. Undoubtedly, he was an accomplished and careful villain, who knew exactly what he was about!

But it was also puzzling! The servants were certainly not afraid nor shy of him nor cowed in any way. It was as though he had suddenly become the master of the house and had so easily slid into her father's shoes with so little ceremony about it and no obvious objection from anyone. Could he be so very clever as to confuse everyone, even Thomas, in that way?

She was not sure that she liked the feeling or approved of the change, but there was little she could do about it, for her mother had been bitten by the same bug and seemed ready to leap to his defense and even to deal with him as she would the son she never raised, and him almost a complete stranger to them all. But then she now needed some support to lean upon, and he was there.

He was perhaps even more dangerous than Lady Seymour may have detailed, if that were possible. Had he not just seen a competitor taken out of the lists? He now had the field to himself. With a houseful of now mostly witless admiring women at his feet, what might he not accomplish? Well there was one that had not lost her wits. What might he be planning?

She decided to keep a close eye on Mr. Devane but would not go so far just yet as showing her mother that most damaging letter or relating any of what she had just found out. She would not be believed, anyway.

Chapter XIII

A Helpful and Silent Observer

Annis noted that by about six o'clock the next morning, a jug of hot water was delivered to Mr. Devane's room, for she heard him thank Molly for it. As she looked out of her door to let Molly know that she would also be stirring, she noticed Captain Cat leaving his room too, even as her sister Sophia was going into it in her nightdress.

Mr. Devane was proving to be very popular with everyone. She would need to have a word with Sophia. One did not enter the bedroom of a grown man before he had had chance to shave and dress, nor even afterward either, and certainly not so carelessly attired in just a nightdress. Mrs. Chepstow's words—unkind as they were—resonated with her.

It seemed that he had almost taken over the house and had the servants attending to his needs, though he had not directed any of them to do so. Even the cat had uncharacteristically made friends with him. Perhaps this was what he intended; to gradually take over everything before he made any other advances.

"A cat can read a man's character better than anyone else, and faster." She heard her own father's words at that moment. Could her father have been wrong? What would a cat know of a man's character? He had been describing, with some humor, the way the cat had mauled the Ibbotson youth when he had thought—like the foolish youth he was—to capture and subdue the cat to try and impress Bella, and to show how clever he was with animals and how inferior to a strong man they were. He had unexpectedly encountered a ball of raging fury with a storm of a thousand razor sharp claws and teeth, dealing with his hands. He had left, somewhat pale and chastened and much bloodied, and had never shown his face again.

No one mentioned the injury to William's hands other than Sophia, who noticed everything, and mentioned it over breakfast that morning. He smiled and shrugged it off with some explanation that it had come up against something rough and hard in the yard, leaving the impression that it had happened while he was helping Thomas somewhere outside.

Annis was also surprised to notice that he was also as careful and silent an observer of them all as she was of him, for she caught him looking at her strangely on several occasions. He did not intrude upon them more than he might, but he stayed close. He could be found about the yard and, if not there, then either in the study, writing letters there or in the parlor, and generally making himself useful everywhere while staying out of everyone's way, yet missing nothing. Undoubtedly, he was biding his time to dig himself in even deeper, as he learned more of their secrets. Eventually, he would strike in some way before they might know what he might have done! She could say nothing to her mother who had seemed to grow even more defensive of him. She would not be believed in any of it, and it seemed that neither Charlotte nor Sophia nor even any of the servants would ever believe her.

Had they known that he was keeping what amounted to a diary of what he saw unfolding around him, just as he had on the Peninsula, and his impressions of them all; they may not have felt so relaxed or comfortable in his presence, though Annis was neither relaxed nor comfortable. Rather, she remained vigilant. Annis discovered it, however, for she had seen him filling it in from time to time and decided that at the first opportunity, she would learn what he was writing in it, and would perhaps learn more of his true purpose from what he wrote.

That afternoon he had carelessly left it on the window seat in the parlor, having been called from the house on some minor task that Sophia had reminded him about.

Annis sat down and looked at it, as she also looked out of the window to see where William might be. He was not to be seen nor was Sophia. There was no-one else close by. Obviously she would have a few minutes to see if there was anything to learn from it that might help her understand his purpose.

It seemed like a bulky kind of portfolio tied with a ribbon. She gently undid it and turned into it, to encounter several letters addressed to families she had never heard of, and spread across the entire country, it seemed—some finished, others not—in the front of it. They were exceptionally clearly written, free of any deletions or corrections, and they were also written in pencil and not in ink. Most strange! She put them aside and encountered what seemed like a diary, with comments on what had unfolded so far for him since he had arrived. Clearly it was thick enough to have been abroad with him, considering the pages that seemed to be filled with both sketches and various writings. He must have been exceedingly well taught to have written in such a careful hand and to express himself as clearly as he seemed to. It was but another strange feature that seemed at odds with his reputation and character. Men—rough and violent men—were generally unable to express themselves at all well, usually, though she remembered that Gideon Thackeray, the father, had also written very clearly in one letter of his she had seen before her father burnt it. His son, on the other hand, had given every sign of being careless and ill educated in that way.

She read quickly about his observations of their family and skipped quickly over the pages.

There were brief notes about them all covering the last few days since his arrival. The more she saw, the more impressed she became. His penmanship showed a surprising degree of scholarship as well as care and neatness, as though he were a perfectionist. Certainly his way of expressing himself was genteel and not as might be anticipated for a soldier just returning from war.

The first entry she read noted that: "All of the girls play or are learning to play the harpsichord and are notable at it and able to keep the spirit and tempo that Mr. Handel demanded in his pieces." Now what might he know of playing the harpsichord or even of Mr. Handel?

In the next paragraph, he wrote: "The middle girl now, Charlotte, is an accomplished artist who draws skillfully, quickly and well, and when her subjects least expect it. She's caught me off guard on several occasions now. She is easily the match of Elizabeth from the little I have been allowed to see when I caught her unawares. I must keep my eyes about me better. They seem to be everywhere and to pop up when one least expects them."

He obviously listened to their conversations and wrote that he had found out that Bella had been the beauty, as befitted her name; Annis, the brains; Charlotte, the artist; and the youngest, Sophia, whatever she would like to be for she seemed to be shaping up to be cleverer than any of them and could often not easily be pried from an atlas or other books more suitable for much older readers. He noted that he would see about getting some of his own books sent over at some stage without letting them know where they had come from.

He described their efforts to pull together and provide support for each other. Noting that their recent tragedy had obviously brought them all closer together and had not so far excluded him too far.

There was a thick section at the back of the portfolio which contained about forty or more most-skillful drawings of scenes that were obviously of either Spain or of Portugal. He seemed to be a good artist himself if he had done them.

She had no time to investigate further, for she heard a horse enter the gateway and only had time to retie the folder as it had been tied before, and to leave it in the same position. It would never do for her to be caught snooping through his private writings. She resolved to watch her opportunity at some other time and look a little deeper if she could.

Chapter XIV

Two Strange Men Arrive, Secretively Confer, and Depart

In the middle of the next morning, Annis saw a small carriage pull into the yard. Two very strange-looking gentlemen were met by Mr. Devane at the door. They were clearly known to him and he, to them. He then took them into the parlor to meet with her mother.

One of them gave the appearance of a clerk, but the other was of a more arresting appearance. He was of less-than-average size but made up for it in his barrel-like chest and long arms. He was a man who would be difficult to forget. He had a most severely misshapen face, and his hands were difficult to regard as hands, for they seemed to have suffered much damage in some way and were mostly scarred and with difficult-to-sort-out fingers on them. When she bumped into him in the corridor, she noticed those details, but especially his eyes. His eyes looked straight into one's own without flinching away and were perhaps small and even beady, but he smiled pleasantly enough at her, revealing gaps in his mouth where teeth were missing. He would not be easy to intimidate in any circumstance she reckoned. She had an uneasy feeling about him. One would not wish to meet him on a dark night, nor would one wish to antagonize him!

They obviously intended to stay for some time, as their horses had been put away. She would have given anything to have been invited into their conversation, but her mother had closed the door after them once they had gone into the parlor.

She persuaded Molly that she would see to refreshments for her mother and the three gentlemen in the parlor, as a means of listening in upon their conversation but found that the conversation had briefly stopped as she entered the room and did not continue, and then only in a lower tone once she had left. The door to the parlor was also gently closed behind her once again. The more rugged and weather-beaten of the two gentlemen had been sitting in the window nursing a beer and playing with a small clay pipe in his fingers as he had watched out of the window. William, her mother, and the other slight gentleman, for he was amazingly thin once he had got rid of his outer coat, were sitting at the parlor table conversing together over several papers when she had intruded with the tea tray.

After about a half hour of conversation, the more studious looking of the two gentlemen accompanied William into her father's study while the other man walked off about the gardens, speaking briefly with Thomas before he then walked off down the lane in the direction of the squire's property. Within five minutes, he had turned about and walked off in the other direction to the small village some distance down the road. He paused often and looked about himself. It seemed that nothing much of any importance would escape his eyes, and yet he had not given the impression of knowing much of anything, for he had not said more than two or three words that she had been aware of to anyone other than perhaps to Thomas. He paused and lit up a pipe with great ceremony at one stage as he looked around himself before he had gone very far, and then rambled on down the track.

The next thing she noticed was that some two hours or more later, the horses were once more harnessed to the carriage; and the two gentlemen, if they could be described as that, loaded two of her father's smaller trunks; brought down from the attic; into it, and then drove off as they had arrived. She had not even noticed the older man come back from his walk, yet she had watched for him.

When she went into the parlor, her mother was gently weeping over a copy of the *Gazette* that the gentlemen had brought.

"What is it, Mama?"

"The notice of your father and Bella, my dear."

"Already?"

"Oh yes. I wrote to our relatives in London to let them know of what had happened that first day when I wrote to William and others. I did not expect them to be able to break away on such short notice to attend the funeral, but they did ensure that it was recorded properly in the *Gazette*."

"So that is why all the blackguards are now suddenly descending upon us."

"And which blackguards might those be? I have seen none yet." Her mother had bristled at her description.

"Blackguards might be the wrong word, but who were those two men? They seemed too secretive and furtive for honest men! What did they want? What did they take with them? Why all the secrecy? You all went very quiet when I came in with the tray. Why was there any need for any secrecy from me?"

"Yes, I thought you were hovering too close and that you'd be itching to know who they were and the rest of it, but you need not be burdened by any of that just at the moment. I will tell you more later. They are Mr. Gilbey—he was once known to your father, Grinder Gilbey—quite a famous man at one time, though it might be hard to believe that, I know. The other is Mr. Diebold, perhaps not so well known. For he is methodical, quiet, and studious. But I think he prefers it that way.

"If he is, as you say methodical, quiet and studious, perhaps that is because he can neither hear nor speak well with those features of his. Was that not a cauliflower ear that he has?"

Mr. Gilbey is the one with the rough features, my dear, though I believe I heard your father also mention him as being very methodical in his approach and quiet enough, without show or bluster so that he often lulled others into not appreciating his true abilities until it was too late for them. He was once a famous prize fighter whom your father followed quite excitedly some ten years gone. He had what was once described as a murderously unexpected left, I believe, and delivered with the speed of lightning and entirely without it being signaled." Annis shivered at considering the violence of it all. "Quite impressed your father, though I was not of the same mind about such brutality!" She had a pained look on her face for a moment. "The other gentleman is the unassuming and quiet one, but quiet in a different way. Very strange men, but I found that I liked them both very much.

"As for the reason they were here, William suggested I meet with them, at least with Mr. Diebold, so I did. Mr. Gilbey was there to protect him and what he took with him. What they took with them might just be the sum total of all of my—our—present problems. If anyone can sort them out, then Mr. Diebold will. I never thought to find things to be so easily dealt with. If they are!"

"Dare you trust them, Mama?"

"I must trust someone, my dear, and I do not have the luxury of time to find out who that might be for myself. I do not trust my own relatives for the most part, but I do trust William. Just as I trust his sister as though she were one of my own. That is all that matters to me at this moment."

It seemed to Annis that her mother had quite lost her senses—to trust their future to such a trio of obvious ruffians and villains!

Chapter XV

An Armed Protectress Disarmed, Rearmed—Confusion! A Revealing Journal

Not much seemed to escape William's attention. By early the next morning, he had noticed that Annis has taken to carrying a bulky and heavy knitting bag with needles poking from it, and yet, he had never seen her knitting to any purpose. It sounded somewhat ominous when she had put it down on the parlor table a little too heavily on one occasion.

He smiled and bided his time. He had noticed one of the large horse pistols had gone missing from the gun cabinet in the study.

That same afternoon, as he was allowing his midday meal to settle, he had sat himself in the window seat of the parlor and opened his journal to continue writing his various letters. Annis was doing a little mending with needle and thread as she sat at the parlor table, intent also on keeping an eye on William as much as she could. He had not spent much time after that first day in their father's study and after the other two gentlemen had left. Annis had watched everything taking place around her, even as she watched William, and was a little concerned to note that her mother no longer seemed worried about the state of their affairs, or almost anything else for that matter, yet she herself could not see that anything might have changed for the better.

She now knew, after a little surreptitious investigation as the opportunity was available, that some of the letters in William's folder were to the families of those who had served with him in his regiment and for whom he had felt responsible, for there were a sheaf of them in the back of his bulky folder along with his sketches.

As a major, he had the responsibility of commanding several men and undoubtedly of losing some of those about him. Her father had spoken of such things as the various news sheets had come across his desk.

William had taken on the task of writing to their families to express his greatest sorrow over the loss of their sons while serving with him in the Peninsula and clearing out the French. There seemed to have been many of them killed in action, and yet, she was not sure just how many men a major might expect to command. She had noticed and read one or two where he had written to those whose son was only badly wounded, to give them news of their son's progress and whereabouts.

He had positioned himself close to Annis's knitting bag, which was beside him and he seemed to have lost something, for he looked through his folder and then beside himself.

"So that is where I lost it!" He had picked up Annis bag as he delved behind it, into the cushions for a pencil that he seemed to have lost there, and seemed surprised to encounter the muzzle of a pistol poking from her knitting bag.

"My! What is this?" He gave every appearance of being bemused as he looked across at Annis. "I did not realize that this was part of the knitting requirements of a young lady. Surely the clacking of knitting needles does not arouse such violent passions in anyone to the point where you need to defend yourself from attack?"

"It isn't!" She colored, even as he smiled and then laughed gently. It seemed that he was able to read her very thoughts.

He smiled at her. "I didn't think it was. You seem to fear for your life. Do you? That is the only reason I know for anyone wanting to carry such a murderous weapon as this!"

She was flustered for a second or two and could not meet his eyes. "There were two strangers here the other day. One of them seemed most . . . seemed the worse for wear and strange, and perhaps with violent tendencies."

"Surely Mr. Gilbey did not scare you that much? Though yes, he does have exceptionally violent tendencies in the right circumstances, as we all do, but I can assure you he is a most gentle man where women are concerned and is even gentle with stupid young boys too in need of his tutelage, as I once was!"

She tried to bolster her case with the pistol. "I also heard that Mr. Thackeray was seen in the area—one of our less illustrious and desirable relatives."

"He was? He is?" His innocent response was as though he did not know that, yet he most certainly did for he had brawled with him, and there was that ever-present smile upon his face as though he were laughing at some inner secret known only to himself. She wondered if he had not also known about the pistol too, and had needed an excuse to disturb her bag, for she did not see him retrieve any pencil that he might have lost. "Perhaps he was just passing through."

It all sounded so innocent, as though nothing need be thought of it. "I can understand your concern over Mr. Gilbey. He has that effect on most people who encounter him. He instills, in some, a great dread of making him angry, as he has the reputation of being unpredictable and most violent if crossed. And in others, he instills a great confidence that trouble will never approach them while he is close by. He is my sister's butler and general factotum, whom I borrowed for that day. As for the taller of the two gentlemen, Mr. Diebold, he is much more to be feared, I think." His eyes sparkled as he thought of that gentleman. 'Yes. Much more dangerous, for he has an incisive and quick mind that nothing will hinder or stop. He is the mightier pen to Mr. Gilbey's obvious sword, but in a violent scuffle my money would be on Gilbey every time!"

Hers would be too. She shivered at that thought, for some reason. "You seem to know only violent and dangerous men!"

He smiled at her criticism. "Violent and dangerous only to their enemies, Miss Barristow! Annis!" She noticed that his eyes smiled at her, and that he did not seem offended by her comment. "Yes, I have lived with such men for the last few years and been thankful because of it! That is what war is all about, and I have survived when too many others did not because I was also violent when I needed to be!"

He continued to smile at her, but then his expression became more serious. "But more to the point over what is dangerous or not." He turned the pistol over in his hands and examined it. "You carry this horse pistol close by you, but can you handle a firearm, or do you pose a danger to everyone about you as well as to yourself?" He looked gently at her, awaiting some kind of explanation, and she found herself blushing at the uncomplimentary thoughts she held for him over his discovery.

"My father taught me to shoot!" She was flushed and even a little defiant. "He sometimes took me out birding with him, so I am also familiar with fowling pieces."

"I see! I regard firearms with great respect and caution, especially . . ." He did not continue his thoughts, but then he had no need to. Especially when in the hands of a foolish woman, he might have continued to say.

"Especially in the hands of a woman?" she filled in the gap.

"No, Annis! Especially when there are impressive and curious children in the house. I was one myself once and very nearly caused the loss of life of a friend with a pistol just like this one. I did not know that with age, they tend not to function as intended."

"Oh!" She digested that admission. "But Sophia knows that she must not touch this, for I had a word with her and warned her of the dangers. She promised not to touch it."

"Good! But safer never to have to carry it. Most ladies I know would not know how to fire such a weapon, never mind be so unwise as to pick one up, to say nothing of loading it and carrying it about with them, for I assume it is loaded." He looked at her for confirmation.

She nodded.

"Especially one so conspicuous and so large and clumsy and even with this vicious blade hinged beneath it." He swung the blade out and replaced it again. "Yes, it would definitely do great injury if it were dropped on one's foot!"

She found that she was feeling stubborn as well as a little angry at him for baiting her and seeming so smug about it all. "Perhaps you would like a demonstration, sir?" She regretted the words even as she spoke them, but he had goaded her.

"Yes, I would!" He smiled at her. "I'm not surprised I touched a nerve! I would be surprised if I had not! But that would be a capital idea! Dare you do that, Annis?" He seemed to be challenging her as his eyes also seemed to smile at her.

She could not back away now, as he well knew. She would show him and perhaps let him see that she knew how to use it and was not afraid to use it if she must. "Yes. I do." She took it from him and cursorily examined the gun. "I will need to recharge the pan, however. The gunpowder has fallen out of it." She blushed at that discovery, but at least, she had discovered it before she tried to show him that she knew what she was doing, and had failed.

"Yes, so it has." He had not taken a second look at the pan, for he had already seen that for himself as he had first removed it from its hiding place. "No danger of that one going off by accident!" Nothing much would escape his keen eyes, it seemed.

He might try to convince her that he had not noticed that, until she pointed it out herself, but it was obvious that he had already seen that her gun would have been totally ineffective had she needed to use it. He did not seem to be gloating at her carelessness, and yet she felt as though he could not have been more critical of it if he had pointed it out himself.

"I think that if you expect to use it with any purpose, and without having to rush around looking for powder to recharge it or to rummage amongst your knitting to find it, it needs a better and tighter cover over the flashpan as well as a little more care in putting it away. That one is a little askew with age and hard use. Quite common, I know, as I found to my cost more than once, and as others did, to theirs. I shall see to it if you like?"

His words were gentle as he looked at her, but she did not answer, feeling embarrassed by that omission despite the fact that he also admitted to having been caught in the same position on one occasion.

"But then we should go outside." He gently took the gun from her. "I doubt your mother would approve of having a loaded gun in the parlor." They walked outside. He carried the gun and handed it to her once they were outside.

He watched as she recharged the pan from a powder horn in her knitting bag also.

"My! What you ladies manage to squirrel away in your bags and purses defies the imagination!"

She knew better than to respond to his gently humorous comment in her present rebellious mood.

"What about the knot in the gate-post over there?" He was challenging her again.

"I do not know my backdrop there, sir. There may be someone walking in the lane."

"Yes, there might." His eyes betrayed that he had already known that, and was challenging her again. "I am also William, remember?"

He had not said so, but that was her second test after she had carelessly failed the first one. Fortunately, she had passed *that* one! She had not known the powder would be shaken out of the flashpan so easily, especially when it was covered, and hoped that the wadding had been secure enough in the barrel not to have fallen out also, and losing the ball and charge in her bag as well. But then that was why she had put it in with the muzzle uppermost. She must make sure that there was no loose powder left in the bottom of her bag. It would be too embarrassing to have it suddenly erupt in flames.

"There are empty fields over there. There is a blemish on that oak, where a branch was taken off, and a weathervane leaning against it. Take your choice. If you miss, there is nothing to come to harm. For the target is a little below you, and a ricochet will go nowhere. Or you can choose a target more suitable for yourself."

"I shall take the weathervane. The middle of the rooster's body will leave a visible mark and a sound, and I shall not miss." She sounded defiant.

He was impressed by her determination and confidence.

She raised the gun purposefully and fired without hesitation at the designated target. There was the dull sound of metal being hit by a piece of lead, and there was suddenly a notable dent in the body of the rooster. She was relieved to find that she had not lost anything from the pistol in her bag other than the powder from the flashpan.

"You hit it! Quite a respectable shot for this distance, but I fear a little light on powder. You are one of only two ladies I know who might decide that they needed to know how to fire a gun and might be capable of firing one in anger, as I think you may be." Her eyes flashed. Yes, she was angry. Angry at being found out. "A little high and to the right, I think, but you would have been most effective anyway. I would have been heading quickly in the other direction after that. If I was still on my feet!"

She was not pleased with herself despite his praise. He seemed to be playing with her if his gentle smile could be read accurately. "It kicks."

"They all do! If they didn't, they would not be very effective at the other end. Please stay there. Do not reload, though I am very sure you have powder, shot and wadding enough somewhere in that knitting bag of yours. I have a better and safer solution to the difficulty."

She watched as he entered the house. She swore at herself in frustration for having been found out to be carrying a bulky pistol and not knowing that it was useless.

He reappeared after a few moments with a small case containing a much smaller pistol, a few lead shot, a little powder, wadding, and some strange and small brass cylinders. She was curious to see that the pistol had no flint and no flashpan.

"This is less bulky and will not lose its powder. It can also be kept in its case and out of the way of children." He began to load it, and she watched attentively as he spoke. "It has a shorter barrel so it is liable to be less accurate too unless you are very close to your target, but then a lady would rarely need take a distant shot—never advisable anyway. Better to wait and be sure of hitting what you decide to fire at with the one shot you can be sure of getting, though that may take some courage. It is also less likely to kick so hard and spoil your aim, but it *will* also kick, so it needs a firm grip. It is one that a lady—well, certain ladies—would not scorn to own. Keep this by you instead. It has a new percussion cap system that is cleaner and easier to use and less likely to misfire."

He placed a percussion cap in place and handed it to her. "Now try it."

She took her time, cocked the gun fully, and discharged it at her selected target. The kick was only a *little* less, even though it had a lighter ball and less of a charge of gunpowder, but she did strike the middle of the rooster, even at that distance and even put a hole in it.

"That will not take up too much room, I think, and you might even be able to carry it with less trouble. It would save you lugging about such a bulky knitting bag to conceal that other murderous weapon. Though safer by far, I think, if you were not to carry it at all."

"Yes. Thank you. I do not knit that much." She recalled something he had said earlier that had stuck in her mind. "You said I was one of only two women . . ."

He proceeded to clean and reload it for her as she watched attentively. "My sister, Elizabeth, whom you all seem to know! She would not be likely to tell you any of that, however. I gave her one like this just before I quit England. It was almost one of the first to use the new percussion cap. She had to use it only once I believe, and to some effect for her protection, *before* she introduced herself to Mr. Gilbey." He was briefly reminded of Julius Maxton. His sister would not have discussed firearms nor have said anything of that misadventure to either Annis or to Bella or anyone else.

"If you do not object, I will see that this horse pistol is cleaned and returned to the gun cabinet, lest your sisters take it into their heads to emulate you. I am surprised that most of the house has not come running to find out whom you have killed, except I saw them heading into the village earlier. So who do you think you need protection from? I know I have a poor reputation in many quarters." He smiled as though he did not believe that of himself. "But surely it cannot be *that* bad?"

She blushed and said nothing other than to thank him for his pistol. Had she been so obvious and transparent? It would seem so.

She was suddenly confused by him. He was obviously a most dangerous individual and very devious and was undoubtedly trying to lull her and the entire family into a false sense of security, including the servants, even Mrs. Rogers, and Thomas. But to what end? He had made no overtures of any kind to either her or Charlotte but rather, had seemed aloof to them, and he was all consideration itself to their mother. But her mother should know enough to see right through him, and yet it seemed that she had become blind. Sophia stood in no fear of him nor should she from what she had seen. He seemed to have everyone else, including her mother eating out of his hand. Either that, or he was far too good to be true, in which case Lady Seymour was much mistaken in her rendering of him. But that seemed most unlikely, for there had been hints of various scandals around him that she had heard of from years before, which her godmother had suddenly breathed better life into, and even that Mrs. Chepstow had known of him.

Over the next hour or so, she began to see him in a little different of a light, still keeping her godmother's cautions in mind, but found that despite that, she was judging him a little less harshly. No brigand or despoiler of women would willingly give into her hands the means to foil him. Or would he? She decided she needed to know much more about him than she had so far read in that letter, though what she had encountered in his own journal began to be seen differently. Perhaps all young men were rogues of that kind. She knew few young men to know *that* with any surety, and those that she did have some acquaintance with were certainly not so very much at ease around women as he was.

She also decided she did not need to carry the pistol, and returned it and its case onto his dresser one morning. He said nothing about it. But shortly afterward, she noticed that it had been placed on her own dresser with a little note on it. It said simply "A gift, to a determined, resourceful, and courageous young lady. Best keep it out of sight of your mother and Sophia."

She was confused again. She decided she would keep a closer eye upon him and try to discover some deeper purpose in his staying, for she doubted it was just to help them in their time of need. Or maybe that's all there was too it, and he was really quite considerate of them all and reserved his predations for other parts of society in which he travelled, and with a different class of female as her godmothers letter had indirectly suggested. Yet he had not been in any hurry to head back to any mistress he might be keeping in London.

She began to take more of an interest in him and to spy on him a little more than she had, though she hoped, not too obviously.

He continued as he had been, busying himself outside quite well, and she could even begin to see improvements in most things, though he said little to anyone other than her mother what he intended to do or had done.

She noticed that he was often in her father's study, mostly in the very early morning before anyone else was up, either writing in his journal; going over the ledgers; or reading through older copies of the various newspapers that her father had collected over the years. She noticed that he had also changed his habits and no longer shaved or washed in the trough now that he had hot water delivered to him whenever he wanted it.

After dinner, he had excused himself for the last two evenings and had sat down and continued writing in his journal or wrote continuations of the many letters, and one in particular that he seemed to add to, from time to time.

One evening, he left his journal again in the window embrasure by some oversight, rather than taking it up to his room as he usually did. As he was not close by but had gone into the village and had taken Sophia up on his horse with him, and as no one else might see her, she picked up his journal again; undid the ribbon holding it all together; and read more of his entries since she had last opened it. He would be unlikely to return unexpectedly as he had before, as she would have ample warning of a returning horse coming up the lane, so she could go through it at her leisure without disturbing anything too much or presenting the impression that anyone had opened it.

The unfinished letter at the front on this occasion was to his sister, Elizabeth. She wondered what he might have to say to her, for she was an especially good friend to them all.

He wrote well and concisely, describing the setting in which he found himself and with some not unflattering viewpoints of her mother and sisters. She turned to entries for the day that he had fought with Thackeray and discovered nothing at all. Most strange, for her own diary had been filled on that day with what she had learned, and enough to spill over onto the following page.

There were many more letters ready to be sent off to bereaved families; there seemed to be too many of them, and the one in progress to his sister.

She looked at the direction on two others but did not recognize either name, though one seemed directed to a law firm. She recognized one name in the list of those on the letter, that of Diebold, and the other, was to a firm she did not know. Both were to go to London. He had sent several such letters to London and elsewhere while he had been here, for the younger stable boy rarely seemed to be doing anything except ride back and forth on such errands. Her mother had said nothing about it, though she must have noticed, and nor did the stable boy who seemed to be rewarded well for his efforts each time, and even from William's own pocket.

She decided not to pry further, but the temptation proved too much, so she picked up the several pages of a letter that seemed directed at his sister. It was still incomplete. It was again, written not in ink, despite there being plenty of ink in the study—which was always fraught with the risk of being spilled and probably not easily available on campaign—but with that most interesting pencil that he seemed habitually to use, that nestled in the edge of the book. The graphite core in the middle of a slim wooden holder, bound tightly to hold everything in place, seemed much harder than usual, leaving a thin easily read line on the paper. It did not seem to easily smudge either, and was totally unlike those graphite sticks from Cumberland that she and Charlotte used for drawing. *They* dirtied one's fingers and even smudged rather easily on the paper and then their clothing if they were careless with their smocks. She would ask him about that some time.

> *Dearest Elizabeth,*
>
> *We continue to miss each other. Thank you for sending some of my better clothing and that little package that I requested. I hope that the sparse contents of my luggage did not too much startle you, but I did not expect anyone other than myself might need to dig into them. The Peninsula was not kind to my wardrobe. I am sorry to hear that you are indisposed, as well as concerned to hear from John, though I can*

assure you that he is safe where he is. I also know how impatient you are to come and visit your friends.

I am slowly recovering from the rigors of the continent, though my other letters revive too many memories of friends now gone. I had not realized I had lost so many of them, though my journal tells me that I did.

I am facing much better fare at table than I ever seem to have remembered. I am finding that the demands of peacetime are much more fatiguing than war, and from my pointless interview with our GM. I still do not know why she wanted to see me, but I do not doubt she intends mischief in some way and was fishing for some chink in my armor, so I gave her a few to occupy her. Of course, I regretted it soon afterward. She will undoubtedly use them too well against me.

I feel the need to write again, for I gave you so little news in my first letter, being as rushed as I was. I appear to be suffering from a peculiar malady, for I am caught up in some rather confusing personal crises (nothing to do with my ill-fated marriage or the aftermath of war—I expect mama must be quite angry, or she will be when she finds out that her plans for me in that direction must have been disrupted or may even have been fulfilled, I am not sure) when I consider the changes that I appear to be experiencing in my own character. I seem to be quite contented for some reason, despite the tragic circumstance in which I landed. This will never do! I have an unenviable reputation to uphold!

I fear I have fallen in love! Do not be surprised by this. She is barely six years old and follows me everywhere just like a shadow. What is even more amazing is that I do not mind. There may be hope for me yet, it seems!

Were it not for the entirely tragic circumstances I find myself in at this time, I would think that I might have landed in a paradise containing some of the loveliest and most charmingly interesting women I have ever encountered, though I am mostly viewed with great reservation, and they all spy upon me! My heart goes out to them for their loss. I am not sure how I will be able to contain or control myself surrounded by such beauty, grace, and gentleness, having been surrounded for the last five years by such horror, violence, and with only rough men, death, and strange and bloodthirsty, and surprisingly violent women for company.

They are all frighteningly intelligent and accomplished and can see right through me (at least one of them can—I suspect you can guess which one)but then you already know all of this, for you could too. The same one seems to have taken me in dislike and was intent on carrying a horse pistol for protection from me! I hope that the next you hear of me is NOT that I have been shot, for she is another just like you and will obviously tolerate no nonsense when it comes to her family. Most interesting! But then neither will I when it comes to a sticking point. I shall have to watch my step. It is a good thing that I was here, for luckily, I was able to save them from an awkward confrontation that would not have gone in their favor.

> *By the way, the younger Maxton is not likely to be a problem for you ever again (RIP), and within hours of my landing. Quite depressing really to think that an individual might bear a grudge for so long and be so all consumed with anger and hatred! It destroyed him in the end. The damned fool thought I would sit still aboard my horse to be shot! At least you may now be able to leave your own pistol at home. More on that topic when I see you.*
>
> *I am not sure what to tell you that you do not already know, for I have learned that you have long been friends with Mrs. Barristow and her daughters and know them all much better than I might. Why is it that no one, you especially, ever mentioned them to me? Alas, I think I might know the answer to that—what a sad pass I must have come to—which means that no one ever mentioned me to them either and for the same reason. Just as well, considering the baggage and sad reputation I am saddled with, and unlikely to be able to free myself of it for some time with what I think I may have to do here.*
>
> *On a lighter note, again. I am more contented and happy, I think, than I have ever been. I even begin to feel useful as well as needed, so you were right about that. For once in my life, I am useful to someone, rather than the constant target of criticism and censure and the rest of it. I am also discovering that though I am following my usual habit of observing everything intently, I am also being subjected to the same intense scrutiny when I might least expect it. There is no possibility of privacy in conversation or anything, thrown together as we are. I find that I must have my wits about me or I am ambushed even as I wake up or retire, in my ablutions, even my bath, I suspect. And it can only get worse, I fear, as they get to know me better, and they seem to be ensconced everywhere where one least expects them or might even see them. I cannot go for a walk or pick up a book or write a letter but that I find I have an observer or a companion, though I do not mind that. I have discovered that I am constantly being spied upon and have little privacy. Somewhat intriguing!*

He seemed to have broken off and had taken up the letter sometime later in the day or even the next day.

> *I did refer to it above, I know, but I had better tell you before you hear about it from others and in a light that does not shine at all favorably on me considering my earlier escapades, which it shouldn't anyway. To wit, I have not lost my touch for brawling, for I found it necessary to turn away one particularly ill-mannered and violent relative (not one of ours—I mentioned an awkward confrontation, but now I shall provide some detail rather than leave it hanging) who had thought to take advantage of their circumstance, and of me—most foolish fellow! I am glad to say that they appear to know none of this or I might not be so welcome, for I really did not feel kindly toward the individual considering what his intent seems to have been, especially when he was a little rough with one of the servants and then thought to bring his firearm into play. Unfortunately, I punished him rather severely for that*

and then regretted that afterward too. Damned conscience! I await with some small trepidation the arrival of yet another, perhaps the vengeful father that I was also warned about by Mr. B.

Tell Mama, if you see her before I do, only what you judge to be reasonable. I will write her when I am able to come to grips with my own feelings a little better. I am beginning to realize that I was an exceptionally poor, thoughtless, and heartless son for her. She did not deserve to be saddled with the likes of me.

No matter, you know how she feels about that side of me and how easily she is set off, so I shall strive to be more considerate and to try to mend fences now that I am returned with a better understanding of what is important in life. I expect I can thank John and our campfire chats and you for that.

Tell our godmother nothing! She can take a minor irritant and make a life-changing issue out of it throughout all of society! I fear she has this nagging dread about me that I might sometime find contentment and happiness and might be able to survive without her patronage, influence, or approval as I have until now, and she is determined to stop that.

More about the daughter who might have shot me. One might almost think she knew more of me than I like. I hope you have not been sharing too many of my secrets. I gave her one of my pistols—the twin of the little set I once gave to you. It had saved my life on occasion. I think she is determined to protect her sisters and mother from some perceived evil in their midst who goes by name of William! Me! I hope that when you next hear of me that I have not been shot. Sorry, if I am repeating myself, but she obviously does not trust me. I do not blame her, considering the general rumors! But I must be careful with my journal and letters, for I fear she might be curious enough to read them if she gets the chance to learn more of me than might be good for her to know.

I did notice earlier that a letter had come for Mrs. Barristow from our godmother. I did not have chance to intercept it and destroy it as I undoubtedly should have done considering her vitriolic opinion of me, and yet, Mrs. B has not seen fit to show me the door just yet nor has locked away her daughters from my corrupting licentious presence. Either she has not yet read it or is aware of more of me than I might expect yet still smiles upon me. I wonder if you had a hand in that by any chance? You should not mislead others about my failings in character you know?

Better let Gossett know to continue managing the estate as he obviously does so well, for I shall need to be here for some time. It is all far too interesting and challenging to leave, for I . . . no, now that I think better of it, I shall not continue my thoughts here. You said I would eventually meet someone that would turn my life upside down. Well, you will be pleased to know that I did. I didn't realize that marriage—especially mine—might prove to be so very interesting despite the tragedy, but then I should have listened to John much more than I did, and I might have learned a little more of this strange estate. There is much more to tell here, but I shall *say no more until I can resolve one or two difficulties, and it may take some time. I may not succeed. We shall see.*

Speaking of John, I am sorry that I was not able to give you better news of him. He thought that he would be able to break away two weeks after I did, but when I think about it more, it could be more like three weeks; for I recall that the weather turns a little more unpredictable in the bay about now. I did bring a letter from him and if I find it, I will enclose it, but I have temporarily misplaced it somewhere.

He had not yet completed it, for it was unsigned. It was an unexpectedly well-written and educated kind of letter as had been the other entries and letters she had read earlier, and portrayed a different picture of him than she had gleaned from other accounts, but it was too early to judge. Men were usually not noted for writing such lengthy, educated letters, but he did.

There was another one he had begun. It was to his mother, for it began simply with "Mama." At that point, his muse had deserted him. He was much closer to his sister than he was to his own mother!

There was nothing else written yet. It seemed he had started and then had run out of something to say.

She wondered if he had not left everything there deliberately for her to read, considering his comments in the letter to his sister.

She gently put the letter back into the place where she found it, along with the two sealed ones, and took herself off, lest she be discovered prying into another's personal affairs when she had no business to do so.

Chapter XVI

Surprising Disclosures— We Are Watching and Learning

The next week had brought never-ending rains, which kept them all close to the house, pouring over books and playing various games, though they soon lost their attraction, and the girls drifted off to find other distractions or settled by the fire to catch up on reading or mending.

"Will this rain never cease?" Charlotte was looking through the rain-streaked window. "Even the ducks have taken to sheltering in the barn with that wind. We can go nowhere in this, and there is no chance of getting into the garden for the raspberries. The birds will get them all again, or they will go moldy or even drop off."

"Oh, mama! Look! Here is that bonnet I was telling you about." Annis showed her mother the drawing of the dress and the bonnet in the ladies magazine she had been reading and took note of the directions for putting one together just like it.

"Well, it is to be hoped you stick at it a little longer than you did your knitting!"

Annis grimaced a little at that criticism. She felt more than just a little foolish the way that had worked out, but William had said nothing about it, and everyone else had been in the village or busy elsewhere so had not heard the shots or had chosen not to inquire about them.

She put the magazine aside. "The weather may intimidate the ducks, and certainly the hens, but it does not seem to stop either Thomas or William, for they seem as busy as ever in the outbuildings considering the hammering, and Sophia does not seem to leave their side. She has become a ragamuffin and does not seem to care how grubby or muddy, or even wet, she becomes."

"Yes, William takes good care of her, doesn't he?" Their mother ignored the unflattering description of her youngest daughter, thankful that she had distractions enough to fill her every waking moment and to keep her mind off the other.

"Is it only a week since the funeral?" Their mother's thoughts were still on that. "Yes, it is!" She stared off into the distance. She would never be free of that particular pain and its constant reminders. She wrenched herself out of that mood as she needed to do many times each day. "I am surprised that we have not received a visit from London, for the Thackeray's must have heard of our loss, and I thought that they would be unable to refrain from hounding us. I have dreaded his showing up. When your father fell ill two years ago, he seemed to express a great deal of interest in that, at least until your father recovered his health and told him to stop his foolishness and to mind his own business and to stop hovering and take himself off."

Charlotte did not raise even her head from her mending to enter the conversation. "If you mention the devil like that, Mama, I hear he is just likely to appear. But Mr. Thackeray will *not* be coming again." Charlotte was too engrossed in mending the hem of a dress at that moment, having become depressed at seeing so much rain, that she did not see the signs and signals that Annis tried to send her way to stop her from relating any such thing.

"And how do you know that, miss?"

"I overheard Molly saying how he had been trespassing and poking and prying here last week while we were in Church but had been sent off in no uncertain way and with a . . ." she paused to get the accent right, ". . . a right proper thick ear—as she said in her Yorkshire twang—and had a rare punishment, a beating that was long overdue and a treat to watch when he had been caught snooping through father's papers in the study. Or so she said. I wonder if those teeth I found by the trough and those sovereigns and watch were his? Who else might they belong to indeed? Well he shan't have his sovereigns back. I intend to keep those. I don't know about the watch: I may give it to William for his pains. But I cannot approve of his fighting like that."

"Really? What beating? What teeth? What sovereigns? Indeed, what watch? What fighting? I knew none of this, miss! I did hear of a slight contretemps when William discouraged some bad behavior about then, but no name was mentioned and no one thought enough of it to say more. I thought it might have been the squire he told off about his letting his cows run loose in our field."

Charlotte glanced momentarily at her mother. "No, mama! You would not hear the full details of it, for the servants were told to say nothing of it for fear of upsetting you. I showed you the sovereigns, and you said I could keep them." Charlotte still had her head in her work and could not see Annis trying to quiet her.

"I said nothing of the kind! I saw no sovereigns! Who administered this beating?"

"Oh, Mama! Need you ask?" She glanced at her mother again in some disbelief that she did not know, and then re-immersed herself in her task. "You noticed the blood on his shirt and cheek at the Church that day, for you wiped it away for him, and his hand was bandaged for a day or so afterward. Surely you noticed it when you sat down with him and those other two gentlemen from London!"

He mother blanched. "Well, yes, I did. But he had a ready explanation for that. He said nothing about a fight!"

"It wasn't the squire. It was that Thackeray man! Have you also not noticed that the squire got his cows out of our field about that time too and has never put them back in there again either and even seems to have repaired the fence that Papa was sure he had weakened deliberately? Surely you have noticed the difference in the servants' demeanor toward William? I have. They cannot seem to do enough for him."

"Well, yes, I have noticed that." Their mother began to wonder what it was that she did not know, that everyone else seemed to know all about. "No more than is his due though. He is a gentleman with them, as he should be, and thanks them most kindly when they do anything for him, and he helps them out too with the more difficult tasks, and he has no need to do any of that. I am sure I don't expect it any more than they do. He even helps Thomas! They have worked wonders, the pair of them, on so many things we seem to have overlooked and neglected." She looked up from what she was doing. "But where is William? I must learn more of this. I have not seen him all morning."

Annis saw a means of diverting her mother. "Best not to disturb him, Mama. He is working with Thomas on a particularly difficult task, I think, if Sophia is to be believed any more. Besides, I have something I need to ask you."

"Very well, I will ask him later. What do you wish to ask, dear?"

"My father was never a violent man, was he?"

"Lord no, child! Your father was a gentle and kind man, at least for the last few years, mostly he was, and quite calmed down a lot when we settled here just after we married, bless him!" Her eyes misted as she looked into the fire for a few moments. "Whatever would have made you think that? Oh, but it was not because he could not be violent when the need was there, for he was not at all gentle when he showed Thackeray off the property that time, but then it never did get too much out of hand, for Thomas was also close by, and I recall he had a pitchfork in his hands.

"It almost degenerated into a violent situation with the squire on that one occasion also. All very minor! It seems that some men will not take a hint and need to see that violence will erupt if they do not change what they are doing. They are just like roosters that way, facing up to each other until one of them backs down or not. If not, then the feathers will fly, and the spurs get used, and the winner can then be declared. I think your father prevailed without going any further than he needed to."

She reflected again upon the question and qualified it a little.

"No. Your father was not violent, unless it was absolutely necessary! So I suppose there were occasions when it was called for but never too seriously." The other still nagged at her. "I must get that tale out of Molly if it was not as I assumed it was! It seems that the servants and my daughters know everything, and I know nothing! Your father always warned me that the servants know more of what is going on about us than ever we might."

Annis then took a part. "But what if there is more to it than just necessary violence, Mama? What if a man seems to be violent for violence's sake and without cause?"

"Oh." She looked over at Annis. "I see you read your godmother's letter to me then? I imagine it did not paint a glowing complimentary picture of William, for I know her opinion of him and her belief that he is an inherently violent individual, even with womenfolk. Well he isn't! You must watch what you believe my girl! Half of what she says is untrue, and the other half is exaggerated or misinterpreted. She has been liberal with her opinion of him every time we saw each other in the last few months, anticipating his return. She does not approve of him and hasn't since he was a boy growing up, nor of what we had been planning in the last year or so—his mother, sister and I."

"Mama! How do you know of what she might have said of him? I was the one who read her letter, and I know you have not seen it."

"I am not entirely stupid, though you may think I am. I know Addie's opinions of William, my dear, and her repertoire of ills and complaints against the boy, for she regales us with them at every opportunity! I set no store in gossip, my dear, and nor should you. I had no intention of reading it until I was better able to deal with it. She can be aggravating and infuriating at times with her opinions of everything, and never sees the need to change or learn what the truth might be where men are concerned. Yet she is one of my dearest friends."

"But it is surely more than gos—"

"No! It is not!" She interrupted her daughter. "All young men are testy and argumentative and sometimes get drawn in deeper than anyone would like. That is their way of preparing for their adult battles with other men. If a man is not prepared to do battle for his rights and property or for the woman he loves, then he will lose both them and his own self-respect and will never be able to hold his head high in society again. It is no different than that rooster we put in the pot. He had lost his place and was incapable of treading hens or of laying eggs, so he had to go, as we all do when we lose our purpose in life."

She heard Charlotte gently repeat her mother's words with a laugh. "Treading hens! It's a good thing Sophia is not here to demand to know what that means!"

"Well, that's what they do! She knows what it means, for she sees it often enough for herself. If they did not, we'd get eggs enough but no chickens out of any of them. I cannot imagine you have not paid attention to that. That's why we have roosters, remember? Sophia already knows more than you think about such things. She's not shy about asking questions of anyone, even about some of the most personal things. She even asks William in front of everyone! Quite embarrassing for the poor man! But he handles it so well!"

She sighed heavily, and her eyes misted over.

"Your father did all that he needed to do on my behalf when we first met and solved a difficult problem that I faced with one particular suitor who did not know what the word 'no' meant and would not be easily put off. I did not approve in the slightest of what he did, but I, nonetheless, was quite impressed in a way I could not relate to anyone, for *that* had been quite violent and saved me from a most awkward marriage contrived by my parents. He overturned all of that!

"No. I shall not tell you any more of that at this moment! We can save it for a time when it is likely to cause less heartache. But I will know where William is and what he is doing." She stared at Annis waiting for an answer while Charlotte concentrated more on her mending.

"He is shoring up the stable, Mama, with Thomas, under the supervision and watchful eyes of our now *never-*present sister Sophia who lives in his pocket and seems far too worshipful of him. She never seems to leave his side and even insists on going off with him on his horse when he needs to head into the village for anything. They have been lucky enough not to get wet so far, but it is just a matter of time."

"I noticed. But I am thankful for that! She was the one I most worried for, with her father gone. I know we all feel it most cruelly, but I feared that she would be the one most upset, and now she seems not to have a care in the world. I was concerned and hurt at first, but now I am most thankful for that! But I did not tell him to do anything, and I certainly did not expect him to look after her so well as he does, and never a word of complaint, and never impatient with her. He does not mind at all for he told me himself that he enjoyed her company, and it is obvious that he does! I should have remembered that he would be repairing out there, for he did tell me what he planned on doing. He usually suggests what needs to be done or asks if I had other tasks for him first and, if not, then . . . and off he goes and does everything."

Annis put her magazine to one side for a few moments, and stretched, while no-one other than her sister or mother might see her. "When you are not here, Mama, he also finds things that need to be done all by himself and says nothing of any of it, as when he fixed those windows and replaced some tiles on the stable roof while Sophia supervised from the pigeon cote. She had climbed inside of it now that it is more sturdy and did not seem to care that she was then covered with droppings. Then he took down that tree that was threatening to block the driveway, or worse, if it had come down across someone. He seems to know how to work with tools. I would probably cut my feet off if I swung an ax the way he does when he was taking those branches off. He says there is another tree to go too that is just as bad. They cleaned out the drains and unblocked the stream too, which was just as well or it would have been running off down the driveway after all the rain we had. He and Thomas work well together, especially on the barn. It settled under the weight of hay last summer, and father never did get around to seeing that it was repaired."

"Yes, I remember. Your father was debating whether or not to pull it all down and rebuild."

"No need now, Mama. It has been raised and repaired. Fresh hay and all, and at least two new support posts, shaped and put in and made from that same tree that he took out, so Sophia tells me. She seemed most impressed by the ingenuity that went into doing it too, with some kind of frame support and pulleys to raise the main beam and even some levers too at work. She was excited to discover that someone as small as she could pull on a rope and raise such a massive beam more than two extra feet into the air while they put in new support posts. They were all singing some kind of sea shanty when I walked in on them with Sophia and Thomas pulling on the rope in time to the song. She was having a rare old time of it. We shall never hear the last of it, I fear, except she does not seem to leave his side for long enough to tell us all about her most recent accomplishments."

Charlotte entered the conversation once more. "She came in earlier and was spouting off at how William had taught her that a little bit of brain work can beat any amount of brawn, and now she knows all about pulleys and levers and such things."

"Harmless enough thing to say, for it's true. Your father used to say the same thing. Now what was it that Mrs. Rogers used to say about that son of Welch's? That great strong lad with no more wit than a fence post!"

"Mother!" Annis laughed. "I do not think it polite to repeat it, for it was not at all flattering to the poor boy, and he did have a little more wit than that. But not much!"

They had not noticed that Sophia had entered the parlor and was munching on something. "Molly said he was 'strong in't back and thick in't head!'" A broad Yorkshire twang was evident in her pronouncement which did not meet with her mother's approval, for she frowned at her as she took in the crumpled state of her dress and hay still attached to it and in her hair.

"Yes, she did, didn't she! My, what a mess you are in! One might think you had been rolling in the stream and then in the hay!"

Sophia ignored her. "Thomas says that too! She is full of sayings like that from Yorkshire, and she must have taught him some when they laugh and cud—" She faltered and colored up a little, but her mother did not ask her to continue what she was saying. Annis was looking at her with an alarmed look in her eyes and a barely perceptible shake of the head to stop any continuation of that particular indiscretion concerning how Molly and Thomas might conduct themselves when they believed that they were alone.

"Yorkshire does not sound like a very polite kind of place, and I hope none of it sticks. But I don't think any of that applies to William, *that* is certain. You should tidy up, dear!"

Sophia ran off outside again at that moment once she saw that William was walking off across the yard and before she landed herself into trouble or was made to go and change. He hesitated and smiled down at her as she caught up with him and took hold of his hand as she skipped along beside him and avoided the mud puddles.

"No. He seems to be a most soft-spoken man with everyone, despite what we have learned about him and Thackeray." Charlotte had put aside her mending and was then was maneuvering her graphite stick at that moment to try and capture a particular thoughtful expression that had just shown on her sister's face as she looked out of the window. "He is so very patient. Do you know that he sings to her at night?"

"Sings? I thought I heard something like that once she had gone to bed."

"Yes. He has some gentle little lullaby kind of songs that he sings in a very low voice so that no one else might hear him. She was singing it to her dolls later while she was playing with them, and I asked her about it. He even reads to her and tells her nursery rhymes too. He is full of them.

"Did you know that Humpty Dumpty really did fall off that wall?"

"Come now, Charlotte. It is a nursery rhyme!"

"Yes, but there is a story behind each of them, you know? They are satirical or lyrical renditions of real social circumstances and political too, as with Jack Horner and pulling plums out of pies—sometimes quite humorous, foolish, or even grisly, I learned, as with Mary, Mary, quite contrary and her garden. Queen Mary! Bloody Mary! It will never sound quite so harmless to me now, for I did not know about her 'garden' or those dreadful cockleshells." She shivered at the memory. "Though he did not tell Sophia the story behind that one, and I am sure he would not have told me either. I knew that one myself from one of father's books that I was not supposed to read."

Her mother looked sharply at her "I thought those were locked away!"

"You cannot shelter us forever, Mama!"

"No, I suppose not. Not now." She nonetheless made a note in her own mind that she would check on where she had put them, along with her sketch books. It would not do for them to be in general circulation.

Charlotte was still rambling along. "Humpty Dumpty was the name given to a very large cannon. When the foundations crumbled under it on the wall, it fell off and they couldn't get it back onto the wall again. So you see there is a real story behind it. He even encourages her to play the harpsichord. For he got her to give him a lesson."

"But she is only beginning herself!"

"Yes. Clever of him, wasn't it? It was becoming harder to get her to practice until he began to show an interest."

Charlotte yawned. The weather was getting to her. "I might almost suspect that he knows how to play himself, the way he was asking her some things and struggling quite creditably to show her how to achieve something while carefully giving the impression that she had shown him, for he asked some very clever questions of her. She also does not regard her freckles with quite as much dislike now that she knows that they are fairy kisses."

"No!"

"Oh yes! She had mentioned that if she could change anything in the world it would be to bring . . . well you know . . . both of them back!" She regretted saying anything of that, even as she said it, for it weighed heavily upon them all much of the time, but continued quickly. "But then had mentioned that she hated her freckles and would change those too! Everyone made fun of her over them, and she did not like to be made fun of. So he told her that she was most privileged to have them and that those who made fun of her were jealous, for they were special, and only very few children ever had them. *That* caught her attention, and she wanted to know why."

Her mother was suddenly interested. "I think I would like to know why too, for I had freckles when I was her age and still have them at times." Her mother brushed a tear from her eye, and Charlotte regretted her thoughtless tongue and thought to steer the conversation into slightly different channels, but Annis took over the conversation at that point.

"I believe he told her that while she was asleep as a baby, the fairies had come in to see her and had kissed her. And wherever they kissed her, there was a small freckle left to show what they had done."

"Well, I never!"

"Oh yes! Now she searches for them in her bath, wherever they are, and points them out proudly. Even to William whom she now insists help bathe her as she chatters along to him artlessly! It is most embarrassing where she manages to find them and is not shy about pointing them out wherever they are, but he does not care in the slightest what Charlotte or I might think about it all nor how embarrassed we are. There are times I wish we were elsewhere when she does that, for she has neither any sense of modesty nor embarrassment, either in her bath nor afterward as she parades about quite naked and cares what no one might think, least of all William, who smiles through it all!

"And why should she? She is but six years old and not at all shy. But then six may be rather old for that kind of behavior. No matter. No one will be offended. William isn't, I am sure. We should leave her with her childhood as long as we can. I was afraid she might have to grow up too fast."

While her mother was distracted a little, Annis continued with their observations. "William has a mischievous side too. He pointed out that everyone living here has one leg and that all of the animals have three legs. Sophia could not believe him with that one, and nor could I, until he went a little further with it and pointed out that though Thomas has only one leg, he also has another, a second one, to go with it. Sophia did not know what to make of it at first and then saw through it all and has been playing that game with everyone now too. He also calls the sheep, bleating chickens. The cows, he insists, are horses with horns and vice versa and gets her quite annoyed with him. I must admit I was quite confounded by it at first too, then she told me what he had said of Thomas . . ."

Their mother's thoughts were obviously far away at that moment.

Just then, there was the suggestion of a rumble of thunder, and there was a general scurrying to join the servants, to bring in the washing before it might rain again and to get it hanging up in the washhouse, where it was at least warm enough to get it dry.

Chapter XVII

Buying Some Time!

"Why are the gates closed, Thomas?"

"I was about to come and tell you, ma'am! Master William told us we might expect a visit from the elder Thackeray today, and suggested that while he was away in London on business, that we should keep the gates closed and to keep Thackeray off until tomorrow when William might deal with him."

"Yes, William took off very early for London before anyone else was up and about after that letter came last evening, and he said he would need to go today as it seemed urgent. He said nothing about Mr. Thackeray being in the area!"

"No, ma'am, he just found out about it himself and asked me to let you know. He said we would need to find a way to keep him out."

"Then we must do that, Thomas!"

"Yes, mum. William said he would be back by this evening no matter how things might go. He doubted that Mr. Thackeray would dare to try and force his way in with me and Ned close by, but he warned us not to say anything to him but to just put him off whichever way we could. Maybe it's time to take that other old tree out too and lay it across the drive a bit, to be sure he cannot get in, and tell him the family is not at home until tomorrow, and I was told that no one was to come in while you were away."

"That sounds like an excellent suggestion, Thomas! Give us warning if you see him coming, and I will make sure that the girls stay in the house and out of the way until he's gone, and you can put him off whichever way you can."

"Yes, mum."

She stopped with an afterthought. "Thomas?" He turned. "Perhaps you would not mind going over to the Davenports and see if we might borrow Sir Licksalot for a while! That might do the trick as well as anything would."

He laughed at her suggestion and walked off toward the Davenport house as she had suggested.

Some hours later, Thomas saw a carriage approaching down the lane and knew who it had to be. He gave instructions to the lad with the ax and went off to the house to warn the ladies to remain out of sight and then returned into the stable where he might hear everything that would go on. The lad was clever enough that he could be sufficiently gormless when required, to put off even the most determined visitor. He could not help chuckling to himself. How true it was that a clever man might easily play a fool, but a fool will never be able to convince anyone that he is a clever man! Ned was a clever lad!

The horses pulled up in the lane as the gentleman driving them realized he could not turn into the driveway with the gates closed, and a tree lying across the drive. He watched the lad wielding his ax for some moments, realizing that it was not likely that he would be finished any time soon. They should have hitched a horse or two to the fallen trunk and dragged it out of the way, but that seemed to be beyond them!

"Ho there! I am paying a formal visit!" He raised his voice and attracted the lad's attention. The lad looked up at him, rested for a few moments on the handle of the ax, and then returned to his work as though he had not heard him.

"I am here to visit the Barristows."

The lad stopped what he was doing again and then spoke. "Not possible, sir! No one is allowed in!" The lad was standing on the trunk, lopping branches off with an axe, but had paused when he heard the man speak again. "Mistress is away at the moment, and I was told to get this old tree out of here while they were away."

"When is she expected back?" He decided patience with the youth might achieve more than any more determined an approach.

"Not till tomorrow at least, sir. Yes, tomorrow." The lad seemed to fall into much deeper thought as he argued with himself. "At least *tomorrow* if today is Wensday, but if it isn't, then I dunno what she might have said!" He seemed confused.

"Today *is* Wednesday!" He watched the lad grapple with that thought but was not inclined to believe any of what he might say. He would assume she was home and had given instructions not to admit him. "You can tell Mrs. Barristow that I am here to convey my condolences over her recent losses and to meet with her. You might consider doing it *now*! I am a close relative and in the area from London, and I desire to speak with her on a matter of some considerable importance and benefit to her."

The lad did not move. He was up to the tricks of gentleman to try and bypass what they did not like. "Not possible, sir!"

"Oh. Why not?"

He looked at the gentleman as though his questioner were a little stupid. Fortunately, the lad was on the other side of the gate and out of reach of his crop so was inclined to be braver than he might have been. "You must be deaf not to have heard what I said the first time." He raised his voice a few notches and spoke slowly. "I already told you. Its a'cause they's not here. And besides, the entire house is in mourning and undergoing renovation, and it's getting a good clean out today too while they are gone."

The older man decided not to take offense at the lad's impudence just yet. He looked about and could see laundry hanging out over lines extending from the house to the corner of the barn. There were carpets hanging over the hedge nearby and being soundly beaten with a broom, kicking dust up into the air and drifting toward him. He was well aware that others might be listening out of sight and was not about to invite more than he needed to invite by trying to enter the property and laying his crop across the impudent lad's shoulders. He had seen his son's condition, and he nurtured a burning desire to correct that wrong, but this lad had not done it, for he was too small, and there was not a mark on him. And not only was he too stupid to live, but also his description did not match the one his son had given.

"Well, where are they?" He sounded impatient to be learning nothing that he wanted to know.

"Not my place to say, sir, even if I knew, and I don't 'cause they don't confide in me with their plans for me to blab to them as arsks. Besides I have me hands full with this tree and then the stable to muck out again, never ending, that. And then lor' knows what after that! Seven days of the week all the same to me, so why should I fratch over whether it's Wensday or Friday or whatever?"

"I do not need a list of your chores! Then I shall leave a message."

"They wun't get it, sir!"

"Why not?"

"Cause I can't remember me own name at times, sir. If my 'ead wasn't nailed on good and 'ard, I'd lose that too. No point arsking me to 'member anything. I have difficulty wiv my own name at times."

"Is there no one else about with more wit?"

"Oh yes, sir. Everybody here has more wit than me, which is why I 'ave the job of cleaning out the stables and not them! I'll let t'gaffer know you're here, if you like." He let out a bellow for Thomas.

Thomas appeared with a pitchfork out of the stable as though he had been pitching hay to the livestock. There was a blank smile on his face as though he were as simple as the vacuous youth.

"I seem unable to penetrate the fog about this fellow's brainbox. I am going to break my journey here." He decided that it would not be open for discussion. But Thomas was wise to this gentleman and his ways.

"Oh. I don't see as how that's possible, sir!"

"Of course, you can see it! You can also see to my carriage! There must be somewhere you can put it out of the way and then you can bring my bags in." He began to dismount from the seat of the carriage.

"Oh no, sir! I wouldn't do that, sir, if I was you!"

A large brindle-colored dog, previously unseen, had raised himself from the ground in the shade of the barn, where he had been gnawing on a large bone that looked suspiciously like a human one and eyed up the visitor attentively as he let out a low growl. Fortunately, he was restrained by a chain.

Their would-be visitor regained his seat on the carriage.

Thomas spoke harshly to the dog. "Down, you devilish brute!" The dog settled himself again with the bone, and his tail wagging, but watched the visitor.

"He's already broken free once this morning! No end of trouble is that dog! I daren't let you in here, sir. It's more than my life's worth to disobey my mistress! She'd turn me off just like that. It is more than your life's worth if you try to come in, with that brute. You can't stay here, sir, with no one home! Not possible today, sir. When mistress says no one is to be admitted, she means it, sir. Told us to keep our eyes open for gypsies and to shoot 'em off the property if we need to, for they'd steal the coppers off a dead man's eyes, they would. That's why we have the dog here too! He doesn't care over much who he latches himself onto, but he seems to prefer gentleman after children." He turned to the lad standing on the tree. "I told you not to give him that bone just yet, Ned!"

"I didn't. I've still got that one h . . ." The lad lost his speech for a second or two, and there was a pale look on his face. "Ooh! Then where'd that one come from?"

"Say no more, Ned. Don't want to scare anyone needlessly now, do we? I'll check in the shrubbery later."

"I am not a gypsy!" The older man did not like to be put off in this way. "Perhaps you should shoot the dog if he is that vicious! Perhaps I should!"

"I think maybe I can see that you are not a gypsy, sir. He's only a bit awkward like with those he don't know, and that makes him the more valuable. But we are doing a lot of cleaning out today while everyone's out of the way, so the house is in a turmoil, and the dog keeps an eye on house and barn both, where he is. Too good an eye, I'm thinking. The inn down in the village could see to you, sir. Highly recommended, I believe, now that they have mostly got rid of their bed bugs, though their fleas might still be a problem. Mistress will be in tomorrow. If you was to come back at noon tomorrow, I expect you'd catch her home then!"

"Well, where is she now? I would like to see her today!"

"Not my business to say, sir."

He was not impressed, and he did not like the belligerent or blockish attitude of either of them. But he could also see a fowling piece laid nearby and was not about to argue with the hired help or the dog.

He was not at all suited. "Very well. Tell your mistress I shall call tomorrow."

"Yes, sir. Very wise. Noon tomorrow, sir! You can turn your carriage down the lane a'piece." He decided not to warn him that the mud puddle where he might turn was quite deep and likely to cause him some difficulty.

After Mr. Thackeray had managed to turn himself around and head back toward the village, Mrs. Barristow appeared from the house.

"You did well, Thomas, and you too, Ned. I was having difficulty holding my laughter in at all of the whiskers you were telling. It's a good job he did not know what a great daft dog that one is and would be inclined to lick him to death, and he has breath that would knock a post over. I am sure the wolves in Ireland left when they saw a dog like that. He must eat enough to feed two men!"

"And some, ma'am." He scratched the dogs belly as it put its paws on his shoulders, almost knocking him off his feet and licked at his face as it drooled down his front. He grimaced. "Ooh! You were right about the breath, ma'am! Maybe *that* was why those wolves left!"

"Perhaps we should have the gate closed all of the time and get an Irish wolf hound of our own!"

Mr. Devane arrived back that evening shortly after dark, mud flecked and tired and hungry, but with good news.

He smiled and was relieved to hear of Thomas's and Ned's successful efforts to keep Mr. Thackeray off the property. They could now return the dog, aptly nicknamed Sir Licksalot, to the neighbor's house with his marrow bone from that butchered cow.

After the girls had been sent off to bed, amidst some complaints from Annis, William sat down in the parlor with Mrs. Barristow and related his day's accomplishments at some length.

He took her hand in his. "One last thing, ma'am. You should be away tomorrow when Thackeray visits again."

"It will not get out of hand, will it, William? Not as it did with his son?" she looked and sounded concerned for him.

He frowned and then smiled. "Yes, I thought you would eventually get a full account of that. But no, I shall try to ensure that it does not, ma'am, but I can offer no guarantees. He is worse than his son if reports of him are correct, but then I suspect age may have slowed him down, and he is more cautious than he used to be, but the more dangerous for it. I think I shall deal with him very gently if I can—more gently than I was initially inclined to be."

"It is to be hoped so! I do not want anything to happen to you after what you have done for us."

"There shall be nothing happen to me ma'am. I know him and what he is capable of, and I do not doubt that he now knows something of me, unfortunately, from his son, so he will also be forewarned and forearmed as I will be. I learned enough of him in town that I think he will easily be convinced of the wisdom of leaving you all alone. Although those papers I brought back with me should do that well enough!"

Chapter XVIII

The Elder Thackeray Countered and Repulsed. A Murderous Listener!

The next day, close to the appointed hour for Mr. Thackeray's visit, Thomas entered the parlor after a brief knock. "I saw his carriage broach the rise, ma'am. He is coming, I believe, and on time it seems. He must have gone further afield after I mentioned the bed bugs and fleas at The Maggot."

"Thomas! You know they have none! Mrs. Fleur keeps a cleaner house than almost any in the village."

"I know that, ma'am. But he don't!" He thumbed over his shoulder at the approaching carriage.

"Who is coming, mama? Are we expecting a visitor?"

"Not one we need to concern ourselves with. Come girls, we must walk out of the back and across to Mrs. Davenport. She is expecting us at this time, and I told you that we would be visiting her this morning. We need to stay out of the way for a while. Oh! Where did Annis get to? Does she not know we were to be out of here when he came?"

"She may be over there already, Mama, and visiting with Ellie. But who is coming?"

"Someone who is not welcome, I can assure you of that! Who it is need not concern you for the moment. We shall be away for a while until he has gone. Is William ready for him, Thomas?"

"Indeed he is, ma'am, but you need not worry, there will be no trouble. I shall be close by."

"I hope you are right, Thomas!"

Mrs. Barristow quickly rounded up the girls, other than for Annis who had taken it in her head to be elsewhere at that moment, and ushered them out through the back of the house, where they would not be seen by the arriving gentleman. She had no intention of confronting a scheming, lying, and manipulative old enemy of her family who had been trying for far too long to see them off the property by any means possible, including one failed legal challenge after another. He had been a constant and persistent thorn in the side of her husband for the last ten years since her husband's elder brother had died and would now be congratulating himself that all he might have to deal with in his way would be several helpless girls and a woman, as well as someone he might feel it easy to remove from his path. He must be even now, congratulating himself on his reviving fortunes.

The Thackeray carriage turned in through the now-open gates and into the driveway before the house. He sat there, looking warily around for the dog he had seen the day before.

William went out to see him.

The description his son had given him of his attacker told him that this was the man responsible for that vicious beating. There were no recent marks on his face or anywhere else about him that he could see, though his son was still laid up with *his* injuries, and his face was still notably marked.

He scowled and looked about impatiently. "No stable hands to see to my horses? The place was awash with them yesterday! They were most uncooperative and disobliging to me. Not the way to greet a visitor!"

"They appear to be busy at the moment. But you can leave your horses there, if you can trust them to stand. You won't be staying long!" There was no mistaking the nature of his welcome!

The man started to respond in a scathing tone to such unwelcoming comments but decided against it. Better to start on a gentle footing until he got to where he wanted to be.

He was a tall man, thin, but getting a little expansive about the waist and with an erect proud bearing. He was dressed in black but with a white cravat, a fashionable hat covering his graying hair, a little jewelry at his throat, and a silver-headed walking stick. He dressed well, considering that rumor had it that he was suffering under a mountain of debt, maintaining a lifestyle he felt entitled to but did not have the means to keep up.

William smiled at his dour expression. The elder Thackeray did not seem to be any more impressed with his lack of welcome today than he had been yesterday from Thomas's description of him, but was intent on getting over whatever rough ground might face him and prevail as he believed he might. His reception left him uncertain of what was going on. He might have been able to bully his way past Mrs. Barristow but the gentleman before him was a different kind of problem. One he had been amply warned of!

The visitor looked William over coldly. "I am here to see Mrs. Barristow, sir. Please convey my condolences to her along with my compliments, and tell her that Gideon Thackeray, a not-so-distant relative, is here to see her and to solicit her hospitality."

William nodded his head to acknowledge the formal approach, but did not respond with his own name. "They are not here, Mr. Thackeray, but I am! You may deal with me. Perhaps you should start by telling me exactly *why* you are here?"

He did not relish that idea and looked about himself. He would have liked to ignore the man. "I was told they would be here today, and they would have been told to expect me."

"No, sir. I am your only welcoming committee." He smiled at his own humor. Nothing welcoming about any of it!

"Considering their recent losses, I am surprised there are no signs of mourning at the gate or the door!" He looked him over with a scathing and contemptuous eye and noticed that he was being smiled at. He expressed himself with cold calmness and detachment, even polite iciness, but it was a struggle. "I think I know who you are. My son told me of you. I want nothing to do with you! It is Mrs. Barristow I would speak with. I should have the law brought down upon you for what you did to my son, attacking him without provocation as you did. He is still laid up and not likely to be about again for some time!" He spoke quietly, but William could feel the anger roiling inside the man, evident in the way he looked at him.

William smiled, but there was no humor in his eyes, which had never left the visitor's face. "That was your son? Ah well, you have my sympathies then, sir! A pity you did not manage to teach him rather better manners when he was dealing with ladies or those protecting them. But then possibly he did not give you an *accurate* account of what happened to him. I, myself, take a dim view of anyone who intrudes onto another's property, forces his way into the house, and then deals roughly with the servant girls, and tries to bully them in order to get his own way."

Mr. Thackeray let out a sound of disbelief. "Dealing gently with ladies is not one of *your* strong points either, considering what I heard of you and your goings-on about town."

"There!" William smiled easily. "You do know me, despite all of that being old history! I thought you might! Just as I know of you!"

The older man did not believe that he would know anything of him at all. "Unlike my son, I am capable of removing those who stand in my way."

William continued to smile at him in a way that the old man would undoubtedly find infuriating. "Bravely said, sir! Bravely said! Let us hope it does not come to discovering which of us might succeed there." He watched him fidgeting with his cane. "A nice-looking sword stick you have there! I trust we shall not need to go down that path. Your son, on the other hand, thought to carry the day by producing a pistol to deal with me, and I, defenseless and unarmed! Quite unnerved me!" His continuing calmness and his smile put the lie to that. "I have that pistol by the way." He seemed to suggest it might be in his pocket, and it could be, for there was a slight bulge there. "I was not of the impression that he was producing it at the time in order to show it off to me, any more than you might be with that stick, though it is quite an impressive little gun. Your son wisely decided to leave any other weapon where it might be, fortunately, or there may have been more serious injuries to one or both of us. He was trespassing without invitation, bullying womenfolk, and poking and prying where he should not have been. I could not allow that!"

"So *you* say!"

"Oh, there were many witnesses to his forcing his way into the house, even after they had told him that their mistress was not at home. She is not home now either! Fortunately, but unfortunately for your son, I then was as I am now. So if we wish to speak of the law intervening in anything, I would be a little more cautious in whom and what you believe!"

"That is a matter that has nothing to do with you, and I will thank you to keep your nose out of it."

"On the contrary. It does concern me now!"

"I doubt it! I do not particularly care how you may have ingratiated yourself with the Barristow's, but I can assure you that it will not serve any purpose other than to delay the inevitable! Clearly, I wish to speak with Mrs. Barristow about this property and its prompt disposition to its rightful owner. Me! It is my property now. I will deal with you later." He had rushed forward more than he had intended to at this stage, but then he was meeting with an unexpected resistance.

"My, oh my! How confusing it has suddenly seemed to become. But perhaps you should deal with me *now*. We could get this over with rather quickly if you can produce a valid deed to the place, and you can then be on your way back to London to finalize everything while I remove myself!" William was smiling. He knew he could do no such thing.

"In good time! I did not come here to either see *you*, nor to be encouraged in any kind of a disagreement with you!"

"Then I am most relieved! But I can assure you that you will not meet with anyone else while you are here. I am *it*! I cannot be bullied or overawed by a loud voice, threats, or bluster . . . as women might be! Your son tried it and did not fare too well as I believe you know. I do, however, respond a little better to an intelligent and rational approach and am even open to persuasion. So unless you can convince me that you have anything constructive to say or have some worthwhile business or legal purpose here, then I shall bid you good day and not waste more of your time nor mine on a fool's errand!"

"I shall not leave until I have spoken with Mrs. Barristow."

"Really? Then you will be waiting here for a very long time! But then, why should I beat about the bush? Do I take it you need to speak with the owner of this property?"

He looked him over with a puzzled look in his face. "Yes, I do. That is what I have been striving to tell you since I arrived! Its temporary and unlawful owner at the moment, who is inhabiting what is rightfully mine. Yes, I do, and not some interfering murderous interloper! I know all about you!"

"As I do about you, sir! It is amazing what one learns when one drops the name of Gideon Thackeray into a gathering of individuals in any tavern at the south end of the bridge and around Saint Olav's. The air suddenly takes on an icy feel about it, and one gets the impression that one might have stepped in something unsavory and had brought it into the company on the bottom of one's boot. So let us say that I am as familiar with your reputation about town as you may think you are familiar with mine." Mr. Thackeray did not like what he was hearing. "However, my reputation is undoubtedly much exaggerated, as it is about five years out of date. I am said to have improved notably in those five years with regard to polish and temperament. For the better that is! At least I hope so! I am considerably more restrained than I was and less likely to act on impulse or the spur of the moment. Although that depends upon the circumstance!" He smiled at his visitor. Mr. Thackeray was obviously not satisfied with the way the conversation or his visit was unfolding.

William continued to look at his visitor with a hint of humor about his mouth. "Yes, I see we do begin to understand each other at last. I am the only one you will get to speak with today or any other day if it comes to that. I would advise you to be brief, however. I have other calls upon my time, and I am losing patience and any feeling of hospitable behavior by the minute in this cool wind."

William noted a stir within the door to the house behind him, and a flurry of skirts, and began to realize that not all of the family had gone off to the neighbors as he had hoped, for the servants were all instructed to be either in the garden or at the far end of the house until their uninvited guest had gone.

"But then I am not entirely ill-mannered or totally inhospitable either. We should discuss this briefly in the warmth of the parlor rather than out in the driveway with the wind blowing everything about, for unlike you, I did not dress for the outdoors."

William saw him dismount from his carriage and ushered him into the parlor, where Mr. Thackeray immediately went over to the fireplace and warmed himself before the blaze. Gideon Thackeray was angry at the opposition he was facing and irritated to find that he was up against someone he could not easily bully. He began to feel out of his depth. He was at a loss and not sure how to go on or deal with this most assured and confident stranger!

He spoke in calmer tones than he felt, from the warmth of the fireplace. "You seem to think you know who I am! I can assure you that you do not! I do not take kindly to those who intrude into my life or make inquiries of me." He was becoming a little more calm, but was still uncertain of what faced him.

"I heard that too! Servants can be rather too expansive of their former masters when plied with a little gentle encouragement and a few drinks. Perhaps if you used your stick a little less often . . . or were less inclined to produce that blade within it . . . they might feel less threatened and thus less likely to betray confidences. But then, reputations—good or bad—are never personal things you know, lying under our own control! I wish they were. They are what the world about us perceives, so my father once told me, and believes it knows of us, and the world is a very vocal place and can be quite cruel concerning those it takes amiss and in dislike." He smiled at the man before him. "I do speak from personal experience! But then I diverge from the subject at hand. I can perhaps roll things along and save you from a needlessly prolonged visit if I tell you that *I* now own Underby outright! Lock, stock and barrel!"

He saw the older man stiffen. He was startled to hear anything of the kind and did not seem inclined to believe him.

"I see you do not find that news at all to your liking, but I assure you, I have a clear and legally notarized title, which I know you have been unable to obtain so far, even with promise of rewards and outright bribery over the years." He looked at him again with a smile still on his face. "Former servants again, I am afraid. As well as the coerced confessions of a beleaguered firm of somewhat less reputable lawyers in the city! Yours!"

He heard a gasp and movement from outside of the door. He stood up and closed it and even turned the key, regretting that he had not thought to do so earlier, but taking care not to present his back to the older man by the fire.

His voice dropped a little so that he might not be easily overheard by anyone else. "And far from it being unlawful, I assure you that as of yesterday afternoon, when I was in the city seeing my own lawyers and making inquiries, I own it legally and lawfully and outright! Rather easily done too, when it is done properly. I ensured that Mrs. Barristow had clear title, which I think you already knew, and then I persuaded her to transfer it to me for . . . various considerations. I have been here only a week or so, but I have grown exceedingly fond of this property and there is very much about it that interests me, and I believe that I intend it to be a somewhat permanent occupation. So it appears that your journey from London was a snipe hunt."

Mr. Thackeray's brow had clouded upon hearing how it had so easily been snatched from him, if it were true, and he looked ready to explode. "I do not believe you! If so, you are a usurper, a thief, a . . ." There were a few moments of stunned silence and uncertainty. It was unsettling to be faced by one so calm and unruffled, who looked at him with a slight smile on his face, but with steely cold eyes.

William heard the door handle rattle a little under some concerted effort to gain entry.

"A usurper? I suppose so, but one who was a little more determined and cunning than you!" He smiled, knowing it would infuriate the older man. "And no, I shall not enlighten you further.

"I know what your efforts with your own lawyers yielded. Who are they now? Yes, Manley, Wrigley, and that other one—Johnson. Strange that they had thought to represent Mr. Barristow all of these years while actually working on your behalf to dislodge the Barristow claim. No wonder settlement never ever seemed possible! Their one true skill is in estimating how much they might squeeze from someone seeking their efforts. You included! Their contrivances on your behalf were not as fruitful as they undoubtedly led you to believe, as they continued to milk you, which is why you are here to try and provoke and frighten Mrs. Barristow into an unwise act of signing that legal-looking paper that sits in your pocket and which is likely to erode a little further, her supposed grip on this property."

His protestations were immediate. "Nothing of the kind! You attribute your own motives to me!"

William laughed gently. "But then I am now the rightful owner, and the family is not here to be browbeaten or cheated by you."

"If that is the case, then no! For it seems that you are the one who has already cheated them!" The older gentleman was becoming more agitated and angry by the minute.

"So it seems?" William sat down at the end of the table away from the fire and removed the small gun from his pocket and laid it on the table within reach as he smiled at his uncomfortable guest. "Damn thing stretches the pocket more than I like! I see you have the same problem."

His guest started, and pursed his lips, but held back any response.

William noted a vague shape walking outside and looking into the window. He recognized Annis and saw her move away.

"I have been here but a few days, and it was not so very difficult to sort out the estate and its succession if you have access to the right documents, and know what you are about, and can employ trustworthy and honest individuals! It seems that you have tried for years now to overturn the legal claim of the Barristow's here, and I achieved in just a few days what you could not in as many years. You really should employ a better class of lawyer, you know, if you wish to achieve anything? Mrs. Barristow was the actual owner after her husband died, for I was able to discover that her brother-in-law had seen to quieting all previous claims more than ten years ago. It made it so much easier for me to step in and scoop it out from under them for a mere pittance compared to what it is really worth."

"My claim was not quieted!"

"You will find that it has been removed altogether, however, when you consult again with Manley, Wrigley, and Johnson. Though I doubt they will meet with you. They feel lucky, I think, to escape with only relatively minor penalties once they fully disclosed—with some gentle persuasion from my own lawyers—their unethical behavior concerning the Barristows, and implicated you in much of it. I believe they are quitting the city and are even now relocating to the North of England as the price for evading a more hurtful legal outcome!"

He continued to look over his guest. "In truth, you were too far off to the side to count. However, I do not and did not expect you to believe me, but you may believe a legal document issued by a reputable firm when you see it."

He tossed a document onto the table for him to pick up and read, and followed it with another.

Mr. Thackeray made no move to pick either of them up.

"Or not! It does not matter to me one way or t'other. I am in possession now, and I intend to stick, and with properly authenticated title and deed. I will be much harder to dislodge than a mere woman, whom you might think to browbeat.

"A tick on a dog's ear has more purchase than you do here! Even that tick can be readily dislodged with a glowing splinter touched to its arse."

William laughed but without humor. "But I am of a little more substance and tenacity than a tick, as I think you know, and as your son soon discovered. It will take much more than a hot splinter to displace me."

The older man was breathing heavily with emotion, and his face was a little too red.

"Go ahead. Read it! I have nothing to hide." The older man picked the second document up and read it, blanching as he did so. It was essentially a full description of the confessed unethical behavior of Manley, Wrigley, and Johnson in the matter of the Barristow estate. He then picked up the first and read it too with mounting anger and agitation. He tossed them both back onto the table and turned away to the fire for a moment to avoid letting his feelings of frustration show too obviously on his face before he regained control of his anger once more and turned to face the man at the table.

"All of this means nothing except to another lawyer! Their way of enhancing their fees for the same simple piece of work. Legal jargon! Used to hide the true state of everything and to confuse the rest of us outside of their tight-knit cabal! They are the biggest criminal class against the rest of us on this earth!"

"The ones you usually deal with are, yes, as you can now see. I thought you would eventually recognize that you had no rightful claim, which is why you tried bribery to achieve your ends. *That* also is illegal, by the way, and is also described in the first document you saw."

Thackeray looked at him from under a frowning brow. "But hard to prove! I put nothing in writing, and it is merely their accusation against me!"

"That is as may be, but I am sure you will recognize the name of the legal firm that drew it all up on my behalf. They have a considerable reputation for knowing what they are doing and for succeeding in it. They do not take bribes, and I would never think of offering them or anyone else one to achieve what I legally and honestly wish to achieve. I do not believe they have ever been wrong in anything they have done for my family! But then they are very expensive!"

Mr. Thackeray was not feeling quite as on top of the world, as when he had at first arrived. "You use the word bribery too easily! Bribery! They are not above it any more than they are above outright robbery when they can get away with it. No one of that kidney is. That's what you are talking about, bribery! These damned legal fellows can manipulate and connive to cheat a man out of everything and anything!"

"Or see that he is not cheated out of it! I know nothing of that. But I share your concerns when it comes to less reputable lawyers. That is why I employed only the most reputable lawyers acting on my behalf and in my interest. I find I can now afford them! But they are cheaper by far in the long run." He looked about himself. "Rather a nice little property this!" He smiled in a needling way. "You should drop in on them, if you dare. I am sure they will give you better advice than your own, who are decamping even now. They may be expensive, but they will cost you much less over the longer haul. On second thought, I doubt they would be interested in whatever business you may think to give them once you tell them who you are. They value their reputations more than that!"

He saw the old man bristle.

"If you like, I will instruct them to provide you with a duplicate of their findings. It will not come cheap, however."

The old man's eyes sparkled with feeling. "What of the Barristow girls and the mother? Did you give no thought of them?"

"My! What a wonderful recovery, sir! I must congratulate you. But strangely enough, I did give some small consideration to their welfare and far more than you might have, I believe. They will be most comfortably settled after all of this. Most comfortably! They will not suffer too much from what I achieved, I can promise you that."

Thackeray's cane rattled on the floor in his barely concealed anger. "You will not get away with this, sir."

"I already have! It is a done deal!" Thackeray could also see that for himself. He had been cheated in much the same way he had planned on cheating the Barristow ladies. "But feel free to have your lawyers—if you can find them now—get in touch with my lawyers and discuss this further. They won't of course, for there is no more reputable or well-known firm in London than that of Stevens, Dellingpole, and Diebold, for knowing their business and how to achieve what needs to be done. Your own are gone anyway by now. I am only surprised that it could be accomplished so well, in so short a time, but then, there was a history that proved easy to follow."

His guest now began to look a little distressed. "But you do not look well, sir!" The older gentleman looked flushed and seemed a little unsteady on his feet.

"I am perfectly well, damn you!"

"I am glad to hear it. I am aware that you have a reputation as a fire-eater and can be a little unpredictable with your stick and that little gun, rather like this one, and are rather more to be feared in most circles than your son. Not too difficult I would think, for he is mostly thunder and roar without substance to back it up! I should also warn you that if you to try to produce a sword from inside of that stick that you are handling, as you now seem more tempted to do, that we will both regret it."

He was inclined to believe him, for he had made inquiries of Mr. Devane before he had ever left London after that incident with his son. It may have been old information for the most part, but he had not liked what he had heard. He habitually carried a small pistol, so the story went, and never far from his hand, so there could be another one in his other pocket too as well as the one on the table.

"Yes. I have heard of you!" His voice was hard and perhaps even more clipped than it had been.

"Of course, you have! Who has not, even after five years? Just as I have heard of you, but then we covered that didn't we?"

"You are not a gentleman but a ruthless, violent blackguard!"

"I freely admit it! There! It takes one to know one. Well at least you are right about that. But I make no claims to being a gentleman."

"And no woman safe in your company either!"

"So rumor has it." He was not generally so agreeable to those painting him in such an ill light.

"That is the general understanding. Obviously the ladies here do not know of your scurrilous reputation!"

"No. Fortunately they don't! Unfortunately, I believe that mine, unlike that of your son, might be too well earned and deserved. I am sure you might feel tempted to look up the Barristows and inform them of my perfidious behavior, but you would be wasting your time, for it is too late for that. A done deal! But none of this need concern you further! I believe our meeting is at an end. You will, of course, excuse me if I do not offer you a lunch or a glass of wine. I gave most of the servants the day off. Besides, I am not known for my hospitality to those I do not know or who appear to be trying to work against me."

He stood up and unlocked the door and opened it. He was relieved to see that the corridor beyond was now empty.

"I doubt you will ever need to approach me again, sir, for any reason. Indeed, I believe I gave your son the same advice, and I see he chose not to accompany you, so I may have convinced him, at least, of the wisdom of it."

"I shall take Joshua's pistol, watch, and other property with me. The pistol is of some value and so is the watch."

William was not about to turn over a pistol to this man! "You should have him apply to me then! A simple letter will do, describing the gun in all of its details, and he can explain to me the meanings of the initials carved into the stock of the gun. I had some difficulty reconciling Joshua Thackeray or J.T., at least two of your son's initials, with those I actually read there—S.B. Unfortunately I have grown to like his little pistol, so I shall not easily give it up, even if it does stretch my pocket a little. I must find out what or who the S.B. is. Perhaps the watch which I have not yet seen is similarly engraved or identified.

"But then, I seem to recall something I read in an older *Gazette*, of a money lender recently brutally murdered in the city and robbed—Silas Bergmann! I believe you once owed him a large sum of money, which you repaid about that time, I heard." He smiled annoyingly. "Yes! Those damned servants again! As he was robbed at the time of his murder, nothing of any money could be found, yet you soon repayed another loan you had just previously incurred for exactly the same amount. Most strange! Come to think of it, perhaps your son might not be so well advised to write that descriptive letter, in case it fell into the wrong hands."

The older man did not like what he was hearing. "The city is a violent place! Someone is murdered there every day or night, I believe. It is also not illegal to borrow or repay money."

William saw that he had hit a nerve with the name he had mentioned, for the older man suddenly began to look even more uncomfortable. No doubt he would raise the subject of that engraved pistol with his son when he next met with him. It had been almost as much a surprise to him, hearing the extent of Mr. Devane's inquiries, even into his own finances, as discovering that he had been effectively blocked from his ambition with this extensive property.

"Perhaps if your sudden concern for the disinheritance of the Barristow ladies extended to a pension or a sufficiently large gift, I think they might feel grateful for it, but then I doubt that you planned on doing that anyway."

Mr. Thackeray recognized that their interview was over and stormed out of the house. He mounted his carriage, wrenched the horses around, and drove off without any further word.

William spoke quietly after him as he left. "No, I thought not!"

He watched him go and then saw Thomas appear from the stable with a saddled horse made ready for him as he had instructed. He followed Mr. Thackeray for some time, to ensure that he did indeed head straight back to London and did not have other business or plans in the area.

He had the reputation of not being a man one might cross and then turn ones back upon. He did not trust the old man, for his extensive inquiries had revealed that he had better be careful how he handled him. He was another that might feel inclined to pay others to see him shot on the highway or to slide a knife or that murderous sword into his back when he least expected it, for it had happened before with others who had crossed him. However, that entirely unexpected comment on attempted bribery and the other on the brutal murder of Silas Bergmann may have shown him the wisdom of not meddling with him in any underhanded way, for fear of what might be revealed.

Chapter XIX

The Revelation and an Embarrassing Reassessment

Some little time later, when Mrs. Barristow and the girls returned from their visit, having seen a carriage leaving their home, they saw Annis pacing up and down the corridor and obviously in high dudgeon. She was steadily fuming and had a drawn and angry look on her face! She rushed over to her mother and blurted out her feelings.

"Oh, Mama! I was right about him! I overheard everything that transpired between them!"

Her mother took in her blazing anger. "So I can see, miss! The intention was that you would accompany us to our neighbors. You were not supposed to be here and listening at keyholes!"

Charlotte and Sophia listened to their sister's outburst but could not make sense of what was disturbing Annis so much. Their visitor must have upset her in some way.

"I wasn't, but I could not help overhearing. They are a pair of rogues, the both of them, and we should never have trusted him. I would have burst in and confronted him with this . . . this . . ." She ground her teeth in anger. "But he locked the door to keep me out! He must have heard me. I overheard one blackguard dealing with another just as bad. I knew he could not be trusted! Oh, why did I not tell you what I knew, *before* we lost everything!" She was close to tears in her desperate frustration. "How could you, Mama? How could you be so easily taken in and be so gullible? Oh, I wish I had shown you Lady Seymour's letter now, for it laid his character out so clearly!" She seemed adamant about that! Yet her mother was smiling kindly at her for some reason she did not understand, and spoke gently.

"I doubt it, my dear. It would have shown you *her* perception of him from many years ago, and I do not always trust your godmother's perception of anything as I have told you often enough. I do trust my own feelings and those of other of my friends however."

"But it did!" She was so agitated she felt like stamping her foot for all the good it might have done. "His character is execrable! We should never have trusted him or allowed him to stay. He worked his way so well into our confidences and look where it has got us! I should have shot him when I had the opportunity and saved us from all of this! If he were here now, I would be tempted to do so. I may still do so, and with his own gun! Poetic justice to pay him back for his treachery!"

Her mother was taking it all so calmly and even put her arm about her shoulder. "Now please calm down, my dear. This is not like you to speak of violence and guns with such animation. I am so glad you didn't do anything so rash. You would have made everything so much worse. Here I thought you might be having second thoughts about his character and his intentions."

Annis was raging on tearfully! "I was! But not anymore! He pulled the wool over your eyes and mine. He was able to fool even Thomas and Molly and even Mrs. Rogers."

Her mother chuckled, but there was little humor in it considering how her daughter had become so exercised over something she really had little knowledge of.

"No, he didn't." Her mother seemed very sure of it.

Sophia's hand pushed into her mother's for reassurance and comfort. She had never seen her sister before in this upset and wildly tearful mood, or so angry. Charlotte stood off to one side and listened, not sure what to believe and not entirely sure who they might be talking about.

Her mother's sober words and lack of anger at what had happened caused Annis to look at her strangely, as though she might not be entirely sane or in complete control of her senses.

"No, I have not lost my wits, my dear, but *you* seem to have. Well. Well. What do you think you know, child?"

She did not take offense at her mother's addressing her as "child" for her apparent simplicity in understanding. "Oh, mama. What will we do?"

"Why nothing, my dear! It has all been done for us and so easily and conveniently and without trouble!"

"It was not done *for* us, mama." Her eyes were flashing with her anger. "It was done *to* us!"

Her mother continued to smile at her in a somewhat exasperated manner. "There was no violence, was there?"

"No! Unfortunately! There was some talk of a sword stick and a pistol and murderous intentions and some other threatening words between two like-minded villains! But why would you be concerned if there had been? One blackguard less, maybe two, and it would not have mattered which one as far as I could see! Neither of them deserves to live from what I heard. You are taking it all so calmly!"

"Yes, I am! So should you be! My, you are bloodthirsty all of a sudden! I do hope your sisters do not become afflicted with this same feeling toward him."

"I won't, Mama!" Sophia seemed to want to rise to his defense, whoever they were talking about.

"I know you won't, my dear."

Annis fumed on. "Papa would not have allowed this to have happened! He can't have known him at all!"

"I fear your father might not have been able to stop it quite as William did! That was his biggest concern also. The Thackerays are rather too well connected in all of the wrong places and have a reputation for shady dealings, and even violence, especially the father! Deviousness, deception, villainy is all they might understand, when it is brought to bear against them. William decided to fight fire with more fire. Nothing quite succeeds with such men like an unanticipated and unexpected excess of something returned to them, whether it be violence or other action. Now, however, it does not matter. So come and sit here and cease your agitation."

She saw Annis was unable to settle down in her present turbulent mood.

"Charlotte, Sophia, get on with you and help in the kitchen!" She stalled their protest with an upraised hand. "No! You are not staying to listen in. You will learn all you need to know of this later."

She watched them reluctantly leave, though they did not leave so very far but lingered to listen.

"Now Annis. We shall sit down. Or I shall, if you are too worked up. What is it that you think you know, and I shall try to explain it to you?"

"Oh, Mama! Please tell me that it is not so, that we have been disinherited by that rogue!"

"Have we really?" She seemed almost to laugh at that thought. "How little you seem to know!"

"That is what I heard. Please tell me that it is not true."

"Of course it is not true! You must be careful what you believe, my dear, no matter what you might hear, especially at keyholes! Nothing is what it seems! Your father told me to believe nothing that I heard from another, unless I knew the source very well, and to believe only half of what I saw. He told you the same thing more than once. He was proved right on many things. Where is William, by the way?"

"He rode out after that Thackeray man. Probably to murder him on some lonely stretch of road like he did that unfortunate Mr. Maxton!"

"You do not know that! Oh I hope not! But then he has a way of cutting through such threats and nonsense and getting to the heart of any problem as he did with the son, and may just feel the need to do *that* to protect us even better!"

"I do believe it . . . !" She faltered. She should not let it be known that she had been snooping in his private correspondence to his sister and knew more about Mr. Maxton than she should. No mistaking the meaning of RIP. "Oh, Mama, he is a rogue of the worst kind!"

"Yes, I believe he might be where the need is there, or almost. But no! Not of the worst kind! Of the best and most effective kind! The kind a woman can rely upon. But whatever he is I am thankful for it. I am also thankful that he would stand no nonsense from either of those Thackeray persons. Very like your father was at that age too! Oh, my dear, you have much to learn about certain men and so little time to learn it I would say now that your father is gone and our situation has changed. Too little time to achieve what we need to see achieved!"

She smoothed her daughter's hair back from her face and wiped the tears of anger and frustration from her face. "The rogues often prove to be the better men, my dear. Your father was! The gentlemen of fine words and apparently finer deeds turn out to be the true rogues, for they too well hide their real purpose. I know several of both persuasions. The younger Thackeray when he first approached us was that way, I remember. All politeness. Simpering and greasing his way into our family as he did, and look how he turned out! He was interested only in finding out what he could to assist his father in his devious intent to put us out. Now we have one of another kind in our midst."

"Yes! Worse!"

"I see that you think so. But easily settled I think." She looked across to the pantry to see that William had left the documents where he said he would. "Pass me that small bundle of papers tucked into the pantry over there. Yes, bring them all over here, and we will go through them one by one. It is time you learned what I know of this man you think to be a villain." She sorted through the documents that Annis brought over to her, to put them in some order.

"A man can deal much better in business and legal matters with those people in London than ever a woman might. A woman can achieve so little with them, for they do not take her seriously, and I would have been at a severe disadvantage. Besides, I do not understand any of that and would have made a mess of it even if I had known who to approach, and I knew nothing about even where to begin. William did!"

She put the first paper into her daughter's hands and watched her read it.

"But, Mama, you confirm everything I said!" She looked up at her mother, convinced she had lost her wits completely. "You sold it to him! This entire property! Several days ago even! Is that what those two men did? They pressured you into this."

"O hush! It might seem so! But I can assure you they didn't!"

"That is what it says." She reread the offending document. "It is a bill of sale to him! But it says nothing of the price paid, for *that* figure cannot be right! Can it? Yet it was witnessed by Thomas and Molly and there are both of your signatures on it. Yours and his! You did this yourself! The servants even helped you!" She seemed thoroughly confused.

"Yes, I did!" She tossed that paper onto the fire, much to her daughter's surprise. She doubted it might so easily be overturned as that.

She produced the next one and opened it up. "William and I had a most enlightening conversation after you had all gone to bed after those gentlemen had left, and he was not at all shy about laying his history out for me to understand; in its entirety I might add—warts and all as Cromwell said to his portraitist! He hid nothing from me. But I already knew most of it. We were lucky to find him, my dear!" She hesitated and thought for a moment or two. "Or did he find us?"

Her daughter was not inclined to believe her, except for the latter.

"He was most busy in London yesterday on my behalf and not on his own, as you seem to suspect."

"But . . ."

"Now what do you think that this is?" She passed the next paper for her daughter to examine.

"It is a full title . . ." She looked closely at the paragraphs her mother indicated, and the legal language, that seemed more easily understood than was usual she thought. She recognized the name Diebold in the Title above it all, as being one of the firm of several lawyers who had drawn it all up. ' . . . to all of that property held by Mr. Lionel Barristow, whatsoever! Father!"

She scanned the paper. It looked disturbingly legal to her. "All of our property—land, house, possessions, everything!" She was pale. "It is now the property of Mr. William Devane of Brooklands. Dated yesterday at three in the afternoon." She opened her mouth to protest but was caught without power of speech for a few moments.

Her mother threw that into the fire also. "No, my dear. Say nothing. It does begin to improve! That was the one he said he would show Mr. Thackeray, to convince him of the worst of his fears, that Underby was now totally lost to him. I think he may have succeeded in that, considering the black look that Thomas described on Mr. Thackeray's face as he drove off. Now this one."

"But it is another deed to all of that property of William Devane, formerly owned by Mr. Barristow of Underby Manor, drawn up by the same lawyers, and it is now entirely in your name. This is also dated yesterday, but the time is at four in the afternoon."

"Yes. The last legal transaction before he returned to us. The London lawyers have copies of all of this and faithfully carried out his instructions and mine, once it was clear what we intended. It is done. Finished! We own Underby again without question!"

There was gentle whispering followed by movement away from outside of the door once Charlotte and Sophia had heard that last of it.

Annis looked confused as her mother knew she would be. That document, she placed carefully back on to the pantry and set a decorative rock upon it to hold it down.

"I do not understand!"

Mrs. Barristow explained it to her daughter. "We now own Underby once more, my dear, and everything that your uncle and father added to it but with no cloud hanging over us ever again. It was William's idea. I told you we spoke at length the other evening for some hours. After that, I gave him title to all of this, as far as I might be able to, so that he could work with his own lawyers in London without question, and bring some clarity to this property ownership. There were other things to do with property that you do not need to know about." She tossed another small document on the fire. "Once it was cleared up, if it could be cleared up, then the intention was that he would transfer title back to me as he did. Otherwise, he would hold it on my behalf until it was resolved. Oh, don't worry! He insisted on other safeguards in there too, so that if anything happened to him, I still had title to it all. You need to know nothing of those."

Her daughter was speechless and undergoing a painful readjustment of her views, which a short time ago had been so violently inclined.

"Are you feeling any better about this, my dear?" She watched her daughter nod her head. There was a pained look on her flushed face. "He is an honest man, my dear! But I was already convinced of that. There are few of them about these days. You have been laboring under a wrong impression as you have been for several days now. The elder Thackeray was shown only the ownership by William. You may have heard part of that conversation that you were not supposed to be here to overhear. Thackeray could not be aware that William had already transferred ownership back to me, nor is he ever likely to find out. We need keep only this one. The others are where they need to be. She watched them consumed in the fire. Far too dangerous to leave those lying around."

Her daughter's anger had drained from her as she had learned of what had really happened, but then the reversal of feeling that suddenly flooded over her was more than she felt she could bear. She flopped into a chair beside her mother.

"Oh!" ·

Her mother smiled at the sudden transformation of emotional feeling. "Yes. Puts him in a different light altogether, doesn't it? From villain to saint! But he was never the former! Nor the latter either! Just a good man! It's a pity you overheard any of it, but then, it could not be helped, I suppose. His thoughts were only of protecting us. Nothing else." At least, nothing else she could easily discuss at this time with her daughter! She watched as the tension and hatred drained from her daughter's attitude, to be replaced by one of puzzlement and embarrassment and even uncertainty, and then guilt.

"But . . . " Annis still struggled with it. "How confusing it all is. It could not have been settled so very easily? Father struggled with this for years! He must still be misleading us somehow! It seems to be part of his nature to be misleading!"

Her hand fell over that of her daughter. "Oh hush. Let go of it, my dear! You appear not to know William as you should!"

"It seems I do not know him at all!" She was flushed, thinking about the uncharitable and even violent thoughts she had harbored. "I seem to have been wrong at every turn! I resented his presence when he first came for some reason, despite what his sister had persuaded Bella of, and I later learned that a deeper animosity was probably justified too, the more I learned of him. I didn't understand how Bella or anyone could be so foolish as to ever consider entering into a marriage with a complete stranger about whom so little was known, and even that little, seemed to be very questionable, considering the tales floating about. In fact, what was known was all either questionable or very bad."

Her mother reached out and took her hand to comfort her. "Bella thought so too at first! Your godmother's views on him are far too pervasive and rather too well known. But then Bella was able to change her mind also, little by little, even without meeting him. His sister, Elizabeth, was able to clarify so much of the confusion, for she was very well aware of so many things that your godmother was not. William also confirmed all of that too when he and I spoke the other night. I don't think I have ever known quite so much of any man, except your father! He hid nothing important from me! I think I would have been most proud to have him as a son, and now I find that I do!

"Bella went from complete antipathy to any suggestion of a union with him, to being prepared to meet him and see him for herself. We could not ask for more. They may not have suited, despite our hopes. Unfortunately, she met with that accident before he might become acquainted with any of our plans or might even meet him. We had not allowed for that! All of those plans and scheming came to a disastrous end before any of it could take place as I had hoped. It is a pity that Bella did not confide in you more after her first confidences.

"Then, after that accident, I felt sure he could not come, not being in England, or would not come if he was. He is not easily either to be cajoled or pushed; no man is. They need to be led but in such a way they do not know that it is happening. Perhaps I was guilty of misleading him there, for I appealed to him in a way I felt sure . . . no, I knew he might not be able to refuse. He didn't refuse. We had not properly set the groundwork as we had originally intended. But then . . . when we most needed him, and when I had despaired of ever seeing an end to any of it, he did come . . ." She shed tears again at that most welcome relief that she had felt at that moment. "I feared for the worst by that time, for I was ready to tear my hair out, and he must have wondered what he . . . no matter, he came. Fortunately for us!"

She wiped her tears away.

"For my part, I held out hope that he would come here myself, but lived in fear that he would not or would not get my letter in time. Everything seemed to depend upon it."

"Oh, Mama! Why did you not tell me all of this before?"

"You would not have believed me! But I did not think of it. There was too much else to occupy us."

"No, I would probably not have believed it! I was sure that he was probably as bad as I feared even without reading that letter, except when . . ."

"Yes, my dear?"

"Nothing, Mama." But she could not hold back her thoughts. "Except when he also shed tears over our loss on that first night. It seemed real and from the heart, when he had no need even to feign any of that. Then, when he kissed . . ." her voice caught as she thought of that " . . . when he kissed Bella in a gentle and loving way after he had married her. I did not expect that of him either. From the little I heard of him, I expected someone remote and untouchable, arrogant, unfeeling, cold. I thought he would be aloof and detached and resentful at being used in that way for our benefit alone, and then would be gone. When he didn't go, I wondered why he stayed and began to suspect his motives for staying. I began to think he was a past master at misleading everyone, including his sister and mother, or so godmother said of him. That seemed better to fit his reputation. What little I had gleaned of him!"

"And what would you know of his reputation from gossip and rumors?"

She decided to say nothing more of Lady Seymour's letter. Some of it was undoubtedly true, but it was difficult to know what was true and what might not be. It had not been a flattering account in any case. "But then I was concerned again, especially after he started wandering that first night. Except he seemed confused and lost, rather than intent on anything . . . worse, like that Joshua Thackeray had been, I think. Then that brawl with Thackeray. I feared for the servants when I saw his bloody hands at church that afternoon, for I had not known Thackeray had been here. And you thinking he had shaved to get that blood on his face and shirt. I had seen him shave earlier, so I knew that was not it!"

"I admit, I knew nothing of any of it until much later my dear. My thoughts were elsewhere."

"I could see that, Mama! I had to reassess him for myself after that and after listening to Molly and Mrs. Rogers and Thomas even. They could not praise him highly enough without breaking down into tears with their emotions. I could not understand them! But what wouldn't I have given to have seen that! They could say nothing nice enough about him and certainly looked after him well after that!"

"And so they should look after him! If he had not interceded as he did, I do now know where we would be, even now, other than that we would probably not be living here! We would have had that grasping ignoramus and his father underfoot, interfering and encroaching in everything we did, and hard to get rid of and would not be quite so comfortable or secure."

Annis tried to reconcile what she had seen with what she had come to believe of him "He seemed kind and good mannered in every way with the servants and with us, especially keeping Sophia occupied as he does. Hardly the attitude of an encroaching villain to enjoy the company of a child! Then there was that incident when he found my pistol, giving me his own. I did not know what to believe."

"I heard of that! I cannot approve of you playing with guns. But not knowing what to believe? Of course you do. You will see it eventually. He is a good man, my dear. He will not judge you ill or hold your honest feelings against you, but may be quite amused by them. What others tell you of someone should not entirely displace what you yourself find out you know? Believe what you know for yourself and see and do not so readily or so easily believe what you hear from others. People are too often mistaken about others they may dislike or are jealous of."

Her mother sighed as she took in her daughter's contrition. "But there is another problem looming before us, Annis. I fear what might happen when he realizes—as he soon will, if not already—that eventually we may be able to manage without him, if we can, for then he might leave to go to his own estates. With both Thackerays now taken care of and difficulties with the title, all needless concerns now and seen to, it seems that our larger need for him is now at an end, but I shall not tell him that just yet."

"Indeed, Mama, why would he stay in any case?"

Her mother felt that she might be able to answer that question if she chose to but could not yet be sure how it might work out.

"I would think that he might want to put as much distance between himself and us, considering what has happened here and what I believed of him. But does he have any estates worth speaking of? You mentioned Brooklands, and I remember that name in one of those papers."

"Yes, my dear, he does! Much larger than this one and a few miles off from here." She stared into the fire. "To think that I actually owned it for a few hours!" she raised her head. "One of those papers I burned!" She recovered from that brief consideration. "His father—late father—Captain Devane was a most respected gentleman, well known to your father and a highly decorated sailor who served with Admiral Nelson. When he died not so very long ago, he left the entire estate to him as the only son, and it is . . . he is quite wealthy. There is nothing here that he could not buy ten times over if he chose. But if he makes that decision to leave, and he will eventually, for there is nothing now to hold him here . . ." She knew that was not entirely true, but her daughter may need a jolt or two to think about that. "I cannot stop him, though I will be more than sad to see him leave. He reminds me so very much of your father at that age. It is to be hoped he will still remember us and visit as he might, for he is not so very far away."

She looked intently at her daughter as she made those comments, hoping to see some indication in her expression of how that eventuality of him leaving, sat with her, but there was nothing to see other than that she was in a downcast mood.

"Mama, you said he reminds you of my father, and I think I recall you saying something earlier about father too, and even eventually admitted about *him* being a rogue at times? Surely, not in the same vein? I find *that* hard to believe. I do not understand."

"Of course, you don't! You do not know the half of it, for I have never told you anything of your father when he was younger, but he and Mr. Devane had quite a few things in common. More than quite a few things! That is why I was not so very defensive about him being considered for Bella. I shall tell you more one of these days but not now. I need to relax for a while and savor what has just happened.

"We will be having a late lunch, and if I do not mistake, William has just returned to join us and will be in from the stable shortly." Her daughter seemed uneasy at hearing that. She probably could not face him at this moment. "You cannot know how relieved I am to see him safely back! I take it you have lost your murderous impulses toward him?"

Her daughter nodded, not trusting herself to speak.

"I shall say no more at this time." She stroked her daughter's hair back from her forehead. "William is very like your father was, and I think your father knew that of him too within seconds of meeting him. A man to be relied upon and not inclined to take nonsense from another like Thackeray. But he had to place his trust somewhere, and so did I."

Her mother met William at the door and, unable to hide her feelings at what he had accomplished, embraced him. "Thank you for what you have done for us, William." He smiled at her as he returned her hug. "You are just in time for a late lunch, sir!"

She watched as Annis somewhat sheepishly excused herself as she moved by them both, toward the sounds from the kitchen, with her head turned aside so that he might not see her tears. Her eyes followed her daughter. She smiled. "Do not worry, she will soon be her argumentative self again, William."

He watched her out of sight. He understood her mood. It must have been quite an unexpected revelation for her to find out that he had not robbed and cheated them. "Yes, ma'am. I must see what else I can do to annoy her and distract her from her present mood."

"As you seem to do so well with all of us! I see you know her too well, William. Indeed you seem to know all of us too, if it comes to that. So what are your plans now? I am sure you must be itching to be gone, but we will be sad to part with you! I was hoping you might stay longer if you can manage it. I am not entirely sure we are out of the woods yet."

"Nor am I. There is still that matter with the squire that should be tidied up, and I still need to define your financial affairs a little better. If the weather stays clear, perhaps a tour of the estates tomorrow will be distraction enough, if I can persuade Annis to go with us, for she will be the one who will need to understand all of that for herself when I am not here!"

Chapter XX

The Tour of the Estate, a Stolen Kiss

The next morning, William approached Mrs. Barristow. "Ma'am, it appears to be a fine day as we hoped and seemingly might stay that way. If you would care to take an outing as we had discussed, we can take the carriage and tour the estate. We might perhaps get over to Nettleshome and perhaps even to Ayles Howing or at least the edges of it. Unless you have changed your mind, this might also be a suitable time to approach the squire about him purchasing that piece of land from you that has been in contention between your two families for some time, or even trading some land for it?"

"No, William, I have not changed my mind on that. That should be the first thing done, and I believe it might be well received if it were to be done by you, rather than me. The squire does not know me well and may still bear a little animosity for harsh words that we exchanged at one time. The more I think about it, the better it seems as a sensible course of action that might bring some peace between us. I think that your suggestion was a very good one and will achieve a lot of good. It will bring an end to that long-lived disagreement that never seemed to go away between Mr. Barristow and him."

"Then I shall approach him first about that, and then we can take a look around and map out your boundaries better after I have that out of the way. It is all well and good to study the books and paperwork, but understanding and managing an estate like this one requires a good deal of getting out and about and meeting your tenants and learning of them. There is a rough map of sorts, and I can follow that well enough, but it appears to be out of date, and I do not know exactly where your boundaries are now, or who your tenants or neighbors might be."

"Unfortunately, William, I would be of no help to you whatsoever. Mr. Barristow saw to all of that. Besides, if I go, then all of the girls will also demand to be taken, and I am not up to that at this moment. Annis is the only one who needs to go."

"Then if one of your servants might accompany us, perhaps Thomas, who seems to know something of the layout and your holdings, it would be of some advantage."

"Yes, Annis and Thomas are the two who need to go with you. She was often out around the estate with her father. It will do her good if she can be persuaded. However, she is down in the dumps after what she overheard yesterday and believing only the worst of you. It was a painful correction, though it will pass soon enough I suspect, with time. I will keep the other girls with me and deal with their protests, for they have also been cooped up too long. Besides, I think Annis needs to get some weighty issues off her mind that have been troubling her for some time now. I suspect her conscience was causing her a little difficulty after yesterday, when she discovered that you had neither disinherited us, as she feared, nor intended to cast us all out, and you were suddenly not the blackguard she had come to believe you to be, though she has been torn backward and forward on that too from time to time."

He understood how Annis must have felt, overhearing him and Thackeray as she had. "Perhaps, ma'am, if you were to ask her, if you do not mind, then she might be less likely to refuse, whereas a request from me at this delicate time might have her seeking refuge elsewhere to avoid a possibly embarrassing situation. I think I last saw her in the herb garden."

"Then as we will need some basil, I shall go and ask if she would help out in that regard and make it clear to her that she has little choice in the matter, for we must know certain things."

She went off to the garden to find her daughter.

They both returned to the house some minutes later with a basket of vegetables for dinner and another of herbs that would be bundled and hung up to dry over the kitchen.

Her mother had explained everything to her, and what the plan was, but she was not at ease with any of it and told him so. She still felt guilty! She had difficulty meeting his eyes. "I do not know why you would wish to have me accompany you. I have not been very trusting of you since you arrived."

He laughed gently. "I find no fault with that! How could you, overhearing what you did? I rarely trust anyone upon first meeting! I gave you little reason to trust me up to yesterday and especially not after what happened then. Nor indeed after my earlier confrontation with the younger Thackeray. Discovering that one has a violent man under one's roof is not conducive to being at ease! However, I do need to have someone who knows something of the estate—your mother's and yours now— to go with me. I would also like to meet some of your tenants and to have someone break the ice so that they will tell me what we need to know to help your mother as well as you, for you will also need to understand it fully too. If I, a complete stranger were to approach them, I would find out very little. From what I have learned so far by going through your father's papers, the estate is in a tolerably prosperous state. I also need to know where your boundaries are. I could guess, but that is not very effective, and the small map that I have is quite confusing and undoubtedly is out of date. I need to know this, so that I may better advise your mother and you—if you can stand me doing that—as you are now the eldest daughter and will likely have to shoulder more of the burden when I need to leave. Your mother candidly admits to having little interest in doing any of it, as she is more burdened with the house and its chores and the home garden."

He smiled at her kindly. "If you might fear being alone with me, we will have Thomas accompany us."

She looked at him sharply at that statement. "I do not fear you!" She saw the look in his eyes that suggested she would have to demonstrate that to him by going with him. He was challenging her again, and she rarely refused a challenge. "Very well, I will accompany you. But I will need time to change and make ready."

"That's the spirit! You have whatever time you may need, Annis. The day is still young. I have other things that I need to do first with the squire, for your mother would like to see the issue of that disputed field put behind you at last. I doubt I shall be very long."

She was ready in less than thirty minutes and patiently waiting for him once he got back from seeing the squire. He told her mother what he had managed to do, and both of them felt that it had all worked out most satisfyingly.

Later, with William on his own horse followed by the mule, Annis on one of the horses from the stable, and Thomas following on yet another; they set out.

Annis noticed that the squire was even then turning his cows loose in that field. His now, in exchange for another piece of land that naturally fitted with the Underby estate, so her mother had informed her as William was getting the horses ready.

The squire tipped his hat to William and his companions and had a broad smile on his face. He could not have believed his luck. When he had first seen Mr. Devane coming up his drive toward the house barely an hour earlier, he began to fear for his safety. He remembered very clearly the day that the younger Thackeray had left the Barristow house in some disarray and pain and had even more recently—just yesterday—seen his father turned off with a black face and in an obvious ill temper, though his leaving had not been accompanied by force or obvious physical injury as far as he was aware. He had begun to fear for the worst. Now, he began to see that Mr. Devane was a man of rare diplomacy who could easily cut to the quick of the matter, and that he had little to fear from him, provided his future dealings with the Barristow ladies were above board and honest. After almost twenty years of argument with Mr. Barristow, he now owned that field that had long been a source of great aggravation and contention. So far, it was all based upon a simple handshake, but considering what he had already found out about Mr. Devane, that was all he needed at this stage.

"William!" Thomas attracted his attention. "I have a lame horse." He dismounted as his companions stopped, and picked up his horses leg to examine the hoof.

"I doubt she is fit to go on, sir, for she is dead lame. I shall have to walk her back."

William dismounted also and examined the mare's foot. The mare was in some distress and obviously not able to go on or to be ridden. They conferred over the situation.

"If I walk her back, she should be all right, but I doubt I'll be able to catch up easily after I see to getting this shoe off and her looked after, for the only other horses are out in the fields, working."

"Then there is nothing for it. You should return, Thomas. We should also return perhaps." He looked at Annis questioningly and smiled at her. "You should not be alone with a violent and unpredictable blackguard such as me, you know?"

She looked startled for a moment. "No. We shall go forward! Considering what the weather has been like for the past week, there might not be another day like this one before we get hit with snow. I am not afraid! I do have your pistol with me for eventualities."

He smiled at her. She saw that he had provoked her into that response, for it was as if he had known that had he suggested going forward anyway, that she would have been more in favor of returning. He seemed to know her too well. "And to protect your honor from the numerous brigands, pirates, and bandits that infest this locale! Excellent. I shall relax then, knowing that I am so well protected with such a good shot beside me."

"You are having fun at my expense, sir, I think." She was still smarting with her feelings of the day before.

He saw that she had been hurt a little by his attitude, and he did not need her to return into her shell. "Yes, I was. I was teasing you just a little. That was not kind of me. I apologize, Annis. It was not called for."

He turned to Thomas. "You'd better explain the circumstance to Mrs. Barristow, Thomas, or else she might worry."

"That I will, sir." They watched as he walked his horse around and began to lead her off back to Underby, looking back at her often to ensure that she would not suffer from that, else he would turn her into a field to rest up and get her at some other time.

They continued to trace out the boundaries as best they could, for Annis was familiar with most of the transactions over the years, for they had been well explained to her by her father. After an hour or two, when they were close to the coast once more, William led the way, and they rode away from the property at a canter.

"But we are not heading around the property at all now."

"No, Annis, we are not! I have seen enough for the moment, and there is nothing in dispute or ill defined for some distance to the North now, for it follows the coast. There are other things I need to see. You can show me more of the property when we return and can pick up above where we left off. We shall not be long. Sophia and I were out this way twice now, and I find I need to go a little further afield." He waited for her to object, but she seemed to have become resigned to accepting that she had objected more than enough about him already and had been shown to be wrong too often.

"In that case, sir, while we are here in this direction, we can visit my aunt, if that suggestion is not likely to sidetrack you too much from what you intend. She now lives with one of the tenants of another holding, not two miles from here, and sees to him and his children since his wife died. She was at the funeral, and I believe she is known to you now."

"I think I remember her. The lady with the slight limp." He did not object.

She followed him and his mule out to a headland overlooking the channel. There were piles of dried underbrush collected there for a large bonfire, possibly for November 5, but that seemed a long time away for such preparations to be underway already. *That* had seemed to be all he was interested in.

They turned back inland, and he then followed her to her aunt's home. After a most pleasant relaxing visit with her aunt, who fussed about them both and plied them with bread and cakes— which only William ate—and tea, they rejoined their planned tour some little time later and continued around the property or examined it from those rare areas of slightly higher ground that afforded a wider view, and from which they could see the boundary easily enough along the lines of trees, well-defined hedgerows, or along a river's edge. It was a large and extensive estate, larger than he had realized, and there was much to see.

It was still early afternoon when they finally turned for home, but the tour had unexpectedly taken its toll on Annis, for she let out a warning cry to him before she swayed in her saddle and almost fell from her horse.

But for her cry, she would have fallen, but that had been warning enough of something being wrong, as he had seen her sway a little in the saddle. He was close enough to reach out and grab her arm.

"What is the matter, Annis?"

"I am fatigued beyond belief and a little dizzy."

"You should have mentioned this earlier! We have been out longer than I intended." He looked at her pale face. "Most selfish of me! When did you last eat a good meal? You only picked at your aunt's cooking."

"I don't know. I cannot remember."

"I seem to recall that I did not see you partake of dinner last night either, for you excused yourself to your room after the soup, and now that I think about it, you did not have much of a breakfast this morning. We need to get some substantial food into you, and Underby is a little too far away. Is there an inn or a hostelry anywhere nearby? Or should we return to your aunt?"

"There is an old inn ahead of us, probably no more than two miles, I believe, and much easier than returning or going on to Underby."

"Then we shall go there. In your weak and unpredictable condition, I doubt you will be able to stay aboard that mare like that and in that saddle. I had better have you up here with me where I can hold on to you to stop you tumbling off." He reached over and, taking her by the waist and her legs as she unhooked herself from her saddle, took her across to his own before she fell off.

"Better hold onto me, if you can."

He supported her about her back and legs as she pushed her hand inside of his coat and behind him. He looked down at her and saw her head so close to his, with her eyes closed and her face very pale. He steadied his horse, leaned down a little, kissed her gently on the neck, and then waited for some response or objection. She appeared not to notice. He frowned.

He looped the reins of her horse around the knee support of her saddle and trusted that the loose horse would be able to follow them. As they rode off, he was pleased to see that she did. His own horse was used to being guided by knee pressure alone or voice, for he had often needed both hands free for pistol and saber when he was caught up in combat.

After heading in the direction that Annis had suggested, and encountering a better-used road, he turned along it, followed by the mule and Annis's horse. As he rode into the stable yard, he was met by the hostler, who had seen him approaching with his awkward burden and proceeded to hold his horse while the rider dismounted, holding the young lady steady on his horse's back as he did so and then allowing her to slide off into his arms.

"I'll let you see to these three. See that the mule is in a stall next to my horse where he can see her, or there will be trouble."

"Yes, sir." He had seen the kind of trouble a mule like that could cause when it took things amiss, and that one had a mean look in its eyes.

William carried her over to the open door where he was met by the landlord who had been alerted to a problem even before they had arrived.

He fussed about as he shut the door behind them to keep out the dust and wind. "Is the young lady well, sir? Why, it is Miss Barristow!"

"Yes, she is well enough, I think. Just famished I believe. She fainted. Hunger! She has eaten little for a week or more since her father died."

"Aye. I heard of that, sir! Nasty accident and not so far from here either. But to lose a father and a sister at the same time . . . nasty thing to have happen to any family."

William ignored him as he saw to Annis and followed the Landlord down the hallway. "I will need some hot water and a cloth, and then soup at first and perhaps some of your coffee. We shall see how she responds to that and see where we go from there."

"Yes, sir. The parlor is empty, and there is a good fire in there, for that wind is none too warm."

He carried her in and sat her in front of the blazing fire and supported her as he took off her cloak and bonnet and then knelt in front of her and placed some cushions to support her head and then saw to himself a little. In a short time, a bowl of hot water and a cloth was placed beside him and he began to bathe her face a little. She slowly began to come around.

She suddenly sat forward and grabbed at his hand for support, wondering where she was and how she had got to where she now was.

"The girl is here with some soup, sir. The rest of it should not be long now."

"Thank you."

Annis was looking at him and what was going on around her. She was clearly not sure what had happened.

"You became faint for lack of food, I believe, and almost fell off your horse," he explained, seeing the question in her eyes. "We shall eat and rest here for a while. Come, take some of this soup. It will help."

He spoon-fed her, and in no time at all, she began to perk up with *that* and with the warmth from the fire.

"Oh! We are at the inn! How long have we been here?" She looked about her and brought her hands to her throat. "My hat? My cloak?"

"Yes, we are at the inn. You are safe." He smiled at her. "You need not worry, you know? I did not take advantage of you too much, if that is what you are afraid of. Your bonnet and cape are on the chair there, and I loosened only the one button at your throat, and I did steal only one kiss."

Most of his words sailed by her without comprehension. "I am not afraid! I don't remember getting here." She was flushed.

"No. I had to carry you, or you might have fallen off your horse. Lack of food is your problem, young lady. Careless of me not to take better care of you! Your mother will rake me over the coals for this, to think of heading out so far, without seeing you properly fed first! It is long past time for lunch anyway, for we have been out more than three hours. They may be worrying for you at home, but no matter. We should stay here for a little time until you recover fully, and I will see that you have something more substantial than soup."

She allowed him to continue feeding her. "Yes, I am hungry, but I have been ignoring the demands of my stomach with all else going on about me."

"Yes. Most foolish, if understandable. Foolish of you for not looking after yourself as you should and foolish of me not to notice! We'll soon fix that!"

He was satisfied to remain there until he saw her recover to her usual self and was pleased to see that she was eventually able to sit up to the table and partake of a good-sized meal, with roast chicken, roast potatoes and fresh garden vegetables. The landlord even had a small beer for them that was of a particularly good quality. She ate as though she had not eaten for a week. It was about time.

When he was satisfied that she would now be able to make it home, he saw her dressed again for the colder temperatures outdoors. He paid the landlord and then lifted her up onto her horse and saw her loop her knee about the saddle support.

"Are you sure you can manage now?" He looked up into her face.

"I think so. If not, I shall let you know—and before I am likely to fall."

He gave a coin to the lad who had seen to the horses and then mounted his own horse and rode beside her. She seemed to have recovered most of her strength, but he was attentive to her.

They arrived back later than intended. Her mother had been worried at their extended absence until he explained the circumstances to her. He helped her from her horse and would have carried her inside, but she insisted on walking in, where she promptly sat at the table. She was still tired.

"She overdid it, and I was too ambitious. We ate at Baldock, at the inn there. I did not notice how little she had eaten over the last few days or we would not have gone so far afield. It was my fault, ma'am, I should have taken better note of what she was and was not eating."

"I think we have all been neglecting ourselves that way, William. She, more than any of us."

Her mother suggested that Annis should get herself to bed to rest for an hour or two before dinner and that she had better see that she ate more substantial meals than she had been, or she would not be going out like that again.

Chapter XXI

Tearful Reappraisal and a Motherly Confession

Her mother helped her upstairs after a light repast and some hot tea in the parlor.

"Oh, Mama, I am so tired!"

Her mother helped her undress. "We all are, my dear! We are all being driven along by nervous energy, and that is the wrong kind. None of us has had time to relax or come to grips with the new reality. We are all being pulled off in a hundred new directions every day so that we do not have time to breathe even, never mind to think. Everything has happened far too fast around us, and none of it seems real just yet. I have had little time to sit and think about any of it, and I never had any expectation of it working out as it has, considering . . .

"I'll order a little more food to be sent up if you wish, for you need to eat something you know, to build your strength up again. I wish I had paid more attention to what you were all eating or not, but I was too wrapped up in my own grief and concerns. That must change!"

"No, mama, there is no need. I did eat well at the inn, so I did not even need to eat as I did downstairs. I am but tired, probably as much from the ride and lack of food earlier as much as for other reasons to do with my own emotions and finding out some things about myself that I do not like. William was kind, and saw that I had a substantial meal at the inn or resolved he would not return home with me but would see me stay there and have my sisters join me. He insisted that he would see that I was quite well recovered before he would think of heading back. I began to worry that you might think the worst, with us away for so long, and after we had seen Thomas turn back."

"I was not worried for you, my dear. You were in good hands! I may have been more worried for William, considering the mood you were in after yesterday! Nothing worse for a man's equanimity than a downcast female for company! Up until then, I think that he was more vulnerable than you might have been!"

She was too tired to note that her mother's comments might have been confusing to her, had she given them any thought.

189

"I think that I would like to be alone and to rest for a while, Mama."

'Of course you do my dear, but I cannot leave you in this mood. We need to get you out of these things and then see to a nightdress for you. I will not rest myself until I know that you are resting. You will recover all the faster with a little quiet rest and sleep." She began to help her remove her dress as though she were still as young as Sophia even.

"How could I have been so wrong about him, Mama? I harbored unkind thoughts and would have done him serious injury at one time, yesterday even!"

"My dear, I told you that you have so much to learn about men, and unfortunately, I cannot be your teacher. They will be! But I can help a little and give you pointers. They all seem to be so easily read like an open book, and then we find that they are not, for they continually surprise us. The scurrilous villains at first blush actually turn out to be heroes and vice versa, and all when we least expect it."

"But it cannot be that simple."

It isn't! They can take years to understand, though *they* say the same of us. When you get to know them, you will find that they are all most complicated brutes at times, or can be, and are the more lovable because of it, as your father was, or the more roundly hated. It is either a greater love or a growing hate, I think, after a few years. But rather than show either one, those who are unhappily married or do not recognize what they have, just become lifeless and aimless and often seek other amusements outside of their family."

"A mistress? I do not want that from my husband!"

"No wife does if she has any sense!"

"I want love in my life. I want the kind of love that you and Papa had. But I am not sure that I will ever find that! I am obviously not mature enough, though I thought I was. I do not know who to trust now, and I dare not trust my own feelings either after being shown to be so wrong. I am too severe a critic of everything!" She absentmindedly allowed her mother to continue to slowly undress her.

"You are learning about life, emotions, and human relationships! A little late in life, I think, but then we made the mistake of sheltering you too much perhaps. It is often a painful experience. William is very like your father, but I told you that. You can trust him. But not too far! You are far too pretty for that." She had seen the way he looked at her from time to time.

"And yet he can be so very violent! Too violent for a gentleman!"

"Yes. Thankfully for us, he is and was. But any gentleman can be violent when it is called for! Mostly, it is we women who help make greater gentlemen or bigger brutes out of all of them. He is a gentleman where it counts and not a gentleman when required."

"I don't think I understand that!"

"Not yet!"

"He dealt so very firmly and calmly yet very violently with Thackeray from what I hear, and with his father, from what I actually *did* overhear, though without the physical violence. But it was all still there, nonetheless, and ready to erupt. I could not believe what I was hearing, and it all seemed so very calmly delivered but with such undertones of hatred and loathing—at least from one of them while *he* stayed calmly smiling, I am sure. I could not see him then, for he had locked the door to keep me out—wise of him I think, considering my mood—but I could sense how it was all unfolding. What I heard completely horrified me. I would have done him injury at that moment, except for that locked door."

"You should not have eavesdropped! One never overhears what one should. Better to have it all out into the open and deal with someone to their face and say what one means."

"I would have done that, but he locked me out! But was Papa ever like that? I cannot imagine it!"

"Do not move so, my dear, I will never undo this if you are so agitated!"

"I am sorry." She stood still and allowed her mother to continue.

"Your father could be very firm! He could be as firm as was needed and as violent as was needed too, but that was when he was much younger, long before any of you were born. Well, not so very long before. After that, we were married and settled, and he had no need then to protect me in quite that way."

She picked up a brush and began to brush out her daughter's hair.

"Oh dear. I never thought to broach any of this so soon, but I must, I can see that now. I shall tell you something of me, my dear, that . . . well, you may judge me very ill for what I will tell you, but it may help you understand a little of me and of your father and perhaps of yourself, for you are human with the same human weaknesses as the rest of us.

"I was the focus of quite a lot of attention—the wrong kind of attention—when I was younger. Like the young fool I was, I encouraged it too, for I was vain and liked to be flattered. I did not know enough to know better not to encourage certain men. I looked a lot like you actually, physically, but I had been brought up in a little more difficult setting. I went out more, for I had an aunt—Aunt Cecilia, almost a sister to me, for she was older only by about four years—that took me somewhat under her wing, and London was not so far. I was very mature for my age, with a figure that men might fight over and did once, even when I was just sixteen. Perhaps we sheltered you all too much, for you have some difficult lessons to learn about men. About just one of them, I think, from what I think I see."

After she had seen to her hair, she continued to undress her daughter as she spoke, and then once she had put all to one side, she opened a drawer on the dresser to find a nightdress for her.

"No nightdress! Oh dear, I thought there was one here. I'll get a warm nightdress from the airing closet and send Molly up with it. No matter, the room is warm!"

Annis picked up the brush and continued with her own hair as she stood before her mirror. "I was wrong on so many things, Mama. I am afraid I let myself be influenced by . . ."

"By Addie's letter?" Her mother continued to fold her clothing out of the way.

"Yes. It was . . . it was dreadful what it said of him, of William! I dare not show it to you. You were upset enough as it was!"

"I will get you to show it to me sometime but not at this juncture. I am sure she paints a most lurid picture of him, but then she long believed he had mistreated her dog by shaving its tail, and that was the start of it all. He did not do it, however, but some other boy did, and he rescued the dog, though she gave him no credit for that. There was also some violent episode with one of her young female relatives, blamed upon him. But she knew none of the truth of that and was not about to believe anything different! Especially when the young lady delivered, sometime after he had gone abroad! He may tell you some of it if you have the courage to ask him!"

"Oh no! I couldn't do that! It is none of my business! There was much more than that, Mama!"

"Yes, I am sure there was! You will learn to put less trust in gossip and rumor as you learn more of life. I know it is difficult to separate truth and rumor, but it is necessary, or we would trust no one. You will soon learn who you can trust and who not! But you can still be wrong!"

"But can any of what Addie wrote be true?"

"I do not know what she wrote, but I can guess. Unfortunately, yes, it can be. Addie does not go out of her way to tell lies about anyone, my dear. Not to us at any rate. But she can often get things wrong or twisted about when she allows herself to do so in anger or frustration. She can sometimes be a little brutal with the truth where others are concerned. She can be evasive and less than honest with the rest of society, especially about her father, but who cares about them? She does it so well too; keeps them all on their toes. But then that is another story. Sometimes, I think she forgets who her best and most trusted friends are and can be quite hurtful of us at times, though she means well."

"You said I had much to learn about men? One man! William?"

"You do, indeed! Perhaps not William." She was loath to elaborate on what she had been happy to have seen when she had noted them together. Annis may not have seen it or understood it yet, but *she* had. "The one you will eventually meet if you have not already. But I think you have even more to learn about *yourself*. It is not so much about someone else as it is about *you*. That is where the greatest change will need to be made, for you cannot, nor should you ever try, to change any man. Women think that once they get married, they can change a man and bring him into line with what they would like to have in their husband, but they can't! That is what leads to conflict between the sexes and creates animosity and unhappiness. Appreciating and loving someone for what they are and who they are now, not as you think you would like them to be, is one of the keys to being happy. Men can be rogues and frustratingly dense, obtuse, awkward, even unfeeling—or so it seems to us women at times in our emotional states. Your father could be when I forgot the rules. But he did not ever hurt me deliberately, though it took me a little while to see that. I hurt myself more than he did! They can be very clumsy in word and deed without intending it, especially when they foolishly insist on telling the truth at some crucial moment, rather than telling us what we most want to hear. Difficult for them to do, as *they* deal with reason and common sense, and cannot read our unpredictable female minds. They can also be magnificent, generous, gentle, kind when one least expects it, and most considerate and thoughtful. We women bring out the best and the worst! But they see far more than we give them credit for, and their feelings can be disturbingly evident all too suddenly and when one least expects it."

"Thackeray?"

"No! Not Thackeray!" She was most emphatic in denial of that. "Nothing to do with Thackeray! Much more personal than that! Oh dear!" She seemed frustrated that her daughter did not understand her better.

"I don't understand."

"No, I suppose not. We did shelter you too well, didn't we? I am rushing you along too fast and expect too much perhaps. As your sisters are not here to learn any of this, perhaps it is time to be a little more expansive of *my* early history. I am sure I will shock you, for I was much younger than you are when I met my . . . your father, but I do not care. Think of me what you will. I am beyond caring at this stage. In fact, I never did care what anyone thought of me once I had married him! Or before!"

"Arabella was born in very early December. The sixth. It was earlier that same year" that I first met your father."

Annis looked at her with a startled look in her eyes.

"Oh yes! We needed no lengthy courtship or engagement. In fact, I am not sure we were ever engaged in the usual way. He was my blinding flash of light into what had suddenly become a most drab existence before he arrived, yet it hadn't seemed that way until then, for he completely turned my life and expectations upside down in the blink of an eye, even as he walked through that door in London in his naval uniform. I can see it now as clearly as though it were this morning, and it was almost twenty-five years ago. We first met in early March of 91, and were married in June of that same year, once I persuaded my mother that marriage was necessary and needed to be soon. Very soon! The same year that Arabella came into the world!" She smiled as she watched the look upon her daughter's face in the mirror and saw her eyes fly to her own as she did some rapid mental evaluation of the dates.

"Yes! Utterly disgraceful that I dare admit such failing of character and moral fiber to my young and impressionable daughter. Bella was an early baby my dear! Yes one of those! A very early baby!"

"Mama!" She chuckled nervously as her mother laughed gently at the amazed look on her face.

"Well! It is often said that babies—later ones, those conceived after marriage—will always be carried nine months, but because of the intense passions of . . . some relationships, first babies may be a little earlier. Or a lot! Bella was one of those!"

"Mama!" They both laughed at the peculiar revelation but mostly at Annis's evident surprise at her mother's unexpected confession and history!

"But what of those who do not marry at all and bear a child?"

"The Trevelyan girl? Yes, they do happen. But that one was a little different. Those pregnancies always go full term. You know that! Many months of denial usually, and then out pops the embarrassing evidence to announce it all so loudly to the world. But there is always a man involved somewhere lurking in the shadows, where they often do their worst as well as their best, no matter how much they—the bruised and compromised young ladies—might protest that there wasn't. Foolish, stupid girls! Better to admit the truth at once, and get it behind them."

She took the hairbrush from her daughter's hands and continued to brush out her hair.

"So Papa forced himself upon you? I would not have th—!"

"No, he didn't! Nothing of the kind! You are fair and far off there! I expect you thought my first admission was surprising enough, so prepare for an even worse one my dear. Had everything been left to your father, who tried to be a gentleman throughout it all, your sister would not have been born until at least a full nine months *after* our marriage, which might have been a year or more beyond our first meeting. Totally out of the question! It was I who decided that I wanted none of that, but I did want him! It was I who rushed things along before my parents managed to sabotage everything I wanted, and before he lost interest in me and found a more accommodating female of which there were many about . . ." she paused, " . . . which I now realized he would never have done. I was the one who set the scene for him to seduce me! He had no choice in any of it, but he did not know that until later, and we often laughed over it since then. I had to do that, I believed, for I feared he would be snapped up by some scheming, immoral . . . perhaps I should say some scheming immoral woman *other* than myself, for I suddenly had very flexible morals where your father was concerned. I was utterly determined never to lose him! I had no need to worry. *He* was mine alone! He stayed that way until the day he died." She blinked back a tear. "There was nothing immoral or wrong in what I did. It was necessary, and I would do it all again! It was essential for my sanity and peace of mind and his! I have never regretted it!"

She paused as she thought about all that had happened years before and even chuckled a little over her recollections. "Unfortunately, my accommodating and kindly aunt got all of the blame for leading me astray when it was all my own doing. She had done nothing of the kind. We were able to laugh at it in later years, but she must have been hurt by the misplaced trust she had placed in me. It seems that I, and not my aunt, was the viperous influence in the family. She was not the kind of woman who would let such a thing affect her for long, for she soon bounced back and married shortly afterward anyway, and we write often and laugh about it all now."

She was surprised at recalling so vividly some of those earlier memories. "No, my dear, your father neither seduced me nor ran off with me nor compromised me . . . in that way, as was the rumor going about at first. I did all of those with him and took him quite off balance. Mind you he did not object too much! That is what I was referring to when I spoke of disturbingly sudden feelings becoming evident when one least expects them. I, who had led a blameless, uninteresting life, trapped your father, my dear. The first and only man I have ever known and loved, and we thanked each other for it with every breath we took. So now you know some of my disgraceful past. My parents relented somewhat quickly, after I told them what I had done and what the outcome was to be. They had little choice if they wanted to cover the scandal over. We married and came to live with your uncle here and away from the prying eyes of relatives. The family was saved from the shame of it all by my moving away with all of the soon-to-be-born evidence of my disgrace. I have never spent a more happy time than all of the years we were here raising all of you. Loving and being loved. There is nothing more that anyone can aspire to I think, than to be as happy as we were. Ah a nightdress! Someone read my mind."

Molly appeared with a nightdress and towels over her arm and a jug of steaming hot water.

"Thank you, Molly."

Annis picked up her warm nightdress. "Mama. I will see to getting myself dressed and into bed. I need time to think and to rest."

"Of course, you do. I gave you much to digest and not all to my credit, but I was honest about my feelings for your father. When you encounter your own, you must make your own decisions about how to go on, but do not shrink from making those decisions as too many do for fear of what others might think. I do not think that Bella would have, had she known that this might come to pass as it did. I shall go and reassure William that you are nothing more than tired. I believe he was quite concerned for you!"

"He was?" She looked startled. "Yes, I think he was, wasn't he? Though why he should be after the dreadful way I have treated him and what I have chosen to believe of him, I cannot understand."

"You will! You are still very young, very naïve, and very inexperienced of men my dear, despite your twenty-one years. They—most of them—do not harbor ill thoughts as we women sometimes do or store up resentment as some might. He forgave you everything. He knew what he had to do, and he knew the risks he was taking and the likely repercussions of it. He knew the burden we all labored under."

Chapter XXII

A Revealing Encounter

It did not take long for her mother to appear downstairs. The other girls had taken themselves off into the scullery and were busying themselves out there helping with the evening meal.

"I think she is not as bad as I might have feared, thanks to you, William. She should be abed by now. She is in need of your company before she falls asleep, I think. Take pity on her, she has had to make some severe re-evaluations of you and of herself in the last day or so."

"I know. I've been doing that of myself too!"

He walked quietly in upon her in his stockinged feet and was surprised to see her standing on a towel in front of her wash basin, facing the window with her back to him, completely devoid of clothing and washing herself. The evening sun shone full in upon her and showed her in her mirror as a fully mature and well-developed young woman. The startling and unexpected vision quite took his breath away and confused him. He took in his breath to mutter an apology and to remove himself from the room, but then he saw that she had her eyes closed with the glare of the sun in her face, and the words died even as they were about to be spoken.

She moved the cloth across her body, unaware that she was being watched. She was devastatingly beautiful in her natural state. Her full breasts gently moved with her actions. She was lost in thought, unaware of his presence. He knew he should leave as quietly as he had entered. He had not been expected so soon after her mother had appeared downstairs. He remained where he was against his better judgment, entranced by such a vision of exciting loveliness that he had never before seen quite so clearly revealed.

She was still not aware that he had entered her room. She seemed deep in thought as she gently wielded a wet cloth across her upper body and tried to reach her back and shoulders but seemed not entirely able to do so, for she gasped and groaned a little at some sudden pain and flinched, almost dropping her cloth as she tried to reach to her shoulders and upper back. He realized for the second time that he should not be there at that moment but discovered that he was rooted to the floor at this sudden stunningly-beautiful apparition that was entirely unaware of his presence and that quite took his breath away and left his mouth dry, with the blood pounding in his ears. He found that he could not immediately leave. He took in as much of her as he could see in the mirror and of her back, and felt both nervous and alarmed at how she might feel when she recognized that he was there and watching her so intently. He should leave!

He noticed then that there was a large bruise on her back and another on the back of her arm and yet another on her upper leg, high up. All of which possibly contributed to her discomfort.

His earlier concerns returned, and he backed gently toward the door and blundered into the edge of it, almost closing it so that he could no longer retreat, and betraying his presence in no uncertain way.

She froze in horror and tensed, with her arms reflexively raising to cover as much of her breasts as she might. She seemed confused and alarmed in that one instant of time as she opened her eyes wide and saw him standing there watching her in the mirror.

He could not escape easily now that he had been seen. He decided to brazen it through and not comment upon the obvious standing before him. "I hope I did not cause those bruises!" He surprised himself at his calmly-outrageous audacity in daring to speak to her at such a moment and not in immediately leaving the bedroom as had been his original intent.

Her eyes opened wider as she watched him behind her in the mirror and took in his unexpected presence and the almost closed door. She brought her hands tighter across her breasts and blushed in her embarrassment, unable to speak or say anything at that moment. Her eyes revealed her near panic at his unexpected presence close behind her, wondering what his intentions might be.

"William! Whatever are you doing here? You should not be here to see me like this!" Was he about to be revenged upon her in the worst possible way, for her untrusting behavior of him over the last few days? The look on his face was not one of anger, however, nor one that might cause her immediate dread, but she could not easily be reassured about why he was here.

He remained calm, though he did not feel it. "Your mother told me to come up, Annis. I am truly sorry to have blundered in on you like this!"

"You should not be here! You must leave! What did Mama say? She should not have sent you up here so soon, for I decided to bathe! You should have knocked! A gentleman would have knocked!" She spoke softly but with deep feeling as she stared at him intensely in the mirror. She had two bright spots of red upon her cheeks. He hoped that she might turn to face him in her confusion, but she didn't. Modesty prevailed, yet she was discomposed with him and almost certainly even angry at his intrusion.

She had not become hysterical and insist he immediately leave as he had at first expected, though she was not easy with his presence. How could she be? He smiled at her confusion and felt overwhelmed by a sudden rush of tender feeling for her but did not betray any uncertainty or embarrassment himself. He recognized that he was walking on dangerous ground and must tread most carefully, if that were still a possibility. He spoke gently. "Then I am excused, Annis, for I am certainly not a gentleman in far too many ways as I think you have suspected for some time and as my behavior has already shown on several occasions. I lost most of my sense of moral values and what few virtues I may have had while I was abroad. They were doing me little good anyway and would have soon got me killed."

She was clearly alarmed but said nothing more.

He walked over to her and before she might further object, gently took the cloth from her hand resting at her shoulder and dribbling water down her back, before she knew what he planned and left her in no doubt what he was about to do as he gently washed her neck and then her back, where she had been clearly unable to reach. She might protest further but could see that he was not about to leave. She was helpless to do anything. She could not fight him from her room without revealing too much of herself or attracting others to . . . She could not scream at him or insist that he immediately leave, for he was not about to pay her any attention in that way. But then she did not immediately fear for herself at that moment either, for some reason.

He saw her more clearly now in her mirror and was not able to tear his eyes away, for her arms defensively crossed over her obvious bosoms did not cover her fully, and there were other areas of similar deep interest to him that his eyes were drawn momentarily to.

She knew that he was fleetingly taking her in, in her naked entirety, and though deeply embarrassed, was surprised to feel that she was not too angry at him but had become resigned to it. She might even deserve his contempt, and yet, he betrayed no such suggestion of punishing her for her earlier distrust. However, she did not feel too threatened by his presence even with her as naked as she was but was somewhat more annoyed with her mother for putting her in this position. She was all drained of anger over the last few days anyway, having been shown to have been wrong on so many fronts about him.

"William. You must leave! Please!"

He ignored her softly uttered plea. "Did I cause these bruises on your back and your arm and leg?"

She swallowed her fear, frustration, and anger. Revenge did not seem to be on his mind. He seemed to be in a strangely gentle mood, and unconcerned by her obvious fears. Her eyes flashed to his. "Yes! I bruise too easily! I think when you grabbed me to stop me falling and then took me across to your saddle, I may have got those. And I pulled a muscle too, using that sidesaddle, for I am not used to it, and that limits my movement a little."

"I could see you were uncomfortable."

"But you must not be here, William!" She was most emphatic about that. She had done everything in her power to try to hint him away, without any effect. He was even smiling gently at her, and there was that mischievous look on his face.

"Yes, I know that I most certainly should not be here, but I am, and I want to be here at this moment. You are so exceedingly beautiful, far more beautiful than I might ever have imagined, and I cannot escape now and would not choose to. But this bruising upon your arms and back! I am a clumsy brute at times and do not know my own strength!" He sounded angry with himself. "I would not have hurt you for the world."

She digested that comment. She did not regard herself as beautiful. Why was he being almost apologetic when she was the one who had done him the most harm by what she had believed of him? He should still be angry with her. Yet he did not seem intent on any revenge upon her. She then began to recognize that she had a strange and unnerving power to attract his attention, and in a kindly way, but was not sure why. Of course, she knew that a poorly clad woman invited the wrong kind of attention from most men, for her mother had told her often enough to protect her modesty at all times, and that men had a strange fascination for a mature and well-formed woman and everything about them and she should be careful never to be alone with any of them if she could avoid it. But she did not know why it might be so, for she could defend her own honor if the need arose. She was strong. She could not see any attraction in her own body, for she did not regard herself as beautiful in that way. Her hips were bigger than she liked compared to those of boys and men, and her body was too soft and not able to do those things that a man might do. Her breasts were a major aggravation to her and seemed to attract the wrong kind of attention most of the time when she had attended the occasional ball in the village.

Men were different, she knew that! She had grown used to their being stronger and much better coordinated in many ways, and they did not have breasts to get in the way of whatever they might choose to do. She had noticed that as she had watched William shaving on that first morning and had found him rather interesting to watch, stripped to the waist. It had been a strange recognition for her, but she had been curious. The cold water had not bothered him nor had he been concerned that anyone might see him as undressed as he was! He had large shoulders and was well shaped with obvious muscles where she, herself, seemed to have none. She had only ever seen her father shave and had even helped him bathe in the past when he had been injured, but that had not been the same. She would never have lingered long enough to watch her father once her first curiosity had been satisfied, nor to have noticed those other things about him that she *had* noticed about William.

Her eyes raised to William's face as she looked at him in the mirror as he gently washed her. She did not feel he should be trusted. She knew so little of him still, and yet she seemed to know everything about him, with too much of it so very confusing and awkward. He seemed to be looking at her with some concern rather than with any other awkward emotion. She recognized—hoped—that he was probably not about to trespass further than he should, which had been her first fear, though his presence at this time was entirely outrageous and far beyond what might be tolerated.

"Sir, you should not see me like this!" She was almost in tears. "I know what it might seem like, but I did not encourage you and I did not plan this!"

He spoke gently. "Please do not be afraid, Annis. I do not think any such thing! I know you did not plan this. Nor did I! A simple mistake. But I am here now, and I would rather be here than anywhere else on this earth! My name is William, remember? But why should I not see you like this? There is nothing to be ashamed of! Nor afraid of! We are both very much as we have been for the past few days, and surely you know me enough to know that I do not present a serious threat to any of your family. Nor to you!

"You are an extraordinarily beautiful young lady, and I am a man who appreciates beauty without overstepping certain limits, though that might be difficult to believe, considering . . . I must confess that I have long wanted to see you like this. To me, you are a very interesting and mature young lady. Besides, I am now family, am I not?" He recognized that his argument would sound very flat and unconvincing, despite her mother having suggested that he was. He was most certainly not family in that sense.

She was angry with him and blushing profusely yet spoke quietly so they she might not attract the attention of others. "It is not the same! You know it is not the same! Oh why will you not leave? You are nothing like my sisters, for indeed, you are a man. And not only should you not be here at this moment, even if you were a brother, and you are not that, but you should also not look at me so intently."

He continued to wield the cloth gently on her back. "You are right! It is not the same! I am nothing like your sisters I am glad to say, though not because . . . you know what I mean! You are a far too intoxicating sight for the likes of me, as I suspect you are now aware, for I would rather not be denied this vision of beauty." She could sense the truth of that statement in the intensity of his glance. "But I will not further betray the precarious trust that I realize I am now in danger of losing. We are both adults. I am still in control of my own actions, and you need not fear that I shall overstep them further than I already have by being here. You are right that I should not see you, so I shall *not* see you! Please do not be too upset. I do not pose an immediate threat to you. I shall close my eyes, if I can, but I shall wash you a little, as I could see that you could not reach your back properly without some discomfort, or raise your arms high enough to do what you need to do. I can at least save you from that. I would like to do so if you do not too much object."

She did object, but he was ignoring her. She resigned herself to say nothing, realizing that he was not going to leave; and though he really should not be there at all, he was, and she began to recognize the disturbing effect she was having upon him. His hand had trembled a little as he touched her at the shoulder as his gentle words had similarly affected her once she had got over her first rush of panic. She would never dare to admit it, but at this moment she was not afraid of him being there and actually even seemed to welcome his gentle words and his strangely admiring presence. Shocking!

She recalled her mother's frank admissions earlier and of suggestions of her own emotions getting out of control. Could she be so much her mother's daughter that she might stand there and not scream in panic or at least object more forcefully?

"As I do not hear any great complaint or further protest over my ill-timed presence, then I will take it that you do not object too much and would like me to help you."

She saw his eyes were tight closed and gradually she began to relax. "I said no such thing! I do object! I also fear any protest I might make would fall on deaf ears in your present mood, for I have asked you to leave several times and you have ignored me!"

"There! You do know me!" Still with his eyes closed, and with his hand touching lightly on her shoulder, he gently washed her back and shoulders where he had seen she could not easily reach. "If you have not noticed, I have now closed my eyes and shall keep them closed until you tell me I may open them." He felt her begin to relax a little more. Undoubtedly, she was watching his face in her mirror to see that he did not still look at her. She did not entirely trust him not to peek and kept her arms where they were, but he seemed resolved that he would not betray her trust at that moment.

"I think I must seem like a . . . a shameful . . . disreputable . . . to allow you to stay in this way without making a much greater fuss than I am!"

"I think nothing of the kind! You did make a great fuss, which I ignored. I, on the other hand, feel a most privileged scallywag. If you were a woman of that stripe, and there is nothing wrong with them either, then neither of us would have our eyes closed. We would both be devoid of clothing, and she would also be washing me as I would be washing her, but neither of us, so gently with each other, or with such gentle consideration."

"I do not think that that is a topic for polite conversation, sir!"

"No, it isn't! But you raised the issue, not I. I should let you know that you had no choice in my presence at his moment, for you did try to encourage me to leave, but I wouldn't. So that is what you must protest if anyone comes in on us. But they won't. the blame is all mine. I do not judge you ill for this. Quite the contrary. I think I shall be forever in your debt for treating me so well when I do not deserve it!"

He was relieved to find that she did not shrink from his touch or complain further at his complete lack of decorum at being there when he should not be, considering that she was now standing before him in a relatively unprotesting manner compared to her first momentary panic when he first betrayed his presence. It was all so very wrong, and so very unexpected.

She watched him as he continued to bathe her. It seemed so wondrously strange and delightful to feel that she excited this man in such a way.

"Not only do I not deserve to be here like this, but I also think I am lucky that your pistol is not so very close at hand!"

She was surprised at his attempt at levity. She had forgotten his pistol, lying to the edge of the dresser and within reach if she chose to retrieve it. But then what? Would she shoot him? She doubted that, now. "Yes, you are! But I doubt I could so easily shoot you now anyway!" She watched his face in her mirror as he laughed gently at that unwise admission and saw that his eyes were still closed, though she recalled that he had waited for some time before doing so, as he had seemed intent on observing her in every embarrassing detail before he did so. She could do nothing about it. There had been no escape! She had been disturbed by his sudden and intense scrutiny, for she did not regard herself as particularly beautiful but had not found it displeasing or threatening for some reason that she began to recognize. She did not feel that he had taken advantage of her, and she certainly did not feel violated in any way by his presence or his actions.

She was puzzled to recognize that she had seemed to want his closer attention in that way, as he had when they were close to the inn, as a sign that he had forgiven her for her previous ill-feeling misjudgment of him, but she had not actually taken any steps to try and achieve it and possibly giving the wrong impression of herself. Of being too forward!

"But what will we do if my mother and sisters come in and find me like this and with me not complaining and objecting as I know I should!" The possibility was a cause of some concern to her, though did not seem to be for him.

"You did complain and object, but I ignored you! I am glad that you are resigned to my staying and are not now complaining too much. Besides, they all seemed to be on their way out of the house to gather roses I think, to brighten up the parlor as I came up here, and have abandoned you to my ministrations, so you need not fear that anyone will come in for the moment. Besides, your bedroom door is mostly closed, so you must let me continue to wash you."

She realized that he was not about to leave her, and besides, it felt so good that he was able to reach where she had not been able to, with her stiff arm and sore back, both of which caused her pain as she had tried to reach behind herself, or indeed to move at all. He reached around her with both arms—a moment of panic did overwhelm her then—yet his eyes were still closed. She felt him breathe gently onto her shoulder and into her hair at the back of her head as he rinsed off the cloth and put more soap on it, and then, before he continued with his task, he gently kissed her on the neck. She stiffened but did not seem to object in any strenuous way to that gentle trespass, though it did startle her a little, as he could sense from her audible gasp and tensing once again for a second or two, uncertain of his true intention for just a moment.

"A gentle brotherly kiss, my dear, nothing more to be afraid of."

"An encroaching kiss! I am not sure what your next trespass may be and it is unnerving me!"

"There will be none! That will be the full extent of it at this moment, Annis. I promise! So far only and no further. Now, please turn around, and I shall wash the rest of you."

"No!" She was suddenly alarmed again.

"Yes. I understand you are afraid." She was about to protest that challenging comment. "But, strange to say, you are safe with me at this moment, and I am not about to leave until I have helped you. My eyes will remain closed."

"Promise me that you will not . . . !"

"I promise whatever you would wish! I also promise you that if you insist I leave you at any moment, even now, that I will immediately, but reluctantly, do so. But I would not like you to do that until I have been able to help you as I want to, so I shall not go beyond what is reasonable at this moment and invite my expulsion."

"Oh! But you have already gone well beyond that!"

"Yes, I have, haven't I?"

"If I were to ask you to leave now, you would do so?"

"I promised that I would!" He began to feel defeat and disappointment.

She could sense the possible disappointment in his voice. She hesitated. "Then I shall turn, but you must keep your eyes closed if I do!"

"Of course, I will! I did promise!" He felt her turn in front of him and then gently touching her only with the cloth, except for the gentle touch upon her shoulder to gauge her position but able to feel every firm contour of her body, he wiped much of her upper body and each arm in turn, as she was able to allow herself to become uncovered in that way in front of him, and move each arm a little to the side so that he might wash her side too. He was not to know that she wished he would lean down and kiss her on the lips now rather than her neck, but he was otherwise occupied. She noticed that there was a bright flush upon his face and his ears seemed a little more flushed and reddish than they usually were, and he was breathing in a more labored way than he might be, as though he were a little out of breath. She even began to feel a similar excitement! She should have felt very guilty at tolerating this, but didn't!

He leaned into her a little, taking her once more by surprise at his closeness. "Sir!"

"I am only rinsing out the cloth behind you again, Annis. Nothing more!"

He was far too close. She could feel his cheek brush upon hers as he rinsed out the cloth and applied soap once more. This time he quickly kissed her on the neck, under her ear. She said nothing. Then gently, as he put a cautious hand upon her waist in front of him, covered by her own hand lest he might not be as trustworthy as he had protested he would be, he washed her upper and outer legs and lower back which, with her stiffness, she could not follow him to do. He rinsed off the cloth again but this time did not steal a kiss as she expected he might, and wiped off the soap left on her naked body and then repeated that action as she turned around, before he put the cloth back into the basin. She was relieved but also she discovered, a little disappointed to note that his eyes had remained closed throughout, and that he had not tried to kiss her again as she would have liked, for she was standing exceptionally close to him and facing him and could feel his warm breath upon her face, but he was not to know that, and could not be told of her suddenly turbulent feelings at his intimate closeness.

"Now the towel, please."

He felt her reach out, noticing her breast gently touch his bare forearm for some moments as she leaned across to the back of the chair and put the towel into his hand.

She felt him hesitate and take a sudden indrawn breath and then tremble as her breast had touched his arm, and he froze for a few seconds at that moment with that sensation, but he did not take advantage of her and give in to the feelings that clearly enveloped him, being so close to her and her without clothing to cover and protect her.

"Thank you." He continued to dry her off, not applying too much pressure but just gently dabbing with the towel, where he knew she was tender and was able to reach her shoulders and back where she had seemed to have difficulty. Once, while he was close to her, she saw that he briefly opened his eyes to see her looking up into his face and then quickly closed them again lest he alarm her. He felt his own color to be heightened at what he was daring to do and could not dispel from his mind the vision created as he had moved the cloth over her body, despite his closed eyes, so he did not notice her smile a little at his almost inevitable trespass and the sudden feeling of puzzled empowerment she felt, able to so visibly disturb him in the way she was now experiencing. But she realized that it was still a very precarious situation.

He was strongly aware of every gentle contour and every part of her body presented to him and yet beyond his visual senses. Nonetheless, his other senses more than made up for it in truly alarming ways, for he was deeply conscious all of the time of a young and vibrantly naked woman in front of him, trusting him not to trespass beyond what he was already doing.

"Your mother has now returned!" He heard voices from downstairs as they entered the house. "I think we may finish this and you in your bed before we are discovered. Now your nightdress, please, to close off this tempting mental vision of loveliness and save me from temptation and trespass if the returning hordes did not!"

"My mother left me *this* for the moment. I decided that I should try to sleep for a while after my . . . difficult day."

"Yes, I was a fool for taking you so far without thinking it through better!"

He could hear voices downstairs as they decided where to put the pots of roses that they had collected. They would not be coming upstairs so very soon.

He felt a thin nightdress placed in his hand. He discovered the neck and its hem and the open front of it, flickered his eyes open for a second to see that it was as he assumed, and then closed them again. She could not raise her arms over her head, so he moved away from her a little and slid the nightdress onto her arms before he gently lifted the back of it over her head, and then brought it down a little around her at the back and then the front, briefly encountering one of her breasts with the back of his hand. She did not flinch and said nothing of that.

"Now that you are covered, may I now open my eyes, please?"

She made a few adjustments before she answered him, ensuring that it had fully covered her. "Yes, William. Now you may." She was looking up at him in a strange way with her nightdress now settled on her body though with its neck open a little and revealing a suggestion of cleavage between her breasts. She did not mind his presence so very much now that she had some covering, as minimal as it was.

He leaned into her and kissed her gently upon her lips before she knew what he was about and then watched for her objection as she pushed him away for breaking his promise for a second time and betraying her trust even a little. It was not there, and she did not seem inclined to push him away. She had not seemed to mind but had momentarily blushed and had then leaned closer to him as she rested her hands on his waist and had even briefly but unmistakably returned his kiss as she raised onto her tiptoes.

He was relieved more than words might express at that simple response and to discover that he was not about to be banished forever for his entirely unforgiveable lapse of judgment and abandonment of moral consideration.

"Now I will leave if you demand it, though I do not want to at this moment."

"Too late now, I think! Thank you for helping me and for not . . .". Her breath caught in her throat, and she turned away to climb into her bed but not before he had seen, he thought, a tear standing out in her eyes. "Thank you for not taking so much advantage of me as I perhaps may have des—" She left others words unsaid, but there had seemed a suggestion that she would not too strongly have objected to a little more bold of a trespass than just a kiss or two, though he knew that she would have eventually, and his place in their secure and welcoming family would not be so welcoming, or secure. He had risked too much and might have lost it all! Yet he hadn't! It was a strangely disturbing recognition. What word had she held off using? Deserved perhaps, or desired? He closed off both of those possibilities as leading along dangerous pathways.

"Thank you for the privilege of being allowed to help you. I did not deserve it. Yes, I did take outrageous advantage of you! I am sorry for that moral lapse, but I am not sorry that I stayed instead of retreating and immediately leaving as I should have done; as a gentleman under your roof would have, but I found that I could not just leave at that moment." He looked both sheepish and apologetic. "You did not immediately banish me from your room or your presence or this house, as I began to suspect and fear would be my fate when I first walked in on you in your . . . wondrous state, but I did not know you were bathing!"

She savored the mood that overwhelmed her at that moment. She felt a sudden elation at his unexpected confession of his admiration of her in her naked state, and at his obvious inability to leave her at that moment as he should have done. Before today, she was sure she had seen what might have been an amused condescension, even remoteness in his dealings with her, though she could have misread him in that too. She did not understand how he might find her interesting in the way that he obviously did. She had been more afraid of his disapproval over her lack of more voluble protest. "How could you have known? Mama should have stayed to help me herself. But then she did not know that I had decided to bathe when she left to go downstairs!"

"Then both your mother and I are excused from plotting anything so very improper!"

They heard others begin to mount the stairs. His hand fell upon hers. "Relax, my dear. Neither of us should feel guilty. I don't! I shall also remove the satisfied smirk that I am sure I have upon my face, but I doubt that I can remove my flush so very easily." *Nor my memories of seeing you as I did!*

"Please William, do not say anything about this, or I shall die of embarrassment! You did mostly behave as a gentleman would have! At least, the one confusing gentleman I have come to know in the last few days—very defensive of our comfort and security, but devastatingly outrageous and most un-gentleman-like at other times. I think that you are more to be trusted than I had at first feared, but in other things you are not to be trusted far at all!" She had clearly come to some understanding of what kind of a gentleman he really might be!

He smiled at her, thankful that he seemed to be forgiven, when he knew he should not be. "You are entirely correct about that! Especially not after the kiss I stole!"

"That was the least of it. Which kiss? For you stole three kisses and were becoming more bold by the minute." She said nothing of her own turbulent feelings at that moment as she had returned that last one.

He said nothing of the kiss she had returned either. Or had he just imagined that? No, he had not! He felt strangely contented.

The footsteps retreated into a further wing of the upstairs. It seemed that Annis was to be allowed to rest, and they were not to be disturbed. Most unusual that no one came to check upon them, although her door had drifted open again somehow. He gently opened the door further and returned to her side. "It seems that you have been recklessly abandoned to my care once more."

He smiled at her. "I know I was too bold by far. But as a man with a poor reputation, I was gently testing boundaries and limits without, I hoped, turning you completely against me. It . . . dalliance, is a fine art, years in the making, and I am long out of practice. Had you objected, I would have pleaded for your forgiveness, blackened my face, and would have promised anything to remain in your trust and good graces. Though I have not been in them much except for the last day or so when I seemed to have gained a most precarious footing. I do hope I have not entirely lost it now again!"

He looked as though he might be entirely cast down if she said anything by way of criticism. She did not answer him at that moment. This was an entirely different William than the determined, serious, and even severe one she had seen over most of the last week and a half.

"However, what just happened between us shall be our secret. But, Annis . . ." his voice took on a cautionary tone, " . . . I should warn you that you must never trust me! I am a mere mortal man when faced with such striking beauty as yours and do not trust myself at times like that, or even like this when I am close by you, especially considering the disturbing state, to me, that you were in. The temptations were most severe, but it would destroy me if I were to hurt or betray *you* or any member of your family who are as dear to me now as my own—perhaps more dear—so you must keep me outside of those boundaries that are comfortable for you."

She continued to say nothing, contented to hear what he had to say, though she did look at him in a strange way. Had he regretted staying, for fear of what he might have done? His eyes told her that he was being sincere.

She spoke then. "I am . . . I know I should not admit this or say anything so very forward, but you *are* family now, in so many ways, looking out unselfishly for our interests as you did and have done and risking your own life to do so!" She now seemed prepared to let him into that select group.

"My unselfishness, as you put it, is not entirely without more personal interest, Annis!"

She realized that she must tread cautiously with him but was also intent on discovering some of those feelings that had suddenly been sparked within herself and what might be those boundaries that he spoke of, not only his, but also her own and how they might be tested without any disastrous consequences to a newfound relationship as well as to her own self-respect.

He spoke again after seeing the play of thoughts across her face as she seemed to become vibrantly aware of her own growing influence over him. "Yes! I see you comprehend more than you are telling me! A sudden sensation of empowerment in a young woman is a force to be looked upon with awe. I saw it once in my sister, and . . ." He held off saying any more. "No matter. Now let us change this dangerous subject. Imagine, Annis, if you can, that I am truly a gentleman, and did delay for ten minutes my entrance. I have just now walked into the room after knocking as a true gentleman should, and being invited in, discovered you at calm and dignified repose in your bed—as you are—and that the delightful interlude we just experienced was merely a figment of my fevered imagination and did not happen. We can imagine also, one of your sisters sitting in attendance to ensure that *all*, proceeds as decorously and as proper as it ought to." He cleared his throat, but not his mind, of that previous few moments that would live with him forever.

Annis knew what had just happened to her, and to them both. It filled her with a feeling of euphoria as well as contentment.

CHAPTER XXIII

Difficult Questions and Foundations of a New Relationship

"How are you feeling now, after this afternoon?" He smiled at her.

He was pleased to notice that she was able to smile at him too, and was seemingly able to put the other matter of a few minutes earlier behind her. She was not too angry with him, but did perhaps give the impression of being a little puzzled and even confused over what she had just learned. It seemed he might be forgiven, though he knew he did not deserve to be. He was relieved far more than words might be able to express.

She thought for a while. "Rested now, content. But also . . . chastened after the last few days! As well as a little confused. Much better than I did, thanks to you. Refreshed a little." She did not mention other feelings that she was still grappling with, or continue with her disjointed recollections.

"Good."

"Will you sit with me for a while, please?"

His eyes seemed to thank her for not banishing him. "Dare I assume that you feel you can trust me after my recent dreadful behavior of just a few moments ago? I am sure that I do not deserve your trust after that." He was smiling at the awkward truth of what he said, yet his eyes were pleading with her this time, rather than challenging. "But yes, I would like to sit with you if you can forgive me for my earlier behavior."

She realized with sudden surprise that he was the one that seemed very vulnerable now, as her mother had said, and even uncertain of the ground he was on. She wondered if perhaps she should not be the one asking him for forgiveness for believing only ill of him for so long, and still not sure what to believe about some things concerning his character, if not his commendable behavior on their behalf. "I think I can trust you a little! Perhaps more than a little! Though I do not know why. I began to fear the worst at first and that I was about to pay the price for not having trusted you as Mama does and for believing only the worst of you. But you did not take vengeful advantage of me in . . . that way, or despise me for not making a more forceful objection of your presence, as I had feared, though your presence was . . ."

208

"Yes, it was, wasn't it? Outrageous, ungentlemanly, and worse! I deserve no mercy, no gentle consideration from you, and will submit to any penalty or penance you demand of me. Why would you think I might despise you for not objecting, for you did object. I think I am more afraid of *you* despising *me* for being so forward myself and so heedless of your modesty. Be gentle, Annis! You now have the power to hurt me far more than you might realize!"

She did not know how to respond to that surprising comment, and let a few moments elapse before she spoke. "I would never despise you now William! Not after what you have unselfishly done for us." She could not meet his eyes as she said that. "When you entered my room and . . ." She struggled to make sense of what had happened. "But then I am dressed now and in my bed, and my mother and sisters are within calling distance." She smiled sadly.

"Thank you! A little trust is all I deserve, but I am glad of that crumb even. But that was why I came up here, to keep you company until you decided to rest or sleep. I had no other motive. I was concerned for you!"

She recognized that he spoke the truth, but he was ill at ease with himself and seemed to be feeling guilty over his previous actions. It was a reassuring sign and gave her somewhat more confidence than she might have felt in finding out more about him than she had so far gleaned and—as it turned out—wrongly, about much of it. "I have been very wrong about you!"

"Most people are! But you? Not so very far wrong, Annis."

"Yes, I admit I have been wrong about you, and now we need to talk, if you do not mind. But first things first . . . the easier questions, for I need to know you much better than I do! You do owe me that much! If you do not mind." She recognized that she was on solid ground with him at this moment.

"I seem to recall you said something to me while we were at the inn, and I was recovering. You said something of you 'almost' being on your best behavior. There seems to be an admission of earlier lapses than the one which we have just put behind us."

"I confess that there were. So you did notice? I wondered if you might let me get away with that, without bringing me to account. Yes, I seem to make far too many little slips like that, don't I? I am such a shambling kind of disreputable fellow that I found I needed to test various boundaries and limits with someone who seemed to hold me in reservation, if not downright disregard! I wonder why I don't have that same trouble with Sophia?" He was pleased to see her smile. A good sign. "You are right, we so much need to talk now that you are able to see me in a little more kindly light, I hope, and can demand a full account from me of various bits and pieces of my scandalous behavior. There is much that I would like to say, though I must slow myself down, or I might frighten you almost as much as I did just now. Myself too! For we have progressed such a long way, I think, in such a short time."

He drew his mind back to the moments at the inn. "I am surprised that you recall that careless comment earlier. I thought it had sailed by too easily while we were at the inn, and I had hoped that more recent and more . . . inconsiderate behavior may have overlain or eclipsed all memory of that earlier dereliction. You have a somewhat inconveniently retentive memory for the likes of me. Obviously, I must confess my inability to fully control myself with you, for I must admit that I *did* steal a kiss after I had lifted you from your horse onto mine. But then that is how we rogues tend to behave."

"That, and ambush ill-clad—disrobed—young ladies in their bedrooms and refuse to leave when they ask you to!" She surprised herself by daring to recall that, and even speak of it so openly.

"Exactly right!" He laughed. "But there was only one of you! You were not ill clad. You were unclad, and a sore temptation for a moment or two until I came to my senses and realized what I stood to lose if I did cause you to despise me by any inappropriate action!"

She let that confession slide by but liked what she was hearing. "But you mentioned that earlier kiss, and I think I recall that!" She blushed. "You seem to lose control often, and yet you don't, in truth. Everything is done with a purpose! You also steal a lot of kisses when you think I might not notice, or even when I might, for you stole several just a few moments ago! Why did you do that?" She looked at him again, in a way that he found somewhat unsettling.

"The earlier kiss when I moved you to my horse?"

She nodded.

"Confession time again!" He drew a deep breath. "I felt a moment of . . . great tenderness and concern for you at that moment, but then I have always felt like that towards you, indeed, to all of you."

"Oh!"

He smiled at her as she digested that confession.

She looked up at him. "And yet, I do not think that a rogue might feel either tenderness or concern for his intended victim."

"You were *not* a victim Annis. You were, you *are*, someone I feel a great deal of affection for!" He could say nothing more without betraying more of himself.

She decided not to pursue that any further. There were more important questions to get out of the way while he seemed to be in the expansive and gentle mood he was in. "Why did you stay with us, William?" She looked at him closely, but he did not rush to an answer. Perhaps he found it too difficult to answer easily. "You had no need to! Yet you did stay with us all here, despite everything and when I did not think you either would, or should, for I tried to hint you away."

"Yes, you did, didn't you?" He decided to be very careful in what he might choose to say. She was quite capable at this moment of seeing completely through him if he were too careless with his words. "You were most off-putting and very cold toward me, I thought! How fortunate that I have such a thick skin and cannot be hinted off or did not run off like a scolded cur. I stayed to help, at least for a few days, where I could. I hope you are not forgetting that I married your sister! There were some things that obviously needed to be done after that, and I could see that you were all otherwise caught up in a most hurtful situation. You all needed to be distracted, if possible. My heart went out to all of you. I could not desert you all in your time of need, even when faced with a determined effort from you to oppose my staying, for some reason." He chuckled gently. "*You* seemed to know me far too well! Besides, I still needed to know far more of the lady I had recently married and of the most unusual, and wonderful family that so calmly accepted me without question and so trustingly despite my well-known reputation. Most of them anyway!"

She fidgeted over that gentle observation, and she colored as her eyes flashed to his face once more, and he instantly regretted making it. He strove to recover. "You were wise to be cautious! I did not expect to be made welcome when there were so many attractive and nubile young ladies present—even your mother, who most needed my support—and all so very vulnerable to the likes of me after all of the trouble I had caused in earlier years, and the hell . . . well, that was all in my recent past. I was not so far removed from the memories and realities of *that* violence, that I began to wonder if the reality was that the battlefield had actually claimed me, and I was now in a most pleasant dream."

She liked the way his attention seemed to be focused upon her. "I do not think you deserve that sad reputation that you hint at, William, and yet . . . there were times when you confirmed all of my worst beliefs in you until I learned more of what had really happened with Thackeray and then his father. Despite what I mistakenly assumed, you have behaved with great consideration and propriety—mostly—with all of us, including me, until . . ."

"But I recovered, remember, and reverted back to my true character, shambling fellow that I am! *Mostly* is the key word. You did notice that my halo had slipped by the time we needed to visit the inn, when I first kissed you then, and it took a further nudge just a few minutes ago when I found that I was powerless to leave when confronted by such mature and poised, if alarmed . . . and most alarming beauty!"

Her eyes sparkled, and she blushed but did not take him to task for referring to what he had said should be forgotten. Neither of them would be likely to ever forget it.

"Also, there was a challenge laid out for me, with three beautiful young daughters and a somewhat more mature yet still very beautiful lady thrown close to me, and all of you actually needing my worthless presence in a moment of great sorrow, even though it may not have been immediately welcomed or obvious. I found it to be most captivating and intriguing. Besides, I have a very bad reputation to maintain or face being drummed out of the Rogues Club. I could not rush off with so much delightful temptation around me, for you are all so very beautiful, each in her own charming way, and so much in need of protection." He sighed. "Alas, mostly from individuals like me!"

"I think you are flattering us a little too outrageously and giving yourself too little credit. However, I am glad you did not leave us!"

He said nothing for a moment but digested that comment with some pleasure, as he could see the sincerity in her shy glance at having dared to admit that.

"So am I. Now!"

She let that sail by, but could not easily ignore that he was looking at her most intently and in a remarkably disturbing way. She felt sure that he might be able to hear her heart beating and must surely be able to see how flushed she suddenly was.

She recovered her composure with difficulty. "So we were a challenge?"

"Yes. I think it's fair to say that! However, to my great disappointment and devastating loss of confidence when faced with so much opportunity, I did not seem to be universally liked or trusted, especially by you or Charlotte, who made a point of staying out of my way most of the time. Very wise of her. Most unusual for me to see, for I am such a likeable, gentle, well-mannered fellow, as you know, and as I continually demonstrate. Sophia recognized it fast enough. All of you should have been striving to encourage me to stay in the most embarrassing and flattering way. But then, if you had, I would have been truly lost, and . . . I may not have behaved as I ought!"

"I think you would have."

"I am gratified that you think so well of me after my most recent lapse! Yes, I think I would have behaved myself too. At least I would always try. The alternative—your censure and feeling betrayed by me and then openly despising me—would be devastating to me now!"

He was being truthful, despite all of the wrong-headed thoughts she had harbored of him and the accusations she would have leveled at him had she been able to burst into the parlor while he met with the elder Thackeray. She liked those words of confession. Fortunately, he did not know how much they affected her own feelings.

"Your mother accepted me easily enough, but then I have that effect on more mature and less cautious ladies, who do not know enough to feel threatened by me."

"Or who know you better than you might know yourself, and place little store by vicious gossip? Unlike her very immature daughter!"

"Perhaps! But there is nothing immature about you, Annis! Not from what I saw, nor from what I know of you in your gentle dealings with me when I did not deserve them. You are a woman, and a very beautiful one."

She blushed. "You know what I meant!"

"Yes, I did know. I think your mother may have been unwise enough, or should I perhaps contradict myself and say, prescient enough, to believe my sister's high opinions of me rather than those of others. Elizabeth is obviously most defensive of my reputation and character as well as most confused about me—obviously—and does not believe so ill of me as others do! However, now I have a true challenge laid out before me—to rise above my hard-won disastrous reputation and prove that I am worthy of a misplaced belief in the nobleness of my character rather than a belief in what is said of me. It may be beyond me, but I will try."

She smiled at his attempted levity. She had every faith that he would succeed.

He sat back, feeling more relaxed and sure of his position. "I am sure that you have noticed that Sophia was quite easy to confuse and has had difficulty tearing herself away from me." He looked around suddenly. "I wonder where she is, by the way? She has never neglected me for this long before!" He shrugged. "No matter. I had come to the realization that I have that effect on very young children it seems, though I have just found that out, for I have never been around them before for any length of time. I always found them to be most wearing and far too able to see completely through me. I find the sudden arousal of family feeling within me to be most interesting and most gratifying! Somewhat sobering too, for I hear that children can be most hard to impress. Now I must work hard to impress those a little older. I am finding that I am sadly out of practice."

"It did not seem that way to me! But Sophia likes you. She even demands a kiss of you before she goes to sleep now and after you have read to her, and she spends far more time with you than she now does with us."

"Yes, I wish you all would do so—demand a goodnight kiss of me! But Sophia is quite a scheming little girl and far too observant of those things she should not observe and sneaks up and gets too close when one least expects it. As I did with you earlier! I like her too. I am looking forward to the time when all of her sisters demand a similar kiss before sleeping. It is the older ones that are more difficult. Charlotte will be a greater challenge."

"How so? She does not hold you in disregard! None of us do now!"

"She is still a little too cautious and unwise to the ways of men like me, but very sharp, and is not sure what to make of me just yet, though I could be mistaken. I think she is guarded of what she sees and believes, and is not yet entirely trusting. Ah well, her defenses will soon crumble when she falls in love with me as all ladies are destined to do." He noticed she was smiling at his boast.

"Well, most of them!" He cleared his throat in embarrassment. "Some of them!" He smiled at her as he had to backtrack on his all-encompassing boast. "I do not read her to sleep, so a kiss will be a little more difficult. But then I find I do not wish to kiss her so very much, except in a protective and avuncular way to comfort her, for she is still very sad and then there is—was—another that is very kissable too."

She remained silent. She knew that he was referring to her, for he was looking intently at her as he said that.

"She seemed to dislike me intensely when I first came here—probably still should, considering how I behave around her while striving to ingratiate myself with everyone—and tried to ensure that I did not stay. It was rather worrisome to find that someone so young could read my character so well! Even took to carrying a pistol to guard against me wandering at night and possibly blundering into her bedroom, with undoubtedly dreadful intentions, and would have had no hesitation in using it, I think, so I didn't blunder as I would have liked. My own pistol too!" He feigned shock at that thought. "Could I have been so madly protective as to work against myself? How lucky I am that she did not have it by her that first night! Or just a few minutes ago!" It had been close by. "I did not think she could have found out about me so well, so soon, for I never would admit to any weakness of character with any of you, and I hoped that by the time you found out about the real me, it would be too late."

"I think we now know you better than the portrait you seem to want to paint of yourself. Besides, you have not blundered into any of our bedrooms again after that first time."

"Really? Except for just a few minutes ago! I shall struggle to decide whether you are relieved or disappointed over that. But then, I do not like to be shot. It is a painful experience!"

"And yet you stole a kiss from her, from me, when I *was* vulnerable. When we were out together. You were not supposed to take advantage of me like that. That was most underhanded!"

"But I must protest in my own defense that it was mostly a brotherly kind of kiss. I really was not taking advantage of you as much as I wanted to."

"It was nothing of the kind!" His later comment had slipped by her.

"No, perhaps not. I must admit that I was relieved that Thomas was not on hand to observe or object or come to your aid as he would have done. But I am being honest. I was concerned. I did not know that you were not one of these ladies who swooned to order. My kiss told me what I needed to know."

"Which was?"

"That you were indeed a little prostrated, for you did not struggle to protest or complain loudly or strike out at me as you should have and as I expected if you had not been in quite the difficulties you seemed to be in. I could think of no other way to provoke a response if you had not been as ill as you seemed. Either that, or perhaps you had planned it, but then that would be a most dangerous thing to do with a man like me, for I would have detected that too."

"So I have become aware! So that was why you kissed me then—to gauge the level of my ability to respond! So it *was* almost a brotherly kind of kiss and nothing else! I think I can forgive that." She almost felt disappointed. "So you thought I may have been scheming in some way. I am not such a dissembler, nor would I be so heedless of the danger I might put myself in by encouraging you. But I was not sure what to think either. I think I may have been wrong about you in almost every way that I could have been wrong." She looked up at him, but he was looking away at that moment.

"I would like to think so, considering what I heard of your initial impression. But in what way might you have been wrong? That I am worse than you thought, or better?"

"I am not sure. Probably more devious, underhanded, and scheming, considering . . . !"

"Yes, I probably am, as recent events have demonstrated all too clearly. I wondered who might shoot me first! You or Thackeray! No matter! There, my character has been stripped bare even down to the bone. But then, the rogue in me has almost achieved his purpose. If I can win over the least trusting of you all and meet with her alone, in her bedroom no less, and her in only a thin nightdress between us—that other does not count, as I am a gentleman—of sorts—and I dare not admit to it and as I had my eyes mostly closed—then surely I can achieve anything I set my heart upon."

"And what might that be?" She did not mind his speaking out so candidly. She liked his present mood.

"My, you are reckless to encourage me in this way! You should not ask, and I dare not say just yet. You would probably . . . no! You would certainly be most critical of me! It is too soon after all of the . . ." he smiled at her, " . . . I am even surprised at myself! My mother and even my sister would also be outraged! I would have to return to the continent! I promise that you will be the first one I will tell, and then you can deal with me accordingly, and as severely as will be merited. Do not ask any more of me. I have said much more than I intended to say already."

He had told her almost everything she might have needed to know! She began to wonder how it might be possible to have him stay with them all a little longer. Perhaps a lot longer! She no longer wished him to leave, but dare not tell him that, as she would have liked.

She took something off her bedside table and handed it to him. "Charlotte decided that you should have this, William." She passed over Mr. Thackeray's watch and watched as he turned it over in his hands. "No engraving on the outside." She watched as he popped the cover and then released an inner one. After a few seconds, his eyes flashed to hers. "Nor inside either! Did you or your sister open it?"

"No! I do not believe so. Why?" She looked up at him, seeking an explanation.

"It is . . . It is an unusual kind of watch." He wound it a little and set the movement into action.

She took it from his hands before he could close it or keep it from her and looked at it. A puzzled frown grew upon her face, and then she blushed profusely at the small naked portraits moving on the face of the watch. She looked at it with widening eyes and reddening cheeks for a few seconds and then dropped it on the covers but said nothing.

"Oh dear! Exactly! Going at it like ferrets aren't they?" He scooped it up and closed it before putting it back down.

She laughed nervously, and was wide eyed at his most outspoken description of what they were doing—going at it like fer—! "I think my uncle even had one, not quite as explicit or as disturbing, for I glimpsed it once fleetingly, though I was not supposed to know about that. It may still be in the back of the desk drawer."

"Yes. Another erotic watch! I saw it. It is still there!"

The silence continued for a few moments as she recovered her composure. She cleared her throat and could feel him smiling at her at the discomfort caused to her seeing that watch and its small inter-acting figures. She changed the subject. "Until recently, I was determined, and had the ammunition, to see and believe only the worst of you since you arrived, and I have had to repeatedly reverse myself, for you behaved in only the most considerate and protective way, though it took a little time to see beyond the first impression that you created. Even just a few moments ago, though you should not have stayed as you did."

"I tried to leave without alerting you to my presence, but I was discovered when I most clumsily backed into the door." He saw a new struggle taking place in her eyes and her thoughts as she built up the courage to ask him more and was wondering what she might decide to ask next.

"I . . . may I ask you some things that I might not dare to ask anyone else, while we are both in this outspoken and candidly honest mood, and without serious barriers between us?"

"That sounds somewhat dangerous, Annis! For me! Have we really come that far, you and I?" He answered his own question. "Yes, we have, haven't we, and in such a short time! So I am not to be shown the door as I began to fear, but am to be asked questions that you dare not ask another one. What things might you dare to ask, I wonder? I am now nervous! I heard you have that reputation of not sidestepping controversial and sometimes risqué discussion. Perhaps I am unlikely to cause you more disturbed feelings than I already did, or you me, but I would not care to gamble on that! You are also outspoken and have more force of character; *much more* than almost any woman I have come across, perhaps including my own sister who is somewhat notorious for her ability to speak out, and even in earthy matters when needed. Your mother warned me! Did you once really engage in political argument on an earlier visit with the younger Thackeray as your mother said?" He was trying to sidetrack her from what she had seemed all too ready to ask. He wished she had not seen that damned watch!

"Yes, I did! My father told me that if I expect to find anything out, I must be direct and ask without any round-about-ness. Thackeray was the wrong one to enter into a discussion with, however, as he regarded all women as needing to find their subservient place in their primping and preening, their crocheting and flower arrangements, their idle drawing room gossiping, and other less intellectual pastimes, and sticking in it, and he told me so. He said *that* to hide the obvious fact that he did not know anything about the subject I wished to open, for he seemed woefully uninformed, and it was obvious to us both. I told him so. He was severely discomposed by that, and he was gone the next day when Father insisted he leave after he had been tempted to wander more than he should. I don't think that you are that way, for you listen most politely to my mother and even very patiently to Charlotte *and* Sophia and never seem to disagree with them or any of us."

"Perhaps I am more cautious about laying my ignorance out before others. I am sure your father did not expect you to argue politics with someone you did not know very well."

"No. I expect not. But he and I did from time to time. Not so much argue, as discuss. He did not ridicule or put me down for anything I said, or interrupt to correct me or try to shut me up as other men might. He listened politely and seemed to value what I had to say. Of course, I was frequently wrong, but then so could he be."

"As we all can be! As for being a polite and patient listener, I always was that. I found that I learned the most when I spoke the least. I was also less likely to reveal my often complete and utter ignorance of any subject." The silence extended for a few moments.

"William?"

"Yes, my dear?" He responded before he had thought about it and even took her hand. She was obviously startled by his endearing words but did not remove her hand from his, or pull back.

"You are evading my attempt at an earlier question!"

"Yes. I am trying to. I am suddenly nervous for some reason. But I did not think that there was a question. I think I heard a statement. We have already made great progress—too much progress—in some ways. I would hate to jeopardize that hard-won ground if you throw more difficulties in my way, especially in discussing politics. I have had to maneuver over some very rough ground already today."

"I do not wish to discuss politics or military tactics with you but something else."

"Yes, I was afraid of that!"

"Liar!"

"There!" He smiled at her new outspokenness. "That is more like the Annis I have come to know!"

He was pleased to see that she did not apologize for that deserved remark! "You were deliberately trying to avoid my questions. I have not encountered anything yet that might cause you to be afraid. Not even, especially not even, a naked young lady standing before you, whether it be me or even Sophia."

"Sophia does not count! I did not and do not terrify her! Nor she me!" She looked at him, finding his comment to be quite strange. Why would he be terrified of a naked female? "Though she also asks some ferociously difficult questions and is quite capable of putting me to the blush!"

"Yes! She does that to me too at times and I am her sister! I saw no embarrassment in you whatsoever at anything she asked you, even in front of the rest of us. How you could maintain your composure when she was striving so very hard to show you every last one of her freckles . . . wherever they might be, so that you could confirm them and count them for her . . . ? Well! Charlotte and I did not know where to put ourselves!"

"I know.' He smiled as he recalled that. "It was delightful to watch you both blush and squirm, recalling where your own freckles might be at that very moment!"

Yes, he had enjoyed that; she could see it now. She continued. "You may have been a little surprised and taken aback, even discomposed, but afraid? I do not think so. You were far too relaxed and assured."

"When you came in upon me earlier, I was not terrified! Well not very much! Not for long! I was shocked! There is a big difference!" At least he had not been offended or disgusted with her at her lack of strong hysterical outrage and protest that she recognized would have been the expected response of almost any other young lady caught in such a situation by a gentleman. Though any other gentleman would also have immediately apologized profusely and left in acute embarrassment, and they both would have been assailed by shame and horror for long afterward at the probable repercussions. He did not display any such guilt or remorse over it and nor did she feel any either. His response had been entirely unexpected, but she soon recognized that it had not been threatening, and she had not been truly concerned for her safety beyond those first few seconds.

"Ouch! But I can assure you that I was neither relaxed nor at ease with the situation. Quite the opposite! But then why would I be embarrassed by Sophia, for she does that quite often when she insists that I get her ready for bed or dress her or bathe her; as I seem to be called upon to do quite often of late? I am amazed that I do not mind doing any of that either, but feel extremely privileged. She has not yet learned to be shy of me, which I find so very charming. Now if only her sisters . . ."

Annis interrupted his thought. "All of which she insists upon most shamelessly, the little wretch! It is not proper, but as no one will be likely to discuss it outside of this house, it does not count. But I was not speaking of Sophia, and you know it! I know that I should not ask . . . but I think that I may trust you to be honest with me as we seem to have accepted you as a valued part of this family, considering what you have done and risked for us. I think we may have gone beyond certain limitations in discussion as well as greater caution in behavior in some ways!"

He responded quite forcefully. "Oh no, we haven't! Not as we might have! There are still behavioral limitations, but I think they took a severe drubbing when you dared to return my kiss and threw the moral responsibility for my actions back upon me as you did! Most clever of you to throw me into complete disarray, and to confound and disarm me in that way!" He watched her expression. "I am sorry. I interrupted you!"

"Yes." She hesitated still to breach that subject she had started to ask. She took a deep breath.

"William?"

"Yes."

"Thank you for coming to rescue us as you did and so calmly submitting to marrying Bella! Mama might have gone mad, I think, without you coming to us. You did not see her before you arrived. She was frantic and almost hysterical. We would all have been depressed forever. We would have been overrun by the Thackerays and probably turned out on some legal nicety known only to lawyers of the kind that we seem to have trusted unwisely."

She continued in a low voice, unable to mask her sadness. "For what it might mean to you, I think you and Bella would have been most well suited. She would tolerate no nonsense, much as our mother would not, once she knew what she wanted." Her eyes had misted over. "What might have been? I shall not be cheated like that, for I think now that you would have been well suited together. Better to have loved and lost—yes, even in the lustful manner displayed on that watch, and even with all of its dangers to a woman—than never to have loved, in that case."

"I think Shakespeare was referring to love, not lust as you say. That is again, a most dangerous admission to make to such as I. But all of that was a statement of the circumstances again. I did not detect a question there. That is the second time you have probably thought better of asking me something."

She blushed and looked at him. "When two people find that they seem to be very suited to each other, *must* marriage enter into it?"

He laughed gently at her daring. "It should! But no! Not always, though it is often expected and prepared for. Sometimes, it cannot happen, where they are already married to others. But that is also dangerous ground to venture upon with the likes of me at this time."

"Thomas and Molly are in love, and yet, they do not marry! When they go off to the market together in the cart, they sit very close together, and I have seen them hold hands. When he helps her down from her seat, they linger together a little and even kissed once when they thought no one might see."

"But you did!"

"Yes. We did! They had forgotten that we had ridden behind them in the cart into market that day. I think that what they have is a love worth having, and yet, I suspect—I know—that they are also very warm for each other in that other way too, though they are difficult to encounter that way, for they know we . . . we saw them in the hay once, making love . . . they were so very tender with each other and loving! I know we should not have watched, but we . . . we were most curious!" She blushed at her most daring admission of that. It was a difficult subject for her to confess. "Yet they are not married, though they have known each other for many years. They were like our parents, who certainly loved each other deeply, and yet, there seemed to be a lustful side to it all too, for there was a good deal of excitement and gentle laughter!"

He felt most privileged that she might already be comfortable enough in his presence to be able to relate such deeply personal and private things.

She continued, unaware of his thoughts. "You did not know Arabella even for a day. How would you know that she could be the one you might love in that way?"

"I didn't! I couldn't! I had never even met her! I knew nothing of her at all. I married her because it was necessary at the time, to solve a greater problem that you all seemed to be facing." He decided to be a little more expansive. "One hopes that between intelligent people of similar interests and aspirations, that love will follow on from their marriage if they do not know each other beforehand, as with some arranged marriages, but I do not think that that is love. It gets it all the wrong way around. Love should come first before marriage, though a general attraction generally precedes them both. But then had it seemed that she would live, such a step would not have been countenanced by either your mother or me without us getting to know each other much better first. One has to wait and see if love might develop between the two of them after that first meeting. Sometimes it will, as it did with my sister and her husband before they were married, and sometimes it doesn't."

"And have you ever fallen in love and encountered . . . ? I should not ask."

"Yes, I have! But I refuse to disclose any more than that, and yes, you should not ask, for I am not sure I dare answer you any further so early . . . we are getting too close to too much revelation of a most personal nature." He cast his eyes ceiling-ward and spoke under his breath. "As if the rest of what we were discussing was not of that kind. For it is!" He returned to the moment. "I am amazed at myself! But yes, my dear, love should prevail! It tends to be more lasting, whereas lust is of the moment and may be fleeting. At least *that*—a lasting *love*—is what one's parents hope for their daughters. Love and marriage should come before any of that other, for children have a habit of sometimes appearing when one least wants them too."

She listened attentively, recognizing that she had asked much more than she should have done and had even risked him refusing to discuss any such thing with her, and even deciding—perhaps—that he should not stay in such an iniquitous situation where a young female dare to ask such shocking things. Yet he hadn't refused to answer anything yet.

Quite unexpectedly, he continued along a similar vein. She had been quite candid with him in relating their observing Thomas and Molly. He decided that he should be at least equally candid. "Males are also given much more freedom than females are. It is expected that a man should approach marriage with some experience of . . . of that other! With sons, it is *expected* that as part of their male characteristics and baser impulses and instincts, that they will, as they say, sow-their-wild-oats in that way with some appropriate and understanding and obliging female, usually one who is much older and wiser and who is not so very particular or needful about protecting her sterling reputation. But such behavior must be conducted out of sight, far from society's gaze and revelation and preferably without ones relatives or society finding out about it! All in secret and in confidence! It is also expected that there will be no repercussions for the family, with distraught young ladies appearing at the door and with an infant in arms, enquiring after their son. Most embarrassing!"

"And did you?—sow your wild oats!"

"My, we are being inquisitive! And brave as well as foolhardy!" He took a deep breath. "Yes, I did. But there were no repercussions."

"Can you tell me?"

"What will you not dare to ask!"

"I am sorry. It is too much of me to expect to learn of that, but how else might I learn of . . . any of that if we do not observe, or if no one is prepared to tell me? And there is no one else that I might dare to ask now."

"Yes. Personal questions best asked of a father or of a husband. However . . . !" He took a deep breath. "You will certainly judge me ill, yet I will tell you, though I am not sure how I dare do so! He did know, but could not explain it to her just yet.

"My first encounter was with a most accommodating, obliging, and most precocious servant girl, who was a few years older than I—I was fourteen—and she was very discreet about it, I am pleased to say, for we managed to hide it for a very long time. Some years! In fact, I do not think my mother found out about it until it was all discovered at the end, though my sister knew. She seemed to know everything about me! And please let us leave it there, for it was a long time ago. I do not regret any of it, but others did judge me ill, though neither of us was harmed by it, and there were no repercussions running around later! I believe my mother still has her on her staff!"

"And were you in love with her?"

"No, I wasn't." He knew what was coming.

"So that was lust, and not love?"

"Yes. I suppose I must admit that, but it is not quite that bad. We were neither of us harmed by the experience. Quite the contrary, I would say."

"Did you first approach her, or did she you?"

He sensed she would not let it go until she knew it all. "She approached me! Most cleverly too! I should say *she* deliberately tempted *me*, as a beautiful and well-developed young woman might, in seeming innocence. But she was far from innocent! She knew exactly what she was doing—as some women seem to know by instinct—where I didn't! I was helping her to lift a bucket of water from the well. She had on a very loose-fitting dress, which she knew revealed quite a lot of her to this wide-eyed youth, as she leaned forward opposite me. I remember that she was smiling at me and was well aware of my focused attention into the front of her dress." His eyes flickered for a moment to Annis's low cut nightdress and smiled at what he saw. She noticed his look but did not feel discomforted or embarrassed by it, but smiled a little. "I was suddenly unnerved, and we spilt water on ourselves. I think she did it deliberately. She was quite concerned about that, fearing trouble from my mother—or so she said—and needed to see me dried off, and herself too. We went out of sight and she proceeded to undress me! Of course, it rapidly got out of hand, just as she intended! That was our first excited and unrestrained encounter of many!"

"Like ferrets?"

He looked at her with some surprise. "Yes, like ferrets!"

"So she was the lustful one!"

"I wouldn't say that. But not far from it! Yes. She was lustful, but it was a mutual feeling and I was more than ready and more than her match in that department, for

I often sought her out if she did not seek me, which she often did! We soon learned how to go about it with the least notice being taken!"

"So it really was mutual?"

"Yes, it was! The standards expected of men are so different from those expected of women. I am sure that it all seems so very hypocritical, for it is. Men always seem to believe that they should wed a virgin, whereas it is expected that a man will have had several escapades by the time he gets married. Settles him down, so they say!"

"Does it?"

What would she not dare to ask next? "No! It doesn't!" He was emphatic about that. "It usually does quite the reverse if he is denied a continuing and fulfilling relationship of that kind! It tends to fire him up more than is good for anyone and makes him more conscious and alive, and even more aggressive to the fairer sex, not less."

She blushed delightfully. "Oh dear. I fear I am not a lady, for ladies do not discuss such risqué subjects, do they?"

"No. They don't! Nor do gentlemen respond to those kind of question quite so openly! Nor do ladies tolerate such discussions or even instigate them! Usually, within the family setting, they do sometimes manage to discuss such things but only in private. As this is a family setting I think, and we do have privacy, we might be forgiven. But then you are still a lady, just as I think of myself as a gentleman, though I have very different standards than others of that breed. You are just not as shy as others are and are the more interesting because of it." He looked down at her and met her eyes. He smiled at her and continued with his thoughts. He resisted, with some difficulty, the impulse to kiss her.

"Do you not find it rather remarkable that though you and I, barely having known each other for something a little more than a week even, are having this exceptionally personal and risqué conversation as though we had known each other for years—our entire lives even? I am sure that if your mother were aware of it, she would be aghast and would show me the door, even unaware of my earlier most dreadful behavior with you, and I would have to leave!"

"Perhaps! But she does not know of this, just as she will not find out the other."

"Just as well! I would hate to think that we were being watched or overheard, though I have had the feeling for some time that I am being watched."

She looked at him with an enigmatic smile. "You are! It is difficult to avoid being watched with Sophia and Charlotte about. And I have a reputation for not shying away from embarrassing topics as you now know. But I do not know who else I might ask, for I was too embarrassed to approach my father for those particularly burning questions I needed to have answered. Mama tries to tell us things from time to time but always avoids the more detailed and interesting aspects and necessary explanations.

She continued with the earlier topic. "And do you have those feelings and impulses? Yes, you obviously must, for you did confess them! Was that Dierdre, you were telling me about?"

He was surprised again. "How did you hear about her? I do not recall mentioning her name!" He chuckled nervously. "Elizabeth! What did she not tell you about me? Yes, that was Dierdre! I am surprised Elizabeth did not warn you never to be alone with me. It is not safe for me to be so close to an attractive and encouraging female that I find so disturbingly attractive."

She blushed at the compliment. "I think I noticed! You seemed a little out of breath and flustered when you encountered me dishabille once you lost concern for my bruising, as you soon did, and were more interested in other things . . . in bathing and kissing me!"

"Was I? Yes, I was, wasn't I? It seems to be part of our instinct and drive. A man, after a certain age, is always attracted to a beautiful young lady. I always seemed to be. I cannot suppress my feelings easily, though I try to control mine rather than have them control me, but the temptations are difficult to deny and fight off at times when the passions, temptations, and provocations are great."

She fell silent for some moments. "Thank you! I think you answered my questions quite well." She put her hand over his at that moment. "I think you might be a gentleman after all for dealing most gently with me and my truly difficult questions. I think I found out what I needed to know. I also learned much more about you than I think I deserve to know."

He was not sure he liked the sound of that. "There, you see, I am working my way behind your defenses and am obviously succeeding in my devious purpose with you, while hiding my disreputable intentions from all of you. But I think that I should keep your mind and mine from dwelling on such unwholesome thoughts by reading to you." He picked the open book from the bedside table and began to read from it.

She yawned. "You should sit up here, William." She moved over a little to make room. "The light is not good there, for you are facing the window and the sun is low in the sky."

"You are being most daring, Annis, after our earlier adventure and after our far too revealing and detailed conversation concerning personal intimacies, lust, and lovemaking. However, I should point out that for me to do so would not be proper. You are in a most becoming but insubstantial nightdress and have your reputation to protect from encroaching lustful males like me! I am possibly the most disreputable member of that clan. I have no such reputation to lose don't forget, but you have. Besides, your mother or one of your sisters may come in and catch us!"

"Is that the only thing stopping you? Fear of being discovered reading to me up here beside me, as lightlydressed as I am? For I don't think you give a fig about propriety or not shocking anyone." He voice dropped. "You have seen me in less, remember?" It was his turn to blush. "You speak of reputation too easily William! Hang proper! I am discovering more about life and about myself at this moment than I might ever have known had you not arrived when you did, and upset our precarious world even more than it was. I know what I want of life, and I do not wish to be robbed prematurely of anything, as Bella was! Perhaps that was why I would not give up so easily on finding out those things that I asked. I really did need to know! I am also twenty-one years old and of age to make up my own mind and decide my own actions." She looked far off as she internally analyzed those words and the thoughts that went with them. "Although that is a little frightening also, and perhaps I am frightening myself over some things I am learning about myself and you! I would not want for you to despise me for not defending myself much better than . . . than I did earlier!"

"We already covered that! There is not the remotest possibility of that, my dear! Unfortunately, we are both vulnerable at this moment, it seems. Those are also not quite the sentiments that a lightly clad young lady should state so forcibly to a man she has invited to sit on her bed after the nature of the conversation we have just had. But I fear that you and they *do not* know *me* just yet, no matter how much *they* or *you* may think you do, so I must at least not try to prove their guardedly positive opinions of me to be devastatingly incorrect . . . if I can avoid it, when faced by so much temptation. Even after some years of being close together, some persons still do not really know each other as well as we seem to even now."

"That would be truly sad, I think." She sighed. "With others, even a few days can achieve the same thing. Perhaps even a single glance as with Romeo and Juliet. Love and lust again!"

"That was a play and not about real people."

"And yet it could have been, and possibly was. My mother is a real person. That is how she fell in love with my father."

She patted the bed beside her. "You do not need to be shy, you know?" *She* was challenging *him*! Oh how their roles had been so suddenly reversed!

He left his chair beside the bed and clambered up beside her, leaning against the headboard. He was in his stocking feet. The light from the window, now more behind him, was better.

She leaned in against him. He picked up the book from the coverlet and began reading to her again.

After a few moments of listening to him read, she reached over and took his hand and then moved further under the covers, snuggling beside him, with his hand against her cheek. With her face pushing into the side of his leg and feeling his warmth, she closed her eyes.

He liked the newfound feeling of trust that she seemed to have in him, despite coming precariously close to losing it, but was not sure he was up to dealing with it as he knew he must. She suddenly knew too much about him and far more than he should be comfortable with, but at the same time, he found that he was feeling very contented. "Well, my fortune has risen in the world."

She looked up at him. "Thank you for not leaving us when you might have, as I think I wanted at first with all that was going on and . . . that other . . . personal things. But that was before I knew you."

He thought he might know about—*that other*—either the violent way he dealt with Thackeray, his revelations of his own weaknesses and failings, or his godmother's likely cautioning of them all about his rakish exploits and execrable character. Perhaps all of them! "You do not know me at all, Annis! But I promise that none of you will ever regret my presence here. I probably should have left when I had the chance, considering the far too revealing conversation we have just had. The situation is far too dangerous in every way, especially for me—a confirmed bachelor, which I once was but no longer—and undoubtedly, for you too. But then I promised your father I would protect you and not desert you. Now what else did I most foolishly promise him concerning my unrestrained behavior with his beautiful and most vulnerable daughters?"

"My father? You did?" She was instantly attentive and looked up at him with suddenly bright eyes. "I did not know that! I wondered what he might have said or discussed with you, for Mama would not tell me with all that was going on. Thank you for telling me that. It makes so much difference if he trusted you. Now I do know that I can too."

"Yes. I did make that promise. *He* may have trusted me, though I do not know why. Something about knowing my father, for he did not know me. *You* should still not trust me, however. I *do* know why you should not and so do you if you think about it. Unfortunately, I am likely to cause a good deal of trouble for everyone before I do leave."

"You've already done that! But in what ways is the situation too dangerous and what trouble? Surely you do not mean the Thackerays still?"

"No. Hang the Thackerays! You have a new and bigger threat looming up over the horizon. I was speaking of me!"

Her mother had been impatient the same way, with her misunderstanding of the same subject just a short time earlier. He meant himself. Her mother had also meant William too!

"Did everything we discuss roll off you like water off a duck's back? I am the one that is far too dangerous for all of you, for I am a confirmed rogue, a libertine, *and* a philanderer, if not worse, as I am sure our godmother let you know, and am extremely violent, as you are now well aware. But only with other men, never with women. At least not on this side of the channel! But the temptations? I may not be able to survive them! Damn! I am too well known by all of you! I have a bad reputation to uphold, or they will drum me out of the club of disreputable scoundrels!"

"I thought it was the Rogues Club!"

"That one too! You are all very interesting young ladies. Your mother too, and all of you far too trusting and most vulnerable as I insinuate myself into your innermost sanctums. I didn't realize such delights, being in the company of so many young women—to be trusted when I do not deserve to be trusted—might ever torment me or come my way as it did. I don't think I will be able to leave so very easily at all."

He sighed. "You know, I think there is only one of your bedrooms that I have not been in!"

She gently hit him on the leg.

"I think I feel as the rooster must feel—let loose in the hen house and not sure where to begin."

She laughed at his metaphor. "You don't fool me, sir. I don't think you would take advantage of any of us quite so casually. Not now!"

There was no responding to that.

He had set her off again. "I *was* afraid that you had betrayed us not so very long ago when I overheard you with the elder Thackeray. But you have had enough opportunity by now to have learned enough of us and to have usurped everything and put us all out several times over."

"Yes, I know. But unfortunately, I listened to my conscience, which has been my constant and pestiferously-confining companion for the last few years! Besides, you now have my pistol, and unfortunately, I showed you how to use it. I needed to find out that it was not in reach before I put any foot too wrong. I must tread carefully and be much more cautious and patient and strike when the opportunity is there or risk being shot or turned out of the house."

"You did not do so—strike and take outrageous advantage of me—this afternoon after I became faint! I think a far better opportunity was there just a few minutes ago when everyone was out in the garden."

"The opportunity may have been there, as you say, but I was not so far lost that I desired to commit complete destruction of myself, although I intended to take advantage of you at the inn, I would have done, except the Landlord recognized you, so I could not plead that my wife had fainted as I thought I might and suggest that we needed a private room *immediately!*" He looked down at her and smiled. There was a strange look in his eyes.

"You had no such intention!"

"Oh really? How do you know that?"

"I told you. I was not totally unconscious of what was happening or what you did. I could still hear what was said, and my thinking was clear enough."

"So you were not totally unaware of what was happening? I thought you were. You gave no indication of being aware of anything."

"No. I did not too much mind your kiss—that was not outrageous or passionate in a way to cause me any concern. You kissed me on the neck, if I recall. You were holding me tightly at the time, hence my bruises, and I think you had a most worried look on your face. When I saw that, I trusted you, despite that minor liberty. I was concerned a little at first, of course, wondering if you might seek to be revenged upon me for my behavior of the previous day, and then, when I saw that revenge did not seem to be on your mind at that moment, I was mostly curious. You were at a loss for a short time. I did not shoot you then. Then just a few minutes ago . . . I am not sure what I felt, though I think I . . ."

"Better stop there, my dear! You trusted me! You were curious? Most dangerous admissions, for they will almost certainly invite another similar trespass when the opportunity is presented, as it is now, I think, with me perched on your bed beside you. I can assure you, however, that if ever any such thing is considered, it will not be because of any thought of revenge. I am a poor specimen, I know, but I am not *that* poor! But your gun was trapped in your pocket at that moment against me, so I knew I was safe. My kiss at that moment was actually giving you notice of my future disreputable intentions toward you, including another kiss and others after that too, so be warned."

"I have been warned, though you do that with Sophia and with Mother too." She turned her face up toward him as though challenging him to kiss her. "I would not too much object at this moment, William!"

"But I would, and you should too! You should not tempt me so mercilessly. I am only a weak man when faced with such revealing opportunities. The kisses I give Sophia are brotherly protective kisses, and the one—just one kiss—I planted on the top of your mothers head was a comforting kiss. She needed to be held at the time. But you . . . there is a difference. You should not tempt me in this way, for you and I are about the same age, and I find you . . . I am no better than Samson confronted with his Delilah, and you should not behave like some siren temptress! The temptations are more than enough to bear most of the time for me, but I do not need to lose your trust in quite that way! I came too close to that as it was!"

"And now I know so much more about you! I think it was providence that brought you to us. I don't think any of us want you to leave now."

"Then I shall stay, permanently, and you will never be rid of me, and serve you right! We shall set the countryside ablaze with rumors of riotous, licentious behavior and outrageously bawdy goings-on, even to eclipse those of the Regent and Byron combined! I shall resolve to behave worse than any Thackeray ever could! They will say worse of me than Lady Lamb ever said of Byron—that he was mad, bad, and dangerous to know. Though I believe I already do behave rather badly. But providence? Perhaps. When I first got your mother's letter, I almost was gone in the other direction, for that was my first instinct, which I suppressed. For once, I ignored my instinct to run."

He became thoughtful for a few moments. "I am glad of that! Though it seems that there were some powerful ladies working behind the scenes here to either see it would come about somehow, or would not. I am not sure either side succeeded quite as they intended. They certainly could not have known what my response would be. Nor I of myself!

"But where is your gun now? If it is not easily within reach, I may be tempted to ravish you just a little."

"It is nowhere within reach at this moment, William. I do think I would like that!" He felt her snuggle more deeply beside him.

He did not respond to that dangerous invitation but continued to read for a few minutes and then she piped up again.

"William"

"Yes, Annis."

She sensed the trepidation in his voice, wondering what kind of shocking question she might now ask. "How is it that you can stay here with us as you have? Surely you must have a life somewhere else waiting for you?"

He was relieved to find the conversation taking a less embarrassing and threatening turn. "Yes, there is. But it has done without me very well for twenty-five years. It can continue that way."

He read further, only to be interrupted yet again.

"William?" He stopped reading and waited. "Do you have any special woman in your life?"

He smiled. "Very searching questions! They seem to bubble to the surface every so often. You are most courageous to ask them of me."

"Well, I felt I had to be courageous somehow, and now was as good a time to continue as we started while you are still here and feeling as you do. I have never been able to ask such personal questions of anyone before without embarrassing both them and me, and not getting a suitable answer, and never a male like you. But I feel that I can ask you, and I am not sure why. I am sorry. I would like to know so much more about you."

"I am sure that you will, and might very well regret it! But considering that I am thrown into the role of protector and stand-in for a brother, and I did marry your sister, then I would say that you do have the right to ask as you have done already, along with some very risqué kind of questions! But I reserve the right not to answer. However, I shall answer you." He took a deep breath. "About a special woman in my life. I had just two until a short while ago—my mother and my sister. Though I am not sure that I let my mother know it. I must remedy that. Then I had three—with your sister whom I married. Now, after losing her, I find I have six of them, and all in the space of a very few days. My cup do indeed runneth over, though there is a certain sadness to it too."

"But is there any one of them more special than the rest? Oh. I should not be asking that, for Bella was that one, I think, even though you never did know her as we did, nor as a husband ought, might . . . of his wife!" Her words tailed off as she sensed she was getting out of her depth again.

"Yes. She was special to me. She became that way when I married her, if for no other reason. You were going to tell me about her, remember?" He tried to nudge the conversation into safer directions.

"Yes, I was." She moved herself up a little more beside him and pulled the covers around herself. "On the dresser there. Charlotte left me her drawings earlier. That is her latest book that she started about a year ago. Please bring them over, and I will show them to you. She will not mind."

He sat beside her again, and she opened the large book as she showed them to him, and provided a description as she turned the pages. It was filled with drawings of her and her sisters, with Charlotte throwing in a self-portrait from time to time, showing off a new gown or bonnet, and she also inserted herself into group portraits that she drew from memory.

"She just needs to see something, look at it for a few seconds, and then she can reproduce it most faithfully."

"My sister too?" He saw Elizabeth drawn most faithfully there.

"Oh yes. She spent many days and weeks with us while her husband John was with you. She was—is very much in love."

He looked sharply at her. With Elizabeth practically living here, no wonder her mother knew so much of him. But Annis's mind was elsewhere. She continued. "She was great friends with Bella. When she was here, they were inseparable." She turned a page. "Here is Bella just two months ago. She has a parasol and is in the garden with Mama."

"The family resemblance is obvious! She was quite tall."

"Almost as tall as you William, but then so am I. She was most happy on that particular day."

She continued to turn the pages and continued to give descriptive explanations as each drawing came up. The last ones included some of himself. He was sitting in the window embrasure downstairs writing in his journal. He had not noticed Charlotte observing him from across the hallway. She must have been sitting at the table in the other room and watching him through the doorway from the shadows.

Another was of him sleeping and must have been done in the very early morning before he was awake. He did not know how that might have been achieved for he was a very light sleeper. There was also the cat on the foot of the bed, stretched out, and oblivious to it all.

"Oh! You are showing him Charlotte's drawings!"

She looked up as William continued turning the pages. "Yes, Sophia, I am. How long have you been standing there watching? What did you overhear?"

"Only a minute or so. Charlotte said I should go and see that everything was all right, for you both had gone silent for far too long and your voices had dropped. She said that those were bad signs and dangerous. She also said that when the children go quiet, they must be up to something! But you are not children, and I do not see why she said that, for you all tell me often enough that silence is golden, not dangerous."

"It depends upon the reason for the silence."

"Oh! But I do not understand!"

"As it was Charlotte that sent you up here to spy on us, and you have now seen that we are not up to any kind of mischief, you should ask Charlotte when you go to report on us."

They both laughed as she went off downstairs again.

"See! Even my own sisters keep an eye on us! I hope she did not overhear our earlier conversation!"

"Yes, for they—you—know all about me it seems!"

"Oh! You were not supposed to go quite that far in the book!" She seemed alarmed.

She took the book from him and closed it firmly.

He had fleetingly seen other somewhat risqué drawings, including one of himself sitting in the copper bathtub. The one doing the drawing had obviously been behind the door leading up to the upper floor at that end of the house, and probably looking at him through gaps in the door that closed it off. He'd wondered about that. There were other candid and detailed drawings of him after that one. He would say nothing of those but decided that he should have listened more closely to Mrs. Barristow when she warned him that her daughters knew everything that was going on around the house. He would take better care over his bathing arrangements in future, considering that Sophia had even blundered in on him the last time and insisted on helping him get bathed, dried, and dressed just as he did with her, so he could not complain or hurt her feelings by suggesting that she should not be there. She had been entirely unperturbed and only mildly curious about his nakedness. It seemed that nothing was secret from these ladies and that they knew far more of life and what went on between the sexes than one might assume.

"You are not such an ogre after all, are you? I don't think you are a threat to any of us as Thackeray would have been, and as I first feared.

"It depends who you listen to. I am biding my time for a better opportunity. Some think I am every bit as bad as it is possible to be."

"Thank you for today. Had you not been there . . ."

He took her hand. "Then you would not have gone anywhere and certainly not so far afield as we did. I should not have done that, and you would not have come to grief quite so badly. So, you see, I am to blame for it all."

"But then I would not have been kissed either."

"I don't know about that. The temptation is always there, even now. But then I would also have been robbed of . . ." He stopped his thoughts in their tracks. "But please do not broadcast it about that I did that, or others may clamor for a similar treatment." He smiled at her. "But then Sophia may come in again if all goes too quiet, so I cannot oblige you at this particular moment."

She yawned again, snuggled against his leg again still holding his hand, and seemed to fall asleep almost immediately. He took the opportunity to turn the pages of the sketch book and took in many more of the drawings she had been loathe for him to see. Many were of Annis herself, with others of him, and most of them were very candid drawings that left little to the imagination. He smiled, closed the book and stood up gently, so as not to disturb her, and put the book back on the dresser.

After straightening the covers up about her neck, he leaned over and kissed her gently on the forehead.

The words he whispered in her ear were inaudible to anyone else, but she was almost asleep and obviously did not consciously hear them.

She mumbled something unintelligible and settled again.

He gently leaned over and this time kissed her on the lips, eliciting no response other than a deep sigh and a gentle turning of her head to make it easier for him. She seemed to want to linger over it, so he did and then retreated quietly.

As he left, he saw Sophia go in and go to her and then return.

"Too quiet again, eh?"

She nodded. She had been standing in the doorway and had seen him kiss her. "Mama says dinner will be late; not for another hour, so we can let her sleep 'till then." She took his hand and led him downstairs.

"I will show you an Eskimo kiss after you have read to me and even a butterfly kiss too."

"Oh. Good! Then I can practice them on everyone. I had better start with Captain Cat. He would like that I think, and it will be much safer for me. He does not have my pistol!"

Chapter XXIV

We Are Forever in Your Debt

William was having such a wonderful dream in serene surroundings with peaceful and charming young women, rather than his usual fare of fighting old battles afresh and losing them in some frustrating way that made no sense and was contrary to what he had experienced.

A feeling of sudden panic gripped him when he awoke to find his room gradually filling with smoke from the corridor beyond, for he always left his door open. There was the smell of smoldering wood.

He threw the bed covers to one side and rushed out, shouting to warn the house of the danger, staying as low as he could to avoid the thicker blanket of smoke in the upper part of the corridor.

Within seconds, there were raised voices from other parts of the house and various sounds of confusion and even of panic amidst the smoke.

There was coughing from the master bedroom, close to that end of the house in which the problem seemed to have begun. He did not bother to knock but burst in to find Mrs. Barristow on the floor and crawling toward him and gasping for air. He grabbed her along with a sheet, which he threw over her, and carried her off to the head of the stairs, where she struggled and fought to return for her daughters. "My children! My children!" He realized she would not submit to be put outside with her children still trapped within. "I will see to them, ma'am. Please just let me get you out into the yard for safety."

She had no intention of being saved with her children still in the house. He chose not to argue with her but carried her off resolutely to find Thomas and the other servants—all awake by then and in the yard. "You will need to hold her here, Thomas, or we will create a worse problem, and I do not need to find that she has re-entered the house. She might be difficult to find. I will see to the others better if I do not have to worry about her."

"Yes, sir. One of the stable lads is off raising the alarm nearby and toward the village for assistance. It looks like it is in the ceiling area and toward that end of the house, for the downstairs is still free of smoke, though I can see some glimmer of flames there, so it won't stay that way for long. I'll see what I can get organized."

"Better if you see to Mrs. Barristow here first. People are the most important thing."

"Aye, reckon your right there!"

"I'll get everyone out. Just the three girls I hope, unless they came out and are somewhere else?"

"No one else is out here yet, sir. No one had time just yet!"

Some water was already being thrown in downstairs through a broken window where the fire appeared to have started and was still growing.

He ran back upstairs to rescue the two younger daughters before they might panic and lose themselves in the house, for it was easy to lose one's orientation in smoke, or do something foolish like trying to get themselves out and losing direction. Easily done, he knew.

He did not notice that Mrs. Barristow had broken free of the servants' restraining hands and had rushed back in behind him, followed closely by Thomas and two others, grabbing at her arms and nightdress as she desperately fought them off. As they mounted the stairs behind him, the entire flimsy structure collapsed under their combined weight.

William was on the top landing when she started after him and did not see the stairway give way. For by then, he was just about up to the girls' room.

Mrs. Barristow was knocked senseless by her fall with the stairs, and the servants were able to carry her out into the fresh air. By then, more men were arriving with buckets and ladders. Fortunately, there was plenty of water flowing in the stream after all the recent rains.

William entered the girls bedroom, relieved to see them huddled under the covers and easily found. He lifted Charlotte into his arms and spoke to Sophia, telling her to take hold of him around his neck and to hang on. They were both coughing and fighting for breath, but Sophia had enough wit to be able to hang onto him. He readjusted his hold on Charlotte to include Sophia's legs against him, trapped by her sister's legs and headed for the stairs. He was having difficulty himself now as the smoke was getting steadily thicker, and he would not be able to move quickly, or move at all if he dropped to the less smoky air near the floor. He was thankful to notice that there were no obvious flames to contend with. He became aware of the problem with the stairs before he blundered blindly over the empty space where they had once stood. He put Sophia down at the edge of where the stairs had been and then set Charlotte on her feet. "I want you both to sit on the edge here, and then I will be able to reach you." He watched them follow his instructions as he climbed over the edge and down onto the remains of the wreckage beneath and out of the smoke. Once he had a firm footing, awkward in his bare feet, he reached up, and Sophia took hold of his outreached arms and slid into them as he turned and set her where she could hold onto part of the remaining banister, and then turned back for Charlotte. She slid to the edge and then fell forward into his arms where he caught her and held her securely. Once onto the even floor at the edge of where the stairs had been, he turned and picked Sophia up in his other arm and carried both of them outside.

In a way, it was a blessing the stairs had gone, else Mrs. Barristow would have followed him in. He could see her sitting off in the dim morning light at the edge of the lawn and being tended to by Mrs. Rogers, as she looked eagerly for her girls to appear from the house. He dropped the two girls off with her, noticing that Annis was now the only one missing.

"Is Annis out yet, Thomas?" He spoke to him as they formed a human chain to fill and transfer buckets of water to throw onto the flames that were still visible in the downstairs parlor.

"No, sir! Just Mrs. Barristow and the two younger girls now. She is the only one left. Up there, that side of the house, sir." He pointed. "No one else went in or came out but you."

He knew where to go. "Make sure no one follows me!"

By then, more men were arriving with buckets and were putting a ladder up to an upper window where the fire and smoke seemed thickest now and had broken in a window to gain access to that level to throw water in upon the fire There was no one residing in that part of the house to worry about.

He quickly returned to the trough, emptied a bucket of cold water over himself, and wet down the sheet that he had picked up with Mrs. Barristow, threw it across his shoulder, and then headed back in to climb up onto the upper floor. He forgot how low the door was and almost knocked himself out as he walked into the lintel in the dark. He swore at his own stupidity, feeling suddenly sick and dizzy. He put the pain aside, climbing easily to the upper floor again. The smoke was thicker now, and he could feel some warmth coming at him.

He entered Annis's room and was surprised to find that she was not there, though the bed covers were in disarray and a water jug recently knocked over. Where she had been lying was warm to his touch. He called her name and looked about carefully to see that she was not hiding out of the way of the smoke. The room was empty. He left that room and closed the door to limit the spread of any flames as far as it was possible to do so.

Staying below as much of the smoke as he could, he could see no one else in the corridor. He shouted again. The thick pall of smoke was still hanging and drifting above his head, but there was no obvious increase in the heat coming along the corridor from where the fire seemed to have started. He rechecked the master bedroom. That was empty too, so he left that and closed that door too. He shouted Annis's name again. There was a faint noise and the sound of coughing from the girls' bedroom that he had recently left. He moved to check that room again and walked into an open closet door before he got there. Through blurry eyes and a curtain of pain following on from his first encounter with the downstairs doorway, he could see a vague shape near the window and coughing in the smoke. Annis had gone looking for her sisters, intent on seeing the other girls out, and was now overcome herself. She was sitting in a tight bundle on the floor and had covered her mouth and eyes with the neck of her nightdress to protect her ability to breathe, but she would soon be overcome if she stayed where she was.

He immediately draped the wet sheet over them both and pulled her fully to the floor where the air was a little clearer. She began to recover her breathing under the damp sheet.

"William!" She grabbed his arm. Her breath caught in her throat as she spoke into his ear. "The girls? Mama? I do not know where they are." She was oblivious to all else around them. Her only concern was for her sisters and their mother.

"They are all safe now! We are the last!" He kicked the door closed to block off a thicker billowing of smoke that had suddenly started to fill the corridor. We shall stay on the floor as we are, where the smoke is less thick for the moment, and crawl to the window. I will see to us getting out. Courage, my dear. I have been in worse predicaments than this."

"William, if we cannot get out of here then . . ." She held on to him and looked pleadingly up at him as she kissed him in the dim light filtering in through the lower part of the window.

He smiled at her. "No need for such a sacrifice yet, my dear! We shall get out! I have seen no flames so far nor felt quite the heat that there normally is with a raging fire. It all seems to be only thick smoke so far, so if we stay close to the floor and avoid the smoke as much as possible, there is no reason we cannot get out. If you let go of me, my dear, and not hold onto me so tightly, I will see to us getting out."

He felt her reluctantly let go of him. She put her nightdress back over her mouth and nose and breathed though its folds to keep as much of the smoke from her lungs as possible. He moved away from her a little as she watched him drape the wet sheet further over her and pull her to the window along the floor. He took a deep breath then stood up and poked the windows and frame out with the chair from beside the bed, feeling a rush of much cooler clear air in upon them, dispelling the smoke a little closer to the floor, and then he pushed the mattress from the bed through the opening to clear off glass and wood fragments and dropped it out so that they would have something to cushion their fall and protect them from the glass outside on the ground.

"The captain! The captain!" Annis was holding his arm and shouting coarsely at him. "Hiding in the corner there. He must have been with them!"

He had not seen the cat earlier. He left her and crawled over to the corner through the thin smoke near the floor and scooped up the cat. He was thankful that he had shut the door, or the cat might have gone off in a panic into the rest of the house and might never have been found alive. He was tempted to drop it out of the window but decided against it. He was not sure how it might fare.

Annis opened the sheet up from around herself as she took it from him, holding it firmly for fear it might break free by grasping the fur at the neck as a mother cat might. It settled uneasily with wild and darting eyes, between her breasts and was obviously ready to head off in a total panic if she were to let it go, yet was trusting enough not to use its claws to escape and lacerate her thinly covered body where she held it to her. William wrapped them both securely in the sheet once more so that the cat could not escape and then covered Annis's head and hair to keep as much of the smoke from her as possible and pulled her closer to the window. Had the cat not been there, he could have put her over his shoulder and made short work of getting out, but this was more difficult.

He noticed, as the air cleared a little, that he was beginning to feel nauseated from the combined pain in his head and the effects of the smoke. His forehead felt like it was split. Damn fool walking into two doors like that!

"I will get you to the window and onto the sill, then I want you to take a hold of my arm as tightly as you can above the elbow, and do not let go. I will need my other hand free to hold on to the frame and get us both outside and to safety. Tell me if I am hurting you."

He bunched up the sheet to trap her securely, trying not to trap her skin or the cat in his grasp, and held it tightly in his fist as she, for her part, held onto his upper arm with one of her own through a gap that was left, and the other hand comforting and holding the cat which had settled uneasily. He picked her up. In that position, he leaned out with her clear of the window. He then let go of her with one hand while she continued holding his arm above the elbow. He held onto the lower part of the window frame with his other hand. Once his upper body and his burden were out of the window, he allowed himself to step out over the sill, followed by his leg from inside the room. Her weight pulled him out, as he knew it would, but he maintained his hold on the window frame to stop them both from falling while being cautious of getting cut by any remaining glass in the frame.

She sensed the desperate strength that lay in his arm as he held her and before she could lose her grip, though he would not lose his on her. He maneuvered himself out of the window to hang down the outside of the building and then dropped the short distance to the ground and onto the mattress. They slowly fell over together as he quickly lowered her to the ground without dropping her. She let go of him and clambered unsteadily to her feet as the cat escaped and ran off into the lessening dark. He steadied her from falling over again as she grasped him tightly in some relief at being out of the smoke-filled room.

He leaned back against the building for a few seconds to be sure of not losing his balance again as he fought for some clear breaths of air. His hand, with which he had held onto the window frame, was most sore. He stood up, gathering her back up into his arms as he let the sheet fall away from her, and they stood together, relieved to be out of it all. She seemed unable to let him go for the moment, so they stood embracing each other for some little time until they recovered, oblivious to everything that might be going on around them in the dim light. She staggered as he let her go for a brief moment before holding her steady again. When she had recovered, he wrapped the wet sheet close about her again, picked her up into his arms and walked off around the corner of the building and into the main yard—a hive of activity at that moment. He placed her gently on the grass at the edge of the drive with her mother and sisters. Only then did he remove the sodden sheet from about her. Mrs. Barristow sat back down in sudden relief that all of her daughters were now safely with her and gathered them close to her.

William could see possibly ten or more people there, bringing buckets of water to bear inside the house downstairs, with another on a ladder up to an upper floor window and dealing with whatever might be visible there. He began to help with the task of filling buckets with water, to put out the fire, but there was little to do that had not already been done, and his help was not needed. There were others close by, who would also keep an eye on the nearby structures if any sparks began to fly. He still could not see any obvious flames.

Thomas met him and spoke, taking in the superficial injuries to his head and hand. "It is good to see everyone is out! It seems to be mostly confined to the downstairs in the wall next to the chimney, and with more men arriving, we stand a good chance of getting ahead of it. With any luck, it may have been nothing more than a bad chimney fire that dropped burning fragments onto the floor. Perhaps even a bird's nest falling down the chimney. It must have been smoldering for some time before it caught fire."

It took almost a further ten minutes and much water to be sure that they could save the structure. Most of the fire damage had been confined to just two rooms, one downstairs and the other directly above it, with some damage to ceiling and walls. The fire had smoldered for long enough to give everyone time to get out before it began to erupt further, and by then, there were enough people from the nearby village to lend a hand and get water onto the situation.

Once there were men inside to receive buckets of water that could be better used effectively, their reports indicated that damage seemed to be confined mostly to the chimney surrounds and from smoke which was rapidly clearing.

"That was a lucky escape, sir." Thomas stood beside him.

"Yes, it was."

"Squire brought all of his men over when they saw the glow of a fire from the top of the chimney and through a window where there should have been none, and then smoke starting to get thicker and heavier. Never thought I'd live to see the day he might be of help to this family, but without him, we may not have got ahead of it so easily. They got on top of it fast enough! I think they've gone now except for a couple of men and the squire himself. I told 'em we could keep an eye on everything now, though how we'll go forward from this for a while, I do not know. But we will. Quite a mess to clean up and repairs to make! I doubt anyone could live here easily for a while, for there'll be a devil of a mess from smoke and a little bit of water damage to clean up!"

He took a closer look at William. "You've got an awful bump raised on your forehead, sir."

"Yes. I blundered into too many things in the smoke! I had to break out of a window at the back with Annis. When the smoke clears a little better, as I expect it soon will, we can put a ladder up where the staircase was and can get in there to get enough clothing to get everyone more warmly dressed. It seems like most of the worst effect is from smoke. Thank God everyone got out including the Captain. I expect we can all get ourselves settled in that wing of the house that is untouched by any of this and decide how best to go forward."

"Aye, sir, you could. But I doubt anyone could sleep for a while after something like that on top of all of the rest of it. I know I couldn't. But then it's almost full daylight anyway. I suspect it will take some good men a while to do repairs here, for the beams might need to be replaced—they were already weak with age and beetles boring into them—as well as those windows we broke to get water in and the one you broke to get out. It wouldn't surprise me if the whole chimney needs to be rebuilt too, for I would be surprised if it was not a soot fire that started the whole thing going. And I would not trust it after that without needed work, for the masonry may be rotten with age too. The years are not kind to buildings or people."

"We were lucky, Thomas! It could have been much worse! I'll go and thank the squire and his men for their timely and most-welcome help before they go, and then see what I can do to help out with the human element now. Quite a shakeup to go through a fire like that and, fortunately, no one too badly injured."

"Mrs. Barristow has a twisted ankle out of it. It's all I can say for injuries apart from your head! When that staircase let go, she came down hard and fainted at the pain, but at least it stopped her following you as was her intent, and getting into harm's way again and creating a bigger problem. The girls are all right and so is Annis too from what I can see."

William turned away and checked up on the ladies. They were all grouped together in their nightclothes, though one of the scullery maids had managed to retrieve some coats, and he saw they had been draped in those before he went off in search of the squire, whom he greeted with thanks enough to warm the older man's heart.

"Well what are neighbors for, sir, if not to help out at such a time and glad to do so? I'll leave one of my men close by to keep an eye on things too, for it looks like you'll have your hands full for a while."

"Thank you!" William returned to the small group in the driveway and could hear sounds of human activity in the upstairs of the house to ensure that the fire was truly out, with other sounds from the servant's end of the house, where there had been no damage at all and where a stove was now sending smoke from its legitimate chimney.

"William, you are all sooty!"

"Yes, Sophia, I expect I am." He put his hand upon her head.

"And there is blood on your hand! Again! There is even a bump growing on your forehead and some blood there too!"

"Not too much damage then for what we managed to do, and the cat may have scratched me in his panic. Well, if that is the extent of our injuries; a twisted ankle and a small cut, bumps, scrapes and bruises, and some smoke damage to our persons, then we can count ourselves lucky. I can see that you and Charlotte are not too badly off, for you were out quite soon."

She threw her arms around his waist, caring nothing for his relative state of undress and held him close, taking him quite by surprise and then pulled his head down and planted a kiss on his cheek as she snuggled her head into his shoulder and then kissed the raising bump on his head. He gently held her there.

"Thank you! Mama says you deserve a big hug for all of that, but I thought a kiss was better." She suggested he pick her up so that she might kiss and hug him again, and properly. He did so. "Well then, young lady, a kiss and a hug are entirely appropriate and always welcomed from you."

"And me." Charlotte came over to him and thanked him with a hug around his waist as she held him close. She seemed to have lost much of her shyness around him after that.

"William!" Mrs. Barristow had hobbled over, leaning on a stick that had been furnished for her. She also gently took his head into her hands as she looked deep into his eyes and then folded him into her matronly arms, neither caring that she was but as poorly dressed as they all were, in nothing but nightclothes and draped by a coat.

"I think truly that providence did bring you to us!" Her eyes were wet with tears. "Where would we now be without you being here? I dare not consider. Too much has happened about us of a dreadful nature, and yet, you have been a pillar of strength to all of us throughout and saved us from who knows what?" She saw a carriage stop in the lane outside of the driveway. "Ah! I see the doctor has come at last! Please, sir, see to Annis. She seems to have been affected by this more than the rest of us, if that is possible."

"Yes, ma'am, I shall do so." He walked over to Annis who was now sitting on the edge of the trough, where she had been washing her hands and drinking a little to ease her throat from inhaling some of the acrid smoke.

"And what about you, miss?" He spoke as he gently touched her face. She was still clearing her throat and looking a little the worse for wear, with her hair askew, though they all had hair like that. There was a scared look still in her eyes. "What might I do to help you?" He gently smoothed the hair from her face.

She was sobbing almost out of control at their escape and captured his hand to kiss it tenderly. "I think you deserve a hug and a kiss from me too, sir, but not just at this moment, if you do not mind! I am still shaking." She reached up and held onto his other hand too, trembling and close to tears.

He knelt before her and leaned into her to see into her face. She pulled him closer and held him tightly between her knees. He looked into her eyes with far more showing in his own than might have been expected upon such a short acquaintance, but then they had grown disturbingly close over the last two days. "That was most brave of you, Annis, to go looking for your sisters like that."

She responded quietly and with a hoarseness to her voice as she looked at him. "I would preferably have lost myself in that fire before any of *them*, especially after our last misfortunes, and might have, but for you. But you . . . Thank you!" Her eyes said more than she could put into words.

He knew the feeling, but it did not surprise him, for it had been his own exactly. "You would even have been prepared to shoot a villain like me too at one time, I do not doubt, and for the same protective reason. Most commendable!"

She appeared not to have heard him. "Will Mama and the others be all right?"

"I believe so. The doctor has just arrived and is seeing to your mother even now, and he can pass judgment about her twisted ankle. It does not seem to be any worse injured, so Thomas tells me. Cuts, scrapes, bruises, and twists. If that is the full extent of it, then we were lucky."

"We were lucky *you* were here to give us warning and to get us out. For you did, didn't you? You got us all out. Mama too. I am glad I did not shoot you now!"

"So am I! Fortunately it seems to have been more smoke than fire, and it is mostly out now, so I am afraid I did very little. We still have a home." We! He smiled at his considering it his own home now. "I think you would all have been safe in any case if a little smoke blackened and hoarse with it all."

"No! Without your warning I don't think it would have finished as it did, for it would not have been discovered so quickly, and the fire would have been worse, and there may have been no recovery from that! I overheard Thomas saying as much to mama."

His head sank momentarily onto her lap as a sudden dizzy moment overcame him. She held his head there and supported him as it seemed he might fall over.

He soon raised his head. "I am sorry. I felt dizzy for a moment." He sat back hard onto the ground in front of her, still unsteady as he tried to support himself and closed his eyes against the pain as she leaned forward and held his upper arm, concern for him written all over her face.

She looked closely at him. "But Sophia was right. You do have a bloody hand and a horrendous bump raising above your eyes. No wonder you almost fell! Oh! Why did I not see it before? The skin is even split a little. Here we are thinking only of ourselves, and you are injured yet again on our behalf. You also cut yourself on the window getting me and the Captain out. Well we are both already damp and grubby, so it can make little difference now. No, do not try to get up. If you have got over your dizzy spell, you can sit there while I bathe your brow and rinse off your hand, and you can hold onto me for support. There is light enough now to see what I need to do. We should get the doctor to see to you too when he has finished with Mama, for you seem as badly injured as anyone, if not the worst."

She sat herself on the ground in front of him with her legs over the top of his and her knees on either side of him to give him support. She gave no thought to how their wet nightclothes were clinging closely to them both, nor how indecorous their position might appear to others, and pulled his head down toward her, placed his free hand upon her shoulder to give him more support, and then picked his bloody hand up and dabbed gently at its lacerated palm with a cloth dampened in the trough overflow, keeping away from the open cut as she did so. "We do not have any hot water at the moment to wash it off better I am afraid, though there soon will be, and then I shall see that there is no wood or glass in it and get you bound up a little until the doctor can see to it."

She reached out and retrieved a basket of wrappings, which had been placed within reach for her use by Sophia, and changed her position to kneel before him. She moved closer into him, not caring how anything might look to others, and sat back on her heels as she took his hand and put it into her lap as she looked it over carefully and dabbed at it a little more. She saw that he had his eyes closed, probably against the pain from his head. "It is a nasty little gash, but I do not see wood or glass in it." She then surprised him by putting his hand up to her mouth and gently letting her tongue touch the wound several times and then licking at it gently as she looked into his face. His eyes were open now. He flinched at the most personal, even intimate aspect of it initially. "No. There is no glass there, or I would have felt it with my tongue. That is the way Mama is able to feel for such things if they cannot be seen. It may sting a little at first. I hope it does not shock you!" She licked at it again.

"Nothing would surprise me now . . . other than the change in myself over the last two weeks!"

His comment was not very clear to her.

"I am also beginning to feel a little better, though I will have a bump the size of a goose egg on my brow very soon if I do not have one already." He touched gingerly at his forehead. "Ouch." He smiled at her and was surprised to find her blushing as she completely refused to avert her eyes from his intense gaze but even returned it. They were sitting far too close together, close enough to feel the heat from each other's legs and even bodies and were not at all suitably dressed for any of this, but they had no choice and neither cared what it might look like to others under the circumstances.

She bandaged him gently and then tied his hand up.

She then surprised him as had her sisters as she reached out and took his head into her hands and pulled him into her, avoiding that tender and swollen part of his forehead and hugged him as the tears ran down her face and then kissed him on his cheek.

"I can do little for that bump other than to bathe it with cold water. That might help a little." She wet down another cloth and then proceeded to wipe around his forehead, staying clear of the raised bruise and the split skin in the middle of it.

She noticed the stubble on his face and had felt it earlier as he had brushed his cheek with her own. "I think we still have a home, so I can think of other things now. You will need to shave soon, William, and with your right hand out of commission and your other injuries, I shall be pleased to do that service for you eventually, if you will not object, but only when there is suitable opportunity, and I see that you also need your hair to be cut. We have been neglecting you dreadfully! I used to cut my father's hair, and I shaved him once or twice when he could not."

"Thank you. I fear that I would be likely to cut my throat if I tried to shave with my left, and as unsteady as I am likely to be for a while, but there is no hurry. We can deal with those things after we are able to decide what needs to be done to give us a home back. I doubt society is missing my carelessly coifed or un-groomed presence any."

She struggled to her feet and then helped him rise also. He was still a little unsteady.

Thomas approached. "We've got your clothes ready, miss, and others for your sisters. They were in the closet or drawers and do not smell obviously of smoke. There was also some still drying in the washhouse, so that's clean too. They will be properly aired out in but a few minutes, I would say, for there is a good fire going in the stove now. After that, Mrs. Rogers says you can all change out of your damp nightclothes in the summer kitchen before you catch a death of cold, and she would like you there now to get out of this morning dampness and off the wet grass.

"We are bringing your clothes down too, sir. Your room escaped most of the smoke. The main damage seems to be to the parlor and the dining room and some of the upstairs rooms where the smoke seemed thickest. The rest is water damage and a few windows gone, but that other end of the house and the back wing is just a little smoky."

Annis took him by the arm. "Come, William. You are shivering as we are. You need to get yourself dried out in a warm kitchen too."

"But I should not, if you and the girls will be changing."

"What! Suddenly shy sir? You are as cold and as wet as we are, so the need is there. Besides, as you earlier said, you are now family. I think you have persuaded me of that now by your unselfish acts. We will trust you to close your eyes again."

"Trust! A very dangerous sentiment that, and no fun at all!"

"Yes, I see you are obviously recovering!" Annis took his hand. "I doubt that they will care overmuch after what you did for them. Well, Sophia won't, nor Charlotte either, and why should I care? We would none of us be here but for you. Besides, I will have you by the stove to get warm, for you are shivering too, and you will be facing away from everyone!"

She led him into the kitchen, where there was a large stove radiating heat into the furthest corners of the small room and sat him by the stove, throwing out its heat. He heard them changing behind him. He sat there with his eyes closed, not from any sense of protecting anyone's modesty, but as it tended to alleviate some of his own personal discomfort which, fortunately, was beginning to lessen as he became warmer.

After the girls had left and the doctor had seen to him and given a few words of praise to Annis's handiwork, which he felt he could not improve upon except for the application of a little powder, which stung as it bit into the wounds, William washed in the basin of warm water left for him and dressed slowly and thoughtfully. He turned over various possibilities in his mind before he pulled on his boots and went off into the morning air to inspect as much of the damage to the house as he could see in daylight. Inside, the damage was not extensive, confined as it was to part of one wing. Thomas was right about beams needing to be replaced and the chimney rebuilt. It seemed likely that the floor and other parts would benefit from being repaired and replaced too. It would not harm to do a thorough inspection from top to bottom, but that could come later. The house would be a mess for some time and would need several days of cleaning and repair where the family had lived, though the servants' quarters had not been damaged.

He knew what he would suggest to Mrs. Barristow. If she agreed, then the servants could continue living there and doing what they would normally have been involved with to keep the animals looked after and the garden and house tended to, but with fewer persons to look after if the family were not there. The diminution in their labor from *that*, would be more than made up for by the suddenly augmented wash load that they had inherited and the need to clean up and down, and inside and out, more extensively. Major repairs were also needed, for it was an old house that had settled in some strange ways over the years, which was one reason why the stairs had collapsed. He would see to that himself too.

Chapter XXV

Change of Plans and Preparations!

William and Thomas conducted an extensive evaluation of that end of the house where the most damage had been done and were both of the opinion that some considerable effort would be involved in making the necessary basic repairs. William was also of the opinion that if one went to the trouble to bring masons and carpenters in, that they should see what they might be able to do to correct decades, if not a hundred years of gradually deteriorating floors, walls, and windows that had been worked upon piecemeal as the need became evident. Those earlier repair efforts had never really addressed deeper-seated problems but had merely covered them up. The roof also needed attention, for some of the timbers there had relaxed more than was desirable. A larger need for focused effort was now all too obvious.

William went searching for Mrs. Barristow when he had formulated his own ideas as to what was needed and how it should be done. He found her in the washhouse with Molly, trying to deal with a mound of smoke-damaged clothing and bedding materials. They obviously did not waste any time bemoaning their suddenly changed state.

"Mrs. Barristow, I think it would be difficult to assume that we can just pick up where we were last evening and continue to live here, for there is now the need for some long overdue work to bring it all back as it should be." She listened to what he was saying, with a sinking heart. "If you do not mind, I can easily see to that work going forward. In the meantime, we can all of us remove to my property, Brooklands, if you do not object, until repairs have been made here." She began to see things more optimistically at that, for there would undoubtedly be other good things come out of such a relocation as a complete family, but she said nothing. "If we were to stay here, we would only be severely underfoot and in their way of that effort. Without us to look after, the servants would also be able to concentrate on what needs to be done rather than be fussing about us and our needs. My home is about an hour's drive from here, and we can stay there until the renovations are completed. I am not sure how long they may take, but I doubt that so many of us being here would help that effort to go forward."

She listened to him as he explained what was likely to be needed and how it would benefit from being thoroughly inspected and gone over by someone who knew what they were doing. "I could also send my late father's carpenters and masons over to see to what needs to be done and to get on with it, as they have a lot of experience in renovating such structures and doing it with expedition. From what I saw, there is nothing that cannot be fixed and done better than before."

She was obviously not averse to any of what he suggested. "You would do all of this for us, sir, on top of what you have already done?" She sounded a little surprised but then realized that she really should not be, for when had he ever responded in any way that was not entirely in their best interests?

"Willingly, ma'am. I have even begun to feel that Underby is as much home to me as anywhere. I am also finding that I would very much like to be of help to a family that seems to have unreservedly invited me into its own existence. I would like to be able to repay that in some measure, if you do not object?"

What he suggested was not at all unwelcome, for it might mean that they would all be able to remain together for much longer, and time was on her side with at least one thing she wanted to see unfold. "Why would I object to such a sensible suggestion? Though you have more than amply repaid us in every way with everything that you have done for us to distract us and protect us all. You are right. We would probably be in the way if we were to stay." Yes, it fitted in quite well with other personal and intimate progressions she had gradually been privileged to observe between William and Annis over the last few days and even more obviously in the last few hours.

He was relieved that she so readily accepted his suggestion. "Over the last week or more, I have never felt so useful or welcomed or contented as I have been in being here and being of assistance, despite the initial tragedy that drew me here. Besides, my own family appears to have forgotten I exist, apart from my sister."

She put a hand on his arm. "By accident, William, not by intent I am sure, and they would soon have expected you to return to your own home! Now you can, but with an entourage of helpless and dependant women! Your mother and sister were both excited at the prospect of having you come home, and we have diverted you from that for too long now. But I must go and let the girls know. They will be happy for the adventure and to be relieved of having to deal with this, as I will be. I am sure that Mrs. Rogers and Molly will be equally happy if we were to go too, for their workload will be suddenly lightened in one direction at least."

Within minutes of finding out this plan—a solution to their immediate difficulties—the fire was forgotten, and the girls were excitedly packing what they might need. The old staircase had been dismantled almost immediately, and a ladder had replaced it to the upper floor so that whatever they might need could be passed down to be packed away if it were not too smoke-damaged.

William went off to find Thomas to let him know what he planned on doing and letting him know that sometime later that day or perhaps within a day or so, his own men would arrive with instructions to do whatever needed to be done. His suggestions, help, and even direction would be most useful in that way, for he would know where wood or other building materials might be locally available and at what price, and which local craftsmen had skill enough to be able to contribute in a meaningful way to the effort. His familiarity with the house and its vagaries would also come in useful, for they would be under his direction if it were needed.

It soon became clear, as the steadily increasing pile of trunks and boxes mounted outside of the house, that they would need a separate cart to transport them.

Annis approached him. "You appear to have solved yet another problem for us, William. But if we are to travel to your home soon, then I would not like you to present an appearance that might suggest that we had neglected you or treated you so roughly. If you do not object, I should shave you now before we change into our travelling clothes, or you may present less of an appearance than might be desirable on your own estate, along with all of your cuts and bruises and bumps. They will wonder what we might have done to you to have inflicted such injuries, and that would not allow us to appear in such a good light at first, as we should."

He smiled at her. "I don't think you have much to worry about, Annis! More likely they will recognize the return of someone who seemed to be forever in such dire straits, so I doubt they would find it in any way out of the ordinary and would not judge you adversely for it in any case."

"And if you do not object or panic at the thought, you would not suffer from having your hair cut too. I told you that I would do it for you." She smiled at him in a way that he was pleased to see, considering how bedraggled, miserable, wet, and even hopeless, they had all been just a short time earlier.

She misinterpreted the look on his face. "Oh, do not fear, I used to cut my father's hair and even my sisters' too, and I did not do so bad a job of it. However, Sophia seems to be unable to sit still for long enough for me to finish it, so do not rush to judgment of my skill based upon her appearance, though I see Charlotte was able to correct what I missed."

He smiled and rubbed his chin, feeling the stubble. "Yes, I expect I do not present even the superficial appearance of a gentleman at the moment. I don't much feel like one, for I have also to wash more of the grime, and smell of smoke off me and out of my hair and will need to change into something better. But a shave first would be a good plan. I shall be happy in that case, Annis, to submit to your wielding the razor and scissors about me, for I am not in a fit state to do it for myself." He held up his bandaged hand.

"I think I am beginning to recover nicely, except for this tender egg upon my forehead, and I am less light-headed than I was, but I dare not shave with my left." He looked about, taking in the changes that had already been started. "Besides, there is little more that needs to be seen too here now. Thomas and others can do a much better job of it, than I might. All of the baggage seems to be piling up nicely, and it will soon be time to put the horses too. Everyone else except us seems to be well enough dressed already to travel. They will soon be impatient to go with us ready or not. Where will you have me sit for you?"

"We can go into the parlor at the far end of the house where we all changed. We will be out of everyone's way, and the sun will shine nicely in there to give me light."

She took him by the arm and led him off through the kitchen and into the end parlor that was used by the servants. At her instruction, he moved a chair over into the window area while she saw to getting hot water, towels, soap, and the razor that her father had used to shave himself.

She sat him down, and then, a little self-consciously unbuttoned the top part of his shirt and moved it away from his neck, folding it under and out of the way. She blushed a little as she touched him in such a closely familiar way and felt his eyes upon her. As she caught his glance, she saw that he was smiling at her shyness, and caused her to blush a little more, for she had never attended so closely to any man before other than her father, and she found it strangely exciting. She worked up a lather in her father's shaving cup and liberally applied the soap over his face and neck. She put the brush aside and then picked up the razor and sat down on the window embrasure in front of him. "You will need to come forward with your chair and bring your legs to either side of mine to get close enough."

He did so and then leaned forward toward her, placing his hands upon her waist at first, as she held his head steady with one hand and stretched the skin with her thumb while she began to gently shave him.

He studied her face as she concentrated on the delicate act of shaving him while not cutting him.

She was conscious of his legs pressing on either side of hers and of his hands now resting gently upon her legs but decided to say nothing, though she found it strangely pleasurable and welcome that he could touch her in that familiar way. They could not easily have done it any other way.

"You are making me nervous, sir." She looked at him, almost severely, with a gentle blush upon her cheeks. Her heart was pounding too, and sure that he might be able to hear it!

"How so? Am I being too familiar?" He took his hands from her legs.

"Not that!" She stopped shaving him, and her eyes met his in a look of censure. She found he was smiling at her in a most disturbing way. "You are staring at me, and I may become unnerved enough to become careless! I would not like to cut you."

"Yes, I am staring. I am sorry, but I cannot help myself, for you are directly in front of me, and you are in control of where my head is to be positioned. I cannot avoid looking at you with you so close to me, and I need to rest my hands somewhere. Besides, you are far too beautiful to ignore!"

She blushed at that outrageously forward compliment. She knew that at this moment in time, he was being truthful with her but decided to respond in a lighthearted manner. "Is this how you deal with all young ladies you rescue?"

"I have not been in the habit of rescuing any so far since my return, other than you and your sisters and mother and before that . . . no matter!" He continued to stare into her eyes. You have the clearest brown eyes—yes, brown eyes with little flecks of yellow in them and the longest, most delicate eyelashes that I had not noticed before. Your eyebrows are . . ."

"Too thick and heavy for my taste!"

"But not for mine!" He slowly reached up and gently traced one with his finger. She did not pull away or comment upon it. "They are in keeping with the rest of your features—striking, intense, straightforward; as befits your no-nonsense personality, but they are also more wonderfully feminine and even delicate than I should admit to you. Not thick! Nothing like mine!" He was right. His were much thicker and heavier, but then he was a man! "You are also smiling more than you did, so I expect your thoughts are more happy now, rather than dwelling on what has just gone on around us, and I like that, for it causes a small dimple here." He gently touched her cheek. "Your lips . . . are most . . . kissable!" He sighed. "But then we already knew that when I have given in to temptation on several occasions now. But I had better not dwell on those as I would like. But oh! how I would like to dwell on them!"

She took his hands and replaced them on her legs where they had been. "I think your hands are safer here and likely to be less disturbing to me!"

He could see that she seemed confused and unsure of what he was about in his present relaxed and expansively pleasant and dreamlike mood. "If you prefer it, I will close my eyes yet again in what may be a delicate situation and not discompose you with unseemly compliments that might be taken amiss or be suspect, to interfere further with your concentration."

She smiled pleasantly "You do not need to close your eyes now. You were right. I was smiling, absentmindedly I think. My thoughts were more agreeable and pleasant than I might have expected them to be after what we just came through and faced with such polished dissimulation from you. Yet we are all safe and unharmed, thanks to you yet again! Circumstances have certainly changed our lives in so many ways and not in quite as bad a direction as they seemed to have been headed, and so easily *could* have done! But no, I should not command you not to look at me, even so closely, and noticing such things as you do. It is a little disturbing and intense, but strangely pleasurable—though I know that I should not admit to that, I think—for you say the nicest things to go with it, and you even sounded sincere about it too!"

"I am sincere, Annis!"

"I believe you, William." She looked directly into his eyes and he could see that she did. "No, I shall have to get used to it, I expect. I hope that does not sound too vain! Besides, you pay outrageous compliments that any woman would be most happy to hear, even if they are not entirely true."

"They are all true!" he protested. "I can add to them if you wish?"

She continued shaving him but did not deter him from continuing his analytical process, though his mind was off in another direction by then.

"Now why did I not meet you five years ago? If I had, my mother and father would never have been able to send me abroad without my returning immediately."

She flashed a glance at him and saw that he had a somber look in his eyes and was all seriousness itself and was not behaving flippantly with her. "Just as well we did not, William. I was only sixteen then and not as I am now, but you *would* have fallen in love with Bella as was intended. Perhaps there would even have been children running about the place to play with Sophia."

"Yes. What a strangely haunting and pleasurable thought—what might have been! I am sure any of my family looking in on me now would be unable to believe any of what I am either saying or dreaming. Contemplating children? But that did not happen five years ago. Instead, I was sent off." They were not pleasant memories for him, but he soon recalled the present, and where he was, and what was happening to him. "I have difficulty believing that you would be any less beautiful or less poised or mature even at sixteen. I think I would like to have met you then!"

"I do not feel very mature, even now. I still am sometimes very stupid where . . ." She paused and looked at him, remembering most vividly her extreme anger with him just two days ago.

"Do not be concerned, Annis. I may be a poor kind of gentleman, but I am still cognizant of what is expected of me no matter how I may test those boundaries from time to time in moments of weakness."

"I meant . . . about other things."

He appeared not to have heard her. "We all are stupid at times. I am noted for it. In fact, I seem to do at least one stupid thing every single day, so I usually try to get it out of the way before anyone else is out of bed to see it and relate it to the world."

She laughed. "I do not think we have seen any evidence of any of *that* since you have been here. Far from it! You have been very supportive of us all and very protective, though it took me some time to recognize that. Had you not been here this morning, I am not sure how we might have fared." She looked at him directly at that moment, and he began to feel how she might be thinking from the way her eyes shone onto him with great tenderness, even promise, and undoubtedly gratitude. He began to feel excited himself, and the blood to race in his veins and pound in his head, at what he saw openly revealed there in her look for some moments before she averted her eyes from his equally intense look. She had looked upon him that same way by the trough as she treated his minor injuries. He had liked it then. He liked it more now. He found he had to close his eyes for a moment or two or risk reaching out to touch and caress her and perhaps of offending her. Yet he had taken much greater liberties with her just yesterday, and he was still here and was still being smiled upon!

"I will now need you to hold still and to stretch your upper lip for me as I get under your nose." She put her hand under his chin to lift his head gently and then unconsciously stretched her own upper lip in the same way as she concentrated on doing that delicate operation without cutting him as he continued to look into her eyes and upon her face. He could not help smiling at her intense concentration. His hands were now on her waist once more as he sat more upright and leaned closer into her. His hands were trembling. He hoped she might not notice, but she did, and thought she might know why. She had learned much of this man in the last few days and was well aware that she excited him in ways that she had not thought possible in any man.

She inspected what she had done and then lifted his chin higher to get at the difficult to reach hairs under that and down onto his neck as she carefully began to maneuver the razor.

"And now I suggest we do not become argumentative, or that you distract me more than you are doing already, for I have your life just a whisker away—so to speak—from being ended!"

"Then I shall remain silent and not provoke you with asking for a kiss." He spoke gently as she tilted his head even further but did not break his mischievous gaze from her.

"William!" She hesitated at his outrageous remark and then smiled at him before she continued to wield the razor most carefully and with intense concentration down his neck and under his chin.

"There! All done!" She closed the razor and wiped the soap off his face with a damp cloth and then dried it a little with a towel.

"I would like to thank you for doing that for me. You were most gentle and thorough."

"You would like to thank me? How?" She already suspected how and was not about to object.

He had a mischievous look on his face and had his hands on her waist now to hold her still. She knew exactly what he intended and did not draw back from it. He leaned over and gently kissed her on the lips.

She blushed red as her eyes opened wide, despite knowing what would unfold. But it had been a different kind of kiss than the one she had expected. It had not been brief but had lingered gently, and had been neither brotherly nor stolen unexpectedly. It had been a lover's kiss—tender, warm, and long. Though she had known what he intended, she was still taken by surprise at the difference that it had upon her, for she felt some alarm at the new and heightened sensations suddenly coursing through her veins and unnerving her from her usual composed state. She accidentally knocked over the shaving cup, which she had placed on the table beside her. She had not felt quite that way when he had earlier kissed her, though they had been somewhat briefer and more brotherly kisses—at least that was how *she* had regarded them, though thinking back upon it, she had no idea what a brotherly kiss might feel like, yet they had all been quite pleasant. That last kiss, however, had seemed different. Very different! The difference, she began to realize, was in herself and not in anything he had done differently, though it had been a longer kiss. She began to blush uncontrollably and to feel suddenly overheated and agitated. She chuckled nervously at the changes she began to feel within herself.

"If you do things like that, William, I will be so unnerved as to be unable to cut your hair!"

He spoke very softly as he looked into her face and eyes. "I would like to do much more than that, Annis!" He remembered where he was, and that he must behave himself. "Alas, that is my hard-earned and scurrilous reputation speaking and beginning to surface again! You bring out the best in me and also the worst! You have the most kissable lips that a man might ever encounter in his entire life, and I would like to kiss you again."

"Oh!" She did not pull back but waited and even seemed to encourage him.

"But I must not!" His head sank to her shoulder and then lifted again as he looked into her eyes with a look almost of apology for his tormenting dereliction and admission.

She felt a momentary spasm of disappointment. He seemed sad.

"It appears that there is far too much trust placed in me by all of you, so I must be a gentleman, when I have never felt less like being a gentleman in my whole life than at this one moment. Despite the need to be more of a gentleman at this time than I think I have ever been before!"

He looked at her with a puzzled look on his face and smiled wryly. "I hope that made more sense to you than it might have done. I must put the safety and welfare of others and of one other especially, before my own very selfish passions and desires."

She found his mood to be strangely sober and serious and, at the same time, very intriguing and not at all unwelcome or even threatening to her safety. This was an entirely new William to her, though he had been that way, a little, the day before. Thought of that previous interlude excited her even more now than it had then.

"Oh! Why could I not have met you years ago?" He sighed but then was surprised by her leaning into him and returning his kiss and dwelling there for a few moments herself, looking deeply into his eyes before she retreated to get the scissors to start on his hair. He sat back, surprised himself, at the sudden turn of events.

She was conscious that he watched every move that she made, and now, she did not mind it in the slightest. She felt as though she were walking on air and was being openly admired—perhaps even loved—in a way that she had never experienced before, and she liked the feeling. She was also suddenly conscious again of her own woman's body—it's intoxicating power over this man and the interest he showed in everything about her when he was watching her. She was suddenly more happy and contented than she had ever been in her life before, despite their recent tragic losses, and began to recognize why.

But there was also a sobering part to it all, hovering like a rather large thundercloud creeping up over the horizon. It was all happening far too soon and far too quickly. There were so many things he did not know and so many difficulties that she could not tell him about just yet. So many difficulties! Among them there was that horrible letter to grapple with. *That* would need to cleared out of the way somehow, with all of those dreadful allegations of outrageous events spoken of and referred to. It could not all be a lie, and yet, the man sitting in front of her was nothing like the person portrayed in that letter. Just a few days ago, she had believed only the worst of him and was quite ready to shoot him if it would have protected her family from what she believed of him.

And all of the time, he had sought only to protect them from their real enemies. He had also saved all of their lives, she was convinced of that, with no thought of danger to himself. If there had been the luxury of time to allow everything to unfold more slowly, there would not have been so many things so poorly understood or done so clumsily or with such little consideration for their after effects. She suddenly felt a little nauseated at the thoughts she had. She was also overwhelmed for a moment by great sadness, ready to break down into tears, but held those emotions at bay and even managed to smile at him from behind a sudden haze of tears.

He did not understand her mood, but accepted that it was tied up with the broader circumstances of the last few days. He doubted he would ever be able to understand the ever-changing moods of women. One just had to accept and to forgive them, no matter what!

Neither of them seemed aware that both Charlotte and her mother had seen into the servants' parlor as they had walked about the herb garden, her mother leaning on Charlotte's arm and walking with the aid of a stick. They had both of them, by accident of timing and position, seen the gentle interchange and even the exchange of kisses, and they had paused briefly.

"He was looking at her the same way before too, Mama, even as she looked after his hand at the trough and neither of them dressed properly nor fully covered! Those wet things clung to them both most revealingly I thought. It was almost as though Annis had nothing covering her, and then him . . . there . . . rather obvious! They seemed to think that there was no one else looking on, but we all were."

"I saw it too, my dear! There was little that could have been done about it, and there was nothing wrong in that! There was no one else at that moment as far as they were concerned. As for not dressed properly, we were all of us in our nightclothes at that moment, though ours were dry! Of course we were not dressed properly! He had just pulled us all out of a flaming house where we might still be but for him! We may not have been as well covered as we might have liked, but he did not care for that and neither did we at the time. At least Annis had her priorities correct, no matter how revealing the situation might have been, for he was as ill covered as the rest of us, and she did not care, but looked after him as she should."

"There, you saw it too, as I did! They were sitting very close together and her with her legs over the top of his at first, and they were touching each other's heads and faces and who knows what else in a most familiar way! She also had her nightdress up above her knees and wide open at the neck, for all that difference *that* made, considering what she had already revealed, and was leaning into him. What he did not see where he was sitting! For even I could see, and I was much further away! He was sitting almost the same way, and . . . he left no doubt to anyone, including Annis, that he was a man! Well, I shall say no more! I shall sketch it all from memory and surprise everyone!"

"You should not, my dear! This is not usual of you, Charlotte to be so prudish! Of course he is a man. He cannot help that any more than your father could, and you saw him that way often enough when you blundered in on us as you often did, and William had no choice about how he was dressed in that wet covering any more than we did! Why, you used to breeze about the house *and* the yard completely naked when you were little less than Sophia's age if the mood took you, and there were no men about other than your father. Sometimes even if there were too, on occasion, for your uncle was there at times! You had no shyness then! We used to laugh about it, for it was all innocent enough. You seem to have forgotten that, but I haven't. I am just glad that Sophia did not find out about it and decide to emulate you in that broader way. Though even if she did, I doubt that William would be put out by it."

"He isn't now, and she does that! She often parades about without a stitch of clothing in his presence when she is getting herself ready for bed. Annis is not six years old mama but twenty-one, and she is most well developed in a way that is likely to attract any man, for I notice that they all seem to gravitate to that kind of thing. And the more that is on display and advertised, the stronger the attraction, as Jennifer Bishop last spring demonstrated at the village ball. And I have seen others admiring Annis that way too, for her breasts are . . . well, they are more prominent even than Jenny Bishop's! William is not immune to it either, for he often admires her in that way and was staring intently at her and down her nightdress as she knelt before him."

"I believe you were mistaken there, my dear! I think his thoughts were elsewhere. In any case, there is nothing wrong with being admired in that way by certain men. Beauty of the kind that she seems now to be becoming aware of rather late in her life, though I am glad of that, should be admired. A young woman is most fortunate if she has those advantages of a good face and figure, delightful complexion, and good sense. Annis has all—most—of those, I am glad to say!" Her thoughts became a little less charitable. "So do you normally! I do not know what has come over you at this time!" She began to wonder if Charlotte was not suffering from a touch of jealousy.

"As for William, he seems mature well beyond his years and well able to handle such minor deficiencies in stride, I expect, without betraying anything improper, even at such an awkward moment. I doubt there are many things that would embarrass him. Not even the dress you have on at this moment either, miss, which shows more of you than it might, although it is not one you would normally choose to wear."

Her daughter blushed. "Well I know he wouldn't be embarrassed, for he wasn't. Not the way he was looking at her as they sat together nor she at him either, so who knows what they may have been up to earlier, for he seems to have no shyness about ill-clad women or girls."

"You do not know anything of the kind Charlotte, and it is unkind in you to say so!"

"Perhaps, Mama! Yes, I know I should not say that, for he had no thought for himself in doing those things he did. But I know what I have seen. He had been here no more than just a few days when Sophia insisted that he be allowed to help Annis and I bathe her. I expected he would gracefully decline, but he didn't! We could not refuse without creating a stir from Sophia and putting ourselves in a lesser light, regardless of how improper it was. He regarded it as a rare privilege, it seems. He was very good about it and not at all embarrassed, as we both expected he would be at first and then tactfully withdraw in embarrassment. But he was not at all embarrassed! I think both Annis and I were both more embarrassed than he was, for there she was busy looking for freckles all over her body and pointing them out proudly to him, no matter where they were. Precocious child! We nearly died of embarrassment ourselves at the little wretch while he just smiled at us as though he knew what we were going through!"

"Yes, Annis told me of that, and you were there too, if I recall. I had a laugh about it, and how I might laugh about anything at all at such a time as that seems most unusual."

"Then what did she do but catch him in his bath in the washhouse and decided to help him too, for she boasted of it afterward at the supper table and broadcast to the house that he had no freckles anywhere on his body that she could see, for boys are rarely kissed by fairies. But that it was difficult to decide because he had so much hair on his legs and everywhere!"

"No!" Her mother had not heard of that episode.

"Yes! He didn't even blush, but took more of the potatoes and just smiled as he usually does."

"I expect we must be thankful that there were not more detailed revelations after that! But how did you know of any of that, miss? Unless you were spying on him yourself!"

"I was sketching, and I followed Sophia's voice and then stayed out of sight. But he does have a lot of hair!"

"There! You spied on him too! I hope he does not find that out. That was most improper of you! As for Sophia . . . at that age there is no false modesty or even shyness once they get to know you. Fortunately, she has no shyness that way for she saw her father and me both without clothing often enough, as you all did, and I doubt that William is any different. Though I do hope she is careful about what she might disclose about that. But if I did not know you better, my girl, I might almost think you were jealous! Since when did you become prudish, for you are sounding more that way than I ever might have thought possible? We did not raise you that way! You never were before, skittering about the house half dressed yesterday before breakfast and even in front of William too, and at your age. You showed enough of yourself at that moment, never mind criticizing Annis under more needful circumstances, though he managed to ignore you!"

"Mama, I am *not* jealous. Honestly. I am not a prude either, but I did not know William was sitting there. I had seen him ride off earlier on some errand, and I did not know he had returned. I did ignore him. I had to! He ignored me, for *he* had to!

What could he have said? What could *I* have said? I was not about to attract attention to myself by rushing off clutching my clothing to me and making a fuss, for I was still well enough covered. I don't think he even noticed, for he had eyes only for Annis, much like now!" She sounded disappointed. "However, I cannot think of him as a brother, for I know as little of him as anyone does, and I doubt I can see him as a father figure either. He is too close to my own age for that. I shall reserve judgment. I don't yet know how I see him, though I do not think that he is a danger to us, as I know Annis first feared when she read that letter."

Her mother did not need to ask what letter she referred to.

"And I do not judge him poorly either, Mama. I like William, and yet how fickle men can be, it seems, with their emotions, for he married Bella just a few days ago."

Her mother turned on her. "*Fickle?* He is nothing of the kind! Do not think such *nonsense*! Well, I suppose we cannot avoid such discussions forever, no matter how painful they still are."

Charlotte regretted saying what she had said and raising that other specter once more.

"No, Charlotte. Had he known Bella for some years before they were married, I would also worry, I think, over this sudden display of . . . partiality toward Annis. But he did not. He is as much a stranger to all of us as we must be to him, but a suddenly appreciated and much valued stranger who deserves a place in all of our hearts. If he has fallen in love with Annis and she with him, and I think he has—though you shall not repeat that to anyone—what kind of a foolish mother would I be to find fault with *that* after what has happened to us? It is not as though he were firmly married to Bella in the usual way. It was more a marriage of convenience for us and inconvenience to him, and too soon ended, unfortunately, or who knows what might have been possible?"

She cautioned her daughter. "Now Charlotte, you shall say nothing of this to anyone of what I disclosed to you about any of this or what we have seen. I doubt that we will lose William so very soon now, if at all. At least, I think I now dare to hope not. I rather think he has found at least one very good reason to want to stay close to us. Despite our recent tragic losses, I begin to feel hope again at last. It is a feeling I had not expected to ever experience again for some considerable time."

"You are right Mama. I think she is in love with him too, and I did not think that possible even just a day or so ago considering what she had said of him." She strolled along beside her mother. "Then what can be done about it, Mama? I feel sorry for them both, especially if he is sincere, for he is a recent widower."

"He is sincere!" Her mother sounded convinced of it. "There is also nothing that I can do about it! Nothing you can do either except stay out of their way! Annis is of age. But he is also a man, and probably inclined to rush things forward as they will, if given any encouragement—fortunately—*if* she gives him any, and I think she may just have done so. Though I have seen no sign of it getting out of hand just yet, as it probably will, if we stay back a little. Men have little patience with courtship or niceties of that kind—your father didn't—but always wanted to rush the gate, once I first pointed the way. Once they find out what it is they want, there can sometimes be no stopping them if there is any—even the slightest, encouragement." She sighed at that memory.

"When I first noticed how he looked at her—*really* looked at her—I was so much shook up that I almost dropped my cup. He did not see me watching him, fortunately, but he could not take his eyes off her. I *did* spill it onto myself, and it was very hot. That was in the parlor on the second evening he was here and after dinner. His eyes followed her everywhere. She was conscious of it but did not like it at the time, for she had determined to take him in dislike. She accepts, and likes it well enough now I think, for she is certainly conscious of it. It took her long enough, however! She caught him once or twice admiring her those first few days. All he did was to smile at her, and she blushed as red as a beet and even scowled at him once! I could have boxed her ears over that!

"I could not believe what I was seeing so soon after welcoming him into our midst, for he looked at her as your father first looked at me—enough to set all the alarm bells ringing as though no one else was in the entire room, and I assure you that there were at least sixty people there. I was lost at that moment, and so was he. I never thought to see that again. My heart can almost sing again." Her eyes misted over. "Come, we should not pry. I almost think I feel jubilant enough to . . . to hope again. But no, I must take care. We shall not spy upon them."

"Yes, Mama, you should be careful. The doctor told you not to walk so very much and to take care for a few days."

"But I will take you to task on one thing, Charlotte. If you think that he should not pay attention to Annis because he married Bella, you would be wrong to do so. He did not know anything of Bella, even as he married her, but it had to be done for our sake, or so we believed. Oh, I hope we did the right thing there!"

The strolled further afield. "But we are in mourning, Mama! William did marry Bella and then was made a widower within an hour of that. I do not see how anyone can easily overcome all of that and *then* turn his affection as he seems to have done—even if he did not know Bella at all—onto her younger sister! Or so soon!"

"Oh, Charlotte, my love. Hush! Now you are being foolish! There was no affection of that kind to return my dear, for he did not know even the first thing about Bella or even of her existence until he walked through the door on that first night. But that was not his fault, nor anyone else's, but a cruel trick of fate. Love does not work to a schedule either, so get that out of your head. When it strikes, it strikes." It had struck! She knew that.

"We may be in mourning, but life does not stop or is delayed because of someone's passing. They will be well remembered by us for the rest of our lives. Besides, William could have been married to any one of you at that moment, and it would have been the same thing to him. He was helping us out of a most difficult situation, that was all! A situation that actually did not even exist, but we knew none of that until later, for it took the efforts of Mr. Diebold to tell us that. Yet without that, I would not have tried to find him that night, he would not have come and would not be here now, and we . . ." She shook her head, disturbed by those thoughts. "No, I shall not think further about any of that! Providence!

"But yes, the situation is strange in the way it unfolded. Perhaps I should dig out those cards again. They started most of it going. Perhaps with the loss of Bella . . ." She kept the rest of her thoughts to herself, but sometimes, tragedies themselves could have unexpectedly happy outcomes. She could not easily explain what fate had conspired to saddle them with, but this most recent outcome of it was something she had seen with her own eyes, and it had surprised her in a most unexpectedly pleasant and comforting way. "No matter. Love conquers all, my dear. They will find a way, I expect, and I shall neither judge them nor say anything about what we have just seen and neither shall you."

"No, Mama. But perhaps Annis does not know what . . ."

"She has much more than an inkling of it! I could see that much for she was not indifferent to him or pulling away. She may not know the full import of it yet. But she soon will. He will show her soon enough. I think she already knows much more about William and men generally, and what moves them along, than I might have given her credit for, from what we both of us saw of her by the trough just some moments ago, tempting him as she was, and writ clear on her face. She will know how to deal with him and how to respond. At least I hope so. We brought her up properly and gave her good values. I just hope she knows enough to dispense with all of that and put them firmly off to one side when the moment is right."

"Mama! What do you mean?" Her daughter laughed nervously and sounded amazed at what her mother was suggesting, for she was.

"Well, if a woman does not know that sometimes she must sometimes be the aggressor and take the lead, how can she expect to succeed in anything she sets her heart upon? Some men can be so tied up with trying to be proper, that they are obtuse to an extreme degree and unbelievably slow at times for fear of hurting us or even frightening us off entirely. There are times when they can be so frustratingly proper when it is least needed, and they need to be led and shown, though not too obviously! They can also be too fast at others and in need of slowing down, but that is more difficult to do and must be done with care. However, in such matters of the heart, they must believe that they are the instigators. Men think they are the stronger sex, but they are not!" Her eyes sparkled with recollection of her own memories. "A clever woman can take advantage of any man, no matter the circumstance. She just has to decide when and how to do so! Mark my words. The same will happen to you one day."

"But leave William out of your plans!"

"He is not in my plans, Mama, for I have none yet!"

Chapter XXVI

Brooklands

"We entered the gates fully ten minutes ago, Mama, and all I can see are oak and chestnut trees, and a few elms. I still have seen no sign of a house!"

Her mother smiled. She had anticipated this. "Patience, Charlotte, we are almost there. I told you it was a large property."

She was interrupted by her youngest daughter. "Mama! Look!" Sophia pointed. She was the first to see the Mansion of Brooklands nestled in among the trees and surrounded by acres of lawns and flower beds. She and Charlotte, who were facing the horses, seemed almost as excited as each other. "Oh, Mama, it is magnificent! Such a large, white house. Why, there must be hundreds of rooms! It must be easy to get lost in it. So this is where William lives and where we are all to stay?"

"Yes, we are! There are more than fifty rooms my dear, perhaps even as many as a hundred all told, so William says, and I have been in most of them at one time or another when his mother lived here. William is now the master of it all!" *As I was briefly just a short time ago.*

Sophia was bouncing with excitement. "More rooms than at Underby, and undoubtedly all much larger too. I hope I shall be allowed to explore them. I do not know how many rooms *we* had, for I did not count them, but I shall do so in my head before I fall asleep tonight! Oh, Captain Cat would so much have enjoyed it too, but I was not allowed to bring him!" She sounded disappointed.

"Cats need to stay in an area they are familiar with, my dear. The rats and mice do not take a holiday at Underby just because we are absent for a while!"

"Yes. I suppose so."

Annis had held her mother's hand on first seeing the property, and her mother noticed her clasp tighten in some surprise, though she had become more attentive to everything about her as she also took in the extent of the massive estate, for it really had been ten minutes since they had bowled into the driveway. The horses had not only kept up their gentle clip but may also have increased it a little, for they had sensed that they were about to find comfortable shelter and food before they would be returned to Underby with Thomas.

Annis looked at her mother with a strange look on her face. "Having lived in such a fine place, he must have found it very confining to have lived with us as long as he has, for our house is very small by comparison. He must have many servants, so why would he occupy himself almost as a common laborer might, for he did when he was helping Thomas?"

Her mother smiled. She had expected there to be some considerable surprise at what was displayed before them. She spoke so that only Annis might hear her easily. "I expect you will find out eventually, if you have not already, that William is a very different kind of man than the usual run-of-the-mill wealthy landowner. He is not so proud that he will ignore a plea for help or refuse to pitch in to help-out where there is a real need as he did for us. Don't forget that he came to us from the continent and the hardships of war. I doubt that Underby presented anything like hardship for him by comparison to *that*, no matter how he may have lived as a boy and a youth." She paused for moment before she continued. "Another thing you and your sisters need to learn is that a house, even a grand mansion, is not a home without children and love and those in it we can love."

She held her daughter's hand and patted it. "I fear he had a difficult childhood, for his father was a strict naval man, though he loved his son dearly. His mother was a nervous wreck while he was growing up. She still can be if things become a little confusing for her! I like to think that we showed him that we welcomed him into our home, despite all of the difficulties we had, and I believe he appreciated *that* more than anyone else might. Before you take me to task for not telling you more about him, I did not have the time or the inclination, for I had greater concerns, but I did assure you that I did know more of him than you might give me credit for, but you chose not to believe me!"

"But where is William?" Charlotte was looking around to see where he might be. "He was following us!"

"Once we entered the gates, he took a shortcut, my dear, and has arrived a little ahead of us to give notice of our arrival, I expect."

William had indeed arrived some minutes ahead of them and was even then being greeted by a servant who well remembered him.

"Master William!" William took the older man's hand and took in the pleasantly surprised look on his face.

"We saw someone approaching, sir, but did not know it would be you. There is also a carriage following you and another cart some way behind that too. I assume they are of your party?"

"Yes, they are, Jerome. But we have a minute or two before they arrive. Too little time to catch up, but we will do that later. I am so glad to see that you are still here. But then I have only been away five years, and though it seems a lifetime considering where I have been, I suppose it is not so very long. I expected to see you in the London house, but then my mother is in Bath, and I thought you might have accompanied her there even."

Yes, sir, I am still here. I did not accompany your mother. She decided that I should stay here and keep everything in order until she was able to return, or *you* did, and to look after your sister when she was here, and she is here now. We—that is, your sister—expected you last week or even earlier, and the next we heard was of your marriage and then your unfortunate loss, and all at the same time! Too much going on, and too fast!"

"Yes. Bad news always travels fast! As for the carriage and cart, they belong to my late wife's family and are carrying them and their luggage. They will be residing with us for some time. Three delightful ladies and a young girl who will set the place on its ear much as I used to I think!"

A stable hand appeared around the corner of the house and saw to the horse and mule after receiving the usual cautions about stabling arrangements. William and the butler moved over toward the house together, reminiscing in the brief moments they might have until the carriage arrived, and then Jerome would then meet the new guests.

"Your father's death hit your mother very hard, sir, and she did not feel she could stay here in such a large house with no one to talk to or socialize with, being so far from London. I believe she and Lady Seymour have picked up their association once more." He did not give any indication of approving of that. "She needed to be distracted, and with friends and other people about her, and to relax better than she might here. Your sister visits her often wherever she is, except that she can't stand Bath!"

"And you say that Elizabeth is still here?"

"Yes, sir. I believe she might be aware of your arrival by now. Excuse me, sir, I need to assist the ladies." They both moved out to meet the carriage and to assist the ladies out of it.

William greeted them all as though he had not seen them for a week or more. "Welcome to Brooklands, ma'am. You must please feel free to make yourselves at home, and we will see to getting you settled in shortly once I learn the state of affairs with our unexpected arrival. I think Elizabeth may be aware of our having arrived, so she should also join us shortly."

He turned back to Jerome. "I know we look a little under the weather and may even smell of smoke, but we had to quit Underby because of a fire—little damage fortunately—and may not have been able to repair the minor deficiencies in ourselves as we might have liked."

Jerome led the way into the house, carrying some of the luggage, followed by William and his guests, who relinquished their coats and bonnets to one of the servant girls, who had been called upon unexpectedly and still had some flour on her apron.

"I am sorry that we have all descended upon you unexpectedly like this, Jerome, but I felt it the best course of action. If we are short on staff for the moment, and I am sure that we must be, then the three girls might share one of the larger bedrooms for this day anyway, and we can get them settled in their own tomorrow."

Jerome helped Mrs. Barristow out of her coat, as the girls got rid of their own or helped each other. "I'll get the housekeeper to see to it, sir. She is still in the house,

I believe, and did not yet head out as she had planned. She will be mightily pleased to see you, Master William."

"And I, her . . . but I would rather not spoil her outing."

"She won't care about that, sir! I know she has much to talk to you about, for as I say, you were expected some time ago. She has been looking for you to arrive any time, and then got news of other things delaying you." He noticed a bandage on William's hand and had earlier noticed a raised bruise upon his forehead. He also saw that the older lady of the party needed assistance by one of daughters to move about on her stick. It may not have been so light an issue as Master William made of it, but then they all seemed healthy enough otherwise.

"No serious injuries, I hope, sir?" He noticed that William had helped the older lady to a chair in the hall to take the weight off her foot. She was obviously favoring it and probably should get it into hot water. He made a mental note to see that a bowl of hot water was brought to her as soon as it might be arranged, and then perhaps a visit to the special bath downstairs that his father had seen constructed to ease his own discomforts in his last year or two."

"Some minor cuts and scrapes, but Mrs. Barristow has a sore ankle where it was twisted during her escape. The doctor said that she will need to rest it for a day or so, and we don't need another doctor to fuss about us. I am not used to giving orders here Jerome, and I would hate to be too brusque with anyone, being used as I am to rough army manners, so I will leave everything for you to organize."

William was relaxed enough in his own setting that he did not seem to notice that he had a rapt audience, where everything he said was being listened to and absorbed most carefully. He treated his butler as though he were a close childhood friend. But then why would he apologize for any possible brusqueness of manner and offending servants when he had never shown either brusqueness or impatience with anyone at Underby, except the Thackerays? But they didn't count.

"I do hope Mrs. Gordon will not feel too put upon too quickly. We still have a cook, do we? Mother didn't take everyone else off with her, did she?"

"We still have Mrs. Abernethy, sir. She was soon made aware of everyone's arrival even as you rode up, and we could see a carriage behind you. We are shorthanded for the moment, but I can send into the village for whatever we might need, and we can soon have other help within an hour or so."

"Obviously, there will be five more for dinner. We require nothing special and will eat downstairs without any formality as I am sure Elizabeth does. No need for any other table staff. None of us was able to eat much of anything today yet. I recall that soup or cold cuts were always available. Fresh bread and cheese sounds very good at this moment after our journey, so we can probably best help ourselves in the kitchen if we will not be underfoot. Mrs. Abernethy is quite capable of putting us out if we become a nuisance." Jerome agreed with him there. Mrs. Abernethy ruled her domain with a kindly but iron hand. "I am not used to the formality that father insisted upon, so I do not expect all of that faradiddle and such, or dining in style, and I never did like it!"

"That might be the best plan for the moment, sir, if you do not mind. But you were never underfoot, for you used to do that often enough yourself when you were a lad, for cook always made sure you had enough food."

William well remembered her kindness to him. "Yes, she did, and yes I did tend to get if for myself when no one else was there, didn't I, and can again! I never did much like being waited upon."

"Please, ladies, I had the freedom of your house and your unstinting hospitality, so now I can offer mine. At least I think it is now mine. We seem to be short of servants at the moment, so we may have to fend for ourselves a little. Wander about as you will and explore, for I fear that food may be a little delayed unless we help ourselves, which I think is the best plan, so I will show you where the kitchen is first, though I am sure hot water will be provided in short order when we require it."

The two youngest girls needed no further invitation to explore such a large house with so many promising adventures and things to see, but headed out.

"We still have Pilmore, do we?"

"Yes, sir. He is seeing to the garden wall at the moment."

"And what about Armitage?"

"No, sir, he is with your mother in London. We have a new carpenter now, and a very good one too. He is re-enforcing a rafter up in the attic, or if he has finished that, replacing a window in the stable. He always has something to do somewhere and knows his job well."

"Good! I will need to see them both when it might be convenient. Probably after they have eaten their own lunch, I would say. I have some challenging work for them. You should do what you need to do, Jerome, with us descending upon you suddenly as we did, and ignore us for the most part. I will see to getting us downstairs and looked after." He looked about himself to refresh some older memories. "My, but it is good to be home!" He recognized some of those memories beginning to come to the fore again—a slight crack in the window over the door and the wood chip missing from the hall table when his father had thrown something at him as he fled laughing, out of the door.

"It is good to have you home too, sir."

Annis attracted his attention. She seemed a little overawed by it all. "If you will tell us what room my mother will be in, William, I will help her upstairs. I think she would prefer to lie down a little before she does anything else, and I can wait upon her. It has been a hectic few hours—even days—for her as well as for all of us."

"That is most thoughtful of you, Annis, but as for you helping your mother to get upstairs, I have a better plan. We shall all go downstairs. I think that can be accomplished a little more easily and with less discomfort for your mother, and I know, at least I believe, it might still be there. There is a most comfortable chair down there that your mother can sit back in and relax by the fire with us, and it will certainly be warm. I slept in it enough myself when I wished to avoid a tongue lashing or more painful punishment from my father, which was often. I used to live in the kitchen when I was a boy and even made myself useful from time to time, so the servants and cook may not completely despair when so many of us appear down there.

"If you do not object ma'am, I will carry you." He stooped, and as Mrs. Barristow put her arm about his neck, he lifted her and carried her into the hallway and then off along it and down the stairs to the kitchen and scullery, to be met by old familiar smells of cooking and of recently baked bread and the gentle aroma of a rack of herbs, freshly-picked, drying off in one corner.

An older lady dropped some cutlery into the sink when she saw him and wiped her hands on her apron to dry them off. Once he had gently deposited Mrs. Barristow in what he regarded as the most comfortable chair in the house, she walked quickly over to greet him.

"Oh, I knew it was you I saw riding, for no one else would dare take a shortcut over the lawns!" She threw herself into his arms and kissed him unashamedly as the tears rolled down her cheeks. It was not the restrained greeting one might have expected from a servant to a master, but more that of a mother to a son!

He returned her affection without reservation and kissed her unashamedly on the cheeks as he gently lifted her off her feet and then held her close as he looked at her. "Mrs. Abernethy! You have not changed but are just as I remembered you! Ah the wondrous memories! I missed you most cruelly, especially your cooking! You kept me alive all of these years! I dreamed of it all of the time I was on the Peninsula, for we were half starved most of the time, eating things I dare not describe to anyone, and not sure what half of it was anyway! I swear it was the thought of returning to your kitchen that kept me going and that brought me home again."

She was not impressed by any tales of hardship considering what she could see of him! "Ye great lout! You don't look half starved! Not the way you can throw me around like a spring chicken! Now put me down, I still have bread and pies to see to. We missed you too, Master William, sir. Though we often heard of what you were doing." She recalled her words. "Oh, sir, I am sorry, I forgot . . ."

"No apologies, Mrs. Abernethy. Now I know that I am home! My name is William or tha' great lout will do! I have not changed, and I am glad to see that you have not either. I have had my fill of pompous formality and want none of it. I shall be offended if you call me sir, too many times. *I* have not changed. I am the same man that went away, despite the changes here in the interim."

The two missing girls had appeared behind them. Annis and her mother had silently looked on, surprised by the outpouring of such affection for the prodigal son, if various hints he had let drop of the events that had seen him sent away were true, and they probably were. Sophia was busy paying attention to a cat by the fire. Charlotte was hungrily looking at a pot simmering upon the large stove and filling the air with a delightful aroma.

He noticed cook looking inquiringly at the other ladies that had invaded her kitchen.

"Oh yes. I had better introduce everyone before my manners totally desert me! This lady is my most favorite cook in the whole world." He kissed her. "She is Mrs. Abernethy, or Cook. She was a second mother to me and used to give me a rare scold when I stole her cooking, though she didn't really mind. This is Mrs. Barristow, my mother-in-law, whom I believe you already have met, though I doubt that you know her daughters." He looked suddenly thoughtful. "My sisters-in-law now." He introduced each in turn with a gentle and even flattering description, and then mentioned that the youngest daughter Sophia had gone again, but from the sounds of it, she had discovered the harpsichord.

"They will be staying with us for as long as they wish and certainly for the next week or more until repairs are done at Underby, their own home. We will help ourselves to food, if you do not mind? You will have your hands full with dinner I expect, and the usual things you do, and we do not expect anything special that we cannot get for ourselves. I expect the room situation will be sorted out soon enough, and then we can get luggage unpacked and everyone cleaned up and changed and settled."

He looked about. "I half expected Elizabeth to have joined us by now."

"She saw you arrive from the garden and rushed off in a panic to change, even as I took that ham down. She was a little put out that you had not warned us of your arrival to have allowed us to have been better organized."

"I couldn't, or I would have done."

At that moment, a tall young lady, a little older than William breezed through the doorway. "William! You wretch! I knew I would find you down here where the food was!"

"Speak of the devil! Elizabeth!" His actions belied his questionable greeting, for he swept her into his arms and kissed her too.

"Devil indeed if you do not have a letter for me, or I am likely to injure you more grievously!" She could see his bandaged hand and his bruised forehead.

"All in good time, my dear. I knew what *your* priorities would be. You may ignore me as you think only of a stupid old letter, but you must not ignore our guests!"

"I suppose not!" She was obviously very well known to all of the ladies and greeted them all and hugged them as though they were family even, which did not surprise him so much considering what he had learned of the friendship that seemed to have long existed between her and all of the girls, including Mrs. Barristow.

Within seconds, the kitchen had become a hive of activity, with the three girls (Sophia had returned yet again.) actually putting on smocks over their dresses and helping out to prepare a luncheon for them all. Far from being offended by any of it, with so many invading her kitchen, Mrs. Abernethy began to be most pleasantly astonished at how readily the girls and everyone seemed to blend in so well and did not scorn to make themselves useful. She also watched the gentle interchanges between all of them and realized that there was much more to be told here, than she might have heard at a distance, bereavement or not.

William saw two plates of food disappear out of the door for Thomas and Ned to dine upon before they returned to Underby with the carriage and cart.

Elizabeth took him to task. "There is a smell of smoke about you. What have you been doing now? Oh I do hope it is not serious!" Her eyes flashed to the girls and then to Mrs. Barristow sitting in the kitchen chair with her feet up. She began to notice little details that had escaped her up until then.

"Bad enough, Elizabeth!" Mrs. Barristow had watched the exchange for a few seconds with considerable pleasure as she watched both the reception that William was getting, and especially the way in which Annis was viewing it too. They were all well enough known to his sister that there might be no hesitation about entering the conversation or even feeling settled in almost immediately, despite the imposing size of the house or it's overwhelming magnificence.

"But fortunately not *too* serious, my dear. There was some smoke and fire damage to our home this morning but, thanks to your brother, we are all safe and sound."

His referring to Underby as '*our home,*' did not escape her. "So, Sir knight to the rescue once more, I see." Her eyes were misted with unrestrained pleasure at seeing him again. "An ingrained habit with you and from which you never manage to walk away without some souvenir of it." She glanced again at his bandaged hand and the bruising to his forehead. "If only our godmother might see you as I do and as you really are!"

"Don't put me on that pedestal, Elizabeth! You know what the Greeks said of that, or was it the Romans? Putting them the higher that they might fall the further or the harder, and there are those who intend to bring it all about one way or another; our godmother among them!"

"Yes, I got your letter about that! Oh never mind that, come here, you foolish boy!" She hugged him again. "It is so, *so* good to see you after all of these years. We waited expectantly forever for that heart-skipping hoof-beat with news of your being wounded, or worse, dead! Fortunately it never came."

"Admit it, Elizabeth. You were more concerned for news of John than of me."

"And why should I not be concerned for my husband as well as my brother? You have been avoiding and evading me, you naughty boy! I waited at Mama's for days, and you did not come with news that I wanted, for you did not come at all! Then I went to Cousin George's for a couple of days and still you did not come, and he had commitments elsewhere, in France, so I had to come here. I knew you would get here eventually. But then I got your news and could not leave. Another day however, and I would have set out for Underby. I am only just up and about after a most dreadful cold, or I would have been at Underby a week ago!

"I couldn't settle anywhere, William! It was quite a shock to hear that you were married! Oh William! Mama has been plotting it ever since you left, but with never a hope of bringing it about and look at what you did within hours, it seems, of your arrival! Marrying as you did and not letting *me* know so that I might be there, but then you couldn't, could you? You were even married to my very best friend too as we had hoped you would!" There was a sad look on her face. "But not as we had planned or with the desirability of you both getting to know each other as one expects! Poor Bella! Poor William!" She brushed a hair from his face and winced at his yellowing bruise.

"Such a tragic loss, for I was friends with Bella for so many years, and I would have been there in a trice had I been able. Had she lived, she would have made you a wonderful wife, and you would have got on so well together, except you knew nothing of her, and she was learning much more of you from me. But this is far too sad and upsetting at the moment and I am sure we all need to get our minds back into other, more pleasant things. Does anything uneventful or pedestrian ever happen in your life, William? You seemed to bounce from one escapade to the next all the time you were growing up, with never any dullness in between that I could detect, and now you are doing the same again."

She mentioned the other things about him that she had already noticed but need to know more about. "I expect you have a perfectly good and most innocent sounding explanation as to why your hand is bandaged and your face is as bruised and cut as it is?" She valiantly tried to get the conversation and thought away from the recent tragedy. She would speak of it more privately to William when the others were not there to be so upset by such a tender subject so recently put behind them.

"No, Elizabeth. It's nothing. I got cut getting out of a broken window and walking into some awkward, uncooperative doors." He dismissed it with a wave of his hand.

"Oh, is that all! Just the usual things then! But you have been home all of ten minutes and you have studiously managed to avoid telling me what I most wanted to hear, and you know what that is! What news of John?"

"Who?"

She playfully struck at him while laughing and crying at the same time as the others looked on in amused amazement at the easy familiarity that existed between them and the freedom she was taking with her brother. This was a side to her they had not seen before and a much more relaxed brother too than they might have expected. But then without brothers themselves, it was all strange, for he had not behaved that way with them, except perhaps for Sophia.

"Oh, him! John! My companion at arms for the last two years. You showed great restraint in not bearding me immediately you walked in upon us, but then you did immediately accost me, didn't you, until I reminded you that our guests come first." He smiled at her. "Yes, Elizabeth, he is as much in love with you as ever, I would say. No. I am wrong. *More* in love with you than ever! He sends you his love, of course. I caught him on many evenings staring into the campfire, and I could speak to him and get no response at all, for it was easy to see where his mind was, and it was not with me or with our predicament."

As they spoke, and with some help from Mrs. Abernethy who let the two girls know where everything was to be found, food had been laid out on the kitchen table for them, by the two elder Barristow girls, with the instructions to everyone to begin helping themselves.

"Is he well? For he is as likely to avoid telling me anything that might cause me concern, as you were. Too tightlipped both of you!"

'Of course he is well. You would soon have learned otherwise by now. I gave him my blessing for your marriage by the way." He looked at her strangely.

"Thank you! But as we are already married, to the devil with your blessing, for I don't need it any more than you needed mine!"

"No you don't, do you? Not now. Does Mama know?"

"No! None of it! I could not tell her for fear of her response at the suddenness of it. I will allow her to make preparations for a proper wedding when he gets back, and I will have told her most of it by then. If she ever comes back from Bath!"

"Best keep it that way, Elizabeth. He was a few days behind me, I think, for I got the last sloop ship out while he was still doing some organizing. He should land anytime, if he has not already."

"We should call a truce, William. The girls have laid out a wonderful luncheon for us, and we should not let it go to waste, though I see that it won't." She watched as everyone helped themselves, with Annis serving her mother. The ladies were eating well by then, but William only picked at the food, for he had more important things on his mind. They were all happy to eat and listen to the interchange between brother and sister. That alone, and the obviously easy relationship between him and the servants, especially with Mrs. Abernethy, told them so much more of their benefactor than they might ever learn in any other way.

After satisfying their immediate needs, they helped tidy things away, and then the girls left William and his sister to themselves, as they gradually drifted off into other parts of the house to explore their new environment. Only Mrs. Barristow remained, and she was ready to fall asleep, it seemed, after the turmoil they had all gone through.

William looked at her in his favorite chair. "Good! It's about time she rested."

He turned back to his sister. "You owe me, Elizabeth. You have no idea how difficult it was to keep that husband of yours alive for you for these last two years. He had no thought of safety nor sense and led me into the worst possible scrapes and into the thick of battle when my instinct was to go in the opposite direction with all possible haste. It had worked so well for me for the previous three years."

"Fiddle! He said the same of you in his letters! Neither of you were so well decorated for shirking your duty, though Winthorpe worked his vicious ways against you both for a while. Fortunately, only a short while, until more reliable voices were heard to relieve our anxiety."

"But I thought I had intercepted all of his letters to you, Elizabeth. As well as yours to him. They were too damned distracting! He was a dull dog and moping to death if he did not get a letter from you every week." He patted his pocket and extracted something. "No. Only the one."

She tried to snatch if from his hand, but he was quicker than she was and held it away from her.

"William! It is not fair to torment me." She spoke gently, but he could see tears lurking.

"Here, my love. He entrusted it to me to give to you personally when I first saw you, but you have led me a merry dance!"

"Thank you, William!"

She gave him a swift kiss on his cheek and a hefty but friendly smack on his rear. She tucked it into her dress. "I shall read it later, in private. I take it Mama still does not know you are home?"

"I don't know. She must by now, I think. I met up with Uncle David just after I rode away from the house. He said that she was still rusticating in Bath. However, I would not be surprised if she may not have guessed that you were married by now with all of those letters John wrote you and with her undoubtedly itching to read them. Uncle David may be married by now too, from what he said. Come to think of it, from what I heard from Horace, when I was in London a few days ago on a lightning visit to the lawyers, I think mother may have seen some of John's letters to you that you left behind on your last visit to her and before she left for Bath."

"Oh dear!" Elizabeth knew that she had misplaced them somewhere. "So now she shall blame us both for disrupting her nerves! I knew I had lost them somewhere! Then she is keeping away from us both and feeling quite angry with me too."

"I would say that you have nothing to worry about. She has had time to consider how she must behave properly to him or risk losing you. I will tell her that myself when I see her, for he saved my life more than once. However, that may not endear him to Mama."

"William! That is not true! She was as concerned for you as I was. No, I am wrong, she was much more concerned for you, though she had but one to worry about while I had two! She will know you are returned by now and I am sure that she is undoubtedly recovering most well!"

"Probably. I hope so. But not if she gets any letters from our godmother to stir her up. Despite that slight negligence on John's part about that marriage thing, without consulting her, she will still deal with him graciously, I think."

"I expect so. She was as afraid of losing you as I was about you both, and fretted about you all of the time. She does love you, you know?"

"I know! As I love her, but like most sons, I could not show it for fear of being thought too soft and a mother's boy. She *is* my mother, but I led her a merry dance. Absence does indeed make the heart grow fonder. It did with me. Perhaps she believes a little better of me than she used to. I think I may not have appreciated how much of a burden I must have been for her."

"You didn't, but you are now in a position to make up for it and let her see that you love her."

"Yes, I do know it. But boys are not so open with their love as girls can be at that age. In fact, they strive to deny any such weakness, and yet, I am discovering that it is actually a most powerful and endearing trait, for a little consideration and thoughtfulness with the gentler sex gains such immense rewards!"

She had seen the truth of that for herself over the last few minutes, as the ladies had been attentive to everything said, and they had all been curious about William in this new setting, but in the nicest way. "About time you recognized that, William! I've been telling you for long enough!"

"I know, Elizabeth, but I was not listening! I was a sore trial for her as well as you. I am sorry for that! But Mama could not understand me any better than I could understand her, and especially when she dissolved into tears when she often did. I think I can make a better job of it now. I shall try to make up for my deficiencies and confess my love for her when I see her. She will be relieved to have succeeded with both of us and so soon and unexpectedly. Though in my case, I had rather it had come to a better conclusion. Married and then a widower in the blink of an eye! I must also thank you for your letters warning me about the various plots that Mama seemed to be hatching around me. She has been matchmaking for me behind my back ever since I left, and I could not understand why."

His eyes flickered to Mrs. Barristow. "I realize that I have no secrets now from anyone, but we should still be cautious." William took his sister's hand and kissed it. "So, what will happen when Mama finds out that we are both married, do you think? She will be most hurt and immensely disappointed to find two of her . . . her only two children married, and she was unaware of both marriages. She will return to Bath instantly and never speak to us again!"

Elizabeth chuckled. "She couldn't easily be present at mine for it was a spur of the moment thing in Lisbon, but at least, John and I had a week together before everything was assembled for war. I don't think Mama missed me from England even. I never dared tell her!"

"Well, she certainly could not have been aware of mine either, not at the time, for that was a complete surprise for me too. I only learned of it about an hour before it happened. Do you think she will wash her hands of us both?"

"No! For we will both of us celebrate proper church weddings when John returns. She will now be able to dream of grandchildren again, for she constantly roasted me about my lack of suitors. If only she had known!"

"You are forgetting something, my dear. I am a widower!"

"Oh, William! I am sorry. Yes I had forgotten! But you are still young. Your life did not end. From what I have seen, you will marry again eventually, and I suspect much sooner than you might think!" She looked at him in a way that suggested she knew more than he might have believed.

"Be careful, Elizabeth! I hope you are right, but I am not out of the woods yet. There are great difficulties ahead of me still."

"Perhaps! Perhaps not! So my eyes and instincts did not deceive me after all. Two marriages for both of us. That must be some kind of a family record when it happens."

His voice dropped. "I suppose I should see all of this tragedy a little differently, for there are still three—well, two—eligible daughters and even Mrs. Barristow herself available."

Elizabeth knew what she had seen. There was only the one daughter—the one marriageable daughter that is—that captivated him, and his feelings there, were returned. Yes, there would indeed be difficulties considering what had already happened.

"I am sure we will manage to think of something to set the tongues a-wagging. I have a reputation with our godmother to maintain!" He looked across and checked that Mrs. Barristow was indeed resting. She was even breathing quite heavily. "Exhausted! Just as well!"

He smiled at his sister, and they quietly got up from the table and walked out along the corridor to the stairs. "She will be all right for an hour or so, and there is always someone in and out of the kitchen to keep an eye on her until we return."

He took his sister's arm and threaded it through his own. They strolled to the stairs and climbed them to the main level of the house. "I was heading well away from London. Our godmother had summoned me for a meeting with her, and against the popular recommendations of everyone, you included, I decided, in a moment of rash bravado, to take the bull by the horns and see what she wanted. I was in one of my more rebellious moods, obviously, and was feeling most brave and decided to get it out of the way. But I was damned if I was going to let any hint of her dictatorial ways and stigmatizing views of me creep into my first day home, so I resolved to say as little as I might. I am not sure I succeeded in that plan, so you will undoubtedly be regaled with some new vicious gossip involving me, I expect. But let us go out into the garden. It is a fine day. But mostly we should be out of the house so that we can talk more easily." He looked about. "Those girls are everywhere and into everything. They miss nothing. They are wonderful! I did not realize that younger sisters might be so very interesting!"

"Wonderful? Interesting? This does not sound like you, William. You have matured and changed."

"I have been away from women too long, Elizabeth, especially such assured and mature young ladies, and beautiful too! All of them! The Spanish and Portuguese ladies are beautiful enough, but the society was most thin and not welcoming to any of us foreigners."

They strolled together arm-in-arm about the flowerbeds. "Why did I not have younger sisters too? I did not realize such young ladies could be so entertaining or even interesting and so damnably tormenting in their ways, and attractive. No, Elizabeth, I have not suddenly lost my mind. Or have I? One was somewhere close by earlier and perhaps not deliberately eavesdropping, but they tuck themselves away and read or write and sketch, and before you know it, all of them know your innermost secrets. They read my journal too when I was not there and even saw some of my own sketches of them and the war."

His sister was satisfied just to listen to him. He had changed and for the better.

"They know everything you do from morning 'til night, for they watch me so closely. I am sure it will be the same here. Most unnerving, but then I seem to have become a stable male presence in their suddenly disrupted lives. Quite a strange role for me! The only time you know for sure where any one of them is, is when they are rattling away on the harpsichord or the piano forte or is arguing with her sisters about something or is sitting where you can see her."

"So what was it that got you out to Underby, William?"

"The usual! A plea directed at me and that I could not refuse. I was at George's relaxing for the first time in five years, when I got a letter out of the blue, and I got dragged into this plot quite without seeing where it might lead, thinking I was helping cousin George. I even married! But then you know that. Willingly too! I could not believe what was happening to me, and I am sure that no one else who knew me might either. When I realized what had happened and how things had happened . . ." He paused and decided to not elaborate on too much. "Gradually, I began to see that there was a strange twist to it all that I may tell you about later, and I could not just rush away and abandon them. Besides, I found the family needed me, and by then, of course, they were growing more and more interesting, and I needed them too."

Elizabeth decided not to comment upon his use of those words—interesting (again) and wonderful as well as entertaining—to describe her friends! She had seen as much for herself. He seemed as much at ease with them as he was with her.

"Will I survive? I am not so sure. Oh dear! I see Jerome is looking for me, so I think he may have me meeting with our carpenter and mason as I requested; or Gossett. Why don't you check in on Mrs. Barristow, my dear, if you don't mind, and I will return shortly."

Chapter XXVII

Time Is the Great Healer

Early the next morning, William saw his mason and carpenter sent off with instructions to do what they might at Underby, and to do as good a job of it as they could, and to give no thought to expense. They were to consult with Thomas and were given funds enough, and to spare, to do anything that they might need to do. He also spent much of his free time with his man of business and learned that not only was the Brooklands estate in good hands, but that it was also thriving, and had been thriving as long as Gossett had been allowed free rein with the decisions that were needed.

Sophia, occasionally was able to intercept William in his plans, and might even expect to be taken up on his horse, as she had been at Underby, and to go on a tour of the estate with the two gentlemen. She was happy to listen to them herself and to see what there was to see.

Gossett, had not known what to expect from this new owner, for some of the tales that he had heard of him, in his absence, were not at all promising, but he soon had reason to feel more optimistic. Master William seemed to have a steady head on his shoulders, was happy to listen and to learn, and even asked some reasonable and searching questions that showed he understood far more than he might disclose. It was also clear that he had no intention of changing anything until he fully understood everything and even then seemed happy to place his trust in his manager, much as his father and mother had done. After viewing the return of the prodigal son with some apprehension, he soon began to realize that he was dealing with an intelligent man who would deal with him fairly and seemed pleased at the current state of affairs and was easily able to tell him so.

William also learned that almost all of the hay was in to the outer barns or had been stacked up into hayricks. As men became available from the urgent business of harvesting the hay crop, and as the season advanced, most of that stored outside as *Ricks*, in the need to see it protected from the frequent wet weather, would be brought in to the home barns for storage and use over winter. It was a late year for haying. At least three weeks late. He learned that there had been some concern that they might not be able to get all that had been planned to get, but the weather had begun to cooperate for once, and the final fields were even then being cut, and the other crops being placed into clamps or brought into storage.

He also took the opportunity of taking the ladies out with him in a carriage on those few fine days, to give them a break from being cooped up too close to the main house, though they found nothing to complain about. Charlotte had access to more paper and charcoals and even hard graphite-core pencils than she had ever dreamed of, and set herself up in the conservatory if it promised rain, or in the garden to draw trees, or the mansion, or barns; for the vistas leant themselves better to being captured than anywhere around their property at Underby. On those rare occasions when Sophia was unable to go out with William, she could generally be found in the library.

The other ladies—Elizabeth, Annis, and Mrs. Barristow—spent most of their days together in gentle conversation or moving through the extensive gardens or the hothouse, where Elizabeth learned much more of what had transpired that fateful day that had brought William to Underby and much of what had happened since then. She listened carefully and began to see much more in everything described to her, than her narrators might have thought possible.

One fine day, there had been an excursion to pick the last of the abundant brambles in the edge of the wood and of the hazelnuts along the hedgerow. Promise of a bramble-apple pie and of making bramble jam and bramble jelly figured largely in their being able to brave the vicious thorns on the bushes, though Sophia did manage to get herself tangled, and needed to have William wade into the middle of them to extricate her with no more than a few minor scratches to her hands and cheek but some damage to his own flesh and clothing, amidst some laughter.

After an hour of good picking, they had filled their baskets and could then relax over the picnic that William had had the foresight to bring. They sat on the edge of an old sandpit that William remembered being the home of a family of foxes for some years. He mentioned that if they were to stay quiet, that they might even see one, though did not expect it, and was surprised to find that they soon had the pleasure of watching a mother fox appear from a nearby den followed by her three grown cubs and to watch her playing with them. They even saw the male fox bring in a dead rabbit for them to play with while they learned what it meant to find food for themselves, rather than continuously nursing from their mother, for she was in process of weaning them away from herself. It had been a little disturbing to watch two of the larger cubs playing tug of war over the carcass until it was ripped into two pieces, with smaller parts of it quickly carried off by the other cub to feast upon, for at that point the ladies tended to become disgusted and to lose interest in the display of nature as red in tooth and claw as it could be. As long as the watchers were silent, the mother fox cautiously tolerated them but did not trust them far. Where there were humans, then dogs were never far behind, though the foxhunt had never been fond of the Devane estate, as it was more likely a place to lose a fox than to find one in all of the thickets and bramble patches, which were unfriendly to both dogs and horses and riders as much as they protected rabbits and foxes and even deer.

After their picnic, they had set too, to pick hazelnuts while avoiding the nettles that also seemed to fill the margins of the hedgerow.

William pointed out other things of interest to Sophia. "Look." He pointed up into the sky. "See those wispy long thin clouds high in the sky? They are called mare's tails. When you see those, you know that the weather is about to change and probably for the worse on the next day. 'In nature's infinite book of secrecy. A little I can read.' At least that is how Shakespeare described something of it."

On those rainy days or where the wind was strong and the weather cool, the ladies remained in the house and pored over maps or played the harpsichord or just read while William was rarely in the house at all, even in the worst weather, but usually took himself off for some hours. They learned from Elizabeth that he was probably off at the dock getting his ship, the Seamew ready, now that he was back, but ready for what, she seemed loath to say, though they knew he probably intended to go across to France and take up smuggling again.

One morning, Annis had found William asleep in the kitchen chair with Sophia curled up with him. He was tired, for he had been out most of the previous night and the one before that too, and that, after working in the fields alongside his men, to try and get another lot of hay in, and she suspected Sophia had not been in her bed either but had watched for him to return.

She took the opportunity to sit at the kitchen table and watched them as she ate a slice of heavily buttered hot bread fresh out of the oven with some of the bramble jam that her mother had made up.

She kept silent and watched as Sophia woke up and reached out to feel the hairs on William's heavy eyebrows and those that Annis—when she last shaved him—may have missed under his jawbone. She investigated a small cut on his chin from a sharp branch on one of their hazelnut outings, and intent, it seemed on waking him up, she kissed it better. By then, he was half awake. Sophia had no shyness or embarrassment over any of it. Oh, the innocence of children! Had she been able, Annis would have swapped places with her sister in the twinkling of an eye!

When Sophia saw that he was awake, she smoothed her hand over his rough cheek. "I am so glad I do not have to shave, William."

He laughed. "So am I!" He gently rasped her delicate cheeks with his whiskers and elicited some mild complaints of discomfort and much squirming and laughter.

"At least you never will need to. But then I haven't needed to shave myself for some time now."

"No, William, for Annis seems most happy to do it for you."

"Yes, she does, doesn't she? I am most happy to let her, for she is so very gentle and considerate and does such a good job of it too, and never a nick worth speaking of, or a word of complaint. Perhaps I should plead to be shaved twice a day. I should go and find her and ask to be shaved now, for it is more than even a full day, I believe."

"You stayed out all night again, so you have only yourself to blame. But surely your hand is healed by now, and you could shave yourself, for you use it to work in the fields. I have watched you!"

"Of course, it is! I keep the bandage on it for a very good reason, called malingering. It healed some time ago, but I can malinger so well and put up a great fuss over how slow it is healing, that she has not yet discovered it and won't as long as I wear this. Don't tell her, will you?"

"I promise to say nothing, William."

"Good!" He noticed a slight noise over at the table as Annis decided to draw their attention by clearing her throat. "But Oh! I see I am mistaken! I am all undone! She *has* discovered it! We have an audience at the kitchen table! Annis! You have been sitting there the entire time and overhearing my candid confession to Sophia! Tarnation!"

"Yes, sir," Annis spoke up. "I would say that you have been found out!"

"Ouch! Ouch! Watch out for my hand, Sophia! I think I was mistaken about it being quite healed."

"Too late, sir! The damage has been done!"

"But, Annis, my eyesight is still not as it should be after walking into those doors, else I would easily have seen you at the table, so I shall still plead that I will need your help to shave."

"Malingerer! But the plea about your eyesight might just save you from the fate you deserve." She tried to look severe but could not hide her smile. She would have been disappointed had she not continued to shave him, for she looked forward to that little adventure as much as *he* seemed to, and there was always a kiss that followed it.

"Thank you!" He smiled at her. She was not sure that he had not seen her, and was just having fun anyway to see how she might respond.

Everything that had gone on over the last few days between William and Annis had been watched and noted upon by both Mrs. Barristow and William's sister. They frequently exchanged knowing glances. Sophia was well aware of everything too, for she still rarely left William's side and could see much more, and understood much more, than the others might have guessed!

Mrs. Barristow was the one most relieved, as she readily confessed to Elizabeth. "I cannot think what we would have done in the last few weeks without him with us. It does not bear thinking upon." She blew her nose and tried to hold back her emotions at recent memories that still gave her nightmares. "He is a brother to my daughters and a son that I never had."

Elizabeth had been well aware for some time that he was far from being a brotherly figure with Annis. The mother could see it too but was not about to discuss *that* too openly, having so recently buried the daughter he had married. What a predicament! Elizabeth's heart went out to her brother and to Annis and was noticeably pleased with what she saw beginning to unfold for them both. It would be the making of him in so many ways! He had changed already, however, and very much for the better. It was a pity their mother and even their godmother were not here to see!

Chapter XXVIII

Truth and Consequences

"William?"

He put his quill down, stood as Annis entered the room, moved the accounts he was dealing with off to one side, and gave her his full attention as he smiled at her.

She noticed with a feeling of inner pleasure that ever since he had arrived at Underby, and now in the days since they had arrived at Brooklands, he always seemed to smile at her and pay her attention, no matter the difficulties thrown in his way.

"Yes, my dear." She liked the way he said that, though he said it to both of her sisters and even once absentmindedly to their mother before he recognized that he was not speaking to one of the girls. "Is it time to shave again already? Oh, good!"

"I shaved you only an hour ago!" She could see what kind of a teasing mood he was in.

'You did?" He had known that of course. He was smiling as mischievously as he always seemed to as he played such gentle games with them all.

"There is something I would like to ask you."

He raised an eyebrow and waited. "I hope it is not too risqué!"

"No, of course not! At least I don't think it is, but it might be!"

"Oh!" He noticed her gradually changing qualification.

She sat down on the settee off to one side of his desk and brought her feet up as she wrapped her dress about her legs and hugged them to her and looked at him in a measured way. He was pleased to note that they were the actions of a young lady who was most at ease in his company and not at all as guarded of appearances as she might be, for what she had just done suggested that she was far *too* relaxed in his company, and *that* might not be regarded as proper if anyone else were to see her. However, what might be defined as *proper* between them, had been redefined in some subtle ways as time had progressed.

He sat back and looked at her face, waiting for her to begin. She noticed that his eyes also seemed to smile at her. Quite disarming!

She seemed hesitant, so he helped her along.

"You may ask anything, you know? Is your room too cold? Draughty perhaps? Are you getting enough to eat now? Has one of the servants offended you? Did the cat move her kittens to your bed? Did anyone tell you that the breakfast ham came from

Cyril, for we used to have a pig of that name that I had as a pet? Never have farm pets that might wind up on the dinner table! It is most off-putting to one's appetite to learn of that. Have I offended you in any way recently or tried to kiss you again when you are *not* shaving me for I have been remiss there I think? Perhaps you are here to allow me to make up for that!" He was in a mischievous and gently provocative mood as he rattled on.

She smiled at his levity. "Of course not!"

"What do you mean 'of course not'? Oh dear, I must be losing my touch. But then you are under my roof now, so I must behave with greater circumspection for as long as I can, so a brotherly kiss is all I can muster at this time."

It was far from being a 'brotherly' kind of kiss, as she was always happy to note. "You seem to steal a kiss or two every time I shave you, by way of thanks, but I do not think that you intend it to be a brotherly kind of kiss, which should be on the cheek as you do to Elizabeth or Charlotte now, and not upon my lips!"

"It should?" He managed to look confused, and she knew that he was nothing of the kind. She would have felt more than a little disappointed if he had kissed her only on the cheek. She liked the various little signs of intimate progress that had occurred almost without being consciously noted, though each one had been disturbingly welcomed and recognized for what it was; notice of others to come, as well as of a progression in their developing relationship.

"William, you are deliberately distracting me from what I want to say! It is none of those things and nothing like that, as I think you already know, for we are all most comfortable and could not have found ourselves in a more congenial or welcoming setting. However, it is somewhat personal!" She could not immediately meet his sudden glance. "In fact it is very personal, and I have no right to ask any of it. Yet I must!"

"Oh? Good! It is time we had another very personal conversation, you and I! Long overdue, considering where we find ourselves and what has already happened to me! To us! Between us!"

Her eyes flashed to his for a moment.

He continued before she recovered. "And if you do not mind me correcting you a little, considering what we have gone through and how far we have come, you have every right to ask even the most personal of questions of me, for I find that I would like you to know me better." He added a little more qualification. "Much better!"

She still hesitated, yet it was not because the tenor or emphasis of his last and very personally-suggestive comment had struck her as strange, because it had gone by her almost unnoticed.

He rattled on more than he usually would, to provoke her *eventually* into asking what she clearly wanted to ask, for she might need some nudging. At least until she got started. "As you feel the need to ask, then I will promise that I will answer honestly. I will be most candid and will not hide anything from you. It is about time you began to ask things of me of a *most* personal nature again, for I have wanted to ask you many things too, along those same lines!"

He was clearly talking along quite deliberately waiting for her to begin and to stop his rambling when it became too much for her.

"Oh! You have? Then please ask them, William. I will also promise to be candid and honest without evasion and will hide nothing from you, for I have nothing to hide from you, do I?" Her eyes said more than her mischievous words did.

He decided not to go there. "But you first, Annis. You raised this topic with me, remember?"

"Yes." She recollected the truth of that. "Oh dear! Where to begin? You are aware . . . I know you are . . . that Mama received a letter from our godmother, Lady Seymour, some two weeks or more ago just after . . ." She fell silent as those memories intruded. "She was busy at the time with all of the . . . arrangements and asked me to see to it." She hesitated for some moments. "I read it." Her eyes flickered to his. "It was quite disturbing! No! It was devastating! I did not tell Mama what was in it other than a few inconsequential little bits and pieces, and I have kept it to myself since then. It said a lot concerning you, and . . ." She fell silent. It seemed to be proving difficult for her.

"Go on. My back is broad you know, and I am well aware of Lady Seymour's poor opinion of me, so I can guess what her letter might say."

"What she said, and I am ashamed to admit it now, shaped much of my earlier behavior toward you. I know now that I was wrong. Very wrong!" She suddenly seemed to become almost angry with him. "Why do you let her get away with telling all of those lies about you? You are not the kind of a person she describes in her letter."

"Yes, our godmother has an annoying habit of cutting through whatever truth there might be and discovering the embarrassing untruths and seeing only *them*. But how do you know they were lies or that I am not the kind of person she described? Though I am sure it was not flattering, if it was mostly about me. I am sure it is a long list of my faults, my violent past, and other and various indiscretions to add to what you already know of me. Unfortunately, I may have, unwisely, responded to her needling and given her ammunition for some more of those when I last met with her just before I got to Underby."

She thought for a while and decided that he was unlikely to refuse to discuss any of it with her, as personal as it certainly was. She opened up to discuss what she had long wanted to find out about what her godmother had written, and she had rehearsed it often in her own mind. "We have all been thrown together for the last two weeks in a most dreadful nightmare. My father, my sister, then that dreadful man and his father . . . who would have forced themselves into our midst, to do what? Then the fire! You have been the only sane spark of life for all of us to hang onto, and without you close by, I dare not think what might have happened on several occasions to us as a family. Then you brought us here into this completely new world where we had chance to get away from all of our immediate problems. If you were the man that she painted you to be in her letter, you would probably have done *none* of those things, but others much worse by now. But you are not that kind of a person!"

"Much worse, eh?" She was not about to be provoked into saying more. "Perhaps I have not yet had the opportunity? But no, I did, didn't I, and at least twice now! What kind of a person? As I have not seen her letter, I cannot answer to any charges she may have laid at my door. However, I see that I must address them and answer them to your satisfaction, whatever they might be, or you will wonder when I am likely to revert to that other dreadful individual that I am sure she described so well for you."

She rummaged in the pocket of her dress and produced the often-read letter. It was crumpled from much reading and being carried on her person. It was even tear stained, but she hoped he would not see that. She would never have dared to put it down anywhere it might be discovered.

"Ah! *The* letter! Well, you are still here and talking to me, and your mother and sisters have not deserted the estate, and earlier, did not cast me out from your home despite our previous revealing conversations and even more revealing exchanges. I refer, of course, to that wondrous unforgettable memory that is now forgotten once more." She wondered which one of several he might be referring to, though there was only really *one* that certainly transcended all of the others. He hesitated, and then prompted her. "The letter?"

She came back to earth again. "Yes, the letter. They know nothing of it! I am the only one to have read it. I have lived with this now for the last two weeks and more, and I cannot but believe it is all a mistake, for I think I know you much better than is shown in this."

He stood up and walked over to sit beside her as she moved her feet off the settee, and then he read the letter she put into his hand, with her reading it yet again alongside of him. She was well aware of the warmth of his legs through her thin dress and of his shoulder pressed against hers and wanted to reach out and hold his hand and even rest her head against his shoulder, but lacked the courage. Far too forward, in such a difficult situation! She held the other side of the letter as they both read it and placed her other hand out of the way, and on her knee, though she had read it several times in the privacy of her room and wondered at it all.

But if she did touch him, she could not be sure what his response might be. Or perhaps she was afraid of what it might be, so she did not take his hand but did find the courage to gently lean her head on his shoulder as he read it. She found him moving a little closer to her and holding it more in front of her so that she would not need to lean over or move her head very far to read, though she had read it many times. She brought her feet up on the seat beside her again and leaned more heavily into him as she straightened out her dress.

She felt his shoulders begin to shake as he read. He found humor in it! She did not understand that. He should be very annoyed with his godmother!

Then she found that his hand had reached out and gently taken hers from her knee and was holding it. She did not snatch it back, which had been her first instinct, but just closed her eyes and listened as he read out loud, drinking in the sound of his voice and wondering how he might deal with the damning charges laid out in the letter, feeling the pulse pounding in her own neck and the warmth of his hand. She let go of the letter and laid her other hand over his as he held hers. She could almost have recited it word for word with her own eyes closed.

> *My dearest Eliza,*
>
> *It is difficult to know where to begin. Too much is happening of a dreadful nature to upset us all. I was devastated to hear of your tragic circumstance and am only sorry that I cannot get there as quickly as this letter. It is to be hoped that it is not as tragic as you fear. I shall come to you when I am able.*

"She is a most untidy writer, isn't she, though she does manage to express herself well so far?"

> *But to get to the point quickly, and I hope I am not too late. In this matter of Bella marrying William Devane that we all of us had discussed when we met earlier—it should never have been considered at the start and must NOT be allowed to happen. The consequences of his continued presence among you and your other girls might be unbearable to you and the entire family.*

"There! Even I could have told you that, for look at what has happened. One thing after another! No end of trouble I have caused for you all!"

Annis said nothing. He read on.

> *I should have laid all of my reservations out to both you and his mother earlier, I know, but I did not wish to cause his mother any distress with my devastating and long-held opinion of her son, though I think she already knows it. I honestly never thought this plan of marriage would ever get this far, or I would have spoken sooner.*
>
> *My objections to this possible connection going forward are numerous and persuasive. I provide details of such disastrous incidents that few in society know about it seems, and those who do know have said precious little about! The less his name is linked with any part of your family, the better it will be for all concerned.*
>
> *Most of my objections come from the time before he was banished, by his parents, but obviously led up to that action. I doubt that warfare and fighting for his country will have improved him any, for I understand it often does quite the opposite. Violent men are for-ever violent! It might have been better for all, if he had not returned, for he was nothing less than a brawler, a libertine, even a . . . . I hesitate to say the word, but it must be laid out without any timidity—rapist, and worse, if that were possible. Yet it is worse, for I have first-hand knowledge of one such affair to a relative of my own. Who knows what else there is that I have NOT heard about!*

> *He will undoubtedly pick up those same propensities when he settles, though five years abroad will hardly have improved his character from what I hear of the dreadful goings-on of the military in their debauching treatment of those foreign women caught in their clutches and passed, I will say it, from man to man.*

"Yes, unfortunately she is right there. There were some most dreadful episodes that the army got up to at times, and it does not reflect well upon any of us." Annis still said nothing.

> *I met with him earlier today just after he landed. He has not changed but seems to have become even more dangerous and hinted, entirely without shame, at some of those scandalous things that I know go on when our soldiers are abroad with . . . other women, whom they hold in no respect, though I gather that much of that is of their own doing. He easily, openly, even defiantly, confirmed what I had earlier heard of bringing a foreign woman back into the country with him, and depositing her in some little amorous situation where he might visit her at his leisure. I must admit that my reservations and opinions are more strongly based now, for I found him to be cold, aloof, and unrepentant of some of what I know, though I did not throw anything directly at him on these most tender issues apart from mentioning the ill-fated Constanza to him, which he readily amplified, though I was sorely tempted to, with at least two other of them.*

"It was my own fault for going on about Constanza to her. Too ripe for her to avoid picking up on it! But then I knew that."

> *To begin:*
> *Some five years ago, he, and another of his kind—a man named Maxton—brawled in one of the clubs over the favors of a lightskirt! It was well hushed up, and I had difficulty hearing of it, but I did eventually. The other "gentleman" involved fell afoul of his own family much more than WD seems to have done with his own, for it seems that he was promptly sent abroad and has not shown his face in London since. It quite surprised me, for that family has so little regard for their social position, that I had thought he would not have been pushed off as quickly as he was.*

"A lightskirt eh? She must have been referring to that Chisholm female whose name somehow became linked with that episode. Just as well she did not know of the other!"
Annis did not trust herself to speak.

> *There was yet another brawl shortly after that in an entirely unrelated incident, I think, except that that also seems to have involved a woman of dubious character. I know that the brawl took place, though I do not have details of that, and could*

never find out who the other man was, or indeed the female, but that incident was also well hushed up.

As if that were not enough, there was an affair hard on the heels of the other two and involving a lady of much better character, who had fallen into his snare. The lady was so upset over it, she has not dared speak of it to anyone since that time, but I know it all. I am reluctant to use a stronger word yet again, but that worse circumstance—*rape*—is clearly what it was, for the lady is well known to me, so I was made aware of some of the details (who could not be, with the physical injuries and those to her sanity too). He did not realize nor care, I believe, that he left her with child—his child!—from that incident, which seemed to have been spread over several days of imprisonment and debauchery as he repeatedly forced himself upon her. The young lady and her infant have been somewhat in my care since that time. She would not divulge any names for fear of retribution from a most violent man—that much was evident to me—but from the startled look in her eyes and her weak protestations and evasions when I threw the name of WD at her head, it was obvious where the blame truly resided. He abandoned her and her unborn child (I took pains to ensure that no one knew she was with child, of course) when he went abroad just some weeks afterward. He had done enough damage in society by then that his parents—who deserved better of a son—could no longer ignore it and forced him out of the country.

What he may have got up to abroad, I cannot say, but some of the shameful and violent things that those troops get up to over there with the local women—young and old alike and even children—is legend and never with their consent, I might add. Indeed, every account of him from abroad reeks of violence and wicked goings-on.

And now, he is returned to pick up where he left off, and with Constanza, whoever she may be. Well, he must be stopped before greater damage is done. I would never forgive myself if I let anything go forward without letting you know of his character.

It pains me to recount this, for his mother and sister are both as dear to me as you are my dear friend. I went along with the plans and plots of you and his mother as they seemed harmless enough with him abroad, and it seemed that they would never amount to anything. Once he did return, if he returned, it seemed obvious to me that Bella—if she ever encountered him—would instantly take him in dislike and see his character writ large as it must be. I could say nothing then without hurting so many others, and there seemed no need. I did not wish to hurt or antagonize his mother and sister, for they have been friends, good friends of mine and yours for many years now as have you.

I just this evening received further disturbing accounts of the only surviving Maxton son having been murdered by a highwayman on the road out of London, near the hamlet of Inchdene, barely three miles from my estate and on the road out to Brooklands that he had to have travelled about the same time after he left my home. It would not surprise me if WD had not himself put paid to him somehow!

Another such incident, and so soon after he returned. It all seems most coincidental and highly suspicious. However, the Maxtons were never well liked, so society will be well rid of him too.

Forgive me for even thinking it, and his mother must never find this out, but I believe that it was a great pity that—if it had happened at William's hands—Maxton had not been able to return the favor at that same moment, for the benefit of all concerned.

Your friend, Addie Seymour.

P.S. I now have the recipe for—from Mrs. Devane. As I have time, as this letter cannot leave my hands now until morning, I will pen it here . . .

"She tears me apart most thoroughly and then calmly switches parts to divulge a recipe for marmalade and tarts! From murder and worse, to marmalade! Yet I still live and even thrive and prosper and am happier than I am sure I deserve to be, despite all of these manifest faults!"

He shook his head. "Most damning and damaging! Especially that Trevelyan accusation! Rather a devastating and full account of me I would say, though she has some of the details and the order of it all somewhat garbled." He laughed once or twice as he read it, but there was little humor in his laugh. "But what do *you* think of me? Of this, Annis?"

She thought for a while, though she already had known the answer for a long time now.

"I think that our godmother does not know you! Not as we know you!"

"I like that answer! But what a villainous portrait is painted of me! So that's what the old beldame wanted to see me about. To throw all of this in my face but then lacked the courage to do so! How I wish she had done so when we met and saved me from this diatribe. Yet even this can have a positive outcome, for at least I now *know* her litany of sins against me. This must have been festering away in her bosom all of these years with her waiting to send a broadside into me I would never recover from, but she did not have the courage to do it to my face!

"I had a most uncomfortable feeling about why she wanted to see me and was warned off by everyone. Yet she asked me none of this nor sought confirmation from me, or clarification when I met with her, but danced around everything, except throwing out her comment about Constanza. The infamous Constanza! She was searching for what she might find out, so I became devious too and told her too much. She clearly knew none of it and chose to take my circuitous and devious answers and comments at face value and spin a disreputable romp out of it. She even danced around that other incident with her niece. A sad piece of work indeed! A direct question—which some ladies seem incapable of asking—which you have now asked on several occasions, would have elicited a better response from me than I was inclined to provide."

"But the truth is rarely simple, William!" She was looking at him strangely, waiting for his denial of it all.

"True." He let the letter flutter to the seat beside them and added his hand to hold hers.

"From what my sister let drop in her letters, I thought that, like my mother, she was striving to find a bride for me, which is something I would have rebelled at. Coming from her it seemed like an act of revenge upon me, especially if it had been the Collishawe woman that my uncle tried to warn be about, whereas from my mother it seemed like an act of desperate motherly concern for my well-being and getting me settled as she would have liked, to raise a few grandchildren.

"But then I did not know what our parents seemed to have planned for me and did not know that it had actually been your sister Bella. I had not met any of your family before I arrived. I find that my views on a few things, most things, have moderated considerably, though I fear that I am not yet become a gentleman in many ways and may never get there.

"It seemed a little out of character for our godmother to do anything out of consideration for me. Now it seems she would have forbidden me instead. Well I am glad she has emptied her budget onto paper for once. It is nice to know what she really thinks of me or thinks she knows. But she missed out on my smuggling career and those later incidents since I arrived. I should take her to task for that, for I worked very hard at smuggling and was very successful at it. In fact, I am taking it up again. There was also that thing about shaving her little dog. Though she found out the truth of that rather late, I heard, or that might have been in here too."

"But none of it is true! Is it?" There was a pained look in her eyes as she waited for his answer.

He moved a little away from her and brought his leg up beside her and between them as he turned his body to face her so that she might see his face and read his expression. He did not let go of her hands but raised them to his lips and even kissed them as he held her eyes.

"Oh yes, my love! I can deny very little of it. It is mostly true, with one or two minor exceptions and the changing of a few details here and there." Clearly, she was not comfortable with that answer. "But I need to be more open with you. Especially with you! Fortunately, our godmother did not know the half of it, and what she did know, she got wrong! Just as well!"

She paled as she looked into his eyes and found it hard to breathe because of his admission that most of it was indeed true, which was unexpected, and he had also absentmindedly called her his love. Perhaps not absentmindedly. It did seem to help.

"I hear that confession is good for the soul. Not my confessions. Hers! She must be most relieved to have put it all down on paper and to have admitted what her true feelings for me are, though I think I knew what those were all along."

She listened and looked into his eyes as he continued. They were still smiling at her. He was obviously telling the devastating truth, for who would ever willingly admit to any of that? She wanted to be almost anywhere else at that moment than where she was but could not just leave. She waited for him to continue as she held her concerns in check.

"So she ferreted out that first brawl with the elder Maxton, did she? I should have known she would have friends there. I am so pleased she didn't learn the whole of it!"

Annis's hand would have flown to her throat at that admission, but he still held it.

"But to think that she believes it was a brawl over a lightskirt! Her sources of information do not seem to be so very robust after all. My sister will be most offended to learn that that is what her godmother thinks of her! I wonder where she heard of that, for my sister obviously did not tell her."

His audience could say nothing at first as she was too choked up with emotion. She did not sound like herself when she was at last able to say anything. "Y-y-your sister?"

"Oh yes! But Maxton—the rest of it. She has that wrong too. He did not go abroad after that. Yes, she was most certainly wrong about that. We dueled after we had brawled. Pistols! He was as dead as any man could be, I would say, even before he hit the ground! His friends and relatives hid that last part most cleverly, whisking him off as they did, for whatever reason, and then they must have started that rumor of him going abroad."

She gently took her hands away from his, only to find that he reached out and took them again. She could no longer look at him.

"And none of his relatives were ever going to tell anyone what they did with his body. They spread the rumor that he had gone abroad for some particular reason that escaped me. Hard to deceive those who witnessed it though, for I think that living men generally do not sport a large hole immediately between the eyes as they fall, to lie prostrate and lifeless on the grass, and bleeding out."

"You killed him?" She was wide-eyed and breathless at the horror of that possibility.

"Oh yes. No doubt of that!"

"But you say your sister knew of this?"

"Oh yes! The brawl was because of my sister! Over her! You should ask her when you next see her. I could not avoid it! Nor could I avoid killing him! He would have hunted us both down in some remote and dark place if I had let him live. She knows it all. Probably more than I do, for she was the reason it took place, and she looked on the whole time. You should refer to her for confirmation of what I will say. A lightskirt indeed! She will be most offended to hear herself described like that, and by our godmother too, for she is nothing of the kind but a respectably married woman, though our mother does not yet know that either.

"I'd better tell you the whole of it—about everything, all of it—so that you may judge me for yourself." He took a deep breath and began.

"Maxton, Julius Maxton, was a notoriously bad character from a family of bad characters. His elder brother had been murdered some time before I came across him—a total rake with an unenviable reputation for gambling and violence, and a loose fish, if you know what I mean?"

She nodded.

"I will ask you sometime how you know that! He even sounds like me on the face of it, but he was nothing like me at all. He was banned from the clubs and polite society generally but had gained access to the grounds at Lady Audsley's estate, having seen my sister arrive earlier, in my company."

She nodded.

"He had decided to take advantage of the situation and that he would pay court to her." His eyes glinted. "Well perhaps not quite so polite or gentle an approach! I think he envisioned . . . the worst kind of encounter with her, and in the secluded garden of the grounds, where one of his friends, the unfortunate Miss Chisholm, whom I never met, had managed to take her on pretense of needing fresh air. He believed that *there*, he might not be interrupted, despite her obvious objections and resistance when he approached her unexpectedly, for she had repulsed him in the past." He looked down at her. "I am not disturbing you too much, am I, by recounting any of this?"

She shook her head.

"He was insulting and even violently rough with her at first when she sought to escape. Elizabeth may decide to tell you more, but I should not. I had stayed for a few moments to renew an acquaintance and heard what was going on in the garden, so I went to see what trouble she had managed to get herself into and blundered onto the scene. She had scratched his face rather deeply, and he was very angry and determined upon revenge.

"He and I then fought. He believed he could beat me easily but found that he couldn't. At least not fairly. My father did teach me something useful from his naval experiences, and one of them was how to defend myself if I wished to survive in the bad company I seemed to frequent. He had some very questionable friends, my father. You met one of those gentlemen who taught me so much—Mr. Gilbey! He is now my good friend!"

She nodded.

"So I dealt with him and one of his friends the hard way as Mr. Gilbey had taught me. No half measures with me when my only sister was involved."

He looked at her pale face and smiled at her. "You should not look so worried or concerned, my love. Your hands are very warm, by the way. I like your hair too." He leaned forward and allowed her hair to touch his forehead as he breathed gently into her neck. "I can also smell lavender. How very pleasant!"

She did not pull away and found his compliments rather pleasurable, despite the charged circumstances of the discussion. How could he deal with all of this so lightly?

"Now where was I?" He sat back, raised her hand to his lips, and kissed it again, recalling where he was and what he had been saying.

"By the time he realized that he was being well and truly beaten, I'd made quite a mess of his face, I think, over and above what my sister had done to him, rather like poor Thackeray's. His friends had gathered by then and some others, fortunately for me, for one of *his* friends tried to give him a pistol. With others there, he could not easily shoot me out of hand as he might have done. Would have done! Except that Sir Alistair, John's father, intervened. John, John Buckingham, my sister's husband, was there too. That was where she first met him. Love at first sight I believe! Much like me!"

Her eyes flew to his face, to see him looking at her with a gentle, teasing smile about his lips. "I am surprised Elizabeth did not tell you!" She dared say nothing.

He continued. "But the gun! That would have been murder, and Maxton would have hanged! The suggestion was made by one of his friends, that honor would be served by a duel there and then. Of course, it was illegal, but that was of little consideration to anyone, myself included, at that moment, for he fully intended to kill me, and if not there, then at some other time, less public and less likely to cause him a severe problem. Also, when I might least expect it!

"He had the reputation of being a murderous shot and basked in the dubious glory of having walked away from two previous duels over a woman, leaving his opponents severely wounded and likely to die. He was too cocksure of himself! Those others who had come upon us there, tried to avoid such a foolish and unnecessary confrontation in that setting, but he was not about to let sober reconsideration take a hand and deny him revenge. It was clear that I could no more avoid a duel with him than I could have avoided the brawl that started it."

He sighed heavily at the thought. "Oh dear, I have not thought of that now for several years. It does not reflect well upon me. However, my father had also taught me something else other than dealing with bullies, that also proved to be of great value and has served me most well over the years. He taught me to shoot well, to shoot calmly, and to stay sober. Maxton was ape drunk, the fool! And angry beyond belief with me and my sister, and she was witness to his being beaten! The outcome was that he was inebriated and roaring angry, and I was not quite as angry."

He thought for a while and reconsidered. "Actually, I think I was the more angry. He had waylaid and been rough with my sister and had intended worse, but I was calm and deliberate and knew what the outcome had to be for the sake of my sister as well as myself. It was all done properly of course, Sir Alistair saw to that. We stood back to back, walked off the paces, turned as instructed, and I calmly shot him between the eyes while he merely grazed me, for he was trembling so much with rage, I think!" He momentarily let go of her hands and ran his finger along a faint scar distinctly visible on the side of his head, in the hairline. Sophia had drawn attention to that too from time to time, but he would not speak of how he had got it.

She was pale, but she also traced the faint scar with her finger and then took his hand again as she leaned weakly against his shoulder. She was pale and wide-eyed.

"Had I not killed him, he would have found some way of killing me later and maybe even my sister, or worse, for I did know of him and his reputation. I was not so very innocent myself. He deserved the beating and his death, for he gave me no choice in either of them. My sister encountered the younger brother some time later and took the wind out of his sails by shooting him in the arm to defend herself from him too. I am surprised our godmother did not have something to say of that! Pity she didn't kill him and saved me the bother of encountering him later when he also tried to kill me, but then I am glad she did not, for it would have weighed heavily upon her, far more than it did me. That was the incident at Inchdene that you overheard, and that the letter related. I did not intend to kill him, but that was how it worked out."

"Oh!"

"There, that is the first and fullest account I have rendered of that incident to anyone, so I expect I should allow you to repeat it as you wish but only with those who need to learn of it. Your mother knows, for I laid out *all* of my checkered history for her some days ago! *All* of it! Elizabeth, and even John, can confirm any of it, I expect.

"Now what else does she accuse me of? Yes, another brawl over a woman of questionable virtue and then a . . . forceful confinement and a rape even!"

He looked closely at Annis sitting beside him. "Are you sure you feel entirely safe in my company?"

"I am safe, I think." Her voice was quiet and a little hoarse.

"Yes, you are! She does not mince her words, does she? Now why didn't she broach that with me when she did see me? The two were related, though Lady Seymour did not seem to know that for she got them reversed. The brawl was the outcome of that confinement of our godmother's niece. There was only the one woman involved. But both were true; rape and brawl, unfortunately, though I can only take blame for the latter—the brawl, another brawl that brought things to an end."

She was not sure that she had heard him correctly.

"Why fate seemed to have singled me out as it did on those two occasions, I still cannot understand. I am sure other young men never got caught up in such violence. Why me? I still cannot understand that, though I am glad that I was there both times.

"To continue: I was walking home fairly late one evening shortly *before*, not *after* that Maxton episode as she believes, when a tearful, disheveled, desperate, even hysterical I would say, and half-clad young lady rushed out of one of the fashionable houses along that street and threw herself at my feet, begging for my help—the unfortunate Miss Trevelyan! She had unwisely put herself into the clutches of a villain. Another villain. Not me. I found out later that she was Lady Seymour's niece. The man involved, I may as well tell you his name too—Viscount Trencham, for he, like the Maxton brothers, is now dead—soon appeared on the scene at the door, afraid of what he might find waiting for him. She had pushed him down some stairs, I believe, to make her escape after he had had her imprisoned in his house for some days before that, so that second part was unfortunately correct about the confinement and the other, but I was not the culprit as my godmother seems to believe.

"He saw what Maxton after him saw—only a stripling. Me. Of no consequence to him, and to be milled down and removed from his path. He was right. I really was of no consequence. He tried to force her to return with him, slapped her once or twice for the slight injury she had done him, and was most insulting to me for presuming to meddle in his affairs with someone he protested was his wife when she clearly was not. What could I not do but help the young lady? He had a little more bottom and skill than Maxton did and was much more calm about it, for he was older too. However, he also underestimated me, for I was but a thin sickly-looking youth, and he did not know me. How could he? Our circles were worlds apart.

"Afterward, I wrapped my coat about her and escorted the young lady—actually I think I carried her most of the way, and a devil of a job I had of it, for she could not walk home with me, and I was not in a fit state to carry her. My parents' house was not too far distant, and I put her in the care of my sister, who saw her properly and suitably looked after, bathed, and dressed, I believe. My part in it ended there, for I never saw her again, but I did not escape the repercussions! Fortunately, my sister was home, or I would have had to have roused my mother and then the entire house would have been in an uproar. It *was*, *later* anyway. Apart from that, I was bleeding quite severely and badly bruised and knocked about, so I presented quite a sight for anyone to see, but he was in a much worse state, I suspect.

"There was uproar anyway, as I said, somewhat later. Difficult to hide with the marks that I was sporting on my face, and a situation with a distraught young lady that was discovered in the house. I was too weak to care what anyone thought, and it could not be hidden. I also could not, and then would not talk of it for some days, so the worst was assumed of me! He had a most punishing left hand, I recall, and that took me a few very painful moments to recognize.

"My sister did not witness the brawl on that occasion, but she patched me up afterward that evening after she had seen to the welfare of the young lady, so she can vouch for the brawling part of it and the fact that the young lady did not object to my presence as she might do if I were her attacker, but had been somewhat effusive in her thanks. As my parents later saw my face, they realized what I had been up to and even assumed much more than that. The young lady was turned over to a relative for safekeeping, but before she corrected the impression left of me. That relative, I later learned, was her aunt, and no less than Lady Seymour. Once out of our safekeeping, she could not undo the impression of me that my parents seemed to believe, and *did not* correct that of her aunt. Then later, that rape was laid at my door. It seems that no one had bothered to ask the young lady what she might know.

"My later protests counted for nothing, but in truth, I was annoyed that they did not believe me, when they should have. The upshot of all of that, and the subsequent

Maxton thing, was that I would have to go. I was out of control. I only recently learned that Miss Trevelyan had given birth, so there is another item to be mistakenly laid at my door by those determined to do so. As her ladyship does!"

Annis reached up and stroked his head without realizing what she was doing. "No. You couldn't avoid helping her! No wonder Addie feels so antagonistic about you."

"I thought I might have deserved being regarded as a hero for that little escapade, but then reality hit home again. I was not the heroic type and certainly not to be believed of any of the finer attributes of a gentleman. I realized that it was time I struck out on my own. No one believed any good of me and more trouble was sure to find me, if not from Maxton's brood then certainly from Trencham's. So I decided to put my latent talents for violence to good use. I joined the military.

"Trencham, unknown to me of course, soon afterward took off for the continent, recognizing—I see now—that Lady Seymour, her aunt, can be a most potent enemy when she is crossed. He had nothing to worry about, for she did not find out his part in it and still does not know. As you can tell from her letter, she is being revenged upon me again for something I did not do." He sighed heavily.

"For the last few years, I have been keeping an eye open for someone in her employ to seek me out—which she does so well—and make an *Il castrate* out of me for that! I have survived so far! When I rashly took her up on her invitation, I only drank her tea, as she also was drinking it, and ate some of her cake only after I had fed some of it to her little dog."

She looked up into his eyes. She could see that he was telling the truth in every sad detail and did not feel the need to hide any of it, but then why would he? By itself, the letter and its accusations were damning, as Lady Seymour had intended, but once the background was revealed, it became nothing more than hateful gossip no matter how true it might seem. No man would leave his sister unprotected. No man could resist responding to the pleas of a desperate woman in such dire need of his help. He had done the same for them, for her mother!

She would be prepared to tell Lady Seymour so, to her face, when she next saw her.

"One final footnote to this story. The one who *did* ferret me out was Trencham himself. I came across him on the continent, or rather, he came across me. He gave me my horse, Boney!" He paused for a few seconds. "That is a slight exaggeration, my dear. He did not *give* it to me willingly, of course. I had to shoot him off it, but then as he was drawing down on me at the time, and I, a fellow officer and an Englishman no less! Fortunately, I recognized him just in time, so I felt justified. He had recognized me earlier and was determined to be revenged for my earlier intrusion into his life and upsetting his continuing plans for Miss Trevelyan! So you see I killed two men up to that time and both of them Englishmen and me barely twenty-two years of age. What a desperate ruffian I had turned out to be! I also, unfortunately, killed numerous enemies in battle, but that is forgivable, I think, and is even expected and commendable, I believe.

"She got the last bit mostly right about me too. Most perceptive of her. I was ambushed by two highwaymen on my way to the North the same evening, a little before I got your mother's letter telling me that I was needed at Underby. Yes, it was the surviving younger Maxton brother that had vowed revenge on me and even on my sister. I told you she shot him in the arm some years ago to disabuse him of that notion and now has the immovable Mr. Gilbey standing between her and others like Maxton. The younger Maxton attacked me, not I him, as with all of them.

"He had been a little young at the time of his brother's death, and I was long gone by the time he felt he had to seek me out. I had to stop him killing me and was hoping to reason with him, but he hit his head when I knocked him off his horse. I had not intended to kill him! I am not fond of people taking shots at me or threatening my sister in my absence. So now the count is three! How lucky I am, that neither of the Thackerays had courage enough to try and kill me also, though the father was sorely tempted, I know. I know even you were at that time too. What a dreadful character is painted of me! You had best wash your hands of me, my dear, I am, beyond hope. The worst part of it is that most of it is true!"

"No, it is not!" She was now very calm and not in any way as tense as she had earlier been. "You said two men attacked you. What of the second man?"

"A most interesting Frenchman with an interesting story that I will tell you sometime. He was not familiar with the role of a highwayman and did not stay long aboard his horse once the guns went off, for the horse reared and got rid of him, so I had no need to shoot him. Which I am glad about. Apart from that, I saved his life in another way, though I am not sure he entirely believed me. Once I had his story, and it *was* interesting, and to do with my horse strangely enough, he decided that he would return to France forthwith, no doubt bemused, and wondering how the English could possibly survive their own stupidity and extreme violence."

"And what of Constanza? You did not mention her." She trusted that *that* would be as easily addressed as the others.

"Yes. Her! The fair and fast Constanza whom I brought back to England and of *which,* not *whom,* I provided some misleading details to her ladyship to think the worst. A ship my dear! Nothing more! A French ship, despite the name! The one my friends and I commandeered from her home port and sailed back to England, before I returned to the Continent. It was well described in the navy gazette and other papers your father had on his desk. I took some pleasure in describing the intimate relationship we had together—for we did—and how she changed hands more than I liked, true also, and then I had left London and her behind! All true. I am afraid my godmother had made up her own mind who and what the fair and fast Constanza was, just as she did with all of the others, so I led her on a little about that and chose my language carefully, knowing she would deliberately misconstrue it, and she did. However, I did just what she seems to do so well. I told her only the truth about Constanza and let her misunderstand it all as she did, for I could see it lodging in her vitals and begin to nag at her. I consider that a small victory! That is the only part of this sordid tale she got entirely wrong!

"Of course, since then, I brawled with Thackeray and might also have come to blows with his father too. My! I have been most busy! I hoped no one else would find out about that so soon and tarnish my already blackened reputation, but the servants seemed to observe it all. Perhaps if they had read this letter about me first, they may have been disappointed by my prevailing over the son and may even have come to his aid to defeat the greater blackguard!"

She flashed a glance at him and found him to be smiling at her for his attempted levity.

"They were afraid *for* you at first. Undoubtedly surprised, and I think I dare say, *pleased* over the outcome. So were we when we heard, though did not express it in quite that way, for you seemed to be—to me—as big a villain, or even a bigger one, than Thackeray!"

"Hence the horse pistol! But as for no one finding out, I suspect that was too much to expect, for I seem to have watchers everywhere about me and find that I am actually enjoying it. I did have a choice over that, perhaps, for I caught him in your father's study going over the papers that I had on the desk. But then, I did tell you some of that. He seemed to think he had every right to do so. I would have liked it to have been more peaceably settled, and he could leave as he came with no one the wiser or hurt. However, he was pigheaded and argued with me when I suggested he should put them down and to mind his own business. I was short on patience at that moment, having been recently bereaved—I think I can use that excuse for not being as patient or as forgiving as I might have been, or more restrained—and I was feeling most protective of some very beautiful ladies who had so suddenly become dependent upon me and of whom I had grown most fond and protective by then. I think I showed him the wisdom of not arguing about that. I also avoided a confrontation of any more serious nature with his father too, which quite surprised me, but then he had got my measure by then and I his, so we dealt with each other like two tom cats circling and wailing at each other."

"I heard!"

"Yes you did, didn't you? But I did show amazing restraint on another matter, for I did not argue, or worse, with the squire as I was tempted to do, much to his relief, I think. For we were able to achieve a suitable compromise that made everyone happy and certainly worked in our favor the night of that fire. He proved to be a very good neighbor after all!"

She remained silent and thoughtful. "I am afraid I may have badly misjudged you again and have harbored thoughts that were not at all complimentary to you. I should have burned this letter!"

"May have? I'll settle for that. However, I did sense your reservations and even guarded animosity! I also began to sense your crumbling defenses against me!"

"I was very wrong about you, William. I know that now. Though I was not as wrong as our godmother!"

"Oh, is that all? I am frequently wrong about many people!" She looked at him in surprise. "Besides, I would rather you thought the worst of me at the outset, as I think you did, and then suffer a painful reevaluation that puts me in a much better light, than have it go the other way. It also gives me a considerable advantage when those who think ill of me suffer from pangs of conscience."

She smiled weakly. "As I must admit to doing. I do not know how I could so badly misjudge anyone."

"You didn't, so do not fret about it! I am as bad a character as you fear I am, I can assure you of that! Your instincts about me were entirely correct, so don't revise them too quickly and possibly prematurely. You do, after all, know so very little about me still. I am not a gentleman as one might define that term, as you well know. At least not just yet! I have to learn again what it is that is expected of a gentleman in this country. That is somewhat difficult when one comes across those like the Maxton's and Thackeray's and others, though my experiences in the Peninsula prepared me well to meet them directly and in ways they did not so soon expect."

He sat back and reminisced a little more. "It is all very well being gentlemanlike in war, but it does not help one to survive, and it is better to dispense with those kinds of genteel preliminary formalities. I am every bit as *bad* as you feared! Just not quite as bad as *you* feared when it comes to either you or your family. At least I hope not!"

Annis was suddenly feeling much more at ease with the situation. "I was wrong about you, for I chose to accept at face value what that letter had said. I could not understand why Mama and Sophia and everyone else seemed to trust you."

"Yes, the older and the very young fall under my spell rather quickly. Do not be in such a rush to think good of me just yet, Annis. My behavior with you so far has not been entirely disinterested or of the most considerate and protective kind in certain directions."

She leaned her head against his shoulder and felt that she might now be able to relax properly. She also could not avoid shedding a few tears of relief. But she hoped that he might not notice that. She found her voice after some moments. "When Bella learned from Mama what seemed to have been planned for her in those meetings with your mother and Addie, she was not at first suited, and was inclined to reject you out of hand."

"Wise girl!"

"After listening to what your sister had to say of you, however, she relented a little and decided that she should at least know more about this unknown gentleman. You! What she learned was quite disturbing, for we were aware of some of the rumors, despite what your sister said of you. However, it seems that Mama was not about to give up so easily, and relied more upon Mrs. Devane—your mother – and your sister Elizabeth for her information and less upon Lady Seymour. I wish I had paid more attention now, and we could have avoided so much misunderstanding, though that letter would still have been damaging."

"I do not doubt it! No matter whom you might consult, it is hardly a rosy picture that is painted of me, for I really did do most of those things, just not in the way our godmother thinks, or with the added embellishments. Perhaps I should consider myself lucky that you did not shoot me when you might have done, twice now, or slit my throat on the many occasions when you have shaved me, and saved your family the disgrace of such a connection, though the damage had been done on that first night before anyone had read that letter!" He looked at her. "So, there you have it, Annis. I am a violent and unprincipled kind of a rogue, but I must deny the violence on a young woman—her niece, or responsibility for her child—laid at my door. I am never violent with a lady, even when she has a knife at my throat or might threaten me with a pistol." His voice dropped. "Not even when she is standing naked before me and the temptations are overpowering!"

She blushed at his smile and his gently suggestive words. "Only *seemingly* unprincipled and only in the deficient details. Not in the broader circumstances, and I find that there is a very big difference." She looked at him with some relief in her eyes. "Thank you!" She found she was trembling with relief and on the edge of shedding tears of happiness yet again!

"What! You believed me against that most damning catalog of my sins?" He laughed. "You are forgetting your Chaucer."

She looked at him and wiped some moistness from her eyes as she smiled weakly at him, clearly much relieved, but waiting for him to enlighten her.

"'Nigh and sly wins against fair and square who isn't there.' I am nigh and sly. Very sly! But I think you know that by now."

"You have it the wrong way round, I think. This . . ." she indicated the letter, " . . . was the 'nigh and sly.' It worked its evil intent upon me quite badly, and from within, over some considerable time until I dared broach it with you."

"Yes. They knew what they were saying, who said that the pen is mightier than the sword. I am obviously a rank amateur. Lady Seymour is a past master at it I now see, yet I cannot think ill of her, for most of what she said was true, if not the whole picture. Had she known all of the details, I am sure she would have been more careful and much more kindly disposed toward me. One day, she may know me better! So you see, it was all a mere misunderstanding! I do not think I have been too severely injured by any of it"

"You are too kind to her. I have now heard from 'fair and square,' I think, who is now there, here! What damage it would have done to any who might have innocently read it, without knowing the full story, or suspecting that it could not possibly be entirely true. But you are right about it being a damning litany against you. Yet, I have seen no sign of any . . . awkward intent . . . against my sisters, my mother, or . . . me."

"My, you do forget so easily! Surely you do not forget when I blundered into your bedroom while you bathed, for I raised it just a few seconds ago? I should be hurt if you did, for it had a most devastating effect upon me! I am unlikely to ever forget that moment. How I controlled myself, I do not know, for my feelings at that moment were very nearly beyond me." He gently touched her hair. "I wanted to take you into my arms just as you were and kiss and caress you relentlessly and . . . well, best leave the rest of it out of this discussion, for it did not happen!"

"No, I did not forget that, but *that* was . . . gentle."

"It might not have been! I scare myself thinking how it might have gone wrong for us both. Especially for me! But the temptation is always there . . . ! Oh how the temptation is there! It can only be a matter of time, my dear." There was a strange look in his eyes. "But as long as you are under my roof and in my protection, I shall strive to behave like a gentleman, and as I think your father might have liked me to behave toward you."

She stood up, retrieved the letter, and then leaned over quickly and kissed him on the cheek, taking him entirely by surprise. Her eyes were still moist and she sniffed. He did not take the opportunity that he had, to capture her for a moment more, for he was looking into her eyes at that moment. He was more than pleased with what he saw.

"As for believing you over this? Why yes, I think I do, sir. Thank you." She avoided his slowly reaching out for her and smiled at him from a little distance, much relieved by what he had confided to her.

"On second thought, now that I am out of reach, I confess that I will reserve judgment on your character, for there are those episodes you described, and other minor deficiencies that I continue to notice, as when you bathed me in my room that day, as you so cleverly remind me from time to time, for you did not leave as I requested, did you? Also, as I have noticed when I have come very close to you to shave you and discovered your hands upon my waist or moving . . ." She blushed and said no more of that. "There are a few other unanswered details and questions. So I now know, I think, the worst of you!"

"I very much doubt it!"

She ignored that. "But you do not know the wors—" She colored up and stopped from completing what she had started to say, regretting even starting to say anything. "I have another question, a difficult question to ask of you, and nothing to do with this, I think." She looked at him and could see that he had not lost patience with her. He was still smiling.

"Yes, my love?"

"What . . . !" She faltered and stumbled over her words and blushed as his words hit home yet again. "What would you . . . what are your intentions—plans for me and my sisters and mother at this time?"

He doubted that had been the question she might have been ready to ask him. "My intentions? My plans? Why, I am going to look after you all if you will allow me, for I am but a sly and ingratiating kind of fellow always seeking the main chance. Can I take it that you now do not object to my intrusion into your personal lives;

this interference in your family's personal affairs; my presence? You did when I first appeared on the scene, I believe."

"That was then, and we just dispensed with that. You seem to have looked after our interests very well as you carefully worked your way into our good graces."

"I did, didn't I?" He sounded smugly satisfied at that.

She thought for a few moments. "I find it most strange. One can live with or close by someone for years and discover that you never really knew them at all. Sometimes I am not sure I know my own mother that well, and I am beginning to believe I did not know Bella as well as I thought I did. I certainly cannot understand my godmother at all after this, and I shall have some things to say to her, I think! Others, you can encounter but briefly and feel quite certain that you know them."

"I hope you do not put me in that latter category just yet, Annis, or you might be surprised and disappointed. I would far rather you believed me a villain worth keeping an eye on. Before you try to place me on that pedestal, there is still something that I must confess to you."

"Oh?"

"I cannot continue to play the role of disinterested 'brother-in-law'—how wounding to me that phrase was when you first used it—for much longer, quite as easily as I had hoped!"

She blushed as he looked intently upon her with a smile on his face. "What role would you prefer, sir?"

"That was a rash question, my dear. But surely you now know the answer to it?" He could see from the reddening on her cheeks that she perhaps did. "My godmother did not totally misinform you of my character, if you can read between the lines a little. No smoke without fire, as the saying goes, and I did tell you of Dierdre! But I find that I am likely to fail in that too, for I think that all of you—your mother, your sisters and even my own—know that I am not as disinterested in one of you as I should be. And find I have too much to lose—my very existence indeed—if I make the wrong step too quickly. So idle seduction is no longer as possible as I had at first hoped."

She faltered for a few seconds as he continued to smile at her. Surely he could see how wildly her heart was beating. She was suddenly flustered again, and her hands were up close to her throat. "I do not follow you. I cannot think that that is a proper topic for conversation, sir."

"I think you do follow me. Of course it is something that needs to be discussed between us. We are both adults, both of age as you once reminded me, and we both know our own minds, so I think it is proper. At least I know mine."

"I do not think that I am supposed to know anything of that subject . . . seduction!"

"Yet you all practice it so well, as women have done across the ages. It happens when a beautiful young lady does not so very violently object when I surprise her at her ablutions, or when she snuggles up close and looks up at you with those large and innocent eyes and does not object when I take her hand and even when I kiss it, or she encourages me to even lean a little toward her and feel her hair on my face, smell her perfume, or I gently kiss her on the neck, or say outrageous things, and call her my love. For you are, you know?"

She seemed a little alarmed to hear that. "I did not encourage you any of those times, for you did all of that, and you did not kiss me on the neck." She was blushing.

"Not just now. I did a few days ago. You did encourage me, even without words, and had been doing so for several days. So you see, there are different degrees of seduction you know, and all of them most pleasant for both parties. Provided they are both of the same mind."

"There are those who might disagree, sir."

"Undoubtedly. I think you should come and sit by me, Annis, for I have some other things I wish to say to you along those same lines."

She was blushing furiously. "No, sir. I think I shall stay over here."

He sighed. "My name is William, my dear. Yes, you should stay over there. Probably that would be most wise with me in my present mood."

"Yes. I think so too. I have another question."

"Oh dear!"

"Men and women see things so very differently. You readily confessed to all of that violence, and as bad as that was, I cannot help but think that you could not avoid being as violent as you were."

"Thank you."

"But how readily would you confess, I wonder, if by confessing something . . . something far more subtle, and perhaps even more hurtful, than killing someone . . ."

He interrupted her progress. "Yes, killing someone is most unsubtle, isn't it?"

"Please do not interrupt. It is difficult enough as it is! A confession that would cause others, innocent of any crime, immense distress! A distress perhaps far worse than killing a villainous man, or even two, who deserved it, and putting an end to it all in that way, for the subjects are still alive and . . . unaware of what has happened just yet . . . but it would all eventually be discovered. How would you deal with that deliberate and plotted deception, I wonder?"

He was surprised to find that she seemed to await his answer with some anxiety, perhaps even trepidation. Might she dare to tell him more? "Yes, deception, deliberate deception is a difficult moral situation to recover from. Sometimes! But sometimes it may be necessary for the greater good!"

"For the greater good!" She had unconsciously repeated his words and seemed to find some comfort in them.

"I can think of any number of times when I deceived my mother and father, especially about that Maxton situation, and before *that*, about the Trevelyan girl, and others too. I undoubtedly deceived Lady Seymour by describing Constanza as I did? No, she deceived herself there. We all deceive ourselves, I think, and that is the worst deception of all."

She absent mindedly responded. "To thine own self be true!" She still seemed anxious over something that she dared not reveal in any greater detail.

He agreed with that! "Yes! But what would be the point of confessing any of it, Annis? I am sure that whatever it is, it is better left alone and even forgotten. It does not sound as though it were a crime against one's fellow man if no life were lost and there was no injured party." He looked up at her. "Is there an injured party in this?"

"No! Not yet! At least, there is, but no one knows of it just yet." She could not meet his eyes at that moment. "Perhaps the only injury is to the truth."

"Oh, is that all! A deep philosophical discussion to balance killing a person with the damage that might be done to the truth. But no person injured. I am confused that you give it such weight. I am sure that the Greek philosophers must have wrestled with this. Perhaps you should consult their writings. But you say that if the truth were told, others might then be injured?"

"Hurt! Not injured. I may have misspoke."

"Then I would say nothing, Annis. Let the gentle deception stand for as long as it will and the scene play through. What would be gained by anyone? Deceptions hurt someone only when they are discovered, and perhaps it will not be discovered, for they sometimes turn out to be true!"

"But it will be discovered! It cannot be avoided!" She seemed sure of that.

"Are you sure? Mine rarely were! They were all what I would call necessary deceptions. Perhaps what you are thinking of might be in the same vein. Necessary!"

"It is. It was!" She was still not easy with any of it. He wanted to help her, but knew that he could not.

"I think you had better let sleeping dogs lie then. By the time it is found out, if it is ever found out, it might not then mean anything. Besides, it may work out the way you would most like it to, with hurt to no one who matters. I hope it does."

"So do I."

He looked at her thoughtfully. "You will eventually tell me the situation behind your question, won't you?"

"Perhaps! Eventually!" She seemed to be relieved by his answer.

"I still believe that my confession was the more weighty. After all murder . . ."

"You did not murder anyone! That is entirely the wrong word. They deserved to die, for you were defending your sister and then yourself and even a woman in need of your protection. Even a mother will commit any number of crimes, perhaps even to kill, to protect her children."

"Yes, and even deceive to protect them too." Her eyes flashed to his face. He recognized that he had come close to a raw nerve. Now what had her mother done to deceive anyone? "No matter! The crime, my dear, is in killing one's fellow man whether deserved or not. That is why we have the rule of law and laws." He kept dragging it back to his own indiscretions, to lessen her own burden!

She did not let it lie. "Laws that were powerless to help you at the time, I perceive. You had to kill, or be killed yourself, so you needed to defend yourself on each occasion as it arose. I do not believe the law regards that as murder."

"You are right. But whether murder or self-defense, I still do not think there is a greater crime than to take a life. Had I been able to avoid doing so in any of those three cases, even in war, I would have done—except for Trencham—but there wasn't. Deception is a mere gasp in a gale by comparison."

She looked a little less anxious.

"My, we have covered some ground in the last few minutes, haven't we? Again! I still would like you to come over here and sit beside me for a few minutes, Annis! I have something most special I would relate to you of a very personal nature."

"No, sir."

"William."

"No! William!"

He began to stand up. She could see a new look and determination in his eyes as he looked intently at her and was not sure she could deal with him at that moment in time, for his purpose seemed to focus solely upon her, and she was not sure quite how to deal with him. Or herself! She turned and fled the room.

He sat down and smiled. He felt that he knew the details of the circumstance behind her quandary, but he could not let her know any of that, or all of their world, his included, might come crashing down. It was in reality, a mere tempest in a teacup, and had been entirely forgotten by all of them it seemed but not by Annis and certainly not by him!

It would be soon enough uncovered and resolved if he had his way, but he would need to tread cautiously. It would never have done, to have let her know that he was aware of any of what she had skirted around, or there might not be a recovery from that. If it were done right, it would work to all of their advantages. Time enough for that to unfold, but it would need to unfold soon, that much was obvious, and for his own peace of mind and sanity.

Chapter XXIX

The Observers and the Most Disturbing Question

"Have they gone?" Such sudden and innocent-sounding inquiry might not have caused any problem had it been made during the day. In the silence of the dark room however, it suddenly became like a cannon shot to the one person there, standing in the dark, especially when everyone else was abed and no one should have been wandering the house at that time of the very early morning.

"Charlotte!" Annis was startled. Her hands leapt to her throat at her surprise at being discovered spying upon those just outside of the house over by the stable. "You should not sneak up on people that way! You robbed me of five years of my life! Keep your voice down, you don't need to wake anyone up or let anyone know that you are here! What are you doing out of bed at this hour? It is barely four o'clock." She took in her sister's white nightdress, brightly contrasted in the moonlight streaming in through the window of the dining room. "You are not dressed! You never know who you might bump into like that and you are standing full in the moonlight!"

"Of course I'm not dressed. Why would I go to the trouble to dress to see what those men are doing out there? They won't see me! Besides, I don't care. But I could say the same of you. You are just as lightly dressed *and* just as likely to be seen!" Her sister did not care either, it seemed!

Annis turned back to watching out of the window. "No, they have not gone yet! They are still offloading their cart." She had been watching them since the cart, showing no lights whatsoever, had come up the driveway making very little noise. She wondered if they had the horses' hooves bound with burlap to deaden the sounds of their shoes. She had heard that those who did not wish to draw attention to their presence in the dark sometimes might do that. They really hadn't needed lights anyway, for there was enough of a moon to see by. She had then watched as William and one of his sailors had quietly unloaded many boxes and what appeared to be kegs into a small tool-shed tucked into the trees by the stable. The cart had then been walked out of sight behind the building, and then a few minutes later, she saw the sailor walking a horse across the lawns. William turned away from seeing him off, walked over to the stable, and disappeared inside.

The sisters stood and watched from the shelter and dark of the house. "Annis, they can't have been out already. They have not been away for long enough, for William rode off just after dark last night. I am sure that it takes much longer than that to go across to France and pick up a cargo and get back again."

"No. They didn't go out last night! They are moving what is left of an earlier cargo out of the way for when they do make a run across to France. For that is what they describe it as."

"How exciting to have a smuggler in the family!" Charlotte was indeed excited. "If Sophia has her way, there will be two of them. If I have my way as well, there will be three, for I would not mind going out with them too! I've never been on any kind of ship, never mind one that is used for smuggling! Sophia has said little of anything else for the last few days now. I think we were both quite excited when we first heard him admit to being a smuggler, as he did that first night when he spoke to Bella and told her all about himself. I wish you had been there, Annis! He was so tender with her and kind. We could not help but cry, for he seemed so sad and even to share our burden at that moment. I was surprised at some of the things he told her about his past, apart from that smuggling. Mama told us both that we must say nothing to anyone of what we had heard, for it had been told in confidence to Bella, and she would be most hurt if she ever learned of us betraying what he said, but she couldn't know any of that, could she?"

"No! Of course not, Charlotte! But you really shouldn't say anything, for he believed he was speaking only to Bella and not to her sisters too."

"Sophia was out at the docks with him the other morning when they were preparing for their next run, I think. She seems to think he will take her out with him, and if he won't, she is determined to dress herself in boy's clothes, as she did already, and smuggle herself on board and go anyway."

Annis was surprised to hear that. "She wouldn't dare!" Charlotte could feel her sister's eyes burning into her.

"Oh, wouldn't she? Much you know! She has been down to the docks once with him already dressed like that. She is too like you in that regard!"

Annis wondered what she might know of *that*, but did not quiz her about it. "But what is that about her wearing boy's clothing?"

"Never mind that, Annis! There is William again." He appeared from the stable, looked around to see what might be stirring, and then walked over to the house.

"You should step back from the window, Charlotte. In your white nightdress and with the moon shining full upon you in the window, you are clearly visible."

"I don't think so. They didn't see you, and you were standing full in the window as they offloaded those boxes and kegs, for I watched you for some minutes before I spoke to you. You were talking to yourself about something. Anyway, he's gone now. He goes in through the conservatory and gets rid of his boots out there so that he disturbs no one."

"You seem to know a lot of what he does and how he does it!" Annis took her sister to task.

"So do you! I am not the only one who is interested in what he does! Sophia told me that when she was down on the docks with him—and the little wretch had no intention of telling me until I cornered her—that they were busy emptying one of the buildings, off behind the headland and were moving an earlier cargo further inland, to clear the space. They will obviously be going out soon, probably at the next full moon, if the weather is in their favor, and that cannot be more than a few days off!"

"How do you know this, Charlotte?"

"I overheard them. I know their whole routine now, and what little I didn't know, Sophia told me with a little encouragement and the threat that I would tell Mama about her. I wish I were a boy! I would dress up, smuggle myself into the back of that cart and into the large box there—where they keep rope and other things in—and stow away on their ship while they are having their meeting. They meet in that little inn on the dockside before they go, to make their plans. It would be easy to sneak aboard then. The reverend is one of their crew, and I discovered that Thomas, was recruited as part of the land contingent, to keep an eye out for the revenue officers and to lead them astray if necessary. I overheard everything one evening in the library when William was explaining it to the reverend." She laughed softly. "They did not know that I was off in the stacks and listening."

"Charlotte, you must promise me not to do any such thing, to hide yourself away like that! That is the behavior of a hoyden and would get you into a good deal of trouble. Some of those men are not to be trusted as we trust William, and if one of them found you . . . Besides, you might put some thought like that into Sophia's head if she were to hear you."

"No, I will not promise! I think it would be fun, and there cannot be so many female smugglers. How romantic! Sophia is already planning that very thing, I think, for you can almost see her thoughts at moments like that. Besides, William would protect me!" Charlotte seemed very sure of that.

"Are you sure? He would more likely put you overboard and would never dare trust you again! He was quite put out that you had drawn him in that bath and those other drawings of him too!"

Her sister turned on her in surprise. "You showed him? How could you?" Her surprise gave way to a mischievous chuckle. "What did he say?"

"Keep your voice down! He did not say anything about any of them. I did not do it deliberately, and it was your own fault. He saw them himself and by accident. I thought Sophia may have told you, for that was when you had sent her up to spy on us when we were quiet. He saw the others of me too, while I was distracted by her, and me not fully dressed either in those, when I posed for you."

"Not fully dressed?" Her sister laughed at her and touched her on the arm. "Annis, you were as naked as a dressed chicken!"

"Yes! I know!" The dark hid her blushes from her sister. "I was so embarrassed! But he said nothing that was critical or censorious. He acted as though he had not seen them, but I know that he had. He could not have avoided them! I don't think he was so very embarrassed at all, but I was so ashamed and my heart was in my mouth there for a while at what he might think or say! So you see the fault can be laid at *your* door for sending Sophia up to distract me from controlling what he might see, for I was showing him your drawings of Bella. I am beginning to think that that was not wise of you to draw any of us that way."

"Pooh! There is nothing wrong with sketching the human form, especially if they are my own sisters, and if they are tastefully done. But you were not supposed to share them with anyone! Mama used to draw a lot of portraits like that at one time, even of father, for I came across some of her sketch books once, but I don't know where she hid them away now. I did not expect you would let him see the *others*, Annis. You should not have let him see them! But what did he say? Was he angry?" She seemed anxious to find out how he reacted to seeing them.

"I did not show him any of them deliberately, and I told you that he said nothing about those of me, *nor* about those of him either, but you were just as revealingly indiscreet about him, and I *know* he saw them!"

Charlotte laughed almost guiltily. "No. I expect he would not be so unwise as to draw anyone's attention to *them*! I could never ask him to pose like that for me, for *that* would be thought outrageously fast of me as well as dangerous to encourage any man in that . . ." she broke off that thought, " . . . and rightly so, and I would never dare do that, but how otherwise might I ever find out what a naked male looks like—apart from father, that is—without risking everything, and getting to draw one! So he knows of them now! Undoubtedly, that is why he has been so difficult to spy upon after that! It is a pity that I do not know this property *nearly* so well as I know Underby and all of *its* hideaways, or I might still be able to catch him unexpectedly! But as for getting myself aboard his wagon or his boat, if I decided to do that, then I would not be found by him or anyone else!" She sounded almost defiant. "At least it all sounds so fine and adventurous when I tell *you* about it, but I realize I must not do any such thing." She sighed heavily. "Oh, if only I were a boy! They have all of the fun! I so envy them riding astride a horse, as you once did, instead of perched on that stupid saddle. They can throw things, wrestle, swim, swing from ropes, and I especially envy them not having to squat to relieve themselves, for they have the ability to pee while they are standing up and directing it where they will, and quite a long way too, *and* high!"

"Charlotte!"

"Well, they can, and they do, and don't get themselves all wet, for I have watched them! I even have a drawing." She chuckled.

"Charlotte, not another one! You do too many like that, and one day you will be discovered and will be made to pay the price. I hope it was of no one that we know or that might be recognized! What Hogarth can get away with, drawing little boys, and what *you* might draw when you are feeling impish, are two different things. But when did you see this? And, if it comes to that, *where* were you to see all of this? I hope you were not seen yourself."

"I went out with Sophia to find that cat in the barn; the one with the kittens. She used to have five, but they took the others away and only left her with the one. They had left the ladder up, and I climbed up to see. It is so cuddly and furry next to my chin, and the mother cat does not mind in the slightest, for she purred the whole time. I was up there in the beams, and there is a little window up there that one can see out of ever so far. I looked out, and there below me was that peculiar misshapen tree. One of the hands was standing there and peeing and . . ."

"No more, please, Charlotte. You should not repeat any of this."

"I won't. Why would I, except to you? But it was most interesting. He knew nothing of my presence far above him. I said nothing to distract him. You never see that sort of thing with having only sisters. How they do that is most interesting. At least they don't get themselves wet, and they can direct it anywhere they like. I tried it and . . ."

"No, Charlotte, please." She tried to silence her sister's further confession. "Spare me that!"

"Well, don't do it! My legs were sore and chapped for some time until I could wash them off! It is not as easy as they make it look! Well at least Sophia did not see him, for she was there with me, and I cautioned her to be silent. She did not know what I could see. Fortunately, she was at the bottom of the ladder, *inside*, and could not see, or you know what she might have blurted out and been far too curious about, and gone to see, and even ask him directly. We would all have to remove back home if that happened! She is too direct at times!"

"I have noticed! But you seem little better Charlotte! It bounces off William, fortunately, but I should have a word with her about that. But I do want to know about the kitten. You shall show me later."

"I would, but they took the very long ladder away, and I cannot find it, and I will not clamber up onto the hay and balance across that narrow beam, and I cannot climb up the other way. There used to be a swing on the beam too, but the rope must have broken off for there is just one small piece left hanging and it is far too high to reach or I might have climbed up a little."

Annis put a hand on her sister's arm. "I expect William will be inside now and settled. We could probably go now without being discovered."

"We should give him a few more minutes, I think. We don't want to blunder into him." She looked at Annis standing in the moonlight and then realizing that there might never be a better moment to broach what had been on her mind now for several days. "You haven't told him yet, have you?" That innocent question shattered Annis's composure.

There were a few seconds of silence over that sudden and extremely alarming statement. "Told him what?" Had it not been so relatively dark, Charlotte might have been concerned to have noticed how pale her sister had suddenly become.

"Oh, Annis! You know very well what I am talking about! We do not have that many secrets! Told him about what really happened? Even what those cards that we made up for a lark really showed and not what we at first thought they showed?"

Annis was far more agitated than her sister might know. "Of course not! You should put all of that from your mind, Charlotte! It didn't happen in any way except the one that was needed! Besides, nothing but trouble would come from opening up either of those issues again! You know that!"

"You should tell him about the cards at least, you know? I am sure he would understand the mix-up and what his fate should have been! He will find out eventually! Better now than later!"

"You make it all sound so sinister—*what his fate should have been*! Better that he not find out at all, Charlotte! Do you not think I have agonized long and hard ever since I found out about those damned cards, and the sleepless nights, and all of the trouble they continue to cause me about what might have been? What should have been?" She sobbed at the thought. "But how do you know about those cards? I told no one!"

"I found out! I puzzled over them for ages after you had thrown them into the fireplace. Fortunately, there was no fire burning then, or all of the evidence would have been destroyed. He will find out if Mama tells him, or Sophia even, for she was there too when I sorted it out, and she will. Although . . . I don't think it made any sense to Mama just yet, but it will eventually, even though she is quite happy at the way everything worked out. It is not the kind of secret that stays concealed for ever. Her motherly concern to see things right will not be submerged for long, for she is itching to do something, and she sees how you cannot take your eyes off him. Off each other even, for it is quite an entertainment now to watch you shaving him and how he responds to you and you to him!"

"You have taken to spying on me too now! On us! Oh Charlotte, that is not kind of you! But Mama will say nothing! She is quite contented with things the way they are, and in truth, so am I. I think! It is better than him finding out all of our secrets and then becoming disgusted with us, as he would, and put us out and leave us. We are in mourning and will be for some period of time. There is nothing we can do about it!"

"But, Annis, Father did not believe in any of that astrology stuff and nonsense! I don't think Arabella would approve of the stupid mistake that has been made, if she had known."

"It is of no matter at this moment, Charlotte. In any case, Mama has said nothing, and she would, if she thought she should, and I think she has also quite forgotten what happened by now and has put it behind her, for it achieved everything she wanted. She has said nothing and hinted at nothing and is still grieving sorely as we all still are. It is not something one gets over in the space of a week or a month or even a year, and while things are as calm as they are, I have no intention of putting it all in jeopardy! I doubt that Mama could take kindly to it being revived to agonize over considering the likely outcome of that! I'm not sure that I could!"

"You should get over it as soon as you can, Annis, and deal with it! If you have a year it won't seem so bad, but you don't! I have seen the way he looks at you and you at him, and so has Mother and his sister. You both are struggling to keep your hands off each other. It's a losing game for both of you. Neither of you will survive a year the way things are, but will be sneaking off to the barn like Thomas and Molly do, and then you *really will* be big with news, but of another kind! The servants all seem to know too!"

"Know what?" Annis had gone pale. "That . . . *big with news* . . . is a most improper thing to say Charlotte! We have done nothing! But . . . you . . . I am sure you are mistaken."

"No, I'm not. You are too blind to see, and think everyone else is too, but we are not. You just have to see the two of you together for a minute, even just as you were, by the trough, that day of the fire. I was most startled by it all, for I was not sure what I saw then, but I do now. Had there been no one else to see either of you, you would have thrown your nightclothes off and have been going at each other like Thomas and Molly were when we saw them in the hay barn, and . . . well you *would* have! Then when you shave him! I keep wondering where he will put his hands next with *you* dressed the way you usually are! I was breathless with anticipation and excitement at what you both seem so ready to do!"

"Charlotte!" Her sister blushed, recognizing the truth of what she suggested, for she had sometimes wondered herself at what he might dare to do next. "You should not be watching at those times! It is private!"

"Oh no, it isn't! But how can we not watch? It is so very tender, and it makes me quite jealous that I do not have such an attentive gentleman of my own. I must admit that I have never felt that way about any male before. It is so obvious that you are in love. I would not hesitate for one second if it were me he was in love with, but it isn't. I would suggest we run off and elope together. Or just ignore what people might say and do what Mama and Papa did! Yes, I dare speak of that! You are far more restrained than I would be! I know where his bedroom is too! So do you! If it were me . . ."

"Charlotte, you must not spy on him!"

"I don't! At least not as much as I used to or would like to. After you let him see those drawings I cannot get as close to him as I used to do."

"You should not say such things! Where did you come up with these notions? I am sure Mama did not put them into your head. They are not proper. It is also impossible! He would never forgive us for the . . . He married Bella! I can do nothing about that. He would hate us all if I were to . . . and then we would be gone from here, and we might never see him again. He would want nothing to do with us."

"Much you know of him! You seem unable to believe your own eyes or your own feelings. I have watched the two of you together. He is in love with you! It is just a matter of time!"

"You must not say that, Charlotte!" But she knew that it were true. The difficulty was that when he learned what they had done, he would not be in love with her any longer.

"Why not? There is nothing improper about being in love and wishing to act upon it. I told you, Mama did! It may not be proper, but life is more important than to be put off by behaving properly, and stupidly I would say, when you know what is important and what should be done! What needs to be done! Love is very important. When I fall in love, I shall know what to do. Provided it is reciprocated in the same way, of course."

"I can do nothing! He would not understand any of that foolishness. Oh surely you can see that! He married Bella!"

"I know that, Annis, I am not stupid! But if she is looking down on you at this moment, she would not wish you to be so restrained or foolish, and stupid even, for it is so very obvious that you were meant for each other! Just a week ago, the night of the fire. You were still in the house. We were outside by then and frantic with worry for you. You did not see him outside, of course, but I did, and so did Mama, for he had just got Mama out and then us too. He did not hesitate for a second with any of us, for we were then safe. He almost ran back after you and in only his nightshirt. He poured cold water over himself from the trough in the blink of an eye—most clever thing to do that, I would never have thought of that—and took a sodden sheet in with him. It's a good job it was still dark, for I know how those cling to your body when they are wet. He saw no one else around him, I am sure. He had a most determined look on his face and would have trampled anyone in his way or knocked them to one side! He was determined to go back in there and drag you out. It was obvious to us all that if he did not come out with you, he would not be coming out at all! Mother was terrified and pale beyond belief. That is the only time I have ever heard mother pray outside of church, and you know she is not that religious."

"I am sure . . ." Annis was pale.

"I am right! We'd all seen it before then of course, even after he brought you back from your ride, with both of you looking like a guilty pair indeed! You are sure that nothing more happened than him just rescuing you when you became faint, are you?" She looked at Annis most searchingly. "One might almost think you had made love then! You had been alone all day, you know? Oh, Annis, we are none of us stupid!"

Annis fell into a deep silence with her thoughts to herself.

"And then after that fire, at the trough, as you did up his hand. Your clothing was still damp, and so was his. Most revealing I can tell you! The way you had eyes only for each other was most telling. I thought you were about to undress each other at that moment!"

Annis blushed crimson. "Charlotte! So you said! You should not say such things! You . . . !"

Charlotte held her hand up to stop her sister's interjection. "I shall say no more on that! But I believe you are behaving very foolishly. Mama will tell him! But if she doesn't, it is only a matter of time before Sophia lets slip something. She and William are as thick as thieves when they go off together."

"Yes. That is the only thing that worries me."

"You should worry at his response when he finds out from someone else rather than from you if you don't tell him. He will never trust any of us again! It is very likely that he will turn us out of here, or if we are at Underby, he will never have anything to do with us again. Men do not like to be deceived. It is better if he finds out from you, and soon!"

"I dare say nothing! It was necessary at the time. At least we thought so."

"We were wrong! Now it must be put right, for there will be no peace nor contentment for either you or him or us, until it is."

Her voice dropped, and she put a hand on Annis's arm "There! We were right to wait. William is just now come back into the house. He will probably go off to his study or will be taking a bath I expect, before he thinks anyone might be up and about to spy on him. But he bolts that door downstairs!" She chuckled. "If I knew he were coming back like this some other time, and you not here, I might just hide in there *before* he bolts the door, and sketch him at my leisure."

Annis tried to change the subject. "I would also like to know when they are going out again." She tried to submerge her other feelings that Charlotte had disturbed so much by her earlier personal revelations and comments. It had not been the kind of conversation she had expected to have with Charlotte. "I shall ask Sophia what she knows of any of this, for she knows more of their plans than I do. She is usually out of bed by first light, watching for him when he has gone the night before. She probably watched everything from one of the upper windows, for there is a telescope up there, though not much good at this time of night, even with a moon, as I found out for myself."

"If she discovers when they are planning on going out, I would not be surprised if she is not out there pestering to be taken with them. Or hiding herself away to make sure she goes. The longer you dither over the other issue, Annis, the more time you give Sophia to empty her mind about everything she knows."

"Please, Charlotte. No more, I beg of you. I am not likely to sleep at all after our conversation as it is." She sighed heavily. "I'll go and check her room. If she is awake, I will speak with her about not revealing any of this."

"She'll be in bed by then, and pretending to be asleep, for she can hear the stairs creaking!"

Chapter XXX

The Unusual Plights of the Kitten and Annis

"Annis! Annis! You must come at once, without delay! Oh please hurry! There is a rat in the barn, and it is going to kill the kitten, I know it! I cannot stop it, for it is out of my reach. The mother cat is gone somewhere! Oh please come, please, before it is too late!"

Annis threw back the covers and reached for her clothes. "It cannot be much after five, Sophia! Why have you not told William instead of me as you seem to be so thick with him?"

Sophia had run over to the door, wondering why her sister was not already following her as quickly as she might. "I tried, and I would have done, but he is not in his bed, and it is cold. He has ridden off somewhere, and I can find no one else, for it is too early. I doubt that Charlotte would help me, for she is barely awake even by nine!"

Her impatience was mounting by the second as Annis searched for something to wear. "Oh please, Annis! We do not have time for that. There is no one else moving about at all, and there won't be for at least another hour or even two." She stamped her foot and was overwrought and close to tears.

"But I cannot go like this! Where are my clothes? Where is my dress? There is no wrap either!"

"We shall be too late." Tearful frustration filled her sister's eyes.

"Oh very well! It is too early for anyone else to be about, except you did say William had gone. I do hope there is no one to see us, though *you* are dressed, I see."

Sophia led her elder sister downstairs and off at a fast clip around the corner of the building and across the yard to the smaller barn. The wind whipped dust about Annis's bare legs and blew her nightdress up around her as she tried to hold it down about her legs, fearful that others might see her in her present state. She regretted having come without taking time to find at least some of her clothes and to get dressed.

They pushed into the dark interior of the barn. It was dusty and eerily still. "This was not wise of you, Sophia. Nor of me, I fear."

"But it won't take long!"

"Now where is this kitten? Or more to the point, where is the rat? I do not like rats!"

"The rat will not stay if you are up there with the kitten, and the mother cat will soon return, I know it. The cat's nest is just under that small window. I dared not come and get you till now when I saw the rat retreat, for I was throwing things at it."

"I see nothing of any kitten!"

"No, it is well hidden as they always are."

"And how am I to get to the kitten, pray? I do not see a ladder except *that one* against the hay, but that is too short."

Oh Annis! You will use *that* one to climb onto the hay there, and then you can go across the hay to that small platform and onto the beam. It is only a short walk from there across to the nest."

"Really? You make it sound so easy. It looks like a remarkably foolhardy venture to me!"

"But it *is* easy. It *is*. I would show you myself, but . . . Please, Annis!"

"No. That is far too high for me, never mind for you. I shall not risk my life by going out there. You should go and get William after I return to the house!"

"But he is not here at the moment! Oh dear! Then I must!" She sobbed in frustration and headed for the ladder to get up onto the first bank of hay.

It was clear that she would too, and would very likely fall from the beam, for it seemed very narrow. "No! *You* stay. *I* shall go." She helped Sophia off the ladder. "But if I fall, it shall be on your head, perhaps in more ways than one! If I get a broken bone out of this, you shall not hear the last of it!"

"Oh *please* hurry, Annis! *Please!* I cannot see the rat now, and it may already be with the kitten!"

"I doubt it. Not after the noise *we* seem to be making!"

Despite the entire escapade being against her better judgment, she climbed the ladder and onto the hay mow and then struggled through the higher banking of hay, scratching her legs in the process. She lost her balance and tumbled back most indecorously on two occasions, getting hay all up through her nightdress and in her hair and mouth, and then maneuvered up to the platform in the top of the barn. It was obviously where numerous pigeons congregated on a regular basis, for there were nests here and there, all empty. *Perhaps the rat had scared them off or . . .* she put that thought from her mind and without looking down, balanced shakily across the beam to the far side and held strongly and with some nervous relief onto the edge of the small window high off the ground.

"Now where is this kitten?"

"The nest is right there. Right in front of you, just below the window. By your knees."

Annis saw with a sinking heart that the small nest was empty. "I do not see a kitten!"

There was a small cry of despair from beneath her. "Oh, do not say that, Annis! It must be there! It must!"

"But it isn't!"

"Look around. It may have tried to escape!"

"I still see nothing, and I do not see where it might have gone either." She decided not to mention that there seemed to be a small spot of blood on the wood near the nest, and even the head of a mouse, but no sign of any rat or the kitten. She shivered in disgust. "I see nothing. The mother cat must have moved it. They do, you know, for we followed one set of kittens to three different hide-a-ways on one occasion. She knew we were looking for her kittens, and she would know of a rat too and would do anything to protect her kitten. I would!"

"Yes. Perhaps that is it. Oh, I hope so! But why would anyone want to drown kittens, for that is what they did with the others, didn't they?"

"Yes, they did I expect. If they didn't, then the place would be overrun by them."

"That is cruel! I would have hidden them myself if I had known."

"Now where did you see this rat?"

"It was over there when I saw it." She pointed to the small platform at the far end of the beam.

"Well, Sophia, I think it must be long gone by now, considering all of activity that you and I both have been involved with here. But now we have yet another problem."

"Oh? What's that?"

"How am I to get down?"

"You can go back across the beam." Sophia seemed to find it strange to be asked so obvious a question.

"I suppose I can. I managed to come across it easily enough, I think, for there was some urgency in doing so, and my mind was elsewhere, but I am not sure it will be quite as easy going the other way now that there is none, and I can also see how far down it really is without the glare from the window in my face!"

"You shouldn't look down!"

"Now why did I let you talk me into this, young lady? If I fall and break a leg . . ."

"But it was *urgent*, Annis! Oh I do hope we were not too late. But you used to climb in the barn at home."

"Yes, I did. But I was fully dressed then, and I knew what I was about and where I could hang onto something. There is nothing here, and I am a little too high for my own comfort. It is higher than the barn at home, and everything is out of reach!"

"You don't look that high to me."

"No. It never does seem that far up from down there, but it is when you get up here yourself. I should have let you do this, and then I could have caught you if you had fallen, but you most certainly cannot catch me."

"No! Then what are we to do?"

"I shall think. Charlotte said something about a much longer ladder. You shall go and find that and drag it here if need be, for I doubt you could carry it." She swore at herself. "Sophia?"

"Yes?"

"Tell no one why you need it, nor what it is for." How Sophia might stand the ladder up for her when she had found it, was out of mind at the moment.

Sophia disappeared from view.

Less than two interminable minutes later, she heard the door creaking. "Sophia! You found it!"

"So here you are. Found what?"

She froze. "William? Oh! You must not see me! You must not!" She pulled her nightdress closer around her with her free hand.

"Why must I not see you?"

He walked into view.

"Well, miss! Not another one after that kitten! What are you doing up there?"

"The kitten . . . the kitten!" She pointed to the nest.

"It is now safe in the kitchen with its mother, by the stove! Sophia and I rescued it this morning when I helped her down from that same perch not thirty minutes ago! I am surprised she did not tell you before you climbed up there!"

"Surely not! She was just . . ." Her voice trailed off. She determined that she would most certainly have a word with her youngest sister about this and find out what the true story was. Unless the mother cat had returned with it as they sometimes did.

William continued as though he had not heard her. "There was a rat about and a little bigger than the cat could handle. We'll get the terrier to find it later. But the ladder that I believe you expected Sophia to find is on its way to one of the outer barns by now. I thought I saw her leave rather urgently and talking to herself about the long ladder, and I know I heard other voices, so I came to find out what was afoot."

"Oh."

"I think you should come down now. It is not at all safe up there, and if you were to fall . . ."

"I would get down! I would if I could! I can't! I got across here easily enough, but it is quite another matter to get back."

"Yes. That's always the way of it. Sophia found that out too! I am here now, and I can always break your fall." He moved under the beam and almost directly below her.

"You must turn away, sir, and hide your eyes."

"Why?"

"Because I am . . . I am not properly dressed!"

"Oh, is that all? Most remiss of you!" He looked up at her. "But a very prettily embroidered nightdress and daringly short too! Or is that because of the angle of view? Yes, you must be quite cold and finding the drafts a little ferocious by that window."

She gasped and gently screamed as she clutched tighter at her inadequate clothing. He was having fun at her expense.

"What made you come out here so ill-attired to rescue a kitten that did not need rescuing and at this hour of the morning?"

"Sophia!"

"You are shedding hay from under your nightdress too!"

"Damn!"

"I did not hear that."

"But I did not know that you had rescued it, and I got the impression that nor did she, and I did not expect to find myself in this predicament. But you must go away or hide your eyes, sir."

"If you expect me to catch you or break your fall, I need to stay here and to keep my eyes open, so I suppose we shall both have to accept the situation. I did not encounter you so little time ago only to see you snatched away from me by this foolishness! If I were to lose you now, I do not know what I would do with myself!"

She scowled down at him, hearing only the first part of his explanation it seemed, or she may have responded a little differently. "Oh, you! You!"

"Yes, my love? Oh, I wouldn't do that if I were you."

She had let go of her support and started out along the beam, holding her nightdress tightly about her legs. He backed up beneath her, ready to break her fall if she did lose her balance.

"You need your arms for balance, my dear, not to protect your modesty at a time like this. Too late anyway, if I recall, for I have seen you in less! Much less! If you fall and hurt yourself, your modesty will count for very little. Why you need to do so escapes me, for there is little that either of us has not seen of the other from time to time, it seems."

She blushed, but he could not see that. "But you are directly below me, and I am up here. I had not intended this!"

"Of course not! Neither did I! But I think I see what you mean, with my looking up . . . up at you. No, I had not seen you quite from this intriguing aspect before! Most interesting perspective . . . which reminds me, the kitten we rescued was also female!"

"William!! Oh, you . . . You . . . ! I can do it." He seemed quite amused at her predicament. "I have done it before, and I shall do it again."

"It is not advisable, Annis. At least not that way. If you will be patient, I will be able to think of something."

"Yes, if I wait long enough!" she protested. "But meanwhile, half of the laborers will be here to ogle me too when they bring hay in. I shall never recover from the shame of it."

"No, they won't! Not for another few hours anyway. Besides there is nothing else for them to do here until more hay is dry, so they will not be in here again for at least another day. Had the rat not been about, this would never have happened this way, for we would not have moved the kitten, and this mow would now be at least half full of hay, and you could just fall off and land safely in the hay."

"Oh!" She stopped and teetered unsteadily.

"What is the matter?"

"I have a splinter in my foot!"

"I'm not surprised! I seem to recall that I discovered a few of those in that same beam many years ago to my great pain and cost, but I did not have your courage to balance across it at that time, and you in your bare feet too! I was astride it and shuffling across it. Most painful! It took a week or more to work some of them out. You are lucky you found out that way first, rather than the other, as I did."

"Now you tell me!" She sounded frustrated and angry. "I found none on my way across. I cannot move."

"Of course, you can. You did very well so far. You are almost to the rope."

"What rope?" She recalled that Sophia, or was it Charlotte, had mentioned a swing.

"There is a rope tied around that beam that we used to swing on as children, and what is left of it hangs down for at least two feet."

"Oh! Can you not get it to hang *up*, sir? It does me no good down there, for I cannot see it." He laughed at her request.

"Oh! This is most embarrassing! But you are a man and would know nothing about that!"

"Yes, it is embarrassing. But do not worry, my dear, I will soon get over it!"

"I meant for me!"

"I had not thought of that!"

He was having fun at her expense. "You are a liar and a rogue, and you are enjoying every minute of my acute discomfort."

"Yes, I am, aren't I? But I am not the one caught in this situation and in a short nightdress. Isn't it amazing how all of my difficulties seem to find me, and not I them! What a pity Lady Seymour is not aware of this as another example of how trouble so easily finds me. You must explain to your mother how I so skillfully managed to maneuver you up onto that beam in just your *short and all-revealing* nightdress so that I might stare up . . . up at you in your present state of interesting undre . . . —difficulty!"

She blushed profusely. There was a certain truth in what he said (and avoided saying) that was not lost on her at that moment. "William?"

"Yes, my love."

"If you dare to mention this to anyone, I will shoot you!"

"Oh! That sounds serious. But that's the spirit! Of course you will! What makes you think I would tell anyone else about this? I told no one about our earlier, even more revealing, and equally disturbing encounter. But there is a solution at hand."

"Where? What is it?"

"Immediately above your head and tying the rafters together, there is a small piece of wood, a brace, going across. If you straighten up and reach directly above you, you will find it. I think it might just be in reach for you."

"But . . . but!"

"You may either continue to protect your modesty, most precariously like that—a waste of time and effort now, I can assure you—and risk a fall for little reason, or you can protect yourself from falling. Though I shall catch you if you do. But if you injure yourself, you will find yourself in a much more revealing state by far and with precious little hidden from prying and curious eyes as we need to assess your injuries. You will need to make up your mind, my dear, for you cannot do both. When I see that you cannot fall, I can come and rescue you."

"But this is a short nightdress and will . . ."

"Yes, it will, won't it? At least I hope so! But no more than it already has! Besides, I need to refresh my tormented memory!"

"You devil!" She let go of her nightdress, straightened up, and felt above her head.

"Almost there. A little higher. Higher, my dear. Yes, it does ride up quite high, doesn't it?"

She ground her teeth at his tormenting her this way. He watched as her hand reached above her and found the wood and grasped it.

"There. That's better." He heaved a sigh of relief. "Yes. Most satisfactory, my love! Now you are unlikely to fall."

"Satisfactory in what way? But I can go nowhere like this and you . . . you . . . seeing!"

"You don't have to go anywhere! But then you can't, can you? Just hold on. I can leave here now—eventually, if I can tear myself away from such scenery—so that you may no longer fear what I might see, and get to you, now that you are at least safe for the moment. Hang on and stay still, I am coming up to you!"

"I cannot see you. Where are you?"

She heard his voice but could not see him. "No. You can't see me now. Don't let go or do anything else! I am climbing up near the window and behind you, and I am no longer beneath you to see anything, unfortunately, so relax."

"Perhaps that is how I should have done this."

"I don't think you would have easily done it in a dress even as short and as loose fitting as that one."

She felt embarrassed over the truth of that and withheld comment. "Oh! But when you get up here, how will we get down?"

"One step at a time, my dear. I shall explain when I get to you. Are you still hanging on?"

"Yes!" She felt the barn sway slightly as he climbed and then felt and heard his feet on the beam behind her.

"Almost got you!" She felt his hand take a secure and tight hold of her nightdress behind her at the lower part of her back and then gasped as his fingers caught some of her skin in his grip. "Ouch!"

"Sorry if I pinched your skin, but I need to make sure that you do not slip out of my hold. It would not do for me to find myself holding an empty nightdress, would it? Now you can let go of that brace and can back up to me slowly. Let go of the wood above you and use your hands to balance."

"My splinter . . ."

"Try! We'll deal with the splinter later. You cannot stay there forever. There is no one down below you now to see your embarrassing plight."

She was able to move her foot. "Ouch!"

"I've got you, you know? You don't have to slide your feet and risk picking up any more."

She moved back, favoring her sore foot, and felt his other arm encircle her waist from behind. She knew then that she was now securely held with his arms across her body just beneath her breasts and backed into him until she could go no further.

"But what are you holding on to if you have both hands on me?"

"I am leaning against the side of the barn, and I cannot slide either way. There is a vertical support by me."

"Now what?"

"I will get you to turn around to face me, and then you will be able to hold on to the supports on either side of me." He put his hands upon her waist, and she turned slowly as she cautiously maneuvered her feet on the narrow beam, and then she reached out and held onto the supports behind him. Their bodies seemed rather too close together as she pushed up against him. But she could not let go, and he was caught in between her arms, though she recognized that she was, in reality, the one that was caught with his arms around her and her with nowhere to go. She noticed that he was also smiling down at her in a mischievous kind of way. "Don't you dare!"

"What? I did nothing!" he protested, but there was still a smile on his face. She had been right about that look.

"You were thinking it!"

"Yes, I must confess that I was. You cannot easily escape me now as you have been doing, staying just out of my reach as you did in my study, and you are a very beautiful young lady, Annis." His hands were on her waist to steady her.

"You are only saying that, as you know I cannot easily escape, with you stopping me from getting down on my own, in the same way that you got up here." She was annoyed with the predicament.

He smiled at her. "We can soon fix that." He gently moved himself off to one side, holding onto the side of the building as she moved her arm out of his way, and then was able to hang on for herself without him between her and the side, though he still supported her by holding firmly onto her arm. "There! I am no longer in your way. Now you can escape from this precarious and personally dangerous predicament." He was leaning away from the beam slightly, still smiling at her.

"Which one? One is as threatening as the other!"

"Indeed!"

She looked down. "I do not see how you got up."

"No. The bright light from this window is blinding you and obscuring the holds which are somewhat in the shadow. But they are there. Long familiarity with climbing up here as a child," he explained.

"But that first one. The only one that I can see is a long way down."

"Yes, it is! You need to hang onto the bottom of the window, lean back a little to see where you are going, and then stretch down with your free leg as you push away from the beam a little with the other foot. It is a big first step. There is also a hand hold a little distance off to the side."

"Too far! It is too big a step!" She could see obvious difficulties with her nightdress riding up onto her legs, and that would certainly make her attempt even more revealing than her earlier precarious situation.

"And that first step is a long way even for me, and I have long legs. I think you would find it quite drafty and perhaps a little too revealing with me here! Though nothing I have not seen before! I would not complain, and I might even close my eyes."

She looked at him with a flustered look on her face. "No, you wouldn't!"

"Well, it would be quite a stretch. You are right. I wouldn't close my eyes! I would need to be ready to grab you if you were to fall."

She could see the difficulty immediately with more splinters likely, if not a fall, never mind the embarrassment of having her nightdress far too high on her legs again. "Is there no other way?"

"Yes, there is. If you look out of the window, you will see that there are several large wooden rungs on the outside of the building leading down to the ground, but they are also very widely spaced. They were not intended for young ladies in filmy nightdresses that the wind might blow around in a most interesting manner." He admired what he could see as she leaned out. She pulled herself back as she sensed his attention on her and took in the smirk on his face.

She blushed. "William!"

He was smiling as she pulled her nightdress closer down around herself and then realized the futility of it. "Some of them seem to be missing too!"

"Yes, probably! There is also a wind to consider, for you will need to hang on with both hands as you reach with your feet, so I doubt that you will present a suitable view for tender young minds like mine. On second thought, I actually think you would!" He painted an alarming picture of horrifying possibilities. "That is how we got back to the ground when the hay mow we are in now gets full of hay. I have not checked them for some years now. But I believe they are all still solid enough. Most of them! Try them."

"No. There is a wind!" She looked at the mischievous smile on his face. "You are enjoying this, aren't you?"

"Not really." He seemed serious. "I want to see you down there safely, more than anything else. Do you want me to go first and help you down and make sure you do not fall? I could also . . ."

"No!" She was emphatic about that, seeing exactly what kind of a display she would present to him immediately beneath her again, with her nightdress blowing about.

"No, of course not. I had not thought of that."

"You had! I know how your mind works! You might almost have plotted this, you and Sophia between you, to get me up here, unwisely clad and revealing . . . I shall need to have a word with Sophia about this! I should have taken the time to dress. Perhaps it was all done on the pretext of rescuing a kitten that might never have been here in the first place."

"Ouch! We have been found out, Sophia and I. You know me too well, young lady!"

"Yes. I should have given more credence to your godmother's observations about you."

"That's it! Enough!" He was smiling at her. "I think I shall go in and have my breakfast with the mother cat and her kitten and let you find your own stubborn way down or until you come to your senses about this! You are unlikely to fall while you are here. I may even be able to see you from the dining room window if you lean out a little, for that is where I shall be. You can wave to me when you want to get down. Except that others might also remark upon it and come out to see what it all means. Or, you could always go back across that beam, but I would not recommend it in your bare feet." He was smiling at her.

"No! Don't you dare leave!"

He would not have left, but she was not to know that. He had moved around her and had swung his foot over the edge of the window beside her. "Why not?" He smiled at her. "All that I am facing here, is abuse at your hands."

"Please, William! I need your help!"

"Yes, you do! So what shall you forfeit for my help?"

"What do you mean?" There was some alarm in her voice.

"After your abuse of me, there is a price to pay!"

She resisted the urge to swear at him. "I did not abuse you. I merely . . . could see difficulties! You scoundrel! What price would you demand of me? You are not a gentleman!" She shivered.

"No, I am not! You already know that, for I told you often enough and warned you about me. Yes, the wind is cool in this window space, isn't it, for someone so ill attired?" He took his other leg over the window sill and stood on the first rung outside of the barn, challenging her to follow him. "Solid enough, that one."

"I shall not follow you out there! If you had only a nightdress on, you would not have dared to have done that, and I will not. There must be some other way." She saw him looking at her with mischief in his eyes. "And what must I forfeit to get your help?"

His eyes twinkled. "I shall think of something." He thought for a while. "I have it. A kiss!"

"On the cheek!" She leaned forward a little and offered her cheek."

"Oh no! Not that *I* should kiss *you*. *You* must kiss *me*!"

"Damn you!" She leaned across to kiss him on the cheek but found that he had receded as he leaned out further and held himself a little way from the side of the building. He had a mischievous smile on his face again. "For that profanity, I shall make you work a little for it; especially after your comments about my character, and then to throw my godmother's accusations . . ."

"All true. Well, most of them."

"After throwing her accusations at my head, you should not expect me to make it easy for you!"

"Well, you cannot lean so very far out that I cannot reach you, can you? But you shall close your eyes, or I shall not do it."

"Why?" He smiled knowingly. "Oh yes, of course! Loose nightdress and female attributes again, and you do not wish to jolt me into losing my grip and falling. Yes, of course, that must be it!"

"Nothing would shock you, you scoundrel!" She was both frustrated at her predicament and angry with him, but not so very angry.

"Very little! Now!"

"But you must promise to close your eyes."

"But where is the fun? Very well. I promise." She was not sure she could believe him. He was still leaning far away from the side of the barn.

He felt her hand on his shoulder and then as she quickly leaned out—for she did not trust him to keep his eyes closed—he felt her lips on his cheek. Before she knew what he was about, he had lowered his head under her and leaned in to grasp her about her upper legs and then had lifted her clear out of the window and onto his shoulder.

She let out a shriek and kicked and tried to hold onto him for dear life!

"You will need to be still, my dear, or you will bruise your toes and get more splinters or even slip out of this loose nightdress of yours!" He waited for a few seconds as he tried to reason with her until she had recognized the precariousness of it all and had settled down. "What are you doing, William?" There was fear in her voice.

"That's better. Now stay still. I am rescuing you. I can get us both down like this if you will stop struggling and just hold still."

"But it is precarious and high, and I do not feel secure. I am also sure it is not proper for you to hold me like this." His arm was about her upper legs with his hand holding her around her leg, above her knees.

"There is no other easy way."

She failed to see the truth of that. "It is a long way to the ground, and I am hanging above it head down with nothing to hang on to, and you are holding me with one hand and with me in a most indecorous position!" She *was* angry now.

"That is a matter of opinion! But alas I am not in a position to see anything!"

She did not mention that it was also drafty. "You cannot climb down with only one hand. This was not a good idea."

"But you are secure for the moment. You are also correct that I cannot climb down with one hand."

"Then this was most unwise! What shall I do?"

"First, close your eyes, my dear. Then, you shall reach under my arm and then hold on to your ankle." She did so.

"The other—my *other* arm and your *other* ankle!" He felt her reach out and struggle to do so. "No objection? Well, we are progressing."

"I do not want to be left hanging up here all day in this indecorous position and the hub of every scathing comment for the next week. "Wait!" She felt the wind lift her nightdress a little. She let go of her ankle and pushed her nightdress between her upper leg and his body to trap it and stop it billowing around and then held her ankle once more.

"Good! Are your eyes closed?"

"Yes, I dare not open them. But why?" She wondered what mischief he was planning.

"It's safer that way. I don't want you to let go in a sudden state of panic, because I am now going to let go of *you*!"

"No!" He felt her tense up.

"But only when you feel secure."

"I feel not at all secure! There is nothing to feel secure about! But I will hang on to my own ankle for dear life."

"But you are secure, my dear. I assure you that if you do not let go, or struggle, you will not fall. You will not fall anyway."

She did not fully trust him. He felt her other hand reach around his body and grasp at the waist of his trousers and shirt and take in some folds of skin. "I do not feel secure."

"Ouch!"

"Sorry." She was not. "A Bon chat! Bon rat! Oh dear! Too apropos in the circumstance!"

"Hold on!"

She felt him begin to descend, and felt them both swaying from side to side as he lowered himself, rung by rung. First testing them for solidity. She felt herself jostled from side to side along with him, but she recognized that as long as she held onto her own ankle, she could not fall.

"Now you can let go of that murderous grip you have on my flesh. We are down on terra firma!"

"We are?" She opened her eyes.

"Yes." He gently put her down and steadied her. "Now let's get you to the house. I am thankful no one else came to see what all of the unladylike complaints and protest was about!"

"I was not . . . But I cannot walk! I am in my bare feet, and I have a splinter!" She was balancing on one foot as she held the other off the ground.

He took her by surprise yet again as he easily lifted her into his arms and carried her back toward the house. She held his neck with one hand and pulled her nightdress about her better with the other to guard against the wind and any other observers.

She was feeling quite put out. "I wonder where that little wretch Sophia got to? She probably took off for fear of what I would say to her."

"She is following us."

"What?"

"She is following us! She watched the whole thing!"

"Yes, I did!" Sophia let her sister know that she really *was* there. "It was very exciting. You were complaining over nothing Annis! It was not so very far up, and he was holding you very securely. But I bet it was drafty like that!"

"Yes, and I shall no doubt have the bruises on my back to show for it and others on my legs. But I shall have some words to say to you later, young lady."

They managed to get into the house unseen, climbed the back stairs without meeting anyone, and traversed the corridor to her room. He put her gently down upon her bed and sat by her for a few moments as she looked up at him with a deep flush on her cheeks as she gathered her nightdress close about her legs and neck. He took her hand and raised it to his lips. She could not wrench it from his grasp, but she did not try very hard. "You will tell no one of this. Either of you." Her eyes flashed from William to Sophia.

"Of course not. I was not even in the barn, Annis, so how could I have played any part in rescuing you? At least my reputation will be safe if no one knows of this." He seemed to have a smug expression, even a smirk on his face.

"Not with me, it isn't! Your reputation? What of mine? You are a scoundrel! You . . . you . . ." She glared at her sister. "Both of you, you tricked me!"

"Yes, I did, for I had to get you out of the window somehow! There was no other way. You did not like anything I suggested—'too difficult, too revealing, too drafty, too precarious'—so I had to make the decision for you. Now the splinter!" He took her foot before she realized what he was about to do and examined it in the bright light from the window. She could not remove it from his grasp any more than she could have removed her hand earlier.

"I see nothing! Do stop struggling, my dear."

"I am covering myself." She was pushing her nightdress to close off the gap opened up by him raising her foot a little.

"It will have to come out, and if I do not do it, there will be more of the painful questions and embarrassing explanations that will be required when you hobble in for breakfast, for it did not come out of any of these floors."

She saw the truth of his statement and submitted. "It is the other one."

He picked up her other foot and examined it.

"Ah yes, a big splinter too! Yes. That one would hurt like the blazes and in the most tender part of your foot too. It is a wonder you did not fall when that happened." He dropped to his knees beside the bed and gently put his lips to her foot as his eyes met hers and closed his teeth on a piece of wood that he could feel with his tongue, and slowly pulled it out. He felt her flinch and squirm as he did so.

She gasped. "Thank you."

He showed it to her. "Quite a respectable splinter. Beats all of mine." He felt that part of her foot with his tongue to feel if there were others, as she had done to his cut hand some days previously, and then inspected it closely. There were no others to be seen, so he kissed it better as he had seen her do to Sophia and let it go. "No more there, and I have now kissed it better."

He looked over at her with a strange look in his eyes. "Are you recovered now, my love?"

She nodded her head. "Not yet recovered but recovering! Fortunately, no one else saw me!"

"Not too angry with me, I hope." He really did seem concerned at what she might think.

She shook her head. But her sparkling eyes said otherwise.

"Shall I see you for breakfast?"

"Yes. As soon as I have got this hay off me and washed and dressed. But there is something I would say." She quickly closed off any attempt at levity, by him suggesting he should stay and help her, for he would not be shy to say anything, no matter how risqué, even with Sophia close by and listening attentively.

"What?"

She looked over at Sophia sitting by the window and looking out, and gestured to him to lean over so she might whisper in his ear.

He did so, expecting that she would strike him for the scoundrel that he had been, and found to his very great surprise and pleasure that she kissed him instead on the cheek.

"There." She spoke softly in his ear. "I have now paid my forfeit to you. I do not like to be behind in what I owe."

Before she was aware of what he was then doing, he had turned his head and had gently kissed her on the lips and caught her by surprise.

She did not pull away as he expected that she might do in her anger. Her hand had raised to his arm to hold him there briefly. There was a look in her eyes that he was relieved to see. Then she blushed a little at her own forwardness and let him go.

"Am I truly forgiven? For I think that I may not deserve to be."

"You know you are forgiven. You have been forgiven many times over, for different things, and no, you do not deserve to be! That last trick to pull me out of the window was . . . despicable. You manhandled me most roughly! I shall have bruises on my legs!"

"I needed to. I am sorry!" He had a look on his face that told her he was being sincere.

"If I tell Mama how I got them, you will have no reputation left with her either."

He sat back and sighed heavily as he looked at her. "But it was necessary, I think. It is to be hoped Lady Seymour does not get wind of any of this harmless little escapade and write your mother another letter, or my reputation will suffer even further. I can see how she would describe it—truthfully, but in the most damaging way with her spluttering pen and much underscoring."

He sat back beside her on the bed and spoke gently so that Sophia would not too easily overhear.

'He was seen to carry a struggling young lady, draped indecorously in only her inadequate nightdress, revealing all, to the world, over his shoulder and out of the

> barn where he had caught her unexpectedly and then handled her rather roughly in order to have his way with her.'

He smiled. "I did, didn't I?" He noticed the startled look on her face at the truth of it. He continued:

> 'What he had been doing in the hay with her, for she was covered with it, does not bear thinking on.'

"Of course everyone will think on it and suspect the worst."

> "He was later discovered with that same young lady in her bedroom where he was unashamedly kissing her, having already achieved what he had set out to do.'

"Whatever that was! The blackguard! The scoundrel!" He sighed. "All true, but not entirely true. Unfortunately! Quite a story line for one of the more lurid novels or a dreadful poem. The entire truth of it, but what a portrait is painted of me, and even of you! She frowned at the obvious truth of that, as she listened further to him. "Of course! That is the nature of such tales. All so very innocent and harmless. Almost, and all to be blamed upon a poor helpless little kitten, and a six-year-old child!"

"I am not a child!" Sophia protested from the window.

He chuckled. "Yes. I thought you might be able to hear more than was good for you miss!"

"Before you leave, William . . . I will ask you to please pass me that other nightdress from the top of that dresser. This one is full of hay, and I would rather not be subjected to a lot of questions at this moment. I cannot easily hobble across there to get it myself, and I doubt Sophia could reach it."

He turned away and retrieved her nightdress from a small pile of them and returned with it.

"And you should not be in my bedroom with me so ill-attired and with this loose-tongued and unsympathetic witness observing it all, for I need to wash and dress, and I see my clothes are now where they should be. No, William, I do not need your assistance for that this time!"

"How disappointing, my love! But you do have a chaperone, or is it a witness? I would like to stay and help. I am very good at washing backs too." He leaned in and kissed her again. As she did not pull away, he lingered over his next kiss.

He was relieved to see she was recovering her composure. "Some protector she is! My sister is a fellow plotter it seems, and you both schemed together so that all of this would unfold as it did!"

"Sophia, we have been found out! Though I must plead innocence, for I did not know what either one of you had planned! Perhaps the pair of you had plotted to get *me* out there!"

Chapter XXXI

A Young Conspirator Is Run to Earth and Expresses Herself Candidly

Some hours later, Annis caught up with her elusive youngest sister. "Sophia! No, do not try to run off again!" She gently held her by the shoulder. "You have been deliberately avoiding me after that episode in the barn!" Annis had tried to get Sophia alone for some hours, but Sophia had seemed to have been avoiding her, recognizing that she was about to be taken to task for what had happened.

"You deliberately plotted to get me out there, as ill dressed as I was, to rescue a kitten that did not need to be rescued at all, with me winding up in a most embarrassing situation! I was most surprised to learn that you clearly knew the kitten was not there at all, for William had rescued you in almost the same way earlier, and the kitten too!"

"Yes. But I was not sure that the mother cat would not return there with the kitten, and I *did* see the rat again, so I had to find you then!"

"I am not sure you are to be believed!" But it had sounded plausible.

"But Annis, William had *gone* by then, so I had to do something! But then he came back again! I do not know what you were complaining about after that, for William would not have allowed you to fall! Besides, I thought it was most brave of you. He did not seem to mind helping you. He seemed to find it all very interesting, despite your fussing and complaints! I thought it quite funny at times, and so did he!"

"It was *not* funny! It was most embarrassing with me in just that nightdress! I guessed what you were up to you know? You must stop trying to throw William and me together! Was he aware of what you were doing? Did you plot it together?"

"Of course not! I would never have dared tell him anything of that. He would have told me it was not proper to put my sister into that predicament, though you and he seem to get into them all by yourselves often enough!" Annis wondered with some growing concern what it was that she might think she knew.

"Why should I not try and throw you both together in that way? He is in love with you, but you seem to blow hot and cold with him, whatever that means. I overheard Mama and Charlotte speaking of how you encourage him one minute and then seem to be too cautious the next, and they think you are annoyingly frustrating for the poor man in the way you behave. I have watched you with him, and him with you. Charlotte even says that you seemed meant for each other, and she didn't approve at first when she saw you both together by the trough, but I did. She also thought that William was moving things along quite fast, or maybe you were, when she and Mama saw you shaving him and encouraging him so outrageously to . . ." She decided to say no more on that. "But Mama approved!"

Annis could not hide her blushes at hearing her youngest sister hint at such deeply personal things. "You must allow others to have some measure of privacy, young lady, and you should not speak in that way Sophia!"

"I know! I won't say anything!" Sophia looked at her sister. "But I like William, and you and he *were* meant for each other, for I think I do know what that means now. If you won't marry him, I will, for I have told him that I love him. I did ask him to marry me too, if you won't, but unfortunately, I am not old enough! Even I know that! But he told me that if I were of the same mind when I was twenty-one that he would most certainly marry me! *You* are twenty one!"

"Oh, Sophia! What would you know of such things? It is not proper what Charlotte may have said . . . well . . ." She was uncomfortably brought to realize that it had all been true. She had encouraged him to be a *little* bold with her, perhaps more than was wise, and perhaps more than just a little! "But he is married now!"

"No, he is not!" Her youngest sister almost stamped her foot in annoyance at her sister's foolishness. "He is a widower and a young man, so Mama said, and he needs a new wife now, and if you are not careful, he will leave us all and find one somewhere else, and if that happened, I would never forgive you!" She was flushed as well as annoyed. "I heard Charlotte say *that*, just the other day too, that he would soon leave us. She said a young man surrounded by so many foolish women and so much temptation denied him, must have a wife to calm him down and to focus his male attention—as Molly does with Thomas—and that if he could not soon attach himself to you . . . but you were resisting most of the time for some reason that no one seemed to understand, and I don't . . . that he would be gone! Though I did not understand all of what she said! He must have a living wife to love! Why is it improper to say what is obvious to everyone? He loves you, and I think that you love him from what I have seen."

"You see too much, and seem to know more than is good for you! What would you know of any of that, young lady, or of what Molly and Thomas get up to?"

"Molly and Thomas do that every Sunday while everyone else is at church, for I watch them whenever I can! It is very interesting! Mama and Papa were in love and did that too! When I could not sleep and came into your bed once or twice, I sometimes woke to see you and Charlotte watching them in their bedroom through that little crack in the plaster when they did not know it, and you thought I was asleep!" Annis listened to her sister in some surprise. "After they had gone quiet, you and Charlotte giggled a lot and thought it quite funny sometimes, and you went very quiet and wide eyed at others and held on to each other just after he had taken off her nigh—"

"Sophia!" Annis interrupted her and stopped the further flow of disclosures. "You must never speak of such things. Nor should you have watched as you did."

"Well he did! You and Charlotte watched! But I did not understand all of what you were saying to each other, except that you thought that what was going on was most confusing, for I could see your faces, and you wondered why mama did not cry out . . ."

"Stop, Sophia!" Annis was blushing quite red. "You must never repeat any of that nor will you ask anyone about it!"

She could see that Annis was quite upset. "I won't! Molly doesn't cry out when Thomas does that to her either! As for not watching mama and papa, you and Charlotte did, and you found it very entertaining from what I could see, for you did not stop watching them! You giggled a lot too, and were silent for such a long time and watched everything that they did."

There was no answering that!

"You and William spend a lot of time laughing together too, just as I remember Mama and Papa doing, and they were in love and were not afraid to show it. Mama says that when two people love each other, it is natural that they want to be together all of the time, and should marry, and that is what I was helping to achieve. I was hoping that you and he might do what Mama and Papa . . ."

"Stop!·Stop! You must not speak nor even think such things! You must not speak of them to anyone!" She looked severely at her sister. "Another thing; that episode of getting me out to the barn to . . . You should not do it in the way that you did, telling lies about that kitten needing to be rescued."

"But it did need rescuing. Earlier! So it was not all of it a lie!"

"And hiding my clothes to get me out there so unsuitably clad while you spun that tale of urgency."

"I didn't! The maid was in earlier and took them, for they were still damp from the water you spilled on your dress just before we came to bed. It did not dry out as you thought it might. But it was urgent! William would soon be gone to the outer fields and would not be able to help you down as he did me, and I wanted him to have to help you down, especially if you were only in your nightdress, for that seems to attract his attention much more than when you are fully dressed. I like to watch you together. Thomas and Molly know what to do when they are alone and in the barn at home, and it is ever so interesting to watch them undress each other, but . . ."

Annis suddenly recovered her tongue after being rendered speechless yet again, over what her sister was daring to tell her. "Enough! Sophia! I am surprised at you! What Thomas and Molly get up to when they are alone, or think they are alone, is none of your business nor mine either, and you must never tell that to anyone else. You must not speak of Thomas and Molly's trysts to anyone else! Nor should you watch them as you do. You will be caught eventually, and that would upset them dreadfully! Yes, you threw William and me together, but I was in my nightdress, and that is not acceptable, no matter what you thought!"

"Why not? The way he was looking at you, it was clear that he likes you in your nightdress, and you didn't seem embarrassed when that was all that both of you, and even *all of us* had on that morning of the fire. He was in his nightshirt when he rescued you, and that was all you had on too, and you were both very wet and it was easy to see—"

"Enough!"

Well it was, and you were very flushed, and so was he. Mama was even smiling, and she should not have been smiling like that, for I know her ankle was hurting her. You have been with him in only your nightdress several times after that fire, and he often helps me on and off with mine when I get ready for bed or need bathing or changing."

"You are six years old, and believe me, it is not the same!"

"I think he likes you even more when you are *not* in it! You had no nightdress on that afternoon after you had come back from that ride with . . ." She stopped speaking, realizing that she had perhaps said more than she should.

Would her sister's perceptive and embarrassing revelations never cease? "And what do you think you know of that? Surely you had all gone into the garden to pick roses at that time?" Annis had an alarmed look on her face with her eyes wide and a distinct blush on her cheeks. Her sister's seemingly innocent observations were most alarming!

Sophia had said more than she had intended. Again! She had a sheepish look on her face and recognized that an explanation was now called for. "Mama and Charlotte did, but I stayed behind and decided I would go up to see if you were all right. I pushed the door open a little. You were bathing in front of your mirror with nothing on, and William was behind you!"

"Sophia! You little wretch! I hope you did not speak of that to anyone else!"

"Of course I didn't! It was all very interesting. He was very gentle with you, just as he is with me! I don't know why you made such a fuss of it all. Why did he have his eyes closed? I see you that way all of the time! He bathes me that way too, but he doesn't have his eyes closed then!"

"That is different!"

"Yes, it was. He was looking at you once or twice when he thought you were not looking at him! But you didn't respond as you should have. He didn't tickle you or kiss you on the middle or blow loud noises on your bare belly as he does me and sets me off laughing and screaming."

"Yes. I suppose there are some things I can be thankful for!" She was surprised to recognize a pang of regret at that moment, which she soon dispelled. "But that was wrong of you to watch us like that. Getting me into that barn under a false pretext was also wrong! If two people are attracted to each other, they will find their own way. It does not help things along if someone else is pulling the strings so clumsily."

"But I do not want him to leave, Annis! Nor does Mama or Charlotte, and I don't think you do either. Do you?" There was plaintive tone in her voice.

"No. Of course I don't. But how can he leave? This is his home, not ours."

"That is not what I meant, Annis! *We* will soon need to leave and go back home when the repairs are finished, for I heard Mama say as much, and they soon will be, and then he may not come with us to stay at Underby, if his interest is not fixed—whatever that means—and I do not want that to happen! He is my friend. I have never had a friend like him!"

"I doubt that we can stop him from coming or going, or whatever he might decide to do. He is a man, and men do what they choose to do, not what a woman might suggest. I have little influence on him! He married Bella, remember? We are all in mourning, though it does not seem that we are at times, for he has a habit if distracting all of us rather cleverly from our grief. But what is more important is that I could not stop him if he did choose to leave us!"

She noticed that Sophia had tears in her eyes. "But, Annis, you could stop him if you wanted to. You could if you set your mind to it! You can do anything you set your mind to! You told Charlotte and me often enough that we can outwit any foolish man if we were to set our minds to it. You just haven't thought about it enough, but I have. He would stay with us if you were to persuade him."

"I was referring to the young men in the village! William is of a different class. You know, if I hadn't seen you being born and helped you into the world, I would doubt that you were really my sister! You must stop this plotting to throw William and me together. It is not proper so soon after Bella . . ."

Sophia had fled the room at that point, in tears, and Annis was left to agonize over what she had said to hurt her sister and how she might have dealt with it all differently, for everything Sophia had said had a glimmer of truth in it. More than a glimmer! She didn't want him to go either!

She decided to give her youngest sister some time to calm down, and she would try to find out more of what her mother and Charlotte had said, for they had certainly not confided in her, whereas Sophia seemed to know everything that was going on. Even about Thomas and Molly. That in itself was shocking enough for Annis to have seen, never mind Sophia! Though she found that she had envied them their tender show of affections for each other, before her conscience got the better of her, and she quietly removed herself from spying on them.

Annis considered long and hard over what Sophia had said and began to see her situation quite differently. What did she really want to see happen in her life? She accepted that Sophia seemed to have a perception and an understanding well beyond her six years, though she had not told Annis anything she had not already seen for herself. She decided that she would try and recover some of the ground she may have lost with her sister.

Chapter XXXII

The Inestimable Value of a Thunderstorm!

The beating of tree branches on the window next to his bed woke William from a peaceful rest. He was surprised that the thunder and lightning had not done it earlier, for it was clear that a major storm, blown in from the coast, was raging outside. His first thought was of the horses. They had been left out in the paddock and would be wet and possibly scared. Then he remembered that they had been put away.

It seemed that the wind might be strong enough to bring trees down. It was very likely that the driveway would be blocked, as there was an ancient copper beech tree at the side of the road which should have been felled for firewood long ago and would very likely come down or, at best, might only shed a few of its branches. He made a mental note to see that it would be felled, and soon.

He heard one of the tiles above his head rattling ominously as it was lifted by the wind. It was obvious that he would not be able to get back to sleep again with the storm raging as it was.

That was when he noticed Sophia standing by the edge of his bed, looking at him. Perhaps that was what had awoken him, for she might have been ready to slip into bed with him to get out of the sudden noise. He yawned. "Well, miss, what are you doing here?"

"The storm woke me. I'm scared! I'm scared for the horses too, for they don't like this any more than I do, and they are *out* in it! I was going to find Annis to help me put them in, but she must have gone to comfort Charlotte, for she does not like storms like this either and. I decided to come to you instead. There is not room for three in Charlotte's bed!"

"There is nothing to be afraid of, you know? I don't think they were left out." He heard the clock strike midnight from the hall below. It was five minutes wanting of twelve for it had been five minutes fast. He had noticed that, when he had retired just before eleven and had forgotten to put it right.

"But they were! I heard Jonathan, the groom, mention that the night was so warm they would be happy to be out."

"But he knows enough to see to them."

"He's not here! You gave him the night off and he went into the village!"

"Yes, I did, didn't I?" He looked at the storm passing across the landscape, illuminating it as though it were daylight each time the lightning flashed, which it did often. He decided that he had better see to the horses himself and then check that no damage had yet occurred to the conservatory attached to the house, for there was a tree not too far away that might lose branches, or it might come down. It was doubtful that it could reach as far as the glass but blowing branches might.

"You say you went looking for Annis?"

"Yes. I was going to her room to slip into bed with her and spend the night there until the storm had passed, but she was not there. She might have gone to Charlotte's room, for she is terrified of the thunder even more than I am. But I dare not go along that corridor with all of those windows and mirrors while the lightning was flashing the way it was, so I came here instead. Then I remembered the horses."

He slipped out of bed and decided not to light a candle, as the lightning was intense enough to illuminate his way, and the wind would only blow it out. Everyone else would be under their covers, if not sleeping through it. He would go as he was rather than wet his clothing and boots, for he could easily change when he got back. "You should go back to bed, Sophia. Or climb in here where it's warm, and I will see to this!"

"No, William. I do not want to be alone in this. I want to come too." She moved over to him and looked nervously about herself as the lightning illuminated everything in the room. He felt her shrink closer to him and grasp his hand very firmly for one so young. "The thunder scares me. I do not like being alone in *this* storm!"

"Very well. But I'll get you to stay in the conservatory out of the storm while I see to them. No point in both of us getting soaked." He could hear the rain spatter upon the tiles above his head and drive hard against the window. At least the Seamew was well tied up with good heavy rope fenders and was not out tonight. The wind was strong enough to tax even the best sailor, with gusts strong enough to snap masts if not to tear sails away. Strong enough to un-hair a dog as his father used to say! It was strong enough even to lay a small boat flat in the water as had happened to him more than once as a boy out in a dinghy, when a sudden squall swept through.

He and Sophia—her hand tucked firmly into his—went down the back stairs to the conservatory, where he let them both in. The door swung closed behind him, driven by a draft from somewhere inside the house. There must be a window open here somewhere. It seemed so well protected from the winds outside, with little movement of the vegetation inside, and was even warm from the dying fire in the stove. It was clear that no damage had yet been done, and it was a relief to see that. But the rain, possibly mixed with hail, began to beat noisily onto the glass above their heads, and ran in small rivulets above them, outlined by the occasional flash of light. He noticed that one of the windows near the floor had been slid away. He closed it.

He counted between lightning and thunder. Fifteen seconds. That flash had been almost three miles away, but which way the storm was headed he did not yet know. It was probably all around him, as the sky everywhere seemed to reflect with light even without the closer sound of thunder to go with it.

He walked across and let himself out into the night, being careful to close the outer door securely behind himself, not realizing that Sophia had come outside with him. Even as he stepped away from the immediate shelter of the building, he felt the wind buffet him strongly and drive the rain into his face and whip his nightshirt flat against his body. There was no hail at all. It was too warm for that. The strength of the wind was what drove it hard, like hail, against everything. The wind seemed to suck the very breath from his lungs.

As he stepped away from the building a little more, the runoff from the roof caught him in a drenching downpour that soaked him entirely, but it was warm and not at all unpleasant. He stood there for a few moments, smiled at the pleasant shock of it, and savored the unusual warmth as it ran down his neck and inside his nightshirt. He then noticed that his young shadow had not dared stay in the conservatory but had stayed close to him and was now holding his hand securely, and also getting wet, but not seeming to enjoy it quite so much.

Ah well, they were both wet now, but it was a warm rain and would do no one harm for the brief time they would likely be out, though no doubt it would soon get cold too, for it seemed always to get cold as a thunderstorm moved through. He could change her when they got back in. A candle could not possibly have been any use out here and possibly not even a lantern. He could hear branches whipping about in the edge of the woods and an occasional dead limb dropping with a crash, not so far off. There might be considerable damage by morning.

Sophia had her hand once more tucked firmly into his as they walked over to the barn. The paddock was empty. Someone must have brought the horses in earlier. He decided that he had better check them anyway, now that he was already wet, and here. The wind was irregular because of the building behind him, but it did not seem that he was in the path of any flying branches from nearby trees, though he could hear the trees complaining loudly as their branches rubbed together or as they were swept into contact with each other. There would be many of them downed by morning, and even now he could hear yet another crash as a distant tree was snapped off by the wind.

"We worried for nothing, Sophia! They must have been put away by someone else. Either that or Jonathan knew a storm was coming and did not go to his mother's house."

He opened the stable door and spoke a few words so that the horses might know that someone they knew was there, but there was no answering snorts as there usually were. Instead, they were all comfortable in their stalls and seemed settled and contented, despite the wind outside. They were intent on eating from the hay nets that had been put up for them late the night before.

"Well, Sophia, it was an empty journey, for I see that everyone is content and not overly concerned about the weather outside, and everything seems secure."

"They are all right." Another voice spoke up from the shadows at the horses heads.

"Annis?"

"I could not sleep either and came to check them too." She saw Sophia with him. "I thought you would still be tucked up in your bed miss!" Sophia held firmly onto

William's hand. "The storm woke me up, and I couldn't stay by myself, Annis! You weren't in your bed, so I went to look for William."

"So you woke William instead! I am surprised he dragged you down here with him."

"I didn't drag her! She insisted on coming! I did tell her to stay in the conservatory and wait for me, but . . . well, she's here now."

"I got scared!" Sophia ran over to Annis and hugged her leg as the lightning flashed and lit a path for her. In the sudden glare, he noticed Annis standing off near the mule, clad, once again, only in her nightdress, as more flashes of lightning, in rapid succession, illuminated the inside of the stable with a flickering light that went on for some time.

"You seem to be making a habit of coming out somewhat lightly dressed! Is Charlotte or your mother not with you too? We could make this a family gathering!"

She laughed at his levity. "No! Charlotte does not like such storms, and Mama will not move when there is one about. But you are also lightly dressed too this time. You seem to make a habit of it too, you know?"

"I knew it might be a warm rain, so I did not think I would be likely to get a chill, and I saw no reason to wet my few remaining clothes. Nor did I expect to find anyone else here. I hope you are not as wet as Sophia and I."

Annis laughed! "But I am sure that I am, for it has not let up since I came out of the house. But you should not have encouraged her to come out with you!"

"I didn't! I told you, she followed me! But it is not cold just yet. We seemed to catch the water cascading off the conservatory roof, but it was nice and warm so I did not mind. How long have you been here?"

"No more than a few minutes. I was surprised to see you two walk across from the conservatory. You seemed to be enjoying it."

He laughed gently. "I was, though Sophia may not have been. I do not mind the rain when it is as warm as this! It reminds me of Portugal."

"Sophia loves rain and thunder and even the lightning, and often sits in the window while a storm moves through! None of us are so very scared of a bad storm, though I must admit we sometimes can be if it very severe like this one is!"

"And here I got the impression that she was terrified of all of that!"

"Not Sophia! Not usually!"

Sophia piped up at that. "I am sometimes scared!" The young lady in question was out of the way in the stall with Pat, the mule, and with the cat fussing about her legs. She seemed unaffected by the turn of conversation that put a lie to some of what she had said to William.

"No matter. Was it you that brought the horses in?"

"No. I expected that I would need to, but they were already brought in much earlier before it began to rain, but I did not know that. They are dry. But William, it seems to be getting worse out there, rather than better!"

He heard the wind pick up even stronger and drive the rain against the side of the stable. "We should probably return to the house. The animals seem settled and contented and are safe here! We are the ones that are wet!" He opened the door and let them out and then closed it firmly behind them as he took her hand. "At least the rain is still warm and even quite pleasurable. We should wait for a while." There was another flash, and he counted again. "Now we can go." Their instinct was to run, to get out of it all, but William strolled almost leisurely across the intervening space with Annis beside him and Sophia tucked in between them, holding close to both of them for shelter from the wind and rain. It was even enjoyable to feel the warm rain against their faces.

"Are you not afraid of being struck by lightning?"

He glanced at Annis and felt her hand holding on to his as though she were not sure what to think. "No. It is still at least three miles away."

"How do you know that, William?"

"I count!"

"But how will that tell you?"

He stopped in the middle of the open space, heedless of the rain beating against them. "I will show you. It is still far enough away that we are in little danger. We will watch for a strong flash." They waited as they leaned gently against each other with Sophia tucked close into them both.

"There?" He started counting immediately out loud when they saw the flash, so they might hear. There was no crash of thunder other than the general rumble of many such strikes further way and all around them until he got to nine, and then there was a loud and strong crash that made Sophia tremble and move even closer to them. He put his arm around her too. He noticed that Annis was also close beside him too and still holding his arm tightly. He could feel her breast pushing strongly up against his arm, and chose not to move. "That was only about two miles."

"How do you know?"

"Light—the lightning—moves very fast. I do not know how fast, but it is exceedingly fast, whereas sound by comparison moves very slowly." The wind suddenly picked up about them and drove the rain hard into their faces to run down them, and to drip down from their hair and faces, and then suddenly whipped about their legs and bodies, sending their wet nightclothes in all directions. They held tight onto each other to stop from being blown over, with Sophia trapped between their legs for shelter as she laughed nervously at the power of the storm. He put his arm about Annis and pulled her close into his chest for protection. He felt her arm go around his back and hold him tightly also.

They were both amazed that he was not as scared as they were. It was one thing not to be afraid of a storm in the shelter of one's home, but outside . . . ? yet he was not afraid of any of it. They took their cue from him. He realized that they probably regarded him as quite strange to enjoy such weather, but he did.

He almost had to shout to be heard over the sudden blast of wind. "If you have ever stood on the cliff top and watched a cannon fired from a ship far out to sea, you can see the smoke from the barrel almost immediately—the flash, if it is nighttime. But it takes some time to actually *hear* the boom of the cannon. One can calculate how far the ship is from where you are on the shore by counting the seconds between the smoke or the flash, and then the noise of the canon reaching you, and can confirm it by using trigonometry and triangular measurements. It is about five seconds for each mile of distance between the flash of the lightning and the time one hears the thunder, for the two are directly related."

"I did not know that."

"It seems to be coming toward us, so we should retreat. I doubt that we will get any wetter than we already are, so we can be most foolish if we like and stand under that runoff and enjoy it while we can. We cannot get any wetter than we already are, and it is most pleasantly warm!"

They walked over to the conservatory and stood for a few moments under the drenching runoff from the roof, feeling its warmth in their hair and down their bodies as they laughed. There was something deliciously sensual about what they were doing! Annis could not help but laugh at his obvious enjoyment of it all. "How strange you are to enjoy such things!" In the poor light, occasionally brightened by much stronger lightning flashes from cloud to cloud far above them, she could just see the rain pouring down his face as he smiled at her. She knew she would present the same sight to him. He leaned in and kissed her gently as the water played over all three of them.

A lightning strike seemed suddenly to hit a tree at the edge of the woods, and within a second or less, there was a sharp and very loud crack of thunder that hurt their senses and threw them together in a moment of reflexive panic that set their hearts thumping. It had been most unnerving, and they quickly entered the conservatory and closed off the outside as they laughed nervously.

"That scared me!" Sophia appeared to be glad to be out of it, but not sure how safe she might be in such an open room, despite the glass covering it all. She seemed to be losing her love of such storms.

"Yes, me too," he admitted. "It was too close and not quite as enjoyable as at a distance. Right on top of us! But we are safe in here, I think. The trees will take the brunt of it as they usually do. I am wringing wet as I know both of you must be too. It may be a warm rain, but it will soon rob us of warmth, so we had better get inside the house and get ourselves changed and back to our beds or . . ." he looked at them and smiled, " . . . or we can get ourselves dressed and come back here to see it all as it moves through, if the mood strikes you, for I doubt any of us will be able to sleep now until it has passed. I think we should be safe enough here for the moment."

Annis took his arm. "I think I would like to do that, for I know that I will not sleep now for a while either." They walked over to the door into the house and tried to open it, but it would not open.

"Strange!" He seemed puzzled. "I did not lock it when I came out, and they are never locked, but it feels as though it is locked now. Ah well, the other door at the rear of house must still be open. Hollis does not usually lock any of the doors unless he knows that the gypsies are about. Maybe that was it. We can get there along the side of the building. We will get more wet I suppose, if that were possible, but at least we will be able to get in unless he locked those too!"

They returned outside and, holding onto each other, walked without any urgency, despite the storm and the wet along the edge of the dark building, noting with some relief that the storm was moving a little further away from them, but with another storm sweeping in along the same track from the coast if the distant lightning was any indication. The wind had died a fraction.

They tried that door too. It was also locked! "I think Hollis has locked them all for once in his life! It's either gypsies, or the storm must have woken him up and he locked all of the doors to stop them blowing open. I seem to remember he considered such a storm as warring between gods and devils and was intent on keeping them out when they were in that kind of a mood. I wonder what would make him think they needed a door to enter by? Damn! I will have to climb into your bedroom window as I did when it was my room! I think I can maneuver the vines in the dark, though I am heavier now."

"You can't!" Annis pointed out to him. "For I closed and latched it against the wind and rain."

"And I did mine too, to stop the wind blowing it open, and allowing the rain to beat in. Back to the conservatory then!" They walked back and let themselves into the conservatory again.

Annis smiled at the sudden predicament they were faced with. "So what are we to do, William?"

"We can stay here all night if necessary! But we need to get ourselves dry first I would say. There is a day bed over there with a heavy coverlet on it. My mother used to spend some time out here. You and Sophia can snuggle yourselves up in that and pass me your nightclothes to dry. There is nothing I can do about it, for Hollis is as deaf as a post, and I would be unable to arouse him, even if I knew which was his room! We can stay out here, and I can make up the stove if there are still some live coals in it, and I am sure there are. We can all sit around that if you would prefer, for the stonework holds the heat for a very long time, and it is still warm." He touched the rocks. "It is not unpleasant here just yet and will not get that way if we can get warm enough to dry out. I used to spend a lot of time out here and even feasted upon figs when they were ripe."

He opened the stove door and discovered that there were still live coals as he expected, and there was a good supply of dry wood nearby. There would be much more after tonight, with all of the trees brought down. He loaded the large firebox up with smaller pieces that would easily catch from the embers and then added larger pieces until there was a blazing fire going.

He noticed Sophia was shivering. "You will need to get out of that wet nightdress first young lady, or you will soon be even less comfortable." He retrieved the coverlet, and as Annis stripped off Sophia's nightdress, he wrapped her in the coverlet, which would soon dry her, and lifted her onto the day bed.

"Comfortable?"

She nodded. "There's room for all three of us here! We could keep each other warm."

"Yes. I expect so, but you and Annis can. I shall stay out here and see to the fire."

He wrung the small nightdress out by the drain in the floor and then hung it on a line strung above the stove where it would soon dry out, for the heat was beginning to rise strongly from it now. He could hear the wood crackling loudly and could see thin fingers of flickering golden light shining out through the air vents onto his legs. He opened the door partially to increase the draft. "You could join her if you wish, you know?" He spoke to Annis. "I would turn my back while you get out of your wet clothing and see that it gets dry for you."

"No. She is warm enough there and wide awake as well, and I am warm enough for the moment, even if I am soaking wet."

"Then you and I can sit here together if you like and talk and keep each other warm. There is a very large kind of straw-filled bed that was used for the dogs when they were kept out here at night. It's a bit scratchy, but I've even slept on it myself once or twice. We can sit on it in front of this stove and get ourselves warm."

He brought it out from behind the stove, sniffed at it suspiciously, turned it over, and dropped it to the floor in front of the fire and up against the wood pile. "It smells clean, and we can lean up against the wood pile here with this behind us and under us and even stretch our legs out and rest them against the stones that we use to hold the heat. Until they get too hot! The cats used to lie against it too until the stones got too warm and then they took off. We'll soon get dry, and it does not matter if this gets a little damp."

She sat herself down beside him, half sitting and half reclining, and leaned up against him as he pulled her closer into him and even kissed her gently once more. She sighed. "I could sleep here, I think. It is so very comfortable against you, and from the sounds of it, Sophia is asleep already."

"No, I'm not! I'm warming up!" Her voice piped up sleepily from the shadows.

"I doubt that you would be able to sleep in all of that wet, any more than I will, but we will soon get dry." His voice dropped as he spoke so that only Annis could hear him. "Be careful, my love, that Lady Seymour does not catch a whiff of this, especially if you find that you can go to sleep in my arms, though how she would find out about that, I do not know, for I shall say nothing!"

"William! How could she possibly hear of any of it?" She struggled to her knees and turned a little as she lay gently with her back onto him. She looked up at his face as she snuggled closer into his chest so that he could put his arms around her, and might be able to kiss her more easily, which he took the opportunity to do, and spoke so that Sophia would not overhear what she said. "To think that both this most indelicate circumstance, and that earlier one, may both have been deliberately planned!" Her eyes seemed to be twinkling with amusement in the dim light.

"Do you think so? Both of them? With what end?" He knew the answer to that for himself.

"To throw us together most shamelessly of course! As we are! We are also most ill-dressed!"

"Yes, for we are again! But it is dark and there is no one else to see us. You may be right about it being a deliberate plot!" He gently stroked her damp hair and wrapped his arms about her as he pulled her closer. "I soon realized that yesterday's adventure was created rather cleverly by her, when she sought me out—for she did—and told me you were stuck up on that beam as *she* had been, and this one fits the same pattern. Now that I recall it, *she* was the one who mentioned having seen gypsies in the home wood. But how did she know Hollis would lock the doors after that?"

"William, if you do not yet know that Sophia knows everything that goes on, even to the habits of the servants, and provokes most of it, you are very slow indeed!"

He tried to imitate Lady Seymour but kept his voice low, speaking softly into Annis's ear as she leaned back against him. *"My dears, the child is obviously beyond saving, leading adults astray and into iniquitous channels, as she does.* She will be fired up to write yet another letter to your mother again about us both! That makes three so far by my reckoning!"

"I do not care if she does, William, and I don't think anyone else will either!" They both laughed gently as she turned and snuggled into him with her arms around him and her face looking up at him. She seemed to be inviting him to kiss her again, so he did.

She brought her knees up to her body once more so that she could lean more closely into him and take advantage of his warmth. As they held each other, he was deeply conscious of her breasts pushing up against his chest and of her nightdress falling away from her legs as she continuously adjusted her position to lie on his chest as she did. She did not seem to care. They had progressed too far for any such considerations of appearance to mar them being able to relax most intimately with each other. He knew that he presented as embarrassing an appearance as she did, and much as they had at the trough that day at Underby as they had sat very close to each other. "I find that I do not want to sleep, William! I like what we are doing, so you have no need to stop kissing me, you know?"

After some moments of such tender affection and with them both becoming a little breathless, she smiled at the obvious effects she was having on his composure and allowed him to rest for a while. She snuggled further down onto him and closed her eyes. She knew that he watched her for some time, fighting with his own turbulent feelings as she was dealing with her own, for she occasionally opened her own to catch him smiling upon her.

He must have dozed off with the warmth from her body, her closeness, and the added warmth from the stove, for he awoke some time later to discover that he was alone and partially covered by a corner of the bedding.

The woodstove had been made up just a little earlier and was throwing out its warmth. In the first glimmer of morning light, he saw that there were two nightdresses now hanging over the top of the stove and seemed to be drying well. He was relieved to find that his own was now mostly dry. He smiled. He looked over to the day bed and saw Annis watching him from under the coverlet. She was wide awake and smiling at him too.

"Well, you were brave to have done that, my love! What would you have done if I had awoken?"

"But you did not awake when I left you and made up the wood stove, and I was far too noisy about it."

"Yes, that was reckless of you. But why did you do that and risk me waking up?" He did not really need to ask.

"I refuse to say for the moment! You are really a sheep in wolves clothing I can see. You are all bluster and not much for a girl to fear!" Her loving smile robbed her comments of any hurtful intent.

"Girls have no need to fear me! Young ladies—one young lady should!"

She studied him. "Yet I don't! I think you fear me more than I might fear you!" She looked at him with a smile on her face, not realizing how true that comment was. "I must have been very tired last night, for I do not clearly remember getting in here with Sophia after that, but it is very warm. Tell me, William, how are we to get back into the house without alerting everyone to this second questionable adventure we have got ourselves embroiled in?"

"Each hurdle in turn, my dear. Hollis will unlock all of the house doors when he wakes, which should not be very long now. We shall hear the lock turn. I don't think he is in the habit of checking out here at all or making the stove up, so when he has done that we can all creep back into the house."

"You will need to pass us our nightclothes first when mine is dry, and we shall get dressed under here."

"That will be no fun for me! I was hoping I might help you again! I need to become practiced at it! Sophia does not object to my helping her in that way, and nor should you! But yes!" he continued. "If he does happen to come out here, you two shall just lie still and say nothing. You will be hidden away under the cover, unseen, and I shall sit here and let him know in a severe tone that he locked me out, but I shall also tell him that I forgive him, for I am most comfortable and contented! He's found me out here before when I was younger, though I was not locked out, so it will not surprise him too much. He laughs at my attempted severity anyway, for he knows I mean him no harm. As well as being deaf, he is as blind as a bat, I think, and will not notice nightdresses drying. At least I hope he doesn't! But even if he does, he will say nothing for he will not see either of you to know that they should not be there!"

She snuggled down lower under the coverlet to join Sophia. She felt contented and safe and very confident in herself at that moment.

Chapter XXXIII

Charlotte Tells a Secret, a Plot Is Born

"William?" He looked up from the book that he was reading by the library fire to see Charlotte approaching him. He had dozed there for some hours after he had returned from the coast, seeing that the Seamew had not suffered in the gale that had accompanied the thunderstorm the night before. It had been necessary to ensure that it was also ready for its planned trip to France later that evening. He had not immediately gone to bed when he had returned in the early hours, for his mind had been far too busy with another, and perhaps even more urgent and pressing problem that he needed to deal with.

"Yes, Charlotte."

"There is something that I need to tell you. It is quite disturbing. I hope you will be able to forgive us!"

He paused and smiled at her. "You too now, eh? I am not sure I will survive many more of these sudden revelations! Nothing to do with a watch or a letter, is it?"

"No!"

"Perhaps Sophia been showing you some things of mine that she was not supposed to find?"

"You mean your drawings?"

"She did show you them! Damn!"

"No! Annis told me of them! She had looked in your journal when you were not there! But you already know that!" He looked sharply at her. How did she know that? These girls really did not miss much of anything! "Sophia was looking at your drawings of the Peninsula when she found them too. That was when Annis stopped her running to Mama with them, for she also draws better than any of us, or telling her of one that you had done of Annis. She said that yours were almost as good as mine, but I already knew that. I looked in your journal once too! We all have! I hope you can forgive us." The signs were not threatening, so she continued. "Your drawings are very good, but I was quite surprised to see that one of them, the one that Sophia had seen, was of you bathing Annis in her bedroo—!"

"Yes, Charlotte! Let us not go there! That was not for general circulation!"

"You will show me the others sometime, won't you? I saw that there were more in there of her too, but I had to put them down when others came in! I'm glad I saw them, for now you cannot criticize me so harshly for doing those of you as you sat in the window seat. Besides, you saw some of mine of Annis that you were not supposed to see, and they were no more revealing than the one you drew!"

She said nothing of those other of her more daring drawings of him in his bath or in other revealing circumstances as he had stepped out of it that he had also seen in her book on that occasion. She probably would not like to admit to those and invite more searching questions about where she had been hiding to have seen him like that. He smiled. "Perhaps! So, not a watch and not a letter."

"No! Not about that embarrassingly dreadful watch!" Her expression showed her feelings at seeing that for the first time, when Annis showed it to her. "Annis is looking after it and may have hidden it away if she did not give it back to you! But what letter do you refer to?"

"Good. If you do not know, then never mind. Yes, she gave me the watch! You said to 'tell' me, not to 'ask' me!" He waited for her to continue.

"Was that the reverend that just came through before lunch?"

Clearly, she was not about to say anything until she was ready. "Yes, it was. He visited earlier. He will come back through here again in a few hours. Do you wish to speak with him?"

"No! Not at the moment. Is he a member of your crew too?"

He glanced searchingly at her. "Yes, he is! How did you learn of that?"

"Sophia!"

"Of course." He saw that she might have difficulty getting to the point and she was hungrily eyeing the cake that he had barely touched. "Do have a seat, Charlotte. Help yourself to some of that cake your mother brought me, if you wish."

"Thank you." She picked up a small piece and ate it as she sat opposite him. "Did Annis go out with you last night too?"

"No, she did not! Why do you ask?"

"She was not in her bed last night at all! Nor was she in the drawing-room chair in the window, waiting to see when you might return. Well! I wonder where she was?"

He had known where she had probably been; waiting for him to return, but he was not about to let her sister know any of that. "Now, young lady, enough beating about the bush. You said you had something to tell me, rather than to ask me!"

She dusted off her fingers on her dress. "Yes, for Annis won't, and neither will Mama, and Sophia does not really know enough about it, so she cannot."

"So you all, except Sophia, know this thing that you say is quite disturbing, and it is not my most revealing drawings of Annis?"

"Yes. But not a drawing! Though Sophia might know. She seems to know everything! But if she does know, I doubt that she would understand! It is quite disturbing!" She paused for a moment. "It is also most tragic! I cannot believe how anyone might think otherwise. Except I think Mama does not think about it anymore. She seemed upset at first when I mentioned it to her, but she said that there was nothing she could do about it now." He let her ramble on. She would get to the point eventually. "She also seems quite happy to leave everything the way it is, and for that matter, so am I, in a way; but in another, I am not happy to leave it be." She moistened her finger and picked up some of the crumbs from the plate as she considered the last pieces of it still sitting there. "Mama says it will all sort itself out eventually, yet it would be wrong to leave it as it is, for it is preying on Annis at times. She is not herself!"

"Yes. I think I had a similarly confusing discussion a little like this one just the other day with Annis herself. But why will Annis not say anything?"

"She does not speak of it, but it is obvious that she is afraid of what you will do when you find out. How you will respond to her? To us! She *seems* to respond to you as she should most of the time, but then at others, she remembers things, and then she becomes remote and goes very quiet and sad, and I know why!"

He had seen the same thing but much less in recent days. "Apart from that, does this involve me in any way?"

"Yes, William, it does! She is not the only one that is afraid. We all are, that you will leave us when you find out."

"How can I leave? This is my home!" He gestured about himself with his hand.

"No, William. Leave us! Turn against *us*!" She stressed that last word.

"Ah! I think I see. But I think you have nothing to fear there, you know?"

"If you were to do that, I think Mama might suffer a breakdown. It has been . . . different . . . with you being with us. We all would suffer most badly, for since you entered our lives, we have been shielded from most things that could have destroyed us, I think. You did not replace our father in any way, but you provided the same kind of support and no-nonsense stability that he did. I did not know that was what a man's role might be in a family, but I do now! You saw Thackeray off. You rescued us from the fire." She took another piece of cake and ate as she spoke. "You even brought us here. As Mama says, you distracted us from ourselves and our dreadful circumstance! For you did! You shielded Sophia best of all. We were most worried for her at first."

"But what about you? You lost them both too."

She did not answer immediately but finished off the cake. "We should have told you sooner, but I am not sure anyone knows how to tell you, for it all seems so very foolish now."

He waited for her to get to the point. She picked up his wine glass and took a sip of that too, to wash down the cake. He smiled at the familiar ease that she showed of him and his presence. He found it quite charming and entirely disarming, for Sophia was the same.

"We made up some of those special cards that we learned about in one of those tarot books that Mama has! We made one up for each of us with our birthdates and other information on them. To make a long story short, your name seemed always to be paired with that of Arabella when we played. That is why this all came to pass as it did, to have you marry Arabella." She fell thoughtful. "There was also the need for one of us—the eldest I think it had to be—to get married before Papa died for some reason. I did not understand that, for I learned that in his will, he had left everything to Mama, though mama did not seem convinced that Father's will might be accepted if it were contested. Then the accident happened and threw everything into disarray!" She swallowed hard, recalling those so recent memories.

"So that is what you needed to tell me? The tarot cards? So what is it that is wrong? Or was that it?"

"No! Annis was looking through those cards again just the other day at Underby before the fire, the day that it rained so hard. She seemed most upset over something, for she swore—I have never heard her swear before—most shocking, and then she threw them into the fireplace. Fortunately there was no fire at that moment, and Mama was not there to hear her, so after she had fled the room, I recovered them to find out what had upset her.

"It took me a little while, but I noticed that there were two cards with Bella's name on them, but only one of them had her information correct with her birthday and all. The one with a smudge of blood from the paper cut that Sophia got, had the information that belonged really to Annis but had Arabella's name written on it in error somehow. There was no card for Annis! How we could possibly have overlooked that, I do not know! I remember that when *that* card was paired with your name, it may have had Bella's name on it, but it was *not* the correct one for Bella. It was the smudged one that should have had Annis's name on it! We had got you married to my sister Bella all based upon that wrong card! Oh William! It has become so obvious to us all in the last week and more, but it was Annis that you should have married and not Arabella!"

She waited for some sign from William that he understood this cataclysm, that what had happened—marrying Arabella—had happened in error, but there was nothing to read in his face though his shoulders seemed to be shaking, perhaps with suppressed laughter. She did not understand that.

"And that is what you wanted to tell me?" He had a strange smile on his face.

"Yes, William! I think that has been rather obvious to everyone by now that you should have married Annis! Perhaps it is very obvious even to Annis herself. No! Most certainly to Annis too, though she will not easily admit it. There seem to be other things on her mind and preying upon her too, for she no longer confides in me as she did. I no longer understand her!"

"Is that all?"

She seemed puzzled that he was neither surprised nor angry over it. "Mama knows this too, for I told her, though she will not discuss it with us now, for she can get upset if she thinks about it, and now it has all worked out wrong in one way, if not in another. So very wrong, and we have ruined two lives and two futures! Yours and Annis's! I do not see how you might forgive us for this—marrying you to the wrong daughter, and you now a widower as a result! It is too large a burden to bear, and I do not know how to go forward with this. I felt that I must come and tell you, and can only pray that you will know how to solve this before we all go mad!"

He smiled at her. She knew he had heard what she had said, but perhaps he did not understand.

"It is not so very bad, Charlotte!" She looked at him in some surprise as he refilled his wine glass for her. "No. I do not feel that I am laboring under any such burden, or that my life is ruined, nor my future. Quite the opposite! We are all still together, are we not? Did you not wonder why?" She seemed confused and unlikely to be able to answer easily. "You forget that when I arrived, I had no expectation of marrying anyone!"

"I expect not! But now I cannot talk to Annis about it for she gets too annoyed and frustrated with me and is afraid of revealing any of it, especially to you! I believe she is afraid of upsetting you, indeed of overturning all of this, for Mama and me and Sophia, and of opening up the will to being contested and setting us all back into the state we might have been in, but for you, if any of it is discovered. But if it is, then what of you? What of Annis?"

"I think we will survive, my dear." He was quite sure that Annis had come to grips with it too and did not care about any of it so much. He moved over to her and put his arm around her shoulders as he gave her his handkerchief to wipe away her tears. He laughed gently. "That is your carefully nurtured secret? This revelation that will turn the world upside down for everyone?"

"Yes, sir!"

"Well! I did not know all of the details of that one! It sounds neither insurmountable nor earth shaking to me! But you say that Annis knows this?"

"Yes. She must! She was the one that alerted me to it by accident some days ago. I told you she was looking through those cards and let out a cry and threw them into the grate and rushed off. I picked them out and wondered what she had seen to upset her so. It took me some time, but then I discovered it too."

"You have nothing to fear, you know. I am not angry over the mix-up, and I do know much more than you are giving me credit for. I am not about to leave any of you either. Not now that I have a family of my own! Not ever, if I have my own way on this! It will all sort itself out eventually!"

"You won't leave us? It will?" She looked both surprised and relieved, but was also puzzled.

"No, nothing will change that much, except for one or two minor things, but they will still be manageable with a little care on my part, though it is getting more difficult and dangerous by the minute, I think. I can assure you that the settlement of everything upon your mother cannot be overturned now. None of it depended upon my marrying Bella or any one of you, but I did not discover that until much later. Under the circumstances, I think it was better that I married Arabella rather than Annis!"

She looked at him in disbelief, not understanding why he would say that, knowing how Annis felt about him and how he obviously felt about her.

"Yes, quite an unexpected thing for me to say! But think about it for a moment, Charlotte! If I had married Annis instead of Bella, what a difficult time we would have had of it, striving to discover and come to grips with each other in the role of man and wife and trying to cope with all of that grief and pain over the loss of her father and eldest sister at the same time!" He shook his head at that thought. "No! No! It would have been far too difficult. Difficult? It would have been impossible! Some marriages do not survive much less than that. Then there was that monumental difficulty created by our godmother's let—! That is another problem that I do not now need to face. No! That would have been too much! I think I should feel lucky that I survived as long as I did in your midst, rather than have all of that hanging over me and a wife who did not know the first thing about me and who would have been ready to see me dead before she allowed me near her after what she found out about me. I far prefer the way it worked out, as unsettling as that has been at times!"

He looked far off as he thought about that. "Though . . ." he struggled with some thought for a moment. "I do begin to believe that it is most certainly long overdue to try and correct all of that, and as soon as possible, considering what has been happening of late!"

She did not understand how he could accept it all so easily and was not sure she was hearing him correctly. It was all so tragic and emotionally draining, and here he was striving to *think* a way through a matter of the heart! Could all men be so coldly unromantic and emotionally unimaginative?

"But let me reassure you of this, Charlotte. I have no intention of deserting any of you, and especially not Sophia nor Annis nor even your mother nor you! I inherited a wonderful and ready-made family all of my own—even a wife and sisters presented to me by none other than your father and with his unreserved blessing! I am so very selfish and jealous of it, as I am sure he was too, that I am not about to jeopardize it or give it up without a fight!" He had a determined look on his face. "All that is needed is a little adjustment here and there, and it will all work out as it should." He sounded convinced of that.

"It will? But what adjustment?" His wonderful and ready-made family was built around a wife that he had almost immediately lost! It did not sound quite as rational or as stable as it should be!

"I am still thinking about that! My mother had a hand in this circumstance too, didn't she? I can clearly see the signs, for she was the one who gave your mother those astrology books and got you all immersed in the occult or whatever it is called these days, with horoscopes and astrology and the conjunctions of planets and constellations and houses in ascendance."

"Yes." There was a look of relief on her face but then a flicker of concern returned. Perhaps he had not understood her. "I know we are in mourning. I know I should not speak about it, but I also know that since you lost Bella, you . . . you and Annis have grown very close together in . . . in that . . . other way, for I have eyes of my own, and Sophia tells me everything."

He looked at her sharply. "I hope not everything!" She would not meet his eyes. He began to see that there really were very few secrets from any of these sisters.

Perhaps it was time for plain speaking and taking the bull by the horns. Charlotte blurted out what she had been thinking for some time now. "She should not be allowed to wait a year, sir, if that is what must happen, for I doubt that she can or will or should! Nor, I think, can you." She waited for him to object to her outspoken utterance.

He looked at her, wondering what she might know. He knew that Annis was not about to wait for even another day to go by, considering what she had already done and had in mind. "Wait for what, Charlotte?"

"I am not sure I dare speak of it, sir. To be married, in that *other way*, of course!" She blushed intensely. But why would he object?

"And what *other way* is that, Charlotte?" He looked steadily at her. He was not about to make it easy for her.

"I am not sure I dare to say! To be married and yet not married! The informal way! De facto, informal, canonical! Not churched!" Her face was red, but she had not faltered to say what she felt was needed to be said.

"Yes! Relax! I understand! I wondered if you would dare say it! The wrong side of the sheets! None of you beat about the bush, do you? But then an informal marriage? I cannot easily do that either! Most strange of me to admit that, for I never thought I might hold back when so much is offered to me, as it undoubtedly was, and is, and yet I *am* holding back!" He recalled the interlude in the conservatory the previous night. Is Annis . . . am I . . . are we . . . *that* obvious and signaling it all to the world?"

"Yes! Of course you are! Both of you!" She sounded quite frustrated that he did not seem to know. "But you both seem to be ignoring it in some grand theatrical way. I sometimes feel that you deserve to be slapped hard the pair of you and brought to your senses as to what needs to be done, and soon, even as immoral as it might seem, before you drive the rest of us mad with how foolish you both can be on some stupid social requirement, that there is no need for!"

"And you but sixteen!" He was impressed by her forthrightness. She seemed mature well beyond her years, but then they all were, especially Sophia. "I can assure you I am not ignoring anything, Charlotte. You seemed worried that when I discovered this it would turn *me* against *you*, yet here am I, trying to find a way through this, that will not turn everyone against *me*, and that most especially will not hurt Annis! For it might, eventually, you know? But what do you think I should do? For I will not hurt any of you, nor her, by any precipitate action if it can be avoided? We are all just recently bereaved! All of us! Including me! I expect we will be in mourning for some time, though it all seems rather pointless!"

"Yes, that is exactly it William! It is pointless! Mama has no patience with any of that. Nor did Papa! But does it matter if certain social formalities are not strictly observed if you both love each other? Happiness is the most important thing in anyone's life, and *that* is what our father told us."

"It is! But how would you suggest I move forward on this?" He waited for her suggestion, for she had obviously struggled with it for some time.

"Why, sir, she must be kidnapped or abducted and, if necessary, *forced* to marry you if it must happen that way! You are both free to marry despite you being only recently a widower! Who cares what gossips might say? You could take her to Gretna Green, or better yet, to France and marry her there, for you will be going there soon, and no one could object or raise a fuss until it is too late, and she could be brought to her senses away from here and us. But even if you do not immediately marry . . . at least you would be happy together in that . . . that other way!"

"Being free to marry and getting married are two very different things, but *forced*, you say? I don't like that word. No. That is not the way. Annis would certainly object to this scheme!" he did not tell Charlotte that her sister had another intent that was just as shocking! He continued, " . . . And so would your mother and everyone about us! But to France you say, and away from here and everyone?" He was deep in thought at that moment but could still devote some of his attention to what Charlotte was saying by way of persuasion.

"But you love each other! You are both eating your hearts out! Oh, why are men so unromantic? It sounds melodramatic, I know, but she has changed! She never did truly hate you! She mopes more than she should, despite . . . and she is moody at times and tearful, and it has not so very much to do with that . . . other. Our loss! Surely any reservations or foolish objection she might make would be swept aside by expeditious action! Then, it would not matter, for you do love each other."

"The expeditious action you refer to Charlotte, is a course that might be more destructive than constructive! I know that it would not matter so much to me. I am only a clumsy unfeeling unromantic man, as you tell me, and yet I am hesitant!"

She blushed at having her own unflattering description tossed back at her, for she had been wrong to have said it.

"Yet I am not really so far removed from propriety that I must thumb my nose at the formalities, or what society might think. I do not care for myself, but I do care for your family's reputation." He seemed to be conducting two lines of thought, one internally and one that he expressed openly. "Although such things—cart before horse—and rushing things along are expected of me I believe, by both my mother as well as Lady Seymour, and everyone who thinks they know me. But it would eventually matter to Annis, and therefore it would to me too, that everything be done *properly*, even if in some haste now, and that is what is important!"

He saw that Charlotte was prepared to listen to what he had to say before she lost all patience with him, but the very act of her broaching this subject presented some interesting possibilities.

"A relationship should be based upon trust. Kidnapping her and against her will, as it most certainly would be, is not an option that I would easily choose, and is not conducive to any degree of trust or happiness afterward. A disastrous start to a relationship!"

"Then she must be abducted much more cleverly, William, and not against her will! There must be a way! She must not recognize that she is a victim of some larger plan until it is too late, and she must approve of what is happening, yet without her knowing that she has been a victim of an abduction. She could be lured into a circumstance from which she could not, nor might want to escape. In fact, it would be better if she never did find out about it all until it is far too late! But then I am dreaming and probably confused with having thought about it for too long."

He looked at her searchingly for a few moments, clearly deep in thought. "One might almost think you were not exactly protective of your sister's virtue or finer interests, wishing that I might abduct her and compromise her, whether with or without her understanding or approval!"

"Hang her virtue, William!" Her emphatic pronouncement startled him, and herself too, but Annis was her sister and she loved her too much to see her abandon her own needs. "I've heard too much of virtue and not enough of what should be done. Once she accepts the finality of what has happened to her, she will recognize that it *had* to be done, just as it *was* done, and everything will work out all right, and she will marry you! A little late perhaps, but it will not matter by then."

"Oh my! I had not realized young ladies might all be so violently adamant about such a decisive and violent course of action! And against your own sister, no less! I am sure your mother would not approve!"

"My mother's views on that might amaze you, William!" The look on Charlotte's face, as well as her words, suggested that she would not place too much weight on her mother not approving it at all. "My mother has her own views on such things!"

"Really?".

"Oh yes! It is just a matter of time before we all succeed. Sophia has tried twice now to bring you closer together but . . . !"

"You heard of those, did you? What do you know of them?"

"Sophia told me! I cannot blame her, for I saw what needed to happen too between the two of you, but you are both holding back when there is no need of it. I watched you both after you had rescued her from the fire as you sat by the trough. I saw everything I needed to know about the two of you at that moment, and so did Mama. Unfortunately, so did Sophia. I did not know it then, but I do now; Sophia is far more of a knowing little schemer than even I might have believed. When she makes up her mind about something, it seems to happen. Then afterward . . . please forgive me, William, for relating this without hiding anything, but you need to know. Mama and I saw Annis shaving you in the far parlor. There was much more going on there between you two then, than we were supposed to see, I think!"

She saw his eyebrows raise in surprise, but he said nothing and let her continue.

"I was not sure what I might believe, for you had just recently married my sister and here you were . . . But Mama soon showed me the way of it and how mistaken I was to think as I did, so she is already quite accepting of what must happen between you and Annis, and it must happen soon! Oh William! How can you not see what we see?"

"I thought I was the only one who did see it in quite the way that I do! So the secret is no longer a secret! It seems that it never was! One way or another, my fate is sealed! I doubt I will survive another night like the last two have been, and they were just the start of it, I think!" He looked at her and saw another determined young lady, much as Annis could be at the time when she had that pistol, and as Sophia had been when she got him out to the conservatory, and before that when she insisted he take her with him to the dock that other morning.

"You are three remarkable sisters! All so frighteningly observant and all with minds of your own and not afraid of being outspokenly direct once you have made up your mind about something! I wish I had known Bella and had been able to speak with her too. I am sure she was just as formidable! My life will never be the same, I am glad to say! But Sophia is only six! Surely she did not dream up those two plots by herself?"

"Sir, she did! At least I think she did! After she told me what she planned, I gave her some help with the kitten, and she was most delighted to hear how things might be rolled along, for Annis never could resist a kitten in a dire plight or anything else for that matter."

"No more than I can."

"But then there really *was* a rat, so she had to try and deal with it herself. That was when you rescued Sophia instead of Annis. She was so downcast to see her plot fall to pieces until it became obvious that Annis would not know that the kitten was not in the barn if she was kept away from the kitchen."

William had to smile. "So Sophia plotted to throw us both together in that way, to ensnare me into a compromising circumstance with your sister, that we might never be able to escape from! Two sisters endeavoring to get me to seduce another! I hope no-one every discovers this about us. I am sure that it is not something that one expects one's own sisters to plot about. Then another clever little scheme that night of the thunderstorm! There was no need for either of those two, you know? Who will get involved next, I wonder? Your mother?"

He looked studious for some moments. "Why not? What is there to lose?" He answered his own question. "Far too much if it were to go wrong!"

She suddenly saw that he was coming around to her way of thinking. "Oh, sir! It won't! Not if we all are involved. Nothing ventured, nothing gained!"

"Or all lost! But then I am in too pessimistic a turn of mind, and I know I should not be, considering what I know. I will need all the support I can get. Perhaps . . . perhaps the time has come then for me to give in to all of these pressures that I am surrounded by and for some rather more decisive action on all of our parts, including your mother's for I think we all see the same thing and desire the same end but do not yet know how to make the best use of what we know, although I am rapidly seeing a way through all of this."

His mind *now* seemed to be working along the lines she had hoped to encourage.

He looked up suddenly. "Charlotte, I think it is time for us to have a word with your mother! I do not think that your presence or that of Sophia would be amiss either, if you can find her. Four heads will undoubtedly be better than one. There is a rational way through all of this that has been sitting under my nose for a long time but which I have missed seeing until now." He felt a small hand slide into his own. He chuckled and looked down at her.

"So! Sophia! Our arch schemer! Where were you, I wonder? No! No need to tell me! Our circle is now almost complete. I knew you could not be so very far away. Sitting off out of sight again eh, as you usually are, and listening and thinking?"

"Will he help us, Charlotte? You will, won't you, William?" She knew the answer to that question by the tearful but happy look on Charlotte's face.

William began to move over to the door with his arms on both of their shoulders, much as a friendly brother might behave with his sisters. "It is not so much about whether I will help you, young ladies, as it is about whether you will help me! Where is Annis at this moment? We need to avoid letting her know what is going on."

"She is gone to the village with Mrs. Abernethy, sir, and should be back by lunchtime. There were some things they both needed."

"And your mother?"

"In the drawing room with your sister, I believe."

"Good. Then you two and I should go and have a meeting with both of them and get all of this cleared out of the way once and for all, and concluded as it should be, starting tonight. Five heads will also be better than four. I think I can see how to do it now. I just hope we have enough time! Bring those cards with you too. I won't need them just yet, but your mother might!"

"But . . ."

"No buts, Charlotte! It will be resolved to everyone's satisfaction and without the feared upset to anyone, including me, I hope. If there is upset to anyone it will be temporary only, but not to any of you, I can assure you of that." He turned back for a moment and looked back to where he had been sitting. "But first, there is a book on my desk over there, would you bring that with us please?"

Charlotte went over and picked it up. "But, sir, isn't this the . . . ?"

"Yes, it is, isn't it? The trouble that book has been to me, you would not believe, though it will be the one thing that will ensure our success! Please bring it, and we shall move things along much better than they have been with your help and that of your mother and even Sophia, who shall play a major role in this. Again! That is, if you all approve of this scheme of mine. Of ours!"

"But why not Annis?"

"The less she knows of this, the better! That is what you said, isn't it? I doubt she would approve the scheme I have in mind anyway, at least not just yet, for it is certainly scandalous and most outrageous and never to be considered even. But then, what isn't, where this family is concerned? Come!"

Chapter XXXIV

That Night! The Grand Deception!

Charlotte had seen the signs developing that a smuggling run was planned for that evening. It would be William's first run across to France since he had returned from abroad, and he had prepared for it for the last two weeks now.

"I watched them earlier . . ." she disclosed to Annis when her sister had wondered the same thing when she returned from the village later that day with Mrs. Abernethy, " . . . and they are even busier now. They are getting ready to make a run tonight. That is the same sailor we watched the other morning. They are getting the cart ready again. I heard William say something about seven tonight, after dinner, and they had to set sail before eight to catch the tide, but they went very quiet when I walked around the corner of the building and they seemed to be talking about something else entirely, and they looked like two guilty little boys for a moment. One might almost think they do not trust us!"

"Oh, come away from the window, Charlotte! You will be seen and upset their plans. Smugglers are always nervous."

"We didn't upset them the last time we watched them, and I know they must have seen us, for William gave me a most strange look over breakfast that morning and asked if I had slept well, for he said I looked a little tired." She perked up. "Look! They are loading some new rope to take with them, so they *are* going out. Did you hear that Sophia was at the docks with William the other morning while they were getting their sloop—I think it is a sloop or sloop rigged, whatever that means—ready for the next of their nighttime jaunts across to France. She had insisted she be taken up with him or that she be allowed to ride Pat, and he agreed, for I overheard her, and then I saw them going off together."

"Surely not! Though I may have heard something."

"Oh yes. She was not about to tell me anything until I caught her putting some boy's clothing away in that closet in your room again, and I demanded to know it all, or I would go and tell Mama what she had been doing. I told you about it earlier. She confessed that she had borrowed some of William's clothing from his boyhood. They were in the closet in that bedroom you now have, and she did some minor alterations—she must have been planning it for some time—and then waylaid him to be taken with him. He could hardly refuse, could he?"

Annis smiled. It was hard to refuse Sophia when she turned on the charm or the disappointment. "Hardly! She can be most persuasive as I have discovered to my cost more than once."

"He took her off with him on that mule and had her back into the house before lunch and before anyone saw how she was dressed. She would provide no more details than that, the little witch. No one would have been the wiser except for me seeing her putting those clothes away when I came to find you. She learned *that* trick from you, I know she did, for you did that with father's clothes when you wanted to go off alone and to ride properly astride the horse, instead of with that stupid saddle and with someone with you to help you when you fall off, which happens to me all of the time."

"I thought no one knew of that!" Annis had an alarmed look on her face.

"Everyone knows I fall off that saddle!"

"No Charlotte, I meant knew about me dressing in father's clothes, for I changed in the stable before anyone else was about, and I made sure that none of you were awake when I did so." She became thoughtful. "Though Bella must have found out somehow for she cautioned me about it later. I only did it the once!"

"You might have been caught by the stable boy, and then where would you have been Annis!"

"But I wasn't! I changed in a box stall and made sure the door was closed, and no one saw me go or return."

"No matter! Sophia knew! She seems to know everything that goes on, for she spies upon everyone! I thought she did that only to William, but no, she does it to all of us! The whole house seemed to know what you had done eventually. She was most impressed by that. No doubt that was where she got the idea. She has now put it to good use I would say, by eclipsing us both. If we don't watch her, she'll be the one slipping aboard the Seamew next, perhaps even tonight, for a nighttime rendezvous with the smugglers. She will come in beaming and boasting of it all tomorrow when they return and after putting us all in fear of her life and her whereabouts!"

Charlotte sighed. "I lack the courage, but I am sure I would enjoy the adventure. William will be out overnight too, for he is going with them this time! I heard that it was to be a big run with a lot of cargo! Perhaps I shall approach William and see if he will take me out with them. I have never been to France!"

Annis frowned. "That will be his second night out in a row! But you must do nothing of the kind, Charlotte! Out overnight with only rough sailors for company? Your reputation . . . !"

"Yes! Always one's reputation! I will not let it hold me back from doing what is needed. Not as *you* seem to do! Life is supposed to have some enjoyment in it I think, rather than confine us to being so mindful of our reputation, and dull. I doubt he would allow me to go anyway, and I am not sure I dare to hide away like that." She changed the subject. "That was a particularly nice dessert we had after dinner. Apple something or other."

"Apple cobbler."

"Oh yes. I think I shall go down and have some more of it."

"It is only half an hour since we ate. Be careful you do not put on any weight, Charlotte."

"You will be putting on weight long before I will, Annis, and it will not be from eating!"

"What do you mean?" Annis felt a touch of alarm at what her sister seemed to be suggesting. What did she know?

"Never you mind! You'll see!"

Charlotte had been right about the preparations. Just a little while later, Annis noticed the carriage pulling out of the yard with William at the reins. So they *were* going out on a run tonight.

"At least you resisted that impetuous impulse to want to go with them, Charlotte."

"Yes, I did! I don't like the thought of being seasick or getting wet! But that is the only reason I decided not to go. At least not this time!"

No more than half an hour after the cart had disappeared down the driveway, a rider approached at a fast clip across the lawns. The horse appeared to have been ridden hard and was all lathered up.

Annis came onto the scene just as the messenger was letting Jerome know that he must see Mr. Devane immediately and urgently, for he had a letter for him and hoped he had not already left for the coast.

Jerome recognized the stable hand from Kellands, where William's cousin George lived. "I'm sorry, but he has gone! He left a short time ago and will be setting sail about now, or very soon, I would say."

"Damn! Beg pardon, miss!" He saw the young lady in the doorway. "I have an urgent message for him. Very urgent, from his cousin! Matter of life and death he said! I was told that I might catch him before he left. But he has gone you say?"

"Yes."

"Then there is nothing I can do!" I will give you this to pass on to him when he returns. If he returns! For by then it will be too late for him I suspect. Master George will not like to hear that I missed him. He told me to say how important it was and that it really was a matter of life or death! I had to make sure that I stopped him setting sail, even if it meant killing this horse to get here."

"And you will kill him if you try to return like that! Get him walked around and seen to. I am sure we will have a spare horse for you if you must return tonight."

"Yes, I must. His cousin will not be pleased to hear that I missed him and needs to be told that. I will be lucky if I am not turned off after this!"

Jerome passed the letter to Annis. It was indeed from his cousin George Devane. It was marked urgent and immediate! Open it now and read it, cousin!"

Just then her mother walked up to her. She seemed a little worried. "Have you seen Sophia, my love? She is not in her bed nor in the conservatory, and all of her clothing is on her bed. She was locked out there the entire night of the thunderstorm in nothing but her nightdress, poor child! She must have been cold and terrified, and here she is gone off hiding somewhere again!" Fortunately, she was not looking at Annis's face as she said that. Or she would have seen a great look of alarm on her face.

Annis tore open the letter and read it. "I thought that was for William, my dear, or did I mishear? You should not open other people's mail! It might get you into trouble!"

"I must, for he is not here Mama! It is from his cousin, and it says urgent and immediate, and he even wrote that William must open it and read it now. Something about life or death! I am sure he will not mind." She read it quickly. Within seconds of seeing what the letter said, she was headed upstairs at a run, heedless of inquiries from either her mother or her sister who was just then heading down to execute her own plan concerning the little that remained of the apple cobbler.

"Charlotte!" She spoke so that her mother might not overhear her. "Sophia has gone off with them!"

"With who, whom?"

"With William!"

"I told you!" She turned and followed her sister upstairs. "I said she would! So she undoubtedly did! She told me that she would be doing so at the first opportunity when she knew they were going off to France, but I thought she was just talking."

"Undoubtedly not, Charlotte! But there is now another reason I must get down to the dock and stop them. I must show William this letter that just came for him. He is in grave danger! They both are! Do not let anyone know I have gone."

"What danger?"

"Revenuers! Customs agents! They know what he is about and of his plans tonight and intend to board him or sink him! He must not go! If Sophia is with him, it is even more important that she does not go either, for that also puts her in danger!"

"She may not be with him!"

"Don't be silly, Charlotte! Of course she is!"

"Yes, she probably is. How will you get down there?"

"I'll take William's horse."

"He won't like you doing that. But if you do, you must also take the mule too don't forget, or you will not get very far! But you should not, you know? William will be most annoyed."

Her sister ignored her. "Yes, and the mule too. He will not be annoyed considering what I have to tell him. I'll saddle the mule up too so that I can bring Sophia back with me, the little mischief! I'll have some words to say to her after this!"

"The side saddle will not fit Boney. The girth is not long enough! You will need to change it!"

"I shall not take the side saddle."

"Well!" Charlotte was shocked to hear that. "Quite a sight you will make careening across the countryside with your skirts flapping at your waist and revealing all to the world!"

"No, I won't! For I shall dress in some of Williams clothes from that same closet in my room that Sophia was at. I tried one set on the other day, but it was not a good fit. It will have to do though!"

"Annis! You didn't?"

Her sister blushed, and was defiant. "Well, I don't see why Sophia should be the only one to have fun, but I realized I shouldn't. Come, I will need your help!"

Charlotte assisted her out of her dress and into a suit of young man's clothing that she sorted from the clothing in the closet. "They are not at all flattering, but they look better on you than they did on me!" She looked approvingly at her sister. "You should have put two shirts on. It would never do to have those obvious parts of you, moving about as they do, and that should not be there if you were a youth! Better do the buttons up as far as you can too! At least the trousers are loose enough to hide your hips!"

"They are a much better and looser fit than the others I had on." Annis sounded puzzled. "I don't remember these! You say you tried them on?"

"Yes. I thought I might try and smuggle away too, but the more I thought about it, the less enjoyable it began to seem. But look! She did go as you thought. There is a gap here where Sophia had those boy's clothes that she wore before, and they are gone again. She did go! The little vixen!"

"Yes. I suspected as much myself when Mama could not find her in her usual places and with her clothes lying on her bed. We don't know the half of what she gets up to! All the more reason that I must now go myself and make sure that she does not come to harm considering what that letter said."

"What letter?"

"The urgent letter that just came was from William's cousin warning him of the revenue officers about to descend on that very wharf sometime tonight after they had departed and await their return in the morning. It also said that they may have a ship out too, to try to intercept them at sea or even sink them! The message said that he must cancel the run at any cost, or he would be risking everything! To think that Sophia is on board with him and he not knowing she was there! I must warn him and stop him, and her, and I have little time to get there to do either of those things! I hope that neither of us will be missed, except that Mama already seems to know that Sophia is not in her bed. But say nothing of the other about the contents of the letter that came, or she would be worried. There, how do I look?"

She did not wait for an answer but stormed out of her door and headed for the stairs even as she was doing up her buttons, closely followed by Charlotte.

"Except for the hair, you might easily pass for a poorly dressed youth. If it were dark! Your complexion is too smooth by far though and your eyes too large and innocent. You don't look much like a youth to me! You are built all wrong! Youths do not generally have such prominent breasts, which nothing will hide you know? If anyone recognizes you, your reputation, even ours, will be lost forever. You will be branded as a Hoyden, which you called me once. Whatever one of those is, but I am sure it is not complimentary."

"It is *not* complimentary and refers to a woman's lack of self-control and thoughtfulness concerning her reputation! I don't care! I *am* a hoyden by that definition!"

"At last! An awakening as to what is really important! But what have you and William been up to? You *will* put on weight if you are not careful, and you are not married either, don't forget."

"Charlotte!"

Annis grabbed a boy's cap from her pocket. She had not recalled that earlier either. It suited the rest of her garb, and as she ran off across the yard, she stuffed her hair up under it.

"There."

"Yes. Better and better. No one would take a second look at you." That was a lie, and Charlotte knew it. "You should not run Annis, or you certainly will be discovered! Boys do not run like that nor do they jiggle like that either." She was having difficulty containing her laughter. "You had better take care of yourself, you know. I only have two sisters left! I shall try to tell Mama nothing until she demands to know, or goes into decline. I hope you remembered to take that pistol with you. It will go into your pocket just in case someone tries to stop you."

"I already have it." She patted her other pocket. "But if they do, I will ride them down! I hope no one sees me leave, or there will be trouble!"

Charlotte could not help wondering for whom there might be trouble. "I shall help you saddle up. At least I can do that. I hope you can manage that brute! He is as much as any man could handle, never mind you!"

Within five minutes, they had the stallion saddled and ready to go, and with the mule saddled too, and turned loose. Annis mounted and she turned off and rode out to get onto the road to the coast and to the wharf where the Seamew was tied up. She hoped she was in time, and that they had not set sail already! Charlotte watched her go.

She smiled as Annis rode out of sight and then chuckled to herself and, in her excitement, almost ran back to the house to report to their mother and Elizabeth that their plan was now underway. What was Annis thinking, to believe she could hide her sex and dress like a youth! No one could possibly be misled by any of it! She might as well have hired trumpets to blare out her coming! Charlotte had to stop in the doorway as the tears of mirth and even of relief ran down her cheeks. She rushed off to capture the images of Annis, burned into her brain. At the same time, she began to feel a slight envy of what lay ahead of her sister. It would be interesting to see how her sister's new outlook on life as a married woman might be reflected in her face when they were able to visit her in a couple of days.

Chapter XXXV

At the Dock

Annis wasted no time once she was on the open road. There was a glimmer of a moon, not yet full, but enough to see by. Clearly, the horse could see far more than she could and was surefooted. He did not seem to mind her on his back. He knew where he was going despite having a strange rider up, so she trusted his judgment.

She rode low on the horse to make sure of avoiding any low lying branches that might sweep her off after the heavy winds of the previous few days.

Within a half hour, she had reached the dock and could see the wharf. She was relieved to see the ship still tied up there with no obvious signs of activity on its deck and, unfortunately, no sign that Sophia might be there either, though she was undoubtedly well hidden by now. They must all still be in the inn, plotting their evening's work.

She pulled up outside, and the boy appeared at the sound of hoof-beats on the cobbles, to hold the horse for her. She lowered her voice and spoke. "I need to speak with William Devane. It is urgent!"

"Yeh?" He looked at the rider suspiciously. Annis wondered what he was thinking. Surely he knew that any customs officers would not be here alone, so he could not possibly mistake her for one of those.

"It alus is on a night like this! I'll get t'gaffer." He went off to find t'gaffer! Whomever he might be. She hoped no one would recognize her as a woman and make a scene, but she was determined to speak with William. If need be, she would break into wherever they were and stand there until he recognized her.

Damn! This was not working out quite as easily as she had hoped. She didn't want t'gaffer; she wanted William. However, apart from a strange look on the boy's face, he said nothing more and merely told her to wait there. An older man took a fast look outside of the door to see Mr. Devane's horse standing there with a strange person on its back and the mule close by and investigating some blades of grass at the edge of the building. He returned inside, and Annis could hear his clogs along the corridor as he went off into a back room.

Within a short space of time, William appeared and took in her appearance in a flash.

She dismounted, relieved to see him at last, and he steered her off out of the way while the boy looked after the horse. "Well. What are you doing here dressed like that? On Boney too I see, and heard. How did you manage him?"

"Easily."

"Then I am surprised and impressed, for he will not let just anyone ride him."

"But then I am not just anyone. I have ridden him before, and you saw me, though you said nothing."

"No, you rode him well then, and I am sure, just as well this time too, and dressed so well for it!" His eyes shone as he looked at her. "I never looked so good in those clothes."

"William!" She liked the way he looked approvingly at her, despite her strange attire. "I could not ride sidesaddle and expect to get here either in time or at all. I would have attracted too much of the wrong attention riding alone like that. So this was necessary! Charlotte helped!"

"She didn't come as well, did she?"

"No! Of course not! But I am not here to pass the time of day. I have some urgent reason for being here." He waited for her to speak. "You have been found out!"

"Oh my! You mean you got another letter, perhaps two, from our godmother?" He was smiling at her.

"You may think it is funny, but it is not! I mean this!" She rummaged in her pocket and passed him his cousin's urgent letter.

He read it quickly. "Yes! Yes. I know all of this!"

"You know of it?"

"Oh yes. I have good informants in London who are able to tell me of the movements of the various ships. I have numerous other friends too, with their eyes open for the wrong people, and anxious to have me renew my questionable habits—that one anyway! I'll read the rest later. I can outrun any ship they might throw at us tonight, and besides that, we do not intend to return here when we are through. George cannot have known that I was aware of this, but it was most protective of him to warn me and most brave of you to have considered doing so as well, and dressed like that too!" His eyes sparkled as he admired her openly. "Most becoming for some reason!" He suddenly remembered where he was. "I am sorry your trip was to no avail, Annis! We already knew! But thank you for the warning. Can you make it back the same way safely?"

"No! I cannot! Not yet. Sophia is gone, and she has smuggled herself aboard your ship!"

That got his attention. "I doubt it! How could she? I checked in the box before we left. I half expected one of you would try that, for one of you did the other night, except we did not go."

"Yet she did, somehow! She is not at home, and her usual clothing is on her bed, and some of your smaller boyhood clothes are missing!" She stored the other about someone trying to go off with them the other night in her mind, to ask about later.

"She must have dressed in your clothes again, for they are gone from the closet. She knows that you check in that box before you leave now, so she would hide somewhere else. You'll not find her if she does not want to be found, you know?"

He was deep in thought. "I know! Especially on board a ship! There are far too many hiding places for a small body to crawl into, and no one will be able to follow her. If I call for her to come out, she will be unlikely to do so if she feels I may put her ashore. She is unlikely to reveal herself to me, but she might for you!"

"I warned Charlotte that it may not be possible for Sophia and me to return tonight, but if we are not back by morning . . ." She looked up at him for help.

"If we do not easily find Sophia, you will certainly not be back by morning, for we must make this run tonight, and we must leave soon, or the tide will shortly be too low to get out of here. We'd better find her, is all I can say." He shook his head. "Your mother will have some choice words to say to me if you are not back home tonight!" In truth he knew she would have some choice words to say to him if she was.

In reality, her mother was excitedly awaiting confirmation that all was going as had been planned.

At that moment, William's friends started to leave the inn and paid little attention to the 'boy' William was with, as his body mostly sheltered 'him' from their view.

Joe appeared from the direction of the ship as the rest of the crew boarded. "Five minutes, William. I told you that fifteen minutes gone! You almost left it too late you know? We need to leave before the water gets too low, or we'll get grounded. So you'd better come now and sharpish like! We have little enough time as it is, if the weather does not cooperate!"

"Then get ready to cast off and leave. I'll be there."

His voice dropped as he turned to Annis and held her close to him by her shoulders. "Very well, it seems that I must take you with us, but if I find Sophia before we leave, I will put you both ashore. If not, then you both will be coming to France with us. If that is the case, you shall stay out of sight in the cabin and be ready to follow my instructions at any time and without question."

"I will. I promise!"

"I hope I shall not regret this. We need to find Sophia! She will be somewhere there, amidst all the clutter, but I will not have time to look, for she was poking about there when she was last here with me. Probably looking for a hideaway if she was already planning this. If we can find her before we put out then I will most assuredly put you both ashore." He had no intention of doing anything of the kind. "Wait here."

He had a few words with the landlord, scribbled a note on a sheet of paper, folded it and gave it to the man, and then led Annis off along the dock. "He'll see the horses and the carriage returned to Brooklands as soon as we leave if we do not find her and get you both ashore. I wrote a note for your mother telling her some of this and what might happen. It will at least save her from too much worry about your absence, and I told her where we will be. I want no evidence to remain here that so many of us shipped out and are not yet returned, and hopefully, they will give up but not too soon and not before the Seamew gets in tomorrow morning.

"I thought you said you were not returning here?"

"We're not." He walked with her over to the ship. "We'll ground this one in dead man's slough, down the coast, and offload her there at our leisure. It's well out of the way, and we'll take the masts off so she'll not be too visible above the shrub and undergrowth. There is another Seamew docked in France at this very moment. *She* will be here by morning for the revenuers to board and search if they can't catch her at sea. My new vessel! Father had her built before he died. Looks much like this one too, but is on her maiden voyage. She will replace this one, for this is her last voyage and shall be retired, a little ignominiously on a mud bank, but nonetheless retired. They won't know the difference. It should be suitably embarrassing for them to come up empty-handed. I shall also rechristen her later. She shall be called the Annabel!"

He smeared at the hub of the carriage standing by the ship and then gently put a thin smudge of the dark greasy mess on Annis face and brow. She did not flinch. "A candle and a cork would have been better and easier to get off, but they are not available at this moment. This will distract from too close a look at you." He knew it wouldn't. "Your complexion is far too white and smooth and gentle for a boy, and your eyes too clear and distracting." He sighed. "Too damned attractive altogether!" He looked about to make sure they were not being watched and then leaned in and kissed her suddenly. She returned his kiss without any hesitation.

"William, someone might see us!"

"No, they didn't! We don't need you identified as a woman on this trip, so it's good that my clothing is so very loose about you." For all the good that did, he could see! "Tie your cap down under your chin. There is a tape there and it will stop it blowing off. I doubt that too many boys have quite a head of well-kept hair as you do either." Nor those other parts that no boy ever had! "It will be a dark night and not so much moon just yet! Some of the men are superstitious and might get a little anxious with a woman on board anyway, and there is at least one other who might recognize you—the reverend! So we will need to stay out of his way as much as we can."

"I thought we passed him as we were going in to the village the other day!"

"You did! Watch for the gangplank, my love. It is very narrow and steep. He was getting ready for this jaunt. Yes, I know what you are thinking. I am a corrupting influence on the poor man. But even the clergy likes its small pleasures and needs a little adventure and to be distracted from hellfire and damnation from time to time. Or as others say, to get the Hell scared out of them! His bishop liked the idea of some brandy as a gift and likes the notion of free trade too, for he preaches about it, or so I hear, so we also have the indirect blessing of the church in our little adventure, my dear. Now if only he could part the waters or even calm them, for it will not be a pleasant or calm crossing tonight, but the better for it, for we are likely to avoid others."

"Better not say the 'my love' or 'my dear' too much, William, or this mess will be for naught, and I shall not be put ashore willingly without Sophia, and perhaps not even then!"

He raised his voice for the benefit of his shipmates. "Come on, Andy, let's get you aboard, cousin." He slapped her on the back, almost knocking her off her feet, and put his arm over her shoulder. He spoke softly again. "You shall be my cousin along for the adventure, and there will be no questions or comments while you are close to me. Speak as little as you can, keep your soft hands out of sight. Put them in your pockets! Follow no orders but mine, and keep out of the way of the men!"

"Aye aye, sir." She saluted, and grinned at him.

He smiled at her levity. "Some of them can be a little rough in their speech and behavior without ladies present and likely will be with a green lad. Do not be overly startled by what you might see or hear. Or at least don't show it."

Chapter XXXVI

Once Aboard the Lugger . . . and So to France

They clambered down the gangplank, which was at a sharp angle to the deck with the low state of the tide, as William held on to her collar to stop her slipping off it. After a perfunctory search for Sophia on deck, they realized that she must be hiding in some inaccessible place, probably below, and would not appear until she was sure they were under way.

By then, they had cast off from the dock and had been pushed out from the wharf as the foresail, once hoisted, began to fill with a light breeze, pushing the bow out from the dock. Two of the several men on the dockside clambered aboard as the boat moved out. One leapt aboard and grabbed at the railing while the other swung easily and gracefully inboard with long practice as the boat heeled over a little, away from the dock. The mainsail was then hoisted up the back mast to provide some forward headway. One of the men on the dock retrieved the gangplank from where it had fallen to the end of its rope and pulled it back onto the dock.

"Joe. You can take her out. I'll see my cousin Andy settled and out of our way."

"Aye, Cap'n. I've got her. I usually do! Don't let it go to your head, William! You're only captain temporarily, don't forget!"

"Watch for that sudden gust as we clear the point."

"I will! Dammit, William! I been doing this longer than you have been in long britches! Too like your father by far with your eye on detail, but you can still read the wind a little better than he could, though not near as well as I can, so you just relax! With this breeze pushing us over, we should still have two feet or more under the keel if we're lucky."

He showed Annis to the cabin set amidships and opened the door. It was quite a small, low cabin and cluttered with sail cloth and mounds of rope and other things that had been placed there ready for their run across the channel. There was weak light from a lantern swaying in the middle of the small dark room, and there was little enough headroom for anyone. With the suddenly increasing gyrations of the ship, buffeted by suddenly changing winds, she lost her balance and found herself pulled into his arms and kissed again. "Not too much privacy on a ship, my dear." He let go of her. "Mind your head. The beams are all low enough to catch even you." He put a hand on her arm and looked closely into her face as he leaned in and kissed her again. "Remember, my love. I need you to be alive and well after this."

"William, I have been on board a boat before. But the same applies to you, you know?"

There was a scuffling and then scurrying of feet as a small body appeared from deep in the shadows and ran to her. "Annis! I thought I heard your voice. What are you doing here? Are you coming with us too?"

She heard William mutter in her ear. "So much for my romantic plans for the crossing."

She squeezed his arm and then turned to Sophia. "We were looking for you, miss!"

"I thought we would never leave."

"Well thank goodness we found where you are. Saves me scouring the ship for you."

"You won't put me ashore, will you, William, now that Annis is here? You promised!"

"Stow it, Sam! Yes I did, didn't I? I promised a lot of things if I recall, but it's too late for putting either of you ashore, young lady—lad." He corrected himself. "We've left the dock, and it would be a wet walk! No turning back now."

"Good."

Annis looked at him for an explanation. "What is this about a promise?"

"I'll explain it later. We have too much on our plates at this moment. Next port of call is in France. You're coming with us now, like it or not, and so is Sophia—Sam!"

"Good." At least Sophia was happy with the arrangement.

He looked at them both. "I may not survive with my reputation intact after this if Lady Seymour gets a whiff of this too. But you had better stick with the part of a boy too, Sam! Sam and Andy! You'd both better come with me before we hit the open sea, and let the crew see that there are two of you with me, so there'll be no surprises beyond seeing two of you now. There shouldn't be any, provided you say nothing and stay in the cabin. You'd better stay out of their way anyway until we are moving steadily and are well out, for it's going to be rough as we clear the point and hit that sea. We'll have to lay her over a bit to be sure of getting out over the bar. The wind is mostly out of the north and will do some awkward things to us for a while. You don't get seasick, do you?"

'I don't, but S-Sam has never been out before, so I cannot venture a guess."

"I won't be seasick!" Sophia seemed very sure of that.

William looked at them both. "Well some of the crew will be, I suspect, and long before we get there, maybe even me!" They both looked sharply at him for that frank admission. A sailor being seasick? "So don't feel bad if *you* do, but don't rush to the rail! Be sick where you are if you are going to be sick. Don't need to see you go overboard until we need to, so if you need to go on deck, which you don't, unless I am with you, make sure you have a tethered rope looped about your hand, and do not explore. If you are near the rail and are sick make sure you are on the lea side of the ship or facing that way," he pointed, "with the wind at your back and with someone to stop you going overboard. I do not have a change of clothing here suitable for you if anything gets blown back onto you."

"Ugh." Sophia did not like the sound of any of that. "I don't see the telltales, William." She was straining to see up into the sails.

"No. Neither can we against those black sails at night, but Joe doesn't need to see them to get the best out of her."

"What are they, William? Telltales? What are you talking about?"

He had his arm about her shoulder to steady her against the increasingly rough tossing the ship was now suffering. Sophia held onto his leg. "Telltales, my love, are little bits of light material, wool usually, attached to the luff of the sails. They show the flow of wind across the sail and tell the crew whether or not they need to bring the sail in more, or slacken it off to get the best out of the wind. With the wind the way it is, we could be across and in France in less than two hours, I would say, give or take, but I can't say which way the wind will be when we leave France, so we will just have to wait and see. Could be from the east in which case we will delay our return and have a nice run back ahead of it, or could be from the west, and hard in our faces, in which case we will have some very strenuous work facing us all the way home."

He looked out across the whitecaps ahead of them and breaking against the side of the ship.

"It will be a rough crossing tonight! Not good! Best to stay off the deck unless I take you, or you might slip, or a boom or a wave may carry you over the side or you may get fouled up in a rope. Not a good place to be even for an experienced sailor in this weather. You will be mostly amidships here, so you will experience the least rough voyage of anyone and won't get thrown about quite as much. We will eat well in France if you have not lost your appetite in the crossing, for it will take some time to get rid of the ballast and then to load us. Timing is crucial, so on the way back, we may have to heave too off the coast for a while, and if we do, it will get very rough. Eat soft foods if you need to eat again before we leave, and you probably will, for we will be some hours. You don't need sharp edges if you bring it back up!" He smiled at the pained looks on their faces.

"What a thing to think about, A-Andy." Sophia looked up at William and saw that he was enjoying it all. "Do you have to talk so much about being sick, William?"

"Ignore him, Sophia—Sam. He's enjoying this and said that deliberately. Take no notice. This is typical sailor humor. Eat what you like, So—Sam. It will make little difference. But do you have to talk so much about being sick, William? S-sam is right, it's enough to make anybody feel ill with all of this buffeting about!"

He grinned. "No, I don't. Come on and let the crew see that there are two you with me, and I will get you to stay in the shelter of the companionway or in here while I try and make myself useful. If you do not feel well, you can lie down on that cot over there or in the hammock, but the way *that* will be moving with you, I don't advise it, or you really might feel ill. Better to be on your feet or sit on that bunk and keep your minds occupied. Talk or whatever. I'll be in to see you from time to time when I can."

"You go, William, and do what needs to be done. We shall watch from shelter."

"It won't be sheltered for long once we get out there, for there's quite a sea running and whitecaps. It will get wet out there!"

He pointed over to one wall of the cabin. "There's heavy coats hanging there. They are dry so far. Put one on if you need more warmth, but they are no use if they get wet, and will be no help if *you* are. Try to stay dry and warm. The stove is not lit, so there is no warmth there I am afraid, and it will be too rough to trust lighting a fire in it. We'll be working hard on this crossing, so we'll be warm enough, where you won't be."

As they moved to the base of the stairs leading up to the deck, they could already feel the cooler and steady wind begin to bite through to their flesh and could even feel splashes of water hitting their faces. "We need to get some running lights out, now that we are further out, though we will dispense with them on the way back."

After three hours of what turned out to be an unexpectedly rough passage, with the crosswinds causing them to corkscrew in the sea and with wind and water coming at them from the port side, they began to approach the French coast.

Both passengers were on deck by then, near the helmsman, out of the way, and firmly hanging on. They had been thrown about in the cabin more than they had liked and needed to see more than just four confining cabin walls moving in a dizzying way around them. *That* alone was enough to make anyone feel ill!

"There Joe! There! Three lights abreast!"

"I see 'em!" He shouted to William who was at the helm at that time. "Head straight for the middle one, William. We'll be ready to drop the sails on my signal."

William spoke to the two figures close by him. "They know what to do and when to do it better than I do. All I need to do is keep her pointed at that middle light. If you look closely, you can see lights from a house or two now, from deep in that cleft. Once we get a little sheltered from this wind we'll be fine, and they can pull us in when we get ropes ashore."

In little time, they still had momentum enough to cleanly enter a small sheltered harbor, shielded by cliffs. The sails were dropped in seconds and ropes thrown off both to port and starboard. The cleft was narrow, only about 150 feet wide, and went in quite far from the opening. Once out into the open area behind the cleft, they could see that there were houses and dock structures on both sides with two ships tied up already and quite a number of men along the side waiting to take over the ropes, even then being thrown out from the stern of the incoming Seamew, to get her turned and berthed by the many bodies that lined the dock side. "We can't turn easily ourselves in such a narrow channel, so we need to be pulled around. Good job there are no others in here but those two, or there'd be no room for us! I wasn't sure we'd get in as easily as we did."

He steered as straight a course as he could as the ship gradually lost way, and the parties of men on both sides of the channel slowly pulled them in. Once much deeper into the little cliff-lined harbor, they put other ropes ashore and crews of men on both banks started to slow them, and to pull them around.

"We need to get her nose pointed out to sea again before we load up, so that's why we have men on both sides, and then we'll tie securely up to that brigantine there. We'll need her to hoist for us. She has the rigging and strength for it where we don't.

"The other boat on the other side" he pointed to a sleek shape across the small harbor, ". . . is the Seamew that will return as expected in our place. They will leave about the same time we will, or a little before, just in case there is a ship waiting offshore to intercept us."

"But she has white sails, William!"

"Yes. We do not mind if she is clearly seen. We would like her to be seen. We are the ones that should *not* to be seen.

"I'll need to go and see her captain before we finish and warn him what his certain reception when he returns, will be like, and that if his crew has any contraband, they had best put it into our care, or they will certainly lose it. Some of our crew will go with them too."

Sailors were already furling the black sails and securing them and moving the booms up and out of the way prior to taking the small hatches off, fore and aft and getting ready to off load the ballast that had given them the weight in the keel to put on as much sail as they dared.

"We have at least twenty tons of granite to offload. Take about an hour if all goes well with two winches going, and then as many tons of cargo, or more, to take aboard and stow.

"We can go ashore once we get tied up. The landlord of the Coq D'Or, Monsieur Planchon is expecting us. We've planned this trip for a while, and he has food organized for us and the entire village. He is a friend and knows us well, so do not be afraid of him!"

"I wasn't sick once, William!"

"I'm proud of you, S-Sam. You'll do. You now have sea legs!" Sophia looked down at her legs but wasn't sure what he meant, for they were the same ones she started with.

"What are those men doing?" She pointed at two men on either side of a device on the deck and both of them working hard at it, with water flowing across and out of the scuppers.

"Pumping us out! We took on a lot of water coming over, with all the corkscrewing we were doing. Loosened the planking that did! If we don't have a sea like that to face on the way back, we should be all right, otherwise we will be pumping continuously, for some of the cargo will need to be kept dry or it will be spoiled. She's an old ship and showing her age. Tiring work and I'll need to take my turn at it too as I did on the way over. Let's get you across to the dock and to meet Monsieur Planchon. I'll need to pay him now once I find out what cargo he has for us and see that there is food and drink for everyone paid for too. That is why we are always welcome here! Nobody works well on an empty stomach." He hefted a weighty little sack in his hands, obviously filled with gold coins. "They'll eat and drink well tonight and even ask about the next run that we plan, so that they can be prepared for us."

"What cargo, William?"

"I think he was getting us brandy, spirits, tea, lace, and silk. There might even be tobacco from Virginia, easier and cheaper from France, for the American colonies will sell to them if not to us. I'll find out more when we get ashore! They are having tough times after the war and they need gold and a few other things that I can get for them easily enough, including wool and cotton goods. The heavier kegs, barrels, tankers, and half tankers will be loaded first for ballast. The last things to load are all of the lighter things that might be damaged by the sea if they get wet—the silk, then the tea, and tobacco if there is any. We'll see what else he may have organized for us too. He always manages to surprise me."

He escorted them across the deck. "We'll need to cross to the dock over that ship, and we should do it now before they start to hoist the granite out fore and aft. Dangerous place to be if a sling lets go, though we try to hoist about half a ton at a time. We don't have big enough hatches to do much more than that of the more bulky materials, and we don't need a hole through the bottom. They have enough carts to move it away and pile it inland a little out of the way, and then they'll load up with what we want from wherever they have it stored and bring it along to hoist across to us."

He lifted them both up to the deck of the brig, a little above them, and then walked with them across the deck and down the gangplank to the dock. "Stay close to me. I'll let the landlord know you are with me and to put you in a separate room if I can, or out of the way a little, away from all of the rough language, smoke, and noise."

Sophia was excited by that prospect. "I'd prefer to listen to the sailors, William. They have some interesting words."

Annis put a hand on Sophia's shoulder. "Words, which you will not repeat in polite company young la—lad! Yes, I bet you would prefer to be with them! You already have enough disturbing ideas without adding to *them* and to your language too!"

William passed the two disguised 'persons' into the hands of the landlord after a few words of French that Annis did not clearly understand. He turned back to them. "I'll join you and eat with you once I see that everything is rolling smoothly along as it should, for there are enough hands to help with all of the transfers. Half of the village at least has turned out to help us, and we'll need them all if we want to get away from here as we should. There are others out on the approach roads to make sure no one else blunders down who should not be here to interrupt us. Well armed too, I might add!" He added a note of caution that only they might hear. "Don't drink the wine unless I bring it to you. Most of it is strong and not of the best and will give you a headache. They save the best for them as will pay for it. We English! There is a good small beer, and he has good water from a spring up on the hillside. He has an excellent roasted chicken, and his beef bourguignon is memorable! I expect he has had a pig spitted and slow roasting now for some time. It smells like it! If you need something lighter and less fatty, he has an excellent ham soup and very good breads and various cheeses."

"No sharp edges on any of that," Sophia noted. She was feeling more at ease about not being ill. "What will they do with the rocks, William?"

"Same as we do. They use them to build with, if they get too many, or they'll use them for ballast on the next ship that offloads and leaves empty and is riding too light.

"With luck, we should be ready to go again in a few hours. We need to time it properly when we get back to England, to get the highest tide of the season, and that will be at about five in the morning, in five hours from now. It doesn't leave us much time. With the wind behind us, the high water might persist until a little later in the morning, but we need to be out of sight by five at the latest, if we can."

He left them with Monsieur Planchon with instructions to keep them apart from the others and to keep an eye on them. Planchon seemed to know all about them, for once, he addressed the elder as "mams . . . —monsieur" before he switched his gender. Annis had an uncomfortable feeling that everyone seemed to know that they were not what they seemed to be, for there were many curious glances their way and occasional laughter.

Over the next few hours, many men and women passed in and out to eat and drink, but spent little time inside before they were out again. They all began to look increasingly tired as the night wore on. Sophia was attentive to everything!

Eventually, more and more of the villagers showed up to rest, and eat and drink in more leisure, and then William appeared and spoke French with all of those who were in his vicinity as he thanked them for their work. They knew they were being well paid for what they had done, just as they were being well fed and would be for the next day or so too.

He escorted his two passengers back over to the Seamew. They were with him as he inspected the hatches, as Joe had already done, and checked that they were well battened down.

"We can now leave. The other Seamew is setting out ahead of us." They could see her departing already, being pulled out and away from the rocks at the mouth of the inlet by a line of many men on each side, and then from small boats anchored further out, to hold them. Once out from the shelter of the rocks and able to raise a sail without fear of the wind driving her back into the rocks, she set her own path and cleared the point.

It was then their turn to leave. "When we clear the shelter of the cliffs, you should get back into the cabin, or you can stay close by me, for I shall not be far from there."

Chapter XXXVII

The End of the Seamew in Deadman's Slough

The wind had grown even stronger, and had veered slightly to the east of North, by the time they had cleared the small harbor. As the channel was almost north-south, the wind was against them getting out cleanly without some clever seamanship. They had been at sea again for at least two hours when Sophia noticed something off in the darkness ahead of them. "What is that light over there, William?" Sophia pointed.

"Where?"

"There!"

He sighted along her arm and saw the end of a trail of sparks. "Damn! You've got sharper eyes than the lot of us! Someone tapping his pipe out on a railing!"

He gestured with some urgency to the helmsman that there was another vessel close by and to change course a little to avoid being seen, but the Helmsman had already taken sharp action to avoid the other vessel and to pass astern of it, for he had also seen Sophia pointing. Neither of the ships had running lights.

"Better get below and hide the light from that lantern in the cabin. They may not see us the way they are heeled over, and we are running quiet, and it's noisy enough out here with the wind anyway."

It seemed that everyone was aware of the other ship. It was also too close for comfort, and they might be hard-pressed to avoid a collision. The approaching vessel was under full sail, heading northeast, with its starboard rails almost under water, which was why they might not be seen as their sails obscured everything to the immediate starboard. They passed with no more than two hundred feet between them, ghostly shapes passing silently in the night. Their helmsman must have been watching other things, fighting to avoid losing a mast or worse, for he seemed not to notice them.

"Are you all right?" He saw Annis and Sophia re-appear from below. Annis seemed scared and hung onto his arm for a moment.

"You mean apart from walking first on one wall of the cabin and then on the other, and seeing water pouring in through the planking. Yes, I think so! That was quite frightening!"

"Yes, I expect it was. We needed to lay her over to miss them by as much as we could and to avoid being seen. They were not watching for us just yet and didn't hear us, or with any luck, they had an earlier glimpse of the sails of the other Seamew and were intent only upon that. There are only two kinds of vessels that go without running lights on a night like this—smugglers and revenuers. That was a revenue ship! Two masted and sloop rigged. Like this one but heavier. Ten guns, I would say. Taking a contingent up the coast to be sure to meet us at sea, almost as if they knew exactly where we would be. They almost ran us down! The other Seamew will be arriving there just after dawn in another two hours, I expect, so she will remain some miles offshore to attract their attention. They were cramming it! I think they did not expect to see us for another hour or so, for they think we are to put in either at our regular dock, or if not, then twenty miles up the coast from that."

Joe came over. "We're running behind our schedule, William, after that near miss. I don't see any blaze on the land yet to show where we are to head for, but I can see a few breakers."

"They'll have the fires going from about two hours before high tide and then into the early hours or until they see us. We'll see them. They should be lit by now. Until then, we heave-too, if necessary."

"No need! There!" He pointed. "I see it! I can see the smaller one too, and maybe another."

"Yes. The small one is exactly four hundred yards due south of the larger blaze. Lets us see how far out we are. Difficult to judge how far offshore we are, in the dark and with no lights, but those two will guide us and give us approximate position and distance, where *one* would not." He took a bearing to each fire and then thought for a second or two. "Looks about right! I can't see the third fire, so it must be directly behind the larger one, as it should be. We are close to five miles out from shore! Aim for about a mile south of the leftmost blaze. You will need a bearing of 260 degrees, but watch the wind. It'll be daylight soon anyway. I scouted it well in the last few days from the land side. There should be at least one long boat with a lantern to mark the midpoint of the entrance, and we'll follow it in."

He turned to his two passengers. "The channel we are aiming for is no more than two hundred feet wide and easily missed, but it's a deep channel that goes inland about two miles. We need the tide and wind to carry us in, or we'll not easily make it against the outflowing river and the mud banks. We'll get some help, for the wind is now with us, coming a little more out of the East."

"We'll come up against their rope when we get where we need to be at four fathom hole, and that's four fathoms deep at low tide, and then after that we tie on and let them pull us up that side branch to the south, with a couple of teams of horses and beach us on a mud bank. After that, we'll winch it the rest of the way in, as the tide lifts us a bit. I hope the water is high enough, or it will be quite a job to get in high enough to get the cargo off without floundering in deep mud. The customs officers will not think of looking for us in there, or believing that we deliberately grounded her once they find the other Seamew."

Annis and Sophia stayed well out of the way. Once they were at four fathom hole and had tied onto the rope across the channel there, they felt a sudden gentle surge as the horses, somewhere out of sight pulled them into the side channel, as quickly as they could, and hauled them until they stuck fast on the mud bank. With no likelihood of getting any further at that moment, there was some urgency to get the masts off or they would be seen from quite a distance once it became fully light, but that process had started even as they entered the channel. The foremast was cut down to lie into the bank, followed by the aft mast to lie nearby, beside it. They were now not so visible to anybody from either the land or the sea. Annis watched as they pulled the two masts closer together and put planking from the freshly opened hatches across them to create a wide ramp to assist with the offloading.

"Where are we, William? Everything is gloomy and unrecognizable in here, and I can see only trees."

"Dead Man's Slough, my love!"

"I've never heard of it!"

"No, I expect not! It's not well known, and it's hard to get to. Sophia and I were here to see it a few days ago. We have a track cut now to it to get the cargo out. As we are lifted higher—if we are—and as we lighten, we will get pulled in a little more, but we are already nicely positioned. Pity we don't have a fog roll in to hide us even better now that we are here, but the wind is still too brisk for that." He put his hand on her shoulder. "We'll be some time my dears, probably the better part of the day, so make yourselves comfortable in the cabin, and we can get a small fire going in the stove for you to keep warm if we don't kick out too much smoke. At least Planchon made sure we had plenty of food and drink, so we will eat well."

There were low sounds of activity from all around them now, and reverberating through the ship.

"We'll be leaving a few men on board until all of the cargo is off loaded. They will be dismantling the ship while they are here. First thing to go is the name. We can't risk anyone finding one Seamew here with another docked thirty miles up the coast. We'll take the sails and other hardware up to the new ship when it is clear to do so. We have a day's hard work ahead of us here, and we cannot leave until it is done. We had a long night and rough crossing, so you can rest on that cot in the cabin or the hammock and get some sleep if you can. There are a few books on the shelf above the cot, and there will be food brought in from the nearby village if Planchon did not provide us enough, though I believe he did."

William saw to the men stripping of the superstructures and everything else that would lighten their weight. They would try to get her further ahead if they could, but if not, then there was another high tide for the next night to take advantage of. Most of the men stripped off and set too with pry bars, to dismantle as much of the superstructure as they might, while others labored to get the cargo off and onto the narrow strip of dry land beside them. They began to offload the more perishable and easily damaged part of the cargo first, to be sent into the nearby village to be hidden away. More and more men arrived with additional horses and helped haul the ship in even further and then set to work on further dismantling, and to move cargo. Others removed the sails and planking and railings to get those out of the way too. That which was salvageable and sound would be used on other boats.

Annis and Sophia watched for a while in the strengthening morning light. William joined them to slake his thirst. "They can get a half dozen cartloads off each night, if not more with that arrangement we built. We're getting more of the heavier cargo off now from the forward part of the ship so that will lighten her a bit more. Come back here in another week or two, you'd never know there was ever a ship here. What wood they cannot use again, they will recover to burn." He went off to help once more.

After an hour or so, the rigors of an extended sleepless night began to catch up with them, and Annis and Sophia retired to the small cot in the cabin and tried to sleep in each others' arms.

Annis awoke as William sat down heavily on the cot by her. She could see that it was now barely daylight outside and was obviously late in the day. He was grubby and had clearly been working very hard, helping dismantle the vessel and to offload cargo.

"Did you get any sleep over all of that noise beside and above you?"

"Sophia did, and then I soon followed her." She yawned.

"I doubt we will be seen from either land or sea now. But it's getting late. Come on, we can go ourselves now before it gets too dark again! We did more than I expected to. There is still a lot of the heavier stuff aboard, aft, but we were able to winch her in further as she was lightened, for the wind kept the water high for us for a while."

He picked Sophia up and led Annis off with him through the clutter and open decking. The only part of the ship not drastically torn apart seemed to be the cabin they had been in.

"Good night, ladies." Joe spoke laughingly to them.

Annis was startled. "William?"

"I know. I had to tell them there would be . . . were two ladies aboard and get their help to see to your safety, or they would have put me overboard for deceiving them." Once they set foot on land, he put Sophia down and walked with them up the busy track.

"When did you tell them?"

He avoided her glance. "Later, my dear, later! Too many things to do now."

Sophia took her hand and pulled her down to whisper in her ear. "He told them before you got to the dock! We were *all* waiting for you, but you were late!" Annis was not sure what she was hearing.

Sophia was swung up and put up onto a cart waiting for them at the top of the bank, and then *she* was assisted up after that, before she might ask for a better explanation of what still seemed to be confusing to her.

"We'll take this cart. It has a full load, and we can at least see it started on its way."

Annis looked closely at the cart and thought she recognized it. William climbed up onto the seat beside her, with Sophia between them.

"I do not know where we are. Where are we to stay?"

"You'll see, my dear."

Sophia listened to everything, perched as she was between William and Annis, and holding onto them both. She seemed to be fighting away her tiredness but could not stifle a yawn or two. "We are going to stay at home, silly!"

"How do you know that? Surely we are miles from there!'

"William told me."

Annis looked attentively into the evening gloom. "But surely this is not the village we are passing through? Though now that you mention it, I think I recognize some of the buildings in the faint light and even the church belfry up there! I do not often come quite this far in this particular direction."

The wind had dropped from the previous night, and there was now a mist drifting inland, and swirling over toward them through the woods. It would provide additional cover for their efforts.

"It is indeed. We are no more than a couple of miles from Underby. The reverend is seeing to hiding most of the contraband in the church and distribution from there each Sunday or on other special occasions. It has a very large cellar and spacious back rooms, and there are plenty of other hideaways in the area."

William pulled the horses in a little. They were keen to be heading home, but he needed to keep as much of the noise down as possible. "He also visits his parishioners from time to time, so we could not have a more ideal courier. A coffin in the back of his cart can hide so much, and not invite close inspection. Especially when there is a grieving widow beside him!"

"I once heard you described as devious. I now see it is true."

"The elder Thackeray probably. I am afraid you do not know the half of it just yet, my love!"

"But surely the masons and carpenters cannot be finished already? It sounded like they had a lot to do, and you brought us on a visit here only last week."

"They finished the rebuilding two days ago. Most of the cleanup should be done by about now. You have a new home!"

Sophia spoke up in excitement and pulled at her arm. "Look there *are* lights on! We *are* expected!"

Thomas walked out of the shadows and held the horses as William dismounted from the seat. "You know where to hide this, Thomas! We got *some* of it offloaded, four loads so far when it was dark enough, but there is a lot left to do. You might get two more loads tonight if you can, before it gets daylight. Rare busy down there, but it's now going faster than it was." He lifted Sophia down to stand by him and then helped Annis down by picking her up at the waist and lifting her down to stand beside him.

"Everything's been ready for ages, sir! Been waiting for you for the past few hours, and was getting worried this morning too, until I heard you had beached as intended. Nasty little storm! I hope it was not too rough of a crossing, for the wind blew hard here for a while."

"No. Mostly uneventful."

Sophia squeezed his hand at such a whisker.

"Did the riders we expect pass on the turnpike as we thought?"

"Aye, about twenty of them late last night and making a devil of a racket, so the lad told me. They took the bait right enough. Pity it was all for nothing, especially as two of their men died for the folly of it."

"What was that?" William sounded shocked to hear that.

"You wouldn't have heard, sir, but there was a revenue ship—the Falstaff—broke up very early this morning near the point."

"That must have been the one we saw and that we very nearly ran into. Full sail and heeling over hard. Fool of a captain to cram it that hard."

"Name of Maxton I heard, sir. Came out of retirement for some reason."

"Revenge on me! I was right! Too juicy a temptation to let pass, and here I thought he and his ship were both laid up!"

"I heard that too, sir. I heard she should never have been put to sea with the condition she was in. He was lost with only one of his men, for the other Seamew managed to get the rest out of the sea and got them ashore pretty fast, so there were some lucky men there, I would say, and some good sailing to get to 'em! It could have been a lot worse!

"Quite a reception waiting for them on shore after that too, as expected, when the Seamew docked, though the outcome of it all wasn't entirely as *they'd* anticipated, I am sure—to be met by their own men, and no contraband to be found."

William shook his head. "A shame anyone had to die, even a Maxton. Another chapter closed, and a new one opened. I hope the Maxton daughters are not as vengefully inclined as their parent and brothers!"

"Is Captain Cat all right, Thomas?"

"Why now, is that our Sophia dressed like a lad?" He looked closely at William's two companions, but he already knew who they were. "So it is! Hard to see in the dark. Miss Annis too, dressed the same way? Well I never! Captain missed you all something wicked he did! He's been waiting for you to arrive now for the last few hours too."

Annis seemed puzzled. "It seems like we were all expected, William. How could that be? Surely no one knew that Sophia or I would be coming with you, for I am sure everyone expected us back at Brooklands." She turned to him, only to find that he was still talking in an undertone to Thomas and had apparently not heard her. But then she recollected that men had been back and forth most of the day from the wreck while *they* had been resting, and they could have spread the word. But that was most unlikely.

"The item I requested, Thomas. Is it here?"

"Yes, sir. He brought it some time ago before he left to join you. It's on the table."

"Is my room ready, Thomas?"

"That it is, Miss Sophia. That was the second one we finished off as soon as we knew you was coming today. I think the Captain might be on your bed waiting for you."

"How did you know she was com—?" Annis was asking too many questions.

Sophia interrupted her. "Good. I'm tired! It's exciting being a smugg . . . , being on board a ship, and in a storm too. I wasn't sick once! France was very strange. I didn't understand much of what they said, but I learned some other interesting words, and it was *ever* so busy on that dock, despite it being nighttime. We almost rammed another ship if I hadn't seen it! The new Seamew is beautiful and graceful, and I will be going out in it soon. Won't I, William?" She had hardly paused to draw breath.

"Yes, my dear, you will."

"Will Joe be on board?"

"I expect so! He'll be captain."

"Good. He has some of the best sea stories I ever heard, for he was telling me some of them before Ann . . ." Her voice trailed off. "Later! I wasn't supposed to say that, was I?"

William was smiling at her. "No, young lady. Not just yet, but it doesn't matter now. There have been a lot of things you weren't supposed to say, but I expect the excitement of the occasion is more than you can bear."

"You should go inside sir, and I'll see to this. Molly has a dinner waiting for you and Miss Annis, and probably for Sophia too if she can keep her eyes open to eat, despite all of that going through her head, but there'll be plenty of hot water for a bath first."

"Good. I'm famished." Sophia rushed off, muttering some newly learned French words that sounded interesting, and that she might never be allowed to say in polite company.

They strolled over to the house. William had taken Annis's arm and threaded it into his own. "What is going on, William? How were we so well expected? Why is everything prepared for us? What stories was 'Joe' telling to Sophia, and when did he have time? She was with me the entire time after we discovered her, and she had been hidden well away before then. If she was!" She began to suspect that all was not as she had been led to believe.

"Yes, my dear! Joe is full of stories. I expect it was on her last visit, for she was on board one other time too, you know, and Joe tells all of the children stories, for he had two of his own on board that time, for we were not going anywhere."

"I am confused."

"Yes, my dear. So is Sophia. You are also very tired. We all missed a good night's sleep. Later, I will explain it all to you."

"Yes, I think an explanation is required."

"But you need to bathe and change for dinner first, and so do I. We've all been in our clothes far too long. Youth's clothing is most becoming on you, but the fewer who see you dressed that way, the better. There is clothing laid out for you upstairs along with hot water for a bath, which is where Sophia is now, if my ears did not deceive me, and you will need to wash a few remaining smudges of that dark streaking off your face." He gently touched her cheek and brow to show where they might still be before he leaned in to kiss her. "I have some things to do here with, Thomas, and then I will join you two to eat."

Some forty minutes later, both Annis and Sophia joined him in the parlor after they had helped each other bathe and dress.

"Well now, that is a big improvement." He watched as they both entered the parlor and welcomed them both.

"You changed yourself!" She looked at him strangely.

"Yes. I felt grubby, and I needed to wash the salt off my skin and out of my hair. I bathed and changed in the wash-house."

"Thomas was mistaken, William. *My* room was not made up but was entirely empty, but my clothing was laid out on Mama's bed in the larger bedroom. That seems to be the only room with furniture, apart from Sophia's. Sophia tells me that Mama and Charlotte, and even Elizabeth will be arriving sometime early tomorrow morning. Is that true?"

"No. My dear. They will arrive no earlier than midday!"

"How did she know we would be here?"

"I confirmed it in my note to your mother, from the dock."

She looked puzzled again. "Confirmed what?"

Sophia leapt in. Annis seemed to be remarkably slow to understand what had happened. "That we would all be here and that we were being kidnapped, silly! She did not approve at first. Then William told us all some things we did not know. Well, we *did*, really, when he *told* us, but before that, we didn't! She thought it ever so . . . I don't know the word, but then she cried. But it was a happy cry for a change."

"I expect it will make sense eventually! Will it?" She looked inquiringly at William.

"Yes, my dear, it certainly will. But let us eat. I have not eaten a suitable meal to sit down to since France, and neither have you, and that was far too many hours ago."

They sat down and helped themselves to the dishes. There were still many questions nagging at Annis. "But why were we both kidnapped? For what purpose? Surely we have nothing that would make us the target of such a scheme. I am beginning to suspect that you were part of this plot too somehow, weren't you, Sophia?"

"Of course I was! But you were the only one kidnapped. I helped do it! I tried to do what I could to make sure that William stayed with us, but you were not being very helpful. I tried to tell you, but you wouldn't listen at first. But this one was mostly

William's idea, except Charlotte and Mama and Elizabeth helped, and I added a few details that seemed to work *ever* so well to get you on board. It would not have been possible without me, except Cousin George did lend a hand."

"I am still confused. What did Cousin George—whoever he is—have to do with this? Although *that* was the letter that came after you had gone. So why are we being kidnapped?"

"That was the wrong word, my dear. You were not kidnapped. You were abducted, although the better word might be 'deceived!'"

"By whom?"

"By me?"

"I was not kidnapped or abducted, but I am beginning to believe that I may have been deceived. No matter. I was determined to come. I had to!"

"I am relieved that you do not believe that you were abducted, but you most certainly were."

"This is all too complicated!"

"Yes, it must seem that way, but it isn't really! It will all soon be very clear to you. I have a particularly good wine I brought back with us—contraband wine always tastes better than any other—and we should discuss the situation over a glass of that. But later! Sophia will, of course, now go to bed, for she is almost asleep at the table."

"I'm not sleepy." She yawned, putting the lie to that, as she propped her head up on her hand at the table and struggled to stay awake to listen to more of their conversation, but her eyes refused to do her bidding, for her eyelids drooped even as Annis and William watched in amusement, and her head slipped off her hand.

"Oh, yes you are! Come on." He scooped her out of her seat. "You have eaten your fill, so I will carry you up and see you into your nightdress and tucked in, and Annis will help too, won't you, my love?"

Chapter XXXVIII

Truth and Consequences Again

They came downstairs after a few minutes, with Annis's arm tucked into his.

"I do not think that I have seen Sophia so talkative, so happy, or so sleepy, and all at the same time! Smuggling must agree with her! Mama will like the new stairs too. They don't creak, and they are very solid. I like the changes!" They moved through into the parlor where the fire needed minor attention. "I think she was asleep before ever she hit the pillow. You will tell me what is going on—kidnapping, abduction, deception, seduction—won't you William?" She looked up at him.

"Of course I will! I don't think I mentioned seduction, though I think that I was the one that was seduced. Seduced by your entire family, and you, even as I walked through your door!"

He helped her clear their dinner off into the scullery, and then they both returned to the parlor where it was warm. They sat together on the window seat beside the fire and savored the wine that he poured for them. He held her hand and kissed her. She moved closer into him.

He looked at her with a knowing look on his face. "What! Now that I am all compliance with your goals . . . are there no complaints, no maidenly protestations, no resistance?"

"Too late! I stopped resisting you some time ago as you well know, and *I* have been the one trying to tempt you and lead you astray ever since! So I fail to see the reason why I have been abducted, and even with the help of my own sister! There seem to be too *many* allied against me for some reason and helping you achieve your dastardly purpose! Which was my own too eventually!" She blushed over that admission.

"But, William, how can I be abducted, as you say, if I am willingly here at my home, with my sister here and all of the servants?" There were no other sounds in the house. "Well, they were here earlier, but now they seem to have disappeared again! No, William, I gave up some time ago being concerned about what others might think of us. I know now what is important for me, for us! I have not been afraid of you for a long time. I wasn't afraid in the conservatory as you well know, but you had decided to be a gentleman for some reason! If I am afraid, perhaps I am afraid of myself at this moment, and of turning you away from me. I find that I am almost a stranger to myself when I compare what I was just a few weeks ago with what I think now. I know it is expected that I should be protesting more, and being more defensive of my honor, but then it is far too late for that. I do not think that I have *any* to defend at this moment either, at least from you, considering what I have dared to admit to you and how far we have come!"

She hesitated for some moments before speaking further. "William?" He answered her by gently nudging his head into her neck. "Where are you to sleep tonight?" She looked at him coyly, feeling sure she knew the answer to that already.

"Ouch! Straight for the throat as usual! I thought we would *negotiate* that at this moment."

"Negotiate? In what way? There is just the one bed made ready upstairs, apart from the one that Sophia is in. After what has happened between us, and what I intended to have happen even some time ago, I doubt that negotiation is necessary!"

"My, you are being rash to point that out! We shall, however, negotiate!" He looked into her eyes and saw that she was not certain what there might be to negotiate. She was here, was she not? They were alone! She was not protesting!

"But let us clear up a few small things first, my love." He thought for a few moments as they clasped their hands tightly together, almost as if they were afraid of drifting apart from each other. "You noticed, of course, over the last few days, that Sophia was quite adamant about throwing us together."

"How could I not notice?"

"And then Charlotte too, for she approached me just a day or so ago and told me of those tarot cards."

"Oh! Those!"

"Yes! Your mother seems to have learned of them too, but did not seem *too* disturbed by what the cards themselves suggested had happened in error. She was happy the way things had turned out and seemed to be turning out. I may have married one daughter, but it was clear to her what was going to happen to another at my hands, eventually. Perhaps she knew it even before I knew it myself, though it had only taken me a few hours in your home to make that decision for myself, though I was not sure how to go about it and not lose all of you!"

"Yes. She would have been quite happy to have us ignoring all of the niceties of social behavior and behaving most outrageously and openly with each other, married or not, and within just a few days of you walking across our threshold! They watched us in the parlor as I shaved you that time and made up their minds about what was happening between us! Mama seemed pleased at what was unfolding, whereas Charlotte seemed rather more reticent at first!"

He reached out and put his glass down on the table before he put his arm about her and pulled her closer into him. "Yes, I heard! By then, they knew what would eventually happen between us, and so did I. But I became a stickler for detail and decided that some things must not be rushed! I enlisted your mother's help in this little escapade when I gave her a much *better* reason why you and I . . . could . . . I'll get into that shortly! Sophia and Charlotte too were getting quite frustrated with us both from an early stage."

"When my own sisters plot against me, as well as my mother, what could I do? With such an army to suggest what my inevitable fate was to be at your hands, and helping you achieve it, and even with my own compliance eventually, what was your difficulty? I gave up quite early on and would have thrown all caution and inhibition to the wind."

"I noticed! I rapidly found that out when we were in the conservatory. I am not sure how I survived that! But I soon discovered that I could not allow you to do that at that moment. No, my love, *I* was the difficulty! *Me*! Not you and not anyone else!" He smiled down at her. "Not at first, mind you, for the circumstance was most challenging in the wrong way. So much grief! Such unexpected trust, at least from Sophia and your mother. Then I found that I had fallen in love with a young lady who seemed to find my presence unnecessary. I did not understand what was happening and so suddenly. Most confusing! But I knew even then, that I must tread very carefully or risk losing everything I had suddenly come to value—a family that seemed to need me. My family now, with one very special person! *You*! What a recognition for the likes of me!"

She leaned into him. "You would not have lost anything, William! I knew what must happen between us. I knew what I wanted! I knew some days ago! I think I was losing my concern about what anyone might think of me that day when you blundered in upon me at Underby! I could sense how disturbed you were at that moment. I felt a strange sense of power over you after that, even though you were the one who had difficulty controlling yourself then!"

He kissed her on the neck. "You are right! How I controlled myself, I will never know, except that I knew I must *never* lose your trust, no matter how close I came to doing just that at that time. I recognized then, the kind of dilemma I was in. Whatever I did *then*, had to be acceptable to *me*, while I protected you from that other me."

"What a strange thing to say, though I remember you saying such a thing earlier! But that is also confusing! I do not need protecting from you! You may need protecting from me!"

"I must beg to differ, my love. You *did* need protecting, and from *me*! So there was a dilemma!"

She looked up at him. "Are you really that much of a stickler for what is proper, William? You did not seem that way in the barn as you watched me as you did, and seemed to derive great enjoyment from it! Your reputation, according to our godmother, did not suggest any such diffidence. But then most of that was misperception on our godmother's part. I shall be sure to tell her *that* when I see her, and tell her how all of her attempts to blacken you backfired with *my* seduction of *you*! *That* will shock her! But then yes, you are more proper than I expected from what I had heard of you, for you had opportunity enough to overpower me and ravish me, or worse, on several occasions now, and to overwhelm me without much resistance from me at those times when my defenses were at their weakest." She paused and then admitted even more. "Even without any resistance at all from me, when I recognized what had to be done to keep you with us! There were other selfish reasons of my own too! Yet you managed to resist the temptations. I began to wonder about myself, and what kind of antidote I might be."

He gently laughed. "You are far from being an antidote, my love! Nor am I that much of a stickler or likely to hold back from you, as you will very soon discover! You were not an idle conquest. You deserved much better than that and were far too important to me to behave . . . to behave as my instincts were driving me to do whenever I was alone with you. They still are!"

She sensed that, as he breathed into her neck as he held her close. She appreciated that comment and liked the way he was looking at her. He had looked at her that way for a long time now, even before the fire.

"So there is hope for me yet, is there, William?"

He smiled at her comment and continued. "It was much more difficult than *that*, for as I said, I had fallen in love with you, as you have known for some time. But everything had to be done, and must be seen to be done properly. At least as properly as it might be arranged, though there were more than enough difficulties to overcome! I could not just marry one daughter, lose her along with her father one day, and then fall in love and seduce another immediately after and expect us to be married, as we so needed to do to maintain our sanity. Even I must draw the line somewhere. Where would it not stop if such a rogue were given such license? Marrying two daughters one after the other? Why stop there? Why not marry them all at the same time? The countryside would be ablaze with scandal!"

"I don't think you care about scandal from what I know of you! But in some societies, I once read that a marriage such as *that*, means that all of the daughters in that family are married to that same man and can expect to share him, for there may be a shortage of young men and an abundance of daughters! I would object to sharing you with my sisters in that way, though Sophia would not care!' She blushed over what she was saying. "Oh, I hope no one can overhear me!"

"No my love. Polygamy is not condoned in our society, even with a shortage of young men after that war! Even I would need to draw the line somewhere. But I am interested—in that deeply, and special emotional way—with only one of you. You!" He kissed her. "I was most surprised and quite shocked to find that your sisters seemed most intent on solving this little problem that lay between us, regardless of moral propriety. Once I knew of their unconventional feelings on the matter, as well as having seen some signs of your own determination, my own soon began to work along in the same way. The plot we eventually hatched between us just a few days ago now, was quite clever I thought, and bypassed so many difficulties. Both Charlotte and I had been thinking along similar lines before that, as we soon found out, though Sophia had anticipated us by some time.

"Charlotte cornered me in my library two days ago when I was approaching my wits end, for I knew what you intended for me, and you even had me cornered." She glanced up in some surprise at his face. He was smiling at her. He had known! "She showed me those cards and told me what I must do! She was all for my marrying you out of hand in France, or even not marrying you at all, and I must admit, that there were some appealing features to both of those plans to a rake like me, but it would not do!

"After a little discussion and clarification of the underlying circumstances, we eventually hit upon a better idea that was acceptable to all, me included, and prepared for it rather well. You would be presented with a desperate situation in which Sophia would need to be rescued from being aboard a vessel that was about to become the focus of revenue agents and could be sunk! Irresistible! Elizabeth was conscripted too, and I persuaded her to dig out some of my older clothing that might fit you, and then Charlotte and your mother and Sophia helped with getting some of the better fitting and loose clothing organized for you with Charlotte as a model. You were out of the way of course! What a woman—women—cannot achieve in an hour or two with a sharp blade and needle and thread! We even got a fine cap for you. Alas, it was still far too obvious that you were a woman when I saw you at the inn, but I did not care! No one else was fooled either! Not for a second! I am surprised you did not notice the grins on the faces of all of those sailors as they tried to avoid us."

He kissed her for a few moments. "In truth, I found that I would like you to go riding with me dressed just like that anytime you would like to. I am sure we can get up to considerable mischief with each other when we get far enough away from everyone!" He blushed and cleared his throat as he recollected where he was and what they were doing there. She laughed gently at his momentary lapse. She liked that idea too, and would remind him of it. He dragged his mind back from that other fantasy and into the present tale. "Sophia was the crucial part of the plot. She met me a little way out of sight down the driveway, so she was not in the box, and I therefore did not lie to you that time. Once we got to the dock, she waited aboard the Seamew with Joe for you to appear, and he told her some very interesting tales of sailing and pirates and smuggling, and the rest of us waited in the inn for you to join us! We cut it pretty fine, but we were not going to leave without you if we could avoid it."

"So everyone was in on the plot? Even the landlord and that boy?"

"Yes. Everyone! The lad almost could not contain his surprise at seeing a young lady—a very obvious young lady, I might add, dressed as a youth and filling out my old clothes in ways no youth ever might! When he came bumbling and stuttering in as he did, we almost could not contain our laughter, so the innkeeper himself had to see for himself. He was no better! If he looks at you a little strangely next time you are at the dock with me, *that* will be the reason, my dear!"

"Oh dear, and I thought my disguise was quite good until you appeared, and then I was quite embarrassed to see you looking at me in the same intent way in those clothes, as you did when I was entirely without clothing! I did not think I was so revealingly dressed!" She blushed and hid her face in his shoulder for a few moments.

He smiled most charmingly. "There are some things that cannot be hidden, my dear!"

"But you did not need to do any of that plotting to kidnap me, William. It was already convinced of what was to happen between us; of what *must* happen, as soon as I could persuade you of it, and I could see that you were already coming to that same conclusion yourself!" She blushed again at that admission. "But what a dreadfully forward thing for a young lady to admit! In any case, we did not marry in France as you and Charlotte intended! I find I do not care anyway! You didn't need to abduct me, you know? I told you I would have been a most willing conspirator!"

"I know! But it is all a little more complicated than I think you know just yet! I really did need to abduct you and to change the scenery and the setting and even adjust the perception of what had happened! Your perception!"

"It sounds needlessly complicated, William!"

"So you already said. But it isn't! It is all so simple! You will see! As for misleading you as I did, leading to your being abducted, you seemed to have preferred things unfolding the other way, and might not easily have come with me if I had not been so devious."

"I would have done! All you had to do was ask me! I would have been a very willing participant in whatever you suggested by then—shamelessly so, for I would have found some way to have caught you alone. Whither thou goest, there will I follow!" She sighed at other memories. She took his hand. "I knew we could not wait a year to mourn Bella. You might have been able to, but I found that I could not! I also could not risk you leaving us, me, so I needed to fix your interest most irrevocably. I saw much earlier than that, that if you were not going to make the first step, out of fear of hurting my feelings or because of social disapproval, then I must do so for myself and damn the consequences! I knew you would never be able to leave us after that! Sophia could see what was needed much earlier than that, though I was still resisting a little, for I was concerned how you might respond, and that if I was too bold, I might turn you from me."

"No fear of that, my love! I was too excited for my own good or yours! I saw the changes in you and your behavior toward me. Most brave of you! But that was the problem. I had to hold you off from doing any such thing!"

"Why?" She had a puzzled look on her face. "I thought if any woman were a perpetrator in such a morally abandoned scheme, by giving herself willingly into the hands of a man, that the man would be quite helpless to resist his own impulses!"

"Yes. You were right about that! I had a devil of a job to keep away from you in that way. I knew that I would not to be able to hold you off for very much longer. You can be most seductively persuasive, damnably tormenting in fact, and becoming more focused and reckless by the minute, and my resolve was weakening by the day. I am surprised I could hold you at bay at all when I discovered how easy you wanted to make your seduction for me that night in the conservatory! Then that following night too when you waited for me to return, and in my own bed! That was why I stayed in the library when I returned. I suspected what you were up to. I hope you did not leave any of your long hair on my pillow to alert the maid, or it will be all about the house by now!"

Annis recognized she had been found out but could say nothing. He did not seem to mind her doing that outrageous thing, for he still smiled kindly upon her! "But then Sophia . . ." He hesitated and then continued. "I should confess to you that Sophia was a little too forthcoming about that conservatory episode. I learned that it was not her idea at all when I cornered her afterward after I had seen her sneak from that bed when she thought we both were asleep and unlocked the house door herself! She eventually confessed that it had been your idea that she would lock us out there all night, and not hers! You can have no idea how utterly bemused, and then happy I was to hear that!"

"Then you know too much already, William! I have no doubt you will be even more shocked to learn that we had agreed, Sophia and I, that she would not be there with us but would be back in her own bed by then! But she found that she was too excited about it all and rebelled at the last minute and decided to stay and supervise us and see firsthand what we might get up to as lovers!"

William laughed gently. "I guessed as much. But then I did manage to survive that plan. But only just, and despite the temptations laid out before me that night! I have difficulty believing some of it even now. I was resolved by then that everything we did together had to be entirely above board, convincing, and believable for me and for everyone else too by then. I think even for you too!"

"Why?"

"I have my reasons. They are very selfish as you will soon discover."

"My abduction and being on board the Seamew with you for almost two days and a night, and being here alone with you now is not exactly above board as you say! Not after the barn incident and the conservatory episode and that other! I think I have been ruined, and I do not care in the slightest!" She even smiled as she admitted that.

"It might appear that way!"

"It most certainly does appear that way, William! I am ruined, and I do not care! I shall broadcast if from the rooftops! I shall write a letter to our godmother confessing all! She will know what to do with it! Weight of opinion of everyone around us will ensure that you must marry me now, you know? If you would like to! Eventually!" She noticed that he had a strangely inscrutable look on his face. "But I still do not wish to wait so long, and I will not, so you may as well drop this notion of being above board!" He was now smiling at her in amusement.

"William, why are you smiling like that? For a confessed stickler about this, you are not objecting very strenuously to my being so forward and so willing to throw my most compromised reputation away so easily! Yet I am! For if you expect me to wait out some mourning period before anything might take place between us in the way that Sophia and I fully intended—except she does not understand, at least I hope not, what any of that means—then I shall behave so outrageously and openly toward you and in full view of everyone that you will be unable to survive! If you think Sophia is the only one who might parade about without . . . ! I will most certainly shock you!"

"No, my dear." He pulled her closer as he smiled into her eyes. "I would like you to do so when we are alone together. I am no longer objecting. We are here alone, are we not? But your reputation is still safe. You are not throwing it away." He reached across to the table and retrieved some cards from the inner cover of the book lying there. "You know what these are, of course."

"Yes." She frowned. "Those damned tarot cards that we made up and that caused all of this confusion and frustration! I thought I had got rid of those."

"I think I see them very differently! They helped make it happen exactly as it should."

"They did?" She was surprised.

"Oh yes! You shall soon see for yourself the delicious twists and turns that they inadvertently caused. It is amazing what leads us astray, isn't it? Here I had married Arabella when, as these cards say, I should have married you, and yet no one knew of it until after it had all unfolded as it did!"

"A tragedy worthy of Shakespeare! That is how I began to see it."

"I know. I've heard it described that way several times now. There was I, struggling to decide how I was to deal with it all. Then we had our little conversation in my study that day, the day when you bearded me and had me explain our godmother's letter detailing all of my faults. A lot seemed to rest upon my answering satisfactorily. I do hope you were not expecting too vehement a denial of any of it?"

"I had hoped! But then your explanation was so much better than any simple denial, for there was a simple explanation and reason for all of it. As bad as it all really was! You could not help what happened. You recovered all of the ground you might have lost in that one interview. But afterward, after your confession, I said much more than I intended to."

"I noticed!"

"You did? Oh! You had confessed it all so well, and now *I* was the one feeling guilty, for those cards were weighing heavily upon me. I was not sure how I might dare to explain to you what the mix-up had been and how dreadfully I felt it. You would never have forgiven us, for we had fallen in love with each other by then and were to be denied full expression of it! What a turmoil!"

"After my unexpected confessions about that letter, my love, you were left struggling with your own burden then, for you spoke of deception and in a most personal way. You seemed to feel much worse over *that* than *I* felt over confessing *my* iniquities. Yes, those cards were nagging at you, but it was not those cards that weighed you down the most at that moment. It was a much greater deception!"

She said nothing, so he continued.

"Your mother and Charlotte—well, Charlotte anyway, not your mother so much—were quite stricken with horror when they discovered the error that had been made in those cards. Sophia didn't care about any of that mere detail. She was intent on a more practical resolution—throwing us together in every compromising way she could think of. I have discovered that Sophia is a most clever young lady, to be able to manipulate that circumstance as she did with the barn, the kitten, and *you*, thrown to the wolf—*me*! Then to help as she did even in this iniquitous escapade. The kitten in the barn was most inventive! I did not know how she had managed that until later of course, though she did get a little help from Charlotte. But it did not work out just as she had planned, for we did not wind up in the hay and in each other's arms, as Thomas and Molly seem to do, but were *outside* of the building!"

"Then there was that thunderstorm, and her deliberately locking us all out of the house according to *your* plan. I cannot level an accusation of being devious against you, though you are, for I am just as devious myself. I am not sure just what was expected of me then, with Sophia keeping close watch upon us both. Had she not been there, then I am sure it might have gone very differently!"

"Yes. I am sure she quite soured the mood for you until she went asleep, and we were then free to learn about each other in a most romantic and tender way, but then you fell asleep too! How unromantic of you, William! I began to despair!"

He smiled at her and filled her wine glass again. "I think it must have been a sudden conversion for you my love, for I did not see any absence of those barriers in the barn. You protested loudly enough when you were on that beam above me in the barn, with me staring up at you as I did and thoroughly entranced! Almost as exciting as when I blundered in upon you bathing!"

She hid her face in his shoulder as she blushed over that memory. "I thought others might come in and see me that way, as ill covered as I was."

"Oh, is that all! I wish I had known that!"

"The conservatory was more private. I did not make too much of a fuss then, did I?"

"No! You did not make any fuss at all, for you snuggled up close to me most warmly and carelessly, and we talked extensively in front of that stove, and you were even in my arms for most of the night! We even kissed most passionately too—many times and sometimes for quite a long time—as we have been doing more frequently now, I am glad to say. I was left at times breathlessly wondering, when you gently adjusted your position with me, whether you were in your nightdress and trying to slip out of it, or were actually out of it and trying to get it on again! I believe I found great courage and took small advantage of you at that moment and kissed you upon the top of your breasts." He looked at her with a smile on his face. "*That* was almost the undoing of us both! But Sophia was wide awake and watching us the entire time, so I could not explore that circumstance as I would have liked."

"Yes, unfortunately she was awake, wasn't she? Until later! But by then, you had also gone to sleep and left me alone with my turbulent thoughts and my own frustrated feelings to deal with. I thought we had agreed, Sophia and I, that after she had persuaded you to see to the horses and had locked us both out of the house to find each other, that she would then go back to bed and then let us both in again in the morning! She was not supposed to be there at all! I had great plans for you! But, no matter! I knew she would soon be dead to the world, but I did not expect that you would be too! You will have to give up these late nights and smuggling William if it is going to cause you to neglect me like that. If you expect to seduce me after that degree of neglect, I will make you work for it. Yes, I did spend almost that entire night with you, didn't I? and with never a word of complaint or protest out of me about any of it!"

"Never a complaint! Though we did have a chaperone for some of it!"

"Yes, we did. While you slept, I made up my mind about a lot of things, and about you, and what would be your fate. I made up the fire and hung my nightdress up to dry and then climbed in with Sophia. So, William. Are those confessions of my outrageous behavior making this unnecessary negotiation any more palatable to you?"

"Almost. We are getting there, my love! There is just one more part to all of this, first!"

She waited for him to speak.

"I need you to tell me something, my dear. Now this part may be a little difficult for you, but I can promise you that you will accept it most happily, and soon."

"I will tell you anything now. You know that!"

He looked at her with that inevitable, knowing smile on his face. "Who did I marry?" He felt her start, at such a surprising and unexpected question.

"You married Arabella!" She spoke softly as she looked up at him with her face a little paler than it had been. That was still a hurtful memory. "You know you did!"

"I thought I did at the time too. I did not question it at all until a little later. It did not take long to determine what had really happened. Will you allow me to explain it to you?"

"Yes. I will do that! Though I do not understand what there is to be gained."

He leaned over and tossed another log onto the fire. "You and I shall go over what I know. I can assure you, however, that neither I nor anyone else *can* or even *wishes* to overturn the marriage that took place. There is no need."

"No. Of course not, for Arabella died just afterwards. It was overturned at that moment. You are free to marry again. I would like you to, provided you marry me!"

"I think you should hear me out, Annis. Without interruption if you can! The marriage was *not* overturned with your sister's death!"

She stiffened beside him. "I do not understand. She died! How can you still be married to her?"

He smiled at her. "Oh, such delicious confusion! Even in your mind! Nothing will change between us. I will still love you as I do, and I do intend to spend the rest of my life with you, so nothing is going to change that."

She seemed to accept that.

"You are here now with me, and we are alone." There were some sounds from above their heads. He smiled at her. She had heard the same sounds. "Almost alone. I still hear the patter of footsteps overhead and they are not mice or the cat, for he is on that other window seat. Sophia is wandering!"

"Yes, she is! No matter. The excitement will soon fade."

"I suspect we will find her asleep in a bed not her own, when we retire. Ah well! We can go to hers instead if we must! But hear me out fully once we have had more of this most delightful wine. Quite warms the spirit!"

"You do not need to get me fuddled to seduce me, William! I am a foregone conclusion for you!"

"You are far from being a foregone conclusion as you so impolitely describe yourself! You will be my pot of gold at the end of the rainbow!" He groaned. "Another bad metaphor!" He threw another log onto the fire and settled with his back against the window seat where Annis still sat above him. He patted the floor. "I think you should join me down here, my dear, and we can sit together in front of this fire and talk, for the night is getting quite chilly up there by that window, and besides, there are others busy outside too and we should not be overseen."

She slipped off the seat to join him as he placed a cushion from the seat for her to sit upon. He pulled the rather embarrassing watch from his pocket and flipped the cover. "Barely midnight!" He ignored the painted figures and their rhythmical intimate activity on its face as he placed it at the edge of the hearth, away from the direct heat of the fire. "Sit here, my dear, and I will protect you from the drafts. She sat between his legs and leaned back into him. "We are not far off a frost, I think. A good night to be laboring offloading cargo though, for I know I heard Thomas come through again a few minutes ago!"

"No, sir! No, William! I object! You shall not desert me at this most crucial juncture in our lives together and rush off to do that!"

"Hush, my love." He kissed her on the neck. "I have no intention of doing any such foolish thing! There are men and women enough involved with that at this moment." He kissed her on the neck again and folded his arms about her to hold her close into him. "There are far more important and very personal and intimate things that you and I need to attend to tonight!"

"Yes. There are!" She was emphatic about that!

He kissed her then upon her lips once she turned her head toward him. "Strange how settled and contented I have become, and so quickly. I am sure I did not expect it, nor Elizabeth either I would say, though she warned me this would happen to me eventually."

"That first night? The night of the marriage, William!" She drew his thoughts back to that.

"Yes, my love!" He waited for her to continue as he nuzzled into her hair and kissed her upon the neck yet again, for she responded so well.

"You confused me more than just a little from the first moment you arrived at Underby. I did not understand why you—a strange gentleman that only mother seemed to know anything about—seemed so calm and accepting of that marriage! You did not seem to be fighting it or resisting it as I had at first expected would be your response to anything so suddenly thrown at you. I do not think that any gentleman would like to be rushed into marriage like *that*, and with a woman he had never met!"

"True, my love! But I was not given the luxury of time to consider any of it as I might have liked. You were all so upset. What could I object to, that would not have created even greater hurt and confusion? It seemed all but certain from what your mother said, that Bella would die, so it would be a minor sacrifice on my part compared to your loss. I could see all of your need and grief before ever I might see the difficulties for myself that I suddenly faced."

"And so you were married to Bella! I hope you have no regrets about that."

"And so I was married! Regrets? Oh yes, there were regrets almost at the outset! I quite amazed myself to discover that I regretted not knowing my bride much better!" She liked that answer. "I regretted not knowing the family much better. But—and this was truly surprising to me—I very quickly found that I had no regrets about that marriage!"

"Thank you! I am sure Arabella might feel some comfort over that if she is able to see any of this. Then you kissed the bride! We none of us expected that, and you cried with us!"

"Yes, I did! Both of those things! I had not cried any of those five years at war, despite losing one friend after another! I was certainly not crying for myself, though I might have done at losing my freedom with so little of a fight if I had thought about it. But I didn't think about it! I never even thought of that until now. No. There were other things preying upon my mind then."

She did not ask him to elaborate. "I do not think any of us expected you to kiss your bride as you did."

"It surprised you?"

"Oh yes! It most certainly surprised me. It was so unexpected. That was the least of it all. I did not know what to think. I was startled almost to the point of saying more than I should have done at that moment. That kiss preyed upon me all night! I could not sleep after that. Of course I could not sleep! I knew when you came into my room, for I was pretending to be asleep. I did not know what you intended, what to expect, or how you might behave, yet I was not afraid of you at that moment. Not after that kiss, or those tears! Fortunately, I had not received our godmother's letter by then or read it or I may have responded very differently! I also overheard you speaking with Thomas after that."

"I wandered because I could not sleep either, and there were too many things nagging at me. I could not think straight. No wonder! I found I was confused, curious, and even overwhelmed. I relived those last few hours over and over in my mind." He stared into the fire, with his chin resting on her shoulder. "I remember the ceremony, but I forget my words. I saw a ring placed on my finger. Your father's, I think. But I remember little else."

She nodded, tears glistening in her eyes.

"I still have it on." He showed her.

"You had it on all of the time after that."

"You noticed!" She nodded, not trusting herself to speak.

"So did your mother! I saw my bride with one on her finger too. This ring!" The one that your mother then gave me the next day for some reason known only to her." He held up his right hand to show that ring too, not on his corresponding finger where it usually should be but where it might fit, on his little one. He wrapped his arms about Annis and held her close to provide some little comfort for her as he slid the ring off his little finger and then gently put it onto her finger on her left hand. She did not resist or protest. "Still as loose as it was! We'll soon get that fixed! Then I kissed my bride—a most alarming kiss to both of us I think—and then signed the register as did my wife. At that time, it was all completed to everyone's relief and satisfaction. Even mine at that moment. Fait accompli! An unfortunate end and a difficult beginning. What a beginning!

"Afterwards, after I had retired, I was so restless and with so much going through my mind that I could not sleep, no matter how tired I might have been. I had to get up and wander the house to be sure I had not dreamed any of it. I hadn't! It was all real enough! I blundered in upon you at first, as you know, thinking you were Arabella, and then went off to find where my wife might really be."

She felt him breathing into her hair as he snuggled his head into the back of her neck. She felt him take the ribbon at the back of her dress in his teeth and pull it, to undo it. "I also had some questions for her!"

She turned a little and looked up at him in surprise, thinking his comment to be most strange. "Questions?"

"Yes. Questions, my love! Questions that only she would be able to answer at that moment, and I was sure she would."

"And did she?" She accepted his strange mood and strange pronouncements.

"Yes. She most certainly did! After I had discovered where she was, I sat with her for a while. I moved back the shroud so that I might see her face for possibly that last time. I told her some things of me and my life as I held her hand. Cold and lifeless at that moment and nothing like the lady I had married."

"Death does that!"

"Yes. But as I said, she was nothing like the lady I had married! Your sisters were there too, but I did not see them at the time nor did I know they were there, for they were as quiet as mice and off in the shadows. When I went to hold her hand, I found it to be swollen to twice a normal size and bruised and broken, as was her arm."

"She was badly injured in that accident."

"It was her left arm! I had watched as my bride had signed the register with her left hand. I had even helped put the ring on her left hand too, yet no ring, not even mine, would have fitted on any of those fingers, and she had not signed that register with her arm broken as it was."

"Arabella was right handed. That was not broken."

"I know! But the lady I had married had used her left arm and hand, and she did it as though that was how she was used to doing it. She was nothing like the lady I had married because she was *not* the lady I had married. One does not marry a dead woman, though I believe it has been done in the past as a means of upsetting the succession and inheriting property, but that is most difficult to do and needs considerable resolve and preparation, as well as a good deal of cooperation from many individuals. But there are many ways to overturn the lineage without murder or marrying a dead person. No matter. The lady that I met with then, in her own bedroom, *that* bedroom, had died even a little before, or just as I had arrived at Underby! *That* was not the lady I had married!"

"No! She wasn't! Yet you did marry her!"

He smiled. He did not find what she said, to be at all confusing now. "We make progress!"

Annis continued. "Bella had died at exactly the same moment as you had walked through our door, William! I heard her breathe her last at that very moment in time! It was most unfortunate, yet it was also an omen, perhaps providential! Almost as though she had waited for you to arrive before she might leave us! I did not question it. I knew what I must do. The marriage had to go forward!"

"Thank you! And *that* was your secret, your feeling of guilt that day you approached me in my study." He sounded relieved to have her admit what he had known now for some time. "I knew as much myself when I thought about it all later. I remember the horrified look on your face as you descended those stairs that first time I saw you. Would you have told me of this if I had not laid any of this out for you?"

"Not so soon! Not willingly! Perhaps not at all! There would have been no need! You did not need to know, except you did discover it! Others still do not need to know. It was important that you marry one of us and it needed to be Arabella, for that is what had been planned and prepared for with the vicar and the license and everything. It had to go forward that way, but with her dying at that moment, I needed to take her place. I was the one in that bed, and yet, it was Arabella that you married." She felt him loosening the ribbon at the back of her dress. "A marriage by proxy! We none of us discovered the error we had made with those cards about you being foreordained to marry *me* as you should have done!"

"So you took her place and carried it all through!" It was not a question.

She was pale. "Yes! But it is not as though such a thing has not been done before, for I did read of that happening when someone was unconscious or so close to death that they could not respond as required. That is what I knew I had to see happen. No one needed to know when Bella had died! So you did marry Arabella as I said. But you are the only one who might know that I was the one taking her place. Except for my mother and Charlotte of course, but they will say nothing, for they knew at the time how important it was that you married Arabella because of the will and because of those cards. Indeed, I think they accepted that it happened the way it was intended to, and so have forgotten what *really* happened. Everyone else believes that you married Arabella too, for you did, and it must stay that way. I did only what I needed to do at that moment. We had not intended to mislead you!"

"I know that! It did not take me long to work that out for myself, so I was not long being misled! Who might possibly discover any of this afterwards, with my bride dead and me a widower? No one!"

She felt a burden gradually being lifted from her shoulders. "You were right about our conversation in your study that day. That was the larger burden of deception that I was still laboring under, though those tarot cards were the start of it all, for indeed, the responses and the body were mine, but you still married Arabella. We were thinking of our own security. I think they have forgotten about it by now. But that is one reason why I am here now, to atone for that error, to make up to you for that dreadful deception, and to make it right! I expected you to desert us soon after that, and of course, you would never learn what had happened and be upset and nor would anyone else. But you stayed, and look what has happened between us! I cannot allow you to wait a year, William, nor will I wait a year myself as seems to be required after such a loss." She could not immediately meet his eyes but blushed over her next words. "I also find that I so much want to have that happen between us now, tonight! It was all of my doing, and the remedy is in my hands too."

"I hope that *that* is not the main reason that you are here with me now, but that you are here for yourself and out of love, as I am, and not because of guilt, or what some foolish pieces of card had to say! You have nothing to atone for. I hope that love, rather than guilt might be the main reason."

"It is!' She looked up at him. "I love you, William, and I know that you love me the same way! That is why we cannot wait to be married!" She turned to him and knelt before him as she held his head in her hands. "I am not ashamed to admit that. But I need you to stay with us, with me, as my husband, married or not. I have never felt this way before about anything! I took Arabella's place once and brought about this marriage, and I want to take her place again! If necessary I will make any sacrifice to . . ." He closed off her further words with a kiss.

"Say no more on that for the moment. There will be no sacrifice here! It will unfold exactly as we both want!" He laughed gently as he looked deep into her eyes. She was relieved to see that he was smiling most kindly at her, enough to set her heart beating furiously in her chest, but then he always did smile at her like that. "I can assure you that Charlotte and your mother would still believe the other, had I not presented them with other realities when I did. What a delicious mix-up! You would all three—perhaps four of you—still be firmly convinced that I had married Arabella, even by proxy, with you in her place, if I had not convinced them otherwise."

She did not fully understand. "I am relieved that you are not offended by it William! But how do you mean convinced them otherwise? You really did marry Arabella! I was so convinced you might never forgive us and would want nothing to do with us or me after that, and yet nothing seemed to dissuade you from this . . . this association with us. With me! I hope that is still true, even now that you know the full extent of it, for it has nagged at me for a long time now. Perhaps you now regret abducting me as you did." Her head dropped, fearing what she might hear him say.

"I regret nothing, my dear! You did what you had to do. I understand. But it did not go quite as you intended, and you do not know the full extent of it yourself. Obviously!"

"So I am beginning to suspect! But how do you mean?"

"One does not need to kidnap or abduct one's own wife. At least I would hope not!" He slid the large book out from the table top, laid it on front of her, and opened it at the page of interest."

"The parish register?" She sounded surprised.

"Yes, my dear. The register! So again, who did I marry?"

"Arabella! Of course. By proxy! That is how it was all legally done." She was puzzled at his questioning something that she had explained clearly enough, she thought.

"That was the initial perception but not the legality of it."

"What do you mean?"

"Take a look at the signature!"

She said nothing for some moments. She seemed to have difficulty focusing upon what she saw.

"But . . . ! I do not understand. I signed Arabella's name. The witnesses saw that I did too, or they would not have . . ."

"No!" He stalled her further words. "You *meant* to sign Arabella's name, but for some inexplicable reason—the heat of the moment, the emotions, the upset, the tears, my kiss—devastating to both you and me at the time, who knows, you signed your own! The witnesses to all of that were as upset as I was, and they saw only what they wanted to see." He looked at her in a way that set her heart beating even more strongly than it had been. "Annabel! It was not a proxy marriage my love, but a real one! *We* are married. *We* are man and wife and have been since that first moment!"

He saw the changing expression on her face as she took in the writing of her name for the first time and began to recognize something she had not been conscious of herself. "I was jubilant when I discovered this the following day! The reverend accepted it too. He had been confused also, but he said nothing. He had certainly been tired, and he asked me what had happened. I told him what I knew. He may have said the names wrong, he could not be sure, as they are so very similar—Arabella, Annabel—but the name you had *signed* said everything."

"But the license?"

"Another wonderful error. It had not been filled in! The reverend, when he applied to his bishop for that license, was mixed up by the similarity of your names and could not remember which daughter was the eldest, for he did not yet know your family as he might. His Bishop did not know either. How could he? So it was left blank as was the space for my name. We filled it in correctly the next day with the name of the lady I actually married—yours, and my own! The entire ceremony was now properly and accurately completed. We, you and I, were married, and you did not know! Neither your mother nor sisters knew either, until I told them just recently, and as I said, *you* did not know until this very moment. I had removed myself willingly and deliberately from the ranks of the widowed to the ranks of the married without lifting more than a pen to write our names on the license. I was elated that I might so easily become married again, and to you of all women, and that I had never been a widower at all!

"How fortunate that it was you, and not some other that I had married. It meant that I was not free to marry anyone else either, not even you, for I was already married to you. So you see I did not need to marry you again in France or anywhere else. The only thing wrong with all of this, until now, was that you did not yet know that you were legally my wife! What a rare pickle! Most frustrating too!"

He continued to loosen the ribbon down the back of her dress and down to her waist. "I had discovered as much the night before, as I had wrestled with what had happened to me and in my interview with your sister—I did not allow for the proxy argument of it. I genuinely believed that I had been the victim of a deliberate but necessary deception! I am relieved that I did not blurt everything out for your sisters to hear as I sat with Bella, realizing that I had married her next sister! I was saddened and jubilant at the same time as I sat with her, and I thanked her for telling me what I so much needed to know. But then, I had fallen in love with a lady I had just kissed. You! I had become married to a lady I had never met before and knew nothing of. Unthinkable! She was also still alive! I was jubilant when I discovered that. Wild horses could not have removed me from Underby after that discovery."

"That kiss, William! I almost started out of my death bed at that moment, for I had never felt so alive!"

"It startled me too, my love! I had never kissed anyone so very far from death and so very much in the living world!"

"But then just a few seconds after that was when my father passed away too, for I sensed that too. It seemed like another omen. But, William, everyone of our acquaintance thinks that you married Arabella!"

"They may have done at first. But then there was so much emotional confusion at that time that it was understandably difficult to sort out what was thought to have happened from what really did happen. There is no doubt about this, however!" He smoothed the page where her signature sat with his. "No mistaking that name, either here or on the license, with mine. I married Annabel—Annis—as I should have done and not Arabella, as was intended. I do not need to marry you again! I was never a widower, even as I seemed to be one! We have been under the same roof ever since, have we not? Everyone knows that too. Even the servants here, which is why they did not mind leaving us to ourselves tonight and with you in my perhaps now not-so-dishonorable company this evening. After all, I am now a respectably married man, am I not? You and I have been married my dear from the very first moment almost of our meeting. But if I were free to marry again, then I would still choose to marry you, if you would have me."

She had no need to say anything at that moment, for her eyes said everything.

"So you see, my love, far from being a Shakespearean tragedy, it is now a true love story as it should be, with a much more reasonable ending."

"So everything with those tarot cards actually did work out as it should!"

"It seems so."

"Are you sure, William?" She was looking up at him, her face full of happiness and with tears running down her face.

"Sure about what? About the way the cards were correct? You signing your own name in error? Or my falling in love with you? For all are true!" He looked at her as he kissed her tears away one by one and passed her a handkerchief from the window seat as he held her close.

"Do you know how difficult things might have been had you really believed that you, yourself, Annis, had married me? You would never have let me get as close to you as a man might get to his wife, though I wanted to from that moment forward. Just as well, under the circumstances!"

"How so?"

"What a short memory you have! It was not always peaceful between us you know? You wanted me gone from your family shortly after the marriage."

"I did not know why you wanted to stay, for I was afraid you might learn too much about us!" Her voice trembled in relief. "We had used you for our own ends, and the longer you stayed the more likely that you would see that! I felt guilty, a little, at first, then much more guilty as time went by, and I began to see what sort of a man you really were and how wrong of us it had been to deceive you. There were other setbacks, of course, to my increasingly uncertain opinion of you!"

"Of course. Our godmother's letter! Not something anyone needs to find out about anyone turned loose upon four most vulnerable and beautiful women, or what a wife needs to find out about her new husband! You wanted my blood after that and did not trust me in any way. You were even more intent on seeing me gone. Not something that a man wants to find out about his new wife either, as I was doing. But I had no intention of going at all by then. You could not have seen me gone short of shooting me—or even then, which you might have done at one time!"

She looked up at him. He liked what he saw in her eyes at that moment. "You confirmed all of my worst fears that our godmother had raised when you dealt so violently with Thackeray, and yet the servants described it all so easily and with obvious admiration. Not that he did not deserve it, for he had long needed to have that happen I think!"

"And then that gun!" He shook his head at thought of that. "I was scared and horrified!"

She laughed at his exaggeration as the tears still ran down her cheeks, and she sniffed and dabbed at her nose with the handkerchief. "Nothing of the kind, William! Admit it! You were amused! You could scarcely contain yourself and stop yourself from laughing at my foolishness!"

"You are wrong! I was most impressed! I began to realize that the young lady I had fallen in love with—and married—would quite happily shoot me to protect her own family from me. What a wife you were turning out to be!"

He nuzzled gently into the loosened front of her dress and kissed her on the top of her breasts yet again. "There! I have managed to kiss you upon both of your breasts twice now! What else might possibly follow that, I wonder?"

She did not resist or complain but held him there and even pulled him closer in to her as she stroked his hair. "Except you gave me your own gun! I began to see you a little differently after that."

He raised his head reluctantly and smiled at her. "But not for long unfortunately. For you overheard my meeting with the elder Thackeray when you should have been over at your neighbors' house with your mother and sisters. I really did think you might shoot me after that. I had to convince him of what I was saying. Unfortunately, I convinced you too, and too well! I imagine your mother told you all of it after I had followed him to be sure he was leaving the area, and did not have a more serious purpose against me, for I told him enough to scare him silly for a while. He will not return! Not because I dealt with him as violently as you had come to expect of me and put his bloody remains in a hedgerow but because of what I had told him. I also had to be sure to be out of your way for a while or risk being shot by you! I dare not return too early!"

She laughed gently. "I felt very guilty after that, when Mama explained it all to me. I began to realize how ill behaved I had been and how wrong our godmother's impression of you was, yet it all seemed so convincing! When you asked to see the estate and for me to go with you, I could not refuse you then."

"I counted on that, sly fellow that I am! Strike while the iron is hot! That guilty feeling! I could not believe my luck that Thomas had to return and that you did not object to go on alone with me, so I began to plot how I might seduce you even then, perhaps on the headland near those bonfires! Seducing my own wife indeed! Then you became faint! It seemed that the gods were beginning to smile upon me at last! There was my first opportunity. I planned on telling the landlord that my wife and I needed a private parlor, as I truthfully confessed to you afterwards in your room, as you rested in your bed, but you laughed at me." He kissed her under her chin. "It would have been true, but I think you would have objected. It was far too soon." He sighed. "The landlord would have objected too, for he recognized you and knew nothing of me, so my courage deserted me! Then my next wonderful opportunity was that same evening when I stumbled in upon you as you bathed. My own wife standing there in all of her naked glory, vulnerable, tempting, and I was unable to take advantage of her as I would have liked, and fondle and kiss her."

"I did not object very loudly, if you recall. But you did not fondle me then!"

"No, for you would have objected most strenuously, I think. That damned gun was also within reach! I saw that! You did not know what I knew about us being married. You were not even at ease with my being there. I do not know of any young lady who might be, apart from Sophia. I had to move much more slowly, for I was moving far too fast for us both. One does not wish *ever* to terrify one's wife that way. Someone else's yes, but not one's own!"

She gently hit him on the arm and laughed. Her eyes were filled with tears of happiness.

"We had a most candid conversation after that, I recall, as I sat with you. I related various things that only a husband might relate to his wife, which is why I was so forthcoming in answering all of them as I did, even about Deirdre, though you could not know that—some irony in that, I thought—though not even many husbands would be comfortable with what we discussed, for you were very pointed in your remarkably personal questions, you know?"

"I know. But I needed to know more about you. I was falling more deeply in love with you too by then. Then we had that fire! I wanted you to make love to me on the floor of that bedroom before we both died, if it were to end like that. I was determined not to be denied, as Arabella was."

"I know. But that was not a suitable moment, for I knew we would be able to get out, and then you might recognize that I had taken advantage of you most grievously. Nor was it a good time after that as we sat by the trough in full view of everyone, though we were both of us aching to do so at that moment, for I could sense it in everything about you as you mercilessly tormented me with everything I most wanted to touch, within my reach, and yet far out of it. I know we confused poor Charlotte! What an education for her! Nor when you bandaged me up or shaved me, though I would have liked to have obliged you even then too, but with everyone looking on, I could do nothing, no matter the promise in your eyes. One opportunity missed after another, but by then, you had fallen under my spell and it was just a matter of time, so I decided to be as patient as I could be. But it was becoming too dangerous for you with each passing day as well as dangerous for me."

"I would not have objected by then!" She blushed at her own candid admission.

"No. But by then, *I* would have! For you did not know we were married, as we were. It was very important for you to know *that* before anything might happen of that nature. I did not wish to antagonize you and lose you!"

"You would not have lost me! So, William, I am not objecting now. It seems that I am a married woman, for you have convinced me of it after everyone else seems to have accepted it! I would say that any negotiation that might take place is now no longer necessary."

"I told you it would work out properly! It is almost enough to have me believing a little in astrology. I think I shall have those tarot cards mounted and framed to hang in our bedroom! Even our godmother's letter too, as a tribute to her atrocious penmanship and for helping with all of this!"

"I like that idea and the sound of that other too—'our bedroom'!"

"And now you are here with me, alone and, perhaps, of a very different frame of mind than you might have been. The servants are gone for the night. Sophia is asleep. I hope. Though where she might be sleeping, we have yet to discover! That child gets around more than one might know and sees far too much! I expect we will have to get used to being spied upon while we make love."

"No, we won't! Not if I can help it! I think I shall close off that little peephole from my former room that looks in on ours, but I shall move a chair to cover it tonight. We used to watch our parents through that while they were in front of their fire and making love. That is how we saw them remove each other's nightclothes and make love."

"She is still very likely to encounter us. It will be unavoidable, my dear. Had she not been close by when you went searching for the kitten and you landed up in my clutches then, there would have been no doubt in my mind how it would all have ended after the way you were tormenting me with that very revealing nightdress that hid nothing of you from me where I was standing. At least I hoped so, if I could encourage you.

"The same was true in the conservatory, except I was much more defensive of your reputation and feelings then, even as you lay in my arms almost without your nightdress at times. Perhaps it was for the better. So you and I have some unfulfilled destiny to catch up on. But only if you wish, my dear."

Her eyes told him all that he needed to know as she raised to her knees and moved forward to press closer into him. "I do wish it, William. I was afraid you might find out all of this, eventually—the initial mistake in those cards and then the deception about your marriage . . ."

"Our marriage!"

"Our marriage . . . and that you would then hate me! Though I honestly remember signing Arabella's name, at least I think I do, and you might never forgive me, trapping you as I did in a marriage to my sister."

"Never a more fortuitous or happy entrapment, my dear!"

"When I changed earlier, I had to search about and eventually found my clothing in the master bedroom. My own was empty and devoid of furniture. Only Sophia's room and that bedroom are finished. I wondered where you would be sleeping if you decided to resist my obvious willingness. Yet, I also saw some of your clothes and a nightshirt laid out there too, so I began to hope."

"I hope that question is now answered for you."

She took his hands in hers and blushed as she looked at him. "Yes, sir, it is. But although the night might be cool outside, as you said, it will be far too warm where we will be, for nightshirts, I think!" She blushed as she said it, but still held his eyes with hers, no longer afraid of her own feelings or of confessing them to him. "There, I am as little a lady as you are a gentleman."

"And will we survive such an admission? But we have been married for weeks now, and I am sure—following that episode in the conservatory—that we are no longer shy with each other. I like you being outspoken in that way and would like you to continue, always! If this devious behavior and subterfuge and abduction, seduction, and my rough male attributes have not turned you off me, it is time we retired, my dear wife."

"Yes, we should do that! I was not sure how I was to encourage you any more than I already had. I was beginning to be frustrated that I seemed not to be able to inflame you as I intended! I was also having some most unladylike feelings concerning what I needed to have happen between us, to make up for those earlier occasions where I was denied. Perhaps it was a good thing that Sophia was there on both of those occasions and brought things to this stage."

"We can always visit other kittens in the barn and even go out into the conservatory during another thunderstorm and build up that fire and fill in those missed opportunities, but we shall make up for that now."

"I believe I can look forward to a marriage as happy and as fulfilling as my parents' was."

"I can but try my dear. But we need to make a start on that. We also have an old Viking custom to undertake with some urgency, common among eager newlyweds I believe."

"Oh, and what is that William?"

"We need to 'christen' every room in the house as soon as we reasonably can! For good luck!" he explained. "We should get started on it as soon as we can, for there are at least twenty rooms here as well as stables and barns, and your mother and sister are arriving tomorrow! That does not leave us much time. There are almost another hundred at Brooklands, and my mother's house has at least thirty, and . . ."

She blushed. "Oh, William! But surely that is not an old Viking custom?"

"It is! But not one that the ladies who were hiding in those out-of-the-way places wished to experience at the hands of those they were hiding from!"

"I shall not be hiding, William! Far from it!" She even managed to blush.

"I should hope not! But at this moment, we are both far too tired to think straight. Your mother will be here with Charlotte and Elizabeth tomorrow! Later tomorrow! Much later! I told them no sooner than midday. We will need to present a suitable appearance to them of a happily married and contented, if exhausted, couple. Now, I think we will!"

He looked into the fire and smiled as he recalled other things. "I had to bribe your mother with promise of lace for her help and convince her and your sister with some silk and some hard pencils. Sophia settled for an outing in the new Seamew—the Annabel, which we will also need to christen properly in that way too—and a few other promises. They were most foolish, for they allowed themselves to be bought off far too cheaply! I would have given everything I owned to achieve what I did. So much achieved so quickly and at so little cost. Come, my love! We should retire. I am curious about just how many freckles you might have too, and where they might be found. I think I noticed at least one on your breast a moment ago!" He gently pulled forward the top of her dress and peered down it. "Yes, I did, and even another too! He kissed her there. "A kiss for each one, as I do for Sophia but not yet for Charlotte, unfortunately, but it is only a matter of time! However, if this present sleeping arrangement does not sit well with you . . . ?" He knew the answer to that even before he asked.

"William! Get rid of that notion! We are man and wife, as you seem to have known forever, and through no fault of mine you have wasted too much time already, for I was willing enough ages ago! We also have so much to find out about each other—what little there is that was not discovered in my bedroom, the barn, or the conservatory—and too little time to do it before Sophia will come thundering into our bed first thing in the morning and wakes us up and asks how we slept and even if we had . . ." she hesitated. "Oh dear . . ."

"Consummated our marriage at last?"

"I would have said it, I think!"

"There will be no doubt of that, my dear, if a little delayed! But she will not need to ask. She will just need to look at our contented smiling faces as we lie entwined in each other's arms!"

"And we should make sure that our nightclothes are within reach, William. It would not do to educate her too much too quickly about . . . all of this!"

"I think she will surprise you there! Not much escapes her—or your sister Charlotte either—about male anatomy or what goes on between romantically inclined adults! I am sure we will be most inventively spied upon, as they do upon Thomas and Molly, and will be the subject of many explicitly detailed drawings, but I can also turn the tables there if I need to!"

He smiled. "Come, my love." He helped her to her feet and held her in his arms. "Let us take ourselves off to our bed. Our bed" He liked the sound of that too. He carried the wine glasses, as she picked the candle off the table and lit the way toward the stairs.

"Oh! One moment, William!" She returned and scooped the watch off the hearth as she held the front of her loosened dress from falling entirely away from her. "We should not leave that for Sophia to find, or there truly will be some most awkward questions. Besides, it does not seem so very improper now, and you may need some prompting as to what is expected of you tonight if you are so tired! Love and lust together! It is also not proper to keep a lady waiting, sir, when she is so excited to learn more than she has ever *known* before. In the biblical sense of the word! About ferrets too, as I once heard you say in an unguarded moment about this watch! Though I *do* know about them!"

She saw he had a serious and surprised look on his face, but he was smiling, even as she blushed over her most daring and unladylike words.

"I see that I married a most remarkable woman!" He put both glasses in one hand, tucked the bottle under his arm, and saw his wife climbing the stairs ahead of him as she gently laughed at the surprised look on his face.

Her laugh soon turned to a gentle squeal, however, and she became suddenly agitated and very nearly lost her footing on the stairs and her hold on the candle as she moved somewhat faster and more excitedly and urgently ahead of him as his free hand rose up under her dress just a little.

"William! Oh, William!"

"Let the freckle hunt begin!" He said mischievously as he followed close behind her up the stairs as her agitation, squeals, and maidenly protestations increased!

They both heard Sophia chuckling softly from somewhere in the shadows above them!

Edwards Brothers,Inc!
Thorofare, NJ 08086
14 July, 2010
BA2010195